The Drowned Realm Series
Book III

I0730514

WORLD ON FIRE

Khalid Uddin

World on Fire
Book Three of The Drowned Realm Series
Copyright 2025 by Khalid Uddin

ISBN: 978-1-7365979-8-9
All rights reserved.
Printed in the United States of America

No part of this book may be used or reproduced in any manner whatsoever without the author's written permission except in the case of brief quotations embodied in critical articles and reviews.

This book is a work of fiction. Names, characters, places, and incidents are either a product of the author's imagination or are used fictitiously. Any resemblance to actual events, or persons or locales, living or dead, is purely coincidental.

Cover Design by Eric Labacz, Labacz Design
Maps by Kaira Marquez

Published by
Can't Put it Down Press

For Mom and Dad.
Through all these years,
Everything you've done has been done with love
And I couldn't be more grateful for that.

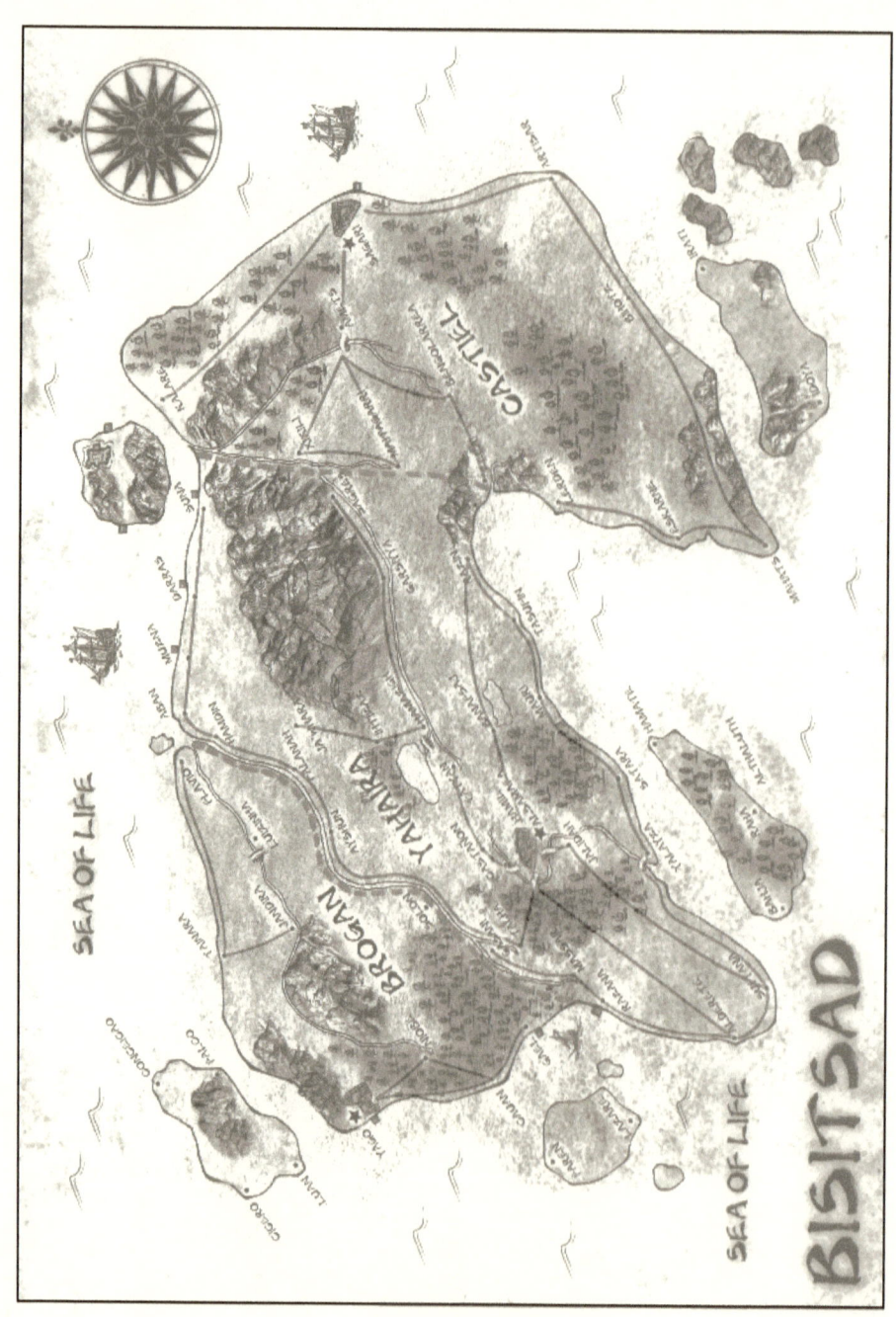

Bisitsad

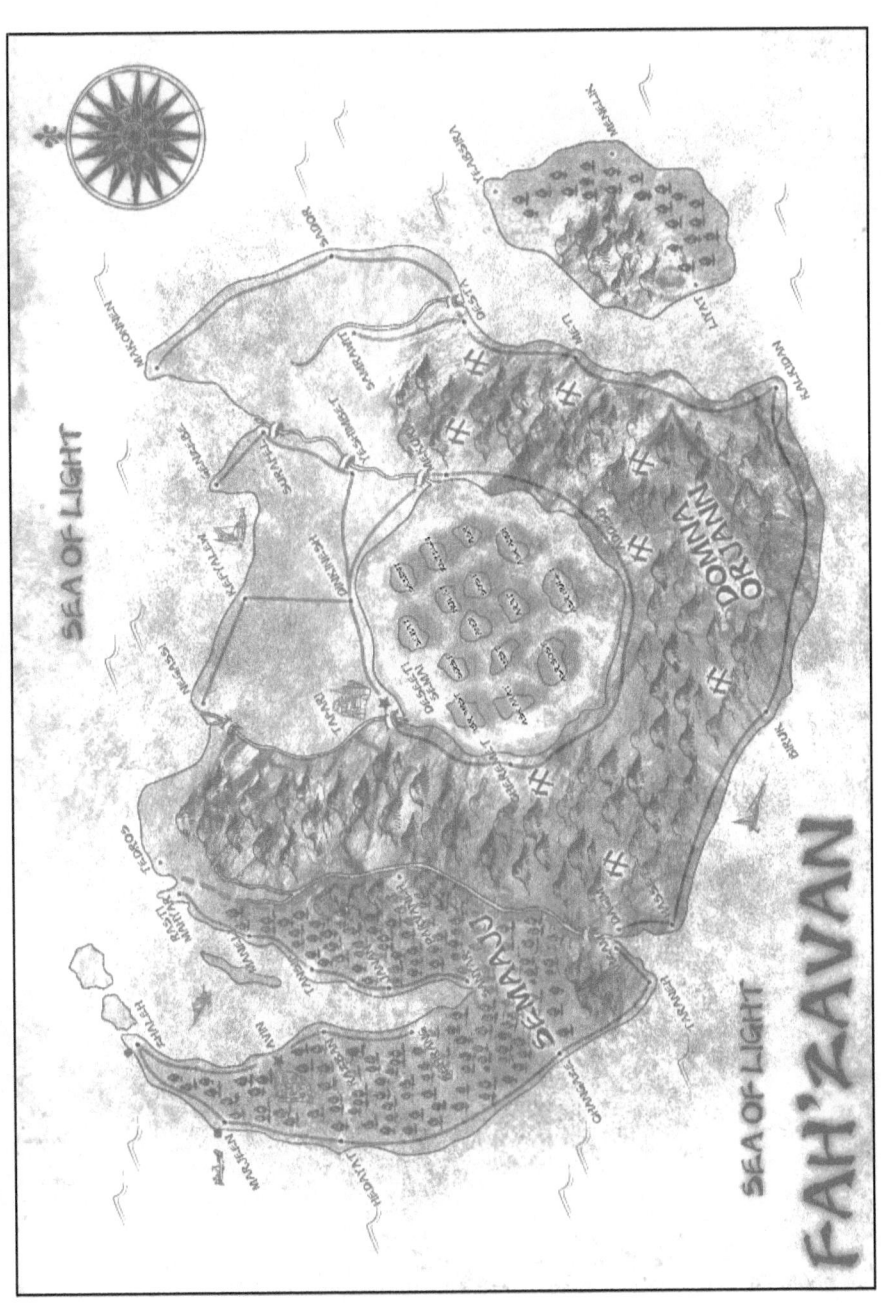

Fah'zavan

PROLOGUE

Abram watched the house from a copse of trees several yards away, hidden in the shadows of early morning. *The man should be out back by now, working with the neighbor. Woman inside with the boys.* He thought about checking on the back of the house, to see if the man had already left, but he didn't dare risk being seen.

For the first few mornings that he'd watched the family and the house, he entertained doubts about whether or not what he was about to do was right. After all, the Orijin had chosen him so many centuries ago because of the goodness that existed in Abram's heart. To do this now, abduct a woman and take her from her family, it broke down those boundaries of good and bad, right and wrong.

Jahmash follows no boundaries. He cannot be defeated by keeping the sides black and white. It's in the grey that he will be stopped. Abram would use the woman to make a request, a noble request that would be the first step toward killing Jahmash. He had come to terms with the fact that even if he appeared right in front of Jahmash with the element of surprise, there was no way he would defeat the Red Harbinger in one-on-one combat. Trying to do so before had almost gotten him killed, and centuries of a combat-free lifestyle surely put him at a severe disadvantage against the man who was once like a brother to him. There would be no duel this time. Abram would use strategy to defeat Jahmash. He would turn Ashur into a weapon, an army, that would stop the Harbinger, no matter how many nations Jahmash recruited to his side.

He had planted seeds centuries ago to ensure that Ashur would be protected, and every now and then, he checked to see how those seeds had grown. Raya Hammersland, the woman in the house, was another seed that needed to be planted.

As the years had gone by over the course of his life, he started to wonder whether he cared so much about protecting *all* of humanity. He knew that if Ashur went to war with Jahmash, thousands upon thousands would likely die. *Perhaps mankind would be less prone to war and violence if the population was smaller. Nothing we did ended up mattering in the long run. Orijin made them this way and then got mad that they've acted according to their nature.* He knew he had to stop Jahmash from killing off Darian's bloodline, but Abram had come to find most of humanity annoying. So many chose to focus on the negative, instead of appreciating life and the world around them. *I suppose immortality allows for a different perspective.*

Abram closed his eyes and softly butted his head against the tree trunk. He had lived for innumerable generations, in a perpetual cycle of making friends, losing friends, falling in love, marrying, having children, leaving his family before questions about aging started, and watching loved ones grow old and die from afar. If anyone else found out about what he was trying to do, they might think he was being brave. Taking a stand. But a big reason for this plan, for this change, was that he was simply tired of immortality and unwilling to take his own life. Rather than just have someone kill him, two thousand years of cowardice and living in shadows would be atoned for by stopping Jahmash from destroying Darian's bloodline.

Orijin, You have not spoken to me in ages, but I have a request, if You still see me. Please forgive what I am about to do. And if it is unforgivable, then please take my intentions into account. If this is irredeemable, then cast me into Oblivion, rather than Opprobrium, as this evil washes away the good I have done.

He stood there, eyes still closed for several moments, and no response came. *Fair enough. I should've expected as much. Perhaps I'll get an answer when we're face to face.* As he ran his hand through his light brown beard and took a deep breath, Abram wondered what the new him would look like, and if he would even have a beard. *That's assuming the Orijin even agrees to any of this. That's assuming the woman doesn't abandon me for the Three Rings.* He looked up from the tree. *Time to find out.*

He looked back at the house and in an instant appeared a foot away from the front door. Just as he extended his hand to grasp the doorknob, the door opened slightly. A pair of eyes peeked through the crack, and as the door opened a little more, the light revealed a face. The fair-skinned woman stepped outside and shut the door behind her. He tensed. *Shit. What is this?*

"You have been vatching our house for days. I vas vondering when you vould finally introduce yourself."

She was nearly a foot shorter than Abram and wore a tattered dress that was clearly not meant for outsiders to see, but she commanded attention. Her slender face was beautiful, despite the black line that stained the left side of her face. Abram shook off the thought; he knew part of his disdain for these 'Descendants' was the jealousy that they were the Orijin's new Harbingers. *Pretenders.* "How did you know?"

She smirked and shrugged slightly, "Intuition, you could say." She stared back at him, her eyes never leaving his. "So vhy are you here? If you vanted to attack, you vould have already."

"How much time do I have to explain?"

"Before I kill you? Or before zhey vonder vhere I am?"

Abram stifled a laugh. Even if he was taking her against her will, it was best not to insult her. "My name is Abram." He paused, expecting her face to change expressions. She didn't disappoint. Her eyes shot up briefly, as if stifling the implications of the name.

"As in, *zhe* Abram, Harbinger of zhe Orijin?"

He could see her trying to work it all out in her mind. He nodded, "The one and only. Look, I know you have your family inside, so let me just tell you my proposal, before things get… complicated." She narrowed her eyes. "I need your help. Jahmash needs to be stopped, and the only way I can sabotage his plans is if I can infiltrate his army and sabotage his plans."

Raya eyed him for a moment. "If you are really you, I vould zhink zhat zhe only vay for you to defeat him vould be to simply appear behind him and impale him vizh your sword. You vould save Ashur in a heartbeat. Vhy all zhese extra steps?" Abram froze, unsure of whether to answer truthfully, or offer some type of contrived excuse. She didn't wait for an answer, "Ah, so zhere is zhe truzh of it. You are afraid of him."

"That's the truth of it," he replied reluctantly.

"Zhere is no reason to feel shame. Zhe whole world fears zhe Red Harbinger. But still, vhy are you here?"

Abram appreciated her encouragement. "If I'm going to go through with it, I need a new body, and maybe a new mind, while still being able to use my abilities. There is only one way to make that happen."

"Zhe Zhree Rings. Zhe Orijin." Her expression remained stoic as she glanced behind her and then back to Abram. "How zid you find me?"

He smirked, "I've had plenty of time to look for the right person."

"I see. And all I have to zo is bring you zhere and back?"

He hesitated, "Of course."

Raya looked at him warily, "No. Zhere's more. Look, I zon't

care *who* you are. You have come to my house and asked for my help. I'm not stupid, so eizher you are honest wizh me, or I vill not help you."

Dammit. She's sharp. She sees right through me. "That's it, I promise. There and back." She stared at him once more, then turned and walked inside, slamming the door behind her. Abram didn't bother with the door and instead reappeared on the other side of it. The room was more spacious than he'd imagined. "Raya, I said that's it. I need you to come with me."

She turned around, already several paces ahead, and glared at him. "And I still zon't believe you. Get out of my house. My husband and children are not part of zhis. And I vant nozhing to zo wizh you, so leave!"

Abram put his palms up and took a breath, then put his hands on his waist. *To defeat Jahmash, we'll have to think like Jahmash. Be more ruthless than him. Do what's necessary. Put the right pieces in place.* "The fate of Ashur depends on this! Depends on *you!*"

Raya clenched her fists as she glowered. She raised her voice to match his, "If *you* cared about zhe fate of zhe vorld, you vould be honest vizh me! You are just playing games, and I zo not have time for zhat. Now go!"

As he was about to respond, Raya's husband entered from around a corner at the back of the room, followed by two little boys no older than a year or two. At second glance, Abram realized they were twins and that one of them was still in the middle of a meltdown, with tears and snot covering his splotchy red face. Raya's husband walked to them and put himself between Abram and Raya, "I don't know who you are, but get the hell out of my house." He held a hammer tightly and cocked his hand.

Abram glanced back at the two boys. The one who wasn't crying stared at him with a deadlocked focus. Abram knew better than to make a move. To get to Raya, he would have to reappear behind her and then disappear again, somewhere far. For a split-second, he thought about where to go, but he realized he already knew the answer to that. There was only one place he knew well, that he could guarantee no one else would intrude. He glanced at Raya, and then looked back at the boy, who was clenching his jaw and fists. As Abram's gaze lingered, he saw the skin near the boy's left eye slowly turning black, forming a vertical line. *Shit. No!*

He disappeared and reappeared right behind Raya before anyone in the room could react, and by the time her husband turned around in response to Raya's gasp, Abram had already disappeared with her. Just before blinking out of the room, Abram swore he saw flames roar up from the ground.

They reappeared amidst a group of serpentfruit trees just next to a clearing. Abram tried to avoid coming to this small island, but it was one of the only places he could come without being bothered and still have some sense of familiarity. *If the fools only knew that I'm not actually buried here. And neither is Darian. At least Lionel wouldn't be offended that his body rests here alone.*

A slap across the face brought him back to the present. "Vhere are ve? Vhere zid you bring me? Ve have to go back! Zid you not see! My house is on fire! I need to save my family!"

Abram rubbed his jaw; it had been quite a while since someone had managed to strike him. He couldn't be upset about the slap, though. He deserved it, and it likely brought Raya some satisfaction. He grasped the immediacy of her concern and traveled back to her house, leaving her behind. In the same room where he'd left Raya's husband and children, a fire had spread throughout the room. He luckily had appeared less than a foot away from a wall of flames, and on the other side of them was Raya's husband. Somehow, the man had gotten separated from the two little boys, who cowered toward the back of the room, near the back door. Another wall of flame separated father and sons.

Suddenly the back door flung open and another man stormed in and pulled the boys out. Abram tried to figure out how to help get Raya's husband, but there was barely any space to reappear without landing in flames. The man was too far from him to reach out and grasp. Raya's husband desperately looked back and forth between Abram and the back door, until finally he dashed through the fire, away from Abram. Abram ensured the man escaped the house before disappearing from the room.

He reappeared exactly where he stood when he left Raya, and saw her kneeling on the ground, with her hands clasped and eyes closed. "They're all safe. I saw them all leave the house myself."

Raya sprang to her feet, "Zhis vould not even be a concern if not for you. Zhey vere in danger *because* of you! Zon't try to pretend zhat you are zhe hero. Vere you not a Harbinger vonce? Vhat happened to you? You vere supposed to be zhe Orijin's chosen vones. First Jahmash killed zhe ozhers, and now you kidnap me? How could zhis be?"

"I didn't kidnap you." He shook his head, "I promise you, this is all to stop Jahmash. I promise you that my intentions are good." *Even if my actions will not be.* Deep down, a sense of guilt lay buried about her husband and sons. But those feelings would stay buried for as long as he needed to see this plan through. "Look, all you need to do is take me to the center of the Three Rings to see the Orijin. Can you do that? Can you bring another person with you?"

"And vhat if I zon't cooperate?"

His patience was starting to tire. "Then I leave you here. You can stay here and keep Lionel's corpse company for the rest of your life. Serpentfruits are rather tasty, but you'll get tired of them if you have to live off them. Might be able to learn to fish. I don't know." Part of him almost hoped that Raya would choose to stay here. It would be a much easier life than what he planned to do with her.

"You zon't plan to…have you vay vizh me? Nozhing like zhat?"

Abram allowed himself to chuckle at that. "Raya, that's not my way. I've lived for millennia. Had a number of wives and lovers. I didn't come to you for that. And while you are a beautiful woman, it would be a lot easier to find someone without a husband and children if I was looking to do that."

His assurance seemed to calm her down. He couldn't tell whether she expected to see her family again, but Abram wasn't about to ask. After a moment, Raya nodded. "I have never tried to bring anyvone vizh me, but it may vork zhe same vay as how you travel. Maybe if ve are in physical contact, it vill vork."

The details of it all made him curious. "How exactly *does* it all work? Do you simply disappear and reappear the way I do?"

She shook her head. "It is not a physical place. Only my soul travels, and my body is left behind. I zon't know how you vant zhe Orijin to help you, but I suppose if anyone can zo it, zhe Orijin can."

"The soul?" *Hopefully I still have one of those.* "Alright, well then let's get this over with. What happens to your body when you go?"

Raya shrugged, "It goes limp. Like I'm in a deep sleep or dead even. I've learned to lie down when I zo it, so I zon't return to any injuries." She laid down on the ground next to a tree and waved her hand as an invitation for him to do the same. "Zhe soul is made up of light and energy. I vill have to see how I can draw yours out." Abram lay on the ground next to her, close enough that she could easily reach him with her right arm. He relaxed his body and watched her, waiting for her to start the process. "Close your eyes. Focus on your life force. Your soul."

He followed her orders and tried to focus. He barely felt her hand on his torso. As the moments passed, he felt as if the energy was draining from his body. He started to feel a certain lightness and began to wonder whether this was what dying felt like. As the thought left his mind, he realized he could see everything around him. He didn't remember opening his eyes, not to mention standing up. As he turned his head, he saw himself lying on the ground, next to Raya. Despite the shock, he felt complete calmness.

Finally, he looked at what he thought was his body. Instead of flesh, he was simply light. His soul resembled his physical self, though completely naked, and there seemed to be a pulse of energy that continuously flowed throughout him. He examined what he assumed was his soul, and the dim light consisted of various white, yellow, and blue hues, all intertwined with each other.

Abram looked around, wondering where Raya was. Her soul floated a few feet away, facing him, except hers seemed noticeably brighter than his. There were no eyes visible on her 'face,' and he assumed the same must be the case for him. Instead, just indentations where her eyes would be. As he focused more on the sensation of sight, Abram realized what he perceived around him was more of an awareness than actually seeing. He could somehow sense everything around him.

Are you ready?

The voice, if that's what it could be called, was all around him, though he knew it came from Raya's soul. He tried to respond by speaking, and mouthed the words, but the sound came from his whole being. *I can't believe it worked. Yes, I am ready. Will it take long to get there?*

Raya floated closer to him and grasped his forearm with her hand. A spark of energy flared up at the contact, but there was no physical sensation. She offered no response. Instead, they beamed away from their bodies, into the sky. The sensation was similar to when he traveled by disappearing and reappearing. They were surrounded by streaks of innumerable colors. He had no idea whether they'd traveled for seconds, hours, or days, but by the time they stopped, Abram sensed a powerful light and energy ahead of him, the same as that which made up his soul.

Ve are here. Zhe Zhree Rings.

Abram couldn't help but wonder again, *Is this the same sensation as dying?* He couldn't be sure whether he thought or spoke the notion, but he supposed there was no difference in this form.

I could not tell you. I have never died before.

He opened himself to everything in front of him. They were massive circles of light and energy, almost as if they were composed of the same light and energy as he was. Abram sensed everything around him again and realized that they were among the stars. Bright spots littered the massive expanse all around him, and he wondered whether any of them were the same as those he looked up at when he took in the night sky. He wondered if the Three Rings themselves were one of the bright stars he saw in the sky.

Raya answered the question that he didn't realize he'd asked. *Yes. Zhe Zhree Rings are visible to every vorld. Vhen ve look up at zhe night sky, ve can see zhem.*

But how? And how could you know that?

Vonce you enter zhe Zhree Rings, you become avare of certain truzhs of existence. I cannot explain it, but maybe you vill experience it vonce ve enter.

Abram focused on the Rings once more. He was surprised that they all intersected one another, though. He'd always imagined that they were placed one atop another. Two rings were oppositely diagonal, while the third was horizontal, and all three intersected at the same point. The pulsating light and energy made it seem as if they were spinning like wheels. Similar beams of light streaked toward the Rings every so often, and they simply absorbed the incoming lights.

Are those...

Raya didn't let him finish, *Yes. Zhe souls of zhe newly dead.*

Let's go do this, then. I don't want to stay here longer than is necessary. Abram decided at that moment that he was in no rush to enter the Three Rings. The sense of finality almost scared him out of what he was about to request.

Raya's hand was still connected to his forearm, and they streaked ahead like beams of light once again. They traveled too fast for Abram to sense anything clearly in any particular Ring. He'd wondered whether he would encounter anyone he knew, and had been nervous about any potential interactions, but Raya was seemingly only focused on getting him to where he asked to go and he was thankful for her expedience.

Again they stopped, and once more, Abram had no sense of the time it took to travel from outside the Three Rings to the center of them. This time, he floated in an empty expanse in the middle of the Rings. The space that he occupied seemed large enough to fit a whole world, if he was sensing it correctly. Only then did he realize that Raya had let go of his arm, and he floated there alone. Abram sensed her behind him, in the distance. He wondered whether, if she left him, he could even find his way back to his own body. He changed his focus to why he was here. *The Orijin must exist somewhere in this expanse. But how do I speak to Him? Are my thoughts and voice still one and the same? Orijin? Are you there?* He waited for a moment. *It is your Harbinger, Abram. I have come to make a humble request.*

He floated there for several moments, unsure of whether he wasn't communicating properly, or whether the Orijin simply didn't want to talk to him. As he continued to focus on the vastness in front of him, a streak of vertical light split open the black nothingness. The line of light expanded and curved until it formed a ring of light, made up of every color Abram had ever seen, and more that he had never even imagined. The ring of light grew again and then spun on its own axis. When it finally stopped, it was a globe of light and energy, similar to that which Abram's soul was made of, except with all of the colors that it had before.

The ball of energy and light could have been its own world, for all Abram knew. The light moved in innumerable patterns and the energy, like that of Abram's and Raya's souls, pulsed throughout the globe.

Abram. The voice boomed, so strong that it paused the movement and pulsing of Abram's soul. It spoke simultaneously in every language Abram had ever known. The force of it was stronger than anything Abram had felt before, and yet, it was almost as if the voice had flowed right through him. ***Abram Feroze, of Our Chosen. You brought peace to your world. And then let it rot. You lived for millennia on Our Grace alone, taking advantage of Our kindness. Why do you come to Us now?***

Orijin. Though I am a Harbinger, I am also only human. With human qualities and faults. I was strong enough to help fix the world, but then too weak to accept death at Jahmash's hands. That's why I'm here before You. I would like to stop him. With Your help and blessing, of course.

We have put new Harbingers in place to stop Jahmash. New creations. Why would they need your help?

Abram paused for a moment before responding. He had expected that the Orijin would question his intentions and methods. *Orijin, I have spent time with him. Befriended him. Come to know him like a brother. And most importantly, I have fought him. That is invaluable experience to anyone or anything You have put in place. I am not saying I can or will do this alone. I simply want to help.*

Why? After all this time? Why should We not keep you here and let you spend your existence in Oblivion?

You are the God of all Creation, Orijin. I cannot argue with Your will. But I only ask for a chance to redeem myself. I lived as a coward for centuries. I have finally understood how to atone for my cowardice. Please, all that I ask of You is to provide me with a new body, so that I would be unrecognizable to Jahmash. I could then form a new identity, with a new name, and infiltrate his ranks. Gain his trust.

You wish for Us to provide you with a new body. And keep the same manifestation.

Yes, Orijin, if it can be done.

You have no concept of what can be done. But very well. We shall provide you with a new human body, built to withstand your manifestation. It shall be delivered to where your current body rests. Once your soul enters that body, you will possess your own mind as well as the memories of that man. It is the only way you will fool Jahmash.

Abram somehow felt relief flow through his soul. But he knew there was more to this. *Thank you, Orijin. But I know this shall come at a cost. What is Your price?*

This is Our price. You will now be a mortal man. Once you enter your new body, you will live, breath, hurt, and age just as anyone else. Once you die, you will come to the Three Rings and spend eternity in Oblivion. That was what you requested before coming here. However, if you abuse Our gifts and stray from the path of Goodness, then you will reside in Opprobrium, where you will be punished for eternity.

I understand Your terms. And I accept. What happens now? By the time Abram finished the thought, he was somehow seized by the Orijin. Streaks of light and sizzling energy extended from the globe and grasped his soul by the limbs, torso, neck and head. Surprisingly, he felt the pain of it, as if the light and energy of his own soul were burning. He felt the sear in every fiber of his soul, and just like when Raya was leading him here, Abram had no concept of whether this was happening for seconds, minutes, or hours. Once the tendrils of light and energy finally released him, Abram knew something was different. He couldn't sense the exact change or sensation, except that he felt redesigned. Rebuilt. Reborn.

Abram Feroze, you are reborn as Adl Maqdhuum. We have remade you so that you may bring justice to your world. In your old tongue, your name means "Master of Justice." See that you live up to it. And remember Our terms. Now go.

Before Abram could think of an appropriate response, a bright light flared from the Orijin and then he was surrounded by all of the brilliant colors he had seen while traveling here with Raya. The colors disappeared as quickly as they came, and Abram realized that all of the sensations he'd felt as his soul were now gone. He felt the physicality of a body and had to make an effort to open his eyes.

Even his mind seemed more full. He remembered the Orijin saying that he would absorb the other man's mind and memories, and it certainly felt like he was sharing his head with someone else. *This will take some getting used to.*

As he looked above, the sight of Raya standing over him made him convulse. She smiled at seeing him startled. "You vere more handsome before. Good zhing you von't have to live forever looking like zhis."

He rolled his eyes and sat up. It would likely be a while before he could see what he looked like. Instead, he looked beside him and saw his former body, now lying lifeless on the ground. "I *was* handsome. I suppose this is rare, though. Not too many people get to actually look at themselves from outside their bodies." He paused and looked up at Raya, "Thank you. I've lived for over two thousand years, and yet, that was a new experience for me."

"I still zon't trust you, but I have some qvestions. Zhe Orijin uses 'Ve' and 'Our' instead of 'I'. Vhy is zhat?"

Abram considered her question for a moment. He wasn't entirely sure how to explain it. "The Orijin transcends a single entity or gender. The Orijin is a part of everything in existence, almost like the energy that makes everything what it is. Orijin is not he, she, or it. The Orijin is everything all at once. I'm not sure if I can give a proper explanation. Words limit the understanding of it."

"I zhink I know vhat you mean. It makes sense. Ve as humans make up so many rules for life, zhat ve forget ve are not zhe only zhings zhat exist." She paused for a moment. "Now you should be honest vizh me."

He finally stood up, glancing back and forth between her and his new body. "Honest about what?"

She stared at him coldly. "Vhat else zo you need from me? Vill I be killed? Or tortured? Or somezhing even vorse?"

He was about to respond when he stopped himself. *No. The time for pleasantries is done. If I want to get anywhere with this mission, I have to be able to be cold. I have to channel that side of me. They used to call me 'The Untamed Harbinger.'" Time to be untamed again.* "I'm taking you to Jahmash."

Raya's smile was gone in an instant. "You cannot be serious? For vhat?"

He put a hand up to stop more questions. "It's not what you think. My first plan is to offer to have you take him to the Three Rings. See if he's interested in making any resolutions with Darian, Lionel, and the Orijin."

"And if he's not interested?"

Abram shrugged. "Then figure out a different way to get him to like 'Adl Maqdhuum.'"

"And vhat comes first? Vill you bury your body, or punish me?"

He looked at her curiously. "What do you mean?"

"Just answer zhe qvestion."

She's starting to make it easy to be shitty to her. "Well, I made a deal with the nurses in Domna Orjann that when I die, they can have my body. I would imagine this still counts. They want to examine it to learn whether there's anything different about my insides than that of a *normal* person."

She cut him off. "Zhis should not come as any surprise, but I zon't care about your ozher plans. So zhis whole plan to use me as a gift, let us get it done now."

He knew she saw through his attempts at friendliness. A thought entered his mind. "Wait. How much time has passed since we left for the Three Rings?"

Raya was visibly annoyed at him, but she turned to look at the water in the distance and answered anyway, "Zhere is no vay for me to know unless ve vent back to my home. Time vorks differently vonce ve leave zhis vorld. Time in zhe Zhree Rings seems to go more slowly. So if ve vere zhere for a few hours, ve might only be gone from here for a few minutes. But, zhis vas zhe longest I've ever stayed zhere, and I zon't know how to measure how long ve vere zhere." She turned back to face him.

Abram nodded and waved his hand, "It *is* still morning, though, just like when we left."

She rolled her eyes at him. "It is morning, but vhich morning? It could be zhe same day, zhe next day, or a veek later. Vhy does it matter?"

"Time matters to me now. I'm a mortal. Everything is limited. Well, no matter which day it is, we'll go to Jahmash tomorrow. I need a day or so to sort out my mind. I have a new person up here," he tapped his head with a finger. "I need to make sure I know how everything works before seeing Jahmash. If he wants to enter my mind and I can't shut my own mind off, then this whole plan will be over before it can even start."

Raya turned back to face him. She spoke calmly, but coldly. "I have come to understand zhat I vill likely never see my family again. Zon't zhink I zidn't see vhat happened in my house before ve left. My son, Baltaszar, gained a manifestation because of you. Two years old, and he has a manifestation. Zhat is unheard of. Most children zon't get zhem until at least six years. Zhat is vhat you created. You gave my *baby* a manifestation. Imagine zhe dangers of a baby vielding fire. And I hope zhat vone day, *before* you die, he manages to find you and burn your new body. Vhat you are about to zo to me is unforgivable. How can you guarantee zhat Jahmash von't hurt me or kill me?"

He was getting tired of trying to be nice. He knew it was a failed strategy, and there was no way to paint his actions in a favorable or noble light. "You are not playing a game with regular people. This is a Harbinger of the Orijin. He is more than human. He is better than you. Stronger. Smarter. And most importantly, he follows no code. He turned on us. We saved the world together, and he betrayed us for it. You, just like everyone else in Ashur, are *expendable*."

Once again, she cut him off. "So zhen vhat are you trying to save? If Ashur is expendable, zhen vhat exactly are you stopping Jahmash from zoing?"

Now he was starting to feel wild. Untamed. "You forget. The Orijin had to step in twice already to try and save humanity. Jahmash and I only exist because you are all so petty, so insecure. My interest is in saving *some* of you. But if even half of Ashur and all the nations beyond it lose their lives in this war, then better for it. Gideon turned himself to stone to set an example, and every life you take in conflict spits on his sacrifice. So perhaps humanity needs to begin again."

She unclenched her jaw. Abram was glad that she had no weapon on her, else she likely would have used it already. "So you are *almost* as bad as him, zhen. Vhat chance do ve have if two Harbingers now vant to kill humanity, razher zhan save it?" She paused for a moment, and the tension in her face eased. "But you know vhat? I vill put my faizh in zhe Orijin. Zhe Orijn could have refused you. But clearly He saw somezhing vorthvhile, because He agreed to your reqvest. So if zhis is ze vill of zhe Orijin, zhen I vill acqviesce. Zhere is nozhing you or Jahmash could zo to me zhat vill break me. So zo vhat you must, *Adl Maqdhuum.*"

He considered her words. *Exactly. The Orijin has to see something redeeming in my plan, to have agreed with it. Or maybe He just looks forward to putting me in Opprobrium. It doesn't matter. No guilt. No remorse. No Abram. Only Adl Maqdhuum. Dammit, that's a stupid first name.* "Just Maqdhuum. And I appreciate your perspective. It will definitely make things easier. To be fair, your son, Baltaszar, will never know who I am or what happened between us. His only memory of all this is of a man whose body no longer exists. There will be no revenge."

CHAPTER 1
BEYOND THE DROWNED REALM

*From **The Book of Orijin**, **Verse One***
O, Mankind. We are the Creator of everything. You are not insignificant. Everything you do, every decision you make, affects everything around you.
Live for what is righteous and good, and know that when you stray, there is always a path back to righteousness.

Maqdhuum eyed the eight men as they cautiously left the table and walked closer to face him. He maintained his wide grin as they glared at him, though his mortal cheeks were starting to hurt from it. He put his foot back down and clasped his hands, hoping that the Vithelegion generals would understand that he was still calm and had no interest in attacking.

Part of him regretted being here, especially because he was pretty sure how this would end. However, with the revelation that Horatio's very existence was his fault, Maqdhuum needed to do this. Either the Vithelegion would agree to follow him, or it would try to kill him for having the audacity to suggest they follow him. Either outcome was a welcome one to him.

Saol Suldas continued slowly toward him, "What did you say? You expect us to believe that you are Abram? The Harbinger of Orijin?" Suldas knelt down on one knee right in front of him.

Maqdhuum finally relinquished his smile. "I am Abram Feroze, of the Five, Chosen Harbinger of the Orijin. I expected that I would have to prove myself, which is why I went through all that trouble of taking your swords. Obviously I could have easily killed you all in the process, but I would rather lead you and work with you than cause more conflict."

Saol nodded and rested both of his hands on his knee. Maqdhuum noticed that all the generals and Saol were in full armor, with the exception of their helmets. Saol met his eyes, "If you are in fact Abram, then why are you alive? Your legend has been passed down for centuries as a hero who died fighting Jahmash. Fighting for the coward Darian, who used you to escape."

They think Darian was a coward? What the hell is wrong with them? "Darian was no coward. He saved countless lives by drawing

Jahmash away from the main cities of Iman Qaja. I chose to fight for Darian. It was the only way to distract Jahmash and give Darian enough of a head start so that Jahmash wouldn't be able to easily catch him."

"Then how is it that you and Jahmash both survived? Surely you would have fought him to the death, my beloved Harbinger."

Maqdhuum nodded his head. Saol had already given away his intentions. "I disappeared before Jahmash could kill me." He paused for a moment, noticing the change in Saol's countenance. The Vithelegion man was making a poor attempt at masking his disdain. "I can see you think that I am a coward. But dying would not have solved anything." As Maqdhuum attempted to explain his cowardice, Saol signaled for the other Vithelegion men to come closer. The other seven men knelt around Maqdhuum, just as Saol did, with both hands resting on one knee.

Saol spoke before Maqdhuum could continue. "You have come here to tell us that you are Abram, Harbinger of the Orijin, but that cannot be true. The man we follow was better than you have claimed. Abram would not have cowered in such a battle. Abram would have died trying to defeat his opponent, especially one as formidable as Jahmash. He would have done everything to kill him. That is why the man we follow could not possibly be you." Saol looked around at the other men, which caused Maqdhuum to do so as well. He put a hand on Maqdhuum's knee, then nodded to the other seven men who knelt around Maqdhuum.

Maqdhuum briefly thought about disappearing, even just to reappear a few feet away, but to do so would prove to them that he was weak. *They need to see that I'm strong. And more importantly, I need to endure this.* As Maqdhuum's eyes shifted around at the others, they inched closer and closer to him. Finally, he set his eyes upon Saol Suldas again. The man met his gaze.

Saol continued, his face a stone, "And if you are here and you are not Abram, then you are an intruder. And you are trespassing upon the most sacred location of this camp. For that, imposter, you must pay." As the last word left Saol's lips, the man flicked his wrist that rested atop Maqdhuum's knee, and a blade stabbed right through his knee. Just as his grimace turned into a scream, seven other blades repeatedly stabbed Maqdhuum all over his body to the point that he couldn't tell where he wasn't hurt. He collapsed from the chair and crumbled to the floor. Saol Suldas nudged him onto his back with the front of his boot, and Maqdhuum lay face-up, groggily staring at the man. "The last time a man tried to get the best of me, it was one of my own generals. I made the mistake of not killing him. He ended up costing me soldiers' lives in one of our sieges. I left him to die and rot in an inn. I won't make the mistake of letting you live." Just as Saol knelt down and put a knee on Maqdhuum's bloody chest, Maqdhuum's heavy eyes closed and everything went black.

**

Bo'az stood on a circular platform with Aric, Hansi, and Deacon in the middle of a circle of robed Casteyan elders. The elders sat in wooden chairs adorned with red and yellow cushions; their platform slowly rotating around Bo'az and his companions. On the ground, disheveled men and women pushed spokes that extended out from the platform at intervals. They slowly walked around and around, continuously spinning the outer platform where the elders sat. *Servants? Slaves? What kind of society is this?*

He writhed his bound wrists, hoping to loosen the knot. Each of the four of them had their hands bound behind their backs, but the Casteyans had assured that it was precautionary, until they were sure that Bo'az and the others wouldn't attack. Almost as bad as the chafing of his wrists was that he desperately wanted to scratch his beard and move his hair from his face. While still with Jahmash, he'd actually had the privilege of regularly shaving and trimming his hair. However, neither of those had happened for the duration of the voyage to Castiel. The beard did help protect his face from high winds out at sea, though. The Casteyans had allowed Bo'az and his companions to keep their black coats on, thankfully. The air held a chill even without the wind, and Bo'az suspected that Castiel was simply a colder nation than Ashur.

The complexion of most of the Casteyans was not much different than the light brown of Bo'az's skin tone, except that theirs was a shade lighter. Bo'az thought of his father, who was somewhat darker than him, and a flashing image of his mother passed through his mind. She had disappeared when he and Baltaszar were around two years old, and he barely had a real memory of her. Every now and then, a glimpse of her would show up in his memories, but never anything much longer than a heartbeat. He remembered her having fair skin and golden hair and understood why his skin was lighter than his father's. He never really bothered to talk to his father or Baltaszar about the glimpses of her. His father avoided any conversations about her and any mention of her tended to put him in a foul mood.

The elders were referred to as the "Hemeretzi", and Bo'az counted twelve of them. Linas stood on the ground outside of the revolving circle, tended to by a few young men and women. He wondered if any of them might be Linas's daughters. He also wondered if this business was actually happening on the street in the middle of a city. One of the young women looked up at Bo'az and held her gaze upon his eyes. Her flat expression didn't allow for any obvious interpretation. *She might want to kiss me or kill me.* Bo'az shook his head quickly but vigorously, trying to rid it of the mild dizziness. *If this whole revolving thing is meant to disorient us, it's working. These elders are not even rotating that fast.*

Focus, Bo'az.

He blinked a few times and shook his head once more. Jahmash's voice sobered him and reminded Bo'az of why he was here in the first place. He let thoughts of the girl slip from his mind. The elders had finally stopped whispering back and forth between themselves. Their accents were strange, but not difficult to understand. Bo'az was surprised that they spoke the same language as the Ashurian common tongue, but then again, up until he'd met Jahmash, he didn't even know there were civilizations beyond Ashur. Even worse, it was only months before that revelation that he found out there was a world beyond Haedon.

The elder directly in front of him spoke first. "Bo'az Kontez. You have proclaimed yourself the emissary of Jahmash, and hail from the Drowned Realm itself. A harbinger of *The* Harbinger. Do you speak on his behalf?"

Bo'az nodded hesitantly. "I do."

The woman next to the first elder spoke, though now she was directly in front of him, as they continued to revolve. "Do you speak for your three companions as well?"

Bo'az nodded again. "Yes."

"Then what do the markings on their faces mean? And why are there none on yours?"

He paused. *Probably shouldn't mention magic right from the start.* "It is common in Ashur to tattoo our faces. That is all. It is a matter of personal taste. I don't care for them, though I pass no judgment on anyone who prefers them."

The next elder to rotate in front of him spoke; this time it was a man. "You have submitted to our demands so far, with no inclination to violence toward us. We have had your ship searched, and there

existed no evidence of an invasion or of any harm intended to Castiel."
By the time he was done speaking, the Hemeretzi had completed a
whole revolution around them, and the man was in front of Bo'az once
again.

The next elder spoke and only then did Bo'az notice that the
twelve Hemeretzi sat alternating between man and woman. "Why have
you come here, Bo'az Kontez? What is it that you, or *Jahmash*, wants
of the city of Sagari? Or have you come with a request for all of
Castiel?" Each elder so far spoke in the same even-keeled tone. The
only differences between them were the actual voices.

They are not surprised about any of this. Bo'az looked up at the
elder who posed the question as she slowly passed to his right. "We
have come on behalf of Jahmash, Harbinger of the Orijin, to request the
help of the Casteyan army." He continued to stare ahead of him, at
whichever elder was in front of him at the time. "Jahmash seeks justice
from the people of Ashur, who chose to honor the charlatan, Darian,
instead of him. He seeks revenge against the descendants of Darian, the
false Harbinger who led him on a chase for days, then cowardly trapped
Jahmash on an island to live for millennia in solitude, instead of
mercifully killing him."

The next Hemeretzi in front of Bo'az didn't hesitate to respond.
"And why does he seek the help of Castiel specifically? Why not other
nations?"

"You are simply the first nation we are visiting. We intend to
ask the same favor in Yahaira and Brogan. Then we will sail north to
Orol Taghdras, to meet with five nations there."

"Only five? Which nation are you omitting?"

"Vitheligia has already arrived on the shores of Ashur to mount
its own attack. However, we cannot be sure whether their motive is
related to Jahmash's or not."

"And what of Fah'Zavan?"

Bo'az had rehearsed all of this almost daily since they'd left
Jahmash. He expected everything they'd asked so far. Fah'Zavan was
another island to the east, which was home to the nations of Semaajj
and Domna Orjann. "Jahmash's sources have told him that Semaajj and
Domna Orjann are loyal to Darian and his descendants. It would be a
waste of time, and perhaps our lives, to go there with such a request."

Another elder responded, "It should be pointed out that Ashur
has done nothing to us. In fact, it is quite likely that they do not know

that we even exist. Why sacrifice our own soldiers to start a war against a kingdom that is not our enemy?"

"Yet."

"Yet?"

Bo'az clarified, "Ashur is not your enemy *yet*. However, in the past year, they have started sending out ships from their eastern shores. So far, these have been peaceful endeavors for the rich and bored, looking to live a life of comfort at sea. However, it is only a matter of time before they see your shores and return home with news of other realms. Ashur is much bigger than this whole island of Bisitsad, and the Ashurian king is petty enough to kill his own people for even the smallest offenses. If he chose to focus his attention on you, he could send an army bigger than yours, the Brogani's and the Yahairans' combined."

"You present a compelling argument, Bo'az Kontez. But more importantly than this *possibility* of a threat, what are Jahmash's terms? How do we benefit from helping him?"

"First, Jahmash only requests half of your army. He understands that your nation must still be protected. He will make the same request of all the other nations, so you need not worry about being overpowered. You would have about six months to prepare before sailing northeast. Additionally, Castiel will stake a claim in Ashur. The seven nations of Ashur will be split amongst the nations who back Jahmash. Ideally that will be eight, but we cannot know for sure until we meet with each nation. You will have all of those resources, riches, and survivors at your disposal. Jahmash wants nothing for himself aside from the satisfaction of victory."

"You mentioned that the Vithelegion is already there. What of them?"

Bo'az paused. That was one thing that had not been discussed. He'd only even found out about the Vithelegion invasion from Jahmash while sailing. *That is up to the Vithelegion and whether they choose to side with us.* He was actually glad that Jahmash was in his head. It took away the need for any improvisation.

"Their fate is in their own hands. If they choose to fight Jahmash's forces, then they will cease to exist."

The next elder nodded, as if satisfied. "Is that the entirety of your offer, Bo'az Kontez?"

Bo'az nodded once more. "It is."

The next elder squinted at him, as if skeptical. "Your offer is enticing, Bo'az Kontez, as long as it is real."

Bo'az cocked his head in confusion. "Meaning?"

"Meaning that you must prove what you say. How can we possibly know that you were sent here from Jahmash?"

Say nothing. I will handle this. Bo'az did as Jahmash told him and just stood there. From the ground, several feet away, he heard a commotion of voices until finally Linas came walking toward the platform without any assistance. Bo'az almost forgot that the man had no eyes and realized that that was part of what would convince the Hemeretzi. Linas walked all the way up to the platform and, without interfering with any of the men and women who were rotating it, hoisted himself onto it. He then walked to the center part where Bo'az stood and patted Bo'az on the shoulder. A din rose from beyond the platform as several bystanders on the ground and street started to chatter to each other.

The eyeless, statuesque man turned to face the Hemeretzi and finally spoke. "Though I cannot see your faces, I am sure that it was clear to you since I arrived that I have lost my eyes. Years ago, Gibreel Casteghar and I were given the honor of helping Jahmash in his quest for justice. He bestowed upon us a special mission in Ashur, in which we were tasked with finding a very special young man who could help Jahmash cross the seas and reach Ashur. However, we were tricked into believing that Bo'az was that young man and brought him to face Jahmash. Gibreel, unfortunately, did not survive the journey. However, while Jahmash was quite disappointed in our failure, he saw the value in Bo'az and kept the young man as an advisor, when he could have easily killed the lad. In my failure and embarrassment for disappointing such a great man, I ripped out my own eyes, which I believed to be a fitting punishment for being tricked so easily. Even then, Jahmash felt my sadness and anguish, and generously sent me back here with these young men, knowing that I would be reunited with my family again. Jahmash is the very reason I stand before you today. It is even because of Jahmash that I was able to get onto this platform to be able to tell you this story." With that, Linas walked toward the edge of the revolving platform, jumped down to the ground, and landed squarely on his feet.

Bo'az shifted his gaze back to the Hemeretzi, who all also watched Linas's departure from the platform. Finally they looked back at Bo'az and he spoke up. "Is that enough proof for you?"

The elder who was currently passing in front of him responded, "Yes. That was quite thorough."

For the first time since they'd arrived, Bo'az smiled. "And you will consider our request now?"

The next passing elder answered, "There is one final requirement. We need to know that you are serious. That Jahmash is serious."

The elder next to her continued. "We need to know that Jahmash is willing to make the same sacrifices that we are being asked to make."

Bo'az furrowed his brow. "Please explain."

The next elder spoke, "Jahmash wishes for our army to sail to war, during which our soldiers could die at any point, from the time they leave our shores. We are being asked to make a great sacrifice."

The next Hemeretzi continued, "We require the same sacrifice of Jahmash."

Bo'az still didn't fully grasp what they were asking. *What sacrifice?*

Once again, Jahmash clarified things for him. ***One of you. They want me to offer up one of you to be sacrificed to them.***

What? As in, killing one of us? That's evil! That's so disgusting! And...

And fair. It is only fair that they would ask this of us. I am asking the same of them.

Bo'az let out a deep breath. "How is this sacrifice supposed to be determined? And if we actually agree to this, do we have your word? You will fight for Jahmash?"

"If you agree, then we will convene with the other cities that protect the Casteyan shores to come to a decision. And you would have an answer within a week."

Bo'az's eyes shot wide open. He would have raised his arms had they not been tied behind his back, and it shifted his focus back to his wrists. They chafed to the point where he could feel the burn where his skin was being rubbed away. "A week?"

Calm yourself. A week is reasonable, given the travel time needed.

Killing one of us should guarantee it, though?

It should, and it likely will. They are about to test the three of you who survive even more. In the next week, you will be their guests and they will be able to determine the true character of each of you. Especially when you are not being bound and questioned.

"It will take time for leaders from the other three cities to arrive here and discuss this weighty decision. Once they all arrive and we have a chance to meet, the decision process itself will not take long."

Bo'az sighed again. "Very well. I understand. So now what? Do you choose or do we?" He could hear and feel the other three growing restless around him. None of them wanted to die as a sacrifice in a land so far away from their home.

The elder before him stated, just as dryly as everything else they'd said, "If you cannot choose, then of course we shall do so for you. You may turn to one another and choose amongst yourselves."

Each of them were already mumbling to themselves by the time they all turned to face each other. Just as Bo'az was about to start a proclamation about why it shouldn't be him, Deacon spoke up over Aric and Hansi. "Let me zo it. It needs to be me. Especially after vhat I zid on zhe ship. Killing all of zhose men and letting you be punished for it. You boys have to let me volunteer."

"But…" Bo'az was surprised at how quickly he realized what was going on. *Don't do this. At least let him decide for himself. Please.*

*You and I both know that he wouldn't volunteer on his own. He is too arrogant. Or would you rather your companions nominate you? I can let it be any of you. And I can already see into that tiny pocket that you've tried to tuck away into the corner of your mind. You **want** it to be him.*

I don't want any of us to die. But I'd rather it be him than me. Bo'az would've liked to think that, given the same option not too long ago, he wouldn't have felt bad about something like this, but even the notion of maturity wasn't enough to make this situation any better. He looked at Hansi and Aric, both of whom shared glances back and forth as well. Surprisingly, Jahmash was attempting to make this process easier for them, and somehow that was only making it worse. Aric nodded to Deacon. Hansi simply said, "I'm sorry my friend."

Bo'az looked him in the eyes, hoping that some part of Deacon's mind heard him and understood. "We won't forget you." He was about to absolve Deacon for murdering all of those men on the ship, but a sharp pain in his mind quickly stopped it. "Thank you for doing this, Deacon."

Bo'az stepped aside as Deacon walked toward the elder. "I volunteer. I honor Jahmash and zhe prospect of your union. Let me be zhe sacrifice zhat needs to be made. Let my zeath usher in a new age for zhe whole vorld."

The elder before him smiled, something Bo'az hadn't known was possible. "Very well. We thank you for your sacrifice." He turned to a group of yellow-robed people kneeling on the ground several feet away, "Morroi! Come. Take our guest here and prepare him for sacrifice."

Once again, Bo'az was stricken with curiosity. *Is this something they do often? There's a procedure to it? We need to get the hell out of this nation as quickly as possible.* The "Morroi" came over to the edge of the platform and helped Deacon down, then ushered him away.

As they disappeared from sight, one of the elders addressed Bo'az, Hansi, and Aric. They had stopped rotating and now sat stationary. "We thank you for your cooperation. We understand that it is no easy decision to sacrifice oneself. For that, we shall provide the three of you with the utmost comfort until our decision has been made." The elders all stood and the two in front of Bo'az waved their hands, inviting Bo'az and the others to leave the platform. As they walked toward the edge, one of the men who had been rotating the platform placed the short wooden staircase on the ground at the edge so they could descend. The Morroi unbound each of them as they reached the ground.

Some of the red-robed men and women who'd been standing with Linas walked over to them. The girl who'd stared at Bo'az earlier once again looked him directly in the eyes. "You. Bo'az. You speak for your companions?"

Bo'az furrowed his brow at the notion. He hadn't put much thought into the idea of "leading," especially because he wasn't sure if the decision had ever actually been up to him. But since they'd arrived in Castiel, he was nonetheless the one who'd done all the talking. It was part of the plan, after all. Finally he answered the girl, "Yes. I speak for them." Now that she was only a few feet away, Bo'az was able to see the girl's features, despite the hood that covered her hair. Her light skin reminded him of Yasaman, and he quickly attempted to put those memories out of his mind.

He hadn't thought of Yasaman since the early days on the ship. The emotions of it all were so confusing, especially because she died. He didn't want to dislike her, but it was hard not to. Bo'az knew that he had lied to Yasaman first, but she'd also used him in order to sleep with him. Perhaps that notion wouldn't have bothered him so much if it hadn't been his first time, and if he hadn't had feelings for her.

"Do you not wish to come with us?" Bo'az blinked out of his reverie and looked at the girl blankly for a moment. She continued, "Have I offended you in any way, Bo'az of Ashur?"

"No. My apologies, I was reminded of something... someone who I would rather not think of. You have done nothing to offend me, or us." He shook off the thought of the girl who'd died so long ago on the other side of the world and smiled at this one before him. "What is your name?"

She smiled in return, a smile that lit up her face and was so big that it caused her to squint a little. "I am Aurkene, daughter of Elder Sei, Sixth of the Hemeretzi. As daughter of the Sixth, it is my responsibility to see that guests from beyond Sagari are accommodated and provided the appropriate comfort and luxuries. As ambassadors of a prospective alliance, I will ensure that you are kept quite comfortable."

He couldn't be sure, but it almost seemed as if she'd lingered on the last few words. Bo'az shook it off. He wasn't about to flirt with an Elder's daughter on his first day in Castiel, especially when the prospect of an alliance rested on how much the Hemeretzi believed they could trust him and his word. If something was meant to unfold, it would find its way.

Aurkene and a few other robed men and women led them down the road, which Bo'az only now realized was made of large flat stones, rather than dirt. They followed the same road for a few moments until they arrived at a huge stone hall. As they approached the oversized wooden doors, Aurkene turned to Bo'az, Aric, and Hansi. "This is *Antxone*, the feast-hall of the Sixth Elder. The three of you will reside in my father's hall for the duration of your stay. Each of you will have a room to yourself. I am sure that, having been on a ship for several months, even the most basic comfort as privacy will feel like a luxury." One of the robed men opened the door to the feast-hall and waved for them to enter. Aurkene tilted her hooded head for them to follow, and walked in. She continued, "While you stay here, our only expectation is that you make yourselves present for suppers each night. Until then, you may do as you wish. If you choose to stay in your rooms and sleep, we shall respect your decision with no offense taken. If you would like to explore Sagari, or wish for someone else to show you around, that can all be arranged. If you fancy wenches or concubines, female or male, of any size and shape, we are happy to oblige as well, assuming you have coin."

The hall appeared more expansive inside than it had from the street. Bo'az looked around the room, taking in the rows of wooden tables and benches, as well as the modest throne on the dais. A few people sat here and there, but Bo'az wondered how full the place would be at night. "Will it be busy here come suppertime?"

Aurkene smiled, "More than you can imagine. Your arrival is an important one, and something to be celebrated. We always celebrate our distinguished guests, especially when a sacrifice is involved." Bo'az flinched slightly, wondering once more how often these sacrifices took place, and whether another one might be required before they left. He had already felt guilty about Deacon, but now he feared what the sacrificial process was actually like.

"We have already sent ravens with messages to the other cities, informing them to ride here at once. It should take no more than a day for them to arrive, once they receive word. Each night, starting tonight, there will be a great feast. Tonight it will be here, and going forward, each night will be in a different Hemeretzi hall. On the final night, assuming a decision is made in your favor, there will be one last celebration in *Koldobike*, the feast hall of Bat, the High Elder, First of the Hemeretzi. That day will begin with a great hunt in the morning. We invite you to join us for that as well."

Bo'az felt his shoulders slump at all of these plans, but shrugged and nodded, "Sure. I've never actually hunted before, though I'm sure Aric and Hansi here have. But I wouldn't dare offend you by refusing. I'm sure it will be fun."

"Indeed it will." Aurkene gave a half-smile, which Bo'az wondered about.

He changed the subject to avoid any awkwardness. "Will you be here in the hall during our stay?"

Her normal smile returned, "I will be quite busy making arrangements for the other guests, as well as the feasts. However, I will surely return often to check on your well-being."

Is she flirting with me? Is this what flirting is like? "That is comforting. Speaking of which, where are our packs? I don't think I've seen them since we arrived on shore."

"They are already in your rooms, along with food and wine. The maids are preparing your baths as well. Come, while everything is still warm." They followed her once more to the right side of the large room, on the perimeter, where another door led to a hallway with five or six rooms. Bo'az realized that none of the other robed people followed this time. "These chambers are reserved for distinguished guests. They are bigger, quieter, and each has its own bath. I hope all three of you enjoy yourselves." She extended a hand for Aric to enter one room, and then Hansi the next. Both of Bo'az's companions entered their chambers without even a look back.

Once their doors were closed, Aurkene opened Bo'az's door for him and escorted him in. A steaming tub sat in the middle of the room, and a maid was there pouring water into it. Along one wall was a bed that was likely twice the size of his bed back in Haedon. A tray of food sat on a table next to the bed, loaded with bread, soup, fish, and wine. Bo'az turned to Aurkene and smiled, "I don't even know which one I want first, the bed, the food, or the bath."

Aurkene removed her hood and a mane of long, curly, black locks flowed down from her head. Her hair seemed to accentuate her heart-shaped face, and Bo'az knew instantly that he was smitten. He attempted to form a word, but a croak barely left his throat. Aurkene laughed, "My face has turned you into a frog, Bo'az? I would strongly suggest the bath first. I find that food tastes better and sleep feels better when I am clean and relaxed." The maid had finished filling the tub and bowed her head as she left the room. Bo'az gulped at the notion of privacy with Aurkene. She continued, with a smirk, "Don't worry, I wouldn't dare intrude on your privacy. Though I think that maybe there is something here? We have the whole week to get to know each other, and perhaps in a few days, we'll have worked our way toward a bath together." She touched the collar of his shirt and lightly slid her hand across his shoulder. Bo'az couldn't be sure whether she expected a response, but he could barely move, much less speak. Aurkene walked to the door and smiled at him once more, before pulling up her hood and leaving the room.

***

He lay peacefully on a cushioned table, dreaming of a little boy staring at him, and in a split second, the boy magically set the room on fire. A different type of panic set in. Maqdhuum felt his mind withdraw from the dream, though his eyes were still closed. He still drifted in a light, weightless sleep for another moment, until his mind processed that he was sleeping. As he exhaled the last breaths of slumber, he suddenly became aware of the world again and quickly opened his eyes.

Maqdhuum knew he was lying down, and looked straight up, quickly realizing he was engulfed in darkness. He thought to spring up from where he lay, but the pain and soreness of more than a dozen stab wounds reminded him of his most recent bad decision. He grunted, more from the frustration of allowing himself to purposely be hurt, than from actually being hurt.

Finally, I am able to speak to you, my friend."

At least I did one thing right and traveled to the right place. While being stabbed and stomped on by Saol Suldas and the generals of the Vithelegion, Maqdhuum knew the only place that he could go to for help would be the floating islands of Domna Orjann. They were known as the Deseeti Semai, which translated to "islands of the sky" in the Common Tongue, and there were fifteen of them. The voice had come from not far beyond his feet and he instantly knew it belonged to the closest thing he had to a "best friend." Maqdhuum grunted, "Eddis Ebaba. I've missed you. I don't know how much conversation I can give you in my condition, though."

Eddis Ebaba stood from where he sat on the ground. Maqdhuum understood at once that his friend had been sitting cross-legged with his feet tucked under his legs, meditating. When he frequented these islands in the past, it was a common thing to see. The Deseeti Semai were populated with healers and nurses, called Nerisi. The Nerisi were the caretakers of the islands, especially because they lived minimalist types of lives and did not want for much. They cared for the islands and had gardeners and farmers to help them maintain crops and vegetation. Aside from the Nerisi and their helpers, no one else inhabited the Deseeti Semai, which allowed them to heal and meditate as much as they wished. "I've not seen you in some time, Meli Ikitenya."

Maqdhuum chuckled at the name. It was the Orjanni term for messenger or prophet, and what Eddis Ebaba had called him ever since Maqdhuum had revealed who he really was. "Been busy, friend. The time is nearly at hand. Lots of preparation." He thought about trying to sit up again but decided against irritating his wounds.

Eddis Ebaba walked to his side, wearing the traditional bright blue tunic and headdress of the Nerisi. "I thought that you have been preparing for decades. Centuries. There is still more to do?"

"Those were seeds that Ip planted, with the expectation of being strong trees by the time I needed them. And those trees are firmly in place and ready for what's coming. But those were institutions. I still have to prepare the regular people for him. They know Jahmash is coming. But they must know how to fight him. Until recently, I didn't think I would need more than what I'd already put in place. But Jahmash is trying to recruit the whole world as his army. He might just get it." Maqdhuum patted his chest and stomach, realizing that he was shirtless, though he could feel the cloth of his pants against his left leg. Only then did he remember that Saol Suldas had stabbed him right through the kneecap.

Eddis Ebaba gently grasped Maqdhuum's right hand within both of his umber-toned ones, then squeezed slightly. "Then why are you here, bleeding all over my house? Many years ago, you promised to let me study your dead body. When you arrived, I almost believed it was that time. I cannot tell you whether I am more excited to see you alive or dead, Meli Ikitenya."

"That day will come soon enough, Eddis. Don't worry, you'll get your wish."

Eddis Ebaba nodded and smiled slightly. "I only wish for it to happen when you are ready. I know you punish yourself for your wrongdoings, but you have also done much good in this world. Do not forget that. This world will not be better off without you. Now tell me, why did you allow this to happen to you? And who did it?"

Maqdhuum sat up slowly as the pain diminished. The Nerisi had the ability to dissipate pain with their touch, though no one could explain why, other than as a blessing from the Orijin. They also lived naturally shorter lives than most others. "The Vithelegion. They've invaded Ashur, already destroyed a whole nation. I never spent much time in their land, but apparently they follow 'Abram.' They thought Ashur was filled with Darian-worshippers and now want to cleanse it."

"And you believed you could sway them by telling them that you are Abram." Eddis chuckled, "Come. You are well enough to walk with me now. Let us go outside and enjoy the view. There is a mist today."

Maqdhuum rose from the table and stood gingerly, expecting at least a trace of pain. Eddis had remarkably removed any trace of it, though the wounds still existed. He followed Eddis out of the wooden house, which sat roughly a hundred feet from the edge of the floating island. Eddis Ebaba lived on the second highest island, Hulet. Having the ability to travel just about anywhere he wanted was a great benefit to Maqdhuum. He'd seen the view from each island and had even traveled up to the sky above the islands to see them all from up high.

They resembled a spiral staircase, as each island floated at a different height in a spiral all the way up to the highest one. In fact, the name 'Domna Orjann' actually translated to "Stairway to the Orijin." Maqdhuum's eyes lit up upon seeing the edge of the island. "Can we sit at the edge?"

Eddis looked at him and smiled as they walked through the bluish-green grass. "Of course! It is something I only do when you visit. Who else could save me if I fell from the side?"

Maqdhuum nodded in agreement, and they reached the edge of the floating island in a few more moments. He gently pressed a fingertip against the stab wounds on his abdomen, but they were numb to the touch. He smiled to himself, "Fair enough."

They carefully set themselves down at the edge of the island, which was a straight drop down. Eddis was right about the mist. It wasn't too thick that it obscured the view beneath them but added a majestic element to the atmosphere. "Why else have you come here, my friend? You speak plainly and simply, but I know there is always much more behind your words."

Maqdhuum looked out at the other islands floating around them. "You don't believe that I just wanted to see my friend, after a long overdue absence?"

Eddis stared ahead as well. Some of the strands from his blue headdress flailed in the wind. "I believe that is *part* of it, but I know there is more. It is impossible for you to offend me, Meli Ikitenya. While we have never been companions in the romantic sense, as you've been with other Nerisi, I am different in that I have always needed friendship more than the others. You have *always* given that to me. You have always brought exotic gifts and foods and shared *life* with me. Knowing you has been a fulfilling experience, my friend, and we both know that I am not long for this world. I have seen nearly forty summers. I dare say I have no more than five or so left. So tell me what you need. And tell it simply and straightly, as you would normally do."

Maqdhuum looked down and fought back a tear in each eye. He couldn't be sure, but he believed that ever since he was given this new body, he'd become more emotional. Still, even Abram, the old version of him, would have been just as sad to lose a friend like Eddis Ebaba. "I suppose only a true friend could say all that. My apologies, Eddis. You know, of course, my intent isn't to trick you or lie to you." He took a deep breath and looked down at his swaying feet. "What I need, it isn't a simple request. There's a boy that I need you to keep here. He needs my help. But I have to work out some other details in order to help him."

Eddis put a hand on Maqdhuum's shoulder. "And what is the catch to this? Who else is after the boy? Or why is he dangerous? It is one of those things."

"It is. About sixteen or seventeen years ago, I can't remember exactly how many at this point, I tracked down the woman who eventually helped me to transform from Abram into Maqdhuum. I never told you all the details of it, but she had a gift that allowed her soul to leave her body and travel to the Three Rings. Once she helped me, I betrayed her. I brought her to Jahmash as a gift. Hoped I could fool him with my new body, get close and find out his plans. Maybe even kill him then. Turns out I was too much a coward. I gave the woman over to him. Hoped that maybe he could use her to see Darian. See the Orijin. Work something out. Turns out he didn't want to. He kept her as a slave. Had a child with her. A boy named Horatio. Jahmash sent Horatio off to Ashur to spy on the Orijin's new Harbingers."

"Before I ask again why this is a dangerous favor, tell me, do you regret these actions, my friend?"

"At the time, I didn't. I saw the woman as just another seed that needed to be planted. Thought I needed to harden myself in order to defeat Jahmash. I regret them now, knowing how much it all cost. The woman had a family that I took her away from. A husband and twin sons. One of those twin sons knows me quite well. Once I tell him the truth of it all, he'll want to kill me. I haven't decided yet whether I should let him."

"Despite all this, I do not believe you are beyond atonement. Dedicate the rest of your days to goodness and redemption, and you may still find forgiveness."

"Jahmash is in Horatio's head."

Eddis turned and looked at him pointedly, "Excuse me?"

Maqdhuum took a deep breath. "Jahmash is still in his head. That's the catch. I need to bring him here and keep him blindfolded and confined."

Eddis stood up and took a few steps back. "Meli Ikitenya, you have visited every single one of these islands, this one specifically dozens of times. You know that we do not keep prisoners here."

Maqdhuum stood and walked over to him. "He wouldn't be a prisoner. And wouldn't even be here long. It would be for his own benefit to be confined. Horatio himself is harmless. It's only when Jahmash is in his head that he is dangerous. And the Harbinger has essentially given up on him. The blindfold and confinement are only precautionary."

"I don't know, Maqdhuum. This puts the Deseeti Semai in danger. It puts all of Domna Orjann at risk."

"I have weighed the risk, Eddis. It is minimal. Once you are ready to keep him here, I will bring him. As soon as I leave, I will procure the other things I need in order to help him. His hands would be bound behind his back. He'd be blindfolded; and most importantly, he'd be confined. Even if Jahmash turned his attention to the boy, there would be nothing he could do to cause damage. Those of us who fight against Jahmash need this boy. He may have important secrets and knowledge that would prove useful. I may have a way to get Jahmash out of his head. And if it works, it may have a hand in saving Ashur." As he finished speaking, Eddis turned and walked back toward the house. "Eddis! That's it? Why are you walking away from me?"

Eddis stopped and looked back at him. "I see you are trying to make amends for your wrongdoings, Meli Ikitenya. You are still a messenger of the Orijin, so I shall maintain my faith in you. We should start building this containment cell immediately. The sooner it happens, the better for you. Right?"

Maqdhuum stared at the man for a moment, amazed at his loyalty, then walked toward him with a grin.

***

Aurkene leaned over to Bo'az, her mouth less than an inch from his ear. In the moment that preceded her whisper, a dozen possibilities raced through his mind about what secret she might be about to tell. Ever since the feast had begun and Bo'az, Aric, and Hansi were introduced as guests of honor, Aurkene had perpetually been at Bo'az's side. He expected that at any point, she might proposition him or suggest they sneak away to his chambers, or perhaps even her chambers. While the thought did somewhat excite him, Bo'az shuddered at the thought of having Yasaman pop into his head if he were to ever be with someone else. He knew that sooner or later, he would have to take that step with someone, but he had no idea when the right time for that would be. He almost wished that things between Baltaszar and Yasaman had never fallen apart. His life would have been so much easier that way. After an eternity of drowning in his own thoughts, Aurkene finally whispered, "Is it true that Ashurians worship

Darian?"

Bo'az squinted in confusion as he turned to look at her. "What?" He tried to maintain a whisper, but a din filled the room and most of the crowd was no longer focused on them. "I don't even know. Hansi and Aric might know better than me. I lived my whole life in my town until Linas and his friends took me off to see Jahmash. Up until that point, I'd never even heard of Darian, or any of the Harbingers for that matter. Why do you ask?"

She leaned back slightly, her eyes suddenly stern. "Darian drowned the world because he was afraid to kill one man. Do you know how many people died in the process of that? This island. Orol Taghdras, Fah'Zavan, Ashur—that is all that is left of the world because of Darian. During his time, the world was so much bigger, and he destroyed it all. If the people of Ashur do worship him above the other four Harbingers, then they truly deserve to die."

Bo'az shrugged. He had no answer for her, at least none that would satisfy her. He turned to Hansi, who was sitting next to him and shoveling food into his mouth and clasped his shoulder. "Hansi, take a break from your food and answer a question for Aurkene." Hansi lifted his head and grunted as he looked at Bo'az from the corner of his eye. Bo'az asked, "Do the people of Ashur worship Darian above the other Harbingers?"

Hansi had finished chewing and gulped down some red wine, as if it was his last drink before dying. He brushed a strand of black hair from his face and looked past Bo'az at Aurkene, "Worship Darian? Hell no. Our *king* could care less about Darian and has trained his army to hunt and kill Darian's descendants. In the City of the Fallen, where Darian and Jahmash lived thousands of years ago, there are giant statues of every Harbinger except Jahmash. In fact, even our days are named after the original three Harbingers, and then four of the Five, excluding Jahmash. Nobody in Ashur *worships* the Harbingers. They focus on the Orijin when they pray."

Aurkene responded from Bo'az's right, "Good! Maybe not all of them will need to die then."

Bo'az stared into his plate; only the bare bones of a few lamb chops remained. Despite technically growing up in Ashur, he had absolutely no connection to it. Aside from Hansi, Aric, and a handful of Jahmash's other captives who'd either died or gone on to other missions, he knew no one from Ashur. He'd never even stepped foot on the ground of an actual nation of the realm. While he felt a certain allegiance to the nation, the more he thought about it, he oddly didn't understand why.

Haedon had betrayed him and his family. And for them to be living in a town that was hidden away in a forest, on a mountain, days away from the rest of an entire continent, it meant that they likely didn't belong in Ashur anyway. *Why do I care so much for a place that I never even knew? How will my life be different, or even any better, if Ashur is saved?* He wondered whether his thoughts were even his, or Jahmash's. *I've barely even felt him since they took Deacon away. Can't be his influence.* He looked back up at Aurkene. "You want to know something funny? I've seen nearly twenty summers, and I've never stepped foot onto the mainland of Ashur. I couldn't even tell you whether it's filled with good people or bad. The only person I know in all of Ashur is my twin brother, because he left to get his questions answered."

"What questions?"

"I don't know. He had this black line scar thing down his face, and supposedly it meant he was special. Someone told him he could find others like him out in Ashur, and that he would get answers about the black thing and our father and stuff. Linas and the other two men who brought me to Ashur, they thought I was my brother. They wanted *him* because of the black line on his face."

"How strange. Perhaps that was the best thing for you, though. If you are successful in all the other nations, then I think you are on the right side of this upcoming war. I'm sure Jahmash will reward you greatly for your role in his success."

Bo'az nodded reluctantly. "Yeah, I'm sure he will. I just want my brother alive through it all. That's all that matters." *Tasz. That's what matters about Ashur. As long as Tasz is there, then he'll be fighting for it. If Ashur loses, then Tasz dies, and I can't let that happen.* He shook the thought away, nervous about Jahmash reappearing in his head while any of those thoughts still lingered. He knew he might have to change the subject before Aurkene could ask more questions. This time it was Bo'az who leaned to whisper to her. "Would it be appropriate to kiss you here?"

She whispered back, keeping her mouth right next to his ear, "Just know that if you do, the expectation is that this shall progress. You cannot just kiss me in my father's hall, in front of everyone, and then cast me aside once you're ready to leave Castiel."

Shit. Shit shit shit. He kept his face next to hers, just in case his expression matched his concern. He needed to quickly decide which was worse, the pain that Jahmash would inflict at even a hint of betrayal or initiating a romance with a girl who might be willing to see his brother die. Bo'az took a breath, then gently nudged his cheek against Aurkene's. As he neared his lips toward hers, he closed his eyes and puckered his lips and softly pressed them against hers. Aurkene reciprocated; her lips were even softer than the skin of her cheek. They continued and, as more people noticed, nearly the entire hall of Antxone erupted in cheers. Bo'az couldn't help but smile in the middle of kissing Aurkene, and he felt her lips curl into a smile as well.

Aurkene's parents had sat at the table next to theirs, facing the rest of the hall. Apparently it was Casteyan tradition for the Hemeretzi to sit and eat with their guests, as a sign that they were one with the people they represented. Aurkene's father stood in excitement. He was a tall man with curls like his daughter, except the man kept his hair short. What Bo'az found interesting about most of the 'elders' was that none of them appeared *old*. They were all old enough to be parents of grown children, but the term 'elder' suggested white hair and frail bodies. At least to Bo'az anyway. Aurkene's father addressed the room, "Friends and family! The arrival of these young men continues to be more auspicious by the hour! Not only is a worldwide alliance on the horizon, but now one of Jahmash's own emissaries seeks to court my first-born! Raise your glasses and let us toast to another prospective union!"

Prospective union? Light of Orijin, he expects me to marry her. And what, am I going to have to take her with us now? Aurkene grasped his hand and gently pulled his hand to stand up with her. "Raise your glass, repeat the toast after he says it, and follow what I do," she told him softly.

Sei, which Bo'az came to understand wasn't her father's actual name, but his Hemeretzi rank, looked over at them and smiled. Aurkene clearly had her father's smile. He held his glass in front of his chest and yelled, "Gora, behera, erdira ta barrura!" As he said the words, Aurkene's father moved his glass up, down, back to the center, and then lastly moved it gently against his chest. As he finished, Bo'az, Aurkene, and the rest of the hall repeated Sei's toast and drank heartily. Back in Haedon, there was rarely a reason to toast, but sometimes at dinner he, his brother, and his father would celebrate a good harvest or a new foal with some local ale at dinner. All it involved was clinking their mugs together, though. Bo'az enjoyed the spectacle of this toast, and although he was hesitant about what might happen with Aurkene, it was nice to be celebrated by a room full of people. He wondered what the toast actually meant.

As they were about to sit, Aurkene's father walked over to them and put a hand on Bo'az's shoulder. "Come with me for a moment, Bo'az. There are a few things we should talk about."

Bo'az's eyes grew wide as they shifted between Aurkene and her father. Aurkene reassured him, "It's fine. He's excited and just wants to congratulate you. Tell you he trusts you, things like that." *Shit shit shit. I made the wrong decision. Jahmash's wrath would've been so much shorter than this!* Bo'az nodded and stood, then let Sei lead him to a table on the dais, behind the Hemeretzi's throne. *At least we're still in front of everyone, even if we're too far for anyone to hear anything.*

He'd barely sat at the round table when Aurkene's father started talking. "I am going to assume that if you have the balls to kiss my daughter in front of everyone here, then you have the balls to properly court her and treat her as a true companion." The man continued to smile, though his tone clearly implied a threat. "If any part of this is fake or disingenuous, then any chance of an alliance will be ended, no matter what the other Casteyan cities agree to this week. And if that ends up being the case, I guarantee you that all three nations of Bisitsad will band together and destroy Jahmash ourselves."

How tempting. Think quickly, you idiot. Once again, Bo'az quickly pushed the thought from his mind. "May I speak now, Elder Sei?" Sei nodded curtly. "If I may be quite honest, I did not come here with the intention or expectation of romance or courtship. In fact, the one girl I'd ever fancied died on the journey from Ashur to Jahmash. I spent much of my journey here thinking about her and whether I would ever be able to move on. *However*, the moment Aurkene even spoke to me, I knew there was a spark between us. And when she removed her hood and I looked upon her, I was smitten beyond return. I am attracted to everything about her. You should also know that, when I asked her if it would be appropriate to kiss her here, in front of you and all of Antxone, she told me that to do so would imply courtship. Do you know what I did? I kissed her right away." *Take that, you ass.*

Aurkene's father smiled at him. It was a tight smile, unwilling. The man gazed into Bo'az's eyes for another moment, as if considering what to say next. Finally he spoke. "And so you swear that your intentions are of your own volition, and not those of Jahmash?"

Bo'az nodded, "I swear it."

"Good. Because this means that Aurkene will travel with you from here. If you truly mean to court her, then I hope you do not expect to leave and have her stay here."

Again, shit! "You must know that we will be gone for a considerable amount of time. Given the number of nations we must still visit, and the time at sea, it will likely be at least four months until we have finished our business in Orol Taghdras. Jahmash will expect us to return after that. What are your wishes for Aurkene after we finish there, Elder Sei?"

The man stroked his long mustache with two fingers for a moment. "The courtship will endure for the length of your travels between here and each nation of Orol Taghdras. Once your time there has concluded, Aurkene and her guardian will sail back here. You will sail back to Jahmash. Once it is time for the Casteyan Armada to sail to war, Aurkene and I will travel with them. After Ashur has been laid to waste, you and Aurkene will wed. Arrangements will be made with Jahmash for you to hold a position of power, such as a lord. Or better. I expect nothing less. Your children will be raised with privilege and wealth, and your bloodline will continue that way through the ages."

Damn. He has this all worked out for generations. Bo'az had to admit, the man's plan was an enticing one, and quite beneficial, if it all worked out. And if Bo'az could stomach actually being with Aurkene. *The first girl I kissed was in love with my brother and used me for sex. The second girl I kissed planned out the rest of our lives within five minutes of kissing her. There's no way kissing girls is this complicated for everyone.* "And what of her responsibilities here, sir? Who will cater to the guests of Sagari in her absence?"

Elder Sei smirked, "Edurne, Aurkene's younger sister, will take on those responsibilities. Assuming some boy from far away doesn't show up and kiss her in front of all of Sagari." This time, the man didn't subdue his laugh or smile. "And my name is Edrigu Ezkerro. You do not have to continue calling me 'Elder' and 'sir.' I approve of you for my daughter. We can move past the formalities. Now go and enjoy your time with Aurkene." He extended his hand out to Bo'az, and Bo'az quickly grasped it with a firm shake.

Bo'az walked back to the table and sat next to Aurkene once

more. They spent the rest of the night engaged in song and dance, with countless toasts and drinks, and kissing each other whenever the crowd demanded it. When most of the room had passed out or returned to their rooms and homes, Aurkene stood up and took Bo'az by the hand. She clumsily walked him back to his chambers and they stumbled through the door. Though mightily drunk, Bo'az knew the direction in which things were about to progress. Before he could process what to do next, Aurkene shoved him onto the bed and straddled his torso. She leaned to him and sloppily kissed him as her hands began to explore his body. Just as her hand slipped under his shirt, Bo'az rolled her over to his side and sat up. He kicked off his boots and sat completely on the bed, doing his best to look into her eyes, despite not being able to see straight. "W-we can't do th…this tonight. Too soon."

Aurkene held a finger up to protest, but her words came a few moments later as she stared into empty space. "Mmm, but we h-have to copu…consummate our marriage."

He giggled for a short while and collapsed on the bed. "We're not married, yet, Y-yas, Aurkene. R-rember?"

Bo'az knew that he'd almost said the wrong name, and somehow she hadn't noticed. "Oh, kaka! Thaaaat's riiiiiight…wow. But can…can't we still do…it?" Aurkene had also kicked off her boots and shifted her whole body up onto the bed. She lay facing the ceiling and every time her eyes closed, it was for a longer moment than the previous time. Bo'az barely realized she'd fallen asleep before he turned onto his stomach and fell asleep as well.

***

By the sixth day of feasts, Bo'az had spent at least a few hours each day with Aurkene. They'd walked throughout Sagari and had even ridden horses to sit and watch the sea. The beach had been so peaceful that they'd just sat holding hands, staring out at the water. During the nightly feasts, neither of them had gotten nearly as drunk as the first night. And while they'd limited their intimacy to kissing, Bo'az had allowed her on the previous day to cut his hair while he bathed, though there was enough foam from the soap that she couldn't see anything. Aurkene had cut most of his hair off, but it was short enough that she gently ran her hand through it when she was all done. Bo'az didn't mind; he'd never intentionally grown his hair out, and she would likely continue to groom him if they were to travel together.

It had been announced at the fifth feast that the leaders of the four coastal cities had agreed to Jahmash's proposed alliance, and that

Castiel would send half of its army to fight for Jahmash. That night, for the first time in days, Bo'az felt Jahmash in his head. There was a happiness and sense of triumph to the presence. It was part of the reason that Bo'az refrained from drinking too much. He knew that if the drink took control of his mind, there was no telling where his thoughts might lead. There was no sense in taking those kinds of chances. Aurkene hadn't accompanied him to his room, as the 'great hunt' would take place on the sixth morning, which was where they were riding to.

Aurkene had woken Bo'az, Aric and Hansi at sunrise. They wore their regular outfits and black coats at her suggestion. Aurkene rode with the three of them in a wagon, one of ten to ride south toward the forest. They'd all been tired from all the celebrating, so the ride was mostly quiet. After nearly an hour, Bo'az finally asked, "What exactly are we hunting?"

Aurkene looked at him solemnly, then glanced back and forth between him, Aric, and Hansi, before finally settling on Bo'az again. "Criminals."

Hansi interjected, "Say that again."

Bo'az also responded without hesitation, "Did you say *criminals*? As in *people*? We're riding to hunt and kill human beings? This is a regular practice in Castiel? Or is it just Sagari?"

Aurkene's eyes dropped to the floor of the wagon. "There are a few cities that do the same. At the beginning of each season, we bring those who have broken our laws out to the forest and have a hunting party. They are hunted and killed until there is one left. The one who remains is elevated to the status of a servant to the elders. You saw them rotating the Hemeretzi platform when you first arrived."

Bo'az was incredulous but refrained from yelling so as not to alarm the other wagons. "And you *condone* this behavior, Aurkene?"

She continued to look down, but her voice was insistent. "No, I don't. In fact, I hate this practice, and I have told my father as much. But traditions do not break easily, Bo'az. It is the Sagari way, and our people are fine with it because crime is something they rarely have to worry about. There are never more than ten or so for each hunt."

Aric finally chimed in, and Bo'az was happy to see that he at least showed some emotion. "How many are being hunted today? How many criminals?"

Aurkene paused for a moment. "Six of them. Seven in total, though."

They each looked at her with squinted eyes of confusion. Aric was the one to ask, "What do you mean?"

"There is one who is not a... criminal. He is... the sacrifice that you agreed to." Bo'az and the other two shrieked and croaked but could barely form words.

Bo'az was glad he was not standing, as he felt the strength drain from his legs and body. "Look, I know this is not your doing. But does Deacon even have a chance out there? Any possibility that he survives and at least lives on as a servant?"

She shook her head, "No. He is an outsider, and the agreement was a sacrifice. They will likely target him first. I know there is no comfort in any of this for the three of you. And the best I can do is tell you how sorry I am that you must witness it all happen. I truly am sorry. It is a way of life for Sagari, but to anyone else, it is savagery. I know how I would feel if the same were to happen to one of my friends. Especially in a strange land, so far away from home."

"Was it your choice to come?"

"No. Because of my responsibility to entertain the guests of Sagari, there is always someone from another city that wants to partake. Even if I didn't have to escort the three of you out here, it would have been expected of me to bring other guests."

They rode on in silence for another hour or so until they reached the forest. Once there, all the wagons stopped, and several other men and women descended from their wagons. The others all carried bows and arrows as they walked toward the trees. A couple of older men came over to Bo'az and his companions and one of them held out a bow. "Will you join us? We would be honored if you participated in the hunt."

Bo'az could barely formulate a response when Aric spoke up for him, "No thank you, friend. We respect your offer, but it is not our way. Besides, the three of us are terrible archers anyway." The man nodded and walked away without protest, and Bo'az sighed deeply.

He turned to Aurkene, who surprisingly didn't walk further into the forest with the others. "So what happens now? Do we just wait here until they return with the 'winner'?"

"Yes. That's basically how it works. They all know how many targets there are, and they help each other keep track of how many have been killed. Once they know there is only one left, it becomes a race to find the last survivor. There is a reward for each kill and for finding the survivor. We'll know they're done when they come back out with the lone survivor."

Bo'az started walking back to the wagon. "I'm not going to stand here just waiting for it to end. I'll be in the wagon, waiting for when it's time to go back. Join me if you want." Aric and Hansi started walking back as well, and he was surprised to see Aurkene also walking back. They sat on the benches in the back of the open wagon for over an hour, listening to shouts and sporadic celebrations. Bo'az counted in his head how many celebrations he heard. After another while, he was sure he'd counted six, which meant they would bring out the 'winner' soon. With a tinge of regret, Bo'az wondered whether Deacon was actually the first one to die, or if he'd managed to outlast any of the others. Surprisingly, the shouts continued on.

He turned toward the trees as he heard the voices getting louder and nearer. "Sounds like they're done. At least we can get out of here soon." Aric, Hansi, and Aurkene all looked up at the hunters returning. Bo'az felt bad for whichever criminal would end up walking out with them. He wondered whether he would rather die as a criminal or live as a servant. Neither seemed attractive to him. After another minute, several men escorted a gaunt man with long black hair. His head hung low with exhaustion. Bo'az squinted, *Is that?* "Aric, Hansi, is that Deacon? Did he make it?"

Aurkene craned her neck to see, "There's no way. I can't believe he managed to outlast the others. It's never happened before." She turned back to Bo'az and smiled at him, "I'm sorry I dashed your hopes. I've honestly never seen this happen."

Bo'az had one eye on Aurkene and the other on what was happening behind her, as Deacon was escorted out of the forest. He had lurched forward, as if he'd been shoved from behind. As he regained his balance and stood upright, he continued to stagger forward. He took a few more steps and collapsed as an arrow pierced the back of his head. "Noooo!" As the word left Bo'az's mouth, he turned, leaned over the side of the wagon, and heaved up everything he'd eaten that morning. Tears and snot filled his eyes and nose as he continued to heave. Even after he was done, he kept himself there to try and compose himself, until finally he rubbed his face with his sleeve and turned to face the others. Their eyes were all glossy, including Aurkene's, which surprised him.

Simultaneously, Bo'az, Aric, and Hansi all jerked. *Remember, he was to be sacrificed. The three of you have done well and I am proud of your behavior and loyalty. Because of that, I will allow you to enjoy yourselves for the remainder of your mission. I will only be present when it is time for these nations to give you their answers. Otherwise, you are free. Unless you betray me.*

CHAPTER 2
DIVERGING PATHS

From *The Book of Orijin*, Verse Three Hundred Forty-Three
Do not let your differences cloud your judgment for what is right. You have been created differently to emphasize your strengths. Embrace those differences and you shall only become stronger together.

Adria stared out at the waves as they died out just before reaching her on the shore. The water crept up the sand in front of her feet, and she'd already decided that she wouldn't move if it got closer. She tilted her head back against General Grunt and closed her eyes. It was her first time visiting the nashorn alone and, as many others had confirmed, just sitting with the animal was therapeutic. He was sleeping and the slow rise and fall of his torso helped to put her in a sort of trance.

Images poured through her head of the attack on the palace in Alvadon. King's soldiers were everywhere, in every memory. She put herself through reliving Blastevahn's death as he stood only a few feet away. At the time, there had been too much to worry about to properly react to it, but tears streamed down her face now. Beyond Blastevahn, her imagination could only fill in the blank spaces of what had happened to Kadoog'han, Malikai, and Reverron.

What could I have done differently? How did I screw this up? Four dead and Lao hurt, and how the hell could I let Garrison's brother die as well? What did Maqdhuum do to Horatio that would have caused that? I knew I shouldn't have trusted him. He didn't change. He's the one who kidnapped me in the first place. She didn't wholeheartedly believe her thoughts on Maqdhuum, though, as it dawned on her that the Harbinger could have killed her and all the others at any time. Still, it only left more questions about why Horatio killed Donovan.

They had only returned a couple of hours before and shortly after being greeted by Asarei, she'd come directly to the shore. Asarei had clearly seen that some of the Ghosts hadn't returned, and Adria wasn't ready to be questioned or beaten down. She knew that this was the last time any of her companions would trust her to be in charge, and she dreaded what might happen when Baltaszar and Desmond let their emotions flow through their words. *Not only did I let people die, but our whole group may be fractured because of me.* In the heat of the moment, Vasher had called her 'Kingsbane,' though now she felt she was more responsible for her friends' deaths than King Edmund's.

To make matters worse, they'd left Garrison alone in Alvadon alone to deal with the deaths of his family. She *had* reassured him that they would return in time for the funerals of his mother and his brother, Donovan, but that was before Maqdhuum had left them and never returned. For them to return to Alvadon for the funerals, they'd have to leave within another day just to be able to get there in time.

Garrison, Horatio, Maqdhuum, Lao. So much going on. People have died, disappeared, and been seriously injured under my watch. Kingsbane my ass. More like 'Friendsbane'.

"Hey, come on." Marshall's voice startled her. She'd focused on only the sounds of General Grunt's breathing and the crashing waves. "That's enough time to drown yourself in your thoughts and regrets. The rest of us are trying to figure out what to do next, and we need our leader there."

Great. I have no idea what the hell to do next and now they seek my counsel? She opened her eyes and looked up at Marshall. She'd barely paid attention to it in recent months, but his dark brown hair had grown out since they'd started training on the island. "I suppose I'm not allowed to refuse?"

Marshall grinned, "What, so you can stay here and wallow in your regrets and pore over everything that didn't go as planned? Not a chance. And before you protest, I guarantee that as soon as you even attempt to question your own leadership skills, everyone down there in that fortress will have an argument about why you are wrong. Adria, no plan goes perfectly. Plans assume that people and life will all cooperate completely. We can only ever hope that any breaks in that cooperation are minimal. Every single one of us knew that risks were involved, and what those risks actually were. And we followed you despite those risks. So come. If I have to carry you back, I will." As she opened her mouth to respond, he cut her off, "No protests. You're coming."

Adria leaned forward and then got to her feet. "I was just going to say that I like your hair. I know I've *seen* you every day for the past however many months, but I don't think I really noticed that it's grown out so much until now."

She spotted a trace of redness in his cheeks. Since their relationship had begun, Adria knew that she hadn't been the type to openly compliment Marshall, though it was never for a lack of wanting to. Their love had blossomed in the middle of a storm, and she'd been so focused on being the perfect leader that she'd sacrificed her ability to focus on other things. She knew she could do better, not just by Marshall, but with others as well. If losing some of her friends in the siege had taught her anything, it was that life was short. If she put off telling people things that mattered, then there might not always be a second chance at saying what was on her mind.

Marshall was definitely caught off guard, "Thanks," he said with a crack in his voice, as if unsure of the best way to respond. He nodded his head indicating for her to follow him, and they walked back to the fortress mostly in silence, but holding hands.

As they entered the meditation room, which usually doubled as the dining room, Adria paused at the sight of everyone. She'd expected that there would be people there, but it seemed that just about everyone on the island was in the room at the moment, except for Badalao and Farrah. "Why is everyone here? Did something happen?"

Asarei spoke up from his usual spot by the far wall. "Of course something happened. The Ghosts of Ashur returned today and we're all celebrating your return and your victory."

She took a deep breath, "We didn't *all* return, though."

"Marshall said you'd be this way, kid. I'm gonna tell you this, and I speak for everyone in this room when I say it. You didn't get anyone killed or hurt. Every single one of you who left understood the risk and understood that they might die in that siege. And they went anyway. And before you start trying to argue, let me pose this question to the room." Asarei walked to the center of the room and looked around at everyone. "How many of you would follow Adria into battle again? Raise your fist if you would!"

Adria didn't want to look, but she knew that she wouldn't have much choice. If Marshall didn't guilt her into looking at everyone, Asarei would likely bully her into doing so. She reluctantly held her head up and glanced around at everyone. She expected that the fists would go up hesitantly, and that perhaps more fists would go up out of guilt. But fists punched the air immediately after Asarei's question, so quickly that less than a second had likely passed before everyone in the room held up a fist. That included those without manifestations, like Baltaszar's cousins, Fariyal and Vilariyal, and even Asarei's daughter, Dafne.

"Does my fist count, as well?"

The voice came from right behind Adria. She turned and saw

the tall, stocky man in the doorway to the large room. His dark shirt and pants blended well with the stone walls and despite his size, his youthful, hairless face put him at not much older than Adria. *Someone that big, how did we not notice him coming?* She opened herself to her manifestation. Not that it would help much in a fight, but it couldn't hurt. "Who the hell are *you*?"

He looked around the room, as if searching for someone. *He's clearly not here to fight.* Adria let her guard down somewhat. If he'd made it this far without being noticed, he could have easily attacked her if he'd wanted to. The man finally spoke, "Figures. None of the 'Ghosts' I met with are here. Usually we're pretty stealthy and knowledgeable about these things, but you laid your siege and left without much of a trace." He stopped looking at all the other faces and finally stared at Adria intensely. "I'm Stream. A Footpad of the Kraisos. Met with Maqdhuum and a few others in Taiju about forming an alliance and preparing Ashur for war. I believe they were Lao, Farrah, and Malikai. Normally we have an idea of where Maqdhuum is. But we haven't heard or seen much in a few days. Probably means he's not in Ashur."

Adria was about to respond to him, but Asarei spoke up from the other side of the room and started walking toward Adria and Stream. She got the feeling that he was trying to protect her. "Kraisos? What's this all about?"

Rhadames Slade had followed Asarei and stood right behind him. "Don't worry. He speaks the truth. One of the things we put in motion before coming here was for a smaller contingent to go to Markos and meet with the Kraisos in Taiju." Slade stepped around Asarei, "Unfortunately, Stream? Unfortunately, Malikai was killed in the siege, and Lao was seriously injured. He is currently on bedrest, under Farrah's care. And we have no clue about Maqdhuum's whereabouts either. He was supposed to help us escape but disappeared with another 'Ghost' who turned on us."

Asarei looked back and forth between Slade and Stream, "Are you sure we can just trust him at his word? And divulge information that only we know?"

Slade turned around to look at all the others at the other side of the room. Some had moved closer to hear the conversation. Adria wondered who Slade was looking for, but then he made it clear. "Tasz, come here." As Baltaszar walked toward them, Slade asked, "Lao reached out to your mind while they were meeting with Stream. Tell them what you discussed."

Baltaszar nodded, "Wind was with him, in the room with the others. He looked similar to what I remembered back in Haedon, when his name was Vikram Bhoodoo, except that his hair was shorter than it'd been back in Haedon. He was excited to interact with me, and it seemed like Stream and the others were all getting along."

Slade looked at Asarei, Adria, and Stream. "We can all trust each other here. Stream, what was the message you intended for Maqdhuum? Surely we can help in some regard."

Stream nodded and walked past them toward the center of the room. "May I sit? I'm going to sit. My journey here was non-stop; I'm tired." He brushed a few locks of hair from his face and sat on the ground in front of a bunch of the others. "Feel free to sit down and join me." He looked back over to Adria, Slade, and Asarei. "You three should definitely sit with me. We have plans to make."

Adria didn't wait for the others; she walked over to the Kraiso and pulled Marshall along with her, then sat next to Stream. She had been in Markos while Maqdhuum and the others had met with him, except she was with her parents while the meeting happened. She'd desperately needed to see her parents again, but a part of her regretted not meeting with the Kraisos instead. She wouldn't have to play catch up now, and it would have made her feel a little better about being the "leader" right now. "What plans did you have in mind?" Asarei and Slade took their places on the floor, across from Stream.

Stream looked at her and then around at the others, "Maqdhuum's request was for the Kraisos to prepare all of Ashur for Jahmash's war by infiltrating the cities throughout each nation and *shifting* them toward that preparation. Badalao informed us that he has made arrangements for his own people to do that very thing in Constaniza. I don't know if Maqdhuum got around to telling you, but Wind convinced our Master to fulfill your request. And now that your siege is complete, the time is right to focus on this."

"With all due respect, some of us have other agendas that need our attention." Baltaszar still stood but was right behind Asarei. "Desmond and I plan to ride to Vandenar. We have loved ones to check on."

Adria took a deep breath. She knew another argument was about to begin. "Tasz, Des, we agreed that we would go back to Alvadon to be there for Garrison. The funerals are a few days away and he likely has few allies there. The least we can do is support him."

Desmond was about to say something, but Baltaszar tapped the back of his hand against Desmond's chest to quiet him. Baltaszar responded instead. "Adria, *you* made that agreement. And while you are our leader, there are some things that should be discussed with the group, instead of making the decision yourself. Des and I spoke with Garrison and gave him our condolences. He also gave us his blessings to go see to our own, as that's exactly what he would do. We're not looking to make this a whole big fight again, but you need to see our side of it. We did *everything* you wanted, the way you wanted. And it's not like we're leaving you for good. We need to go there and see about our loved ones. By the time we get there, Lao should be in good enough condition that he can relay messages for us as well as tell us where you all are. We can meet up with you when we're done, wherever you are."

She looked at Baltaszar and Desmond, then around at the others. Baltaszar wasn't wrong, and Adria wondered why she was so adamant against them going. She was somewhat afraid of what the two might find in Vandenar, as well as what the consequences would be if things didn't go well there. But sooner or later, they would have to deal with it anyway. "You're right, Tasz. It's unfair to stop you two from going. Stay the night to get some rest and leave in the morning. We'll all leave here at the same time. In order for the rest of us to be back in Alvadon in time for the funerals, we must leave by sunrise. And for what it's worth, I have faith that your loved ones are still alive."

Much to her surprise, Baltaszar shook his head. "Then your faith is stronger than mine." He glanced down at the ground and then back at her, "The way I see it, luck only lasts so long. We found a new leader after the House of Darian was destroyed. We succeeded with the siege, which should secure the Anonymi alliance." He nodded his head toward Stream, "Looks like we've got the alliance with the Kraisos. Not sure about the rest of you, but in my experience, life has a way of making sure that you don't stay happy for too long. I know we lost some of our friends, but being on this island has been one of the best phases of my life. It sure seems like the winds are about to change for me. The Orijin has a way of keeping me in check." Baltaszar twisted his mouth, as if trying to avoid showing any emotion in his face and then stepped away from the group. As he walked toward the doorway, he called back, "I'll see you in the morning," and then left the room.

Desmond hurried after him and murmured to Adria in passing, "Don't worry Mouse, ya didn't do anythin' wrong. We're just on edge."

Adria took a deep breath and looked around at the rest of the group. "Alright. Well, does anyone else have a different agenda than me? Might as well figure it all out now."

To her surprise, Delilah stepped closer from behind a few of the others. The woman was a few years older than Adria and certainly looked much more like a woman than Adria felt she ever would. "Adria, I know it may not be the best time but given what's in store for us and all of Ashur in the near future, I *need* to go back to Sundari. There are some personal things that I must attend to before I can truly focus on fighting Jahmash. Sindha will accompany me as well, as she would like to see her family at least one last time. We will travel with you to Alvadon for the funerals and then leave from there."

Adria glanced around to find Sindha and noticed her trying not to look at Adria for very long. Adria wanted to be offended by all of these decisions but knew that none of them were about her. Surviving the siege impacted all of them and made them question their own mortality. They wanted to be able to focus on who and what they were fighting for. Who they were protecting from Jahmash.

"Look, none of you should feel like you owe me an apology for wanting to sort out your affairs before we fight Jahmash. I went to see my parents before the siege, and I would be surprised if you *didn't* want to see your families and loved ones before it's too late. I feel we should be there for Garrison, but if your needs are more pressing, then use your best judgment. We're all exhausted. Sunrise will be here sooner than we'd like. So let's all get to sleep in actual beds, and I think we'll all feel better in the morning."

The group nodded and dispersed. As Adria turned to follow everyone out of the room, she felt an arm wrap around her side. The familiarity of the touch brought a much needed smile to her face. She turned to Marshall at her left side and put her head against his chest as they walked.

***

Delilah Fakhri sat at the side of her bed. The mattress was much harder than the one back at the House of Darian, and neither of those beds compared to back home in Sundari. Even still, after days of sleeping on the hard ground, even this bed was like sleeping on a cloud. She pushed her hands down against the edge of the bed to stretch her muscles and let out a soft groan. Surprisingly, that was enough to wake up Sindha, whose bed was only a few feet away, right next to Delilah's.

The girl from Itarse turned to her and blinked her eyes a few times. "Just sitting there in the dark?" she whispered, "You think she's actually fine with us leaving, or just pretending not to be mad?"

Delilah shrugged and spoke softly. "I think the old Adria would have been angry about it. But she's changed since we've gotten back. I don't mean that in a bad way, but I think she was insecure about her leadership up until recently. And rightfully so. As Marked Descendants, of course we have all seen hardships and tragedies in our lives. However, we were all so pampered at the House of Darian. Nobody challenged us, not in ways that we'd ever fear for our lives, anyway. None of us would have been ready to lead the others into something like that. If I'd been in her place, we would have been lucky that there weren't more than four casualties."

Sindha sat up and faced her, waving a few curly locks of hair from her face. "You should tell her that, you know. I think she needs to hear it. Adria's already so hard on herself; I think that would ease some of her stress."

"Of course I will. We should ride with her up to Alvadon as well, ahead of the others, and have some girl time without the boys around. She even wished for it only a few days ago, and now we've told her we're going to abandon her." Delilah had felt some guilt over leaving Adria, especially because of Adria's desire to spend more time with them. The world's dire need for people like them had caused them all to become so close, but they barely ever had the opportunity to have any kind of sustained fun with their friendships. There was always something serious to focus on.

That had also prevented Delilah from focusing on herself. She knew that, in a sense, she had used Lincan for her own personal fulfillment, even if he had enjoyed himself with her. But in doing so, she had hoped to find some clarity on whether to continue to pursue a life with the Daughters of Tahlia. Being one of them meant that she could only lay with a man for the sake of procreation, *not* for pleasure, even though she knew there were some Daughters who bent those rules from time to time. Bedding Lincan only confused things further, though, she realized that she enjoyed being with men and women alike.

She'd felt bad about being so abrupt with Lincan. He was younger than she, had gotten roped into sleeping with her so quickly, and before they'd even had a conversation about defining what was going on between them, Delilah had told him it was over. At the time, she had thought that things would be easier that way, but all it had done was make things more uncomfortable and awkward. He'd handled it surprisingly well, though, considering the circumstances.

Part of the reason for traveling back to Sundari was to have some time away from the others and sort things out for herself. She'd confided her dilemma to Sindha, who had been ready in a heartbeat to travel back with her and help her find some clarity. A part of Delilah convinced herself that Sindha might even be attracted to her, but the more she thought about it, the more unlikely it seemed. Sindha was simply a good friend and, if anything, seemed to want to eventually go to Markos to find a husband. Something Badalao had told her intrigued Sindha about Markosi men.

Krissette walked into the room with a lantern, barely making a sound and startling Delilah. She looked around the room, specifically at Adria's empty bed, and then at Sindha. Adria had gotten up nearly an hour before and crept out, though not quietly enough. Delilah had woken up at the sound of Adria leaving the room. Krissette was likely looking for her friend and finally spoke sheepishly. "I'm sorry to interrupt, especially so early. Sindha, do you mind if I have a word with Delilah alone?"

The request surprised both of them, as Delilah and Sindha glanced at each other quizzically. Delilah wondered what business the girl could possibly need to discuss, but assumed it had to be important for her to be here so early and still in her nightgown and slippers. Sindha rose from her bed, "Of course, Krissette. I'll take a walk and see if anyone made breakfast yet." She glanced back at Delilah, "Any requests?"

Delilah smiled and shook her head. "No thank you. I'll be over when we're done here." Sindha left the room and Krissette walked toward the bed and placed the lantern on the cabinet between Delilah's and Sindha's beds. There was an awkwardness to the girl that Delilah hadn't noticed before. She was beautiful and somewhat petite in stature, though her body still showed curves through her nightgown. Whatever Krissette needed to talk about was heavy. Delilah smiled and waited for her to speak.

Finally, after twiddling her fingers for several moments, Krissette spoke. "Sorry, this is difficult for me to do. But let me just say it before I run out of time." She glanced at the door and then looked Delilah in the eyes, and promptly lowered them to her hands. "I would like to come with you and Sindha to Sundari."

Delilah lowered her head so far that she basically had to look upwards to see the girl. "You want to do what?"

"I know, I know." Krissette's voice gained some conviction. "I know how strange that sounds. The thing is... I... there is something I've been going through, and I don't think I really started to understand it until you all came here. Until I got close to Adria and spent more time around all of you."

Light of Orijin, tell me she didn't fall for Adria. "Are you saying you have feelings for another girl? For Adria?" Delilah had to keep herself from shouting, despite how surprised she was.

"Well, sort of." Krissette continued to shift her eyes between Delilah and her clasped hands. "I don't think I was necessarily attracted to *Adria*. But spending so much time with her kind of gave me a confirmation within myself that I'm not attracted to boys. Look, Delilah, I don't know if it works the same for... everyone who goes through this, but I've felt... different for a long time now. And for most of that time, I didn't know exactly what it was. I thought that maybe it had something to do with being marked, with having this black line and manifestation. But then I met others who had it and I still felt this way."

Delilah put her palms up, as if to stop her. "Hold on a moment. Don't you think that maybe you're getting ahead of yourself? It's one thing to prefer women, but to want to become a Daughter of Tahlia is a hell of a difference. You can still be with a woman and be accepted for it without traveling all the way to Sundari and adopting a whole new lifestyle. To be a Daughter you eventually have to be with a man, you know."

Krissette finally fixed her gaze upon Delilah's eyes and kept it there. "I don't think you fully understand me, Delilah. I want to travel with *you*. I have so many questions, not about the Daughters of Tahlia, but about being attracted to women. About what it's like. And even besides all that, I... I don't know how exactly to say it..." Krissette moved from the bed and before Delilah could comprehend the girl's meaning, Krissette had already reached out her hand, gently grasped Delilah's cheek, and kissed her on the lips. Delilah froze in exasperation for a few moments while the younger girl kissed her, and thought for a moment that she might have even kissed her back.

In all the confusion of it, neither of them realized that the door to the chamber had opened. "Oh my gosh, I'm so sorry! I didn't realize that you two... I should have knocked! I'm so sorry Delilah and Sindha!" Adria's voice was unmistakable, and Delilah finally managed to pull away from Krissette. "Krissette? Is that you?" Adria's confusion finally dissipated. "What's going on? No, I'm sorry, that's none of my business. I'm just so surprised; I don't really know what to say. I should probably let you two be alone. Of course, that would be the smart thing to do, Adria."

As Adria abruptly turned to leave, Delilah was about to stop her when Lincan and Vasher arrived at the door. They both had to have heard Adria's confused outburst and Lincan stepped into the doorway. "Everything alright? Anyone hurt?"

Adria attempted to respond, "Yes, Linc. Everything's fine. I just... it's just..."

Krissette spoke up, though Delilah was hoping she wouldn't. "Everything is fine, Lincan. Adria walked in on me kissing Delilah and obviously had a lot of questions. As I would imagine most of you will. Phew, that feels good to say."

Lincan's eyes widened immensely, as did Vasher's behind him. Lincan looked at Krissette and then Delilah in the dim light. "Wow, definitely a lot of questions. But that's probably none of my business. So, anyway, we were actually tracking you down, Adria, to tell you that the two of us plan to travel with Sindha and Delilah down to Sundari. Vasher wants to see his mother, and I'm going to head to Fangh-Haan from there. I haven't been back to see my family in Xuyen in a while, and I might as well risk it while there's still time."

Before Delilah could protest or even get a word in, Krissette spoke up again. Kissing her must have emboldened the girl, as now she wouldn't shut up. "I'm going to travel with them down to Sundari as well. Which means I will also accompany you up to Alvadon."

Adria seemed to compose herself and looked at Delilah once more. "That all work for you?"

Oh for the love of all fucks. What in Opprobrium is going on here? A nice personal trip with Sindha just turned to hell in a matter of a shallow breath. Fuck. Fucking fuck. Delilah took a deep breath and tried to hide her disappointment. "How could I say no to any of that?"

***

Adria kept her horse's pace to a trot. They had ridden for most of the day and would need to stop for another break soon. The biggest issue with riding from Shipsbane to Alvadon was that there was no true road that connected the two cities, or even that connected Shipsbane to Maradon, which was where they intended to stop on the second night.

For tonight, they would have to make camp out in the open, as barely a tree stood in the open plains of Cerysia.

The other reason to slow down was because Krissette had finally ridden up next to her. Adria was hoping to be able to talk to her friend during this ride, but she didn't want to push Krissette if she was uncomfortable. "Hey." Adria wasn't really sure how to start, but she knew that if Krissette was willing to ride up to her, then the girl was willing to talk.

Krissette replied, "Hey," with a slight smile.

Adria looked at her for a moment. The two of them were physically very similar, except that Krissette was a hair taller and a little curvier. Ever since she saw Krissette and Delilah kissing, Adria couldn't help but wonder if Krissette had ever had those types of feelings toward her. *Did I lead her on to believe that I was interested? All I ever talked about was Marshall, though. She had to have known that I didn't feel that way.* Adria shook off the thought. Krissette had never given any indication that she'd felt anything toward Adria. One thing that was for sure, though, was that the two of them were rather honest and open about everything they *did* talk about.

"Krissette, you know I'm not mad at you, right?"

Krissette nodded, "I know. It's just, I've wrestled with this whole thing in my mind for a long time. Before all of you came to the island, I wasn't really that close to anyone there. Obviously we all got along, but I just never felt comfortable sharing what I was going through, mostly due to fear of them not understanding. I mean look at us," she put her finger to her left eye and touched her Mark, "we're already outcasts. The last thing I want is to be outcasted *from* the outcasts."

Adria thought for a moment about her parents. She'd always felt similarly, having parents from two different nations. It wasn't necessarily frowned upon, but definitely not common. Growing up, people definitely looked at her a moment longer, trying to determine her background. "I understand. I appreciate you talking about it now, though. If I acted awkwardly, I think it was mostly because I wondered…"

Krissette cut her off, "You wondered if I'd felt that way about you? That was one of the other reasons why I was nervous to talk to you about this. I didn't want you to think that I'd felt that way for you. Don't get me wrong, you're beautiful and wonderful, but that feeling was never there. Besides, you were smitten with Marshall the whole time. What did happen, though, was that I think becoming so close to you helped me to know for sure that I prefer women to men. I don't know why, to be honest, it just seemed to make more sense to me."

"That's fair. I can appreciate and understand all that. So…you and Delilah, then?"

Krissette laughed nervously. "Who knows? I kissed her because I was feeling brave this morning. I took a leap of faith, and before we could really talk about it, all of you walked in. I feel I may have sprung too much upon her in too short a time. She likely doesn't even want me to go with her."

Adria wondered something, but was hesitant to ask, for fear of sounding like she was trying to dissuade her friend. She decided to ask anyway, "Krissette, I'm not questioning your decision in asking this, just curious about your intentions. What sparked this decision to go? Why do you want to? Is it specifically to pursue something with Delilah?"

Krissette brushed her black hair from her face, and Adria wondered why she hadn't tied it up. "It's not so much to pursue something as it is to be able to talk to someone who's gone through what I'm experiencing. I just want to be able to talk about how I've been feeling and, I don't know, get some validation for all of it? Delilah seems so strong and sure of herself. And I figured Sindha wouldn't mind, because, well it's Sindha. I knew after one conversation with her that she's one of the nicest people in the world. I didn't think she would mind if I tagged along."

Adria eyed a few trees in the distance ahead, that seemed full enough to provide shade. She turned back to the rest of the company and shouted, "Trees up ahead! We'll break there!" Most of the others either nodded or grunted in agreement. This had been their longest stretch of riding for the day, and she knew all of them needed a break from the saddles. She turned back to Krissette, "Sorry. I was listening. You *should* go, then. From what I know of Delilah, she actually might be dealing with some confusion of her own, so if anything, you might even be able to counsel *her*."

After riding for another few minutes, they reached the group of trees and dismounted. Bam had already shoved a wooden stake into the ground near a tree for them to tie their horses. Adria secured her horse and then pulled two apples from her pack, holding one in her mouth and offering the other to her horse. Most of the others stretched or sat at the trees once they'd done the same for their horses. Adria walked amongst them, making sure all were in decent shape.

She passed Farrah, who was helping Badalao settle down next to a tree. Badalao had shared a horse with Farrah; she took the reins while he held onto her. Adria had to admit, despite her resentment toward Farrah, she had been by Badalao's side ever since he returned from the siege, and had waited on him hand and foot. She'd even made sure that his hair was done up in his traditional style. Adria overheard him talking to Lincan and Vasher. "Honestly, that's the only reason I'm alive. I think I did just enough inside his head to fight him off."

She stopped in her tracks and the hair on her neck and arms prickled up. "What are you talking about, Lao?"

Farrah, Lincan, and Vasher all looked at her, while Badalao turned his head in her general direction. She briefly forgot that he couldn't see and composed herself before any panic in her face became noticeable. Badalao responded, "Linc asked me about what happened with Raish in the castle. How I managed to survive, even though he killed Malikai."

Images of the siege and the deaths of her friends started to flood Adria's mind, but she pushed them all back and focused on Badalao. "You mind starting from the beginning again, Lao?"

He nodded, "Not at all. You didn't miss much. Linc asked about it and I said that when I walked into the ballroom, Vermillion soldiers littered the floor, but the strange thing was that there weren't any apparent wounds as if they'd died in combat. They were all killed quickly, likely at the same time. That was when I saw Raish and Kai lying next to each other on the floor. Kai... well looked the same as when you all saw him, and Raish was breathing heavily, with blood coming out of his nose and ears. He'd definitely been pushing himself too hard with his manifestation. And the strangest part was that he looked right at me and told me to kill him.

"As soon as he said it, the first thing I did was enter his mind. I was hoping to be able to grasp whatever it was that was making him so erratic. The thing is, though, he was already wrestling with something, someone else in his mind. The Red Harbinger, Jahmash. Except his presence was much stronger than when I felt him in Farrah's mind. I think it was because Jahmash was actually in there at the same time as me. He was trying to fully control Raish, and it was taking all of Raish's mental strength to fight him off. For Raish to tell me to kill him, he knew he wasn't going to be able to fight off Jahmash for very long. The only reason he wasn't able to kill me was because I was already in his head and was able to parry some of what Jahmash was trying to make him do against me.

"Honestly, I'm lucky that I escaped that fight only losing my eyes. Jahmash is supremely more powerful than I imagined, and I have no idea how Raish was able to keep him from completely controlling him for so long. We got lucky. You guys said Maqdhuum and Donovan appeared between us and Raish. If Donovan hadn't been in the way, I think all of us would have been struck down. I mourn for Donovan, but his sacrifice saved all of our lives."

Adria processed what Badalao was saying, but one thing didn't make sense. "I understand how Jahmash was able to get into Farrah's and Maqdhuum's heads, but how did he get into Raish's? We have yet to even encounter Jahmash in person. Can he reach our minds from far away now?"

Lao shook his head, "I think the issue here is that perhaps we do not know Raish as well as we thought. I'm not saying he is one of Jahmash's disciples, but clearly there is some part of his past that connects to the Harbinger."

"Horatio is Jahmash's son."

They all turned to look at the familiar voice, and a collective gasp ensued at the sight of Maqdhuum, his hair wet and stringy, and dressed in his usual all-black attire, though his clothes were ripped in various spots. Adria opened herself to her manifestation, and she was sure all the others did as well. "You. You took him away and promised us answers. You returned to the castle with that whole thing about Gideon's sword and then disappeared again. You'd damn well better have more than just that to tell us."

The Harbinger shrugged and took a breath. "I don't have a lot of time, but fine." He looked around. "Where's Baltaszar? He should be here for this."

Adria looked at him flatly. "Tasz and Desmond are headed to Vandenar. They're not with us. What is it?"

"Damn." Maqdhuum looked at the ground for a moment, as if pondering his next move. "You all dislike me enough already, so here goes. Keep in mind that I am now trying to atone for all of my mistakes. Jahmash had a woman imprisoned on his island sometime around sixteen years ago. I know this because I brought her there as a gift to get into his good graces. Her name was Raya Hammersland; she was

Baltaszar's mother."

Asarei came storming from several feet away, with Slade right behind. Asarei walked to within inches of Maqdhuum's face. "What the fuck did you just say? *You're* the one who abducted her? I'm going to beat the bloody piss out of you, and I don't give a shit how much you can disappear!" Asarei attempted to grab Maqdhuum's neck with his tattooed fist.

Maqdhuum disappeared and reappeared several feet away. "Look, do you want me to finish telling you this or not? I don't have much time, so the choice is yours."

Adria strode up to Asarei, then stood in front of him. She nodded to Slade to keep his heavily tattooed friend at bay, especially because Slade was big enough to keep Asarei back. "Go ahead, finish what you were saying."

"Thank you. Raya's manifestation was that she could leave her physical body to travel to the Three Rings. She's the one who made it possible for me to see the Orijin and transfer my mind to a new body. Anyway, I thought that if I brought her to Jahmash, he would be able to travel and see Darian, then get some closure or clarity, maybe even make a deal with the Orijin. Jahmash wasn't interested. My backup plan was to infiltrate his ranks, so I offered Raya as a gift to him. At some point, he decided to have a child with her, hoping to use that child as a spy in Ashur. Well, as fate would have it, that child ended up with a Descendant's Mark."

The air filled with murmurs and the chatter of everyone there. They all had questions, but Adria asked the one that was pressing in her mind. "Are you saying that Tasz and Raish have the same mother?"

The Harbinger lowered his eyes again, "Yes. Horatio knows this now. Baltaszar does not. I plan to tell him of this when I have a chance. I only just learned all this in the past few days."

Asarei stepped from behind Adria, "That's not why you're bloody here, though. What the fuck do you want?"

"You're right. I'm here because I'm trying to fix things. I have Horatio in captivity. I want to try and rid his mind of Jahmash's presence."

Adria's eyes went wide, "And to do that, you need Lao."

"Precisely. I will return him as soon as it's finished."

"Absolutely not. We can't trust you anymore."

Maqdhuum tilted his head slightly, "Can't trust *me*? If not for me showing up, Horatio would have struck you *all* down. The only reason any of you are still alive is because of me. Remember who singlehandedly went from house to house to rescue the survivors of the attack on Vandenar? That was me. And besides, even though *you* lead the Ghosts of Ashur, this is not *your* decision."

Badalao walked up to Adria's side, led by Farrah. "Right; it is *my* decision. After all, it's my services that you need. I was in Raish's mind while Jahmash was in there. I'm lucky all I lost were my eyes."

"You're right, Jahmash is not to be trifled with in that capacity." Maqdhuum dared to step closer to them again. "However, Jahmash is done with Horatio. Now that the boy's identity and treason have been discovered, Jahmash has abandoned him. You were able to rid him from Farrah's mind and my mind rather easily, because Jahmash was absent at the time. This would be just as easy."

"Where is he? Where would I have to go?"

Farrah spoke up, "We. Where would *we* have to go? Don't think for a second that I'm letting him out of my sight."

Maqdhuum casually waved his hands, as if to say he didn't care. "I wanted to do it right here, but I don't want to risk Raish or Jahmash knowing where all of you are. We can take no risks about giving him extra advantages. I have created a holding cell... somewhere. But I cannot disclose that information at the moment. I am certain that Jahmash is finished with Horatio, but that doesn't mean he can't pop into the boy's head at any moment. If that happens, he would know where Horatio is. And while it is impossible for Jahmash to get there any time soon, there's a good chance that his influence has reached the nations and governments beyond Ashur by now."

Badalao nodded, "I understand. It's smart to be safe. It would be even smarter to get it taken care of quickly, so that the possibility of Jahmash re-entering his mind is no longer a concern."

"Can we leave now, then? I can't imagine that it would take more than several minutes. I could return you before your company is ready to depart again."

Adria put her hand on Badalao's shoulder, "Are we sure about this, Lao? You know I trust your judgment, but you seem ready to jump into this with no hesitation."

Lao turned as if he meant to speak to the whole group. "Look, I was *in* Horatio's mind while he was struggling. He wanted me to kill him because of what Jahmash was doing to his mind. I take that to mean that the whole time we all knew him, Raish was doing everything he could to fight off Jahmash and prevent him from taking control. He might get on our nerves from time to time, but he is one of us."

"Oh, shit," Lincan exclaimed from behind Adria.

She turned to him, "What?"

"Nothing. Just a conversation I had with Tasz about… actually nothing. I just realized something. Don't pay me any attention."

Adria shrugged, "Right. Anyway, then."

Maqdhuum walked all the way up to Badalao and Farrah, despite a growl from Asarei. Maqdhuum rolled his eyes and addressed Badalao. "Look, aside from being a genuinely good person, Horatio *knows* Jahmash and has shared intimate details with the man much more recently than I have. There has to be some good information we can get from him in terms of strategy and weaknesses. I promise you all, my intentions are good. I could have easily just appeared and taken Badalao without explaining any of this."

Adria's face twitched as she remembered Maqdhuum doing that very thing to her and Gunnar. Except while she had survived, Gunnar was killed shortly after by Farrah. Adria attempted one last protest, but Maqdhuum had already grasped Badalao's and Farrah's arms, and the three were gone in an instant.

CHAPTER 3
A NEW FIRE

From **The Book of Orijin**, **Verse Four Hundred Seventy-Five**
Adversaries will present themselves in various shapes and forms.
Know their weaknesses before attempting to defeat them.

Baltaszar squeezed his feet into the sides of the mare, urging her to ride faster. He and Desmond had ridden for most of the day, taking only two short breaks, as Maximillian had given their horses enough energy to ride all the way to Edgeboro without stopping. Maximillian had advised them to stop every now and then anyway, as the horses still needed water and food.

Thoughts of Anahi continued to bombard his mind, and Baltaszar knew he wouldn't be able to properly rest until he knew that she was safe. He was sure that Desmond felt the same way about his family.

Desmond had kept pace with him the whole way, though they mostly rode in silence. The few words exchanged between him and Desmond were to confirm when to take breaks and when to start up again. They both understood the solemnity of their journey and were trying to prepare themselves for the worst. Baltaszar had spent so much time and energy consumed in his own mind that he barely even looked at Desmond. "Hey," he turned to his friend and yelled. "Hey! Break?"

Desmond nodded in agreement, and they gradually slowed their steeds to a stop. They dismounted and gave their horses water before letting them graze. They'd tested the beasts a little during the first break to see whether they would stray, but both seemed to be obedient. Baltaszar lay down in the grass and stared up at the afternoon sky. "Damn, we've been riding forever. My ass and thighs are killing me."

Desmond sat down a few feet away. "Yeah. I'm sore an' only goin' ta get worse as we go on. Still prefer it ta the alternative."

"You mean taking longer? Hell yeah. As fast as we're going, it's still not fast enough. How you holding up?"

Desmond shrugged, "Eh, my head's in knots. Can't stop thinkin' bout what we'll find there. Can't stop the dread, either. As much as I want ta hope that it won't be bad, somethin' deep down tells me there's no hope."

Baltaszar sat up and nodded in agreement. "I feel exactly the same. And I think that's exactly what I'm afraid of. Getting there and having it confirmed and not knowing how I'll deal with it."

"What ya mean? What would ya do?"

"Des, I haven't really handled crises well in my life. When my father died I left my town. I'm sure the people there probably would have killed me if I'd stayed, but I still left. Once I got out of the Never, though. You know that river that separates Mireya from the Never?"

"Yep. Best place fer fishin'."

"Also a great place for dying. I remember being on the shore, after getting out of the forest, and I had no clue about how I was going to get across. It was at that moment that everything I'd been going through finally just caught up with me and it nearly broke me. Des, I've never told anyone this, but I was ready to die there. I actually walked into the river and accepted the notion that it might've meant my death."

"Oh shit. An' so how'd ya...not die then?"

"Got bit by a snake in the water and a couple of fishermen must've seen me go down. The next time my eyes opened, I was at the Elephant, staring at Anahi. Even after that, though, you all saw what happened when I returned to Haedon and found out about Yas. I almost burned down the town and I set myself on fire. Munn Keeramm gave me a prophecy that I would kill my own brother. For a while, it sounded like such a ridiculous notion. But given how I've acted in the past, it doesn't seem beyond my capabilities."

"Tasz, ya need ta slow down fer a moment. We've both handled things poorly. Why do ya think I looked like a walkin' corpse the whole time we were on Asarei's island? I used all that power ta keep the House o' Darian up, an' then it caught up ta me. But I did the same thing as ye. I let it turn me inta an asshole. All o' us have shit that's too hard sometimes. At that point, it's up ta us ta decide how we're goin' ta handle it. When we get ta Vandenar, if it turns out that Anahi didn't make it, then ya have ta stop yerself before ya act. Ya don't have ta be the same kid that did all those things, or who tried ta fight me at the Elephant because ya were jealous." Desmond grinned for what seemed like the first time all trip and tossed a small rock at Baltaszar.

Baltaszar couldn't help but laugh as well. The act seemed to chip away at the boulder weighing down his neck, shoulders, and back. "That's pretty good life advice. Think first and don't be an asshole."

"Damn right it is. An' Tasz, don't let that be an option again. Givin' up on yer life. Especially now. Especially if things are fer the worst in Vandenar. We still need ya, an' there's still lots o' us who need ya around."

Tasz looked down and nodded. He gritted his teeth for a moment to stop a tear from forming. Bringing up everything to Desmond made it all more real for him as well, and it was the first time he'd really acknowledged his intentions at the river. "Thanks."

"He's right, there are more people than you realize who need you." The familiar voice came from several feet away, behind both of them. Baltaszar turned to see Maqdhuum walking toward them.

"What the hell are you doing here? I thought you abandoned us after Alvadon." Baltaszar stood up, as did Desmond.

Desmond joined in, "Yeah, dick. Where were ya when we could've used a quick trip back ta the island? We laid siege ta the castle an' then rode all the way back ta Shipsbane with barely any sight o' ya. Except when ya swooped in ta grab Adria without any notice. What the hell do ya want now?"

Maqdhuum walked closer and put his palms up, seemingly hoping that would stop Baltaszar's and Desmond's anger. "I know, I know. I'm sorry. But there are some things going on within and beyond Ashur that need my attention. I actually just ran into Adria and all the others. I needed to borrow Lao for a short while, and they told me that you two were headed to Vandenar and I thought that I could help you get there faster.

Baltaszar and Desmond looked at each other suspiciously. It was like being offered a free apple at the market and wondering what was wrong with the apple. Baltaszar's eyes thinned. "Why? What do you need from us?"

"Nothing. I need nothing from you. The only thing I need is to get back to Lao and Farrah quickly so we can handle our own business. It's like you were just saying, Desmond. Just because we might've been shitty in our lives before, doesn't mean we can't change that. If you must know, I left all of you to save Horatio. He isn't our enemy, he's just been used against us, and I'm trying to fix all that. So do you want to be in Vandenar in an instant or not?"

They both said "Yes," simultaneously. Baltaszar wondered what he meant about Horatio, but he couldn't focus on that at the moment.

"Good." Maqdhuum disappeared for a moment, then reappeared right in front of them with their two horses. "I'm sure you'll still need these." He handed off the reins to Baltaszar and Desmond. "Where should I bring you?"

"How bad is it there?"

Maqdhuum put his hands on his hips and glanced at the ground. "I tried to get as many survivors out as I could without getting killed. I went in and out until I was physically unable to keep going, so there's a possibility there are still survivors, but who knows if they're still there. Anyone sensible would have left for somewhere with more protection. Honestly, I wouldn't get my hopes up if I were you, but that doesn't mean there isn't a chance."

Desmond patted his black mare, "Bring us just inside the main gates."

"Very well. I should warn you, I don't know that I can come back for you. You'll be on your own once I bring you there."

Baltaszar bit his lip and nodded. "That's fine. There's a strong possibility we won't want anyone else to be around anyway." He and Desmond mounted their horses once again. Baltaszar opened himself to his manifestation as soon as he was in the saddle, ready for anyone who might be waiting in Vandenar.

Maqdhuum rested his hands on the two horses and in an instant, Baltaszar was surrounded by innumerable colors racing toward him, many of which he hadn't known existed. In a blink, they were on the main road of Vandenar, surrounded by lifeless bodies strewn about everywhere on the ground. In the confusion of it all, Baltaszar had released his manifestation only to realize that there was nothing here with enough life to attack them. The stench of rotting corpses and char was a punch to the nose.

He looked all around him and despite all the bodies, there was no sound to be heard save for the cool autumn wind. Maqdhuum broke the silence, "I must leave now. I hope that your time here is with as little difficulty as possible. And Baltaszar, there is a conversation we must have when we meet again, which I hope is soon. But for now, I know you must focus on this."

The Harbinger's words had barely reached Baltaszar's ears, though he'd taken in enough to be confused. He felt frozen in place by the utter destruction of the city that felt almost like a second home. Pillars of smoke billowed at various points in the distance. Desmond finally broke him out of his daze. "I'm goin' ta check on my family. This might all be easier if we both have our space. I'll meet ya back right here when I'm done."

Baltaszar nodded, "Yeah. I guess I should start with the Elephant. I know I have to go in there, I'm just afraid to."

"I'm scared, too. But we have ta do this, Tasz. The sooner we know the truth, good or bad, the better fer us."

"Right. Meet back here then." Baltaszar dismounted from his horse, removed his black cloak and draped it on the saddle, then walked toward the Happy Elephant. His black boots felt heavier than ever before. With every step, another memory of Anahi flashed before his eyes. He shook them off to evade the emotion, and also to be able to pay attention to where he was stepping. Bodies of Vithelegion, Vandenari, and Vermillion soldiers littered the road and the last thing he wanted to do was trip and fall into a bunch of corpses.

The entryway to the inn was wide open, as both doors had been broken off and were nowhere to be found. Bodies of various origins continued to litter the ground. The entire inn was filled with bodies, from the common room to the stairs that led up to the rooms, in most places the floor was barely visible. Baltaszar knew what he was looking for though. He focused on the outfits of the bodies, rather than the physical features. To the right, at the counter where Cyrus usually worked, he saw two figures on the ground, propped up against the side of the dark wooden counter. Both of their heads drooped down and they were each wrapped in grey cloaks. "No. Orijin, no." He rushed over to the one on the right and dropped to his knees, then gently lifted her head with his hand under her chin. "Anahi, no! NO!!!" He brought her lifeless head to his chest and held her there with his face against her head. His immediate tears flowed into her hair like drops of a powerless elixir.

Millions of thoughts ran through his mind as he held her, especially the name of her murderer. He moved her a few inches away from him and slid the cloak down, hoping to find where she'd been wounded. Almost immediately, he saw the gash on her pale neck and his tears flooded down his face once more. Baltaszar felt the urge to retch but composed himself. *Someone placed her here. Someone who cared about her enough to not want her to just be a body on the ground.* "But who?" He whispered to her unhearing ears. "Who killed you? And who put you here and covered you up?" He grasped her hands in desperation, hoping that maybe her ghost might appear and give him answers. As he put his fingers through her left hand, he felt something rolled up within her grip.

A note? Baltaszar desperately pulled the small parchment from her hand and set Anahi's body back against the counter, then unrolled the parchment. His eyes shot wide at the sight of it being addressed to him.

> *Baltaszar,*
>
> *I know one way or another, you're going to get this letter. I'm sorry about Anahi. We arrived too late to be able to stop it from happening. I hope you're not mad that I didn't bury her. I thought that if I did, her body wouldn't be discovered, and I wanted you to know for sure what happened to her. I know who killed her. He is a Vithelegion general named Khurt Everitas. We have his son with us and he confided that it was his father who killed her and Cyrus. I am with Avenira and Fae and the Vithelegion boy. By the time you read this, we will either be at the Tower, or have convinced someone there to bring us to the Anonymi Fortress. If everything goes to plan, the next time I see you, I will be behind an Anonymi mask. The Vithelegion also killed Munn. I mean to avenge him and will not stop until I do so. Please tell my cousin Desmond that I survived. He likely knows by now that the rest of our family did not. I apologize that we couldn't do more.*
>
> *For Ashur,*
> *Farco*

Farco. At least he made it out with some others. Baltaszar wiped away the remaining tears and looked up at Anahi's corpse. He knew he had come to a lull between crying fits and would need to use his time wisely before the next wave came. Baltaszar tucked the small parchment into his boot, then wrapped the grey cloak back around Anahi's body. Gently, he hoisted her onto his shoulder and walked out to the back of the Happy Elephant, then found a spade in one of the sheds and walked back to where he'd set her down. He knelt down next to her and held her hand once more, just before the next deluge of tears began. Glimpses of a whole lifetime raced through his head as his whimpers intermittently broke up the sobs.

As he stared into nothingness, he saw kisses and hugs, laughter, hand-holding, smiles, glares, and somehow the visions transformed into a wedding ceremony, being surrounded by friends and family, a home down the road from Munn Keeramm's house, and eventually children running around that same house, with only the sounds of laughter filling the air.

Why? Why did this have to happen? She was harmless. A maid at an inn. The only thing she ever did in her life was be nice to people. He'd kept his thoughts inside, knowing that his voice would likely crack and spill out only broken words. But his anger got the best of him. "Khurt Everitas. I'm going to fucking kill him. Only a coward would storm an inn and kill helpless people. And then I'll burn every last Vithelegion until the whole world is rid of them."

He stood and grasped the spade handle, digging away at the ground with reckless abandon. Every time the spade hit the ground it was a strike against the Vithelegion. Baltaszar didn't stop until the entire grave was dug. Once again, he sat next to Anahi's body, only this time he pulled her up next to him as if they were sitting together. He hugged her tightly, knowing it would be the last time he would ever do so. After several moments, Baltaszar knew that he would have to go through with burying her, or Desmond would eventually return and do it for him. He wanted to be able to have this to himself, so he kissed Anahi's forehead one last time and slowly set her in the ground, then covered her head with the grey cloak.

The spade felt heavier in his hand than before. Baltaszar stopped to take a deep breath and felt the void growing inside him. There was a coldness in his body and chest that he'd never felt before, which was especially noticeable considering that the wounds from the Jinn in his chest and face were always warm. He struck at the pile of dirt and began covering Anahi's body. *It is just her body. That's what Slade would tell you. And he would be right. She's up in Omneitria, looking down at you right now, waiting for you to join her.* He looked up at the sky, "Not yet, my love. There's too much evil in Ashur and coming to Ashur for me to leave this world just yet. I cannot see you again until I've avenged you. And I promise you, I will live my life well enough to be able to see you in Omneitria when I die." He paused for a moment to fight back another sob. "I promised you that I would look out for Fae, too. If she's training to be an Anonymi, then this world is in for some real trouble." His chuckle wasn't as forced as he thought it would be. He tightened his grip on the spade handle and continued to bury his love.

Once again, Baltaszar shoveled tirelessly without stopping. He knew that the Vithelegion had already wiped out most of Mireya, at least the northern cities. Once he finished honoring Anahi, he would talk Desmond into riding south to track them down. Together, they would kill any and every Vithelegion soldier they encountered. If Badalao and the others checked up on them, he would just tell them this business was more important, no matter how hard Adria tried to convince him otherwise.

The pile of dirt was finally down to nothing, and Anahi's grave was complete. He thought about leaving something there to mark it or place for symbolism, but there was nothing on him that was meaningful enough to matter. *It's not her anymore, just what she left behind.* He sat down next to her grave and wiped his brow. The sweat on his sleeve surprised him, but didn't detract his focus. Baltaszar clasped his hands in front of him and closed his eyes. *Orijin, I know we don't have many of these conversations, and in all fairness, I don't really ask much of you. But I need your help now. Please help me avenge her death. You know better than I that she was as pure as a person can be.* He could feel the tears flowing from the corners of his tightly closed eyes. *Please let me come face to face with her murderer. I honestly don't know if it will bring me peace to kill this Khurt Everitas but I need to face him. If you can do this for me, I promise I will do everything in my power to protect Ashur and stop Jahmash from succeeding.*

After several deep breaths, Baltaszar felt a familiar warmth grow inside his mind. He wasn't sure if the Jinn or the Orijin were responsible, but at least it was confirmation that someone was listening to his prayer. He remained there and opened himself to his manifestation, though he didn't know why. It simply felt right, and he wanted to feel the melody course through his veins. The sensation allowed him a few moments of clarity, free of any emotion. He finally stood up again and blew a kiss to the clear afternoon sky, hoping Anahi's soul could really see him from the Three Rings. He realized that the sun was starting to get low and walked back to where they'd left their horses.

Desmond was already there, sitting at the side of the road. He'd moved a bunch of the dead bodies and created a clearing around him, but he stood at the sight of Baltaszar approaching. Baltaszar reached down and grabbed the parchment from his boot. "Farco left a note. In Anahi's hand. He told me about your family, too. I'm sorry, Des." No more words were exchanged between them. Instead, they approached each other and embraced in a tight hug. Despite all the crying he'd already done, somehow the shared grief between the two of them made the tears flow even stronger, and the sobs even louder. Baltaszar cried for Anahi and Cyrus and Desmond's family, and continued to cry for Malikai, Kadoog'han, Reverron, Donovan, and Blastevahn. He cried for his father, the rift with his brother, for the guilt of being on the other side of Ashur when Anahi was murdered, and for the deaths of hundreds of Mireyans who likely never had a chance to defend themselves against the Vithelegion. And with it all, Baltaszar cried at the acknowledgement that he'd once wanted to end his own life. The thought of all of the people and experiences he would have missed out on made him cry even harder.

Each of their right shoulders were soaked and neither of them cared. Desmond sobbed just as loudly and Baltaszar knew it was for the same things, as well as for whatever personal demons his friend had been holding in. When the waves of tears and sobs finally subsided, Baltaszar looked up, as did Desmond. He knew that his friend's splotchy and snot-dripping face was a mirror image of his own, and Baltaszar surprisingly let out a small laugh. "Your face and mine probably look exactly the same."

Desmond wiped his face against his own sleeve and then smiled. "Thanks. I think we both let out about two years o' cryin', huh."

Baltaszar nodded, "Maybe even more."

"Oh shit, what happened ta yer eyes?"

"What you mean? I don't know? Red and bloodshot from crying?"

"No, not that part. Yer pupils. They're different from before. Yah used ta have brown eyes. Now they're…they're like fire. Swirls o' red an' orange an' yellow."

Baltaszar took a step back. He didn't feel any different but knew that Desmond wouldn't make something like this up, especially given the situation. "I don't know. I buried Anahi and then got lost in my thoughts for a while. Prayed to the Orijin and then opened myself to my manifestation. Maybe that did something."

"Holy shit, Tasz. That's weird. What ya think it means?"

Baltaszar shrugged, "Maybe it's a sign that we should ride south and kill the fucking Vithelegion." He raised his eyebrows, waiting in anticipation for Desmond's response.

"They killed my whole family. I'm goin' ta send 'em flyin' so far, they'll be back across the sea." They walked to their horses and Baltaszar donned his black cloak once again.

"Here," He still had Farco's message in his hand, "you should read this, too."

Desmond took the parchment and read it over. "I hope they didn't kill Everitas, so we can do it ourselves. Maybe his son, too. Knowin' Far and Avenira, they've already made it ta the Anonymi fortress. I'm so thankful at least they made it out."

"That just reminded me that Munn is dead."

"We should head over ta his house."

"You think so? Farco probably would have given him a proper burial before they left."

"Not fer that. All his books. They're useless ta us because we can't read 'em. But we can check on 'em, save what we can an' come back ta bring 'em ta the Tower."

***

The sun barely hung over the horizon by the time they rode out of Vandenar the next morning. Neither of them had slept well, despite the comfortable beds at Munn Keeramm's home. Before leaving Vandenar, Desmond had made it a point to go inside the Happy Elephant and see the chaos for himself, then pay his respects to Anahi. Until then, Baltaszar had almost forgotten that she and Desmond had known each other for so long. They had spent their entire lives in Vandenar, while Baltaszar had only arrived here for the first time two years before.

After the storm of emotions he'd faced the day before, Baltaszar felt mostly numb since waking up. His mind barely processed anything but superficial thoughts.

Save for a few abandoned wagons here and there, the Way of Sunsets proved to be barren for quite a while, to no surprise. If the Vithelegion had wiped out most of Mireya, if not all, there would be no signs of life.

After riding for most of the morning and some of the afternoon, they saw Khiry on the horizon, and more plumes of smoke. Baltaszar turned to Desmond, who kept his horse to a trot next to Baltaszar. "More smoke. You think that's just destruction, or somebody there? The Vithelegion have to be camping out somewhere, right? They sure as hell aren't in Vandenar, and Maqdhuum said Gangjeon was empty as well."

Desmond looked at him with barely any emotion in his face, "Only one way ta find out. What's a bunch o' soldiers against fire an' levitation? They may be great fighters, but they're just human beings. You an' me are more than that."

They slowly rode on, cautious of their surroundings and constantly looking around for an ambush. Baltaszar allowed his manifestation to course through him. If the Vithelegion were hiding, then they were brilliant at it. Baltaszar could see the entryway, and the main gate to the city was completely destroyed. Almost no sign of it remained, save for one post at the side of the entryway. A shout came out of nowhere, but Baltaszar and Desmond couldn't find the source. As they looked up, a volley of arrows hurtled through the sky toward them. *Shit.*

"I got it. Don't worry." Just as Desmond spoke, the arrows stopped in mid-air, high above them. He glanced at Baltaszar with a smirk. "I'll hold 'em there fer a moment. Let's ride closer an' find 'em. Then you can set 'em on fire an' I'll return 'em."

"You can hold them for that long?"

"We've come a long way since the House o' Darian, huh."

Baltaszar nodded, "You can say that again. Alright, let's go." They cautiously neared the entryway to Khiry. Baltaszar knew that, despite their need to be cautious, whoever shot those arrows had to be scared at the sight of them still hanging there in the sky. He kept his eyes up, knowing that even if the archers weren't high up, there had to at least be a lookout somewhere on a rooftop. Then he caught the scout's mistake. On the rooftop just to the left of the main gate, a man stood somewhat hidden by the chimney. Baltaszar only noticed him once he raised his arm to point to the arrows. "There. To the left on the roof. You have enough focus to be able to send one arrow at him?"

Desmond smiled without turning his head; his eyes were locked on the scout, who was now looking down and shouting something. "Easy." One arrow turned in the sky to face their target, and Baltaszar focused his attention on it. Within a heartbeat, the arrow was in flames. "Here we go. Have ta do it fast so he can't react." The flaming arrow zipped downward toward the unsuspecting scout. In another heartbeat, the man collapsed with a scream. They couldn't see his body from their vantage point, but Baltaszar knew for sure that the man didn't stand up again. "Let's go. Quickly while the archers are still near. These arrows are a waste if they get away."

They rode confidently to the broken-down entryway and saw nearly a dozen men, looking either up at the sky, up at the roof, or toward the entryway. They shouted at the sight of Baltaszar and Desmond. Without a word, Baltaszar set the floating arrows on fire and Desmond sent them streaking down at the archers. Most hit their mark, though with varying success. Most of the archers wore breastplates, and some helmets, which made Desmond pause. "Wait. Des, those are Vermillion soldiers. Look at the red crests on their helmets. Those aren't Vithelegion."

"Yeah, an' they still tried ta kill us."

"Fair point. Let's return the favor.."

"Only hurt some o' them, though. We're outnumbered. Gion' ta have ta stick ta the manifestations."

Desmond had barely finished speaking when Baltaszar heard the voice in his head. *We have given you a new knowledge. Trust your manifestation. Focus your eyes on your target.* Baltaszar blinked several times, trying to process the words and their source.

I thought you were done speaking to me.

We were never finished. We told you that you must prove yourself worthy. You have carried yourself properly so far and have made wise decisions. We have rewarded you as such. Focus. And heed our words.

Baltaszar nodded and focused on the Vermillion soldiers in the distance. He wanted to ask Desmond whether he was sure this was the right thing to do. Surely if the Vermillion were here, then they were tracking the Vithelegion and fighting them. What confused him was why they would attack him and Desmond. *They've been hunting and killing us for decades. Even when they're protecting Ashur, they're only protecting some of Ashur. Besides, the Jinn even told me to kill them. That leaves no room for doubt. Right?*

As the remaining soldiers got back to their feet and reoriented and rearmed themselves, they stalked toward Baltaszar and Desmond. *What did they say again? Focus my eyes?* He concentrated only on his manifestation and focused on the handful of soldiers running toward him. The pressure in his face and head built slowly, but not in a painful way. It almost felt as if something was trying to force itself out of him. He silenced his thoughts and let the manifestation take control. The pressure grew warmer, and he no longer tried to fight it. Streaks of flames shot out of his eyes, straight at the oncoming soldiers. The fire moved so quickly that the Vermillion had no time to react. Baltaszar shifted his head to ensure that he hit all of them, and in a matter of seconds, every one of the soldiers had crumpled to the ground.

"What the fuck was that?"

Baltaszar smiled at Desmond, "I guess that explains why my eyes changed." He stared out at the charred heaps on the ground and his smile faded. "Let's go find the Vithelegion. I'll find Khurt Everitas, confront him face to face and send fire through his eyes and out the back of his bloody skull."

***

Badalao walked out of Eddis Ebaba's home, led by Farrah. She gripped his arm firmly and stayed as close to his side as she could, without being too close to make him stumble. Ever since losing his eyes, Badalao had tried to focus on letting his other senses guide him. He tried to judge proximity with his ears and use his nose to help understand who or what was around him. The trouble was that his face was in terrible pain, despite Lincan's attempts to heal him.

While Farrah led him, Badalao attempted to enter her mind and use her eyes to see their surroundings. When he'd originally suggested the idea to her, Farrah consented instantly without hesitation. Still, Badalao didn't want to make a habit of it, as doing so too often would border on intrusion.

Ever since Badalao had found out about her history and involvement with Jahmash, he'd been overly cautious about how much to trust her. However, since then, Farrah had provided absolutely no reason to think she was being disingenuous about her feelings toward him. If anything, she had been nothing but devoted to him. Badalao had been tempted to delve into her mind to probe whether that devotion was genuine, but he thought better of it. He wondered whether part of her behavior was due to guilt or a desire to prove herself. Regardless, she had waited on him hand and foot and tended to his every need ever since they'd returned to the island from their siege. And along with that, she hadn't acted like she was trying too hard.

He heard Maqdhuum and the other man talking several feet ahead of them, and assumed they'd stopped walking, as their voices felt closer. He'd briefly spoken to Eddis Ebaba while waiting for Maqdhuum to return. The man was kind and hospitable and offered medicine to help with Badalao's pain once he was finished with Maqdhuum's business. Badalao had happily obliged and looked forward to anything that would dampen the pain in his face.

"Horatio is only a few feet in front of you, Lao," Maqdhuum whispered to him. "Once you are ready, I will open the holding cell and grant you entry. I warn you, do only what is necessary and be done with it. No reason to tempt fate."

Badalao nodded in agreement. "I understand. Don't worry, I'm eager to get back inside of Eddis's home and take the medicine he promised me."

"Good." He felt Maqdhuum grasp his forearm. "Let's go. Don't use anyone's eyes while you're inside his mind. Just go in, push out Jahmash's presence, and then you're in the clear." Badalao heard the lock open and the chain clink against a metal bar. Maqdhuum continued, addressing Horatio. "Raish, it's me, Maqdhuum. I have Lao here to help you. He's going to get your father out of your head. End your suffering."

"Thank you. He hasn't been in my mind since that conversation he had with you, but still. I'd like to make sure he doesn't come back. Hey Lao. Thanks for doing this."

Lao choked on a laugh, "Are you kidding, Raish? It's the least I could do. I don't know how you fought him off for as long as you did. I'm sorry you've had to struggle through this on your own for so long. Rest easy, though. It shouldn't take long." Badalao let Maqdhuum guide him.

"Lao, you feel that? There's a bale of hay right in front of you, grazing against your shin. Turn and sit on that, then Raish will sit on the ground right in front of you. Once you're ready, you can start the process." Badalao turned and slowly sat on the bale then felt Horatio's shoulders against his shins. Maqdhuum had blindfold Horatio, as well as bound his hands behind his back. Hopefully there was no way his friend could hurt him if Jahmash tried to force it.

He took a deep breath. *This shouldn't be difficult. It took mere moments to clear Farrah's head of him.* "Ready, Raish?"

"Ready."

Badalao heard the clink of metal and assumed that Maqdhuum had left the holding cell. It made sense just in case anything went wrong. He opened himself to his manifestation and rested a hand on Horatio's head. It wasn't necessary to make contact, but it was easier, especially without being able to see anything. Badalao reached out with his mind and entered Horatio's. The sensation was almost like walking into the ocean. There wasn't much resistance if the person was willing to let him in or was unaware. Badalao barely felt Jahmash's presence, like the slight discomfort of an out-of-reach itch. But remnants of the man were still there.

Every mind looked different after Badalao initially entered it. After many years of experience, Badalao assumed it had to do with specific factors such as imagination and emotion. Some minds were wide open to wander freely, while others involved compartments such as walls or caves. He hadn't spent any time delving into Horatio's mind before this, but the setting of a fishing town quickly materialized.

Badalao found himself standing in the middle of a rock-paved road. He looked around, trying to see if Horatio's mental representation was within sight. Once they'd returned to Asarei's island and he'd had a little time to recover, Badalao began experimenting with his ability to see through Farrah's eyes by entering her mind. He realized then that he didn't need his physical eyes to "see" when in someone else's mind.

The distant itch that he'd felt before instantly became more present, and Badalao heard a voice, as if in his own mind. "Horatio didn't bring you here. I did. This is where he grew up, with his adoptive mother." Suddenly, a tall, slender man with short black hair appeared in front of Badalao. He put a hand to his chest and smiled, "We haven't met yet, Badalao Majime, but my name is Jahmash."

Badalao took a step back and almost stumbled from the panic. "Why are you still using him?"

Jahmash laughed as Badalao scampered a few more paces backward. "Don't worry, boy. I cannot extend my will upon you here. Much like I imagine it works for you, I have to have physical contact to create that bond with someone. I will not be able to link our minds here, unfortunately." The man continued to smile at him, as if unaware that he was the single-most feared man in all of Ashur. Badalao took a breath and stood back up, several feet away from Jahmash. The Red Harbinger continued. "He is alive, which means he still has purpose. But I am not here for him. I am here for you. I have been checking in every now and then to see when you would arrive. And here you are."

"You knew I would be here? How?"

"It was the predictable thing to do. Abram found out the true nature of his mind and confined him to an uninhabited island. I must say, the parallels of it all are rather ironic, don't you think?" He paused, and continued after Badalao didn't laugh, "But why *wouldn't* Abram ask you to free Horatio's mind? Imagine everything you could learn about me. Now, 'Lao', here is my proposition. Help me."

If this conversation had been taking place in the physical world, Badalao knew that he would have choked or fallen to a knee, or something of the sort. His mental fortitude was much stronger. *Help him?* "What?"

"You know what. I want you to join my cause. You would be a valuable asset in this war. And your allegiance would guarantee a place for you and your family in Ashur. I would ensure that the Majime family would be in power until the Orijin has had enough of humanity."

Badalao was about to ask why, but he stopped himself. He didn't care about why. The reason was that Jahmash just wanted another piece he could use, just as he'd used Horatio and Farrah. "And if I do not?"

Jahmash's smile grew thinner and wider. "Then there will be no Majime family left once I am done with Ashur."

Badalao looked at him flatly as he attempted to loosen Jahmash's grip on Horatio's mind. *Let him get worked up and distracted.* "What is with you and feeling the need to massacre everyone who disagrees with you? Even back to Darian. The man simply told you that you were mistaken, and rather than see reason, you had almost all of his wives and children murdered. And if that wasn't enough, you swore revenge on the rest of us because we saw those actions as monstrous." He felt his mental reach growing slowly and steadily throughout Horatio's mind.

"You do not get to judge my life, you *infant.* You know nothing of what I lived through. How many lives I saved and tried to save. How many people I allowed myself to love and care for, only to watch them suffer or die because they refused to heed my word. Or because I refused to enter their minds and change their perspectives for them." As he continued, Badalao focused on navigating Horatio's mind and finding every point in which Jahmash's presence had extended. The grip was more in depth than it had been in Farrah's mind or Maqdhuum's.

Jahmash continued, "Had I followed the Orijin's directives, I would have been successful, but at odds with my own conscience. How can God himself command you to do something that goes against your morals? And do you know who got blamed for the death and chaos? Not the Orijin. I did. Me. Gideon gave his life for our cause. Darian, Abram, and Lionel were much more likable than I. Of course the world would not find fault with them.

"Everywhere I turned, another woman would fall in love with Darian, including my own wife. All I needed was one. One woman. And that was too much to ask. And in all of that, the world wanted Darian as its king. The whole reason that Orol Taghdras fell to shit in the first place was because people fought to be the sole ruler of it. Everyone wanted the throne. So much so that it caused a civil war. They do not teach you that part, though, do they? They only tell you that the Harbingers saved the world and evil Jahmash turned on the others and killed them. What a ridiculous summarization of it all. Do you really think it would be so simple?"

Got it. Badalao wanted to think of something clever or profound to say but doing so would cost him the moment and the element of surprise. The mental representation of Jahmash still stood before him in the middle of the street, about to continue his rant, when Badalao pulled strongly with his mind against Jahmash's grip and ripped it from Horatio's mind. In an instant, Jahmash vanished before him, and the surroundings of Horatio's mind were blank once again.

He withdrew himself from Horatio's mind and was once again aware of his own body. At first, Badalao wondered why everything around him was still dark, and only after a moment did he remember that he no longer had eyes. *Must be getting used to the pain for me to forget.* "Raish? Did it work? Do you still feel him?" He still felt his friend's shoulders against his knees; it seemed as if they were shaking or shivering. "Raish, are you alright?"

"Y-yeah. I just don't know what to think. I don't feel him in my head, and it feels pretty strange. My mind always had that…boundary around it and I was used to it. Now the freedom seems kind of scary. I don't think I've ever been able to admit it before, but I've never had a free thought in my life." As Horatio grew accustomed to his freedom, Badalao heard the clink of the lock opening and then the door itself open.

He knew it must be Maqdhuum checking on the outcome. "I did it." He was about to elaborate, but Maqdhuum cut him off.

"What took so long? You were in there for nearly a half an hour."

Badalao's natural response was to raise his eyebrows, but the motion hurt his face, causing him to reach for his forehead. "Ow. Dammit. I was in there that long? Jahmash was in Raish's mind as well. He's been expecting this. The weird thing is that it was rather easy to get rid of him. I managed to distract him by asking about his motivation in all this, and he went on a rant. While he got lost in that, I just worked on loosening his grasp wherever I could and all of a sudden, I just pulled it all away from him."

He heard Maqdhuum sort of snort air out of his nose. "He's a tricky one. If he was expecting you or us, chances are he wanted it to be that easy. He tell you anything?"

Badalao nodded, "That is the craziest part. He was trying to recruit me. He asked me to join him; he even promised that my family will have a prominent place in Ashur after he kills everyone. I suppose it's nice to know that I have options. Then again, he promised to massacre my family if I refused his offer, so we're going to have to make sure that Markos is ready."

"Yeah. He'll attack there first. Taiju is well-positioned as the northernmost city, but it is ill-equipped for an attack by sea. We will have to fortify it. Otherwise your family in Constaniza will be an easy target. That being said, he's afraid of you and your potential, Lao. Only reason he would recruit you is he's worried about how strong you are. You said you kicked him out of Farrah's head without issue."

"That's encouraging."

"It is. But don't get overconfident. Jahmash isn't a two-bit soldier that you can just outduel with a sword. He's smart. He thinks steps ahead of what he's currently doing. He *wants* you to dwell on how easy that whole process was. He wants you to let your guard down, tell everyone that you're stronger than he is. And while there's a possibility it's true, Lao, it's still too dangerous to assume it. We need to get you back to the others."

Badalao stood up. "No. If he's steps ahead of us, then I need to go directly to Garrison. Before we left Markos last time, I provided my sister with detailed instructions on how to fortify and prepare the nation. I had a feeling even then that Markos would be a target. And still, that might not be enough. We need to prepare all of Ashur *now*. That means working with the Kraisos and the Anonymi to reach every city of every nation. Take me and Farrah to Alvadon, and I'll just mentally tell Adria that we're there already."

"Let's go. No time to waste." Maqdhuum patted him on the shoulder, then led him out of the cell and back to Farrah. "I'm going to leave Raish here for now. Let him get used to his new mind. Also make sure that Jahmash is definitely gone."

CHAPTER 4
ENTER THE ANONYMI

*From **The Book of Orijin**, Verse Three Hundred Fifty-Eight*
You will find help from unexpected allies. Trust that you are not alone
in your fight and you shall find success.

Khurt Everitas sat down on the cool stone ground, sweat dripping from his brow. The motion of wiping his face caused the shackle to press into his raw, chafed wrist, making him wince. He'd been in the dungeon cell for several days, chained to the wall with shackles around his neck and both wrists and ankles. There had been enough give with the chains for him to move around a few feet or so, but Khurt had spent most of his energy trying to break the chains from the wall. His efforts had only resulted in sore shoulders and severely chafed wrists and ankles.

The cool stone felt good against his back, despite the fact that he'd been stripped down to his smallclothes. His captors had barely spoken to him since he'd been brought here, though they hadn't been unkind. Khurt had received food and water consistently, and his waste bucket was changed regularly. One man in particular came to check his progress often, a golden-skinned man with long blonde hair like a lion. The man had yet to speak to him, despite Khurt yelling and screaming at him, demanding to know what happened to Khenzi. The last thing Khurt remembered was the same man striking him and knocking him down a flight of stairs. When Khurt had woken up, he was in this cell, already in shackles. He couldn't fathom how they could have moved him all the way to a dungeon cell without him waking up.

If Khenzi had been taken by them as well, there was no evidence of it. Khurt regularly spoke aloud to see if anyone would answer, and the lack of response proved he was alone on this level of the dungeon. As a Vithelegion captive, he could understand why he would be separated from the others, though he wondered whether Khenzi might be in the same dungeon, just in a different part of it. The most favorable outcome would have been that Khenzi escaped with the other Vithelegion and was safe with Khurt's battalion.

All he'd thought about since then was his son and the desperate hope that Khenzi was still alive. He'd hoped that the Ashurians wouldn't kill a child, but the thought brought him back to the first city that the Vithelegion had raided and the boy he'd stabbed through the stomach, who'd known nothing about worshiping Darian or anything of the sort. *I'm no better than these people. If they spared Khenzi, then I'm actually worse.* He remembered the little boy, lying innocently in his bed, asking questions and oblivious to Khurt's intentions. What made it worse was that Khenzi knew nothing of it and assumed that Khurt had killed some violent attacker.

Every time the lion-maned man came to see him he walked down a flight of steps on the other side of the corridor. It was the only evidence Khurt had that he was in one section of a larger dungeon. He heard the faint clack of boots on stone coming from those same steps, except the frequency indicated more than one set of boots. He craned his aching neck to the right to see if it was the lion-maned man once again, but the pain of stretching away from the wall again convinced him to sit back. The two sets of boots neared and echoed through the corridor. Khurt continued to look down; if he attempted to watch them walk all the way toward him, it would make him look eager and weak. He took a deep breath and looked at the floor between his raised knees. The clack of the boots stopped right in front of his cell. "Khurt Everitas of the Vithelegion," the deep voice sounded urgent, but not angry. Khurt looked up, at first confused about how they would know his name, but then remembered his desperate pleas to be reunited with Khenzi when he first regained consciousness. He couldn't remember exactly what he'd said, but surely his name was the bare minimum of what he'd shared in his despair.

Khurt stared at the source of the voice, a tall figure, at least a hand taller than Khurt. The voice was a man's, but it came from behind a red metallic mask with eye holes and a slit for a mouth. The statuesque man was sheathed in a cloak that was so off-putting that he heaved up some of his breakfast after staring at it. The cloak was almost indescribable—a blend of colors that changed as it moved, and yet, he couldn't identify a single color on it. Khurt stood to make sure none of his vomit had landed on him, then licked his teeth and spat. He looked back at the two men; the other was the lion-maned man that he'd seen so frequently already. "You know my name. Good for you. Who are you?"

The blonde-haired man nodded and spoke first, "I am Wendell Ravensdayle, commander of the Royal Vermillion Army. I defeated you in combat. You are far away from your people. We have treated you well in the hopes that you might be open to sharing information about the Vithelegion and how we can… get you to leave Ashur."

Khurt put a hand on his head, which still felt foggy from time to time. Still, there was something familiar in what Wendell Ravensdayle had just said. *Vermillion?* "You said the Royal Vermillion Army?" Wendell nodded. Khurt's eyes narrowed as he glared at Wendell in the eyes. "What hypocrisy is this?"

Wendell cocked his head in response. "What do you mean?"

Khurt paused for a moment to try and remember all of the details of their original encounter with the Royal Vermillion Army. "Yongradae. Mireya. Easton…Grey?" He mumbled to himself to put it all together. "The first city that we laid siege to in Ashur, it was a place called Yongradae. I only know that because your army arrived, attacked us, retreated, and then approached us to form a pact. Is Easton Grey not one of your generals?"

Wendell turned to the other man with a quizzical countenance, then looked back at Khurt. "He is. Explain this encounter to me."

His general is a traitor and he doesn't know. "After your army realized it could not win, one of the Vermillion generals halted the battle and requested to speak with us. His name was Easton Grey. He told us that he would allow us to destroy all cities in the nation of Mireya, as long as we didn't burn anything down. Something about killing all 'Descendants of Darian.' And that we could claim the nation of Mireya as our own once we helped to cleanse Ashur of all of these Descendants. The Vermillion stayed out of our way as we decimated the next few cities; in fact, they even showed us how to get to each one. We laid waste to the western coast of Ashur and your royal army allowed it. So I find it strange that you would imprison me for the very thing you allowed me to do. Have you changed your mind, Commander Wendell Ravensdayle of the Royal Vermillion Army?"

Ravensdayle glanced at the taller, masked man, and then glared at Khurt. "You said it was Easton Grey who negotiated this… *arrangement*?"

Khurt nodded and flicked a piece of regurgitated food off his pant leg. "Indeed."

The blonde-haired man's chest rose and fell with a deep breath. He looked down at his hands and muttered quietly, as if to himself more than Khurt or the other man, "How? How did we let that happen? Edmund's loyalists were never supposed to be that far from Alvadon. All that blood is on my hands." He balled his hands into fists and looked up at Khurt. "We need your help, Khurt Everitas. We barely stopped them in Vandenar. We need to know how to get rid of the entire Vithelegion without more bloodshed. If the Vermillion army has been compromised, then our forces will definitely not be enough to defeat them."

Khurt balked and a gasp escaped before he was even aware of it. "*My* help? What concern do I have if you cannot drive us out? I am not of your people. I am Vithelegion. Helping you means I would be responsible for my own people's failure."

Ravensdayle looked at him flatly, "And what about your son? Would you sacrifice the rest of your people to be reunited with him?" Khurt punched his palm, uncaring of the scrape and burn of the shackles against his wrists.

Dammit. Khenzi for the whole Vithelegion. Khurt disregarded the two men and turned to face the stone wall behind him. He pressed his head against the cold stone, allowing it to relieve some of the ache that pervaded his head and body. *Khenzi for the rest of them.* Khurt took a deep breath and cleared his mind. He'd already come to terms with the notion that his captors would most likely not return him to his people. If he didn't help them, he would either die or live out his days in this cell, but it wouldn't just be his own life at stake. If he did help them, he would be a traitor to his people and his whole existence. *The same people that turned on me. The same general that demoted me and left me for dead while no other general stood up for me.* He held on to those thoughts for a moment while they fully digested, then turned around to face Ravensdayle and the masked man again.

"No killing, right?"

Ravensdayle looked at him with raised eyebrows. "Of course."

Khurt didn't fully believe him. "I need to know that you are true to your word. No killing. I cannot be complicit in the genocide of my own people. I understand why you would want to wipe us out; I would feel the same way. We arrived on your shores with that same impetus. However, we were misinformed about your ideologies and..."

"And yet your people continue to kill ours." The masked man cut him off. "Don't worry. We are true to our word."

Khurt punched his palm again. "Fine. I will make them accept defeat and retreat back to the ships. But that can only happen one way."

"We're all ears," Ravensdayle crossed his arms impatiently.

"If I challenge the Master General, Saol Suldas, to combat. One on one. I have sparred against him before and won. I can defeat him again. If I defeat Suldas, the rest will return home. This war is Suldas' war. Not all of us agreed to it, not all will continue with Suldas defeated."

Ravensdayle squinted at him. "You do not want to be a traitor, but you would kill your own commander? No wonder you all got on so well with Easton Grey."

"It is not that simple. I was Saol's First General. There are eight ranks after Saol. I was the highest rank next to Saol Suldas. On our voyage here, I pleaded with him to extend mercy once we arrived. His goal was to kill anyone who was unwilling to relinquish their faith as a worshiper of Darian. I do not necessarily have to kill him to defeat him."

Ravensdayle interjected, "We do not worship Darian. We worship Orijin and celebrate *all* of the Harbingers except Jahmash."

"I am aware of that now," Khurt nodded. "Regardless, I lobbied for us to take captive anyone who was unwilling to readily convert. I didn't see the point of killing everyone in our path. Understand that invasion is not the Vithelegion way. But Saol is overzealous. He thinks he is unstoppable. I didn't even tell my wife what our true mission was, because I knew she would try to shame me into standing up to Saol.

My point is, after attempting to be firm with Saol Suldas and the other generals about being merciful, Saol demoted me to Eighth General, then manipulated me and threw me overboard, leaving me for dead. My feet still ache and burn from the impact of the sea. My own commander already tried to kill me. I have no love for him or loyalty to him. I do, however, believe that the Vithelegion would be more than willing to return home if Saol is killed, especially by me. Then they will not need to avenge his death by continuing to besiege Ashur."

Wendell Ravensdayle stared at Khurt for a few moments, as if processing everything he'd just been told. He glanced at the man in the red mask, then looked back at Khurt. "You are sure that this will work? That you would go through with killing your own general, and that the Vithelegion would retreat as a result?"

"I am certain that I can defeat Saol in a duel. But not certain that I must kill him."

The masked man spoke up. "Khurt Everitas, you realize that if your plan does not work, we will have no choice but to engage them in battle. Even if it means we would lose, war would be the only solution. That means more of your people would die."

"It will work. So what now? How long do I stay in this cell? And when do I get to see my son?"

"I will bring you to him shortly," the masked man replied. "However, there is more to it than simply releasing you and trusting your word. From this point on, you fight for us. I belong to an order known as the Anonymi. We will train you and adopt you as one of our own. Your son has already begun his training and has shown promise in combat, despite his size."

Khurt was about to argue when the man put a hand up to quiet him. "Save your protest. The very people in Vandenar that you Vithelegion attempted to eradicate saved your son's life and brought him to us. The Anonymi fortress is literally the safest place in Ashur for your son. No one in Ashur besides members of the Anonymi and a select few, know the location of the Anonymi fortress. You are Vithelegion no more, Khurt Everitas. Today, you enter the Anonymi. When you face Saol Suldas in combat you will do so as an Anonymi. Wearing the gold mask of an Anonymi soldier. You will only be allowed to remove your mask and helmet in order for him to know who you are. You will no longer be Khurt Everitas once you begin your training."

Khurt stared at the man, and only after a moment did he realize his mouth hung open. "And what of my wife and daughter? I have a life back in Vitheligia! A good one!"

The masked man nodded. "You came here accepting that death might be an option. Accepting that you might not return home. Would you rather us kill you and your son?"

He closed his eyes and shot breath out through his nose. Even if the question wasn't rhetorical, the man had to know Khurt's answer. "When do I face Suldas?"

Despite the mask, Khurt knew the man had to be smiling behind it. "Tomorrow. You will be fed well today and tomorrow morning, and fitted for your Anonymi armor, robes, and mask. Once you have been properly looked after and prepared, you will travel with me and a squadron to meet the Vithelegion at their camp. Then you will do your part."

His palm was growing sore from hitting it so much. He would have to be conscious about not punching it. Khurt tried his best not to think about being stranded in Ashur and focused on seeing Khenzi again, as well as coming face to face with Saol. Those were the only things he could think of looking forward to.

***

Savaiyon stepped through the gateway at the top of the dungeon steps and closed the yellow-fringed rectangle behind him. He'd refrained from using his gateways where Khurt Everitas could see, saving the shock of it for when Khurt would walk through one for the first time. He descended the stairs, where Wendell Ravensdayle awaited him, holding a short prisoner's shackle in his hand, just as they'd arranged. Outside, the sun began its descent, but Savaiyon understood that Khurt's sleeping patterns were different from their own. Vitheligia was far enough to the west that the night fell at a different time there than in Ashur.

As he neared the Vithelegion's cell, he saw that the man was already awake, sitting against the wall as if expecting him. "Are you ready?" Savaiyon asked. Khurt simply nodded and pushed himself up to his feet. "Good. Everything that you had with you when we found you has already been brought to your quarters at the Anonymi fortress, including your sword."

Khurt raised his eyebrows at the mention of the sword. "You would trust me with a weapon already?"

Savaiyon smiled behind his red mask. The beauty of the Anonymi masks was that they hid all expression. If one was able to compose themselves quickly, no emotion would ever be noticeable to others. Composure was definitely one of Savaiyon's strong suits. He wiped the smile from his face and responded. "No. But should you be with us long enough to establish a life in Ashur and commit yourself to our cause, then you may eventually be trusted with field assignments. In that case, your own sword may prove helpful. But that will not happen for quite a long time. In the meantime, if you were to ever use it against any Anonymi in the fortress, your life would end swiftly." Savaiyon turned to Wendell and nodded.

Wendell nodded in return, then lifted a ring of keys from his belt and used one to open Khurt's cell door. He held the short-chained shackle in both hands and looked at Khurt, "Turn and face the wall. Put your arms behind your back. If you try anything, even so much as scratch me, Savaiyon will detach your head from your body with his manifestation."

Khurt abided but turned his head in confusion. "With his what?"

Wendell smiled, "It's better that you don't find out the hard way."

Khurt nodded and turned his head to the wall. "You must mean the magic that Easton Grey spoke of. The reason your King's army hunts down sympathizers of Darian." Khurt pressed his head against the wall. Wendell went through the process of switching out Khurt's shackles from the ones connected to the wall to the short-chained version that would keep his arms bound behind him. Savaiyon found himself somewhat surprised that Khurt complied the entire time.

Once Wendell finished, he took a step back. "We're trusting you enough to leave your ankles unbound. Again, the moment you break that trust, Savaiyon can easily remove your foot so that shackles are not necessary."

"I appreciate the leniency. Look, what I want more than anything is to see my son again and ensure that he is safe and healthy. I understand that anything I do to break your trust will put that in jeopardy. So you don't have to continue to warn me."

Wendell nodded and unlocked Khurt's ankle shackles. Savaiyon eyed Khurt closely as the man followed Wendell out of the cell. It was one thing for the Vithelegion man to speak genuinely and sound it, but his actions and countenance would determine his trustworthiness. As Khurt walked up to him, Savaiyon also got a better look at the man's skin, which had intrigued him from the first time Savaiyon saw him. Some parts of it were light tan while others were darker, almost like Savaiyon's brown skin. He found it curious, as he had yet to encounter anyone in Ashur with variegated skin such as Khurt's. It dawned on him that the Vithelegion all had black patterns painted on their skin, and that this must be indicative of their people. He would ask Khurt about it once he was able to let his guard down a little. Which reminded him of what he intended to do next.

He formed a wide gateway in the corridor between the two rows of dungeon cells. As Savaiyon walked slowly toward it, he beckoned for Khurt to follow him. Savaiyon didn't intend to actually go through it, but he wanted to show Khurt why the Vithelegion were wrong about Ashur. "Khurt Everitas. Come look. I have the ability to create gateways to anywhere in the world. If you look through this one, you will see the City of the Fallen, which is the only city in Mireya that your people have not destroyed yet." Khurt walked up and stood next to him, looking through the gateway. Savaiyon focused on the man's expression, and it did not disappoint. Khurt's eyes shot wide open as he looked down upon the city from high above. "Just under our feet, you can see the top of this statue, which is of Darian. But if you look around, what else do you see?"

He waited as Khurt evaluated the view. "Those other three in the distance. Other Harbingers? But there are five. Who is missing?"

Savaiyon rolled his eyes. *Not the smartest.* "The other three are Abram, Gideon, and Lionel. We do not celebrate Jahmash, which I assumed would be obvious. He murdered Lionel and Darian. Up until recently, we believed he murdered Abram as well, but it turns out that Abram is still alive under a different identity and in a different body. My point, though, is that we are not 'Darian-worshippers,' as you like to put it. We celebrate Darian, of course, especially because many of us in Ashur descend from him. The very reason I can create this gateway is because I am of Darian's bloodline."

"You said Abram is still alive?" Khurt looked at him incredulously.

"Indeed. He only made it known to us about a year ago. But he is working with us to prepare Ashur for Jahmash's return."

Khurt dropped to one knee. His head hung low for a moment and then he looked back through the gateway. "My people. Many of us descend from Abram. Our nation was founded by the Greatmother Ashota. She descended from Abram as well. All this time we spat on Darian's memory because we believed that Darian allowed Abram to die. It's the whole reason why Saol began this invasion in the first place—to defend the honor of Abram. This all…we were *wrong* this whole time." Savaiyon watched Khurt patiently as the man came to terms with this new reality. He knew it couldn't be easy, believing that they were on the side of justice, only to realize that they were the villains.

"I know it must be difficult to fathom. But focus on the bigger picture. We all descend from Harbingers. The Orijin's chosen messengers who worked together to save humanity. Only recently I was part of a company of people whose motto was 'Salvation as One.' Lately I have been thinking of that phrase often, and I believe it applies to all of us. Your people, my people. We must come together. It is our only chance of salvation against Jahmash."

Khurt stood up and looked at him right in the eye slits. "We did terrible things here. We killed innocent people. Children. I need to meet Abram. I need to atone for what I've done in his name. He should reveal himself to the other generals. Convince them that he is our ancestor and the Harbinger of Orijin. It would not be easy to do so, but that would guarantee that the Vithelegion would return home without a quarrel."

"Easier said than done. Abram now goes by the name 'Adl Maqdhuum.' However, he lives up to the title, the 'Untamed Harbinger.' He comes and goes as he pleases, and answers to no one. He has explained to us that he is focused on a great deal of preparation, which I imagine involves many moving parts beyond our comprehension. Khurt, you should know that Maqdhuum is not Abram. This version of him has definitely blurred the boundaries of right and wrong in order to stop Jahmash. He has his own agenda and we are just pieces in it. We cannot rely on him to entertain our wishes. We must stick with the plan we agreed upon."

Savaiyon sensed that there might be doubt in Khurt's mind about what he'd said about Abram. "I promise, the next time Maqdhuum comes to us, I will request that he meet with you. I don't know if he will definitely *listen* to me, but I will ask."

Khurt took a deep breath and looked back through the gateway. "So now what? This Anonymi fortress?"

"This Anonymi fortress. The sooner we go, the better." Savaiyon closed the gateway, then opened a new one that led to the dimly-lit first chamber of the fortress. "Follow me. And don't say a word if you would like to keep your head." As they reached the seventh chamber, two black-masked novices awaited Savaiyon and Khurt. "Is the Komytii ready for us?" The taller of the two novices nodded in affirmation, then turned with the other to walk away. Savaiyon gripped Khurt by the forearm and led him behind the novices. The walk to the Crucible was familiar, even in darkness. He wondered what might be going through Khurt's head, and how many questions were piling on top of each other. After a few minutes, the two novices turned and stood on either side of them as they entered the Crucible.

***

As the doors closed behind them, a voice boomed. "Welcome acolyte. Welcome Khurt Everitas of Vitheligia." The man in the red mask escorted Khurt to the center of the room where a large torch stood, held in place by a wooden case on the ground. The man who'd brought him here walked away and joined dozens of other dark-robed figures standing on platforms of different heights forming various circles around the perimeter of the room. It was impossible to tell any of them apart, aside from the fact that some wore red masks while others wore silver. Once his escort reached one of the platforms, all of the robed figures circled their respective platforms several times until a rush of air blew out the torch and all Khurt saw was darkness.

"Khurt Everitas of Vitheligia, why are you here?"

The man who had brought him here had told him not to speak. *Surely that doesn't mean now. They are addressing me.* He decided to take the chance and respond. "Here as in this room? Or in Ashur?"

"We know why you and your people have come to Ashur. We ask why you are here in this room that we call the Crucible."

Your people brought me here. I don't know. I'm guessing that answer won't do. Khurt sighed. "I am here to carry out a plan that was agreed upon with one of your...acolytes?" *Hopefully that's satisfactory.*

The voice boomed again. "And you have given your word that you shall comply. We have not set in stone whether we shall require you to stay in Ashur or release you back to your people once you have fulfilled your oath."

What? "So there is a chance I can return home? What of my son?"

"Your son will make his own choice. He joined our ranks of his own volition. However, that scenario is hypothetical as of now. There is no need to pore over various possibilities. You must first do what you swore." It was impossible for Khurt to determine where the voice was coming from, not just because of the darkness. The voice filled the room. He wondered whether the same person spoke every time.

"Very well." *Of course Khenzi would choose to return home with me. Thank the Orijin that they would even give him the choice.* "When will I have this opportunity?"

"Tomorrow. In the time leading up to that, you will be fed, bathed, stretched, and briefly trained with some of our sparring tactics. You will also be provided a personal chamber for comfortable sleep. Everything you will need to be prepared for your part of this plan will be provided for you. Do you understand?"

"I understand. Thank you."

"We accept your gratitude. This concludes our business until the pact is fulfilled. Acolytes." The darkness remained, but Khurt heard the shuffle of several sets of feet. He barely remembered where he stood and wondered whether he was expected to leave the room.

After another moment, a hand grasped his arm. "Come." Khurt followed where he was led. The total darkness somewhat evaporated after they left the Crucible. The halls and corridors were dimly lit, with only enough light to barely make out other figures around them. He was led around many turns and down two flights of stairs, and Khurt sorely missed his boots with how cold and hard the ground was.

The figures in front of him finally moved out of the way after several minutes of walking. One of them opened a door in front of him while another led Khurt through and removed the shackles from his wrists. Three torches on the walls made this room much brighter, and noticeably warmer. Khurt looked around and eyed a wooden chair, a dresser, and a large bed with his belongings sitting atop it. His black boots had been placed on the floor next to the bed. The door shut behind him and Khurt looked at where his escorts just had been. They'd left him alone in these quarters and Khurt used the time wisely to look over his things. His black armor and helmet were still intact, aside from dents and scratches, and his sword was laid next to them on the bed. Khurt sat down and gently rubbed his aching wrists, then lay back on the soft mattress. It was the most comfortable thing he'd been on since back home in Vitheligia.

The aggressive nudge against Khurt's shoulder forced his eyes open. He blinked for a moment, forgetting where he was and sprang up. Four figures stood before him, all wearing those strangely colored robes that Khurt found so nauseating, as well as expressionless black masks. Khurt almost reached for his sword until he remembered that he had agreed to come to the Anonymi fortress, and that these acolytes were likely providing some of the promised hospitality.

Sure enough, two of the figures revealed a cart with several plates and bowls of food, as well as a pitcher and glass, and a mug with steam billowing from it. Those two figures left the room while two others stayed, but stood at the door, as if guarding it. "Eat while your food is hot. Then we shall escort you to the bathing chambers."

Khurt couldn't tell which of the two had spoken because of the masks. As strange as they were, he imagined the experience must be much different from behind the mask. Khurt almost looked forward to it. He pulled the cart closer to him and sat down on the bed once more. The aromas coming from the food were quite different from what he was used to, but it still smelled appetizing. Being hungry helped. He poured himself some water first and drank, then eyed the food in various small plates. Nothing resembled his own cuisine, but he recognized chunks of charred fish with sliced onions over rice. One of his favorite dishes in Vitheligia was roasted fish cooked with a sauce of peppers, mint, and onions in oil. He salivated at the thought of it and picked up the bowl. He looked around for a fork or spoon, but none were in sight. "I do not seem to have any utensils." One of the Anonymi walked over and pointed to two thin wooden sticks that rested beside a small plate. Khurt nodded, "Can you demonstrate for me?"

He silently applauded the guard's patience with him, as the robed guard picked up the two sticks with a gloved hand, then held both between his index and middle fingers and used his thumb to stabilize the sticks. He then moved his fingers to widen or narrow the gap between them and grabbed a chunk of fish. The guard then held the sticks closer together and used them in a sort of shoveling motion to scoop the rice. Khurt watched intently, and the guard then handed him the two wooden sticks. He modeled the guard's strategy by placing the sticks between his fingers, and was surprised at the dexterity it took to control them. He moved his fingers around for a few moments to get familiar with the movements and then picked up a piece of fish and brought it to his mouth.

As the guard went back to his post at the door, Khurt devoured everything in the bowl. He used the wooden sticks more to shovel everything into his mouth, rather than take the time to pick pieces up individually. The fish had been seasoned with lemon and garlic, and there was a hint of spice, which Khurt enjoyed. Vithelegion cuisine involved many seasonings and flavors but tended to lack spice. Sometimes, when Khurt was still friends with the other generals, he would travel to Nachtoveel with Hector and Raiza just for the food there. It was heavy with spice and pepper, while still being extremely flavorful. Khurt paused for a rueful moment, knowing that those days were over. Even if he did make it back to Vitheligia, there would be no camaraderie with the other generals. *Maybe when I kill Saol, all of their true feelings will come to the surface and they will finally admit that they can't stand him either.* It was his only hope for redemption.

Over the next hour or so, Khurt finished eating, was led to the bath chambers and allowed ample time to bathe in the steaming hot water. He'd never been one for overindulging, but the opportunity to take a hot bath for the first time in several months could not be passed up. Khurt thought could spend a whole day soaking the warmth into his bones; his aching feet benefitted the most from the bath. He only considered leaving once the water cooled, and his guards escorted him to another room with cushioned tables situated in several rows. The room, like most of the others, was nearly pitch black. The only evidence of others in the room was the occasional groan, and Khurt knew for sure that once they started stretching him, he'd likely be the loudest.

The guards led him to a table and one of them tapped his arm and gently pinched at the fabric of Khurt's thick robe. Khurt took the hint and disrobed, then lay face down on the table. He waited quietly for a few minutes, the only sound in the room the occasional grunt or groan. Finally he heard footsteps quietly nearing him, as if the owner's feet were either barefoot or in socks. He welcomed this quietude much more than that of the dungeon he'd just been in. Especially because those footsteps stopped next to him, and two hands pressed firmly into his back. At first he arched at the pressure, but Khurt quickly got used to the sensation. Over the next hour, the pair of hands worked a magic that Khurt couldn't believe. He knew his whole body had grown increasingly tense ever since leaving Vitheligia, but either he'd been too busy to pay attention or he'd just gotten used to the pain.

Regardless, by the time the two hands were done, he felt like he was in a new body. As ready as he'd been to confront Saol before, Khurt was even more confident and excited now. Releasing the tension in his muscles had helped to do so in his mind as well. He knew Khenzi was safe here, and he knew that he could be safe here if he came back. One of the two hands clapped against his shoulder three times, and Khurt assumed that his time was done. He arose from the table and donned his robe once more before his guards escorted him back to his chamber. Inside, the food carts had been removed and his Vithelegion armor had been placed neatly on the floor in the corner, next to a cabinet. A new all-black outfit was laid out on the bed, complete with new smallclothes and a hip scabbard. To his surprise, Khurt also saw a black metallic mask next to the clothes.

"Get dressed. And put on your mask." One of the guards instructed him. Within moments of Khurt getting the new clothes on, he heard a rap at the door. He donned the mask, which he found to be a curious thing. The top of it fit over the crown of his head, and the part that covered his face was connected to the crown by hinges on both sides.

At least they didn't just barge in. "Come in." His voice with the mask surprised him. It sounded deeper than his own, and he knew he should have expected that.

Two more silver-masked acolytes walked in, one holding a sword much different than his own. The acolyte outstretched his arms, as if presenting the sword to Khurt. Khurt gently took it with one hand on the hilt and the other under the blade. "Thank you." The acolyte nodded and took a step back, then tilted his head toward the door. *He wants me to follow him. Time for sword training I suppose. I wonder how receptive they would be to learning my own sword techniques. Maybe another time.* Khurt nodded and followed as the two acolytes left the room. As he exited, the other two who were guarding him followed and one of them gently grasped him just under his right elbow. They walked in near darkness until finally they entered a door into a large room that was empty save for a gigantic spherical boulder sitting in the center of it. The two acolytes in front of him walked toward the boulder and the other two escorted him to it. The two in front looked at him and then back at the boulder and then repeated the process a few more times. He wasn't sure what they wanted him to do, but then both of them touched the boulder in unison, and Khurt's jaw dropped as both of them disappeared in unison. Khurt's two escorts nudge him closer to the boulder. *What the hell is this thing? Surely they must be safe if they've already done it, but where did they go?* His escort gripped his arm a little tighter, as if growing impatient. *I'm sure I don't have a choice in this.* Khurt punched his fist, which he realized was no longer sore. He took a step toward the massive rock and pressed his left palm to it. Before he could even begin to process a thought, everything around him faded to black, even the ground.

He looked all around, and the lack of any landscape disoriented him, and almost made him dizzy. Khurt could feel himself moving forward quickly, but not in a way that really felt like moving. It was almost as if the blackness around him was moving. He blinked several times to try and find anything in the utter darkness to focus on, and after another moment, he was thrust back into the physical world, but in a different place. Khurt took a few breaths to regain his bearings. He looked around and realized he was outside, on the corner of a large square platform. Other masked acolytes were there as well, in all shapes and sizes, sparring and going through various stances and strikes with their swords. They all wore the same black outfits and masks of various colors, including black like his own, silver, red, green, and gold.

One of the acolytes that had traveled with Khurt walked up to him and faced him, then drew his own sword. "Draw yours." The command took Khurt somewhat by surprise, but he wasn't sure why. They had told him that he would engage in sparring training, among other things, and sparring was the only thing left to do. Khurt drew his sword from his hip scabbard and examined the blade. The longer he held it, the more he appreciated how it contrasted from his own sword.

Vithelegion blades were heavier with wider blades and thus, required more strength to wield. The acolyte waved him on to follow him toward the middle of the training grounds. Khurt followed and the acolyte immediately shifted into a ready stance, which Khurt found surprisingly similar to his own. His own stance required the legs to be farther apart, and the sword held closer to the body rather than in front of it, but Khurt saw the advantages of their strategy since their swords were lighter.

Many of the sword forms and stances that the Vithelegion employed were meant for attacking *or* defending, but not both. As he mimicked and followed his new mentor, the acolyte explained to Khurt that their stances, or what they called 'lap truong' were meant for both. The stance was pointless if one could not attack *and* defend from it. Over the next few hours, Khurt learned the basics of swordsmanship. His prowess with his own sword had allowed him some advantage in learning their skills, especially because he didn't try to diminish what they were teaching him with his own knowledge. After a while, he requested a second sword to use in sparring. He wasn't sure how they would react, but he felt confident enough, especially with the Anonymi swords being lighter, that he could impose his will with two swords. The acolytes entertained his request and the advantage was immediate.

As the acolytes realized Khurt's prowess with the two swords, many of them took the opportunity to spar with him. Some used one sword while others attempted two. Khurt entertained dozens of acolytes in sparring sessions, and by the time he was too exhausted to continue, he'd only been beaten by his final opponent. He'd defeated most of the others and reached a stalemate with a few.

***

By the time Khurt woke up late the following morning, he was well-rested and incredibly hungry. The intense sparring from the previous evening had tired him out so much that it had overpowered his hunger. Now, the grumblings of his stomach were loud enough that he was glad to be alone in the room. Still, Khurt wondered whether those grumblings were loud enough to be heard outside, as a knock came within minutes of him sitting up in his bed. "Enter."

The door opened to a silver-masked guard in black robes. "Breakfast. I must show you the way. Don your mask and robes. Then follow."

Khurt heeded the guard's words and put on his black mask and robes, then followed. The walk was short and followed a few unfamiliar corridors, and ended in a giant mess hall filled with scores of long, rectangular wooden tables. Khurt's guard extended an arm, indicating where Khurt could get his food, and then departed. Khurt looked around the room, curious about how so many masked acolytes would eat in front of each other. To his surprise, they all had their masks lifted while they ate.

His first thought was to look around for Khenzi, which, considering Khenzi's stature, would have been an easy task, except that nearly everyone else in the room was bigger than his son, so he could be easily missed. Khurt slowly circulated and scanned the tables again, focusing only on shorter acolytes. At the table just next to where he paused, a boy and girl who had seemingly known each other previously, found each other and sat across from one another. Khurt briefly overheard the boy call the girl "Near", and the girl refer to the boy as "Far" but shook off the curiosity of those names so he could continue his search for Khenzi.

As he alternated between navigating through the tables and stopping to look around, a silver-masked acolyte grasped Khurt by the arm, catching him by surprise. "Now is the time for eating. You will leave shortly to fulfill your obligation. Once that is complete, you will be reunited with your son almost immediately, and you will have ample time to reconnect."

Khurt punched his fist, knowing there was no protest he could make. Since leaving the Crucible Room, this was the first time he'd felt any frustration. Still, the Anonymi had been true to their word every step of the way, and he had to take it in good faith that he would see Khenzi soon. He reminded himself that he was set to duel with Saol Suldas later in the day and after that, he might once again have some say in how he lived his life.

He walked over to the counter where the cooks, who wore dull grey masks, were putting out more bowls of steaming hot soup. Khurt had seen some of the others eating it while walking around but had been too consumed in his search for Khenzi to acknowledge his grumbling stomach.

A few other acolytes arrived at the counter around the same time, but enough bowls had been put out for everyone. Khurt carefully carried his bowl to the nearest table, along with a spoon and a pair of the wooden sticks he'd used before. He pulled up his mask, which surprisingly stayed in place like a visor that some Vithelegion women wore when the sun was too bright.

He stared at the soup for a moment, which consisted of a tan beef broth, long thin white noodles, thin slices of different cuts of beef, small circular slices of an unfamiliar vegetable, and sprouts sprinkled on top. He tried to watch how others ate it, but there didn't seem to be a consistent way. Some acolytes just slurped up the noodles with their wooden sticks and let the broth splash freely. Others loaded up their spoons and ate by the mouthful. Khurt noticed the spoons were wider and deeper than a typical spoon, so he tried the latter method. He used his sticks to put the noodles in first, then topped them with a piece of beef, followed by the sprouts. Finally he gently dunked the spoon back into the broth and then put the whole spoonful in his mouth. He'd forgotten that the soup was freshly made and thus, quite hot, but not enough to burn his mouth. The taste of everything together brought a sense of bliss that he hadn't felt since before leaving for Ashur.

By the time Khurt was done with it, there was barely a drop of soup left in the bowl. He'd heard that in some nations on the island Orol Taghdras, where Vitheligia was situated, it was offensive to finish everything you were served, and now he hoped that wasn't the case here. As he returned his bowl to the counter, he noticed that most of the other dishes there were empty, just like his, which brought some comfort.

He flipped his mask back down just before a silver-masked acolyte beckoned for Khurt to follow. "It is time to prepare. Your battalion will leave soon." Khurt nodded and followed the guard back to his own quarters. He wondered how long it took others to learn their way around all of the corridors.

Once he arrived inside his room, Khurt sat on his bed and stared at the floor in front of him. He thought about how the day's events would unfold and, somewhat to his surprise, he felt no fear or hesitation about facing Saol. He knew there was a chance he might lose, but he also knew that he'd beaten Saol in a duel rather recently, and that would be fresh in Saol's mind. All the pressure would be on Saol.

He stood, changed his smallclothes, and slowly put on his new armor, which had been placed on a wooden stand at the back wall of the room. He inspected each piece and ensured that it fit correctly and felt comfortable while moving around. His wrists and ankles still ached from the dungeon shackles, but he'd grown used to the pain.

Once he was fully dressed, Khurt took his swords and practiced a few stances and forms, making sure that no part of his armor restricted him. He felt satisfied after going through each new stance and form a few times. He sheathed both of his new swords in the scabbards on his back. Someone knocked on his door after a few moments, and an acolyte opened it. "It is time." Khurt didn't wait for another command; he fastened his new cloak, which was becoming somewhat more tolerable to his eyes and stomach and donned the new gold mask that had been placed upon his bed while he was at breakfast.

Khurt followed the guard through several corridors, to the point where he assumed he'd never learn his way around the Anonymi fortress. To his surprise, the halls were mostly empty despite acolytes normally bustling through them. Khurt's escort finally stopped at a door and opened it for him to enter, then walked in after him and stood next to him.

Several acolytes had already gathered in the room, and were armed just as Khurt was. A tall, red-masked acolyte stood on a platform at the front of the crowd. The acolyte on the platform didn't speak but used several hand gestures to seemingly communicate with the crowd. Khurt softly asked his escort, "What is he doing?"

"Seasoned acolytes do not use words to communicate with one another. We use a silent language with our fingers, hands, and arms to 'speak.' It is a measure that further protects our identities."

"How will I know what to do, then?"

"Your instructions are not the same as the others in this room. Once they have been briefed, the officer up there will take you with him through a gateway. Your only responsibility is to face the Vithelegion leader and defeat him. Do not worry about the other acolytes. Every man and woman involved in this mission has a responsibility. As long as everyone focuses on their own responsibility, everything will work. Do you see?"

"Yes, I understand." After standing and watching for several moments, the group dispersed through various yellow-fringed gateways that hovered in the spacious room. Khurt realized that the red-masked acolyte was the same who'd been at his dungeon cell and had arranged this whole agreement.

The acolyte looked directly at him and addressed him. "Come. I must show you something." Khurt walked onto the platform as the red-masked acolyte created a new gateway. Khurt looked through it and the view startled him for a moment. The gateway opened to an aerial view of a city. Khurt hadn't realized that these gateways could be created anywhere; he'd assumed they were always on the ground level. *What a gift to have.* He scanned the city and noted the Vithelegion tents set up in the middle of the town. *Saol will be in the middle of all of those. There, that big one in the center.*

The acolyte spoke up again, "We have been studying them for several days now. Every day, your Commander comes out of that big tent in the middle to survey his troops. After a few minutes of walking the perimeter of the tents, he returns to his own and seven other men go into his tent."

Khurt cut him off, "Those are his generals. I used to be a part of those meetings. I have to tell you, though, judging by the way the soldiers are oriented, the army will be on the move soon. Possibly today, definitely by tomorrow."

"How likely is it that Suldas will be willing to fight you?"

"As soon as I show my face, he will be ready."

"Good. Remember that that is not a normal practice. We are making this exception because it justifies the outcome. I will make you a gateway that leads directly to the perimeter of the tents, shortly before he normally comes out. You will have two Anonymi soldiers with you, with several more behind the mass of Vithelegion soldiers. However you choose to engage him is up to you. As long as he is defeated and the Vithelegion retreats, that is all that matters."

He looked at the red-masked acolyte. "What if I get attacked in the aftermath? Will I have the protection of more than two soldiers?"

The man continued to look down through the gateway. "Make sure you do not get attacked, then. You were a general once, use that to command them. Also, your armor is stronger than you think. It is imported from the mines of Semaajj. You can afford to be aggressive."

Khurt nodded. *'Make sure you don't get attacked.' Thanks. I'll do that.* "I am ready when you are, then. Where is my escort?"

The acolyte raised his arm and used his fingers to beckon two golden-masked Anonymi to come over. Once they were abreast of Khurt, the red-masked one turned to him. "As soon as the gateway is open, you are to walk through. I will close it immediately but will be watching from above. If anything unexpected arises, such as an ambush, I will have other gateways opened immediately for reinforcements to help you."

"Understood."

The red-masked acolyte turned back and a new gateway opened next to the first. This one led directly in front of the tents that housed the generals. Khurt walked through with his two companions in tow. He turned to see the gateway closing as the last of them walked through. The wind gusted strongly, causing their cloaks to flail aggressively. Khurt looked around at the familiar surroundings. A part of him considered killing his two companions in the golden masks and spurring the Vithelegion on to fight the Anonymi. He wondered how Saol would feel about that, whether the man would welcome him back with open arms. More likely, Saol would see him as weak for losing in battle and getting captured and being in this situation. He wondered if Saol had even considered that he was still alive. *I suppose I'll find out soon enough.*

The other part of him knew he would never see Khenzi again if he dared to be so bold. He would make whatever sacrifice was necessary to be reunited with his son, even his own nation. Khurt was sure that sooner or later, he would manage to find a way to get back home to his wife and daughter, but he had to take things one step at a time. And just as he finished surveying his surroundings, the first step appeared in the distance. Saol Suldas' silhouette was unmistakable, as if a tree trunk had uprooted and was walking toward Khurt.

All seven of Saol's generals followed closely. One of them must have suggested an attack, as Saol put his hand up in the air with just his index finger outstretched, signaling for everyone to remain at ease. Saol continued toward Khurt and his two companions with his mouth tight, as if offended that they were there. When he finally reached Khurt, he didn't bother with pleasantries, though Khurt imagined it would be worse if he could see Khurt's face. "Who are you? And why would you be so brazen as to infiltrate my camp, as if you would not pay any consequences? Do you know who I am?"

Khurt was glad for the mask. He usually found Saol's hubris to be annoying, but now it was more comical, given that they arrived in the middle of the Vithelegion camp without anyone knowing. "You are the *great* Saol Suldas, Commander of the Vithelegion. And with you are your generals, Raffa, Hector, Thiel, Raiza, Davala, Bragha, and Ezera. All great men, but none with quite the legacy as you, Commander. We simply arrived here with barely any notice from your men. Such an easy camp to infiltrate." He knew that would agitate his former commander.

"Impossible." Saol's surprise at the names of his generals was tangible, and he sneered at Khurt. "Tell me your name and purpose, or we will kill you. Slowly and gruesomely."

Khurt smiled again. "We are acolytes of the Anonymi. We have no names. And we have come here to demand that you yield."

A hearty laugh cracked Saol's tight-lipped mouth. "Surrender? We have taken every city that we have attacked, with barely any resistance. We will not yield."

"You have mistaken my request, Saol Suldas. We demand that *you* yield. Once you surrender, we are sure that your army will follow."

The man looked confused now. "That makes no sense. I am the Commander of the Vithelegion. If I yield, the entire army yields."

Khurt shook his head, "Not if I am only challenging *you* to duel. When I defeat you in front of all of your men, you will agree to return to your ships and sail home."

Saol looked incredulous. "*When* you defeat me? In a duel? Up to now, I have given you the opportunity to peacefully state your business. I do not have the time or patience any longer to entertain you. Generals, apprehend these men and detain them. We will skin them, starting with their toes."

Saol was about to turn and walk away, when Khurt lifted his mask. "Yes, Saol, when *I* defeat you in a duel. You have left me for dead more than once, and now I shall return the favor." Saol and each of his generals collectively gasped at Khurt's face and voice. Khurt pulled back his hood and unsheathed his swords from his back. "Surely that little hand wound I gave you isn't still bothering you?" This time, Khurt was glad that Saol could see his smile.

The man hurtled himself toward Khurt and swiftly pulled his sword from his hip scabbard. Khurt reset his mask and immediately assumed one of the Anonymi stances, *lap truong moi*, spreading his feet wide and holding one blade in front of him with his right hand pointed toward his charging opponent. Most stances were meant for one sword, but it was easy to adapt the second sword to them. He held the second sword in his left hand out to his side.

Saol charged quickly with the expected aggression. He initiated the attack and swung with an overhand diagonal strike. Khurt deflected it with one sword and used the momentum to spin away and create more space between them. Saol turned and advanced once more. He proceeded with more caution this time, and Khurt knew that Saol wouldn't make the mistake of being too aggressive again, especially with Khurt wielding two swords.

In his haste, Saol hadn't bothered to put on full armor. He wore only his breastplate, tasset, and helmet, but nothing else. Khurt knew immediately that he wouldn't win by going for Saol's head. Saol came with another attack, this time with an overhead strike. Khurt used both swords to defend the assault. Because of Saol's two-handed strikes, Khurt would have to defend with both swords each time and then figure out how to counter. He deflected Khurt's swords away from his body and backed away a few steps to create some distance.

By this point, there was a circle of soldiers around them, all yelling and screaming. Khurt couldn't tell if some might be cheering for him, but he hoped so. And he hoped that Saol heard it. He entered into *oisong odai* stance, in which both swords extended out in front of him at face level, one horizontally and one vertically. Khurt didn't wait for Saol to initiate this time; he opened his stance and kept his arms and swords in place. Doing so held Saol in place, as Khurt had several options about where to strike. Khurt lifted his right arm and feinted a strike at Saol's neck, then struck with his left down toward Saol's unprotected shin. Saol dodged the attack at the last second and swung his heavy blade into Khurt's side. The sword clanged against his armor and the force knocked him down, but he held onto both weapons. There would be a bruise on his ribs later, but Khurt realized that Saol's blade couldn't pierce his armor. He glanced down at it and there was no evidence of even a scratch. He spied Saol attempting another strike and rolled out of the way, then regained his footing.

He re-entered the *lap truong moi* stance and stalked forward. It would be a huge advantage if Saol couldn't get past his armor, but Khurt would have to be faster in order to actually strike Saol. He set forth with a flurry of strikes, most of which Saol was able to parry. The rest were off the mark, as Khurt realized it was impossible to strike accurately with both swords simultaneously. Trying to do so would also leave him exposed and off balance. Surprisingly, Saol didn't waste his breath on trying to goad Khurt, but Khurt assumed that the man was focusing even harder because of the two swords.

That doesn't mean I shouldn't antagonize him. Khurt pulled up his mask, "You made it seem like this would be a shorter fight, Saol. I'm surprised I haven't lost yet." Khurt circled with both swords in front of him, the blades set in a crossing pattern.

Saol took the bait. "If you fought like a Vithelegion, you'd be dead already. But it's different with a traitor."

"If you can only defeat Vithelegion and unarmed Ashurians,

how good of a fighter can you truly be? Besides, I already defeated you as a *Vithelegion*." Khurt smiled, then pulled his mask back down. He knew Saol would be relentless now.

As expected, Saol grimaced and advanced without a word. *Have to end this quickly now. He'll be careless early on, then he'll come to his senses.* Khurt processed all of the possible angles from which Saol could attack, and set in his mind the proper counterattack for each. Saol hefted up his sword and moved to another vertical attack but changed his angle at the last moment and switched to a diagonal overhand strike, aiming for the left side of Khurt's neck. The misdirection slightly threw off Khurt's strategy, but he got his swords up in time to block the strike. The impact was so strong that it knocked the sword out of Khurt's right hand. *Improvise. Quickly.* Using the momentum of Saol's attack, Khurt spun to the right, then swiped his blade at the back of Saol's knee. He was close enough that he felt the blade cut through significant flesh.

Khurt didn't waste time in looking for his other sword. Saol was now lame and every second mattered. While Saol yelled, Khurt struck the back of Saol's other knee, slicing through muscle and tendon alike, ensuring that the man wouldn't be able to stand. He walked back around his former commander to face him, and heard the chatter get louder around him. He lifted his mask once more and looked Saol in the eyes. "Do you yield?"

Saol scowled, still clinging to his sword but clearly wanting to reach back and grasp his wounds. "I will not yield so long as I can hold my sword. You'll have to kill me, coward."

Khurt shook his head and spoke loudly for the whole crowd to hear. "That is the difference between you and me. Mercy. You see it as a weakness, while I see it as a virtue. Imagine how much bargaining power we would have had in Ashur if we had spared lives. And after all of it, it turns out that we invaded a people that celebrate the four virtuous Harbingers equally, not just Darian. They have a statue of Abram in one of their most sacred cities. You were wrong, Saol. I knew it from the beginning. You brought us on this journey for a futile war. Allowed our people to die for nothing."

Saol spat at his feet. "Save your mercy for other cowards and just kill me." He looked around at all of the soldiers and generals watching. "Kill me here in front of everyone, and the Vithelegion is yours to command, and you can allow all the mercy you wish. But you'll have to let go of that mercy to do so."

Khurt nodded. He knew that Saol's current wounds wouldn't be enough of a message. He would have to further insult the man, in a permanent manner. He walked a little closer, wary of Saol's ability to still swing the sword. "Do you know what I like about these Anonymi blades, Saol?" Saol swiped at him and the blade clanged against the greave of Khurt's left leg. The impact was minimal because Saol was kneeling, and the momentum caused Saol to fall forward. Khurt simply ignored the attack and continued. "I like them because they are light enough to wield with one hand, but strong enough to cut through the same things as our Vithelegion blades. Let me demonstrate." Khurt lifted his sword above his head and struck down at Saol's sword hand with perfect precision. The strike separated Saol's right hand from his wrist. While Saol screamed in agony, Khurt kept talking to him matter-of-factly. "Do you see what I mean? I just cut off your hand with one swipe of this light sword. Let me show you how it feels."

As Saol writhed in pain, holding the bloody stump where his hand had been, Khurt found his other sword and brought it over to Saol. He stepped on Saol's bloody arm, causing the man to cringe. At that moment, Khurt placed his fallen sword in Saol's left hand and slightly backed away. "Do you see what I mean? Do you see how light the blade is? Imagine how well you would be able to fight with such a weapon. In fact, Saol, you will *only* be able to imagine such a thing from now on." Before Saol could process Khurt's words, Khurt promptly sliced Saol's other hand off. Khurt immediately kicked the armless hand away from Saol and retrieved his other sword. He then lifted his mask and walked over to hand it to one of the other golden-masked Anonymi.

Surprisingly, none of the Vithelegion showed any signs of advancing upon him or the other two Anonymi. Khurt spoke loudly again for everyone to hear. "As you requested, Saol Suldas, I have relinquished mercy upon you, though I obviously did not kill you. Khurt looked toward the seven generals, who had rushed to help their commander. "Generals, you should cauterize his wounds immediately and ensure that he doesn't bleed out. The proposal was that in Saol's defeat, the Vithelegion would return to your ships and sail back home. Raffa, while Saol is currently unfit to lead or command, the decision and responsibility falls upon you. *You* are the acting Commander of the Vithelegion. Will you comply?"

Raffa removed his helmet and stepped closer to Khurt. His hair, the traditional shaved head save for a thick stripe of long hair extending from front to back, had lightened since the beginning of the voyage. The darker patches of skin on his face were less symmetrical than most others, but one patch enveloped his right eye while another covered only the left half of his mouth, which made for an intimidating look. Raffa was quite a few inches shorter than Khurt, and also younger by about five years. Khurt hoped that his age and stature might hold an advantage with the younger general. "Khurt, why are you doing this?"

"When we attacked that inn, I engaged in a fight with one of the Vermillion's generals and he beat me. Knocked me down the stairs and the fall knocked me out. Saol left me for dead and that same Vermillion general took me prisoner. The people I fight for now have my son but have not let me see him. This was the agreement. Defeat Saol, get the Vithelegion to leave without any more death or bloodshed, and then I would be reunited with Khenzi." Khurt waved his arms at his sides, "This whole thing is the only way I get to see my son again. So please. Go. Ashur is not for us. We have everything we need in Vitheligia. Our people care nothing for conquest and expansion. Don't you want to get back to your wife and family?"

Raffa nodded slowly, as if understanding Khurt's betrayal. "And if we leave, would you come with us?"

Khurt smiled sheepishly, "I do not think they would let me. Maybe one day? But if it means that Khenzi is safely back with me, then it is a worthy sacrifice." He heard Saol screaming as the other generals carried him back to the tents. "Besides, I'm sure that I would be dead within a day if Khenzi and I dared to board our ship."

This time, Raffa smiled. "Don't be so sure. Your men are still loyal to you. They loved you and fought for you. In their eyes, *you* were their leader, not Saol Suldas. You know, I never liked you very much. I respected you until you tried to undermine Suldas. Don't get me wrong, I don't like our Commander much either, but he is still our Commander."

"If you don't like me, then go home and forget about me. Let me ask you something, Raffa. Are you afraid of Saol Suldas?"

Raffa looked at him and was about to say something but paused. "Of course not. But he is our leader."

"If I had killed him, then that would not be so. And if he is unable to lead you into battle, that would also not be so. I have made it so that Saol will never wield a sword or any other weapon again. He can no longer lead you. *You* are the Commander now." Just as Khurt finished his sentence, two Vithelegion soldiers broke free from the crowd and ran toward Khurt wielding their swords. Even with their helmets and armor on, Khurt recognized them to be Saol's two sons, Salken and Saymon. As they were about twenty feet away, a yellow-fringed gateway opened in the ground and swallowed up the two boys. Khurt wasn't able to see where the gateway led to, but he was sure it was somewhere far away from any other people. He turned and looked up into the sky, then raised a hand in thanks toward the open gateway.

Raffa looked at him incredulously, "Greatmother, what the hell was that?"

Khurt smiled at him and put his hand on the younger man's shoulder. "There are people here who can wield all kinds of magic. You see that doorway in the sky? There is a man standing up there, watching *all* of this. He can open those gateways wherever and whenever he likes, and he decides what the destination is on the other side. I have no idea where he just sent Saol's sons, but I firmly believe that you will never see them again. I believe that was also a message meant to help you make up your mind."

Raffa's eyes pivoted back and forth between Khurt and the gateway in the sky. "And what of Saol Suldas? We must still answer to him, one way or another. Eventually his wounds will heal and he will be able to get around again. Even if you've taken his hands away."

"Then leave him behind." Khurt shrugged, "Join the other generals in his tent and tell them that you are leaving him behind. You command now. Saol will only hinder you. If he poses a threat to your leadership, then leave him here. And if you think my advice is faulty, remember that Saol attempted to do the same thing to me on our voyage here. He threw me overboard, fully expecting me to die, because he saw my insubordination as a threat. Do the same to him if you must. Or the rest of you may face the same fate as Saol's children."

Raffa took a deep breath, looked around at his surroundings, and then back at Khurt. "Fine. You win. We shall leave. I will need to speak to the generals privately to determine the details and timeline. I may take your advice about Saol, but I have not decided yet. But the only reason I am giving in so easily is because of two things. First, if I was in your position, I would have done the same. And second, all of the circumstances regarding what just happened to Saol's children are terrifying. The fact that there is a glowing doorway in the middle of the sky. And that we didn't notice it. Then there is also the problem of those two boys disappearing in an instant and no chance of any of us knowing where they went. I cannot risk having that happen to any more of my men."

Khurt looked at him sternly, "Thank you. But you're wrong about me *winning*. I have not won. As the entire Vithelegion sails home, I will be stuck here with my son in a strange land, forced to fight for strange people, with no idea of if or when I will ever be able to return home. You agreeing to leave is the victory of a small battle in a war that I have lost. Aside from being able to see Khenzi again, the only comfort is that all of my people will be able to return home without any others dying. Speaking of which, it is time I left you. I would like to return to the fortress so that I can finally see my son."

Raffa nodded and clasped Khurt's forearm, then turned and walked back to the tents.

CHAPTER 5
AN EMPTY THRONE

From *The Book of Orijin*, Verse One Hundred Forty-Nine
We have blessed you with free will. You alone have the power to control your actions and your reactions.

"Perhaps it would be best to take things one step at a time, Garrison." Wendell Ravensdayle sat on Garrison Brighton's bed, his elbows resting on his knees and chin resting on one hand wrapped around the other.

Garrison had mostly confined himself to his former princely quarters in the northern tower of the palace, ever since Maqdhuum had brought him back to Alvadon nearly a week ago. He had been surprised at the extent of the destruction to the palace, but knew he shouldn't have been, considering the manifestations of his fellow Ghosts of Ashur. The tower that held the princes' quarters had been unaffected by the siege, though the smell of smoke and ash lingered in his rooms.

He'd barely paid attention to Wendell since returning to his former home. Wendell's signature golden hair had grown longer, and he always had it tied up these days. It only made the pain in his face more obvious. Garrison had to remind himself that losing his brother Donovan wasn't his pain to endure alone. Wendell had been close enough to both of them to be like a brother. If anything, Wendell and Donovan had grown even closer after Garrison's departure, considering they were left to command the Royal Vermillion Army.

The funeral ceremonies for his parents and brother would happen in one more day, and Garrison would have to lead the procession to the crypt where all of the royal family's tombs were located, just northeast of Alvadon, where legends stated that the Brighton family's sword was found. Garrison snorted at that thought. *That sword didn't even belong to this family. Our whole legacy is built on something that was never ours.* He looked up and realized that he'd been staring down at his boots as he leaned against the wall. Wendell was looking at him, awaiting a response.

"Sorry. Just lost in thought. But some things have to be figured out now. The moment my father is placed in his tomb, I guarantee you that every single wealthy family in Alvadon is going to try and stake claim to the throne. And how am I to stop them? My father publicly renounced my princehood and labeled me a criminal. I wouldn't be surprised if someone tries to kill me the moment I walk out of the crypt."

"We have enough loyal soldiers in our new army who will protect you. But very well, let us entertain this concern for a moment. Do you even *want* to be king?"

Garrison pulled the chair from his desk and turned it to face Wendell, then sat down. He leaned back and clasped his hands over his legs. "For a while, it wasn't even something that could be possible, so I let go of it. But now? I... this is going to sound extremely shitty of me to say, Wen, but I don't think anyone else in Cerysia, much less Alvadon, can prepare Ashur for Jahmash the way I can. No one else who would be seriously considered for the crown would even think of aligning the throne with Marked Descendants. Even me, think about all of those out there that still see me as the monster who was hunting them and killing them. Then there are the alliances with the Kraisos and Anonymi that are just about to blossom. It *has* to be me."

"I agree. It *does* have to be you. So if you are sure of it, then how do we secure the throne for you? How do we stop anyone else from claiming it?"

Garrison shrugged, "That's the trouble in all of it. I would say use force to keep others at bay, but do I even have that as an option? How many soldiers are loyal to me? How many of my father's advisors are loyal to me?"

Wendell clasped his hands, mirroring Garrison's posture. "That raises another concern. One that I was hoping to save for later but might as well tell you now." Garrison looked up at him, but Wendell didn't wait for a response. "One of our generals, Easton Grey, has taken it upon himself to make decisions on behalf of the throne, as well as on behalf of the entire Vermillion."

"What do you mean? I remember Grey. Very quiet."

"Quiet. Well, his treachery has certainly been very quiet. He somehow struck a deal with the Vithelegion. Told them they could sack Mireya and that our armies would stay out of the way. He apparently agreed to let them have Mireya once they are done with it."

"Is he here, or still dealing with them?"

"I believe he has returned for the funerals. What should we do about this?"

"What proof do we have? How did you uncover all of it?"

"We had a Vithelegion general in captivity. He told us

everything. He was being honest; in fact, he was confused as to why he was a prisoner when our armies were supposed to be working together. He knew Grey by name."

"Do you still have the general?"

Wendell shook his head. "No. We made a deal with him. Savaiyon took him to the Anonymi fortress, where his son is under their watch. The man's name is Khurt Everitas. He agreed to fight as an Anonymi and engage the Vithelegion commander in a duel in order to convince the Vithelegion into leaving. In return, he will be reunited with his son."

Garrison pushed a breath out audibly, "Light of Orijin, that is… something. You're all sure that this will work? That this man can win the duel, and then the Vithelegion will just leave?"

"Khurt assured us that would be enough. If it doesn't work, he doesn't get to see his son."

"I'm skeptical. Give me updates as soon as you hear anything. Regarding this whole agreement between Grey and the Vithelegion, our only source of proof is now at the Anonymi fortress. Which means we have no proof. We cannot accuse Grey without real evidence. Keep an eye on him, try to put trustworthy ears around him if you can."

Wendell nodded, his eyes squinted in frustration, "Damnit. Fine, but if he gives me a reason to punch him in the face, I am going to do so."

Garrison shook his head, "Be careful with this. You know his family is rather prestigious and influential. These are delicate times. People will find any reason to challenge my legitimacy to the throne. We don't need to give them more reasons. Our best bet is to keep Grey close and monitor his actions. Sooner or later, he has to give us something incriminating."

Garrison. It's Lao. Where are you? Maqdhuum is bringing me and Farrah to you.

Garrison paused for a moment. If Badalao was coming to him without the others, then it was important. *Lao, I'm in my chambers at the palace. It's the northern tower, the highest room.*

Wendell looked at him curiously, "What is it?"

"Lao is coming. Must be important." Within seconds, Maqdhuum, Badalao, and Farrah appeared in the room, standing in between Wendell and Garrison. Garrison twitched at the sight of Badalao's face. Back on Asarei's island, he knew what had happened to Badalao, but didn't stay long enough to see the extent of the damage. His eyes and the areas surrounding them were all blackened, with more purple and red discoloration surrounding the blackness. "That was fast."

Maqdhuum smiled at him. "Would've been faster, but I glanced through the window to make sure we didn't appear in the same space as either of you. Defeats the purpose of coming here if we kill you in the process."

"Fair enough. So why the urgency? Did you come to tell me exactly why Horatio killed my brother?"

Badalao turned to face him though kept his head down. "Well technically no, but we can do that for you. Horatio was a vessel. He was being controlled by Jahmash and was acting through Jahmash's will."

Garrison cocked his head, glad that he was still sitting, "How exactly would that happen unless Raish was working for Jahmash?"

Badalao turned his head back to Maqdhuum, as if expecting the former Harbinger to answer. Maqdhuum took a step closer to Garrison and then took a deep breath. "Jahmash is Horatio's father. I found all of this out after I stole Horatio away from here, after he killed Donovan. Long story short, I brought a woman to Jahmash when I first intended to deceive him. Brought her as a gift to him. He ended up impregnating her. Horatio was the result of it all. Jahmash had him sent to Ashur as a baby to grow up here but mostly maintained a grip on his mind. We believe that at a certain age, Horatio started pushing back and limiting Jahmash's influence."

"You believe? You haven't interrogated him yet? Found out everything?"

Badalao responded, "We just came from Raish. I managed to remove Jahmash from his mind, but Raish's mind is very fragile right now. We stayed with him for hours after I removed Jahmash from his head, and he's mostly been sleeping the whole time, or staring off into the distance. There's a lot for him to come to terms with. I understand that there is for you as well, Garrison, but pushing Horatio into an inquisition would be dangerous right now."

Garrison slumped in his chair and sighed. "I don't mean to be short with you. I would just like some answers."

"It will take time. Believe me, we all want to know what's in that boy's head. That's why I saved him, despite him begging for death multiple times." Maqdhuum looked around at all of them, "Which reminds me, I should get back to him. But first, I'm going to bring the other Ghosts here. Least I can do for them. And Asarei and his disciples. You'll need their help here. Wendell, Garrison, where do you want them?"

Wendell stood up from the bed, "My personal barracks. Behind the building. Instruct them to go inside and rest; they can tie their horses up there. I'll be there shortly to meet them."

"Got it." Maqdhuum nodded to each of them and then disappeared.

Garrison looked back at Badalao, "What was so urgent? It couldn't have been the news of Horatio. What else is going on?"

Farrah pulled Badalao over to the bed and instructed him, "Here, sit on the bed."

Badalao did as she said and then lifted his head. "Right. Jahmash appeared while I was in Horatio's head. He wanted to recruit me to his cause. Obviously I refused, but the price of that refusal is going to cost me. It's going to cost Markos. I have a strong feeling that he'll be sending armies there soon, if he hasn't sent them off already. Maqdhuum said that Jahmash is smart, tactical. Always steps ahead. He had to have known that I would refuse. I always had a feeling that Jahmash would target Markos, especially after I freed Farrah's mind of him. Now I'm sure of it. I had my sister, Kiryako, take steps to prepare all of Markos for a large-scale attack, but I fear that it will not be enough, now that Jahmash wants to punish my defiance. Is there any chance you can send soldiers there?"

Wendell sat back down on the bed, a foot or so away from Badalao. "We would love to help, especially if it means protecting Markos. The only issue is that your assumptions are absolute. If Jahmash is sending another army here, there is no guarantee that they will simply arrive on the shores of Taiju. Or even Fera or Darling Harbor, for that matter. The Never is unguarded, and half of the river that divides Cerysia and Markos runs through the Never. They have many options if they want to attack. Remember, they wiped out the Taurani without so much as a squeal from a village of trained warriors. And they were in the *middle* of the forest."

"So what are you suggesting then, Wen?" Garrison asked him curiously.

"I don't know if it's truly a suggestion or just an idea, but I think there may be a common solution to Lao's concern *and* to yours,

Garrison."

Garrison nodded, "I don't know if I already know it because of how long I've known you, or because it makes the most sense. But I agree."

Badalao pivoted his head back and forth between the two of them. "What do you mean? What's your issue, Garrison?"

"When my father deemed me a criminal and relinquished my princehood, I lost my claim to the throne. With my whole family... gone, it means the throne is vacant. However, I intend to claim the throne for myself. The only issue is that there are several others in Alvadon alone who will surely contend for it. And legally, they would not be wrong."

"Your father had no other family? Or your mother for that matter?"

Garrison shook his head, "My father had a brother who died years ago. And my mother has one brother, though he doesn't have a family of his own. However, I don't know that my uncle would have any interest in being the King of Ashur. He doesn't seem the type. Anyway, what Wendell is suggesting is that we *move* the throne to Markos."

Wendell cut in, "Hold on. It wouldn't be that simple. We would have to destroy what's left of this palace to make it inhospitable. And we would have to make sure that Markos is on board with it as well, then determine an appropriate location *in* Markos for you to stay. We would also have to make sure that you are connected to the other cities, and that we can transport enough soldiers to fortify the existing Markosi militias."

Badalao chuckled, "Lucky for you both, you have a highborn Markosi in the room. My parents essentially control Constaniza. I will connect with them shortly, but it is not out of the question to use our estate, at least as a temporary home for the throne. That's assuming that Constaniza is conducive to the rest of our plans. Pyrrha may be beneficial as well, given its proximity to the Never, but it is considerably farther from all the other cities of Markos. The other thing we can work on is our alliance with the Kraisos. Remember that Maqdhuum set that up before we even got to Asarei's island, and they agreed. I'll also have to check in with Maqdhuum about that, but the Kraisos can help us greatly with surveillance from our shores as well as from the Never. This is a good idea, Wendell, with a great many benefits."

"Glad that we all agree. Now the question remains, how do I keep my hold on the throne secure?"

Wendell's eyes widened. "Why do we not wait and discuss this with the rest of the Ghosts?" Garrison was about to ask him why, but Wendell was too passionate about his idea to stop. "You said that the use of force might be the best bet in keeping yourself safe against other claims to the throne. If the Ghosts are here, then you don't need armies as a show of force. You can do that with a handful of people who are the equivalent of an army. Let them rest today, and then after the procession tomorrow, we can discuss it as a group. It will help to get our minds off of the funerals anyway."

Garrison nodded. "That makes sense. Assuming that they are willing. You three should go and meet them. I will join you shortly. I just want to reflect on some things for a little while." Wendell nodded and beckoned for Farrah, who was sitting off to the side, to come help with Badalao. Wendell helped him up and then the two led him out of the room and down the winding staircase.

Once they were gone, Garrison looked around the room. Garrison had slept here for the past few nights, but his mind had been in too much of a haze to take in his surroundings. The smell of smoke and ash hadn't reached the tower, but his room still smelled musty. He imagined that his father had prohibited anyone from maintaining the room after his departure.

He walked over to his bed and sat on it, remembering the last time he'd been in it before being banished. *Vanna. She was with me the last time I was here. I wonder what she's doing.* Garrison rubbed his back at the memory, remembering how she'd thrown a candle at him, and that it had had something to do with not wanting to bring her with him to the House of Darian. *Probably saved her life, not bringing her along.* He stared off into space as he got lost in the thought of who he might be able to trust. He would need to assemble a set of advisors to report to him, but trusting anyone aside from Ghosts would be tricky.

Despite the old smell of things, the bed itself was more comfortable than he remembered. He shifted and reclined so his head fell back into the pillows. Garrison knew he'd said he would meet the others soon, but his eyelids seemed to have other plans, as they closed within moments.

***

Garrison woke to the sound of a familiar voice, and a hand

pushing his shoulder. He slowly rolled to his side and blinked his eyes a few times. It took a moment for him to be able to focus, when he finally realized his Uncle Roland stood at the side of his bed, wearing his usual long, hooded robe.

"Uncle Roland! I haven't seen you since... since the dungeons of the House of Darian. Wow. That was so long ago. Have you been back in Alvadon ever since?"

"That's complicated." Roland Edevane brought a wooden chair over to the side of the bed. The man looked somewhat thinner than Garrison remembered, but then, anyone could likely have said the same of Garrison not too long ago. "Indeed it has been some time, boy. And I apologize that our reunion had to come at such a terrible occasion."

Garrison sat up to face his uncle, nodding in agreement. "The apology is not necessary. I'm sure that you have been busy with your own affairs. However, I agree that the occasion is the worst possible situation. The good thing at least is that we have each other to get through this. You know, you were a big help to my mental state while I was imprisoned in that dungeon. The truth is rather ironic, however. If the House of Darian hadn't been destroyed, I would likely still be in that cell. How obtuse of me to think that I would have been accepted there."

"Ah, but you *have* been accepted by them, or so I have heard. Even if it is after leaving the House of Darian, it still counts. The truth is a fickle little thing that has a habit of helping some and hurting others, Garrison. And yes, sometimes it is ironic. In fact, here is some irony for you. I would have told you this in the dungeon, however, it was too sensitive and secret a topic at the time to divulge. And it might've put you in danger. Now, though, the truth will not matter to anyone else. Garrison, the only reason that you were spared and allowed to live in a dungeon cell there is because of Zin Marlowe."

Garrison's nostrils flared, "Marlowe? That coward could have used me to help defend the House of Darian. He put me on trial and then sent me back to the dungeon, where I was useless."

"And yet, he did not kill you. And why would he? He was your great-grandfather. My grandfather and your mother's. And the first time he'd ever met you was when you arrived at the House of Darian, begging for acceptance after years of your army hunting and killing the very people he was trying to protect."

Garrison stared at the ground for a few moments. *Great-grandfather? How could that be? My mother said that all of her grandparents died long ago.* "Why wouldn't my mother have told me the truth? Especially with me being a Descendant with this Mark down my face. Why didn't *you* ever tell me?"

Roland looked at him flatly and took a deep breath. "Boy, your father had already started brainwashing you by the time you could wield a sword. There would have been little we could say that would have made you see things clearly. Besides, Zin Marlowe was at the House of Darian long before your parents met. Obviously in Cerysia, it is a death sentence to be seen with this Mark. Why do you think you saw so little of me? Especially once you started killing Descendants? Once Edmund ascended to the throne, it was best to avoid letting anyone know of your mother's relationship to the headmaster of the House of Darian."

Garrison nodded to himself, as if that might allow him to absorb these revelations more easily. "So he was protecting me the whole time? Then why didn't he ever try to talk to me? You would think he would have made an effort to come to the dungeon and at least tell me the truth. Put me at ease and help me understand why things happened the way they did."

Roland nodded as well. "Another way in which the truth is a delicate thing. What would it have done for you to learn the truth while locked in a dungeon? Do you really believe that you would have taken that calmly and reasonably?"

Garrison ruminated on the question. While his mind chewed at the scenario of Zin Marlowe actually coming to him to share such a bold truth, Garrison slowly saw his uncle's point. Given how emotional and determined he'd been to get to the House of Darian, he realized that learning such information would only have made him angrier and more desperate. "I don't know. You're right; it isn't something I would have handled well. Still, though, it's something I should have known. Something I should have been told. You came all the way to the House of Darian to speak to me and counsel me, and you could have prepared me for such information, but you chose not to."

Roland raised his eyebrows at Garrison. "That is not entirely true, I'm afraid. The nature of my manifestation means that I do not have to physically travel to places to *be* there."

"What do you mean?"

"It is a sort of projection of myself. A vision. I can see the entire environment, interact with it, and even touch things if my energy is strong enough. So despite what you might have thought, I did not actually physically travel all the way to the House of Darian to see you. I know it is a technicality, but you may as well know that truth now."

Garrison stared blankly at his uncle. His shoulders grew tense and his head started to ache. "And now? Are you actually sitting in front of me now? Or was it too much trouble to come here for your sister's and nephew's funerals?"

Roland reciprocated Garrison's stare. "I understand that you might be frustrated or angered about it, but *you* and your father made Ashur unsafe for those of us with these black lines on our faces. Judge me if you like, but I have spent so much of my adult life hiding because my own nephew led the charge to hunt and kill Descendants. And Garrison, I do not put the blame *completely* on you, because of the type of person that your father was. However, I do find it remarkable that you never had the common sense to stop and wonder why you were killing people who bore the same Descendant's Mark as you.

"While you may have changed your ways, you have no right to judge people or criticize us for living in fear when it is *you* who caused that fear. You forget that Ashur was mostly a peaceful place aside from the conflict between Galicea and Fangh-Haan. At least that conflict was kept between them and then rectified with their wall. Even when Shivaana seceded from Cerysia, there was no *fear*. The Shivaani stood up for themselves and stopped fighting only when they were able to create their own borders. But what your father started—that was terror. We feared for our lives based on something beyond our control. We were hunted. Tortured. Captured. Killed. All because one man feared the worst part of what we *could be*. And you were a part of it. I understand how you could have bought into it as a child. But you were almost a man and still committing such a grave sin. And you know what, Garrison? I have forgiven you for it. You have tried to become a better person, even if later than I'd hoped. But *you* do not get to judge anyone for their shortcomings or fears. Especially when those fears exist because of your actions."

Garrison only realized after his uncle stopped speaking that his mouth was hanging open. He closed it and licked his lips. "I…" He thought about defending himself or countering with something to shift the blame, but his uncle was right. It had taken him way too long to see the truth of things. "I agree with you. My head was so far in my own ass that I conveniently forgot about my own Mark. By the time I saw the truth, I had already ruined so many lives. But I also wonder if I had known who my great grandfather was at an early age, maybe I would have acted differently." He looked down at his hands, which he'd unconsciously clenched into fists. "None of it matters at this point in time, though. None of us can go back and change our actions. But we *can* do our best to atone for our mistakes. Which is why I must ascend to the throne and ensure the safety of everyone with a manifestation."

Roland nodded. "Very well. Let us look to the future. If you take the throne, all of Alvadon's high houses will turn against you. There will be no one with any influence who will support you, at least not within a day's ride. You will have no allies to protect you, save for some loyal soldiers here and there that hold you in high regard because you trained them."

Garrison stood up. He wanted to walk around a bit to help him process his thoughts. "Actually, my allies have just arrived. Remember how you said that the House of Darian finally accepts me? Well those supporters are loyal to me and have already sworn to be my personal king's guard. Wendell has nearly half of the Vermillion behind him, which means they are also loyal to me. And this palace is no longer suitable for a king, which means whoever rules will have to either quickly rebuild or relocate. I have already made arrangements to relocate the throne and rule from somewhere else."

Roland nodded his head, but the bald man's furrowed brow showed skepticism. "And what if they *do* rebuild here? Surely there is enough manpower here for at least one wealthy family to throw their support for a strong, young nobleman. Alvadon could be swayed by anyone who is brave enough to question the legitimacy of your kingship. And once that person has the proper backing, then a new palace and army will follow rather quickly. What will you do then?"

Garrison turned to Roland from looking out the window, "Squash them like an insect. The Ghosts of Ashur are my personal guard now. They would take down any imposter who tries to establish a false throne."

"I see."

"I understand that you have your doubts, Uncle. But your doubts do not concern me. The moment we leave this tower and begin the funeral procession I will expect just about anyone who is not family or a Ghost of Ashur to oppose me or even try to harm me. I will be on my guard every moment that I am in public."

Roland nodded again, but with acquiescence this time. "Very

well. Speaking of the procession, I have brought a traditional barongan for you to wear. I doubted whether you have a great deal of garments here, especially anything formal. I placed it in your standing closet there. It would be in our best interest to go and get everything started. Which reminds me, your father's royal council has already begun infighting just outside the palace. They all seem to think that they or their children should be the next to occupy the throne. I would wait until the ceremonies have finished to squash them all."

As Roland left the room, Garrison scurried over to his closet to get the ceremonial outfit his uncle had brought him. The barongan consisted of a long sleeve white shirt, adorned with intricate embroidery, and matching embroidered white pants. Cerysians traditionally wore white for their funeral ceremonies to symbolize the peaceful state of the dead, as they finally rested in Omneitria. The notion made Garrison wonder whether his father had truly been accepted into Omneitria, given his crimes. However, Garrison also wondered from time to time whether repentance would be enough for him to even be accepted, or if he was destined for one of the other Rings. *It should have been me instead of Donovan.* Garrison shook off the thought. He knew he didn't have the luxury of wallowing in self-pity. *All I can do is continue along this path, and hope that, by the time I hear the Song of Orijin, I've done enough.* Once his scabbard and sword were in place, Garrison rushed down the tower stairs, skipping steps as often as he could. He unhitched his horse as soon as he got outside and rode toward the front of the palace.

Sure enough, just as his uncle had warned, a throng of his father's advisors had interloped the patio that led to the front of the palace. They hadn't gotten violent yet, but the shouting and angry countenances suggest that violence wasn't far off. All twelve of his father's old advisors were there, as well as some of their children. He reluctantly remembered getting along with some of them years ago. That had been a different version of him, though. Once Garrison had broken free of his father's influence and realized his hypocrisy, he'd spent less and less time around these men. *Interesting that he only chose men for his council. Interesting, but not surprising.* Some of them had been tolerable, and Garrison dared to say that some might even have been good people. But he also knew that power can corrupt even the best of people, and the fact that all twelve of these men were here and were actively arguing with each other proved that they were susceptible to corruption.

What bothered him the most was the presence of Malcolm Hailstone, his father's Proxy. Hailstone was the one who was the living word of King Edmund. He was the personal advisor to the king and would travel at the king's request when Edmund could not be present. There was supposed to be a bond between King and Proxy, an undying loyalty. Hailstone's presence itself was not the insult, but unless the tall silver-bearded man was doing his utmost to stop the bickering amongst the others, then he was surely here for the throne. Either for himself or for his son, Courtland. Garrison remembered Courtland growing up as a rather quiet boy, despite his grand stature. Courtland was older than Garrison by a handful of years, and any remnants of the quiet boy were currently gone as he yelled alongside his father.

The target of their ire appeared to be Oswald Midwinter, the King's Envoy to Cerysia. The position itself was a thinly veiled courtesy to Midwinter, as he and Edmund had been childhood friends. Anyone with enough sense knew there was no point in an envoy to the same nation in which the throne resided. Garrison remembered his father trying to rationalize it at first, and after a while just punishing anyone who attempted to criticize Midwinter's position. What piqued Garrison's interest was that Oswald Midwinter, despite his short stature and rodent-like mannerisms, was a decent man. It would have been easy to assume he was just like the King, having grown up together and likely sharing similar ideologies and perspectives, but Garrison remembered always enjoying his talks with Midwinter. The man was rather sensible and self-aware. He knew what people thought of him and accepted the position mostly to ensure that his family could live comfortably. *What man wouldn't do the same?* Midwinter had a daughter of a similar age to Garrison, though he didn't see her in the throng before him. *Smart to leave her out of this. What was her name? Kayla? Kyra? Kyla. Her name was Kyla. That has to be the nature of that argument right there. They don't think Kyla is a serious candidate for the throne. Joke's on them; none of them are.*

Garrison put an end to his spectating and rode his horse right up to the spat. "Attention!" He circled around the whole group and halted his horse once he was between them and the crumbling palace. "Friends and *former* members of my father's council. I urge you to stop! This day is for anything but fighting, and by doing so, you shame the memories of my parents and brother." It took a few moments, but the arguing died down and all of the council looked at Garrison sheepishly.

Hailstone responded first, "My apologies, Garrison. We meant no offense. We all arrived for the procession, but these are confusing and tenuous times. There is no heir to your father's throne, and it would be dangerous for the throne to remain empty for too long. We let our emotions get the best of us, indeed. However, a decision must be made quickly about who will take the throne next."

Garrison eyed him flatly, "I appreciate your directness and your apology, Master Hailstone. I take it then, that you believe Courtland should ascend the throne? Or do you intend to sit in it yourself?"

Hailstone cleared his throat. "I would not dare betray your father's trust. However, my son has the qualities to be a good and fair king. And all of King Edmund's other advisors say the same for either themselves or their children."

"Do you all believe that whichever of you shouts the loudest will inherit the throne?"

This time, Arundel Fernsby responded to him. Fernsby was the Envoy to Mireya, a square man with an equally square jaw. His personality, however, bore little shape or interest. "With all due respect, Garrison, this is unprecedented. Your family was murdered with no trace of the murderers, and your father has no living relation that could be considered an heir. While we all respect you, Garrison, he publicly denounced your right to the throne and labeled you a criminal. Unfortunately, once the procession is over, we must have you arrested and imprisoned."

Garrison used everything he had to stifle the laugh. He looked over at Digby Bloodworth, another square-shaped man who had been his father's Master of Law. Bloodworth had advised King Edmund on the legal aspects of all of the King's decisions. He was well-educated in just about every legal matter that existed or that could potentially arise. "Master Bloodworth, in your legal expertise, is this true?"

Bloodworth lived in absolutes, so Garrison knew that the man would answer him directly. *He's too analytical to intentionally be an asshole.* "Master Brighton, I'm afraid Master Fernsby is correct. The last decree that your father made about you was that you were a traitor to Cerysia and a criminal, and we must adhere to that order. You understand that it is nothing personal."

"I see that your son did not accompany you. Did you not come here to advocate for Kenley as the next king?"

"No. I did not. As Master of Law, and as a friend to your father, it is my duty to be a part of his funeral procession."

"I see. Unfortunately, I must disappoint you all. You see, I will not be arrested or imprisoned. However, I *will* be your next king."

Bloodworth responded again, "Master Brighton, surely you do not understand that that is illegal. We cannot and will not allow that to happen. As a criminal, you are susceptible to a forceful arrest if you refuse to comply. The more you fight and resist said arrest, the more forceful the soldiers will be. In such a situation, we cannot guarantee the state of your health in the aftermath."

"You would be willing to kill me, Master Bloodworth?"

Bloodworth answered, his tone matter of fact. "It is a possible and legal outcome. It has happened before." Garrison noticed the man's eyes glance away to Garrison's left, just behind him. He turned his head, curious as to what had caught the man's attention and saw Adria leading over a dozen others, including his Uncle Roland and Wendell on horseback toward Garrison. Except for Wendell, who wore his traditional armor, and Roland, they all wore full black armor, with shields on their backs, and held their helmets in their hands.

Garrison looked back at Bloodworth, and then at the whole group of his father's former advisors. "Dear *former* Royal Council, to prevent me from the throne, you will *have* to kill me." Adria and the others led their horses so that they all stood behind Garrison and faced the crowd. He continued, "The people you see behind me are known as the 'Ghosts of Ashur' and they will comprise most of my own Royal Council, as well as my personal guard. While you may have soldiers at your disposal, the Ghosts of Ashur are strong enough to counter a whole army. Think about that before you unwittingly send hundreds of soldiers to their deaths."

Bloodworth responded again, "What you speak of is treason."

"Is it? My only *crime* was having this black line on my face. Digby Bloodworth, what crime did I commit?"

"That fell under your father's jurisdiction, not mine."

"So then you do not know what makes me a criminal, except for the word of a dead man, whom the lot of you are so desperately trying to replace."

"They were the words of the *King*, Garrison. It matters not whether he has perished since. Perhaps the new king shall be willing to pardon you."

"I, King Garrison, hereby pardon myself. There. I am officially pardoned."

Adria urged her horse a few steps forward. "Enough arguing. It is my understanding that you are all *former* members of the Royal Council. Which means you have no authority. My name is Adria Kingsbane. I lead the Ghosts of Ashur as well as King Garrison's Royal Guard. This conversation is done. The funeral procession needs to begin, so if you intend to be a part of it, then you may follow us."

She turned to Garrison. "Come, King Garrison. Let the procession begin." She turned behind them, "Trevor, Marshall, Sindha—you three accompany this... mob. If any of them tries anything, they are to be forcibly removed and detained." With that, Adria clucked her tongue to get her horse to a trot, and Garrison followed. Wendell rode alongside him, while the other Ghosts formed a tight perimeter around them.

He exhaled for what felt like the first time in an hour. He was glad that Adria had spoken up and was also surprised at her declaration that she was the leader of his Royal Guard. As he thought about it, he realized there was no better candidate. He glanced at Wendell and was reminded of where they were going. The throng of advisors had distracted him from what he should have been focusing on, and his thoughts immediately reverted to his mother and brother. *Their bodies have already been prepared and await me at the crypt. At least this whole disaster of a council cannot accompany me inside. Orijin knows they would squabble in there as well and likely wake my dead ancestors.* Garrison realized that he'd only sparingly gone to his family's crypt. He knew his father had gone from time to time, but Garrison never felt the need or desire to go. His father had never really talked to him about any greatness of his family or anyone in particular who'd been inspiring or larger than life.

Any time he felt the need to talk to someone who wasn't there, Garrison found solace in the Stones of Gideon. They were about the same distance away from the palace, and it was easier to feel separate from the world there. There was a certain perceived judgment that came along with speaking to dead family members. However, dead soldiers who'd been turned to stone over two thousand years ago were less likely to pass judgment. Especially when those soldiers were responsible for a Harbinger sacrificing himself. He wondered what Gideon and the other Harbingers would think of the state of the world right now. *Well, I guess two of them actually know about the state of the world. Which is why we're in this mess in the first place. Why my family is dead.* He gritted his teeth to push back against the surge of emotions and managed to keep them at bay. *Just need to make it into the crypt. Then I can let it all out.* He would let Wendell enter with him and his Uncle Roland. Wendell had been attached at the hip to Garrison and Donovan from the time they were small boys. If anything, Wendell was more of a family member to Garrison than his own father had ever been.

After several more minutes, they arrived at the steps that led down to the crypt of the Brighton family. Adria and the other Ghosts opened up a path for Garrison to proceed without others following. "Uncle Roland. Wendell. Accompany me." He dismounted the black mare and descended the stairs. At the bottom, two knights guarded the large iron doors that led to the crypt. They opened the doors without waiting for a word or signal, and saluted Garrison, Wendell, and Roland as they entered. Garrison saw a group of handmaids near the back and walked toward them. The crypt itself was an impressive piece of architecture. While underground, the vast room was filled with rows of ornate columns and arches. Even the tiles on the ground were intricately engraved in complex patterns of flowers and geometric shapes. Sconces rested on the walls of every arch, making the crypt surprisingly bright.

Three uncovered tombs waited ahead, and the handful of handmaids gave Garrison sorrowful glances and quickly scurried away. *I wonder if they grieve for all three of them. Or just my mother and Donovan.* Garrison walked up to the tombs and placed his hands on the center one. They had been given their own alcove, with room for at least one more. *Not for a long time.* He glanced down into the one in front of him and saw his mother's crown resting on the wrapped body. Garrison's face twitched instantly. He didn't care to subdue his emotions any longer. Despite the sounds of his sobbing, he kept his words to himself and went down on a knee. *I'm so sorry, Mother. I'm sorry I wasn't there to protect you. I'm sorry for everything my father was and everything he did to you, and most of all for never standing up to him to protect you. I promise I will be a better king than he ever even dreamed to be. I promise I will mend Ashur and fix every last piece of it that he broke.*

And beyond all that, I promise that I will find a queen who will make you proud, and I will treat her like a queen should be treated. Mother, I'm so sorry for all of the hardships you faced, and I hope you can forgive me for letting it all happen. Please, Mother. Please forgive me. I was too weak. Too cowardly. Too much like him *to do anything about it and now there's nothing I can do for you to make it better. Mother, I'm so sorry I wasn't there.*

He took a deep breath and pressed his forehead against the cool stone of the tomb. *Orijin. Please watch over her and protect her. Please let her be at peace in Omneitria, and away from him. Please don't let them have to cross paths ever again and let her be surrounded by everyone else that she loves.*

Garrison stood up and took a few deep breaths. He'd forgotten that Roland and Wendell were with him and were grateful that they'd given him some space. He took a step to his right and saw Donovan's crown in the tomb to the right of his mother's.

Despite the moment of clarity, seeing Donovan's crown and body elicited more heaving sobs. This time, Garrison fell to both knees and barely held himself up by clinging to the top of the open tomb. *Donovan. Donovan, I'm so sorry. It should be me lying there, not you. It's all my fault, Donovan. If I hadn't left, then none of this would have happened and you'd still be here. Please forgive me, brother. I'm so sorry that I couldn't protect you. I failed you. I failed you as a big brother and now I'm all alone. Donovan, this is all my fault. It's all because of me and I'm so sorry. I've failed our whole family, and I'm so lost now. It should be you taking the throne now, not me. You were always better suited for it, and I screwed it all up. Please forgive me. I promise I'll do everything I can to be a good king and try to make you proud. Please, please Donovan, please don't be mad at me. I know I can't undo any of this, but I promise I'll make things better. I promise I will. Please. I know you're at peace in Omneitria. And if by some chance I can convince the Orijin that I'm worthy of going there by the time I die, please don't be mad to see me. Orijin, please take care of him and let him and my mother be happy together. Please, Orijin, I beg of you.*

A part of him could have stayed there for hours, even days, but Garrison knew he would have to get up at some point. He continued to press his head against the side of the tomb and kept his eyes closed. After a moment, he reluctantly pulled himself up and took one last look at Donovan's wrapped body. He wiped his eyes and leaned in and touched Donovan's foot with his tear-soaked fingers. Garrison turned and stepped away so that Roland and Wendell could have their moments as well. He walked toward the front but stopped halfway so that Wendell and Roland could have their privacy, and also so that the guards wouldn't think to open the doors for him.

After several minutes Wendell walked toward him, and then eventually Roland did the same. Roland gave him a knowing nod and walked toward the doors. Wendell hung back and clasped Garrison's shoulder. "You know you're not alone in all this, right?" He paused for a minute to compose himself, then continued, "Garrison, I know this may sound forward, and I apologize if it sounds…insensitive. But we both lost a brother in Donovan, and while I could never replace him, I want you to know that you have a brother in me as well."

Garrison once again felt tears well up in the corners of his eyes. The ends of his lips curled downwards as he attempted to speak. He gave Wendell a tight hug while he composed himself, and finally muttered, "I know, Wen. I know."

Garrison let go and turned back toward the entrance to leave the crypt. He kept his head down through the whole process of returning to his horse, mounting, and then leading the procession back to the front of the palace. The Ghosts still maintained a perimeter around the three of them. Once they reached the front patio of the palace, Garrison led his horse to face the growing crowd. Wendell flanked him on the right while Adria stayed to his left, and the Ghosts and Roland all formed a line behind him. The people of Alvadon respected him enough to provide some distance between them and Garrison, as the closest ones stood twenty feet away from him. Among them was a girl who looked to be close in age to him, with the olive hue to her skin indicative of a Markosi. Her oval face bore no blemishes and her long brown hair only enhanced her beauty. She wore black pants and a black riding coat, though her whole outfit seemed too elegant for her to be a commoner. Garrison wondered who she might be and his gaze lingered a little too long, as she looked directly back at him. He averted his eyes immediately. *No time for that. More important things to focus on.*

Garrison didn't bother to wait for anyone to speak up or ask an unwanted question. "Citizens of Alvadon, citizens of Ashur. It is a sad day. To lose one family member would have been enough to crush our hearts, but to lose all three is truly shattering. While I have done my best to maintain my composure, I know that it will be a long time until I am able to find any joy in the world." He paused for a moment, unsure of whether to actually say what he wanted to say. *Go ahead. Chances are there are many who feel the same way.* "I feel it is only fair to share the truth with you all. And if anyone feels the same way, then you are free to agree. If you feel differently than me, then I harbor no ill feelings toward you. It should be known that I mourn my mother. I mourn my brother. However, I bear no sadness for my father's death." He paused, unsure of how his words would be taken. He could hear gasps as well as cheers from the growing crowd. "My father used me from the time I was a young boy. Manipulated me to think that I was evil for bearing this Mark on my face, and he told me that the only way to atone for it was to hunt and kill anyone else who bore the same Mark. Then, once I dared to question that directive, he labeled me a criminal and disowned me—his own son, his chosen heir. And even worse, he turned you all against those of us who bear the Mark and split Ashur in half. Let me ask you. How many of you will join the fight against Jahmash once he returns?"

Someone from the crowd shouted, "Jahmash is a lie!"

Garrison nodded curtly. "A lie? Do you know that Donovan's death was Jahmash's doing? Do you know that Jahmash infiltrated someone's mind and struck Donovan down with lightning? Yes. That is how my brother died. There are people behind me who have seen Jahmash in the flesh. He is coming. And that is why I have renewed my claim to the throne." Within a second of Garrison finishing his sentence, a clear bluish dome encircled him and those around him, and an arrow bounced off of it. Garrison looked beyond the crowd for the bowman, as it came from higher up, but there were too many windows from which it could have originated.

Much of the crowd gasped at the sequence of events, though he wasn't sure if they were more surprised at the attempt on his life or by Sindha's manifestation. "Good. You have all witnessed firsthand the benefits of having a Marked Descendant on your side." In his periphery, Garrison noted random flashes of yellow here and there in the distance. He stayed on his guard and continued, "Ashur is no longer safe. Every nation must prepare for Jahmash's return, and as king, I can and will oversee that that happens. Before you all protest, remember that you once loved me. And remember how many family members you lost because of my father's decree against those of us who bear the Mark. So unless you are currently living a life of criminality or hatred toward those with the Mark, then nothing will change for you with me as your king."

As he waited a moment to take in the crowd's reaction, a yellow-fringed gateway appeared about ten feet above the ground between Garrison and the crowd. A tall, middle-aged man fell out of the opening and landed face-first on the patio. Despite him breaking his fall with his forearms, the man was clearly in pain already. Garrison recognized him as Nigel Thundercliffe, his father's Master of Coin. The gateway closed and then another opened the same distance away, but at the ground level. Savaiyon walked through, which led to another round of gasps, this time from the crowd as well as those who stood behind Garrison. He wore a long hooded black cloak and approached Garrison. "My deepest condolences for your losses, King Garrison. This is the man who fired upon you. I took it upon myself to *discipline* him a bit before bringing him before you. What do you want done to him?"

"That is an interesting question, Master Savaiyon. Thank you for bringing this man before me. He is a stranger to you, but he was my father's Master of Coin. His name is Nigel Thundercliffe. It would seem he does not approve of me as his new king, nor does he have any interest in reprising his role on the King's Council. As I have yet to officially appoint my own council, I will need some time to determine a fair punishment for him. In the meantime, he will reside in the dungeon. In the lowest level, please." Savaiyon nodded and created another doorway, Wendell dismounted and helped Savaiyon carry Thundercliffe through.

Once the doorway closed, Adria brought her horse up so that it was even with Garrison's. "Fellow Ashurians. You may not know me, but my name is Adria Kingsbane. I say 'fellow' Ashurians because I hope that with Garrison as our king, it ushers in a new age of harmony between *all* citizens of Ashur. I have lived my whole life in fear of being seen in public with this Mark on my face, and I am tired of hiding. The first thing you should know is that the group of people behind me are known as the Ghosts of Ashur. We were charged with killing King Edmund in order to restore balance to Ashur. Doing so was the first step toward preparing for Jahmash's coming." The shouts and gasps grew, and a din rose through the crowd for several moments. However, people were hesitant to act after seeing what Sindha and Savaiyon had done. Garrison glanced at Adria, who patiently waited to continue. "Yes. We are the ones who sieged this palace, and *I* am the one who killed King Duncan. His death came only moments after he killed his Queen out of fear and selfishness. Garrison had no part in any of it. How could any of *you* support a king who would murder his own wife just to save himself?" The crowd still murmured audibly, but Garrison could see the nervousness on many people's faces. Adria had stopped talking for a moment and, to Garrison's surprise, her silence caused the crowd before them to become silent as well.

Adria continued, "You have seen a sample of what those of us with manifestations can do. And there are more of us throughout Ashur. If you dare threaten King Garrison, or any of us, then you will suffer for it. In case you have foolishly forgotten my name, it is Adria Kingsbane, leader of the Ghosts of Ashur and Commander of his Royal Guard! Now that Edmund is dead, we hope that violence will only be needed again once Jahmash and his armies arrive. If you have any *reasonable* questions, I will gladly answer them now."

Garrison looked around at the crowd, as did Adria. Nearly everyone whose face he could see stared blankly ahead or looked down at the ground. *They're scared of her. Maybe more scared of her than me. I suppose that's good, since she's in charge of protecting me.*

Garrison continued to survey the audience. Even those who wore frowns and scowls refrained from speaking up or asking questions. Garrison took the opportunity to send them back to their homes. "Thank you for your time, fellow Ashurians. I promise that I shall reward your trust and faith in my abilities as king. One last thing before you return to your homes. As you can see, the royal palace is broken down and falling apart. Also, inside is still quite smokey and the air makes it difficult to breathe. Therefore, I will entertain grievances and requests on Gidsday, two days from now, in this very spot. However, after two days, we will relocate the throne until the palace has been rebuilt. Thank you. You may go now."

With that, the crowd slowly dispersed. Garrison watched them as they walked away in every direction, wary of another attack. The Markosi girl who'd previously caught his eye remained where she stood, looking toward Garrison and Adria. He dared to look at her eyes, and realized that she wasn't looking directly at him, but in the general direction of him and his company.

The girl looked around her and then straight again, before walking toward Garrison and the others. Her gait was marked with intent, but not so fast as to be alarming. *She's walking toward us. Could she be so bold as to just walk right up to me?* As the girl neared them, Garrison placed a palm on his sword's hilt, just in case. *There's no way she would come here to mourn my family and then attack me in front of all these people. No Mark on her face, so she couldn't try anything that we wouldn't see.* He noticed Adria grasp her sword hilt, as well as her horse's reins.

"Kiryako!" The shout came from just behind Garrison. He turned and saw Farrah leading Badalao forward, with a broad smile on his face. "You all can relax; that is my sister. Kiri, you made it all the way here!"

The girl ran toward Badalao. "Lao! Light of Orijin, what happened? What happened to your eyes?" The others moved out of the way as she reached her brother, and she wrapped her arms around him tightly and put her face into his shoulder.

"I'm so sorry you had to find out this way," Badalao said to her softly as he stroked her hair. "We ran into some trouble when we laid siege to the palace. Things got… complicated, and this was a result of it. It'll be alright. I'll be alright. Did you come alone, or did mother and father accompany you?"

Kiryako gently pushed herself away from Badalao and looked upon his face with concern. "Your beautiful eyes, Lao." She paused and looked down, then looked back at him. "They stayed behind. I am not staying long; most likely I shall ride back today. Is there anything I can do for you?"

Badalao shook his head to refuse any pampering. "No, I'm much better than I was when it first happened. Trust me. Also, this is Farrah. She has seen to my every need since then. I'm in good hands."

Garrison eyed the interaction between Kiryako and Farrah. He also noticed Adria slightly tense at the attention shifting to Farrah. Kiryako took Farrah's hands into her own. "Thank you for caring for my brother, Farrah. It is a pleasure to meet you, and Lao is quite lucky to have you."

Farrah smiled at her, "It is my pleasure, Kiryako. The very least I could do."

Kiryako looked around at the rest of them and then settled her eyes upon Garrison. "I apologize for approaching you all so abruptly. Once I saw my brother up here with you, he was the only thing I could focus on. Excuse me, my King, for not introducing myself at first."

Garrison smiled at her and walked to her to extend his hand. He responded as she shook it. "Think nothing of it, Kiryako. It has been a long and emotional day for many of us. There's no need to worry about those trivialities, especially when family is concerned." She maintained her grasp of his hand and even placed her left hand against the back of his, so that her hands were sandwiched around his. Garrison didn't let it alter his mindset. "You mentioned that you are returning home today.

Those of us who are here have some ideas to discuss regarding an agreement with Markos, and possibly specifically Constaniza. I would greatly appreciate it if you would join us. Also, please let me know if there is anything I can provide when you are ready to return home."

Kiryako looked down and then into his eyes and smiled. "I am intrigued. Business with Constaniza? I would definitely be willing to join you. When will you hold this discussion? And thank you for your generosity and hospitality, my King." She grasped his hand a little more tightly before letting go.

Garrison looked around at all of the others, "Can we do this now? We have the luxury of having Savaiyon here. Stones of Gideon?" The rest of the group agreed with nods and various affirmations, which allowed Garrison to look back at Kiryako with confidence. He was just over half a foot taller than her, but her presence commanded attention. "How about now?"

She nodded with a smirk, "Now would be perfect, my King."

As she gently grasped his hand for another brief moment, Garrison corrected her. "You can just call me Garrison, please."

Garrison suddenly felt a firm presence in his head. *Hey! King Garrison. I might be blind, but it is clear as day what you're doing with my sister. If you don't stop fucking flirting with her, then I'm taking Constaniza off the table!*

CHAPTER 6
ERUPTIONS

From **The Book of Orijin,** **Verse Four Hundred Sixty-Nine**
There is no set way to love purely. Love shall manifest itself in several shapes and forms.

From the time Bo'az had learned that he would be Jahmash's envoy to the world beyond Ashur, he had assumed the rest of the world to be beneath Haedon. Growing up, there existed a comfort in the mountain village, especially because no one new ever arrived. Everything had maintained its familiarity from his earliest memories. However, after traveling through Castiel, and now Yahaira, Bo'az understood just how mistaken he'd been in underestimating the rest of the world. *I wonder what I missed by not going off into Ashur. There had to have been so many beautiful things that I didn't get to see. Things that Tasz got to experience without me.*

They had traveled across Castiel, so they'd only seen the middle portion of the nation on their way to Yahaira. They had just departed the town of Garsiyya, and it was another place that Bo'az wished they could have spent more time. The streets were filled with amazing food stands, dancing, and music. One of the instrument vendors had allowed Bo'az to try a stringed instrument called a sitar, which he fell in love with immediately. It was used in just about every song that the musicians played for the street dancers.

A mountain range filled the horizon to the north of Garsiyya, and two enormous volcanoes overshadowed the mountains. Despite growing up in the mountains, Bo'az had never seen or even heard of a volcano before. Aurkene had explained to him that volcanoes had the ability to erupt, and when they did, it proved a dire situation for any nearby towns and cities. Bo'az hadn't understood at first, but then Aurkene told him that when they erupted, the volcanoes poured out a liquid called lava, which was exponentially hotter than fire. Apparently the smaller of the two volcanoes, Murelaga, had erupted two generations ago and laid waste to a city at the southern base of the mountains. Most of the people had evacuated in time, but there was nothing left of the city itself. Beyond just the lava, thick clouds of smoke hung in the air for weeks, requiring most nearby towns to also seek refuge in other places.

Aurkene had said that the other volcano, Infernua, hadn't erupted for as long as anyone could remember, but at more than twice the size of Murelaga, it would likely destroy any city close to the mountain range. Bo'az couldn't imagine living that close to something so deadly. The threat of Infernua erupting would be in the back of his mind every day.

"You're thinking about the volcanoes, aren't you?" Aurkene put her hand on top of his left hand. He continued to stare out of the window of their carriage at the volcanoes. "Lucky for us, they are not a threat."

He turned to look at her, "I wouldn't sleep at night if we lived here." Thankfully, Aurkene hadn't been overbearing or even slightly annoying since they'd left Sagari. He had looked for things about her to be annoyed at, just to continue the narrative in his head that their union would be a bad idea. However, the worst thing about her was the amount of time it took to brush her hair in the mornings. And since she looked stunning once she was done the wait was always worthwhile. He smiled at her, "I'm glad I kissed you back in your family's hall. I'll be honest, I was nervous about the prospects of it all for a while, but I've enjoyed everything about you since we left Sagari."

Aurkene laughed, "Just wait, I'm sure you're bound to find something wrong with me. I'm quite close to perfect, but not completely there."

"I highly doubt that. Even after this is all over and we can settle down, it's not like anything will be different."

She cocked her head and grasped his hand a little more tightly. "That reminds me. I have been curious about something. Linas Nasreddine stated that he was tricked into thinking you were of great value to Jahmash, and that they were looking for someone else. What exactly happened that led you to Jahmash?"

Bo'az turned to look out the window again for a moment. *Great. I guess I might as well tell the truth.* He turned back to look at her, then stared down at their hands. He clasped his fingers into hers, "It's not a very heroic story. There's a chance you will be disappointed."

"How long ago was that?"

"I don't know, maybe two years? More?"

"Look," Aurkene shrugged, "two years can bring a lifetime of change for some people. If you are embarrassed by it, then that means you've grown from it. So you aren't the same person anymore. I won't judge you."

Her insight and maturity surprised him and, if anything, eased him into wanting to tell her. "Very well. As I've told you, I have a twin brother named Baltaszar. For as long as I can remember, he's had this line on his face, the same that Hansi has and that Deacon had. We assume Aric has it as well, beneath his tattoos." He nodded toward Aric and Hansi, who sat across from them. "That Mark apparently means you have some type of magical power."

"Why does your twin brother have it, but not you?"

"Hansi explained to me that one receives that mark as a young child. You must be in a dire situation and put your utmost faith in the Orijin to help you out of it. So either he was in a situation that I wasn't a part of, or I just don't remember the situation. I don't think he really even knew the full meaning of it. We both grew up believing it was a scar that he got from getting burnt. That's what our father told us, anyway.

"But going back to Jahmash, Linas and his two friends came looking for Tasz. However, Tasz wasn't at our house. I was. I managed to convince them that I was my brother, and that the line on my eye had disappeared. They were skeptical but eventually accepted my explanation. I didn't realize that we were going to see Jahmash until we'd been sailing for a few days. That being said, I never knew anything about Jahmash or Darian, or the other Harbingers while I was growing up. We knew of the Orijin and that was it."

"Still, how did you go from that to all this?"

"Well, that part isn't so great. Jahmash is bent on returning to Ashur, and I guess my brother can help him do that."

"How?"

Bo'az shrugged, "He talked to others a lot about burning away the seas. I've been thinking about it a lot ever since being with Jahmash. I know there were a few instances of fires happening in our village growing up. Over time, they were eventually connected to my father, which was why he was killed, but I've started to suspect that maybe they had something to do with Tasz." Bo'az paused for a moment. It was the first time he'd ever actually shared these thoughts with anyone else, or even allowed himself to fully believe in his suspicions. "I don't know how realistic any of my suspicions are; it's all pretty complicated. And there's a lot of other things to process along with it. Anyway, the point is, Jahmash still needs my brother, and I guess he figures that I'm leverage for my brother to eventually come to him and fulfill Jahmash's wishes."

Aurkene squeezed his hand a little more tightly, "He seems to have a lot of faith in you, then. Assuming you would just return to him?"

Bo'az chuckled, "Faith? No. At least not very much of it. He is in my mind, as well as Aric's and Hansi's. He had been maintaining a presence quite regularly until your leaders agreed to support him. Then he told us that he would allow us some peace unless we give him reason to tighten his grip on our minds again."

"That seems… excessive." Aurkene let go of his hand and shifted to face him. "Does it hurt? When he has control of your mind?"

Bo'az examined her face for a moment. He'd somewhat expected her to support Jahmash's mind control, given her hatred for Darian. "It depends on the situation. Most of the time, it just feels like there's another presence in there besides my own thoughts. Kind of like we know there's a voice in our head even when it's not talking. It feels like there's an extra one of those. But if we've done something wrong or if he's angry, then it can feel like anything from a bad headache to a crippling vice grip in which we can't even control our own movements. There have been times in which I've bled from my nose and ears because of how tight his control has been."

"Grace of Orijin, that's terrible." She paused for a few moments as their carriage rolled on toward the city of Hamil Alsamaea, the capital of Yahaira. "What is he like? Jahmash? Is he always so controlling?"

Bo'az noticed Hansi and Aric looking at him. He wondered if they were worried about his response. In truth, there wasn't much embellishment needed. "He can be cruel to those who defy him or don't fulfill their obligations to him. But I think Aric and Hansi here will agree that he has treated us rather well, especially while we resided in his fortress. I don't recall ever feeling like I was a captive or anything like that. Deacon did something stupid on our voyage to Castiel, which summoned Jahmash's wrath, but that was probably the worst we've faced. He has waited thousands of years for all of this to come together, so I would say that patience is one of his stronger qualities."

"What does he look like? Is he… you know, normal looking?"

Bo'az chuckled, "What do you mean *normal?*"

"I mean, does he look like a regular person?"

"I guess. If you're that curious, he's tall and thin, but in a muscular way. Very methodical in taking care of his looks. He has someone on hand to regularly trim his beard and keep his hair short.

It's kind of a reflection of his whole personality, I guess. Very meticulous. Even when it seems like he's made a mistake or misjudged someone, it tends to turn out that he knows what he's doing. *Except* with the three he sent out looking for my brother. I'm not sure how or why he put so much trust into them, but they failed him in a huge way. Gibreel is probably lucky that he died. Linas has no eyes now and Slade lost an ear out of Jahmash's anger. Not sure if you know Slade as well, but he definitely was working against Jahmash the whole time and Jahmash didn't know about it. Like I said, he's usually on top of these things, even if he doesn't let on, but somehow Slade tricked him. It's weird; that's probably the one instance where I don't think Jahmash was as careful as he normally is." He lowered his voice so that only Aurkene could hear him, "Can we talk about something else, though? I don't like to think about these types of things for too long. Even though he told us he would stay out of our minds, I'm sure that he pops in every now and then to check up on us."

Aurkene nodded, "Understood. What do you want to talk about, then?"

Bo'az pondered for a moment. "Tell me what I need to know about Yahaira. About its leadership. Is it anything like Castiel?"

"Not really. They have a ruling council, as we do, but they are randomly selected. I don't remember exactly how many there are, but there is one representative from each Yahairan city, so likely over twenty. They vary in age, from anywhere between thirteen to sixty years old."

"Are they forced to be on the council? What if they are chosen but refuse?"

"Refusal is a crime. Criminals in Yahaira are outcasts."

"Outcasts? So then where do they go?"

"They are provided with a boat and instructed to sail away. Where they go from there is up to them, as long as they don't try to return to Yahaira."

"Wow. That's… something. Not sure whether that's worse than sending them into the forest to be hunted down." Bo'az slightly cringed. He realized immediately after the words came out that he might've offended Aurkene. "Sorry, I didn't mean to offend your culture. I'm just not used to it."

"You don't have to apologize. There are many Casteyans who find it to be extreme."

"So why not ask the elders to change it?"

Aurkene shrugged, "Honestly, Castiel does not have much crime. Whether that speaks to the morals of the people or the punishment as a deterrent, I don't know. But as far as the elders are concerned, the process is effective and it's difficult to prove otherwise."

"Fair point. It just seems like more effort to do all that than to just execute them outright. Sending people off in a boat is even worse. Do they think they're giving people a chance at survival by doing that?"

"Given how long you sailed to get to Bisitsad from Ashur, I would wager that it is much farther away than we are to Fah'Zavan and Orol Taghdras. Both of those islands are somewhat easy to reach with a larger vessel. With a small boat, the journey is obviously much more difficult to survive, but not impossible. And you'd be surprised at how many things are no longer *impossible* when one's life is at stake,"

Bo'az took a moment to absorb her words. "I couldn't agree more. That being said, I wouldn't be surprised if some of them made it all the way to Ashur. There is definitely some resemblance between some people I saw in that last town…Garsiyya, and some of the people in my hometown of Haedon. I don't know if that's an extreme coincidence, as I don't know what most people in Ashur look like, but there has to be a reason behind it."

"Who knows," Aurkene shrugged. "Remember that before Darian drowned the world, all of our islands were one giant continent. It is quite possible that Ashur has many cultural and ancestral similarities to us."

"That makes sense." He felt the carriage slow down to a stop. "Are we here already?"

Before Aurkene could answer him, the carriage door next to her opened and the stocky driver appeared. "We have arrived at the gates of Hamil Alsamaea. There are two Yahairan Senators waiting to greet you."

Aurkene smiled at Bo'az and then quickly tilted her head, nudging him to follow her. Aric and Hansi waited patiently for her and Bo'az to exit first. He followed her out of the carriage and stepped down onto the dirt path. A few feet next to them, the path transitioned from dirt to white and turquoise stones, which led to two ornate white gates that stood at least three times as tall as Bo'az. Though he wasn't close enough to see the specific details, Bo'az knew the gates had been intricately designed. There were images worked into the design, and what looked to be symbols or patterns, which he suspected might be the native language of Yahaira. On each side of the gates, a tall, white, stone wall with several turrets sprawled out and behind as far as Bo'az could see.

The gates opened and two hooded figures in loose-fitted clothing approached them as all four fully exited the carriage. As they neared, Bo'az saw that the two were a man and a woman, both older than him, but likely not by much. Once all of their packs were unloaded, their driver commanded his horses to turn and the carriage departed, leaving small clouds of dust behind.

The woman walked a few paces ahead of the man, who was just a hair taller than her. Both were taller than Bo'az, and their muscular builds were apparent through their billowing earthen-hued clothes. The woman acknowledged them first. "Good day, visitors. I am called Taali of Ihtizaz, Senator of Yahaira. My companion here is Magallan of Hamdin; he is also a senator. We were informed of your travels and have prepared accordingly. Please come with us; I am certain you are hungry and would like to relax."

Bo'az hesitated a moment, unsure of whether he should be the one to speak up. He wasn't sure if Aurkene had the same thought, but she initiated a response. "Greetings Senators. I am Aurkene Ezkerro of Castiel, Daughter of Elder Sei, Sixth of the Hemeretzi. These are my companions, Bo'az, Hansi, and Aric, all of Ashur."

Taali's head cocked slightly sideways. "Ashur, you say? Bisitsad is a *long* way from the Drowned Realm. Not many of us from other nations look highly upon your motherland. You are fortunate to have a Sagari Elder's daughter as your guide."

"Indeed," Bo'az nodded. "While we hail from Ashur, we do not necessarily represent all of its people or ideals. We come on behalf of Jahmash, and I think you will appreciate the proposal that we have come to make."

Magallan took a step forward. "There will be time for all of that soon. First, let us show you to your quarters. The food will be served shortly, so please follow us." Taali and Magallan picked up their packs before Bo'az and his companions had an opportunity to do so. They carried a pack in each hand and led the way through the gates, where the path continued and split into two, both paths leading straight ahead. Each path was sandwiched between areas of lush green grass.

The two senators walked Bo'az and his companions over to a few men who sat at a bench beside one of the pathways, smoking pipes and laughing at something one of them was saying. Behind them were carts that Bo'az assumed were for horses, except that no horses could be seen. Magallan spoke to them in a different language and two of the men stood up, still laughing. He dropped something into each of their hands, which Bo'az assumed to be coins or payment of some sort. The two men waved over Bo'az and the other three, when Magallan spoke up, "These men will take you to the feast hall of the Yahairan Senate. Taali and I will deliver your packs to your quarters and ensure that everything is ready for you in the meantime."

Bo'az looked at the two men curiously, wondering where their horses could be, when one of them smiled and beckoned for Bo'az and the others to come to him. He slowly walked over to the two men and his company followed. "Good day, sir. Where are your horses?"

The man, clad in reddish-brown pants and a black vest, continued to smile. His arms weren't overly muscular, but they were incredibly toned and defined in places that Bo'az didn't know were possible. "You truly must be foreigners. *We* are the horses."

"What?"

"You and your lady can sit in this cart," he waved a hand toward the cart closest to him, which Bo'az realized resembled giant wheelbarrows with seats, "and your other two companions can take the one that my friend here will commandeer."

Bo'az shrugged and walked over to the cart. As Aurkene sat down next to him, he glanced at her and asked, "This is new to you as well?"

"Yes," she nodded. "I've never actually been *inside* the city before. They don't have these things in the couple of other Yahairan cities that I've been to. And I can't imagine that anyone wants to *commandeer* one of these from here all the way to another city."

"Right. I sure as hell wouldn't. I hope they are paid well for this. Wait, are *we* supposed to pay them?"

The man walked up to the wagon. "We are paid by the Senate. Employed by them as well. It is a grueling job, especially in the heat of summer, but we are well cared for, as are our families. I am called Fadel. Sit back and relax; I will take you to the dining court of the Senate."

Bo'az did as Fadel suggested and took in the scenery. The cart had a canvas canopy over it that thankfully provided shade as they traveled. Bo'az took in the sights on the sides of the two paths. Buildings of magnificent architecture lined each side, all white with ornate gold trim. "Are we actually *in* the city? Do people actually live inside all of these massive buildings?"

Fadel turned his head and then looked straight again. "This part is for our government. You met two of our senators, but there are thirty-one in total, one for each city in Yahaira. Each of them needs their own quarters, and there are several bath houses, kitchens, and dining rooms as well. There also must be space for other needs, such as any interests and hobbies they may have. Each senator serves for three years, and they can be as young as thirteen years old. Our government provides private teachers and instructors for them, not only because they are young and might be missing that education at home, but they must also be aware of the world around them if they are to make decisions with Yahaira's best interest in mind."

"That's amazing. So everything we're passing by right now all belongs to the Senate?"

"Yes. The residents of Hamil Alsamaea live in a different part of the city, away from the affairs of the Senate. It is a nice separation; this way everyone has their peace."

"Are Senators required to go back to their cities once their terms are complete?" Aurkene asked. "Have there been instances of them being attacked by angry civilians?"

Fadel nodded, "Good question. They are allowed to stay here if they choose. The younger ones tend to return home, as they have people and situations they prefer to return to. Many of them do choose to stay here in the Capital, as they enjoy the solace that comes along with this city."

Bo'az wondered if any places in Ashur had similar systems in place. Haedon had only had Oran Von, whom most people seemed to like. He had liked the man for a time as well, until Von turned on his father and had him hanged. He clenched his teeth rather than his fist, not wanting to hurt or alarm Aurkene, whose hand was in his. He changed the subject quickly, "I must ask, Fadel. Why no horses? Wouldn't it be easier for you to sit up front on a wagon and drive from there?"

"It depends on what you mean by *easier*. It would be less physical work for me, individually. However, horses require maintenance, especially food. Look at these paths and grass. You see how pristine they are? Now imagine them covered in horse shit! Who would want to spend their days cleaning that?"

Bo'az hadn't thought about that. "That makes a lot of sense." He saw ahead that they were nearing a group of men dressed in the same attire as Fadel and the other man who pulled the wagon with Aric and Hansi.

"Of course it does. My friends, we have reached the end of our journey together. At least for today." Fadel set down the wagon so they could depart. Behind the other men stood another ornately crafted gate, with two figures standing in front of it. They wore the same billowy, earth-hued clothing as the two senators who had greeted Bo'az and the others outside the city.

As soon as the four of them departed from the wagons and thanked their wagon drivers, the two figures approached them. Once again, it was a male and female, though this female looked older than Taali and was notably shorter. The man spoke first, "Good day, guests. I am called Sagrajas of Aban, Senator of Yahaira. My companion is Ibarra of Jalidah. We shall escort you to the Great Hall, where the four of you shall dine with the entire Senate. Please give us your names."

Bo'az smiled and responded before Aurkene had the opportunity, "I am Bo'az Kontez, of Ashur. This is Aurkene Ezkerro of Castiel, and behind me are Hansi Huu and Aric Taurean, also of Ashur."

"Thank you. Please follow us." The gates opened as they turned, and they walked through without hesitation. Bo'az followed first and the others filed in behind him through the gate. They walked across a stone patio inside, and the two senators led them to a set of wooden double doors, almost as intricately decorated as the gate. Sagrajas opened the door for them and Ibarra led them through.

As they walked in, Ibarra raised her voice, "Senate of Yahaira, I present Bo'az Kontez, Aric Taurean, and Hansi Huu of Ashur, and Aurkene Ezkerro of Castiel."

Bo'az had thought that Aurkene's family's hall was enormous, but this room was at least double the size. Long tables of food lined the perimeter of the room, and in the center was an enormous circular table that looked like it could seat all of Haedon. Each seat had cushions sewn into it as well as a servant standing behind it. Some senators already sat at the table, while others mingled about the room or surveyed the food. Ibarra led them to their seats, though surprisingly she had them all sit separately from each other.

She must have noticed Aurkene's discomfort. "Do not worry. We separate you to give you an opportunity to mingle with the senators. Also, it prevents any dishonesty, as you cannot confer about anything by whispering to one another. But if you have nothing to hide, then there is nothing to worry about." Ibarra maintained a smile even as she finished, though the threat was clear. She then showed Bo'az and the other two to their seats. Bo'az was only a few seats away from Aric, but Aurkene and Hansi sat on the other side of the table.

The servant behind his chair was a skinny young man, likely of an age with Bo'az. He pulled the chair out for Bo'az, then pushed it back in as he sat. "What can I pour for you, Master Bo'az? We have a large collection of wines, ales, and juices. Or water if you prefer."

"I'll have some wine, thank you."

"Very well, master. Do you prefer red or white?"

"Oh. Um…white please?" His experience with wine had been limited to what he drank in Castiel, which had been minimal. The locals there had had more of a liking to ale, and Bo'az hadn't wanted to offend them by asking for something else. The ale had filled him up quickly and made him drunk more easily. It also managed to make him retch when he'd had too much, whereas the wine didn't. As it was only the middle of the day, he hoped this event didn't lead to such a crazy occasion. Bo'az looked around the table as the senators took their seats. *They definitely don't look like the type to turn this into some wild drunken festival.*

The servant returned with his wine, and whispered to him, "Do you have a preference of what you'd like to eat, Master Bo'az? We can cater to nearly anything you might have an appetite for. Within reason."

Bo'az almost chuckled at the overly lavishness of it all. "I'm not picky and I'm rather hungry. So anything you bring me would be fine."

"Very well, I shall return shortly."

As the servant departed once more, Bo'az noticed several of the other personal servants doing the same. One of the senators from across the table cleared her throat loudly. "Good day, everyone. Guests, we welcome you to the Great Hall of the Senate. I am called Alamar of Talha, and I am the eldest senator. Please share with us your purpose for this visit."

"Very well," Bo'az took a deep breath. He was hoping they might ease into the business part of the meeting. Still, it was better than the way things started out in Castiel. *At least we're not tied to a rotating platform.* "My name is Bo'az Kontez and I hail from the nation of Ashur. My companions from Ashur are Hansi Huu and Aric Taurian," he opened his palm and pointed his hand toward Aurkene, "and this is my intended, Aurkene Ezkerro of Castiel."

Alamar raised her white, bushy eyebrows, "*Intended* you say? You cannot have been in Bisitsad very long, and you already plan to marry one of our own. Was that your decision, Bo'az of Ashur?"

"Yes, it was my decision, and not a strategic arrangement, if that is why you ask," he answered instantly. "I was stricken by Aurkene from the moment I saw her."

"Very well," Alamar's long braid hung in front of her shoulder and swayed as she nodded. "Go on then, share with us why you are here."

It occurred to Bo'az that this whole reception had to have been planned. There would be no way to prepare all of this food and gather this many senators together without any planning. He would gauge the course of the conversation before asking about that. He took a moment to go over the speech in his head, that he'd practiced innumerable times while they'd sailed. "My two Ashurian companions and I have come on behalf of Jahmash, Harbinger of the Orijin, to request the help of the Yahairan army. Jahmash seeks justice from the people of Ashur, who chose to honor the charlatan, Darian, instead of him. He seeks revenge against the descendants of Darian, the false Harbinger who led him on a chase for days, then cowardly trapped Jahmash on an island to live for millennia in solitude, instead of just mercifully killing him. On his behalf, we respectfully request soldiers to aid in his attack on Ashur. In return, Yahaira would be given a claim to parts of Ashur to expand its dominion."

A din rose amongst the senators around the table until the man next to him put up a hand to quiet everyone. The stocky man, who looked old enough to be his father, turned to face Bo'az, "Good day, Bo'az. I am Durr'an of Alderete. There have long been rumors of Jahmash's existence as well as of his desire to exact revenge upon the descendants of Darian. Do you mean to suggest that Jahmash is alive and that this is the start of his return?"

Bo'az nodded "Indeed. The three of us have seen him ourselves and lived on his island for quite some time. He already has a backing and hopes to expand his armies, so that all of Ashur's population is laid to waste."

Durr'an continued, "And as citizens of Ashur, you accept your hypocrisy?"

Every nation is going to ask this, aren't they? "I wouldn't call it hypocrisy. I lived my whole life in a village hidden away in the forest. I never stepped foot onto any populated area of Ashur. In fact, in my lifetime, I've met more people from *beyond* Ashur than I have who've lived there. I only state that I am Ashurian because nobody would understand my situation. But you cannot be loyal to a place that you have never seen."

Durr'an stared at the table for a moment before responding dryly, "Yet you ask us to pledge our loyalty to Jahmash, though we have never seen him."

Another senator spoke up, who sat farther to Bo'az's left. "Good day, Bo'az and guests. I am called Alange of Sagres. I would like to know how you expect us to trust your word? You simply arrived at our gates and while we have welcomed you in, that does not mean that we are allies."

There it is. That's my opening. "We thank you for your hospitality, Alange of Sagres. You are implying that we arrived out of nowhere. However, the only way this whole feast could be possible is if you knew that we were coming. You had to have had someone following us, at least from Garsiyya, if not even longer. I would like to believe that, if we had proven to be a threat at any point in our journey here, you would have had us either killed or taken prisoner. So while we are not allies, my companions and I are not here to make threats. Jahmash knows that not every nation will back him. However, we are here with a request, not a demand."

Bo'az's servant returned with a plate of food, as did several others. He looked around the table and noted that everyone had a plate in front of them. Just about all of the senators switched their focus from Bo'az to their food. He looked down at his plate and saw that the servant had brought him what looked to be seasoned fish dressed with herbs, along with roasted vegetables and tiny grains that were smaller than rice. The room went quiet for a few moments until one of the senators broke what felt like hours of awkwardness. Bo'az wasn't sure what it meant that his rant went without a response.

The senator responded as if no time had passed at all, "Good day, I am called Lobaton of Massar. Let us say for a moment that you are telling the truth about your purpose here. What do we have to benefit by sacrificing a portion of our military for a fight that is not our own? And before you repeat yourself, what guarantee is there that Jahmash will be victorious in Ashur? What happens if he loses? We will have lost countless soldiers in vain, in a land far across the world. Even if we *are* on the winning side, what good does it do for us to expand our dominion in a land so far away? I can only assume that Castiel agreed to your terms, especially considering the presence of your *intended*. I mean no offense, Aurkene, but Castiel has always been more aggressive militarily than we have. But look at how many soldiers you lost when you attempted to conquer Vitheligia. That may be before your time, but it is a legendary example of underestimating your enemy."

To Bo'az's surprise, one of the younger senators spoke up. "Good day, I am called Rabarrah of Razin." *For the love of Orijin, must they all greet me that way? There is no way I will remember all of their names.* Rabarrah continued, "I must agree with Lobaton. My father is a soldier, and my older brother plans to become one soon. I support everything that they do, but to send them off for this type of war would be a grand mistake. Why would I want to risk losing my family for something like this?"

"Your family would not be forced to stay once the war ends. They would be more than welcome to return home to you."

"You mean if they survive. Nothing is guaranteed in war."

Another senator joined in, "Good day, I am called Lucena of Banafsaj. As you might be able to tell, Bo'az, I am one of the older senators. I heard rumors of the existence of Ashur from when I was a little girl. My parents believed that it was real and saw it quite unfavorably. They blamed Darian for drowning the world and creating so much distance between nations, just to stop one man. I grew up embracing that resentment. However, while I have never liked Ashur, I do not think that it is enough of a reason to sail there and attack them in order to fulfill someone else's sense of justice. Jahmash's war is simply not worth risking our own people."

Just as Bo'az's servant came to him with another plate of food, another senator responded to Lucena. Bo'az took the opportunity to put a chunk of grilled lamb in his mouth. "Good day guests, I am called Massi of Garsiyya. Lucena, and those who agree with her, I ask you to stop and consider something for a moment. We live in a nation that is home to two volcanoes. While I am one of the oldest senators, I was not alive the last time one of them erupted, but it did destroy a whole city. And that was the small one. If Infernua was to erupt, or both of them, my whole city would cease to exist. I'm sure that several other cities would perish as well. I write to my family in Garsiyya quite often. They have mentioned feeling the ground slightly shake in the recent past. Joining this war would provide an opportunity to escape this land should another eruption happen. Even if not for us, what of our descendants who would suffer?"

"Good day Bo'az and guests, I am called Azar of Fatyan. I must agree with Massi." Bo'az glanced at Azar and then couldn't help but look again. He was a boy who clearly had not started the process of manhood or perhaps had barely started. Still, the rest of the Senate looked at him as they'd done the rest. "We should consider what is in the best interest of our nation in the long term, and what will benefit Yahaira for generations to come. An eruption of Infernua alone could cause enough damage to even affect Castiel. If both volcanoes were to erupt together, imagine how many lives that would take. It would likely be more than that of any armies we would send to Ashur."

Dammit. I knew those volcanoes would be trouble. Did he say the ground is already shaking? What the hell is wrong with these people? Why are they not panicking about this? As the rest of the senators started to mumble, Bo'az's servant whispered to him once more. "Master Bo'az, may I get you another plate? More wine?"

"Yes, please," Bo'az whispered back.

"What would you like?"

"I'm not sure. Perhaps anything I have not tried yet?" Bo'az had grown up being somewhat picky, especially about trying new and unfamiliar foods. He'd always known it was an inconvenience for his father, as many meals came down to what they could trade for from their own farm. He was doing his best to change that now.

"Very well, sir. I shall be back shortly."

Bo'az focused back on the senators as his servant left. The din quieted a moment later as Alamar, the eldest one, spoke up once more. "Senators and guests, we will have no choice but to have the Senate vote on how to handle this situation. Clearly we are divided on the matter. But first, Bo'az, how many soldiers does Jahmash request of us?"

"Half of your army. But I believe that can be negotiated, if you have concerns."

"Half? That sounds lofty, especially considering that Brogan, our neighbor to the west, could easily decline your offer and then attack us, knowing that our army has been reduced. But that is my sentiment, not the Senate's." She looked around the table at everyone else, "Servants, please leave us." The servants all immediately filed out of the room without asking questions or looking back. Once they were all gone, Alamar continued. "Now. Bo'az, Hansi, Aric, and Aurkene: there are thirty-one senators at this table. Two-thirds vote is required for anything to pass, which means at least twenty-one senators must vote either way for a decision to be made. Do you understand?" Bo'az and the others all nodded in agreement. *This isn't going to go well. She basically just scared them all about the possibility of getting invaded.* "Good. Senators of Yahaira, once I indicate that it is time to vote, those of you who vote to deny this request will stand. Those of you who accept will remain seated. If there is any confusion on the matter, please state it now." Alamar paused for a moment to allow for any questions. "Very well. Senators, I ask that you now show your votes on the matter."

To no surprise, Alamar rose out of her seat. Bo'az looked around the table as many of the senators also stood. He tried to count in his head those who remained seated. *Seven. Shit. I hope he doesn't punish me for this. It wasn't my fault.*

Alamar spoke again, "The vote stands as twenty-four to seven, in favor of refusing our visitors' request. You may all be seated again. Azar, please inform the servants that they may return now. Guests, unfortunately, this means that your business here is complete. However, it would be rude of us to ask you to be on your way so quickly. We shall finish our meal as friends and you are welcome to stay in the Senate's guest houses for two days' time, after which point, we shall expect you to continue on your journey. Should you choose to leave earlier than that, we shall bear no grudge nor attempt to stop you. During your stay, if there is any hospitality that you need, our servants shall be more than happy to help. So please, continue to enjoy this delicious meal and converse with the senators."

"Thank you for your hospitality. We accept your offer to stay." Bo'az tried to sound as genuine as possible, though a hint of anger pulled at the back of his mind. What unsettled him was that he knew the anger was his and not Jahmash's. *Have I truly become his disciple?* He hadn't felt Jahmash's presence at all throughout the whole process of meeting with the Senate. *Does he trust me that much to not even see how things are going? Then again, it wouldn't take very long for him to know what happened. And if he's angry, then I'm sure I'll bleed out of my face, wherever blood can come out of it.*

He blinked a few times and his plate reappeared before him. Bo'az looked up and saw that the rest of his companions had taken the opportunity to talk to the people around them. He wondered what they thought of everything that had just happened, but there would be plenty of time to converse later. He took another bite of the grilled lamb and then asked the servant for a mug of ale. The wine wouldn't be enough to dull his senses. He turned to the senator next to him, who had spoken up earlier. "Excuse me, it…you are called Durr'an, right?"

"Yes Bo'az. I apologize that we will not fulfill your request. Please understand that it is not meant as a slight to you or to Jahmash."

Bo'az nodded, "I do understand. As I'm sure Jahmash will as well. I was wondering, once we have had a chance to rest and perhaps bathe, where might we be able to go during the evening, perhaps for dinner or even just to have a drink and unwind?"

"Ah, of course. That is completely up to you. The usual practice is that the Senate returns here for dinner, and any family and special guests of the Senate join us. As grand as this room is, we have another room that is meant for more informal things. We Senators are not *always* concerned with business. Please feel free to join us tonight. The Banqeta, which is where these festivities occur, is not far from the guest houses. You can simply ask the servants tending to you to escort you there. There is no bad blood, we shall welcome you with open arms."

"Thank you. I'll be honest, the Senate decision is disappointing, but I think some good drink can help with that."

Durr'an smiled, "Drink can help. The *hashah* will help even more."

"Hashah?"

"Yes, yes. Do you have pipes that you smoke out of in Ashur?"

Bo'az was curious now. "Yes we do. My father, when he was still alive, used to smoke from it every now and then. I tried it once or twice, but he would never let me do so regularly."

Durr'an patted him on the shoulder. "Do not worry. Tonight you shall be my special guest. You look young enough to be my child. How old are you, Bo'az?"

"I have seen roughly twenty summers. With all this travel, I have forgotten," he surprised himself with a chuckle.

"Ah, then you are younger than my own children. Not to worry, my wife and I will introduce you and your companions to the hashah tonight. It will be an evening to remember for all of us!"

***

A servant had escorted Bo'az and the others to the guest houses.

Each of them had their own bedroom with a bathtub, though Bo'az was disappointed that he wasn't sharing a room with Aurkene. *I guess it doesn't matter that much; we can share a bed if we really want to.* The bed was large enough that it could fit him and Aurkene, with plenty of room to spare. He pulled some clothes from his pack, which had been placed at the foot of the bed, then disrobed to climb into the steaming bathtub. As he eased himself in, he couldn't help but let out an audible "Ahhhh."

The journey from Garsiyya hadn't been bad, but the stress that led up to the Senate meeting as well as the outcome had manifested itself into knots in his shoulders and back. It would have been nice to have Aurkene with him to massage his back, but perhaps he would make those arrangements with her later. He stayed in the bath for what felt like an hour, occasionally pouring in more hot water to maintain the temperature. When the aches finally dissipated, he stood and dressed for the night. As he was finishing, someone knocked at the door.

"Who is it?"

"Your future wife."

He smiled and opened it right away. "I just got out of the bath. I was thinking we could take one together later."

Aurkene walked in and sat on his bed, "We can definitely do that, and maybe some other things." She smiled at him and raised her eyebrows suggestively. Bo'az walked closer to her and just as he was about to gently push her back to lay on the bed, another knock sounded at the door.

"For the love of Orijin. Seriously?"

Aurkene took a deep breath, "Your friends have impeccable timing."

He opened the door and saw Hansi and Aric waiting. Aric looked at him, "Are we all ready?"

Bo'az turned and walked further in so they could follow. "I suppose. We'll just have to find a servant to walk us over. I'm not sure which building it is." He sat on the bed next to Aurkene and noticed Hansi's eyes go wide. Hansi mouthed an apology and he nodded. *At least one of them understands what's going on. Aric is so fucking oblivious right now.* "You're both ready?" Aric and Hansi both nodded in agreement. "Good. We might as well go then." He stood and led the way out of the room. All of the guest rooms connected to the same hallway, and servants moved about between rooms to keep everything in order. Bo'az patted the shoulder of a younger man, "Excuse me. We were wondering if you or someone else might be able to escort us to the Banqeta? The Senators encouraged us to go and suggested we ask one of you to walk us there."

The servant nodded and set the two pillows he was holding down onto a small chair next to him. "Good day, sir. Of course I can do that for you. Please follow me. You shall be surprised as to how close it is. You should be able to get back here without any assistance, but any servant can escort you back if you require it." They walked out of the guest house and turned in the opposite direction of the Great Hall. The servant had been correct about Bo'az's being surprised. The Banqeta was an enormous building next to the guest houses, less than thirty paces away.

"You were right. You could have saved yourself the time and trouble by just telling us where to go."

The servant smiled, "It is no trouble. The night is agreeable and the fresh air feels nice. I would strongly advise against any deceit or attack, if that is something that any of you have in mind. You would be outnumbered rather quickly, and I have no doubt that you would all lose your lives."

"We are not here to cause trouble. Our meeting did not go as we'd hoped, but it is not something that we can control or change. Besides, it is not a total loss. We have met several nice people here and it will be nice to enjoy an evening with them."

"Very well, Master Bo'az. We are here," he gestured to the large wooden doors and opened one for them to walk in. "I hope that you enjoy your evening. As I said, if the ale and hashah end up getting the best of you, there are plenty of servants who shall be willing to escort you back to your quarters."

Aurkene responded, "It seems like this happens frequently?"

The servant smiled, "Without fail, every night that they celebrate here."

"Wow," Aric's eyes went wide; he looked nervous to go in. "We sure are in for a hell of a night, then."

Bo'az thanked the servant and entered with the others in tow. He grasped Aurkene's hand and then looked around at the spectacle of the room. Durr'an was right in that the Banqeta put the Great Hall to shame. Circular tables filled the right side of the room, clouds of smoke hanging above them. Bo'az could see large round silver platters in the middle of each table. Several small bowls lay on top of each platter and people sat around in a circle and smoked from pipes. A huge candle was in the middle of each platter. He imagined that Durr'an was probably at one of those tables with his wife. He turned to Aurkene and noticed that Aric and Hansi had already left them. He wondered if they'd gone to smoke, or if they were in another part of the room eating or drinking. "You ever smoke hashah before?"

"No," she shook her head, "my parents never let me. They never liked smoking anything, but I have always been curious. Shall we try it?"

"I'm curious myself. And Durr'an, the senator who sat next to me, promised to take care of us tonight, so we should try to find him." He searched the tables for the stocky man with short, curly, black hair. They walked between a few of the tables when he caught Durr'an's profile amidst a dissipating cloud of smoke. Bo'az yelled once they were a few feet away, "Durr'an!"

The man heard him despite the noise surrounding them. He perked up when he saw him. "Bo'az! Aurkene! I am so happy to see you! Where are your companions?"

Bo'az noticed a gloss in the man's eyes. *Wonder how long he's been here.* "They went off to do something else. We came to you to try the hashah, if we can sit with you."

"Of course! Like I told you, you two are my special guests tonight! Ah, how rude of me, this is my wife; she is called Maarida." Maarida stood to greet them and Bo'az realized that she was a good deal taller than Durr'an. Bo'az sat down next to Durr'an to avoid staring at his wife. He didn't want things to get awkward or have her think he was staring for the wrong reason. Aurkene squeezed next to him on the bench.

"Should we ask for some ale before we start?"

"Oh no, dear boy. The hashah will dry you out." Durr'an raised his arm and beckoned someone over with his hand. "Please bring water over for my two guests here, and two pipes as well, my dear." The maid nodded and left. Durr'an turned back to him and Aurkene, "Water for now. We will smoke first and you will drink plenty of water while doing so. Then you will wait a short while and we'll eat something. *Then* you can drink your ale. This is the order of things, otherwise you will end up back in your room within the hour."

Bo'az smiled at him, "You are the expert. I will follow whatever you say." The maid returned with their water and pipes.

Durr'an took one of the bowls from the center of the table, as well as a thin rod that lay next to it. "First, you take the hashah and pack it in with the rod. The more you pack, the stronger the pull, do you understand? I am going to start both of you off lightly. Then you can decide how you want to proceed from there. Once your pipe is filled, you will take a spill, those are the very thin candles at the foot of the giant candle, light one, and then light your pipe. Like this." He took the thin spill and put its wick to the larger candle until it was lit, then lit his own pipe with it. While he was lighting his pipe, Durr'an put his mouth to it to inhale. He exhaled a small puff of smoke as he spoke, "Pulling from it while you light it helps to light the hashah. Sometimes it will stay lit, but often you will have to light it again. Now you try."

Bo'az looked at Aurkene and they both put the pipes to their mouths at the same time, then put the stills to their pipes simultaneously as well. Bo'az inhaled cautiously; he was afraid of taking in so much that he might choke, but also worried that he might not like the taste. He pulled it in and let the smoke flow through his mouth, then into his lungs. The hashah tasted sweet and a bit sour, and there was a relaxing sensation of drawing it in and then exhaling the smoke. "Wow, that feels really good. I didn't realize that it would taste like that!"

He took a few more drags over the next several moments, though Aurkene went at a slower pace. Durr'an nudged his arm, "The key is that they mix the hashah with Yahairan *altaba*. That makes it sweeter and also less potent, so you can enjoy it for longer."

"What is altaba?"

"It comes from a leaf that we dry and then use for smoking. The process is the same as the hashah, except that altaba does not affect your mind the way hashah does. Altaba relaxes you. Hashah alters your mind."

Bo'az thought for a moment, "That is what my father used to smoke. Except he called it *tambaku*. It had the same effect, though. He smoked it in his pipe to relax every now and then."

Durr'an smiled, "Yes. That is the best feeling, to sit back after a long day and smoke some nice altaba. You start to look forward to it."

"I'll have to try some by itself, without the hashah." Bo'az felt himself swaying a bit, but he enjoyed the sensation. He still had his faculties about him, but he knew he would have to pace himself if he wanted to enjoy the night for a while. He and Aurkene finished what was in their pipes over the next half of an hour or so. Durr'an offered to fill their pipes again, but Aurkene refused. She preferred to sit for a short while, and then she would traverse the room to see what else it had to offer. By the time Bo'az started on his second pipeful, Aurkene had left them. He knew she wasn't upset with him and just wanted to take things in. He giggled for a moment, "I, Durr'an I am a lucky man. I kissed that girl in front of all of Sagari and I didn't realize it was a marriage proposal. But, but it was, oh man it was the best thing I ever did."

"I am very happy for you, my friend," the elder man chuckled and clapped his shoulder. "She is quite beautiful and also intelligent. You are right, you are a lucky man," he turned to look at his wife and then kissed her, before turning back to Bo'az. "As you can see, so am I."

"What…what did you do before you were a senator?"

"My wife and I both stopped working about four years ago. We actually own an altaba farm; it is quite a lucrative crop in Bisitsad. Now my daughter and one of my sons take care of it and have forced us into a life of leisure. We are from Alderete, which is at the southwestern-most part of Yahaira. It is a beautiful city, especially the views of the sea at sunrise and sunset. By the time my term is done, my oldest son will have fulfilled his duty to our military. He is a captain, you know. That is why I had to reject your offer, my friend. Sending half our army would almost guarantee that my son would have to leave. I have two years left as a senator, and then our whole family can be together again on our farm."

Bo'az grinned so widely that he could feel his cheeks and eyelids touching. "I unders… I understand, Durr. I would feel the same way. And if I, if I end up in a similar position when Aurkene, when we have a family, I would vote the s… the same way. It's so beautiful what you have." Bo'az knew they continued to talk for a while longer, but at a certain point, he realized he didn't remember anything that they'd said. In the midst of it, a moment of clarity hit him, "Wait. You own a… an altaba farm. Now that we are great friends, may I buy some from you to take with me? I would love to have some and a good… a good pipe throughout m-my travels."

Durr'an grasped his forearm, which was resting on the table. "My friend, you do not have to buy it. I will arrange for someone to bring it to you before you leave. It would be my pleasure."

"Really? That might be the, the nicest thing anyone's ever done for me. Thank you so much."

"Think nothing of it. It shall be a nice gift for you to remember us by. I shall also make sure to give you some hashah as well. You enjoyed it so much that we have finished all of it! Drink some water. You should eat something shortly."

Bo'az nodded slowly and then gulped down water from his mug. "Maybe I should sit, just sit here for a moment."

"Yes, that would be wise." Bo'az turned around on his bench and looked around the rest of the room for what felt like hours until finally Durr'an nudged his shoulder. "Come, let us find some food at the banquet tables. It would do us all well to eat something."

"Wait, we're still here?" Bo'az looked at him with a furrowed brow but got up to follow him and his wife. Durr'an waited for him and put an arm around him as they walked. They arrived at one of the food tables and Bo'az eyed Hansi and Aric with two girls not far in the distance. He attempted to say something but just smiled to himself and nodded while putting a few skewers of lamb on his plate.

As he moved to the next tray of food, he looked around for Aurkene, and finally spotted her along one of the walls, talking to a man and woman who he assumed to be a couple. The man looked familiar and ended up staring at him until Durr'an startled him. "Do you have an issue with Senator Sagrajas? That is his wife next to him, so if you are suspicious, there is nothing to worry about. He would not try anything with Aurkene."

Bo'az shook his head. "No not that. I, I've met him before. I think he walked us into the Great Hall."

"Indeed he did. He sat at our very table as well and voted in your favor. He is a very nice man. Like I said, there is nothing to worry about with him." Bo'az wondered why Durr'an felt the need to repeat that. But then again, he'd likely been staring at the man for too long. Durr'an signaled to a maid and mouthed "three ales" to her. Within moments, Bo'az had a new mug, this time with something better than water. He ate and drank more throughout the course of the evening, to the point that everything melted into a long blur of time.

***

Bo'az snorted a puff of air from his nose and forced his heavy eyelids open. His chest felt heavy with the remnants of smoke, and he coughed lightly at the thought of all the smoking he'd done the night before. He craned his neck off the pillow and was grateful to be in his room. *Oh no, did the servants have to bring me back here?* He looked at the ceiling to try and recall the previous night when he realized that Aurkene's leg was resting on top of his. He smiled and turned to look at her while she slept, and somehow jumped back out of fear while still laying down. "What the fuck?" He looked again to confirm what he thought he saw, or *who* he thought he saw. Lying next to him was a woman with blondish, brown hair, though only her head and neck were uncovered. *Please don't be naked. Please let both of us have our clothes on.* He already knew what the answer to that request would be, but he slightly lifted the blanket anyway. Sure enough, he saw her naked light-skinned body underneath and let the blanket fall back down immediately. *Fuck. What am I going to do? I don't even remember meeting this woman or talking to her. How did she end up here?* He sat up and leaned back against the headboard, noticing another body next to the strange girl. He looked again, as he couldn't be sure whether to trust his blurry eyes and knew for sure that the thick, curly hair belonged to Aurkene. *What the hell happened last night? Did all three of us sleep together? How would that have even happened?* He tried to rub the sleep out of his eyes with both hands, hoping that some type of clarity might come to him.

He heard a groan come from under Aurkene's pile of hair and tried his best to whisper without waking the strange woman. "Aurkene." His dry throat caused it to come out broken. Bo'az glanced at the other woman who lay between them. Luckily, Aurkene stirred and rolled over to face him. She brushed her thick hair back and blinked a few times before smiling at him. He couldn't help but laugh upon seeing the crusts at the corners of her eyes and a trace of dried drool on one side of her mouth. *I probably look the same way, but she's still stunning.* "Good morning," her voice was also scratchy.

"Is that…are you sure? Who is this?"

"You don't remember? She came back with us last night; I met her at the Banqeta. Her name is Suriiya."

"And the three of us…we…did things together last night?"

Aurkene braced on her elbow and leaned her head on her hand. She then gently rested her right hand on Suriiya's arm and smiled widely at Bo'az, "Oh, we did things. Honestly, Suriiya and I did most of the work, but you made sure we were both satisfied."

He could feel himself blushing, "And you…you are alright with this?"

She squinted her eyes in confusion, "Bo, it was *my* idea. As I was speaking with her and her husband, I realized that we had a connection. She couldn't take her eyes off of me and when I started flirting, she returned the favor. Somehow her husband was oblivious to the whole thing; I'm not even sure if he knew when she left. I just hope that he hasn't sent out a search party for her or something."

"He wouldn't," the voice startled Bo'az, as he hadn't realized that Suriiya was awake. "It would be a great disgrace for him to have to tell people that he doesn't know where his wife is." She looked up at Bo'az, "Good morning, by the way."

"Indeed," Bo'az exhaled deeply. "So now what?"

Suriiya sat up and the blanket fell, exposing her bare chest, which made Bo'az blush once more. "Now, it is wise for me to leave the two of you. I will have to return to my husband at some point. However, the danger of being caught makes it more exciting." She leaned close to Bo'az and kissed his cheek, then turned to Aurkene and kissed her as well, before climbing over her to get out of the bed. She searched the ground to find her clothes and got dressed. "Bo'az, I've gathered that you do not remember all of the details of last night, so you should know that my husband is a senator; he is called Sagrajas of Aban. If you happen to see the two of us together before you leave Yahaira, please do not react strongly."

Bo'az processed what she'd said for a moment, then nodded. "I think I remember seeing the two of you talking to Aurkene. I understand, though."

"Thank you." She looked at Aurkene seductively as she finished dressing, "Shall we do it again tonight?"

Aurkene looked at Bo'az as if asking permission. He pursed his lips and shrugged, leaving the decision up to her. Aurkene looked back at Suriiya, "Absolutely."

Suriiya smiled at them both and blew them kisses, then left the room. Bo'az immediately turned his gaze to Aurkene, "Look, we should talk about all of this. I'm sure that we all had fun last night, but you're fine with all of this? We haven't known each other for very long, but I think fancying women as well as men is something that you should have mentioned."

Aurkene sat up in the bed and sighed, "The thing is, I don't think I really knew I fancied women until last night. I don't know if it's women in general, or just Suriiya, but I'd never felt like that until last night when I was talking to her. It was just something about her that turned me on. Bo'az, I am sorry if it's made you feel uncomfortable. If she *does* come back tonight, I can always explain to her that we are not interested in doing it again. You're right, it should have been a conversation first, and last night neither of us were in our right minds. I was acting more on lust than anything else. And please don't think it changes the way I feel about you. It wasn't about that at all."

He grasped her hand and moved closer to her. "I'm not *mad* at you. I was just confused about where that all came from. One of the fun things about us not knowing so much about each other is that we get to learn about each other every day. I think, more than anything, I'm surprised that you're willing to share me with someone else without any jealousy."

She squeezed his hand and kissed him, "I enjoyed watching you get pleasure from her. I enjoy seeing you happy. It was as simple as that."

"It's a shame that I don't really remember any of it." He blushed once more.

Aurkene laughed, "Then I think that means we need to do it again tonight. We'll have to reenact everything we did last night, as well as try some new things." She hung her arms around his neck and pulled him down so that they were laying down again.

"I think that's probably the best solution. It's probably the only way to know for sure whether I enjoyed it."

"I completely agree. And perhaps we'll have to continue to do it until we know without a doubt whether you like it or not."

Bo'az snickered, "I appreciate how concerned you are for my happiness. Hey, we actually have nothing to do today and we don't have to leave until tomorrow. What should we do?"

Aurkene inched closer to him, "I have a few ideas that involve not leaving this bed."

He wondered if he continued to blush this frequently, whether his face would permanently stay red. "You'll have to show me what these ideas are."

***

Bo'az sat at the side of his bed and rubbed his face. Aurkene had left a few minutes ago to return to her own room so she could take some time to bathe and freshen up. Bo'az requested the servants bring steaming water for him to do the same. *Wow, last night I slept with Aurkene and another woman, and then slept with Aurkene again afterwards. Maybe the Orijin has decided that I've suffered enough in my life and is now balancing things out.* He slapped himself lightly to make sure he was awake. "Definitely awake." He reclined back onto the bed while he waited for the bath water and tried to remember the details of the night before. *I was smoking with Durr'an and his wife. Damn. I hope I didn't do anything to offend them in the process of leaving. That hashah was good, but wow is that stuff dangerous. Hopefully I'll run into him today so I can apologize for anything I might've done. I wonder if he'll still give me the… shit, what did he call it? Dammit I don't remember.*

Someone knocked at the door and Bo'az immediately responded without bothering to sit up. "Come in!" He tilted his head forward to see a few servants enter, carrying giant metal pots steaming with hot water. "Oh, thank the Orijin." Bo'az sat up as they filled the tub for him. "Excuse me, would any of you happen to know how I managed to return from the Banqeta last night? Did any of you or the others have to carry me back or anything?"

One servant looked at the other two and then back at Bo'az. "No, there was nothing of that sort. You returned with your lady friend and the other woman. However, the three of you had to brace each other to keep from falling or swaying too much."

Bo'az sighed, "Great. Did we cause a scene or embarrass ourselves? Or worse, did we insult any of you or treat you poorly?"

The servant smiled sheepishly, "You do not have to worry, Master Bo'az. At the time of night during which you returned, even most of *us* are sleeping. My shift had just begun and I happened to be in one of the rooms near the corridor. There were barely any people around for there to be an audience." He looked over at the other two again. "And if I may, we do not engage in any gossip with the other guests or senators. We do talk amongst ourselves about certain *notable* things that occur, but we have a code amongst ourselves that we do not share any of that information with others. That being said, the identity of your extra guest last night will not be revealed to anyone."

Bo'az laughed louder than he expected to. "Thank you. What is your name?"

"I am called Andujar." The short, greying man looked at him curiously.

"Andujar, will you be here for a shift tomorrow morning?"

He shook his head in affirmation, "I am here every morning."

"Good. I will leave a generous amount of coin inside the wardrobe over there before leaving tomorrow. You can keep it all to yourself, share some with these two gentlemen, or share it with anyone you wish. But I am grateful for your honesty and hospitality."

"Thank you, Master Bo'az. That is very considerate and generous of you." Andujar seemed to realize in the moment that he had a towel draped over his shoulder. He set it down on the bed next to Bo'az and then turned to the other two servants and beckoned for them to exit. "Thank you again. Enjoy your day."

Bo'az smiled and nodded and put up his palm as they exited. He eyed the steaming bath and disrobed before easing himself in. The water was always a little too hot at first touch and then became comfortable after a moment. He closed his eyes and lowered his head until it was completely submerged. *I like this place. I like it better than Castiel, and definitely better than Haedon. I wonder if Aurkene and I could return here once all of our business is done. I wonder if we'd be allowed back.* He brought his head back up. *Between the hashah and the Banqeta, and obviously Suriiya, I don't think I would ever get tired of being here. I guess if and when Suriiya's husband were to find out, it might be a different story, but still.* The ground beneath him shook, or at least he thought it was the ground. It continued for a few moments and some things around the room shook as well. The bath water sloshed around a bit. "What the hell was that?" He grasped the sides of the tub.

The rumbling and shaking stopped and Bo'az looked around the room to see if anything had broken or fallen. He heard voices from outside the room as well as from outside the guest house. People were shouting all around. *Light of Orijin, couldn't even enjoy a bath. Gotta see what's going on.* He pulled himself up and hopped out of the tub. He dried off and dressed in a matter of minutes, then flung the door open and hurried down the hall toward Aurkene's room. Other guests and servants were rushing through the corridor as well.

She opened her door just before Bo'az reached it and noticed him coming toward her. "What *was* that? Sagari is a good distance from here, but we've never felt anything like that!" She grabbed his hand and they headed outside with everyone else. Once they were out of the guest house, Bo'az saw that people all around were standing around and looking toward the sky. To the northeast, dark clouds loomed. "Those are strange looking clouds," Aurkene commented.

Bo'az noted that the "clouds" stemmed from a pillar that was the same dark grey. *Oh no.* "Aurkene, those aren't clouds. It's the volcanoes. That's why the ground was shaking. They're probably going to erupt soon. We should go to the Senate and see what the plan is.

Come on!" Bo'az moved quickly toward the Great Hall while keeping Aurkene's hand in his. He hoped that at least some senators would be in the Great Hall to provide some answers about what to do.

As they neared the large, round building, the crowd grew denser as more and more people either stared at the sky or yelled in panic. Bo'az noticed some senators squeezing through to get inside and decided to follow suit. He was about twenty feet away when the ground shook again and the world itself sounded as if it was thundering. Most of the people around them were either losing their balance or dropping down to shield themselves. Bo'az stumbled but held tight to Aurkene and pushed through into the Great Hall.

Inside, several people stood around talking urgently. Most were senators that Bo'az had recognized, with several unfamiliar faces. He eyed Suriiya and Sagrajas talking to Alamar, the eldest senator, and a handful of other people by one of the walls. *This room looks much different when it's not set up for a feast.* He turned away from the group and looked at Aurkene. "Suriiya and her husband are right there. Will this get uncomfortable?"

She cocked her head a bit and shrugged, "Only if you make it so. I talked to them for quite some time last night. Sagrajas departed before she did, so he wouldn't have known that she left with us unless someone specifically told him. Can you handle this? If you think you'll mess it up, then you should go talk to other people."

"No. I've got it. I can be normal. I'm pretty sure I can, anyway." He started walking toward them, thinking of how to open a conversation. *You're an idiot, you know that? Just ask about the cloud and if it's the volcanoes.* He nodded in response to his own thought and proceeded. "Pardon us, but Senator Sagrajas, it is nice to see you again. Is it safe to assume that all of this is from the volcanoes?" He did his best to not even glance at Suriiya.

The senator turned to him and smiled. "Good day, Bo'az. Good day, Aurkene. It is nice to see both of you again. Your assumption is correct. We are nearly positive that one, if not both, of the volcanoes is acting up and that an eruption is coming, though we cannot be sure when. Our scouts reported several wagons racing here from the northeast, most likely from cities closer to the volcanoes. We are waiting for some to reach the gates so that the Senate can meet with them. Unfortunately, once they arrive here, we will have to ask everyone who is not a senator to leave."

Bo'az glanced at Aurkene and then at Suriiya. "Is that necessary?"

Suriiya spoke up before anyone else could, and looked back and forth between Sagrajas and Alamar, "Surely an exception can be made for these special guests of ours. This could largely affect their ability to travel, as well as their departure from here tomorrow."

Sagrajas looked at Alamar, as if asking permission. She nodded, "This is not something that needs to be kept secret from them. I have no objection to having them sit in on this discussion. They have posed no threat or given us any reason not to trust them."

"Thank you," Bo'az smiled at her. The ground rumbled once more, this time more strongly than before. Bo'az dropped to his knees and braced himself with a hand on the ground while Aurkene fell into the wall. Suriiya stumbled into Aurkene while several others wobbled around or fell. More shouts came from outside and Sagrajas raced to find out the reason. Bo'az followed him, curious about what could have changed from earlier. He reached the doorway and saw streaks of red and orange mixed in with the white, grey, and black plumes. "Light of Orijin, if it looks that big from here, then it must be *massive*."

Sagrajas stood next to him and agreed, "Yes. Even if this is only Infernua, it could wipe out at least four cities. That volcano is vast and who knows how far it might shoot out that fire. Look, here come senators and knights escorting a group that I would imagine are people fleeing the cities near Infernua." They let the group pass them and then Sagrajas closed the doors to the Great Hall. Bo'az studied their fearful and weary faces, then followed Sagrajas back to where Alamar and the others were regrouping. "Alamar, they are here. Riban and Gharza just escorted them in with a few knights."

Alamar nodded and walked over to the travelers and spoke to them for several minutes. Bo'az checked on Aurkene to make sure that she wasn't hurt, and then they both watched Alamar intensely. The whole room seemed to slowly quiet down as more and more people realized that the travelers were present and speaking to Alamar. As everything completely quieted, Alamar walked to the center of the room and the few knights hurried out of the room to go back outside. "Everyone, please stop your conversations and listen. I have some important information and instructions for you all! Please sit on the floor for now so that you can all hear me." She waited a moment for everyone to get situated. Bo'az sat and leaned back against the wall, next to Aurkene. Suriiya sat next to her, with Sagrajas on her other side.

Poor man has no idea.

Alamar continued. "It is as we feared. Infernua has become unstable, and it seems that Murelaga has also activated again. As we can see from here, the smoke coming from them is an enormous amount, and it could make it difficult, or even impossible for the northeastern cities to breathe. I have already instructed our knights to send riders out to Sagres, Garsiyya, Ihtizaz, and Suna to evacuate everyone from their cities. I have instructed other riders to head to Darras, Muzna, Ja'whara, Aban, Hamdin, Fatyan, and Hamazigh. Those cities shall be instructed to let in the refugees from the cities affected. If other cities are needed to provide shelter and accommodations for the displaced, then we shall send more riders out. The guests that we just welcomed in have reported that the tremors are far worse in Ihtizaz. These will be difficult times, and we must work together to make things as easy as possible for our citizens. Once this meeting has ended, senators, I shall leave it up to you to decide if you would like to return to your families for a week. If so, you would depart tomorrow, after we have settled any final business regarding emergency plans."

Wait. Perhaps there's a chance for them to reconsider their vote on Jahmash's request. Bo'az stood and walked closer to Alamar. "Senator Alamar, I have a request, if you would be so kind to let me ask?"

She flinched at seeing him but composed herself. "Very well, Bo'az Kontez. What do you need?"

He took a deep breath, then raised his voice for the room to hear. "I would like for the Senate to reconsider the offer that we originally put forth yesterday and revote on whether to send a portion of the army." As he suspected, murmurs littered the room.

"I am sorry Bo'az, but we gave you your answer to that. Please, we have more pressing matters to address."

"Hold on! Do you not see how this could stand to benefit you?" He started to move around the room so that he could connect with more people. "Your volcanoes have the power to wipe out at least five of your cities in a short amount of time. And while I'm sure other cities will be willing to help, they certainly cannot have been built to accommodate so many more people for the long term. By helping our cause, you may be able to directly help your citizens as well. Along with soldiers, you could send willing and able citizens to fight for

Jahmash. Think about it! They would depart here and then be able to directly stake claim to Ashurian lands once Jahmash's conquest is over! You would not have to send anyone out right away. It would be expected that your army would depart in six months, which would be plenty of time for people to decide for themselves, as well as build enough ships to sail out."

As he walked around and stated his case, he noticed many senators pondering his words. He saw Aurkene out of the corner of his eye and noticed that she bore a grin. "I simply ask that you consider my words and also take into account what is happening in the northeast. This arrangement could benefit you immensely. If you would be willing to revote." He stopped walking around again once he was in front of Alamar. "Please?"

She looked him in the eyes, "As I said, we shall think on it."

To his surprise, Aurkene walked over to his side. She spoke loud enough for the room to hear. "Senators, as someone who is more familiar with the way Yahaira works, please consider what I am about to say. As a Casteyan who has been in charge of catering to guests and visitors for years now, I understand of how societies tend to work, as well as the finances. You are about to evacuate four of your cities and will displace those citizens into seven other cities. While that might seem manageable, imagine how much more food each of those cities will need, as well as clothing and shelter.

"Those four cities are not just being evacuated; there is a strong possibility that they will be destroyed. And if that happens, all of the land that exists between the volcanoes and them will also be destroyed. That means a loss of crops, mines, wood, and meat. Your people will be rushing to leave—there will be no time to pack enough resources to help remedy that. Your northeast is about to face a great deal of hardship, and I understand that these are times when people will step up to help. *However*, these are also times when people become desperate. Parents will take risks to steal for their children. Good people will bend laws to care for their sick and elderly. Selfish men and women will challenge rules and regulations that you set in place. All of this will happen within the next two months or so, and then you will be dealing with an incredible increase in crime. What will you do with all of these criminals? Hire them to make their own boats? Consider Bo'az's offer. This is the perfect time to offset those difficulties by allowing people to leave. The prospect of more land, especially to those forced to leave their homes, will be quite an attractive one. If not, you risk having them turn on you and blaming you for not doing more."

To Bo'az's surprise, Durr'an stood from a few feet away and spoke up. "Senator Alamar, Bo'az and Aurkene may have a point. Our circumstances have changed. I originally voted against his request, but I think several of us may have had a change of heart in light of this new development. Let us vote again on this offer." As Alamar considered Durr'an's words, several other senators offered support for Durr'an's suggestion. Bo'az sat down and signaled for Aurkene to do the same.

"Very well. Senators! We shall vote again. If you are in favor of fulfilling this request, please stand now!" Alamar sat down, which surprised Bo'az. In the next moment, several senators stood up. Bo'az tried to count but couldn't see if some people were standing behind others.

After another moment, Durr'an looked around and then looked down at Alamar, "Twenty-six! There are twenty-six of us in favor of sending soldiers and willing civilians to Ashur!"

Alamar stood to address the room once again. She looked down at the ground and waited a moment before speaking. "You all have your answer now." She looked over at Bo'az and Aurkene, "I hope that this decision is satisfactory. We shall do as you asked. Half our army and as many civilians as are willing to go. You two have the luxury of leaving here tomorrow morning and moving on to the next place. If Yahaira disagrees with our decision, we senators have to sit here and deal with it. That being said, I will make sure that every ship we send out has an image of you with it, Bo'az, so that if Yahairans are cheated out of the tiniest little thing, they will know who to find."

Bo'az stood, "On behalf of Jahmash, Harbinger of the Orijin, I thank you, senators of Yahaira. I promise you we did not come here to lie to you or cheat you."

"We shall see. The Senate has more to discuss with these travelers from Ihtizaz. I ask that anyone aside from them who is not a senator to please exit the room. That includes family members of senators."

Aurkene arose with him and whispered as they departed, "It looks like we ruined their party. But we still got what we wanted." He grasped her hand and smiled, and they walked out of the building. Scores of people stood outside, in awe of the distant sky.

"I don't know how we managed that, honestly. That was amazing! We have to go straight to the guest houses. Aric and Hansi won't believe it."

"Do you mind if I join you?" The voice came from right behind them. Bo'az turned his neck slightly to see Suriiya with an arm around Aurkene's shoulder. "Now that my husband is indisposed for some time, I thought that we could start our fun a bit earlier. Unless you have business that you must attend to?"

Bo'az blushed at the thought of what they would be doing soon. "We do have to briefly speak to our other companions, but it will not take very long. Suriiya, I am curious, though. First, are you not concerned about being so visible with us? Surely more than one person out here knows you and will take note of how... affectionate you are with Aurkene?"

She smiled, "It is of no concern to me. I have certain plans in mind that shall make all of that irrelevant. That is my problem, not yours. Do not worry, Bo'az, nothing will happen to you because of my actions. Now what was your other question?"

"Very well. Please don't get the wrong idea in my asking, as I am not saying that I have an issue with our arrangement. However, do you not feel bad that hundreds of your countrymen are in the process of losing their homes and so much more?"

"Of course I sympathize with them. My city, Aban, is one of the cities that will be taking them in. I have dozens of family members there who will be asked to take in these refugees. However, one thing has nothing to do with the other. I am allowed to feel sorrow for them while also engaging in pleasure, but they are independent of each other. It will not change anything for them whether I lay with you and Aurkene or go to my quarters and cry. So why not do what makes me feel better?

"Bo'az, life is sickness. Pain. Suffering. It is difficult and frustrating. Yes, it can be amazing as well, but have you ever noticed how quickly the greatest amount of joy is overshadowed by the tiniest hint of something negative? Sex is the antidote, Bo'az. Sex is the remedy, and it cures everything."

He could have sworn that his face had gone from pale to blushing in a matter of moments. "Wow."

"Have I offended you?"

"No, not at all. Just surprised me. But I *am* looking forward to the 'antidote' very shortly.

Good. Enjoy yourself, Bo'az. I am beyond proud of your efforts here. I would have been upset about leaving her with nothing,

but I would have understood. For you to stand up and convince them so quickly, I am impressed. Your loyalty is no longer in question.

Bo'az stopped walking for a moment. Despite Jahmash's positivity and encouragement, hearing his voice still made him uneasy, as if punishment could come at any moment. For as many times as it had happened already, Bo'az would never get used to the intense crippling pain that caused him to bleed from his nose, mouth, and ears. He was thankful to now have Jahmash's trust, especially if it allowed him the comfort of having his mind to himself more often.

"Are you alright, dear?" Aurkene put her hand on his upper arm.

He shook his head to get rid of any remnants of Jahmash's voice. "Yes, sorry. It was *him*. Jahmash. He told me he was proud of how things unfolded so it wasn't bad or painful. I'm fine, we can go."

"Are you sure?"

He raised his eyebrows at her, "Aurkene, considering what we are about to go do, I am *quite* sure."

She giggled, "Do you mean sharing the news with Aric and Hansi?"

"Of course that's what I mean. I am thrilled to go tell them!"

"Good, we should hurry then. It *will* be exciting to tell them, but it will be even more exciting to get it over with."

Suriiya leaned forward to look at Bo'az, "We should definitely get that part over with."

The ground rumbled once more and all three dropped to a knee. Once it stopped, they continued walking. A thought formed in his head, that he knew he might regret asking if Suriiya took it the wrong way, but he needed to know. "Suriiya, I don't want to ruin this, but I need to know," he quieted his voice, "what would happen if your husband found out?"

She answered without any change in her expression or tone, "Well, let's put it this way. My husband is a good man, and honestly a good senator as well. However, for some reason he is too timid to stand up to me. He would likely ask what he did wrong and what he could change or do better. Perhaps ask me if I still love him."

"Do you?"

"Of course I do. Sex and love are also separate things. I would do anything for my husband, and I honestly do treat him very well. We get along swimmingly, *however*, he is a giant bore. I don't mean in the sense that he is not entertaining or funny. I mean that he wants for nothing. Before being chosen for the Senate, he was a fisherman. But that is all there is to him. He doesn't talk of goals or hopes or dreams. He is content to just fish all day every day. Every now and then, he will come home and bathe and lie with me, but even on those *exciting* days, there is barely any passion in him. I even suggested finding another woman for us to share, and he was not interested."

Aurkene seemed to grow curious as well. "Would you ever leave him?"

Suriiya laughed at the question, "Leave him? What would I do? I love him too much to want him to be alone. He has only seen twenty-five years, but he wouldn't have the courage to find someone new after me. He is too timid and it would break him if I left him. I could not do that to him. Besides, I am also a fisher, and my boat docks at the same place as his. I was trying to convince him to sail away together and live on the seas for a while. We are both excellent at catching fish that we could live on a boat for months, if not years, with no trouble. But he does not want to leave."

Bo'az could understand the reluctance, "It is a big change to leave everything you know. Especially your family."

Suriiya shook her head, "The only family he has are a couple of cousins and their parents, who all live in the next city, Darras. Darras is where the soldiers dock to return to the mainland. There is a small island off the north shore where the army trains. Both of his cousins are in the army. So he doesn't even see them much. There is nothing holding him back."

They were a few steps away from Aric's and Hansi's doors. "I'm sorry to hear that. You live with a great deal of passion. Hopefully you can find other options to keep you happy after we leave."

She smiled at him and winked, "I will be fine, don't worry."

They knocked on both doors at the same time, and Aric opened his just after Hansi. Both seemed to have difficulty talking. Bo'az peeked in and thought he saw a woman inside. He also caught someone peeking out from inside of Hansi's doorway. "Sorry. I didn't mean to interrupt the two of you. Clearly you are both busy. First, we wanted to make sure you were alright, with all of the tremors going on."

Hansi nodded, "Yeah, we're fine. Things are shaking, but anything that could have fallen, we just put on the ground, so now it's just waiting for the tremors to end."

"Good. The main reason we came is to tell you that Aurkene

and I convinced the Senate to vote again on our request. The tremors and volcanoes have changed their minds, and Jahmash is happy." He paused for a moment and realized that things were awkward now that he'd finished speaking.

"Really? That's amazing!" Aric finally spoke up.

"It is, and the longer we stand out here, the more I realize how strange this is, so I will leave you both to get back to your…business."

Hansi nodded quickly, "Great idea. Thank you." He turned and walked back into his room, and Aric followed suit.

The three of them walked over to Bo'az's door. "That probably explains why we didn't see them when we were all fleeing the guest house." They walked into his room and Suriiya immediately sat on the spacious bed.

"You know, it would be fun and a little exciting for the three of us to be a huge tangle of arms and legs in this bed while a tremor is happening. Imagine the three of us clinging to each other as the world beneath us shakes and convulses." Bo'az didn't say a word, but he looked at Aurkene and in a matter of moments, both of them had disrobed and were in the bed with Suriiya.

A couple of hours later, the three of them lay in the bed, disheveled and out of breath, but all smiles and giggles. They all agreed to get up and separate in order to bathe and change, then meet back here to eat. One or two more tremors shook the room while they had their romp, but they seemed to be less intense. However, Suriiya informed them that there would be less people out and about, and she doubted there would be many people in the Great Hall for dinner, or at the Banqeta in the evening. They agreed to stay in the room after dinner and celebrate their last night together.

Bo'az wasn't sure how he felt about leaving Suriiya behind. The three of them got along well, and not just physically. She was passionate and full of energy, and quick-witted as well. More than anything, he liked the way she looked at Aurkene, as it was the way he felt about Aurkene as well. It filled him with joy to know that Aurkene could be spoiled and celebrated by two people. It didn't hurt that Suriiya was amazing at pleasuring both of them. He wondered if he'd be able to experience this type of situation anywhere else or ever again. Bo'az rose from the bed after both women left and sought out a servant to request hot bath water. He also asked the servants to change his sheets once he was in the bath. Andujar happily obliged, likely at the prospect of the generous coin that Bo'az had promised.

By the time he was done bathing, the servants were long gone. He dried himself off and lay in the clean bed. He knew the other two would be much longer in bathing and prepping, so he dared to indulge his heavy eyelids and fell asleep almost immediately.

He woke to the sound of quiet voices on the other side of the room. "How did you two get in here? Have you been here long?"

Aurkene walked over to the bed and sat down, "You slept past sunset, my dear. We must have worn you out. I'm glad you rested though; you'll have more energy for tonight." She smiled at him and then at Suriiya as well. "And you didn't lock your door, so we walked right in. We honestly didn't know you were sleeping, so we were talking loudly when we arrived. But you slept through it, and through the tremor that we had not too long ago." He sat up and realized that he'd never even put any smallclothes on. He stood to get dressed. It amused him that only a day before he was blushing every other moment around Suriiya and now he was completely comfortable getting dressed in front of her.

She didn't flinch at it either. "Bo'az, where you are from in Ashur, does everyone share your skin tone?"

Bo'az inspected his brown flesh, "Well, actually no. I came from a town hidden in the forest and on a mountain. So I cannot speak to a whole nation such as Yahaira. However, in Haedon, there are actually many different skin tones and features. Many actually resemble the people of Yahaira. There was a girl I fancied back home who could honestly pass for Yahairan. Perhaps her parents or grandparents were criminals and managed to sail all the way there. Why do you ask?" He was briefly reminded of Yasaman and her father, Ihsan. He pushed the memory down so it wouldn't ruin the moment.

"I was simply curious whether all of Ashur bears similar features. I have seen visitors from Semaajj who look similar; however, they were usually a shade darker."

Aurkene chimed in, "Tell me more about this girl you fancied who resembled a Yahairan."

Suriiya sat next to her, "Oh yes, what was her name?"

He rolled his eyes, "Why do you want to know?" They continued to stare at him with expectant smiles. "Fine. But you should know that she was with us at the start of the journey to Jahmash. She died along the way."

"Oh my, I'm so sorry Bo." Aurkene looked at him with regret,

"You don't have to continue. I'm sorry, I didn't realize."

"Of course you didn't, I'm not mad at you. It can still be difficult to think about from time to time, but it was about two years ago. I have come to terms with it. Anyway, her name was Yasaman Adin. Her parents were rather controlling. I remember her father well; he also died shortly before we left. Ihsan. I hated him. But Yasaman, she was beautiful, in a different way than you, Aurkene. Her hair wasn't so full and her body was not…voluptuous like yours. She had tan, almost light brown skin like you, Suriiya, but her hair was black and sometimes straight, sometimes wavy." Both women smiled at him. He was surprised that they let him continue to speak without getting jealous. He supposed they might have felt a little guilty and realized that it was difficult to be jealous of a dead person. "You don't have to feel pity for me. She turned out to be manipulative and selfish. It's sad that she died, but it doesn't change the type of person that she was."

"There was a senator a generation or two ago whose name was Ihsan," Suriiya explained. "It was before my time, maybe twenty-five years ago. But they tell the story from time to time because he was the only Yahairan senator to be banished."

"All this is starting to change the mood. Should we eat, and then engage in some festivities between the three of us?" Aurkene grasped Suriiya's hand.

Bo'az nodded, "Yeah, let's do that. We should see if Aric and Hansi are free to join us for dinner. We should talk about what we'll do tomorrow." Suriiya and Aurkene agreed. "How about you two ask the servants about meals, and I'll go get Hansi and Aric."

The five of them met back in Bo'az's room a short while later, and their food arrived just after. They sat in various spots around the room. Bo'az had been surprised that the girls that Hansi and Aric had met were no longer around. But Hansi explained that all of them agreed that it was all just temporary fun they were having and not meant to develop into anything. The two girls had departed in the morning without any complicated goodbyes, or so Hansi said. Bo'az wondered if it would work out as easily with Suriiya. He realized that regardless of her desires, he didn't really want to part from her, and he didn't want Aurkene to have to part with her. *Should be an interesting goodbye. Speaking of which, I guess we should figure that all out.* He finished chewing a cube of grilled lamb, "We should decide the arrangements for tomorrow. These people have a lot going on and I honestly don't want to be in their way any longer than necessary."

Aric agreed, "Yes, that makes sense. I say we eat something early and then depart. Do we know how far our next destination is? Or how long it will take to get there?"

Suriiya responded, "Brogan itself is less than a day's ride away. However, the capital city, Yago, will take a few days to get to. Unfortunately, there is not an easy or direct way to get there. The fastest would be for you to head west to Razana, which is right at the border. Once you cross into Brogan, you will immediately face mountains. From what I have heard, they are not treacherous, but they are still mountains, and you will need to be cautious. That will slow your pace a little. Once you get past those southern mountains, you will have an easy path along Brogan's southern coast. If I remember correctly, there are at least two cities along the coast on the way to Yago. So at least you will be able to stop and rest more than once."

"I have a crazy idea, "Aurkene looked up from her plate sheepishly. "Suriiya, what if you escorted us, at least to Razana? It would be nice to have a guide, especially someone we trust." She looked around the room to gauge what the others thought.

Bo'az stayed quiet, as did Hansi and Aric. They all looked at Suriiya, who paused a moment before responding. "I think I can do even better. What if I just escort you all the way there?"

That's what you wanted, isn't it? More time with her? "Your husband wouldn't mind?"

She shrugged, "How could he, or the Senate, turn down a request to be a proper ambassador to distinguished guests? Besides, they wouldn't want to anger the emissaries of Jahmash, would they?"

"Good point." *We may have to make this journey last a bit longer than necessary, just to get the most out of it.* "I suppose that settles it then, right? Tonight we'll gather our things and leave just after breakfast." They continued to eat and bantered throughout the meal. The women asked Aric and Hansi about the girls they'd met and teased them as well. Once everyone finished and the servants cleared away the food, Aric and Hansi returned to their quarters. They seemed to not want to impose by staying longer than necessary, and Bo'az suspected they might be seeing the girls they'd met one last time.

Suriiya stood up and casually paced about the room. "Bo'az, Aurkene and I have a proposition that we have been discussing on our own."

He raised his eyebrows and looked at her with anticipation.

"Well, go ahead," he smiled.

"It's a lofty suggestion, which is why I am hesitant. And I don't want to make things strange between us if your answer is no. So please understand that however you respond, there will be no ill will or hard feelings." He nodded and she continued, "I don't want this… thing that we have to end in Brogan. I don't know how you feel about the three of us, but Aurkene and I were discussing the idea of perhaps me traveling with you to Brogan and then afterwards as well?"

"Ah, so that's why Aurkene suggested that you escort us out of the city. Well played, I must say. I guess the simple answer is, of course I want you to come with us. I enjoy your company, and I think the three of us have something special. You make both of us quite happy. My concern is that you will be abandoning your husband, without telling him the truth, I assume. I hope I'm not coming off the wrong way. The decision is completely up to you and what you think is best regarding the people you leave behind. I imagine that by the time Sagrajas or anyone else realizes that you aren't returning, we will be long gone. I just hope that they don't come after us as a result."

"Your concerns are warranted, but there are ways to ensure that he doesn't come looking for me."

"What do you mean?"

"When we arrive in Razana, I could easily pay a messenger to come here and report my untimely death. Perhaps we will decide to swim in the sea and I drown trying to save someone else. He knows I am too strong a swimmer to drown on my own, but if it happens trying to save someone who is panicking and it prevents me from returning to shore, then that is quite believable."

Bo'az smiled, "Wow, that is incredibly crafty of you. It's almost as if you had this plan in mind already. Very well, though. But I must warn you, if you put any of the four of us in any danger along the way, then we will have to leave you behind. I'm not saying that to threaten you, but Aric, Hansi, and I answer to someone else and at the heart of it, we still have a mission. That is the most important thing, otherwise none of us would live long enough to enjoy any of this."

"I understand."

"Good. Honestly, I think Jahmash would like you."

CHAPTER 7
PROXIMITY

From *The Book of Orijin*, Verse Four Hundred Ninety-Nine
There will be no peace until each of you is at peace with yourself.
Master your emotions and still the torment within. Only then can you
guide Mankind.

Baltaszar rode alongside Desmond toward the outskirts of the City of the Fallen. He could see a mass of cloaked figures ahead, though they all stood in place with their heads facing the same direction, as if watching the same thing. As they drew closer, Baltaszar got a better look at the cloaks the figures were wearing and, for some reason, he found them so unsettling that they made his insides turn a bit. He looked at Desmond, "Uhck, you see those cloaks? I can't look at them. I don't know why but I almost want to retch."

They had stopped not too long ago to eat before reaching the city. Khiry had proven to have few soldiers remaining, and somehow all of them wanted to fight Baltaszar and Desmond. It still made no sense as to why the Vermillion soldiers wouldn't want their help against the Vithelegion, but Baltaszar didn't bother asking questions while setting them all on fire. He didn't know whether he'd always been able to shoot fire out of eyes and just didn't know how, or if the Jinn actually had the power to do that for him. Either way, it had proven to be a fun way to use his manifestation. It also allowed him to get caught up with something and not dwell on Anahi's death the whole time. *Khurt Everitas. I will find him.*

Desmond swallowed hard, "Yep." He paused for a moment. "Anonymi. Munn used ta tell us stories o' them. Cloaks are meant ta throw off their enemies. An' I guess anyone who's not used ta them."

"Wait. Munn told you about them? Munn Keeramm, who couldn't see?"

Desmond rolled his eyes, "Ya know he spent time at the Tower o' the Blind, right? An' who trains the servants there? The Anonymi."

"Whatever. Why do you think they're here? Did they finally leave their fortress to fight the Vithelegion?"

"Yeah, it's got ta be somethin' like that, right? Dare we ride closer an' find out?"

"We definitely should. I've never talked to or even met one

before. Then again, I guess if you count Savaiyon, I have. But that's different. I don't count him as one of them during the time he was with us."

Desmond laughed, "I completely agree. It doesn't count if he wasn't actin' like one. I honestly couldn't believe it when he told us, though. Crazy that one o' us could be an Anonymi."

Baltaszar urged his horse forward, "Also rather helpful, though, to have an ally in their ranks has to be of some kind of benefit to us, right?"

"Let's hope so," Desmond shrugged as he kept pace.

As they reached within a few paces of the Anonymi, one of them turned to face Baltaszar and Desmond and put a hand up to halt them. To Baltaszar's surprise, they wore a gold mask that bore the slits for eyes and an opening for their mouth. Regardless, the Anonymi didn't actually say anything to him, but kept their hand up. Baltaszar assumed it was a man but couldn't be sure.

"The acolytes only speak when necessary outside of the fortress. His hand is doing the speaking." Baltaszar turned to look behind him, where the voice came from. The statuesque figure in the red mask startled him. "Greetings, Baltaszar and Desmond. Before you get ahead of yourselves, I have no identity when wearing this mask. Which means you do not know who I am. If you need to address me, you will call me *acolyte*."

Savaiyon? When did he show up behind us? We were just right there. "How? When? Your voice sounds different with that thing on."

"I was just in Alvadon to attend the funeral. Garrison plans to take the throne and has appointed the Ghosts of Ashur as his Royal Guard. However, there are many in Alvadon who dispute his claim to the throne, so it is quite a tense atmosphere. One of his father's former counselors shot an arrow at him. Luckily, Sindha stopped it. You two should return there. Your help will be needed."

"We needed ta go ta Vandenar first. See ta some things."

"I understand that. But you are a long way from Vandenar."

Baltaszar scowled, "We're trying to track one of the Vithelegion. Did you know that some of them were still in Khiry? And what's even stranger is that there were Vermillion soldiers that cared more about killing us than killing them."

Savaiyon nodded, "Yes. Wendell and I had a Vithelegion soldier in captivity and he told us as much. A Vermillion officer made a deal with the Vithelegion and allowed them to lay waste to Mireya."

"Why didn't the Anonymi do anything about it? Why wait until they got all the way here to do something?"

"The Anonymi Komytii had the bigger picture in mind. They also didn't know about the pact. They thought that the Vermillion would stop them. Once we all realized the truth, we prepared soldiers to come here. However, we managed to force the Vithelegion to retreat and return home."

Desmond's jaw dropped, "How? Ye were able ta overpower them so easily?"

"Not quite. I am only telling you this because of our history together. It turns out that the Vithelegion soldier we captured is an outcast. He was willing to fight his former general and the terms were that if he defeated his general, then the Vithelegion would leave."

"An' it worked? That's what everyone is watchin'?"

"It worked. He cut off his general's hands. The Vithelegion are boarding their rowboats and returning to their ships." The Anonymi soldiers moved into a structured formation as Savaiyon spoke.

Baltaszar nodded to himself, "Good. If this soldier is still here, maybe he can help us. He can point out the man we're looking for. His name is Khurt Everitas."

***

Khurt Everitas ruminated over the conversation with Raffa as he watched him walk away. The man hadn't shared the same views as Khurt regarding taking prisoners instead of killing. He didn't completely trust the new First General to be true to his word. While it had been so enjoyable to watch Saol's sons disappear right in front of all of them, Khurt realized that it might have actually done more harm than good. If Saol didn't know where they were, he would not agree to return home. He hoped that there was even a small part of Raffa that might be tempted to kill Saol and take command. There would be a better chance of the Vithelegion actually returning home that way. With Saol still alive, Khurt knew there was a chance the Vithelegion would attack again.

I'll have to tell the Anonymi to be ready. Although, if there's any doubt about their retreat, then I may not be allowed to see Khenzi. To hell with them, then. Khenzi is more important. He turned and started to walk back toward the Anonymi soldiers waiting for him. Once he reached them, they got into line formations and continued to face the Vithelegion. *Clearly they aren't taking any chances.* Another faction of

Anonymi had already positioned itself on the other side of the city by the shore, to ensure the Vithelegion leave. Other soldiers flanked the Vithelegion as they walked. *I can only imagine how tempted my people are to fight the Anonymi. Most of them would lose, I think. My men might have had a better chance, with all their varied training. Who knows. It would be a good battle, likely with great losses on both sides. Not worth it for my people, though.*

He punched his palm, angry at Saol for not listening to him in the first place. If anyone else had been Commander, everything would have played out differently and Khurt likely wouldn't have been left behind. Khenzi wouldn't have been taken from him either. *Maybe I should have just killed him.* He entertained the regret for a moment, before laughing under his breath at the thought of someone having to feed Saol for the rest of his life. *Big bad Saol Suldas having someone else put the spoon in his mouth for him. Having someone else have to wipe his ass for him.* He almost laughed loudly at that thought. The Vithelegion were far enough away now that an acolyte up front gave the signal to turn around and march. *We couldn't be very close to the fortress if we had to get here through one of those... doorways. How far are we going to march?*

As the battalion exited the gates of the city, Khurt noticed two men talking to a tall, red-masked Anonymi. He was almost certain it was the same one who came to him in the dungeon, judging by his height. He wondered what they could be talking about.

***

Baltaszar noticed columns of Anonymi soldiers starting to walk past them out of the city. Savaiyon turned and walked alongside the outermost column and Baltaszar and Desmond followed him on their horses.

"I am sorry Baltaszar, that will not be possible."

"Why not? I can't live with myself knowing that that man is going to be allowed to get on a ship and go home to his own loved ones after he destroyed my happiness. Sa..." Baltaszar almost said his name and then caught himself. "Same for Desmond. He knew Anahi before I did, not to mention *all* of the people in Vandenar who perished because of these savages who showed up out of nowhere. Acolyte, I know the man's name. I could simply charge through the city and yell 'Khurt Everitas' until the right man steps forth. And then as soon as he confirms who he is, I can send fire right through his skull."

***

Khurt thought he heard his name coming from one of the two strangers. They were just about even paced at the moment, and the two men who rode alongside them wore black cloaks and bore black lines down their left eyes. *Interesting design. There were others who bore that design in one of those cities we sacked. The same one where I lost Khenzi and where Saol left me behind.* He tried to steal glances as often as he could without turning his head too much. He wasn't sure if eavesdropping was a crime, but he didn't want to draw any attention to himself. The darker skinned of the two men did most of the talking, and Khurt was almost positive that it was him who said his name. *How could he know me?*

***

Baltaszar had grown so frustrated that he opened himself to his manifestation. Savaiyon must have sensed his tone. "Because Khurt Everitas is the Vithelegion soldier that we captured. In fact, he was a general. He made an agreement with us and he has honored that agreement. I know you have vengeance in your heart right now, but there are bigger things at hand than revenge against one man. Because of him, we just managed to turn the Vithelegion around and send them on their way with the most minimal of bloodshed."

He clenched his fist, but Desmond spoke up before he could. "Wait. Yer sayin' that the man we're lookin' for is most likely marchin' among all these soldiers?"

"Precisely. And what will you do? Attack every single Anonymi soldier here just to find the one you are looking for?"

Baltaszar knew he was right; there would be no way to find Everitas now. Anonymi didn't talk, and they shed their names once joining. Everitas likely wouldn't even respond to his own name. Baltaszar's shoulders slumped. "That isn't fair, Acolyte. I came all the way here to kill him. To be so close and not be able to do it makes it so much worse."

***

What makes you think you could kill me, you little boy? How many times have you even used that sword? I wonder who I killed to make you so mad. Khurt almost wished he could break rank to fight the man, who was barely that. *The beard isn't bad, but it doesn't hide your baby face very well. You can't have seen much combat, though you talk like you've seen dozens of battles. How many men have you even killed, boy?*

***

"Believe me, Baltaszar. I understand your frustration. You were not there when the House of Darian was attacked. You had already been banished because you couldn't handle your emotions then. But the rest of us were awakened in the middle of the night to attackers that we were not prepared for. And despite all of our manifestations, we were not enough. Despite every shred of magic we were able to conjure up, we lost so many people. Anahi was special to both of you. I understand that. I knew Zin Marlowe from the time I was younger than you. I practically grew up with several of the Mavens on that island. And by the end of it all, the only thing that made sense was for me to find anyone who was still alive and get them out of there. There was no opportunity for revenge against any of them for what they'd done. Do you know how frustrating that was? Not only did I lose dozens of loved ones, but I couldn't even *avenge* them. I had to run away."

Baltaszar tried to slow his breathing a bit. He had been more worked up than he realized. He knew Savaiyon was right, but the difference was that he was so close to the man who caused all of his pain and wouldn't be able to confront him. "If any of those attackers were this close to you now, would you confront them? Would you attack them?" He wondered what Savaiyon's expression was under that red mask, in response to the question.

"I would want to confront them. *But*, if that person was a tool that could be used to help things in the bigger picture, I would swallow my anger. I am not saying it would be easy, but it would be for everyone's benefit that I would be doing so."

I wonder if he's just telling me what I want to hear, or if he really believes that. It's such an easy answer to give. "And that's what you expect me to do."

"It is."

***

Khurt marched on. *Wow. This boy really wants to kill me quite desperately. It's still so strange that he would know my name to be able to get revenge. There's no way the two men in the dungeon would have sent him, even if that red-masked man isn't the same one I originally met. They were the only ones who knew my name, but it doesn't make sense for them to set him on a path for revenge against me. I wonder if it was that boy.*

His mind brought him back to the little boy he'd killed in the first city they invaded. The boy was so innocent. So calm about it all. *He didn't know a thing about Darian or Abram or any of that shit that so many of us have been so caught up with. Ashur doesn't even worship Darian.* He thought about his conversation with Saol back in Vitheligia, before they'd even sailed for war. Khurt had had reservations about sailing all the way to Ashur just to eliminate infidels. He didn't agree with their ideologies, but it didn't make sense to sail so far to face an unfamiliar foe. *And look, after it's all said and done, they don't even worship him. I killed that little boy for no reason.* He'd thought about that boy often ever since waking up in the dungeon. The parents were lucky that they were killed as well. Khurt considered the prospect of losing Khenzi and having to deal with such a life-crushing loss. He wondered if he'd be able to move on, or if he'd take his own life from the inability to deal with the pain.

Someone from their ranks behind Khurt shouted, "Turn! Attack!"

***

Baltaszar heard the command and saw Savaiyon turn around at the same time. "Acolyte, come! Get on my horse! Let's go!" Savaiyon took his advice and mounted the horse. As soon as he put his hands on Baltaszar's shoulders, Baltaszar turned the horse and pushed it to sprint, while Desmond kept pace. He held the reins with one hand and created a fireball in his left palm. "You think the Vithelegion are stupid enough to attack while they're outnumbered?"

"Stupid? No. Confident enough? Yes. They are skilled fighters. The Anonymi will match their skill, but the advantage will come from me, you, and Desmond."

They strode past the columns of running Anonymi and back into the city. It wasn't until they'd almost reached the other side of the city that they saw the skirmish. Baltaszar slowed the horse and Savaiyon hopped off without warning. Before the tall man hit the ground, a gateway appeared where he landed and then disappeared. *That was pretty incredible.*

***

Khurt turned with his column and followed them as they ran in line. The men on horseback rode past him with the red-masked officer on the horse as well. Khurt almost thought his eyes deceived him as he noticed the bearded man's left hand on fire. *Wait. No. Could she have been telling the truth?* He remembered the maid he'd killed at the inn. He hadn't wanted to kill her or the other maids, but Saol demanded it and if he'd shown mercy, Saol likely would've had him or Khenzi killed. *She said she was betrothed to a man who could summon fire. It seemed so stupid at the time. That's why he wants to kill me. But how could he have found out my name? And how would he know I killed her?*

***

Baltaszar dismounted and drew his sword. Desmond ran past him and immediately joined the fray. Vithelegion soldiers started hurtling through the air as Desmond got closer to them. *Smart. Show them that we're not normal soldiers. Put some fear into them.* Baltaszar used his new eye trick against the first Vithelegion who ran to fight him. The man crumpled to the ground as smoke billowed from his head. *Getting a little tired. We should've eaten more. I may have to go easy on the fire.* He wondered whether they'd actually be able to scare the Vithelegion away. Just as his concerns started to get the better of him, Baltaszar noticed a mob of Vithelegion soldiers simply disappear from where they'd been standing. He realized almost immediately that Savaiyon must have created a gateway beneath them, just as he'd done for himself moments ago. *Wonder where they'll end up.* He got his answer right away as he saw a cloud of flailing figures falling from the sky in the distance. He heard their screams as they fell on another mass of Vithelegion soldiers. *So glad he's one of us.*

***

Khurt's column and all the others around him broke formation and joined the fray. He slowed his pace as he got closer to the fighting. *Shit. By the Grace of Orijin, what the hell do I do here? I can't fight my own people. Saol was different. But they will definitely attack me on sight. Honestly, it wouldn't even help if I took my mask off. They'd probably be more likely to kill me.* He allowed the other Anonymi to run past him as he looked around for a place where he could go unnoticed. *Besides losing Khenzi, this has to be by far the worst situation I've ever been in. The only good thing is that the Anonymi don't know that I'm... me. Would they know immediately if they saw me, though? I'll have to risk it.* He eyed a building on the side that hadn't been completely leveled and ran to hide behind one of the broken walls.

***

More Vithelegion ran toward them and away from the shore. Baltaszar fell back a bit and tried to create fires in front of him to slow the onset of the Vithelegion. *Would've been nice to have armor on.* He wondered where Savaiyon was, but figured the man wouldn't be close enough to help him again. He'd probably continued toward the larger faction outside the city. Baltaszar fought off a few Vithelegion soldiers with more fire and as others noticed what happened, other Vithelegion soldiers tried to avoid him. He saw a giant yellow fringe as tall as a building outside the city. *He's got to be walling them off from advancing past the coast. Why not just kill them, Savaiyon? What could there be to gain by sparing their lives?*

He created four fireballs that rotated around his body, then turned around to see how the Anonymi behind him were faring. There were significantly less Vithelegion remaining. While they were good fighters, their spirits had to have been broken by what they'd seen him, Desmond, and Savaiyon do. As he surveyed the area, he thought he noticed one of the nauseating Anonymi cloaks from behind a broken wall. *Are they hurt? Dead?* Baltaszar rushed toward the injured Anonymi, confident that the other Anonymi soldiers would eradicate the remaining Vithelegion shortly.

As he reached the wall, which was the only thing left standing of a building, he realized the injured Anonymi was still upright. He looked the gold-masked soldier up and down, trying to pinpoint the injury. *He's not even clutching anything. Tired then? No way, unless their training standards have seriously dropped, there's no way one of them would be tired already.* Baltaszar continued to stare at the Anonymi, and finally it clicked. *Not injured. A fucking coward.* "It's you, isn't it! You can't fight the Vithelegion because you *are* one! He swooped his leg behind the soldier's legs and slammed his torso backwards before the man realized what he was saying.

***

Fuck. Khurt's back smacked against the stone ground, right before the back of his head smashed against it. He tried to blink away the black fogginess several times, and realized he could barely form a thought. In the few flashes of consciousness, he felt the bearded man's knee against his chest. He couldn't tell if his brain had been damaged, but he swore the man had four fireballs hovering over Khurt. The man was shouting at him, but Khurt couldn't differentiate any of the sounds. He was mostly surprised that his mask hadn't become dislodged.

***

Baltaszar knelt on the man's chest and stopped his fireballs from rotating so that they hovered just about Khurt Everitas' head. "You stormed an inn up in Vandenar. Innocent people were hiding there. One of them was a maid who worked there. She was one of the purest people in this world and I was going to marry her one day. Her name was Anahi. My name is Baltaszar and I'm going to kill you." He ripped the mask from the man's head and stared at him and was caught off guard at the man's skin, which consisted of patches of different hues. The pattern seemed random, but Baltaszar wondered if it meant something, the way his Descendant's Mark signified his manifestation. He focused back on Khurt Everitas' eyes. "A maid. You killed harmless maids that could never have hurt anyone. You fucking coward." He wanted to summon as much fire as he possibly could to turn the man into a blackened crisp that would flake away with the wind and scatter across Ashur.

"I… I didn't…"

Baltaszar glowered at him, "You didn't what? You didn't do it? I don't believe you."

Khurt managed to lift a hand in front of him, to plead with Baltaszar. "N-no. I didn't want," his eyes refused to focus and he took a deep breath. "I did not want-t…"

"I don't fucking care about whatever you're about to say, you bloody coward. You sailed all the way here to kill our people, even the helpless ones. Even the best of us. And what? You want mercy now? You want me to take the time to listen to you?" His lip trembled and he shook his head. Baltaszar was about to push the first fireball into the man's face, when he felt himself lifted off Khurt and into the air. He was so disoriented by watching himself float and flail without any control, that he released the fireballs and they fizzled out without any harm. Once he was a few feet away from Khurt, he stopped moving around and hung in midair in one place. *Des? He's the only one who could be doing this.* "Desmond, what the hell are you doing?" He tried to look around but he was facing the ground and found it nearly impossible to crane his neck enough to see anyone.

He heard another voice from a few feet away, "Desmond, you may release him now!"

"No! Don't drop me!" In a split second, Baltaszar was released from his hold and fell. Right before he hit the ground, a yellow-fringed gateway appeared beneath him and he fell right through it. He found himself still staring at the ground, except from much higher up. He continued to fall and the ground grew closer and closer. His scream was swallowed up by the wind as he fell faster and faster. Another gateway appeared just beneath him. *No. Please.* He fell through it and, once again, he was higher in the air. The process repeated a few more times until he vomited what little food was left in his stomach.

Finally, the gateways stopped and he just continued to fall until he was several feet from the ground. Desmond must have taken hold of him again as his fall slowed. Once Baltaszar was about five feet from the ground, he heard Savaiyon's voice once more. "Hold him there." After a pause of a few moments, Savaiyon continued, "Now drop him." Before Baltaszar could process the command, he fell to the ground on his forearms and knees. The scrapes hurt, but they were better than falling from higher up.

He got to his feet and narrowed his eyes at Savaiyon and Desmond. "What the hell is wrong with you two?"

Desmond put his palms up in defense, "I was just listenin' ta the acolyte. No way I'm goin' ta disobey if he gives me an order."

All Baltaszar could do was throw his hands up and shake his head. He looked around for Khurt Everitas and saw two Anonymi in the distance walking with another one between them, his arms over their shoulders. "Why? *Acolyte.* Why?" He could feel Savaiyon's stare coming from behind the man's red mask.

"Because you are still acting on impulse. Killing him will not bring back any of your loved ones."

Baltaszar scowled. "That's it? You stopped me because you think I'm too emotional?" He spit on the ground in front of him, "You were supposed to be on *our* side. You were supposed to be helping us. Looking out for us. And this is what you do?"

The tall man took a deep breath, "No, Baltaszar. It is vastly more than that. However, you should keep something in mind. You are a warrior; but that is starkly different than being a killer. Warriors fight for honor. They fight when they must. Killers kill because they enjoy it. They do not need a reason. But before you protest, let me share something with you." Savaiyon walked closer to him and Desmond as the remaining Anonymi resumed their formations and departed the city. "I am not fully convinced that the Vithelegion will return home. Everitas dueled their Master General and cut off the man's hands rather easily. Also, I made the man's sons disappear through a gateway that led to the Never, not far from where I dropped you when you were banished from the House of Darian."

Baltaszar rolled his eyes, "Fine, but what does any of that have to do with anything."

"I firmly believe that Everitas could sway the Vithelegion into helping Ashur against Jahmash. He was once their second in command until he fell from grace with the Master General. And do you know why? It is because he wanted the Vithelegion to show mercy. To take women and children captive, rather than killing everyone."

Desmond cut in, "Then why did Farco leave a note sayin' he killed Anahi an' the others? Doesn't sound very merciful ta me."

"That is what he was trying to tell Baltaszar. He did not want to kill Anahi. He wanted mercy. It is the Master General who made the command to show no mercy and take no prisoners."

"And you believed him?" Baltaszar shook his head. "He was your prisoner. He would've told you anything to get out."

"Why lie about that? Also, he is the one who informed us that there is a traitorous faction of the Vermillion that is working with the Vithelegion. He even gave us the name of the man who made the pact with them. Look, I understand and I expect you to be skeptical of him. I am keeping my guard up as well. However, we currently have control over a man who has a claim to lead the entire Vithelegion. I do not want to throw that away, Baltaszar, so you will have to maintain your grudge, if that is what you really want to do. But remember, the Anonymi focus on what is best for *all* of Ashur. I will track the path of the Vithelegion to see where they go. If they return and try to attack, we shall be prepared."

He put his hands to his hips and looked at the ground. His mouth churned, trying to form a response. "If he gives you or anyone else any reason to doubt him, or if he turns on you, then I am the one who gets to kill him. Do you understand?"

"I can give you that much. Agreed."

Baltaszar was about to respond sarcastically, but he changed his mind. He was too tired to play games. "Thank you. So now what? Are we all honestly walking all the way back to your fortress?"

"No. Now that we are positive the Vithelegion are leaving, I will send them through a gateway first."

"Them?"

"Yes. Them. I am going to bring the two of you up to the rest of your group. King Garrison could use your help.

He and Desmond responded simultaneously, "*King* Garrison?"

"Indeed. See, you have both missed quite a bit. I was just there for the funeral processions. But there is much to plan. Your presence will be useful. And it will be good for you to be around people with whom you can let your guard down. Let them lift your spirits. They all need it as well."

He nodded. He knew the man was right. Killing Everitas would have brought satisfaction but would have been fleeting. It would have done nothing to heal him. But being back with his friends would do just that. "Thank you." He was sure that Savaiyon was smiling and relishing hearing that.

CHAPTER 8
DISPLACED

*From **The Book of Orijin,** Verse Four Hundred Eighty*
*We have created Mankind to be a social creature. Depend on one
another, love one another, create with one another. Remembering this
will ensure the peace and survival of your race.*

Garrison dismounted his horse, tied it to one of the stone
soldiers, and walked straight to Gideon. It had been so long since he'd
been to the Stones of Gideon, and being in the presence of the dead
Harbinger always put him at ease. He knelt before the stone figure,
closed his eyes, and took a deep breath. *Orijin, please bless his soul
and allow him peace in Omneitria. Please protect us and guide us so
that we may defeat our enemies.* He stood up and looked around at
everyone who'd followed him here. He was somewhat surprised that
Asarei had joined the pilgrimage from his island, and even more so that
the heavily tattooed man had attended the funeral, as well as his address
to the Alvadonian citizens. *I'll need everyone I can get to help us with
what comes next.*

He stood up and turned to face the rest of them, who seemed to
be patiently waiting for him to finish. "My apologies. This place,
despite its violent history, has always been a place of solace and
contemplation for me. My brother and I used to come here all the time
to get away from things. I like to talk to Gideon every time I come here
and say a prayer for him as well." He eyed a yellow-fringed gateway
forming in the distance. "Oh. Looks like we have more company." The
gateway reached its full size and Desmond, Baltaszar, and a tall, red-
masked Anonymi walked through.

Wendell, who stood next to him, uttered to him, "That's
Savaiyon. He must have come straight from the fortress or something."

Sure enough, the man removed his mask to reveal Savaiyon's
brown ovular face. He acknowledged the group with a nod. "I hope we
have not missed anything important. We have just come from the City
of the Fallen. We managed to turn the Vithelegion back and send them
to their ships. I will continue to monitor them to ensure they don't
decide to turn around. I wanted to drop off Baltaszar and Desmond, as
we ended up crossing paths down there and they helped us with
overpowering the Vithelegion."

Garrison eyed the two to gauge their emotions, but their faces bore barely any expression. *That can't be good. If their experience in Vandenar had been good, there's no way they would have traveled south to the City of the Fallen.*

Savaiyon continued, "I know you all have many things to plan and I did not want them, or myself, to miss such an occasion."

Garrison walked over to Desmond and Baltaszar immediately and hugged each of them. "I'm sorry. If you made it all the way down there, then I already know what the outcome was. I'm sorry for the losses of all your loved ones." He paused as he noticed Baltaszar's eyes. "Your eyes, Tasz. It's like they're on fire. What happened?"

Baltaszar nodded, "Thanks. Yeah, I figured out how to use fire through my eyes now. More importantly, we're sorry about your brother and mother, Garrison." Garrison was glad that Baltaszar was as astute as he was. He appreciated his friend not mentioning his father.

"Sorry fer yer losses, Garrison."

Adria walked up to Desmond and Baltaszar and gave each of them a long, tight embrace. She looked twice at Baltaszar's eyes as well. Garrison heard her apologize to both of them; he knew she must have felt guilty, given all the arguing that had happened on the island before the siege. Once the others realized why Adria had gone over to them, the rest of the group did the same. Included with all of the hugs and condolences were even more tears. Garrison himself felt tears forming at the corners of his eyes and let them run their course.

It took several moments for everyone to compose themselves, but there was no judgment about the show of emotions. They all knew that it was needed and would only strengthen their bond.

"What of the cities of Mireya?" Adria looked toward Savaiyon.

He blinked slowly. "Gone. We tried to evacuate anyone we could from the City of the Fallen, but all that is left of Mireya is whoever Maqdhuum managed to get out on his own. Otherwise, Mireya was laid to waste." A silence overtook the group for several more moments.

"Look," Garrison took a deep breath and made sure his voice wouldn't crack. "One of the reasons we are out here is to start the process of defending the honor of the people we lost. Tasz, Des, Savaiyon, you missed some important happenings after the funeral procession. You should know that I have reclaimed my throne, much to the chagrin of some of my father's counsel. Also, the Ghosts will assume the role of my Royal Guard, with Adria as its leader. But I suppose the biggest thing of all is that we are planning to move the throne to Markos."

Desmond squinted at him, "Markos? Fer what?"

Garrison turned to all of them. "There is a traitor in the Vermillion Army. Savaiyon and I had a Vithelegion soldier captive in the dungeons of Alvadon. It turns out that one of the Vermillion Generals, Easton Grey, formed a pact with the Vithelegion. They allowed the intruders to destroy every city in Mireya, and told them that they could settle there. We know we cannot trust the Vermillion any longer. And it's only a matter of time before one of the high families of Alvadon challenges me for the throne. I wouldn't be surprised if they tried to kill me sooner rather than later. So, to be cautious, we are going to move the throne to Markos, specifically Constaniza. Lao, and his sister, Kiryako informed us that their parents' estate is large enough to hold us for the time being. We will go there with Wendell's portion of the army who are loyal to him and me."

Vasher stepped forth, "Well, not exactly all of us. Some of us have other missions."

"Right," Garrison agreed. "There is a faction heading south to Shivaana and Fangh-Haan. Which reminds me, please remember your missions while you are down there as well. We need to go to *every* city and build armies and militias. We will send soldiers with you to help train those willing to help. They must be combat ready. I am not doing this simply so we can have numbers to defend Ashur. I want to destroy anyone who would dare arrive on our shores expecting to conquer us."

"What if they also have manifestations in other nations beyond Ashur?" The voice belonged to one of Asarei's followers from the island. *What do they call him? Av...Dool? Ahvedool? I think that's it.*

By the time Garrison made up his mind about the name, Kiryako responded. She stood directly across from him, which he guiltily appreciated. Looking at her somehow put his mind at ease. "What do you mean other nations? What is beyond Ashur?"

Once again, Garrison was about to speak, but Rhadames Slade interrupted. *He's probably better qualified to speak on this anyway.*

"There are several other nations beyond Ashur. We currently know of three islands besides Ashur. They are Fah'Zavan, which is where my nation is, then there are also Bisitsad and Orol Taghdras. Each island holds multiple nations with very different kinds of people. The legend goes back to Darian, saying that all of us were part of a large mass of land, and then we became separated when Darian drowned the world. To be honest, there is merit to that thinking. From what I have experienced so far, we all speak a common tongue, even if we speak other languages that might be older or more native. Granted, there are different accents to this common one, even here within Ashur, but everyone I have encountered from other nations speaks it."

Garrison eyed Kiryako as she processed what Rhadames said. "I see. And what he asked about, are there others out there with manifestations? Or something entirely different?"

Rhadames shrugged, "I do not know, to be honest. I have not encountered people from every single nation, but I have not seen any magic or anything miraculous from the nations I have seen. My nation is called Semaajj, and the nation next to us is Domna Orjann. There are some of us who have long suspected that there is magic of some sort in Domna Orjann, but that is only speculation, as no one has ever seen it. However, the swords of the Harbingers—the myths of my country state that they were made in that region during the time of the Five."

"No offense, Rhadames, but I think the best source of information for that would probably be Maqdhuum. Is he not here?" Savaiyon looked around at the group and clenched his jaw after not seeing him.

Garrison shook his head, "No, he is not. He is tending to Horatio at the moment." He noticed a few people slightly glancing at Baltaszar, but he dismissed it. "He was here very briefly, essentially just to bring everyone to Alvadon swiftly. Look, right now it doesn't matter what people from foreign lands can or cannot do. The Vithelegion were not magical and yet, they caught us off-guard and decimated all of Mireya. More than anything else, we must be prepared."

"Do you have a plan to prepare Ashur?" Asarei asked.

"Well, we have a plan. I don't know if it's the best plan, but I don't know if there's a better one. As I mentioned, Vasher, Lincan, Delilah, Sindha, and Krissette will leave soon to travel south to Shivaana. I know Vasher, Delilah, and Krissette all plan to go to Sundari, but you may have to eventually split up to get this done."

Vasher responded, "I don't plan on staying there too long. I want to see my mothers, but the next step after that is to speak to the Shivaani army about their help. My mother will likely have advice on who to speak to, as my father was a well-respected soldier."

Garrison looked at him curiously, "I thought your father was still alive. Would you not be able to talk to him?"

"No. He boarded a giant ship that was created to allow people to spend months, if not longer, at sea. He was excited about it and despite me wanting to stop him, I didn't want to take that away from him. Regardless, there's a possibility that I'll have to admit to people in Shivaana that I know who my father is in order to get the army's support. I'm not sure how that'll go."

"I know that won't be easy, but I think we'll all have to make some uncomfortable choices in order to make this work. Do what you have to do but be careful." He focused back on the rest of the group. "Aside from them, Sindha will travel down to Itarse and Linc will head to Fangh-Haan. I'll need people to go to Galicea and the Wolf's Paw, and then others to travel through Cerysia as well. That may prove to be treacherous. If anyone has better or other suggestions, I am open to them."

To his surprise, Kiryako responded before anyone else. *Oh no, she thinks my plan won't work.* "If I may, I would also like to help. I have already overseen the training of soldiers in Markos and have appointed officers in each city. We have established protocol for several possible scenarios regarding an attack. I think I could be an asset for your plan."

Garrison hesitated, and wanted to look at Badalao, but remembered that his friend could no longer see. *It's better that I don't look at him. He doesn't make her decisions.* "Thank you, Kiryako. Is there a part of Ashur where you would feel most comfortable?"

She half-smiled at him. "I have spent my whole life in Markos, though I have traveled to Cerysia many times. It would make the most sense for me to start with the eastern cities of Cerysia, then if needed, head west."

"Very well; Cerysia it is. I can prepare you for the various cities as well. Who else would make sense to travel with you in Cerysia?"

An unfamiliar voice answered him. "I believe we can help." Everyone looked around for the source of the voice, until two figures appeared from one of the rows of stone soldiers. Two brown-skinned men wearing grey cloaks pulled down their hoods and revealed themselves. The taller of the two acknowledged the group and spoke, "Greetings everyone. Some of you have met us before; I am Stream and this is Wind. I know we told you we would meet in Alvadon, and I apologize for our late arrival. Sometimes things come up. However, we are here to help."

From the other side of Garrison, he heard Baltaszar yell, "Vik! Sorry...Wind!" He ran over to the two of them and clapped Wind's shoulder. "Sorry, please continue. I was just excited to see an old friend." Baltaszar stepped aside to let Stream continue.

"It is understandable. As I was saying, we are ready to help you with your endeavor. Please let us know what you need us to do. Obviously, you have more than the two of us at your disposal. We Kraisos cannot spread ourselves so thin that we can send many of us to every city in Ashur, but we can help quite a bit."

Garrison considered Stream's words for a moment. "Thank you. How many of you can be sent out? And what exactly would you be able to do to help us?"

Stream paused to fiddle with his fingers as if working out a solution to something, "We have just over fifty Kraisos ready to help you. With the loss of Mireya, and Markos not needing any support, there are nearly forty cities left in Ashur. I don't know that it makes sense to send one Kraiso to each city. We are better used when we work in numbers. King Garrison, if I may offer a suggestion, I believe we would be of the most help in Cerysia and Fangh-Haan. Those two nations are notoriously against you, and we could infiltrate them well enough to change how things work there."

Savaiyon interjected before Garrison could respond, "In addition to them, the Anonymi are ready to mobilize. Garrison, if you are looking for the best strategy, then the largest contingent of soldiers would be most effective in Cerysia. They would be able to remedy this Vermillion problem."

"Is it safe to assume you would get them here the quick way?"

"Of course. Unless you prefer the long way. I doubt the Anonymi will, though." Savaiyon chuckled. Garrison appreciated the levity. He looked around at everyone and took the time to just appreciate the moment. The last time they were all together they were planning the siege on his castle. *Donovan and my mother were still alive as well.* Once they finalized these plans, it would be another while before they would all be together again. *I wonder if that will actually happen.*

Maximillian stepped forward to speak. As one of the shorter members of the group, he likely wanted to ensure he was heard. "I would also like to help in Cerysia. While I haven't been back in some time, I would like to be one of the people responsible for waking these people up."

"That makes sense, Max. And if Kiryako is going to brave the cities of Cerysia, then I think Trevor and Neraiya should accompany her as well," Asarei offered. He turned to her, "I do not mean any offense, young lady. But the benefit would be two-fold. It will help to have Marked Descendants with you. It will show people that you have formidable support beyond Markosi soldiers. Remember that Cerysians will not fall in line with these plans very easily. They will argue, fight, and refuse. You will have to be forceful with them to get them to fall in line. Kraisos, I know you mean to help, but your specialty is in the shadows, not in punching people in the face, which is what many Cerysians will need. At least while you are affecting things without being seen, Kiryako will have help with her at all times. Master Stream, how soon would the other available Kraisos be able to leave Markos for the rest of Ashur?"

"I suppose it depends on when you want to meet with them. It can be arranged for them to meet you in Constaniza and travel with you the whole way, or they could meet you at any destination of your choosing."

Garrison didn't wait for Asarei to answer, "Constaniza. I would prefer for them to travel with our people, and I want everyone to meet before heading out. That means all of you."

To his surprise, Delilah challenged him, "Why? Is time not of the essence? I would imagine that every day matters at this point."

"It does. I am sure Savaiyon could help us travel to Constaniza rather quickly, so we would not be wasting a matter of days. But still, the Vithelegion did not come here on behalf of Jahmash. While they created so much chaos here, one thing we are fortunate about is that their fight is different from Jahmash's. I don't think his armies would arrive here without him, and he would have to find a way to get here without sailing. As of right now, that seems unlikely. My point is, I think we have some time to prepare. And one thought that I can't seem to shake is that all of us are together right now. And my hope is that we will all be together like this again, but there is no guarantee. I think we should take at least the next day to enjoy each other's company and allow ourselves to let our guard down, even if for a short while. Does everyone think they can do that?"

Slade responded first, "That is well-said, Garrison. And you are right. We are all about to go in several different directions to prepare Ashur for war, and we have no idea what will happen to any of us in that time. I was a soldier a long time ago in my own nation, and while I know you *all* have more than enough motivation for this fight, it's always nice to be reminded of what we're fighting for."

To Garrison's surprise, every single person there was in agreement. Adria's immediate agreement surprised him the most, but he wasn't going to ask anyone why they'd agreed so quickly.

Slade continued. "That being said, I think we should sort out all of these details before we allow ourselves that fun."

Garrison walked more to the center and knelt on one knee, then waved the group to come closer. "Very well. Markos is covered. As far as Cerysia is concerned, I honestly think you will be better off splitting into two groups. You can have more Kraisos in your faction, as well as knights. But if you all go to one city at a time, especially with how difficult they will be, it will take forever."

Maximillian sat across from him, "Agreed. I can manage with just a few knights and Kraisos. Kiryako will travel with Neraiya and Trevor, as well as the Kraisos and knights. My manifestation should protect me well, anyway."

"Very well. Then Cerysia is settled. What of Galicea?"

Asarei put his arm up, "Rhadames and I will handle Galicea. We'll take Bam and Ahvedool. We can split up as well and should still manage." He looked around at the three men he'd just named, and they all nodded in agreement. "Glad we got that squared away."

"Good. That was easy. While we're in that area, what about the Wolf's Paw? If anyone invades from the south, the Wolf would be vulnerable. They need to be ready."

Baltaszar walked up next to him and sat down, then put a hand on his shoulder. "Can Desmond and I handle that? Maybe Wind as well? I'd like to see where Raish grew up, maybe meet his mother as well."

Once again, some of the Ghosts looked at Baltaszar longer than Garrison felt was normal. *They know something. What could it be? Both times, it has been when Horatio's name has been mentioned.* He let the thought go quickly so that no one would suspect something. "I don't have a problem with that. Wind? Is that acceptable?"

"As long as my superiors are in agreement. It would be nice to be able to catch up with Tasz as well."

Stream affirmed his concern, "No one will have an issue with that, Wind. Enjoy your time with your friend."

Garrison smiled. He remembered first meeting Baltaszar back

in the dungeon of the House of Darian. Baltaszar was probably the only one at that time who wouldn't have judged him. Along with Marshall. All three of them, in their own ways, had been outliers of Ashur at that time. *Both of them came from remote villages that existed away from the rest of Ashur. And I finally opened my eyes to the truth only a few years ago.* The thought of Marshall reminded Garrison that Marshall hadn't offered to go anywhere yet. "That only leaves Fangh-Haan, then. Linc, I can't expect you to cover the whole nation on your own."

Lincan nodded, "One good thing is that Fang already has an army, so there wouldn't be as many people that need to be trained. But I don't mind company."

He hadn't heard from Adria in a while, so her voice surprised him. "I wouldn't mind going along, if you approve, Garrison? I know that I now command your King's Guard, but I figure you should be safe for a while in Constaniza. Marshall and I could travel with Linc."

***

Shit. Marshall realized he was running out of time to speak up. *She's going to kill me.* "Wait." He bit his bottom lip and moved toward Garrison so that no one, especially Adria, would think he was hiding. He looked around and stopped at Adria most frequently, "I'm sorry to do this, but I think I need to be on my own for a little while. I know it's selfish. I know it isn't going to help our cause right now, but it's something that I need to do."

Adria narrowed her eyes at him. He knew she was hurt, and possibly even felt betrayed that he hadn't told her about this before anyone else. "Why?" Adria asked. *For her to only be able to muster one word, she must be furious with me.* He took a deep breath, more to stall a response than anything else, but Asarei saved him the trouble by answering Adria instead.

"Because he wants to figure out his manifestation. Isn't that right, boy? It's been no secret that you've been having trouble with it since you were at my home. I even tried to help, but to no avail." Marshall hung his head and nodded in agreement.

"So you'll stay back and work out how to fully use your manifestation?"

He almost hoped that Asarei could read his mind to answer Adria again. *No such luck.* "I don't know. I prefer to return to my village so I can sort it all out by myself. No distractions, no observers. I tried to work on it when we were all together and I couldn't get past releasing my shadow and reflection. Even during the siege, the only time I used it was down in the corridor to the king's chamber. I know you all think I am abandoning you, but I truly believe that I'm capable of using it to a much further extent. And if I don't sort it all now, then I'm afraid it'll be too late to do it once we're finished militarizing Ashur." He looked around at the group again, hoping that the rest of them wouldn't be as angry as Adria. "You all remember how the whole sky went dark a few years ago. That was *me*. Remember? I'm capable of that and I don't know how to do that again. I promise you, I'm not being selfish just for the sake of it. I'm doing so because I think it will benefit all of us, all of Ashur, once I have a better handle on things. I just have this feeling that it will be needed in our fight against Jahmash."

"At the risk of offending you two, let's just address the uncomfortable part of this first," Asarei responded matter-of-factly. "Marshall, you and Adria can sort out your feelings about this later. As far as this decision goes, I firmly believe that Marshall is right. I can empathize completely, having also been raised as a Taurani. We were even worse off with our manifestations than most of you, as we didn't even know that we had them. While many of you were able to work on yours as you grew up, Marshall and I never knew what we were capable of. He is much further behind the rest of us in terms of his potential, and that is not his fault. I think it is in our best interest to be supportive and let Marshall figure things out for himself. We *all* know that no one else can really tell us how to use our manifestations, as they are specific to each one of us."

Marshall nodded at Asarei to show his gratitude and appreciation. He wasn't sure what he could possibly say in response, so he kept it simple. "Thank you."

Garrison rose from the ground and stood next to him. "I have no issue with what you're asking, Marshall. You're right, you'll be more valuable to us if you have full command of your manifestation. Adria, I think you and Linc can handle Fangh-Haan with the help of Kraisos and some knights."

Adria briefly glanced at Marshall, then looked at Garrison. "I believe that would suffice. Do we have everything covered, then?"

Garrison looked around at the whole group again. "I think we do. All of the nations are accounted for. I will leave it up to each group to determine where to start and what each faction will cover. That doesn't seem like something that the whole group needs to discuss together. Besides, it might make more sense to discuss strategy with the

Kraisos once they arrive in Constaniza."

Marshall looked down at his feet while Garrison addressed the group. He dared to glance at Adria out of the corner of his eye, but she was focused on Garrison. *Is that a good sign or a bad one? Damn, I should have said something to her. But when? Would she have understood? Or would she have tried to talk me out of it? I need to do this; she has to understand that.*

Savaiyon broke him from his panic, "If the business has been settled, then we should go. You mentioned that there is a portion of the army that is loyal to you. Are these soldiers ready? Or should I only make a gateway for you?"

"I will have to prepare them to mobilize, get them packed, all that stuff," Wendell responded. "Should we all return to our own quarters first, and then we can meet back here to travel to Galicea? Perhaps those of us who are here can go tonight, and in the morning the soldiers can use a gateway?"

"Yes, that would work. We don't have long until sunset. Let us return to the city now and then we will meet back here about an hour past sunset. That way the darkness will offer some protection."

Great. This won't be uncomfortable at all. Knowing my luck, she won't forgive me and will be mad at me the whole time we're in Constaniza as well. Everyone affirmed Garrison's decision and returned to their horses. Marshall saw Savaiyon and the two Kraisos talking in the distance, and Savaiyon then created a gateway for them to go through.

***

Marshall finished unloading his pack into the standing closet. Badalao's home was the fanciest place he'd ever stayed in, and it was likely the nicest place he'd *ever* stay in. He turned away from the closet as Adria walked into the room. They hadn't talked yet, but he was surprised that she was willing to share a room with him. There was plenty of room in the estate for everyone to have their own room. *At least she doesn't hate me, then.* He walked over to a desk, pulled out the chair, and sat. "I know I messed up, Adria. I'm sorry. I was afraid to tell you about what I wanted to do. I knew you would be upset about me wanting to leave and I didn't want it to turn into an argument or a fight. We had just come back from the siege and all of our emotions were raw and fresh and I didn't want to put that on you, or make you think I was abandoning you when you were feeling vulnerable. It's just that this is important for me to figure out, and…"

She cut him off. "And you were an absolute idiot about it."

Damn. "Yeah. That's the best way to put it."

"Marsh, you're also being an idiot about your apology. I'm not mad at you for wanting to fully understand your manifestation. Why would I be upset about that? You're right. You should be able to have complete control and understanding of it before Jahmash comes. That isn't what upset me. I'm annoyed that you didn't tell me first. We're *together* now. That means something, assuming this is going somewhere?"

He took a deep breath. *Shit.* "Of course it's going somewhere. I wasn't trying to end our relationship or anything like that. Light of Orijin, I was just worried you would be mad, and I didn't know how to tell you."

She stood in front of him a few feet away, "Anything would have been better than finding out like that. I would rather you have told me on the shore with General Grunt while I was falling apart than to find out with everyone else! We're supposed to be able to confide in each other about these things. I'm not saying that we have to tell each other every tiny little detail about what we're thinking, but you leaving is important and a big deal. And you handled the whole thing like a jackass."

"You're right, I did. And I'm sorry."

"You should be, Marshall. You understand what happens tomorrow, right?" He knew he was supposed to know exactly what she meant, but there were so many things happening the next day that he had no idea what she was referring to. He bit his lip and slightly nodded his head, hoping that would be enough to not require an answer.

"There's a chance that, once we all go our separate ways to militarize Ashur, we may not all end up back here. I don't mean that we'll die, but we may end up having to stay wherever we go, just to make sure things go as planned. Or, even worse, what if Jahmash arrives while we're all separated. That means that this war for Ashur will happen while we're all in different parts of the world. And that's the scariest option, because what if some of us *don't* make it?

Light of Orijin, that's what she wanted me to see. She's right, I am a jackass. I've got to make this up to her, but how? Damn, I'll have to sleep on it and figure something out. Or, maybe I should just ask her?
"You're right, Adria. I understand. I was trying to think of the grand scheme of things, but I didn't think about all of the details. I know I

messed up and hurt your feelings, and on top of that, I embarrassed you in front of the group. I don't think I have the words to explain how sorry I am. Please, what can I do to make this up to you?"

She crossed her arms and glared at him. "Well, when you told everyone this afternoon, my first thought was that I wanted to punch you in the face. Or at the very least, slap you."

Her tone was sharp and he couldn't detect any sarcasm in it. *What the…how am I supposed to respond to that? Should I just let her?* "Um, are you sure? I know those kinds of things can help, but is that definitely what you want?"

"I think you can take a punch. It's not like it would put you to sleep. Besides, I'm sure everyone else would know *why* you have a bruise on your face tomorrow morning. Would you prefer to close your eyes or keep them open?"

Blessed Taurean, she has changed. Was it the siege? Did all of that make her violent? Maybe she's using this to get out those frustrations as well. He looked into her eyes, resigned to the idea that she would punch him. "Open is fine," he responded dejectedly. Her eyes gave nothing away, so he just pressed his lips together, clasped his hands, and looked at her without focusing on any particular thing.

Adria stalked closer and cocked her right fist. Marshall tried not to look at the fist, as he didn't want to flinch or instinctively move out of the way. She stood in front of him for a few moments, her face stoic and her mouth tight. He felt himself breathing heavier, knowing that things would change drastically between them once she hit him. To Marshall's surprise, she unballed her fist and brought her open palm lightly to his face. She slapped him hard enough to get his attention, but not enough to hurt. "You're an even bigger idiot if you think that I would ever punch you in the face. Especially just for being an idiot. The thing is, I know you men can be dumb, and I've come to understand how you all think. It was an easy study being surrounded by so many of you at the House of Darian. Marsh, I accept your apology. I was never as mad as you thought. I was definitely annoyed and a little embarrassed, but I've come to realize that we can't let such little things make us crazy anymore. So that's why all you got was a slap. *But*, I have some other things to say."

"Of course, what is it?"

"I was thinking that you should start getting your tattoos back before this war begins. The Taurani need to be represented with pride, and the only way for you to do that is for you to look like a Taurani. I think tomorrow, before you leave for your village, you should at least get the other line tattooed on your face, you know the one that was on your right eye? It mirrored your Descendant's Mark. I'm sure you can find someone here or in town to do it."

He coughed to stifle the emotions that were starting to stir inside, then paused for a moment to compose himself. "Wow, you amaze me. That's a great idea. I'll find someone tomorrow and that's exactly what I'll do. Was there anything else?"

"Of course," she smiled. Adria walked to him, straddled his legs and then kissed him. Before he could even kiss her back, she spun herself around on his lap and placed his hands on her shoulders. "You've put me through a lot of distress. The only way to fix that is to give me a backrub to remove it all. If I'm convinced that you've done a good job, then you can massage the rest of me." She glanced back at him and smiled. Marshall smiled back at her and swore he heard faint giggles from outside the door, before light footsteps got quieter and quieter.

* * *

The elevated patio in the back of Badalao's parents' manor spanned almost the entire length of the house itself. Over twenty of them sat about outside enjoying the cool autumn air and taking in the calm of the Markosi River, which could be seen from the patio. Garrison stood at the railing of the patio, turned sideways so that he could enjoy the view of the river as well as appreciate the company around him. They had all just finished eating what felt like a feast. Despite not being at his own palace, he had eaten like a king. Everyone seemed to have had their fill, and were now relaxing. He was somewhat surprised to see Marshall and Adria enjoying each other's company. There had definitely been tension between them at the Stones of Gideon. *Guess they worked things out last night.*

Despite the relaxing morning, Garrison was disappointed that Savaiyon wasn't present, though he hoped that the man would return to them soon. Badalao had informed them that Savaiyon had reached out to him through their mental connection. Something had come up at the Anonymi fortress that would keep him there, though he didn't know for how long. *That's exactly what I was worried about and what I wanted to avoid. Who knows what things will pop up to prevent us all from being together again.* Wendell had already informed them that he would ride back to Alvadon later in the day to lead his soldiers to

Constaniza. Garrison had been tempted to go with him but knew that the risk would be too great to return there.

"Am I interrupting? You look lost in thought."

He blinked a few times to clear his mind and realized Kiryako was standing a few feet away from him. "No, not at all. I'm sorry." He smiled at her, "I was just thinking about how it's unfortunate that Savaiyon couldn't be here. I was hoping we would all be able to enjoy this company together today."

"Ah, that is kind of you. It *is* unfortunate. I mean no offense to your friend Savaiyon, but don't let his absence prevent you from appreciating the people who *are* here. I know that if I were in his position, I wouldn't want everyone to stop enjoying themselves just because I couldn't be here."

"You are rather wise beyond your years." *That sounded stupid. Was that a dumb thing to say?*

Kiryako laughed, "I am a Markosi highborn. My parents literally run Constaniza. There has been no shortage of educated and experienced minds in this house for my whole life. I suppose I've just absorbed all that wisdom over the last eighteen years."

Garrison couldn't wipe the smile from his face. "So you essentially have your own manifestation, then."

"If you want to call it that. I just call it being smart and doing my best to learn from every situation. Speaking of which, I only wanted to come over and see how you're doing. I know the past few days have likely been heavy, and despite my enhanced wisdom and empathy, I couldn't begin to imagine how difficult things have been for you." She placed her hand over his, which was resting on top of the railing. Garrison almost forgot about the sympathy she was offering.

"Thank you for being so considerate. It has definitely been hard these past several days. I'm trying to just experience each moment as it comes and not get too ahead of myself. I think as time goes on, things get slightly less difficult to bear, though I don't know if it will ever completely go away."

She grasped his hand tightly. "I don't mean to be forward, but if you need to talk or share anything, I don't mind being your audience. I know you could very well do so with any of the friends you have here, but if you prefer to talk to a fresh set of ears, then I'm here for you."

"Thank you. I'll try to take you up on that before we all part ways."

"Good. Speaking of which, perhaps we should get back to the rest of the company. I wouldn't want to steal your time when the whole idea was to share this day with everyone."

Damn. She has a point. "That's true. Come, let's have some fun." He led her to where most of the others were lounging and sat on a thick-cushioned wooden chair big enough for two people. He waved a hand for Kiryako to sit next to him, then looked around at the others. "Can I have everyone's attention? I was informed that the Kraisos are on their way and should be here by the afternoon. I was thinking we could enjoy some levity in the meantime."

"What did you have in mind? A jousting tournament or something?"

He couldn't tell whether Lincan was being serious or not, but he didn't bother to entertain the idea. "That's a terrible notion. I meant something that would allow us all to stay out here and lounge around like the rest of the world doesn't exist."

Baltaszar sat up from his reclined position, "Garrison, can you answer something for me?"

Great. Another stupid question? "What is it, Tasz?"

Baltaszar smiled widely at him, "What's a stupid thing that you're afraid of?"

"What?"

"Just answer it. We can go around and share our own, and see whose fear is the worst one, or at least the silliest thing to be afraid of."

He couldn't help but let out a small chuckle. "Fine. That's not bad. Let me think about it for a moment." *Guess I should be honest. I wonder what Kiryako will think. Oh well, it couldn't be that bad.* "Big birds."

"What?!" Kiryako pushed his shoulder and looked at him with an open-mouth smile.

"The big ones, you know? Eagles. Hawks. Falcons. Wendell, you remember what happened when we were little? What was it, a grey huntsman falcon? Swooped down and carried my mother's pup away right in front of all of us. Ever since then, they've scared the shit out of me." He laughed at himself and looked around at the others, wondering what they'd think. Wendell was laughing to himself and nodding, and all the others were doing the same. "Now what Tasz? Who's next?"

Baltaszar shrugged, "It's up to you. Pick someone."

Garrison eyed the group. No one looked like they were shying away from being picked, which came as a relief that he wouldn't embarrass anyone. "Marshall. What about you?"

Marshall tried to whisper under his breath, but everyone heard him say "Fuck," and then they all broke into laughter again. He'd never seen Marshall's face turn that red, but he looked forward to what the Taurani would say. "If anyone beats this, then I feel so horrible for you. Oh, none of you will let me live this down." He looked around at the group, hesitant to answer. "Fine. The dark. I was terrified of the dark as a child. And even though it's not as bad as it used to be, it still makes me uncomfortable from time to time."

Lincan looked at him with a furrowed brow, "Wait, didn't you make the whole world turn dark? You said that was you, right? Why do that if you're afraid of it?"

Marshall put his palms up, "I mean, I was more concerned for my life, and I didn't even realize I was doing it at the time. All I cared about at that moment was staying alive because Maqdhuum and his army were ransacking my village."

Garrison couldn't help but laugh at the irony of it. "What a cruel joke from the Orijin to give you that manifestation despite your fear. Sorry, Marshall. Who are you choosing to go next?"

Without hesitation, Marshall said, "Adria."

She rolled her eyes at him but smiled. "Here's more irony for you. I'm deathly afraid of mice." Most of the group broke out into hysterics, though Garrison didn't know why.

"Wait, why is that so funny? Or ironic?" He assumed it was an inside joke that he hadn't been a part of.

Badalao stopped laughing long enough to answer him, "Her nickname at the House of Darian was 'Mouse.'"

"Wow. So then that had nothing to do with your fear?"

Adria shrugged, "Well, yes and no. Savaiyon gave me that name because of my small stature, but he did know about my fear. I just never told anyone else that it was part of the reason. On my first day at the House of Darian, he walked me to my chambers and witnessed me jump about as high as my own head when a mouse ran past us in one of the corridors. That was the hardest I ever saw him laugh. But he never told anyone else about it, as far as I know."

"Eh, it's not like anyone calls you that anymore anyway. Right, *Captain*?" Badalao's tone seemed harsher than his expression. He bore a big smile, and Garrison remembered the two of them being close while on Asarei's island.

Adria smiled as well, "Pssshh, you're just jealous, Lao. Why don't you tell us about your fear?"

"I should have seen that coming." He paused for a moment, "Get it? I should have *seen?*" Garrison nervously smiled at Badalao's joke and his eyes darted around at the others. Adria was already laughing, which put the others at ease enough to laugh as well. "Mine is boring, as Marshall already took it. I'm also afraid of the dark. Only thing I've ever really feared."

Adria replied, "You're right. That is rather lame. Next?"

"Don't worry, even though I can't see, I'm sure I can find a mouse somewhere to put in your room. Anyway, go ahead Farrah."

Farrah shook her head, as if in denial that she would have to speak. "Ugh, mine is really stupid. And embarrassing. It's rabbits."

Badalao turned to her, "Really? Rabbits?"

"Obviously it's based on a reason. Just a stupid reason."

Garrison couldn't help but laugh, "As your king, I hereby demand that you tell us!"

His decree made her laugh, and she relented, "Fine. but if mine ends up being the dumbest one, then I should win a prize."

"Tell us first, then we'll see," Badalao nudged her to tell.

"So when I was little, too young to even have a manifestation yet, we couldn't find my cousin. He had run off or something, and he was missing. So my father, uncle, and aunt went to look for him and I sat there in front of my house waiting, hoping they would find him and bring him back. While I sat in the grass, I noticed a few rabbits several feet away nibbling at something. As I looked at them longer, I noticed their mouths were coated in dark red and I swore that they had eaten my cousin. I ran inside crying and yelling to my mother that the rabbits had eaten him."

Garrison shook his head in disapproval, "You can't stop there. Why were their mouths like that? And what happened to your cousin? No way a few rabbits ate him."

She rolled her eyes, "Fine. He was hiding in the house the whole time. I think he had gotten mad at his mother over something, but I don't remember exactly. As for the rabbits, they had gotten into a berry bush and had their fill of raspberries. I swear they looked murderous. It was the most frightening thing. Especially at only a few years old! Can we move on to someone else? Um, Kiryako, I think it's your turn now."

Garrison found her frantic reaction to be hilarious, but he stifled his laugh to avoid embarrassing her further. He was also intrigued about

Kiryako's answer, so he stayed quiet and tried to act like it was anyone else's turn.

Kiryako spoke without hesitation. "I don't mind. Farrah, if it's any consolation, mine is just as irrational and the story behind is... well *almost* as crazy." She looked at Garrison and then around at the others. "I'm afraid of lying. Yes, you heard correctly. Lying is my fear. Lao, you may or may not remember the whole story, but it's because I got caught in a lie with my parents and the punishment was *bad*. Many of you may not know, but Lao and I were educated by a number of learned men who came to our house and gave us lessons in various subjects. I always appreciated the lessons and *loved* to learn, but it can be tough when many of your friends don't have to do the same thing. Well I think I had seen roughly six or seven summers, and a few of my friends were planning on going off into the Never to explore. They wanted me to come, but I was supposed to have a lesson that day. So when it was time for my tutor to arrive, I rushed to the front of our home and met him outside and told him that my parents were taking me to Taiju for the day, so he did not have to stay. It wasn't unprecedented, as my parents had done that sort of thing before, and I was always enthusiastic about my lessons, so there was no reason to believe I was trying to get out of it.

"As soon as he left, I ran to the shallowest point of the Markosi River to meet my friends and we swam across into the Never. I didn't even think about what I would look like when I returned. We explored the Never for a couple of hours and then swam back across. I was still soaked when I returned here, and I must have brushed against some poisonous leaves or bushes, because I was so itchy by the time I got in the house. My parents were waiting for me, and Lao was curiously peeking out from behind my father's legs. They asked me what I'd been doing and I lied and told them that my lessons had been outside that day. I told them that my tutor wanted to teach me some things that could only be shown outside. They knew I was lying, but didn't bother challenging me, as they could see the rashes forming on my face and knew it was only a matter of time before I fessed up. And to their credit, I went running to them that same night crying that my skin was on fire and I couldn't stop scratching it. That's when they told me they knew I was lying. I have not lied to them or anyone else since, at least not intentionally. I'm too afraid of the consequences."

Garrison looked at her incredulously, "Wow. That might be the worst one so far, but also the most incredible story."

Badalao couldn't stop laughing. "I remember that so vividly. Your face was covered in red splotches when you got home, and your clothes were pasted to your body with how wet they were. You also stank, and you still swore that you were with Master Karyme the whole time! But you're right; you've always been honest since then."

"Well thank you for the confirmation. I'm with Farrah here, though, what's at stake? Whoever *wins* has already had to deal with the embarrassment of their admission, even if most of you are good friends. Perhaps there should be something to compensate for that?"

"I think we could let the winner decide that, right? Within reason." Garrison glanced at her for approval.

"Fair enough. So who shall I choose to go next? I think one of the older folks should have a turn. Asarei, let's hear from you."

The tattooed man stroked his brown beard, which had gotten longer since Garrison had last seen him. "I don't know if mine has a shot of winning. It's a stupid thing to fear, but I doubt it has anything on rabbits or lying." He looked at Farrah and Kiryako and smiled, "Mine is elephants."

Baltaszar perked up, "Really? Elephants? I've eaten elephant; it wasn't scary at all."

Asarei belted out a laugh at that, "Yeah, they're not scary when they're dead, you fool! But when you see them for the first time and they're walking down the main road of Khiry, and one panics and starts going wild, that's a different story. I was about ten feet away when one stomped on a man and crushed his skull. Those creatures are gentle and friendly when they're not threatened, but you remember their size instantly once that changes. Vitticus Khou used to have some when he still lived in Galicea. I never made a point to get too close to them then either. That's enough about mine, though. Rhadames, enlighten us about yours."

Slade put his palms up in resignation. "I don't even know if mine is something you would all understand. It was based on stories my grandmother used to tell me when I was small. Do you have quicksand here in Ashur? I feel as if I have traveled this whole continent and have never experienced it."

Garrison shook his head but found himself rather curious. "No, I have never heard of it. But now I'd love to know what it is. Maybe we have a different term for it."

"There are certain areas of sand that have too much water stuck in them, and somehow it sucks you in if you step in it. The scary thing is that if you start getting sucked down into it, the more you struggle to get out, the more it sucks you in."

Garrison was intrigued, "So did you know someone that got stuck in it?"

"No, that's what makes it pretty irrational. I've only ever heard stories of it from my grandmother, and maybe a few other people her age. They swore they'd seen someone drown in it, but nobody else ever spoke of such a thing. But as a little boy, it used to scare the shit out of me. Especially considering I grew up near the water, so there was a lot of sand around. After a while, I figured it was either just a myth, or something that didn't last very long so I just never saw it."

To Garrison's surprise, Manjobam spoke up. Despite his large stature, he was incredibly quiet to the point that Garrison had forgotten he was there. "I get that it might seem irrational now, but I could see how that would scare the crap out of someone. If I had heard those stories as a little boy, I would avoid sand for the rest of my life! Damn, now I'm going to think about it for days. Anyway, should I just share mine then?"

"You definitely should," Slade agreed.

"Great. Mine is stupid, to the point that I'm sure everyone was afraid of it up to a certain point. But the thing is, it *still* sort of scares me. I know, I'm too old to be afraid of thunder, but it's true and I just can't seem to shake it."

Most of them laughed, but not in a mocking way. Lincan responded, "You're right, I think we've all been afraid of that at some point, some later than others. But Bam, are you afraid of the thunder itself, or because you know that lightning is coming as well?"

"Both?" He laughed, and so did everyone else. "I grew up in Agralun, off the coast of mainland Shivaana. We spent a lot of time on boats, and it's terrifying to be on the water when a thunderstorm is raging."

"Yes, I can attest to that as well. Especially if you're a child; it makes you want to piss your pants," Lincan agreed.

Manjobam laughed, "I won't say whether that happened or not. There's a chance, though." He looked around for a moment, "Tasz, what's yours?"

Baltaszar rubbed his short beard, "Oh great. If you want to talk about stupid fears, mine is definitely high on that list. Seeds. I grew up being terrified of seeds." Everyone gasped, as did Garrison, but they all let Baltaszar continue. "Not in the sense that if I saw seeds, I would run away. Oh man, that would be even more embarrassing. But, my father used to tell us when we were little that if we swallowed the seeds while eating fruit, then more fruit might grow inside of our bellies. That's one of the reasons why I love apples so much. You know where the seeds are and there's not much risk of swallowing one."

Desmond laughed with his head tilted backwards, as if it was the most ridiculous thing he'd ever heard. "Seriously? I know yer from the middle o' the forest an' everythin', but how did ya avoid seeds? So many fruits have 'em?"

Baltaszar shrugged, "Not sure, I just avoided eating them, I guess. It's not like the fear stayed with me. Eventually my father told me he was joking about the whole thing. Still, it took me a while to stop being picky about it. Since you're so vocal, Des, what about you?"

"Pepperflies."

Badalao perked up, "Really? You never mentioned that you had an issue with them."

"O' course I didn't. Why would I want ta be picked on about that. Those things are nasty, though. Tasz, ya know the river that separates Mireya from the Never. I used ta go there often when I was little. Thought I'd play a prank on my friends by hidin' behind some shrubbery. Turns out there was a swarm o' pepperflies in it. Don't know if any of ya have ever been bit by one, but it's a nasty bite. Gettin' attacked by a whole swarm, though, I was layed up fer days. Probably looked just like ya, Kiri. Had welts all over my body forever. An' I didn't go back to the river fer years. Honestly, I still hate 'em. I know they're supposed ta be good fer ya all crushed up an' everything', but I don't like 'em when they're alive." He looked around at everyone, though the rest of the group was mostly quiet with disgusted expressions.

Garrison felt bad for him, so he tried to inquire further without embarrassing Desmond, "I don't think we have them in Cerysia. At least not in this part."

"Alvadon isn't near water. Ye can usually find them near rivers an' such. But I wouldn't mind if they found their way there now. Let 'em go on a spree of bitin' everyone there. Anyway, Vasher, yer up."

"Oh man, this is going to be a tough one to explain." He surveyed the group to read everyone's faces. Garrison sat forward. He'd enjoyed everyone's responses so far. It was nice to see this side of everyone and even better that everyone was being honest and candid with their answers. Vasher continued, "Mine is the sun." He nodded vigorously, "Yes, I know. The friggin sun. I kind of wish Savaiyon was here for this; he would never let me live this down. So, when I was in that phase of childhood where I was curious about everything and how everything worked, I asked my mother what the sun was. She told me she thought it was a huge ball of fire somewhere in the sky, and that it helped to keep us warm."

Baltaszar chimed in, "That seems pretty reasonable so far."

"Yeah, so far. But the more I thought about it, I assumed that maybe the sun could fall into our world and then we would all be on fire."

Garrison laughed, and he noticed Kiryako doing so as well. "That still doesn't seem so unreasonable for a child."

"Hold on, it gets better. So I cried to both of my mothers about how I was too scared to go outside because I was worried that the sun would slam into us and that I didn't want to be set on fire. My second mother reassured me that the sun had followed the same exact pattern from the time she was a child. And at no point did it ever seem like it was getting closer, or close enough to hit us. So then my mind got fixed on the notion that maybe the sun might disappear one day and then we would never be warm again. Or have any sunlight."

"Yours might end up being the worst one, Vasher." Delilah commented from her reclining position. She barely moved a muscle in passing her judgment.

"It might just be. But let's hear yours then, Del."

She shook her head slightly and looked up. "Mine is dumb, but not *that* dumb. I saw a huge branch fall from a tree once. It narrowly missed my mother and obviously scared the hell out of me. I must have cried for at least an hour after seeing that. So of course the idea of falling trees and branches crippled me with fear at times. I avoided being anywhere near trees. Didn't play in them, on them, near them, nothing. I swore that any tree could fall at any time, and I was always alert when walking near any. I'm not as afraid of the idea now, but I still hate traveling through forests."

Vasher stared at her with a smirk on his face, "Damn. That was nowhere near as bad as mine."

They continued on until everyone had shared, and they all agreed that Vasher's strange fear of the sun was by far the most irrational of everyone's. He asked if everyone could pitch in for a pouch of tambaku for him to buy before they all departed, and they all agreed to give him some coin once they returned inside.

Garrison was grateful for Baltaszar's suggestion. He'd wanted everyone to get together and lighten up for a short while, but he hadn't been sure of what would help them do that. Baltaszar had come up with something at the right time. He looked around at everyone and was glad they'd had the opportunity to get their minds off of everything. The mood made him bold, and he slid his hand to Kiryako's, which was somewhat tucked under her leg. Garrison gently nudged his fingers against her palm and she immediately moved her hand to his and intertwined their fingers. He liked the feel of hers, as they were slender and elegant, while his were much thicker. Kiryako smiled slightly, as if hesitant about others catching on. Garrison just tilted his head back and looked at the sky.

Hey. King. Remember how I said not to flirt with her? I know what you're doing, even if I can't see.

Garrison's eye shot open. *Lao? How could you possibly know? More importantly, why is it such a problem? What do you think I'm going to do to her? Break her heart or something?*

"It doesn't matter what my reason is. I said no. Hmmm, you seem to be feeling really tired all of a sudden. Rather sleepy. Your head doesn't want to lift itself from that cushion. Your... eyes are... getting... so... heavy. You're... too... tired... to... lift... them.

Garrison's sight faded into blackness until he woke up after what felt like an hour. He blinked several times and saw Kiryako, Wendell, and a few others standing over him. "What? What are you all looking at? I just dozed off."

Wendell's chest heaved with laughter, "Just dozed off? You were energetic and wide eyed all morning and all of a sudden you just fell asleep? That doesn't make sense, Garrison. Are you sure you're alright? Did you eat enough?"

Badalao shouted from several feet away, "He probably needs more food. Or some water. Have the servants bring him something."

Within a blink, Kiryako was gone from his sight. He heard her yelling but wasn't sure at whom. Upon trying to lift his head, Garrison realized that he was still sitting on the couch. He shook his head and focused on where Kiryako's shouts were coming from. Badalao was still sitting, but had his forearms in front of him, attempting to protect himself. Kiryako stopped trying to hit his chest and switched to slapping his shoulder. After a few successful tries, she stopped and just stood in front of him. "You need to stop meddling. I can take care of myself! You were fine with me going all around Markos to prepare them for war, but holding hands with a man you call a friend is something I *cannot* decide for myself? Lao, I am a grown woman, and for some reason, you cannot see that. Even if you had a *thousand* eyes, you wouldn't be able to see it!" She turned to Garrison, "I am sorry for that, Garrison," and stormed back inside.

Garrison looked down at the ground, "Thanks Lao. I just wanted for everyone to be able to relax for the day, without any conflict or trouble before we all separate. And that's what you turned it into."

"I know. You're right, Garrison. I have more difficulty thinking about her in a relationship than her on a battlefield. I'm sorry; I'll go talk to her. Farrah?" Badalao sat up and was about to stand, but Garrison stopped him.

"No. Stay for a moment." Badalao sat back down. "What should we expect from Savaiyon? Is he coming back or not."

Badalao gently touched the edge of his giant black scar on his cheek, that started at his hollow eyes sockets. "Hold on." Garrison and all the others waited a few moments, hoping that Badalao would get a response from Savaiyon. "He wouldn't elaborate much on the incident. One of his acolytes attacked another one before he even opened the gateway for them to return to their fortress. He's the one responsible for sorting it all out. He said something about having personally recruited the one who was attacked. It doesn't seem like he'll be able to get back here anytime soon."

Garrison took a deep breath. "That means your soldiers should be on the march here as soon as possible." Wendell nodded and excused himself from the patio. Garrison looked around at the others. "I don't mean to be selfish, but I don't have a choice. Without most of you here, I will not have much protection. Therefore, I ask that you all wait until Wendell returns with our army to leave for your own destinations. If he leaves now, he should return by tomorrow afternoon. I hope that doesn't inconvenience your plans too much. It also means that you will have to make the actual journey to your destinations, which will take *days* for some of you, Please be careful on those roads."

"Any other plans until then, or are we free to spend our time as we wish?" Adria had been standing up since Garrison woke up from his forced nap.

He stood up to address them. "I did have another idea in mind, but something a little more…active." He looked around at the group. Their eyes were all on him, but none of them seemed to suspect what he would say next. "I think we've all been dealing with various emotions that have put us on edge. We're strung out and perhaps spread too thin. Before we relax, there's something we should do to get all of those emotions and aggression out." He scanned his audience again to gauge their interest. "How would a sparring tournament sound?"

A murmur overcame the group, though most of them were smiling. "I'm going to have to sit this one out. I'm still figuring out how to use other people's eyes to see, so I wouldn't be a very good opponent." Lao grasped Farrah's hand.

She spoke after him, "I'll pass as well. That way I can tell him what's going on. I wouldn't want Lao to get lonely."

"Very well. Anyone else?" Everyone looked around at each other to see if someone else would back out. Garrison counted them in his head, *seventeen.* "Good. If Kiryako is willing to participate, that means there are eighteen of us. To start, we will all draw stones. Nine of us will have a certain color that will allow us to choose our opponent. That means nine of us will move on to the second round. I think from there, perhaps the person who won their first match the fastest will be exempt from the second round. From there, we can decide how to proceed."

Marshall stood up as well, "When do we start?"

"How about in an hour? Lao, is there a sparring ground on your property or anywhere else nearby? A nice open space?"

"Yes. We have a sizable training ground on the north end of the estate. It is outside, next to the house."

"Perfect," Garrison smiled. "Then we'll meet there in an hour. A couple of rules: leather armor only; I don't want anyone's good armor getting damaged. No shields, just swords. And no manifestations. We fight until someone yields. Linc, are you comfortable healing anyone in the event of an injury?"

"That's fine," Lincoln nodded.

"Good, then we're all set. Everyone can do what they need to prepare. I'll gather the stones for the selection process and see you all at the training grounds." The murmur continued as everyone went back inside. Garrison was glad to see them all excited about something. While there would be room for levity once everyone left, he doubted they would all be able to have fun together like this for some time. If it happened to be the case that they could, he would welcome it, but he knew that realistically, it was unlikely.

CHAPTER 9
SPARRING GHOSTS

From *The Book of Orijin*, Verse Three Hundred Forty-Four
It is your duty and responsibility to challenge and uplift one another.
In doing so, you shall make your friends and allies better.

Garrison had arrived at the training grounds several minutes before everyone else. He'd gone to check on Kiryako first, and she assured him that she was fine. Badalao had already had a conversation with her in her mind and had apologized. He knew that he was wrong and promised her that it wouldn't happen again. Garrison told her about the sparring, and she immediately stated her intent to participate. He knew she might be receptive to it, but he was surprised at just how enthusiastic she was.

After leaving her, he'd gathered the stones he needed, nine white and nine black, and placed them in a coin purse so that no one would be able to see inside. Everyone arrived at the same time, as if they had all met each other along the way. Garrison smiled at the thought that they'd all embraced this idea and that they were all excited about it. Everyone had their swords at their sides and wore their black leather breastplates. "Glad everyone made it back. I was nervous that some might chicken out."

Marshall smiled at him, "Who exactly were you concerned about?"

"No one in particular," he laughed and nodded his head toward Asarei and Rhadames, "well, maybe the old ones over there."

Asarei raised his eyebrows, "Old, huh? Better hope we don't get matched up first, *king*."

"We'll see. Speaking of which, everyone line up along that wall and face me. I'll come to each of you so you can take a stone. No peeking and don't reveal your stone until everyone is done. I'll just take the last one remaining." They all stood shoulder to shoulder in front of a wooden wall that bore racks of armor and weapons, while Badalao and Farrah remained on the side of the entryway. Garrison went down the line and let them all take their stones. Kiryako drew the first one and balled her fist around it immediately. The others followed suit until he reached Rhadames at the other end, and then Garrison reached into the purse and took the last stone. "That's it. Everyone can look at theirs now. If you have a black stone, that means you get to choose your opponent. As you look at them, walk over to the adjacent wall so you can see everyone who doesn't have one." He looked at his stone. *Damn, white. I really wanted to have a go at Marshall, just to see how it would turn out.* He watched others gradually walk over until nine of them formed a new line. "Kiri, since you're at the left end of the line, we'll start with you and then move on to the next person until everyone has picked their opponent."

She looked at him and nodded, "Easy enough. I choose you, Garrison."

What? Did she really just say my name? Light of Orijin, what the hell do I do? "Are…are you sure?"

"Positive," she smiled, "And don't hold back. I want to see if I can defeat you fairly."

"Very well, if you insist." He shrugged, resigned to the idea that he had no choice. "That means you're next, Adria."

She smiled widely as she looked at the other line, "Marshall for sure." Garrison looked over at him just in time to see Marshall's mouth drop. Adria continued, "Don't worry, Marsh, I'm not mad at you. But I do have some stress that I want to take out on you."

Desmond stood next to her and waited patiently for her to finish before announcing his opponent. "Tasz, yer my pick."

Baltaszar looked at him in shock, "Really? Why?"

"I figure I already kicked yer ass back in Vandenar a few years ago. So I kinda want ta see if anythin's changed since then."

Baltaszar bit his lip and nodded, "Alright, bring it then."

As they continued down the line, Vasher selected Manjobam, then Delilah chose Lincan, much to everyone's surprise. After her, Trevor chose Maximillian because he wanted to fight a fellow Cerysian, Krissette also surprised everyone by selecting Delilah, then Neraiya chose Ahvedool. Given that it was either him, Slade, or Asarei, her selection made the most sense. By the time it got to Rhadames, only Asarei was left.

Asarei turned to Garrison, "I guess no one wanted to fight the old men, huh? It's easier for one of us to eliminate the other. Sorry, Rhadames, but I'm gonna have to defeat you. So now what, Garrison? Who fights first?"

Garrison looked at the two lines, "Why not just fight in the order that we chose in? Kiryako and I can go first, then we'll just go down the line." He eyed her from the corner of his vision to see how she would react to that. To his surprise, she smiled. *She really wants this fight, huh?* "Is that acceptable to you?"

"Sure, I can live with that."

"Good. I'm sure you'll appreciate the extra rest anyway." He smiled widely at Asarei as he walked back past both lines and collected the stones, then left the pouch on the ground next to one of the walls. Garrison then walked into the sparring circle. Kiryako had already walked to her place and stood with her hands behind her back. She wore a red breastplate and had tied her long hair in a high ponytail.

She looked at him expectantly, "Who is going to start us off? Or do we just start fighting now?"

Garrison drew his sword and assumed a ready stance. "We can begin when you are ready. Once you draw your sword, we'll start." She nodded and reached over her shoulder for her sword, then entered her own ready stance. They both stayed in place for a moment or two, each waiting for the other to make the first move. Garrison feinted an attack to see how she would respond, and her reaction time surprised him. He stepped into an attack and kept his hands high, hoping she would defend high as well. Kiryako took his bait as he shifted the angle of his wrists and swung diagonally low instead. She jumped back to avoid the swipe and attempted to spin in anticipation of Garrison attacking again.

Instead of striking with his sword, Garrison dashed toward her and swept her legs out from under her mid-spin. Kiryako managed to break her fall with her forearms instead of her face but lost her sword in the process. Garrison put a knee into her back, being careful not to hurt her, and then brought his blade close to the back of her neck. "Do you yield?" He knew it couldn't be easy for her to have lost so quickly, but he hoped that she didn't try to fight back.

Kiryako hesitated for a moment, then the words finally came, "Yes. I yield." He helped her up and looked at her sheepishly. To his surprise, she smiled at him as she got to her feet. "I know, it was a stupid move. I swore you were going to strike again while I jumped away, perhaps trying to end the fight quickly while I was off balance."

"No, it was smart. I definitely understood the logic in what you were trying to do. The problem was that I knew from your first flinch that your reaction time was fast, so I had a feeling you would be ready for something. The spin was where you got reckless, but if I *had* actually struck at your jump, then you would have had me." He picked up her sword and handed it to her as they walked out of the circle. "Alright, Marsh and Adria, you two are up next."

They walked over to the one wall where no one was lined up and sat against it. Despite the fight being short, Garrison was sweating a bit. He wiped his head with his forearm and slightly turned to Kiryako, who wasn't sweating or breathing heavily at all. She looked at him and smiled, "I'm disappointed that I lost, but I'm also a little relieved. It would've been rather embarrassing for you to lose right away."

He chuckled, "Oh, thank you for your consideration. Well, anytime you'd like a rematch, let me know. We can spar until you win, however long it takes."

"Don't underestimate me. I'm a quick study. It might be sooner than you think."

"I can't wait. But I'm extremely curious to see who wins this one."

"Me too. I think Adria is going to clean the floor with him. You?"

"See, now you're underestimating Marshall. How about a wager?"

"Absolutely. What are the terms?"

"Hmmm," Garrison thought for a moment. "How about if Marshall wins, I get to kiss you when all this is done. If Adria wins, you can have your rematch as soon as this little tournament is over."

"Ohhhh that's an interesting deal. Fine. But don't be a sore loser when I defeat you later."

Garrison nodded and smiled. He leaned his shoulder closer to hers as they watched Adria and Marshall spar. Adria was the aggressor as soon as they began. He remembered her sparring sessions while at Asarei's base; she tended to only attack this much when she was either frustrated or had something to prove. Marshall remained patient against her attacks, though, and parried them rather easily. However, Adria put together a series of strikes that caused Marshall to focus more to his right, and Adria used the momentum to spin the opposite way and strike him in the chest with her elbow. Marshall stumbled back a few steps because of the blow but regained his composure quickly before Adria's next strike.

"Damn, her spin move worked better than mine."

Garrison laughed at Kiryako's comment but remained focused on the match. Adria maintained her attack, even after several minutes, while Marshall deflected every move and kept his eyes locked on hers. Garrison noticed that her attacks started to seem more labored, as if she was slowing down. Marshall must have noticed the same, as he went on the offensive with a flurry of strikes that seemed to be directed more at Adria's sword than her body. The tactic caught her off-guard, as her parries all came just in time until Marshall finally struck the sword out of her hands. He stuck his blade out as she tried to reach for it, and then he kicked her sword away to put himself between it and Adria. She yelled in frustration, but Marshall didn't fall for the distraction. He stalked her down until she had no room to escape, except to leave the circle, which would have disqualified her anyway. "Say it!"

Even from the wall, Garrison could see Adria's face get tight, until she finally relented and said the words. "Dammit! Fine. I yield." Instead of turning and walking off the mat though, Adria clapped her hand against Marshall's chest, then put her hand behind his neck and pulled him in to kiss her.

Garrison turned to Kiryako, "Don't worry, I won't make you do that right now. We can wait until everyone is..."

Before he could finish, Kiryako copied Adria's move and pulled him in to kiss her. She pulled away after a moment and looked into his eyes. "There. You win, my King. And if it's any consolation, it's not much of a punishment." She smiled at him and turned back to focus on the mat.

"Good. Then we can still do it again later. And if you still want a rematch, I'm game."

"That sounds like a good deal. I'll take it."

Adria and Marshall sat down next to them, and they all nodded to one another. "That was a good fight. I bet Kiri that you would win, Marsh, but honestly, for a while it looked like Adria had you."

Adria half-smiled, no doubt frustrated about losing a match she chose. Marshall put his hand on hers and turned to her, "You were too eager, too aggressive. You were tipping your strikes with the positioning of your hands. I knew where your sword was going. I have to admit, the elbow was a great move, though."

"Wait, Garrison, you bet *against* me?"

Ah shit. "I did so because Kiri said you would win. I thought she was underestimating Marshall, so I figured I'd disagree for the sake of it. It was nothing personal."

Adria nodded at him. "All I heard in what you said was that you thought Marshall would win. And fine, he did. This time. But if you ever bet against me again, I guarantee you'll lose."

"Understood. It won't happen again. Can we watch Tasz and Des now?" They all turned their attention back to the sparring circle. Desmond and Baltaszar had already begun, but both were tentative in attacking. He didn't know much about what Desmond had referred to about their previous fight, though it had been brought up when they were all still training with Asarei. The only thing Garrison really knew was that Baltaszar had initiated it, and Desmond had ended it, but clearly the two had resolved things quickly enough that they got along well.

They were currently fighting a balanced fight, with both attacking and defending evenly. Neither seemed to press or let emotions get the better of them. *Much different than sparring someone you're romantically interested in.* Garrison knew that Desmond and Baltaszar were both still dealing with the deaths of their loved ones, and while they had likely dealt with their emotions on their own, he knew there had to be things they were still holding onto. He hoped the sparring might rid them of even the tiniest amount of stress.

Desmond caught some momentum and started a flurry against Baltaszar, but Baltaszar's timing was surprising. Every one of Desmond's strikes was defended at just the right time for Baltaszar to be ready and in the right position for Desmond's next move. In fact, Baltaszar seemed to see Desmond's next strike even before Garrison, as he kicked Desmond in the torso just as Desmond raised his arms to start an overhead strike. The hit sent Desmond crashing to the ground and no doubt knocked the wind out of him, as his breathing came in gasps. The kick was so perfect in its timing and placement that everyone watching also gasped.

Somehow, Desmond was still holding onto his sword, but Baltaszar walked over and kicked it away while Desmond tried to regain his breath. "Do you yield?" Baltaszar pointed his sword toward Desmond as he got to his knees and braced himself on one hand. He nodded his head in affirmation as his heaving breaths slowed, and he finally closed his mouth. Desmond stood up gingerly and clutched his torso. "Fuck, that was a perfect kick, Tasz. Saw the overhead strike comin' next, did ya?"

Baltaszar smiled and clapped Desmond's shoulder. "I saw it coming about three moves before it happened. I knew you were setting me up for that, but you were more focused on my sword than anything else. Figured it would be easier to beat you without it."

"Damn. I really thought I had ya." They walked over to Garrison and the others sitting at the wall and joined them.

"That was a good fight, you two. I think we all gasped as loud as you did, Des," Garrison said. I just realized something, though. So far everyone who got to choose their opponent has lost. I guess you need to be careful what you wish for."

Kiryako waved a hand at him dismissively. "Does that mean you think Manjobam is going to defeat Vasher this round?"

"I wouldn't be surprised, and that's not meant to insult Vasher. Bam is nearly a foot taller and despite his size, he is quite fast."

Kiryako shook her head in disagreement, though most of the others sitting with them agreed with Garrison. Baltaszar held out hope that Vasher could pull off an upset victory. They watched as Manjobam walked Vasher around the sparring circle. His reach was too long for Vasher to be able to get close enough to attack. The two continued on for a while, doing the same thing, until Vasher grew desperate and charged in for an attack. As he ran toward Manjobam, he leaned forward and held his sword with both hands and raised the hilt to shoulder level.

Smart, Vasher. He's too tall to be able to strike low. Garrison thought Vasher might be able to surprise Manjobam with his sudden burst of aggression, but Manjobam slashed down diagonally at Vasher's blade and sent it clanging on the ground. *Wow. That was quick.* Garrison shook his head as he watched Manjobam pivot to let Vasher's momentum take him past Manjobam. The taller man then turned and slashed at the back of Vasher's breastplate, which sent him sprawling past the boundary of the sparring circle. Vasher didn't bother to go back for his sword. He crawled to the wall that he was closest to and sat against it as his chest heaved. Manjobam walked over to him and extended his arm for Vasher to shake. Vasher reciprocated and Manjobam took the opportunity to sit next to him. They both laughed as they discussed their fight.

Garrison looked at Kiryako and raised his eyebrows. He decided to just smile and not say anything, which led to a punch on his shoulder. He laughed as Kiryako then rubbed where she'd hit him. He felt a thought creep into the back of his mind. *Donovan would have loved this. He and Wendell probably would have sparred for an hour until they could barely move.* He smiled at the thought, more to push his cheeks up and avoid tears forming than anything else.

"Are you alright?"

Damn. She must have caught my awkward expression. "Yeah. It just made me think of my brother and how much he would have loved being a part of this." Kiryako put her head against his shoulder and clasped her fingers in his. His mind wandered and reminisced over the next few sparring matches. He barely noticed how excited everyone was about Delilah defeating Lincan, though Kiryako mentioned something about her breaking the trend by selecting her opponent and still winning. His daze remained as Trevor defeated Maximillian, Sindha handily beat Krissette, and Ahvedool defeated Neraiya. The only reason his mind returned to what was happening before him was shout from Asarei. He'd missed most of what the man had said, though. Garrison leaned to Kiryako's ear, "What did he say? I was kind of lost in thought."

She whispered back, "You have been for a while. But I understand. He said that you should watch how it's done, because he'll have a go at you sooner or later."

The threat brought a smile to Garrison's face, "You have to win first, old man!" After delivering what he thought was a witty comeback, Garrison realized that a few people were standing around Ahvedool, as if he needed attention. He turned to Kiryako, "Did I miss something with Dool? I must have been in more of a daze than I thought."

"He took a slash from Neraiya during their bout. Got him on his sword arm. Honestly, I can't believe he continued, much less *won*. I wonder if he'll be able to continue."

"I'll go check it out. See how bad it is." Garrison pushed himself up from the ground and walked around the sparring circle to the small crowd. He peeked over a couple of people to try and see what they were doing. "Dool, how bad is it?"

"It's a pretty good cut. I don't think I'll be able to keep fighting. I mean, if we were in an actual battle, I would. But this isn't really worth the risk. No offense, of course, Garrison."

"None taken. You definitely shouldn't fight anymore. Since Linc is also done, perhaps the two of you can go back into the house and he can heal you."

Neraiya poked her way through to see Ahvedool. "Doolie, I'm so sorry. I swear I didn't mean to hurt you. At least not *that* bad. Lincan, is he going to be alright?"

Lincan had been caught up in the throng that surrounded

Ahvedool but managed to push his way out. "Yeah, he'll be fine in no time. I've healed much worse. Don't worry."

To Garrison's surprise, she hugged him tightly. "Thank you so much. Please take care of him; he's like a brother to me."

Garrison noted Lincan's awkward expression, as he attempted to reciprocate the hug. "You're, um, very welcome. We should go, though. I don't want him to keep bleeding all over the place, or he'll pass out before he can walk out of here." He recruited Vasher to help him get Ahvedool up, and the two of them walked him out. By the time Garrison remembered there was still another sparring match going on, he turned around and saw Asarei standing over Rhadames, his sword point poking the man's breastplate. He didn't ask Slade to say the words, however. The two men just nodded to each other and then Asarei helped Slade to his feet.

Once Slade was standing again, Asarei looked over at Garrison and mouthed the words, "You're next."

Garrison walked to the coin purse to get the stones, then past him to the center of the circle, "Well hold on a moment, old man. We have to sort some things out." He looked around at everyone and cleared his throat to get their attention. "Unfortunately, Dool needs some medical attention and will be unable to continue. So instead of giving the fastest win a break for this round, we will be able to have four matches without a ninth person." He collected four black and four white stones, then dumped the rest and placed the eight stones in the small bag. "Those of you who won, gather here. He placed the pouch before each person for them to draw, then took the final one. "Once again, we'll just start at the end of the line. Open your palms to reveal your stones."

They turned toward each other and opened their hands. *Damn.* Garrison looked over at Asarei, who also had a white stone in his palm. *There's no way Asarei and I will be able to face off already. Especially not with Marshall picking.* Garrison noticed that all the others who had been eliminated were now standing around the circle, eagerly waiting to see the next matchups. "Marshall, out of the four of you who have the black stones, you won first. You get the first choice."

Marshall smiled, "Bam. I want to face Manjobam. No offense to the rest of you, but I'm excited about the challenge of fighting him."

Garrison laughed, "Have at it. And good luck with that. Tasz, you're next."

Baltaszar looked around at the five of them who were still available to fight. Garrison wondered who he might pick, as none of those remaining had much history with him in terms of fighting or animosity, or anything else. "Sorry Garrison, but Asarei is going to have to go through me before you two can fight."

"Boy, you think you can beat me? I nearly made you shit yourself in a choke hold not that long ago."

Baltaszar laughed and nodded, "Yes, that's true. But I was also incredibly emotional at the time. You'll find I'm a much bigger challenge when I have my wits about me."

Garrison applauded Baltaszar's bravery. There weren't too many in the room that would have willingly chosen Asarei. "You'll just have to beat him, Asarei. That's all. Trevor, what about you?"

"I choose you, Garrison. Another fellow Cerysian, and possibly the greatest fighter out of all of us. If I can defeat you, well then who can't I beat?"

"I think you're giving me too much credit, but obviously I still hope to win." He looked at Delilah, who held the final black stone. "Sorry, Del. I guess that means you and Sindha have no choice but to fight each other."

Delilah shrugged, "I don't mind. I'd rather fight my dear friend than one of you nasty boys anyway."

Garrison turned so that everyone around them could hear. "If you didn't catch all that, the matches are set. Marshall will face Bam first, followed by Tasz and Asarei, then me and Trevor, and finally Sindha and Del. After this round, it stays even and there will only be two matches." He turned back to the remaining fighters, "Are you all ready?" They nodded in agreement, and everyone left the circle save for Marshall and Manjobam. Garrison eagerly wanted to watch this fight, as he thought Manjobam might be the best suited to match Marshall evenly. He wondered whether Marshall had held back against Adria, but he wouldn't dare ask.

The next matches went quickly, with Marshall defeating Manjobam first. As Baltaszar joined Asarei in the circle, Garrison noticed that his eyes looked different, almost as if his pupils were tiny fireballs. He didn't want to ask at the moment, though; it might distract from the fight. The two men acknowledged one another and started their strategic dance inside the circle. Baltaszar quickly won the match.

Garrison walked alongside Asarei as he left the circle. "Sorry we won't get to fight one another. We can always have our own match before you go, if you'd like."

Asarei eyed him suspiciously, "I'll think on it."

"Don't worry, we don't have to tell anyone if I win," Garrison whispered.

Asarei raised his eyebrows at that. "Tomorrow morning. We'll meet right back here after breakfast."

"You're on. Now excuse me; I have my own match to take care of." Garrison patted Asarei on the shoulder and then walked to his starting marker in the circle. *Shit. I wasn't paying attention when Trevor fought before. I didn't get to see any of his tactics or tendencies.* He drew his sword and nodded to Trevor across from him. Trevor nodded back and they began. Garrison knew that since his match against Kiryako was so short, Trevor wouldn't have had much to learn about his fighting style either. Garrison went on the offensive with a series of strikes, but Trevor's timing was just as impressive as Baltaszar's. Everything he offered was perfectly defended.

Once Garrison let up on his attack, Trevor sprung his own series of swipes and strikes. Each one was precise and calculated, and he was already moving into his next move by the time Garrison blocked. They took turns being the aggressor several times, to the point where it was the longest match of the day. *He's leaving himself the tiniest bit open once he's ready to stop his attack. Sword gets a bit low before he gets defensive. How do I take advantage, though?* He refrained from starting another sequence and tried to strategize how best to capitalize on Trevor's one small weakness. *Got it. Just have to be patient. Not let on that anything is different.* He stepped forward for another attack and went at Trevor once more. Trevor blocked and deflected each of his strikes. Garrison stopped just before he became tired and waited for Trevor to reciprocate.

Trevor attempted his own series of attacks, with more urgency. Garrison did everything he could to keep up with the man, until finally Trevor let up and let his sword dip low horizontally in front of him. Garrison dashed forward and to the left of Trevor, then pivoted his torso to knock the sword from Trevor's hand. He put everything he had into the move and watched the black clang to the ground right as he struck.

Caught by surprise, Trevor looked down at his sword instead of at Garrison, and Garrison took full advantage. He stepped between Trevor and the sword and extended the tip to Trevor's chest. "Yield?"

Although Trevor shook his head in denial, he accepted. "I yield."

Garrison realized that Trevor was likely a better fighter than any of his personal knights from back when he was still a prince. *That's my fault, too. If people hadn't been afraid of these black lines on our faces, Trevor easily would have been one of my best knights.* Garrison watched Delilah and Sindha take their places in the circle. *Me, Tasz, Marshall, and either Sindha or Del.* Garrison found these final four or five intriguing, though he thought that if the first matchups had played out differently, things would have changed. *Trevor, Adria, Bam, Asarei. Any of them could have easily still been fighting if their opponents were different. I guess that could be said of some others as well, though.* Delilah won the match and patted Sindha's shoulder. "You were already getting desperate. Hacking at me like that isn't a sign that you were about to win. You thought you could beat me with brute force. The problem is that you were being too simple with your strategy, and then to make it worse, you started tiring yourself out. You were better than that before. Why did you resort to that?"

Sindha shrugged as they sat down just beyond the sparring circle, next to where Garrison was standing. "I don't know. Once you kicked me that first time, I got desperate. It was a smart move and I just thought that if I let the fight go on for too long, you would get the best of me. It's fine, though. If I was going to lose, I'm glad it was to you. I just hope you take down one of the boys next."

Garrison retrieved the pouch of stones and left two black and two white inside. "Alright, Tasz and Marsh, you two come here and join us." Garrison placed the pouch before each of them so they could draw their stone. Once again, Garrison took the last one. "Now open your palms." He looked down at his—white. *Damn, white every time. I haven't gotten to choose my opponent at all.* Baltaszar and Delilah had drawn the black stones. "Tasz, you won first, you pick first. Although, I guess once you make your selection, then it doesn't matter, as Del will fight who's left."

Baltaszar nodded, "Makes sense. I choose you, Garrison. I don't think we ever sparred on the island. It would be nice to finally have the opportunity."

Interesting. I can't underestimate him. "Very well. That means Tasz and I will fight first, then it will be Delilah against Marshall." He was somewhat glad that Delilah's fight with Sindha hadn't ended quickly, giving him time to rest after his own fight. Barring some type of random luck, his fight with Baltaszar wouldn't be short. He looked around at everyone who was still there, "None of you are bored yet? This has taken longer than I thought it would. If anyone wants to leave, please feel free."

Adria responded, "With all due respect, Garrison, you organized this to help shift our focus for a bit, and it has done that. It's also reinforced our bond. I think we were all falling apart after the siege and we needed something like this. So thank you. And there is no way in Opprobrium that I am leaving, especially since I want to watch Del wipe the floor with all of you."

That caused the room to erupt in laughter. Garrison wondered whether Asarei would want him to win or lose. Losing would allow the man to make fun of him, but it would also diminish Garrison's standing as a fighter, which might make it less desirable for Asarei to fight him. *Whatever. He already lost, so if anything, he's proven to be less of a fighter already.*

Once again, he took his place in the sparring circle. Baltaszar looked into his eyes, reminding Garrison of how his eyes had changed. "Your eyes, Tasz. I still can't get over them. When did that happen?"

Baltaszar looked at Desmond and back at him, "Sometime while we were either in Vandenar or on our way to Khiry. Desmond noticed it and told me. It's a pretty neat thing. I'll have to show you some time."

Murmurs started around the room until Slade finally addressed Baltaszar, "Was it the Jinn? Did they have anything to do with it?"

"Actually, yes. They were in my mind and told me how to do it. I had no idea until then. How did you know?"

Slade shrugged, "Just a hunch. But you'll have to show us later. I'm rather curious to see what it looks like when you do it."

"With pleasure. I managed to take out a bunch of Vithelegion and Vermillion soldiers with it. Even more fun than using it was seeing their expressions when I did."

Garrison was equally as curious to see Baltaszar use his newly discovered ability. "Why don't we get this fight started then. The earlier we finish, the earlier we can all go see what you can do, Tasz."

"Challenge accepted. Let's go." They assumed their starting stances, then made eye contact to ensure each of them was ready to begin. Baltaszar took small cautious steps from side to side, but didn't actually advance on Garrison. His left handedness would likely be an issue, but Garrison would have to deal with it. Baltaszar was used to fight right handed swordsmen, so he might even have a small advantage.

They studied one another, waiting for the other to pounce. Baltaszar hadn't attacked first in either of his previous fights. *If I wait him out, this fight may go on for days. Have to find a way to disrupt his timing.* Garrison thought of how he'd fought his Royal Guard back when his father had deemed him a criminal. He moved closer to Baltaszar, and once he was close enough for his sword to reach, he leaned in with a diagonal strike to Baltaszar's left side, causing Baltaszar to move his sword away from his body for the deflection. Once Baltaszar committed to the parry, Garrison launched a fist at Baltaszar's midsection. However, his opponent's timing and reflexes proved quick, as he lowered himself enough to let his chest take the brunt of the punch.

The hit moved him back a step or so, but it wasn't enough to knock him off balance. Baltaszar countered with a straight stab right at Garrison's torso, which almost caught Garrison off-guard. He spun out of the way and readied himself once more, holding his sword diagonally in front of him. Baltaszar came to him this time and attempted to undercut his sword. Garrison steeled his arm and his grip to defend the strike, but Baltaszar pulled back just before their blades clashed, and stepped past him. Before Garrison could turn to protect himself, Baltaszar somehow switched his sword to his right hand and offered a backhand strike to Garrison's upper back. He lunged forward a bit and slightly stumbled but stopped himself from falling. *Damnit. He's sure of himself with his right hand as well.* He turned to face Baltaszar once again, and his opponent nodded at him and smiled. Garrison smiled back, knowing that Baltaszar was having fun with this. "Right handed, huh?"

"Figured I'd give it a try. I guess it worked."

"We'll see. Come on." They both took a step closer to each other. Garrison started the volley and Baltaszar deflected each shot while pivoting to Garrison's right. *Have to stop him from moving that way. It's harder to hit him.* Garrison attempted to cut him off by moving in the same direction more quickly. In response, Baltaszar pivoted so that Garrison was between him and the edge of the circle. *Smart.* Garrison stalked in for another attack. They traded advances for several moments, but neither of them managed to gain an advantage. *I wonder if I can use his own strategy against him. I am a bit bigger than him. I wonder if I can use my strength to my advantage.*

Garrison started another attack, leading a series of strikes that Baltaszar continued to defend with ease. He then borrowed the move that Baltaszar had just attempted on him, feigning an underhand strike. Baltaszar took the bait. Once he readied himself for the contact, Garrison stopped his momentum and took two steps past Baltaszar, switching his blade to his left hand in the process.Finally, Garrison swung a backhand strike to Baltaszar's lower back. Baltaszar fell to one knee. Garrison dashed forward to put his sword into position just as Baltaszar turned around, and had the tip just inches away from Baltaszar's neck.

"You have got to be fucking kidding me. I fell for my own move? Light of Orijin, how stupid could I be?"

"I'll take that to mean you yield?"

Baltaszar bit his lip and shook his head in denial. "I don't want to, but I guess I have no choice." He rose to his feet, "As angry as I am, it's at myself for being so dense. Brilliant tactic to use my own strategy against me. Are you actually skilled with your left hand, or were you just hoping it would work?"

Garrison smiled and clapped his arm, "I was trained to use both hands from the time I was a boy, but in combat I rarely ever had to resort to it. I don't like using my left; it's uncomfortable. I thought I would give it a try on you, as I just had to swing low enough to get your lower back."

Baltaszar sighed as they walked to the perimeter of the sparring circle. "Well, congratulations on your win. I guess you're one fight away from being the champion. I may have to come back here with Asarei later to get some revenge, though."

"Gladly. Anytime you want a rematch, I'm here." Garrison eyed Kiryako and smiled at her. He walked over and she put her arm around his waist.

"That was impressive. He fought you really well, to the point where I wouldn't have been shocked if he won. That's not meant to be a slight against you."

"Are you kidding? There were numerous times during that fight where I thought Tasz might win. He's that good and his timing is impeccable. Fighting lefties is awkward and, quite honestly, I likely would have lost if I didn't have some skill of my own fighting left-handed." He turned his attention back to the sparring circle and saw

Marshall and Delilah take their places. "It's crazy that I'll fight one of these two for the final match. I've always taken pride in my combat skills, but I didn't think it was a guarantee that I would make it all the way to this point."

"It's only fitting that the King of Ashur would be there at the end, right?"

"I suppose that's a good point. Maybe one day I can have a grand contest for all of Ashur to challenge me. I could even have a prize for anyone who can defeat me." Delilah and Marshall began their match, and Garrison shifted his attention. "I should watch these two. Hopefully, I'll find something to help when it's my turn."

Delilah started the match similarly to her fight against Sindha. She looked tentative, but more patient than nervous. She fought admirably, but Marshall quickly stunned her by knocking her down. The fight ended when Marshall rushed toward her as she arose and butted his shoulder directly into her chest. The blow sent her straight to the ground again. Marshall knelt and put his foot on her sword. "I'm sorry if I hurt you, Del. That shoulder was probably excessive. Are you alright?"

Delilah looked annoyed at his question. "I'm fine, you fool. Is this our fight? Casual talk while I simply lie on the ground?"

Marshall smirked, "No. I just felt bad is all. I wanted to make sure I didn't hurt you. Anyway, if you want to be like that about it, do you yield?"

She rolled her eyes at him, "What the hell do you think? I'm somehow going to fight back from this position? Of course I yield." Marshall got to his feet and offered her a hand to help lift her up. Garrison found no surprise in Delilah's refusal for help. She arose from the ground on her own and punched him in the chest. "I don't know why I let up on that charge. You threw me off once you got into your ready position, and it made me rethink my strategy."

"Yes. You definitely should have maintained your charge. As soon as I saw you let up, I knew you were disoriented and no longer had a strategy. I barely even formed a thought once I made the decision to charge at you. It was a good fight, though. You definitely gave me a good wallop with that sweep of the legs. Why did you bother running to get your sword? You probably had a better chance if you had tried to take mine."

"I wasn't sure how quickly you would recover. I thought I'd just knocked you down, the way you did to me. Even after I retrieved my blade, I swore you were already rushing in for an attack. I was baffled to see you still getting to your feet. That's why I charged again. I thought I could finish the match right then and there. But then you recovered."

Marshall nodded, "Then I recovered. Listen, "It was a good fight. My head still hurts and now I have to fight Garrison. He probably has an advantage now."

Garrison laughed, "Don't you dare make excuses already. When I defeat you, I don't want to hear anything about how your head was hurting the whole time. Or, if you think this big injury of yours will be an issue, you could always forfeit the fight. Clearly your health is more important than some silly sparring match,"

Marshall smiled at him. "Get your ass into the circle and take your position. I don't even need a rest."

Garrison looked over at Kiryako, who pursed her lips as if to blow him a kiss. He smiled and nodded at her. "Ready when you are."

"Good. Let's go." Marshall nodded to him and Garrison returned the acknowledgement. They remained cautious for several moments, moving side to side to gauge their reaches and who would be the aggressor. Garrison didn't feel like waiting around for Marshall to plan and launch a strategic attack. He feigned swinging at Marshall's legs and turned his wrist and forearm slightly upward, but Marshall was ready. Garrison continued his attack, slashing from various angles and positions, but Marshall deflected everything with ease. Marshall let one strike follow through as he spun out of the way, which sent Garrison a couple of steps forward. He knew a strike was coming to his back, so he followed his momentum and rolled forward, then sprang up and turned. Sure enough, Marshall's sword had just finished swiping through where Garrison had stood.

Phew. That was close. Marshall continued forward, confident in his attack. He came at Garrison like a whirlwind, swinging and moving faster than Garrison expected. He managed to deflect most of Marshall's attack, but one strike caught him on the breastplate. Luckily, it was only the tip of his sword that got past him and cut a small nick in the leather. *Not sure if I got lucky or he did.* Garrison took a step back after Marshall finished his follow through.

Garrison attempted to counter with his own series of strikes. He walked down Marshall as he swung his blade as quickly as he could, but once again, Marshall evaded him by somersaulting out of the way.

Garrison shook his head. *You have to be kidding me. He can do all that in the middle of a fight? Light of Orijin, I may have to make a sacrifice if I'm going to beat him. Bait him in. I'm the king, I can't lose to anyone here. Hopefully Lincan will be free by the time we're done.*

For him to trap Marshall, he wouldn't be able to prepare in advance. It would come down to reacting at the right moment. Garrison shook his head again, this time a bit more vigorously hoping Marshall would translate it to losing confidence. He attempted to look tentative about going on the offensive by biting his lip and glancing at the ground every now and then.

After a few moments, Marshall inched a bit closer to him and Garrison shifted to a defensive stance. His opponent took the move as an invitation to close in and start an attack. Garrison deflected each strike, waiting for the right moment. Marshall continued on with his flurry until finally, he thrust his sword toward Garrison. *Now.* Marshall threw his left hand in front of him to catch the sword and the tip of the blade sliced right through his palm and out the back of his hand. He gritted his teeth and gripped his sword more tightly, forcing himself to keep his hand in place so that Marshall couldn't free it.

Marshall's mouth dropped open in horror, but before he could get a word out, Garrison put his body behind his left arm so that Marshall's blade was positioned vertically between them. Garrison pushed Marshall back as he swept the man's foot, forcing both of them to the ground, crashing their bodies to the floor. The move shifted Marshall's blade and it cut more deeply into Garrison's hand, but he focused on completing his plan. As Marshall tried to orient himself and grasp what was happening, Garrison placed his sword at Marshall's throat. "Yield."

Marshall closed his eyes for a moment, then banged the back of his head against the floor. "You sacrificed your damn hand just to beat me. You really took it that far?"

Garrison watched as his blood flowed down the sword and onto Marshall's leather breastplate. *Damn. That's going to stain.* "I was willing to make the sacrifice to win, if that's what you're mad about. So do you yield? The longer you take, the more of my blood spills on you."

Marshall glared at him, "Fine. I yield. I sure hope Linc is too tired from healing Doolie to work on you today. Let you deal with the pain for a while. That would make all this so worthwhile."

Garrison slowly stood and pulled his bloody hand from

Marshall's blade. He winced as every little movement caused him more pain. As he got himself upright, Kiryako rushed over to him with a few cloths and wrapped his hand. "That was a brilliant and completely stupid idea."

"I agree," he laughed. The tight wrapping helped ease the pain a little, but he knew he would either need Lincan or some medicine soon. He turned to Marshall, who was on his feet as well, "I hope your soreness from losing eases before the pain in my hand. It would be a shame to linger on this for too long. If you want another round, let me know. It seems like Asarei and Tasz are ahead of you on that line, though."

Just as Marshall was about to respond, Lincan and Vasher walked back into the sparring room. Lincan looked around and addressed everyone, "Ahvedool will be fine. The cut wasn't as deep as I thought. It's mostly healed, but he'll just rest until it's time for all of us to go. What did we miss?"

Marshall glanced at Garrison and then turned to Lincan and Vasher. "Garrison beat me in the last match. Let me put my sword through his hand just so he could trap me."

Vasher's eyes went wide as he and Lincan looked at Garrison's wrapped hand. "You sacrificed your hand in order to win? That's incredible and also irrational. What if Linc wasn't here? Or is too tired to heal you?"

Garrison knew Marshall had to be laughing on the inside. "Well, that would be less than ideal. The only reason I did it was because I knew Linc would be able to heal it. Besides, I'm the king. I have to do what it takes to win. If people knew I lost the competition that I created, how would that look?"

Lincan shook his head, "Wow. Just taking advantage of my manifestation, huh? I think I *am* too tired for more healing today."

"Honestly, I could manage that as long as someone was willing to get me some tea and medicine to help with the pain. Linc, don't feel obligated to heal me today. I'm sure the Kraisos will be here soon and everyone will want to bathe and relax after all of this sparring. My hand can definitely wait until tomorrow." Garrison did his best to subdue a wince. *I definitely can't wait until tomorrow. I really hope he's bluffing.*

Lincan walked over to him. "Here, let me see it." He unwrapped the blood-soaked cloth from Garrison's hand and inspected it. "Whoa. Sliced right through. Honestly, this won't be that difficult to heal. But if you could let me rest for an hour or two and maybe have someone bring me a nice big meal to restore my energy, then I could get to it in a little while."

Garrison nodded as Lincan rewrapped his hand, "Very well. That can be arranged." He took a few steps back and made sure he could see everyone. "Listen, I have some important news that I want to share. And I want to do it now, before we get caught up talking strategy with the Kraisos and then everyone departs tomorrow. As a matter of fact, it's something that you can tell all of the nations as you reach your destinations in the coming days." He looked around at everyone; their eyes were all locked on him. "Any nation that agrees to militarize and help us defend Ashur against Jahmash will be granted autonomy after the war is over. One thing I've never understood is why the Cerysian Throne has to rule *all* of Ashur. Every nation should be able to govern itself. Therefore, after we rid ourselves of the Red Harbinger, no nation outside of Cerysia will have to answer to me."

The room filled with murmurs and a range of different countenances from confusion to happiness. Garrison continued, "I'm serious. It's not a ploy. If there weren't so many other things going on right now, I would set those wheels in motion right now, but it would endanger our ability to recruit every nation and every city. Please deliver that promise for me. It's important that the people of Ashur have something bigger to fight for and to hope for in the aftermath of all this.

CHAPTER 10
UNFORGIVEN

From *The Book of Orijin*, Verse Thirty-Seven
There shall be times in which you must look to others to heal. Look to those who love you and do not forget about Us, for We love you more than any of your kind ever could.

"I know you *want* there to be something, but he never confided in me like that. I was never a confidant for him; I was a vessel. I left my adoptive family in Damaszur because I wanted to travel Ashur before going to the House of Darian. He knows what Ashur looks like even though he hasn't stepped foot on this continent in over two thousand years. He knows what everyone looks like as well. So when he finally gets here he won't have to wonder who his enemies are. You *know* him, Maqdhuum. You know how smart he is. He does everything for a reason." Horatio looked at him as if pained.

"Fine. I'll stop asking if there's anything he shared with you. But he never even spoke to you? Like casually, conversationally, nothing like that?"

Horatio laughed for the first time since Maqdhuum had brought him here. "What, you think he sent me away across the sea to literally be a means to an end for him, then wanted to build a relationship with me, so he checked in regularly and asked how my day was? Asked about my interests and talents, and if there were any girls I fancied? Or asked me to give my fake mother a kiss for him?" He'd raised his voice the more he talked. "Stop! Please, just bloody stop for the love of Orijin!

"All he needed me for was to learn about Ashur and how things work here. I don't know if he got lucky or unlucky that I developed a manifestation. Yes, we all know about him now and were able to get him out of my head. But he also learned so much about his biggest threat here. He saw how everyone trained and what their manifestations are. He knows who we love and what's important to each of us, and he didn't even need to arrive here to be able to do all that. Because *I* did it for him. I asked you all to kill me for a reason. What purpose could I possibly serve now?"

Maqdhuum leaned back on his arms as he looked out. His favorite thing to do on these floating islands, the Deseeti Semai, was to sit at the edge and hang his legs over and take in the scenery. "You can let everyone else know that. Tell them that he knows how they all function. And you forget that you also have a manifestation, and a lethal one at that. He can't control you anymore, which means that he can't force you to fight or kill anyone you don't want to. Also, Horatio, you forget that you have a brother. Technically a half-brother, but you still shared the same mother. And that means that Baltaszar's cousins are yours as well, because they are from your mother's side."

"Have you told him any of this yet? Does he know what you did?" Horatio shifted his gaze to Maqdhuum. "I'm guessing you haven't, because you haven't started your whole self-pity thing yet. You should know that I don't forgive you for what you did. You took her and knew you were stealing her from her family. And then you left her to the mercy of *him*. Who the hell does that? Light of Orijin, you were a goddamn *Harbinger* once. How could the Orijin have looked into your heart and chosen *you* to save mankind?"

He returned Horatio's gaze. "I ask myself that question every day. But to be fair, I was a good man a long time ago, when I had to carry out the Orijin's commands. I was good and pure and admirable. It was Jahmash that ruined everything. Who changed me. I don't know if I was already capable of those evils before Jahmash turned on us, but it changed all of us. Darian quite literally sacrificed the lives of thousands just to trap Jahmash. Changed the whole landscape of the world because of one man. There's no way he would have done that before Jahmash turned on us. Raish, I had four friends in this world. Gideon turned himself to stone because of what we were tasked to do. Jahmash turned on us and killed Lionel and would have killed me as well if I hadn't vanished like a coward. Then Darian killed himself in the process of stopping Jahmash. Do you know how many friends I've had since then?"

"Over thousands of years? What, hundreds? Thousands?"

"None. Sure I've found love from time to time and had children and all that. But after what happened with the other Harbingers, I couldn't bear to have friends again. I was always afraid that if I did open myself up like that, anyone could turn on me. It was easier to be an asshole to everyone so I wouldn't have to worry about being betrayed. Look, I know the severity of what I did to your mother. Even when I was doing it, I convinced myself that it was for the greater good, just to go through with it. And I'm doing everything I can now to protect Ashur from Jahmash, I promise you."

"It doesn't really mean shit until Jahmash has actually been stopped. You know that, right? Say whatever you want, but if Ashur falls to Jahmash, then it's all on you. Why even let him get to Ashur? Why wouldn't you just go to him and kill him?"

Maqdhuum shrugged, "Fear. Cowardice. Remembering that the only reason he didn't kill me the last time we fought was because I ran away. Raish, I am an amazing swordsman. Jahmash is exponentially better than me, even without his mind control. It's something I considered a while back, but I don't know if it's worth the risk. I've set a lot of things in motion in Ashur toward stopping Jahmash and I need to see them through. I don't know that fighting him one on one will be the best thing for Ashur. If I fight him face to face and he kills me, then I can't see through the things that I've set in place."

"What exactly are we talking about here? What things have you done to prepare Ashur? It's not like there's some grand army ready to defend us against invaders. The Royal Vermillion is a joke; they spend more time hunting down Ashur's biggest assets than worrying about what's best for Ashur."

"I created groups a long time ago for the purpose of defending Ashur when the time came. And I did so long before Jahmash would be ready to return so that there was enough time for them to prepare, so that they would have generations upon generations to be ready. They work in secrecy and in the shadows so that they can't be taken advantage of by the masses. As for the Vermillion, they will be handled as well. Your friends should know of the Vermillion's treachery by now, and they have a portion of the royal army that is loyal to them. They just have to make sure it stays that way."

"Speaking of them, I never even bothered to ask. Were they successful? Did the siege even work?"

"Well, they did what they set out to do. Once you were compromised and Malikai…well, you know…Adria apparently took it upon herself to hunt down King Edmund. She killed him, but he killed the queen before Adria could get to him. The palace has been ruined as well. Filled with fire and ash and smoke. I doubt anyone could breathe in there." He glanced at Horatio from the corner of his eye.

Horatio hung his head. "He killed his own wife? What the hell? Then again, I guess I'm no better. I killed Malikai and Donovan."

"No. Jahmash killed them. You know that wasn't your fault, and no one else is going to blame you for it. Trust me."

"I'm still the one who did it, though. And you're right, it's not my fault. It's yours. *You're* the reason I was even created. If not for you, I wouldn't have been there. Those two would have still been alive."

"And if not for you, Zin Marlowe wouldn't have been killed either. Do you think any of the others would have been able to kill him on purpose? You did your friends a favor by killing him, even if it was by accident. Without you, *everything* would be different. But you're right, their deaths are on my hands, and I have to live with that."

"You're good at doing and saying all the easy stuff. If you really wanted to take some accountability, you'd make it a priority to find Tasz and tell him the truth. He deserves it even more than I do. You fucking stole his mother away from him. He told me that he remembers her being taken away and that there was a big fire surrounding them when it happened. And guess what Tasz's manifestation is? Fire, you asshole. You are directly the reason for his manifestation. And somehow Jahmash knew about his manifestation, and sent men looking for him to be able to burn away the sea so that he could finally return to get his revenge. You're almost as bad as my father."

Maqdhuum leaned forward a bit and looked down at everything beneath the floating island. A few decades ago he wouldn't have cared about being called a villain. He probably would have laughed off being compared to Jahmash, but now that he'd taken strides to try and be better, the words hurt. *He's got a point. Everything about me screams villain. Even when doing good, I don't come across as likeable.* He turned to Horatio, "Do you want to come with me?"

"Where?"

"Don't be an idiot. You know what I mean. I'll go find Tasz. Do you want to come? He might need you there after I tell him everything. Only if you're up for it, though. I know your head has been through a lot these past few days."

"Yeah, I can be there for him," Horatio nodded. "But I'm doing this for my friend. My brother. Not for you."

"Understood. Alright, let's get up. All of your friends were in Constaniza, but I don't know if they're all still there or not."

"Why? What's there?"

"New base for Garrison. He proclaimed himself King of Ashur in the wake of his father's death. But with his palace destroyed and a lot of people in Alvadon not too happy about all of that, he's safer somewhere else. So they all headed over to Constaniza and they're staying at Lao's family's estate. That being said, many of them were planning to leave after a couple days to different destinations throughout Ashur. They want to militarize it. Train people to be able to fight for when Jahmash eventually arrives. So we'll check Constaniza first. If he's not there, we'll have to do a little bit of work to track him down. Are you comfortable with seeing everyone again?"

They started walking back to Eddis Ebaba's home and Maqdhuum grasped Horatio's shoulder. Horatio shrugged and brushed Maqdhuum's hand away. "Eh. I don't know. I'm not sure if I'm ready yet. I don't know what I'd say to anyone besides 'Sorry,' you know? It's one thing to see Tasz; I didn't hurt him. But to have to face Garrison or Lao? I don't think I can do that yet. Even if they're willing to forgive me, I haven't done that for myself yet."

"Understood," Maqdhuum nodded. "Then let's go back inside. You can just rest up while I figure out where he is, and then I'll come back to get you when I find him. If he's not in Constaniza, it may take a little bit of time to track him down, as I'll have to try and locate him while I'm falling from the sky. Easiest way to cover a lot of ground at one time."

Horatio chuckled and shook his head, "That actually sounds like it's fun. I might be willing to do that if you have to resort to it."

"Then I guess I'll have to get you if it comes to that. I'll go now, though. Either way, I'll be back for you shortly." He watched Horatio go inside and then closed his eyes. *I told his mother that he would never know about me. About what I did. God I was so stupid back then. So arrogant. Just for the sake of making sure people wouldn't like me. Two thousand years later and I'm still too daft to learn from my mistakes. Maybe I should go fight Jahmash. At least if he kills me it would be the last stupid decision I make. Then I can just rot in Opprobrium.*

He shook away the negativity of his thoughts and opened his eyes again. Instead of simply disappearing, Maqdhuum turned and ran toward the edge of the floating island and jumped off the side of it. Just as the arc of his jump ended and he began to fall, he pictured his destination and traveled there. He reappeared on the road that led to the estate of Badalao's family. *The Majime family has done well for themselves. Nice to see that they're still prospering.* He walked toward the front, and noted four guards standing outside. *Interesting, this place has never been guarded before. Must be because of Garrison.* Maqdhuum approached one of them, "Greetings. I'm here to see Garrison and his company. My name is Maqdhuum. They know me."

The tall and muscular guard remained quiet but turned back toward the front doors of the estate. It opened a moment later, and a golden-haired man walked out who Maqdhuum recognized as Wendell Ravensdayle. Wendell walked up to him and smiled, "Good to see you again. Sorry for all the formality. Garrison has set up the Majime estate as a temporary palace. And now that just about everyone is about to leave to start militarizing Ashur, our soldiers are the main form of protection."

"So everyone is still here? All of the Ghosts? Everyone?"

Wendell nodded, "Everyone. Some will be heading out soon, others will go later. They're all traveling pretty far. Garrison wanted to wait until our whole army arrived, but Savaiyon is apparently caught up with something at the Anonymi fortress, otherwise he would have been able to move everyone much more quickly. As a result, it took days for the army to get here. The same goes for everyone who is traveling. We were hoping Savaiyon would return and provide gateways for everyone, but now it will take a little more time for them to get there."

"Well, I think we're all lucky that I arrived when I did, then. Wendell, I need to speak to Tasz privately. He knows that I've been intending to have a conversation with him. However, once we're done, I don't mind bringing everyone to their intended destinations, as I'm assuming that will make things easier for all parties?"

Wendell's eyes shot up, "Yes, of course that will make things easier. You'd be cutting down on days of travel for everyone! I can't see why anyone would refuse. Hold on, I'll go get Baltaszar. Actually, where would you prefer to speak to him? Out here? There's a beautiful patio out back, with lots of space. No one is there now, so you'd have your privacy if you prefer. Probably much better than just talking in the middle of the road?"

"No one would interfere?"

"We can make arrangements for you to be left alone. Come. Follow me. I'll bring you out there and then I'll get Tasz for you. I believe he's waiting to spar Garrison, so he may be a little fired up." Maqdhuum followed Wendell inside and up a set of winding stairs, then through a few corridors. They finally reached a set of glass-paned doors that blended in with similarly shaped windows along the same wall and walked outside. "Take a seat somewhere and I'll be back shortly."

Maqdhuum surveyed the patio, noting that there were several chairs of all different varieties. He didn't want to look too comfortable, so he chose a plain wooden chair and sat. After several minutes, Wendell returned with Baltaszar in tow, then returned inside and left the two of them alone. Baltaszar furrowed his brow, "What exactly is this supposed to be about, anyway? You mentioned you needed to speak to me, and I'm guessing it's pretty important if we need to be alone."

"It's the most important conversation I'll ever have with you. And things won't be the same after we're done. First, though, I have to get someone else to be here. I'll be right back, so please don't leave. And don't move from where you are." Maqdhuum disappeared from the patio and returned to the Deseeti Semay to retrieve Horatio. He walked into Eddis Ebaba's home and found Horatio reclined on a chair. "I'm ready for you. Come on. Unfortunately, I already found him, so no floating in the sky for you. But I'm sure I can let you do it another time."

Horatio stood up and walked to him, though his lazy gait indicated reluctance. "Fine. But if I have to see all the others against my wishes, I swear I'll hit more than your hand with lightning this time."

Maqdhuum clenched his fist, remembering the near-perpetual burn of being hit with lightning. "We have a private space to speak. No one will bother us. So come." He grabbed Horatio's arm and they disappeared together, reappearing just in front of Baltaszar. "Sorry to keep you waiting." He sat down in the chair he'd previously chosen, and Horatio sat next to him. "Horatio is connected to all of this as well. I told him the same night as the siege, because I needed him to understand where he came from and how valuable his life is."

Maqdhuum took a deep breath, looked at the ground and then back at Baltaszar. "Tasz, what I'm about to tell you. It's heavy and it's complicated, and most importantly, it's my fault. So however you choose to respond, I'm not going to stop you."

Baltaszar glanced at Horatio and then looked back at Maqdhuum. "Just get on with it. I'm already a little thrown off by Raish being here after everything that happened. So stop stalling and just tell me what's going on."

"Very well. A couple of decades ago, I caught wind that there was a woman in Ashur who could travel to the Three Rings. I spent a couple of years tracking her down, hoping that she could bring me there to be face to face with the Orijin. I'm sure you've deduced that I'm talking about your mother, Raya Hammersland. She agreed to take me, and that's when the Orijin agreed to transform me from Abram into Maqdhuum. He gave me a new body. Anyway, that doesn't matter.

"I thought that if I brought her to see Jahmash, maybe he would agree to go to the Three Rings and confront Darian, Lionel, the Orijin, and make some type of peace or amends. So I did. I took her to Jahmash. I'm sure you remember the day of that fire in your home. It was the last time you saw her. She knew I wasn't planning to bring her back and there was nothing she could do about it. She had faith that the Orijin would set things right. That in the grand scheme of things, justice would serve itself." He could see Baltaszar's mouth starting to twitch. "Jahmash had no interest in going to the Three Rings. Instead, he had a baby with your mother, then sent that baby off to Ashur, hoping that it would be his eyes to learn about this place before he was able to arrive. It turns out that that baby ended up with a Descendant's Mark and became friends with you. As fate would have it, that friend is also your half-brother and he's sitting right here."

Baltaszar stood up. His mouth was turned downward and tears poured down his cheeks. "What happened to her? What fucking happened to her after you left her there? After he was done with her? Did you leave her there with him? Leave her there to die?"

He looked at the ground once more and then up at Baltaszar. "As far as I know, she died shortly after Horatio was born."

Just as Maqdhuum finished his response, Baltaszar sprung at him and toppled him out of the chair. Maqdhuum landed on his back and Baltaszar pounced on him and sat on his torso. "Don't you dare fucking disappear, you bloody coward!" He punched Maqdhuum in the face. Maqdhuum felt his cheek split open as Baltaszar continued to wail away at his face and chest. "You brought her to him so he could rape her and then left her there to die! You couldn't even go back for her and save her life? Fuck you!" Maqdhuum felt one of his teeth dislodge and he couldn't be sure whether he swallowed it as he gulped down a mouthful of blood.

Blood seemed to cover him inside and out. Maqdhuum had always known this was would be the outcome of the conversation. He stayed and allowed himself to be thrashed by Baltaszar, knowing that he deserved much worse. As blood started to blind his vision, he noted Horatio standing over them, just watching. Even that didn't bother Maqdhuum. Baltaszar was doing what Horatio probably wished he'd been able to do when Maqdhuum had told him the same story. Maqdhuum assumed his face was a bloody ball of meat and bone, because Baltaszar changed his focus to Maqdhuum's chest and ribs. The pain in his face was too intense for him to be able to focus on his ribs breaking. He faintly heard the voices of other people in the distance.

His head lolled about with every punch to his chest and midsection, until he felt the weight of Baltaszar's body ease from on top of him. He knew someone must have pulled Baltaszar away, though a part of him wished that Baltaszar had stayed and just killed him.

***

Baltaszar flexed his left hand and opened and closed his fist. He was sure he'd broken a knuckle or two on Maqdhuum's face. *Definitely worth the pain. What a piece of shit.* He wouldn't have minded breaking the rest of the bones in his hand, but Garrison and Marshall held him in place. He was still so intent on the bloodied Harbinger lying on the ground, that he didn't realize they were talking to him. Garrison startled him out of his daze by shaking his shoulder violently. "Tasz! Tasz! What the hell is going on?"

He shrugged himself free of the two of them and put his hands up to show them that he wouldn't do any more damage to Maqdhuum. "It was him! My mother! *He's* the one who fucking abducted her when I was barely older than a baby! And do any of you know what he did with her? He brought her to Jahmash! Jahmash! He thought the Red Harbinger, hell-bent on destroying all of Darian's descendants, would welcome her in and treat her like a welcomed guest on his island. All these years, I thought she'd either died or abandoned us. All those years my father spent breaking his back, and Bo'az and I wishing we had a mother. And he left her to be... to be raped and rotting with Jahmash." He fell to his knees and doubled over. He looked up as Garrison and Marshall both crouched down to comfort him.

They helped him back to his feet and he wiped his face, "He robbed me of my whole family. Everything that has happened in my life, including this bloody manifestation, was all because of him. You fucking prick. If you had just left her alone, they'd all still be alive and Bo would still be here, and *we'd* be the people we're all rushing off to prepare for Jahmash." He looked around at the others, finally able to see clearly. None of them seemed to be as angry or surprised as he was. Most of them, save for Garrison and Wendell, looked down at the ground or at Maqdhuum.

Finally, Lincan spoke up. "Tasz, I don't want to lie to you about this, because I think it would make it worse to pretend. He," he nodded to Maqdhuum, "told us about this while we rode here. You and Desmond had already departed. Maqdhuum appeared, looking for Lao to help with Raish. He told us about what he did, because he wanted us to know that Raish wasn't acting of his own volition. I'm sorry. I think we all wanted to say something, but how could any of *us* tell you something like that? We also made it clear that we didn't trust him anymore."

Baltaszar fell to a knee once more. He put his forearm on the other knee and rested his head on it for a moment. "You all knew. Of course you did." He couldn't be sure whether he was mumbling or speaking loudly enough for them to hear. "You all knew and nobody said. Nobody said a fucking word." He shot to his feet and looked around at everyone. "You all knew! You all fucking knew! We've been together for *days* now and nobody said a thing! You didn't trust him, but you had no problem letting him bring you all here, right? To hell with all of you then! I'm heading to the Wolf's Paw now, and you all can keep him around and be best friends with him. I'm sure you'll heal him up real good, Linc."

He shouldered past Garrison back inside, and felt the slightest bit guilty about it, as Garrison most likely hadn't known anything. But the anger consumed too much of him to want to go back and apologize. He stormed through the house, retrieved his pack and then ran outside past the guards to get a horse. Within seconds, he secured his pack and mounted up, then rode off. He thought he heard shouts behind him, but there was nothing more for him to say to any of them.

Thoughts of the Jinn somehow ran through his mind, and he wondered what they would think of his reaction to Maqdhuum or his outburst. He rode on past the city gates and the words seemed to form on their own. *I'm sorry. I know we're connected and that I need to be able to control my emotions better. I couldn't help myself. I was blinded by rage and there was nothing in me that was able to stop myself from doing any of that.*

We understand your reaction. While we were not created in the same manner and therefore do not share bonds the way you do, we understand how mankind works. This is not something you should have been expected to control. And therefore, we do not judge you for your reaction to such a matter. However, you are not to physically direct your aggression toward anyone else.

I understand. That's also why I left. I'm infuriated with the others, but I didn't want it to turn into something else. I know I can't always control my emotions, but I'm doing my best to control my reactions. Thank you for understanding.

Remember that we are always watching.

***

Garrison stared at the bloody mess of Maqdhuum's face and then looked around at the others. *That's why there were all those awkward glances.* "You all really knew about this? That's cold. The least any of you could have done was to tell him *something* was up, even if you couldn't bring yourselves to tell him everything. I was wondering why you all looked so suspicious around him. Desmond, you're supposed to accompany him to the Wolf's Paw. Go and keep pace with him. Don't catch up to him right away; he'll need his space. Horatio, you weren't part of these original plans, but you are now. You're going with them. Go with Desmond, I'll make sure there are extra clothes and supplies provided for you. Wendell, send six knights and six Kraisos with them. Because it's an island, it will be easier to have one Kraiso per city there." All three of them acknowledged him and left the patio. Garrison looked at the rest of them and then stared down at Maqdhuum. "As for you, I think it would be wise for you to return to wherever you were staying."

The battered man slowly pushed himself up to a sitting position. He tried to mumble something, but Garrison couldn't discern the words. To his surprise, Adria responded to the man. "No. We don't want your help anymore. Coward. I would rather take a few extra days to get to Fangh-Haan than in an instant with your help. You've done enough, so please leave us now. Lincan is not going to heal you, and none of us feel sorry for what you've just been through."

Garrison watched as the man disappeared before them. *He could've vanished before it got that bad. He let Tasz do that to him. Why? He knew he deserved it? That would be the only reason.* "Look, for him to stay for Tasz's whole tirade, he knew he had that coming to him. The man is a bastard, but if he knew enough to let Baltaszar beat the piss out of him, then I don't believe he's completely irredeemable. Maybe I'm just speaking from the experience of being a hypocrite, but it takes a lot to sit there and take that kind of punishment. He knew he deserved it."

Lincan stepped forward, "You're right, though, Garrison. And so was Tasz. We're shitty friends for not having said anything. Even when Maqdhuum showed up out of nowhere while we were traveling to Alvadon, he told us everything he did and we were mad at him for what, an afternoon? And then he showed up again later and we forgot about it all because he got us there much faster than we would have on our own."

Adria shrugged and sighed audibly, "No, I didn't forget. I just pushed it aside because he was doing us a favor. But even as I was allowing it to happen, I knew it was wrong. And still didn't say anything. I know it's selfish to say and I'm not doing it to excuse or defend myself. We've all been through so much recently that I think the easy thing has been to focus on what we've individually been going through. I think we've all been rather caught up in our own personal miseries that perhaps we've kind of lost sight of doing what's in each other's best interest. We all need to be better. If we can salvage any type of lesson from what just happened with Tasz let's promise to not let that happen again to any of us."

Garrison hadn't realized that Badalao and Farrah had joined them outside. Badalao spoke from next to the doorway, "Should I reach out to him? Let him know that we're aware of how bad we messed up?"

Garrison shook his head, "No. It won't help right now. He's emotional and probably a little irrational. I know I would be. Let him have some time and space. That is why I told Desmond and Raish to follow him for a bit and then join him eventually. He'll calm down in time, I'm sure of it. And if anything, those two are likely the best suited to help him see things clearly again. I think the best thing for us to do now is for those of you who will be leaving to get everything in order. I would imagine you will all want a good night's sleep before heading out. It will be time for dinner soon. Why don't you all get your things in order and then we'll eat together before turning in early. I also want to make sure that the knights and Kraisos who are traveling with Tasz have enough food to last a while." He led the way by turning and walking inside, and the others all followed. *Never thought I'd see a Harbinger of the Orijin get such an ass-kicking. As much as he's helped us, though, he's definitely had that coming for a while. Good for him.*

***

Baltaszar slowed his horse to a trot. He knew he was starting to think somewhat rationally again, as he started to question whether he should have ridden off in such a rage. *It was the only thing to do at the time. To stay there and harbor all of those feelings would have led to another situation like what I did back in Haedon. No need to make it rain fire again. I'm better than that. More mature than that.* He continued to ride southwest on the road that led to Saphria, rather than turning back, and couldn't shake the thoughts of what his life could have been like if Maqdhuum had never interfered. *Mother still alive. Father still alive. Bo still around. No Haedon. No bloody line down my face. Just a normal life and by this point, I might have even settled down with a wife and family. With a simple life.*

Those thoughts led him to a new train of thought. *That also means I never would have met Anahi, though. I wonder if I would have met someone just like her. I wonder if things would have ended up the same way for her. Things would have to have been different. Damn. I never would have known about her, would I? I probably never would have had a reason to travel to Vandenar. No Anahi. No Cyrus. No Munn Keeramm and his prophecies and books.*

Thoughts of Munn Keeramm brought a smile to his face. He remembered how Anahi had walked him through town and how they'd walked past the Blind Man's home, and he called out to Baltaszar, knowing the whole time that Baltaszar would walk by at that moment. He remembered seeing Farco for the first time and being led into the house, then waiting for a prophecy. Suddenly, a troubling thought dawned on him. *Oh no. Oh no. No no no no no. The prophecy said I would kill my brother. But Bo isn't my only brother. Shit. Shit shit shit. Who the hell am I going to kill?*

CHAPTER 11
TWO RANZAS AND A SCORPION

From *The Book of Orijin*, Verse One Hundred Forty-Seven
Fortitude shall be the key to your success. And your success can only be defined by you, not even by those whom you love.

Savaiyon stood in the small, barely furnished room. He was exhausted and starving, and one of the two chairs in the room was calling for him to sit, but he didn't want to do so until the acolyte whom he'd requested arrived. Sitting would make it look less formal, and Savaiyon wanted the acolyte to understand the formality of the situation. The person had attacked Khurt as he was being helped, or more like carried, back into formation. If he was to be honest with himself, Savaiyon was rather impressed by the acolyte's precision in attacking Khurt. Given their smaller stature, Savaiyon was almost positive that it was a woman who was responsible for the attack. *This had better be worth my while, especially being called away from the others in Alvadon. This business is likely costing them days of travel, since I can't transport them instantly.*

After several moments that involved pacing, standing still, and looking longingly at the cushioned chair, the door finally opened and the acolyte in question was escorted in by two others. The two silver-masked escorts nodded at Savaiyon and then exited. As soon as the door closed, Savaiyon addressed the much shorter acolyte. "You have committed a serious infraction, acolyte. You attacked one of your own. Anonymi do not fight amongst ourselves. Explain yourself."

"The acolyte that I attacked has committed an even worse crime. He is a Vithelegion invader who killed three o' my friends right in front o' me as he an' his army invaded an' destroyed my town. They killed everyone they saw with no mercy. The few o' us who survived managed ta take his son inta custody. We brought him here with us. I want revenge. The Anonymi hold Ashur's best interests dear. I would think eliminatin' the Vithelegion falls under that directive."

A Mireyan accent. She must be from Vandenar. That's where Khurt was captured. "If he is wearing the Anonymi garb and walking in our ranks, then he is now Anonymi, not Vithelegion. His former identity no longer matters. Furthermore, you would be willing to leave his son without a father?"

"Are ya really arguin' with me on this? I thought ya had Ashur's best interest in mind. How many Mireyans did they leave childless? As orphans? Or even worse, how many bloodlines did they just completely eliminate? His son doesn't even like what they're doin'. Told us himself that he doesn't want ta go back ta that."

"He is the only Vithelegion captive that we have. You saw what he did; he fought his own Master General and dismembered him. He did that because he has agreed to become Anonymi and shed his Vithelegion identity. He understands that he most likely will not return home. He has more family there that he will never see. He has accepted drastic sacrifices in order to be able to see his son again."

The acolyte pulled her hood down, ripped off her mask and flung it to the ground, then walked to one of the chairs and fell into it. Her dark brown hair was somewhat matted against her slim face before she pulled it out of the way. *So young. She has to be of an age with everyone I just left in Alvadon, if not younger.* "Fer what point? Do we really need *one* more soldier that badly? Is he somehow goin' ta turn the tide fer the Anonymi?" She stared straight ahead and didn't bother to look at Savaiyon.

I suppose I should be mad at her disrespect, but at least it is giving me the opportunity to sit down. Savaiyon sat in the chair across from her but kept his mask on. "I am only going to tell you this in confidence. If somehow word gets out, I will know it was you who told. And now that I know your face, it will be quite easy to identify you. I do not completely believe that the Vithelegion are returning home. Their Master General was just embarrassed, and his children are missing somewhere in Ashur. All of that suggests them biding their time and attacking Ashur again from a different vantage point. Therefore, it is important that we keep this particular Vithelegion man alive, as he will be able to help us if and when that happens. He was a general and may still have significant influence over those soldiers. Especially after they saw him humiliate their Master General in front of everyone. Do you understand?"

Her face remained solemn, but she nodded in agreement. "I understand what yer sayin'. But that doesn't mean I like it. That was Baltaszar who attacked him when we were still out there. He wanted ta kill that man fer the same reason. The longer you keep him here, the longer that line of people who want ta kill him will be."

"If it turns out that he fails us or betrays us, I will let you and

Baltaszar rip him apart together. Fair?" He wasn't sure what response to expect out of her, but all she did was purse her lips and nod. "There is something else. Did you have any fighting or combat training before coming here? I understand you worked at an inn, but perhaps a father or brother who trained you in combat?"

She shook her head. "No. Never picked up a sword until I got here. If I'm bein' honest, though, I like using these swords. They're different than what I expected swords ta be. They're light an' easy ta wield. When I'm usin' 'em, I feel like they're just an extension of my arms."

"That is what I was alluding to. You seem to have become skilled with the blade rather quickly. The way you defended yourself against the other acolytes after assaulting our Vithelegion friend, I honestly assumed that you had been trained. Fighters like you are uncommon, in that you have natural skill. If you are interested in advancing up our ranks, I could recommend you for more rigorous training and officer training as well."

She looked tentative, as if considering his words carefully. She looked down at her hands as she fiddled with them for a moment. "What would that mean fer me? How would that look?"

"Less free time and more training. Learning how to command and lead by example. You know the formations as a soldier but you will also learn how to use them properly and when." He paused for a moment to consider his words, "If you want revenge, this is likely your best path. If it turns out that the Vithelegion do return to attack us, then you could be on the front lines to fight them. And then if our captive cannot turn them to fight for us, then we could arrange for him to be turned over to you. And Baltaszar Kontez if you like. Does that sound like a fair agreement? You are a valuable asset to the Anonymi; you could help us and all of Ashur in a meaningful way." He was almost positive that that would sway her. After all, she had come to the Anonymi willingly. There would be no point in being here if she wasn't willing to fight for Ashur.

"Well, if yer goin' ta butter my bread like that, then how can I say no? It's a fair deal. All I want is justice fer my friends. An' ta stop it from happenin' again. I'm doin' this fer Anahi an' Sadie an' Cyrus, an' all the other Vandenari who died fer no reason. I would hate ta see anyone else have ta go through that."

"Very well. Then you will resume your duties as normal for the rest of the day and tomorrow. After that, you will receive instructions in your quarters at waking time. That is when your officer training shall begin. Until then, salvage your energy as much as you can. You will need it for what's coming."

The girl smiled for the first time. "I will be ready."

***

Farco reached the sparring grounds and surveyed the area for a few moments. He knew Avenira would arrive sooner or later, or perhaps even be there already. As he looked around, he realized that so many of the acolytes had distinctive walks to them. That was how he and Avenira had managed to recognize one another. They had both agreed to stand and walk a specific way once they realized that everyone wore the same attire, and the only distinctive part of them was their masks. Even with those, most acolytes that he had been exposed to wore black or gold masks, so that didn't help. Even with their strategic gaits, Farco had come to understand that their tactic likely wasn't something new. While not so common that an abundance of acolytes were walking strangely, it had to be a common way for acolytes to recognize one another without blatantly exposing their identities. The two of them had agreed to keep their toes noticeably pointed inwards while standing or walking.

Definitely wish I had asked Munn about this place. The thought of his former mentor soured his mood. He hated the notion that Munn Keeramm had to die in an invasion of all things. The man had left the Tower of the Blind because of how much he loved his home and the people of Vandenar. He was beloved by everyone and should have died of old age. *Instead, he was murdered in his own home with no one around to protect him. And I was off with Avenira when it was all happening.*

He knew that if he'd been at Keeramm's home, he likely would have been killed as well, but that didn't take away the sting of regret. Part of the reason why he'd survived was because he was with Avenira and she knew where to hide to keep them safe. It also helped that she had a manifestation in which her bones didn't break. His memories shifted to the first time she told him about it, and how he didn't believe her. Instead of trying to argue with him, Avenira had handed him a club and told him to swing at her. He had refused, but then she threatened to hit him with it instead, so he acquiesced. She instructed him to swing hard, so that she could show him the full effect.

Summoning the courage to swing the club had proven near

impossible, but he had done it and Avenira blocked the club with her arm. The impact left a bruise on her skin, but she showed him how nothing was broken and aside from a sore, tender spot on her arm, there was no pain. She was so excited about Farco hitting her that she kissed him and he dropped the club immediately. It had been the first time he'd kissed a girl and he knew at that moment that they had something special between them. She didn't get in the way of his responsibilities with Munn, in fact, she encouraged him to spend time with the man.

"Takin' a nap while ya wait? What're ya thinkin' about?"

He'd gotten used to her voice being different with the mask on. "Thinkin' 'bout the love o' my life." He smiled, hoping she was aware of it despite the mask.

"Oh that's so nice o' ya. She's a lucky girl; I hope I can meet her one day."

"Ya wouldn't like her. She's bossy an' likes ta fight. She even made me beat her with a club once."

Her shoulders and chest inflated enough that he knew he'd made her laugh. "She sounds like my kinda girl. I'll have ta become friends with her."

Farco always enjoyed their banter, "I missed ya. Mostly because I want ta fight ya. Are ya ready ta lose another sparrin' match once our instructor arrives?" They had been receiving regular sparring sessions and combat training ever since arriving. Their lessons included starting stances with their swords, as well as various defensive forms called *katas*. Their instructor had informed them that the Anonymi employed five fighting styles in combat. They started all acolytes with Snake style, which was more defensive and patient. They learned to gauge the distance between themselves and their opponent, then use their reach as an attacking strategy. The biggest reason why he'd been able to defeat Avenira so many times was that his long arms provided a longer reach that she often couldn't get past.

The next form they learned would be Ranza, which was more attack-focused, but also patient and tactical. Their instructor had informed them that they would start Ranza in this session. After Ranza would be Nashorn, then Scorpion, and finally Monkey style. Anonymi soldiers were not allowed to go into combat until they had mastered the first three, Snake, Ranza, and Nashorn. Farco felt some despair in the idea that he would have to master three styles before being able to fight, but he knew he controlled how quickly or slowly that happened. He only hoped that he and Avenira would stay on the same timeline. It would be embarrassing to either of them if the other progressed to combat.

She punched him in the shoulder before turning to face him. He had beaten Avenira every time they sparred except for two instances. Despite the lopsided outcome, her two victories had come recently, and he knew it was only a matter of time before her skillset matched his. Knowing how competitive she was, Farco hoped that she wouldn't try to embarrass him in front of the others. He wouldn't be mad, especially since no one's identity was known amongst the Anonymi, but he didn't want her to be able to hold that over her. He walked over to face her and she drew her sword. "Remember, I won the last one, so yer streak is over again."

I'll just have ta start a new one then, won't I."

"How many times have we even fought? We've only been here fer a few weeks. Yer actin' like ye've beat me a hundred times."

"My longest streak was twenty-six. Then ya won fer the first time, and then I won about ten more before ya won again. I'll have ta try fer thirty this time."

As they continued to argue, another acolyte in a gold mask walked over and stood a few feet away, but equally close to both of them. *That's not our instructor.* The acolyte was a bit shorter than both of them, although Farco knew that that might not have been the case a month or two ago. He'd recognized that he'd gotten taller lately, as had Avenira, though he was still a few inches taller than she. *Is that Fae? Looks ta be about her height.* Avenira turned in the direction of the visitor, expecting the acolyte to address them.

"Did either of ya happen ta see what happened on the way out o' the City o' the Fallen? Assumin' ya were there?"

Farco glanced at Avenira and then back at Fae, "Fae, that you? I wasn't there, we're not ready fer combat an' things like that yet."

Fae waved them in to come closer to her, "They have Khenzi's dad here. The one who killed our friends." Farco's jaw dropped open, even with his mask on. Fae continued, "They worked out some kinda deal with him, an' have turned him inta an Anonymi. I know neither of ya know anyone else here, but please don't tell anyone."

Farco cocked his head, curious about the news. "An' how exactly did ya come ta get this information, then? Why did they trust ya?"

Fae looked around and then stepped closer to them. "That's a fun little story fer ya. First o' all, I saw Baltaszar an' Desmond at the City o' the Fallen. They were there an' I guess they know one o' the red-masked Anonymi. They were talkin' ta him fer a while. Anyway, Baltaszar attacked one o' the Anonymi an' guess who it turned out ta be?"

Farco was at a loss for words. *Could be anybody. Jahmash? Holy shit, was it Jahmash?* "Jahmash?"

The way Fae slowly turned to him, he could see her judgment even with her mask on. "Are ya that dense? Really? Ya think Jahmash arrived an' I'm casually tellin' ya *here*? C'mon, Far, don't be an idiot. The question was rhetorical. It was *him*. Khenzi's dad. Baltaszar knocked him ta the ground an' looked like he was about ta kill him, but then Des stopped him by makin' him float in the air. I'm near positive that the red-masked one made Desmond stop him. An' then the one in the red mask took him an' Desmond away. Once they left, I attacked Khenzi's father as well. Completely left formation an' knocked him over. Now, he was already hurt, so it's not like I woulda been able ta do that if he was healthy. Like I said, Baltaszar knocked him ta the ground pretty good. His head hit the ground hard, he had ta be stunned. But still. I wanted ta finish the job. All I could think a was what he did ta Anahi an' Sadie. Anahi was right there in front o' him, an' she even told him that Baltaszar would come fer him. I remember it so well; he hesitated like he didn't want ta do it, an' then his leader came in, told him ta kill them, an' that was that. Coward."

Farco hoped she'd forgotten about his dumb question by now, and responded, "So the other Anonymi soldiers stopped ya from attackin' him?"

"Yeah, they were on me rather quickly. Another red-masked one got us back inta formations an' we continued marchin'. Then after a long while, the other one in the red mask returned without Baltaszar an' Des, an' created this gigantic strange doorway fer us ta walk through. Just outta thin air. Led us right back here inta the fortress. One moment we were walkin' through a field an' in a second we were back here. Crazy. An' I didn't know Descendants could be Anonymi, but that's the only explanation that comes ta mind."

Avenira cut her off, "Fae, in case ya fergot, *I've* got the Mark as well. An' they let me in. I don't think it matters ta them. As long as we can help 'em, I doubt that they care."

"Oh my, yer right. I'm sorry, I fergot about yer Mark."

Farco interrupted, "That's all fine, Fae. But what's yer point in all this? We all want revenge on the Vithelegion; that's part o' why we're here. But what do ya want us ta do?"

She nodded in agreement. "Sorry, I got caught up in the wrong part o' it. I'm almost positive that the one who made that yellow-fringed doorway is the same one who met with me last night. He wants me ta start trainin' ta be an officer. Said my fightin' skills are advanced fer someone with such little trainin', an' thinks I'm a fast learner. I don't know why ya didn't get ta train together with me, but somehow I flew through Snake an' Ranza quickly. Took another week or so fer me ta master Nashorn. Now I'm in the middle o' Scorpion. The focus there is fightin' with two swords at the same time. If I can become an officer, then I can lead armies, an' eventually lead a charge against the Vithelegion. So I want both o' you ta take yer trainin' more seriously and keep gettin' better. That way both o' ya can be under my command. I know we'll have ta wait a bit fer it ta all unfold, but if we can have some patience an' prepare ourselves in the meantime, then we can get back at Khenzi's father an' the rest o' them. Wipe 'em all out so there's no one ta return home. Give 'em what they deserve fer what they did ta our people."

Farco and Avenira looked at each other simultaneously and then at Fae. He smiled at the prospect of being able to fight the Vithelegion on the battlefield. "Definitely. We'll get ourselves up ta form an' ready way before the time comes fer that. But wait, ya can't just casually mention it an' not explain. How did ya get through Snake so fast? An' then Ranza as well? We've been here about three weeks an' we *finally* just got done with Snake. How could ya have mastered it in a week?"

"Told ya, I can't really explain it. It just makes sense ta me. The swords, the motions, everything. Besides, I'm a good five years older than ya both. Maybe it's just the wisdom I've carried all these years, helps me ta understand all this faster. Anyway, my officer trainin' is supposed ta start tomorrow." Another acolyte approached as she spoke, who was much taller than she. They wore the blue mask of an Anonymi Master and nodded to Fae as they walked up and stood next to her. She took the hint and turned to walk away. Before departing, she nodded to Farco, "I'll find ya."

Farco nodded in return, then turned his attention to their instructor. "I apologize. Are we forbidden from association' with others? Like talkin' ta them? Havin' friends an' such?"

"No. This fortress is sacred and it is expected that you shed your name and identity from your former lives. However, the Anonymi are only as strong as our weakest acolyte. If we do *not* associate with one another, then we will not *fight* for one another. The only rule is that we do not use names. As you have seen and apparently adopted, there are ways of contriving a certain level of individuality here. Whether it is a limp or a tic, or another identifying marker, the acolytes know how to stand out without using names. You are expected to have friends. However, as informed when you first agreed to our ways, you no longer have a name. And remember, you wear your mask at all times, except in your own quarters. If you are a guest in another acolyte's quarters, remember that they must grant you permission to remove your mask before doing so."

"Yes, I remember. An' I take that very seriously." He was glad for wearing the mask at the moment, as there had been several times in which he and Avenira had been in each other's quarters and their masks were off without a word even being said. *Then again, I guess if the host doesn't complain, then who would know anyway?*

"Good. Now let us begin your Ranza training. Go to your starting points." Farco and Avenira both walked to their respective lines on the sparring square and assumed their ready stances. "No. Ranza begins differently. Shift your weight to your back leg so that it supports all of your weight. Your front foot should only be touching the ground with your toes. This is called 'cat stance', as it allows you to pounce upon your enemy from your back leg. Do either of you know what a Ranza is?"

Avenira shook her head and Farco did the same. She responded, "We've heard o' 'em, but mostly just as myths. Never seen one."

"Ranzas are large wildcats. Stealthy, patient, deceptive. They wait for the right moment to attack their prey and normally do so when their target is distracted or unaware. That is the basis of this fighting style. By the time you see the Ranza, you cannot stop its attack. It moves too quickly and already knows that it has you. Do you understand?"

"Yes. It makes sense."

"In this instance, both of you shall be patient. Take the time to study one another's movements and mannerisms. Do not attack simply because you feel you must. Attack because you see a weakness. An opening. Attack because you know you will be able to strike your opponent. And when you do strike, you must continue to do so. Once a Ranza attacks the first time, it rarely needs to regroup and pounce a second time. Once it has struck its prey, it continues through with the attack until the prey is dead. So must you be with your enemy. Let the first time you commit to an attack be the last one in the fight. See your movements in advance. Know where you will strike and how many times you will strike before you even initiate it. If you can think so many steps ahead, your enemy will never have a chance in the fight. But first, you must study them. So begin."

Farco heeded the instructor's command and turned his attention to Avenira. She did the same and kept her focus on Farco. They both assumed the cat stance and pivoted here and there, trying to find an opening in the other's defense. Farco knew he had to be patient, but the biggest issue was avoiding frustration and engaging too early. *We're not bein' judged on our fightin' skills here. We're bein' judged on how well we can execute this form. Have ta keep that in mind.* His instinct was to rush at Avenira and be aggressive, but that would contradict the whole point of the Ranza style.

He inched closer, hoping that proximity might throw her off somewhat, and make her wonder what he had in mind. He noticed that Avenira's back knee was bent more than his, and wondered whose stance was in better form. The instructor hadn't given them precise instructions on exactly how the cat stance should look. He assumed it came down to comfort as well as balance. It didn't make sense to bend too much on the leg if it threw him off-center. As he thought about it more and more, Farco started to test how much he bent his back knee, to see whether it was easier or more difficult to balance, depending on how much it was bent. Just as he decided that his original instinct had been the correct one, he realized that Avenira was already upon him. She was merely a few feet away by the time he thought to react. She held her sword strangely so that the blade extended from the outside of her fist and was parallel with her outer forearm. She slammed it into his padded chest as she hooked her leg behind him and sent him crashing backwards to the ground. Before he could even attempt to counter or get to his feet, she was kneeling on his chest and had her blade to his throat.

"So much for yer streak, Far. Looks like I'm startin' my own."

The instructor even chimed in as Farco got to his feet, "It is perfectly acceptable for one of you to advance more quickly than the other. Neither of you should allow the other to hold you back from your potential. Remember, it is only when you master Snake, Ranza, and

Nashorn that you can join the ranks of soldiers."

Ah shit. He's encouragin' her ta go on without me. That would really suck fer that ta happen. He paused for a moment. *Eh, I shouldn't be the one ta hold her back. That would be shitty o' me an' I don't want ta be like that. So what if she turns out ta be a better fighter than me. Besides, this is Ranza now. I owned her at Snake an' we just started this style. Plenty o' time fer me ta get better.*

***

Fae knelt on the floor next to her bed, tucked her feet beneath her legs, and closed her eyes. She placed her hands on her lap and made a triangle with her thumbs and index fingers, then pushed away any thoughts and focused on the black emptiness of her mind. She pictured a point in the distance, took a deep breath, and put all of her concentration into that point. She stayed fixated there for several minutes until she felt satisfied that her mind was clear. As a result of the meditation, Fae also felt some of the tension ease in her shoulders and back. *Trainin' starts today. Have ta be ready.* Before she got up, she continued her morning ritual with a prayer. She spoke lowly, not wanting anyone outside of her chambers to hear, "Orijin, please bless the souls o' my friends an' allow 'em passage inta Omneitria. Please look out fer Anahi, Cyrus, Sadie, Munn, an' all the others who perished because o' that stupid attack."

She took a few more deep breaths and then rocked on her knees to get the momentum to stand up. As she got to her feet, Fae surveyed the small room. It wasn't much, but the days had been mostly busy with training and other responsibilities to maintain and upkeep the fortress. Regardless, it was enough for what she needed. It had a serviceable bed, and comfortable chair, and enough storage to keep the minimal things she'd brought with her. She was more concerned with what she'd received once she got here. Once she was elevated to Scorpion style, she received a second sword. Her room, and she imagined all rooms, had two wall mounts for her swords over the head of the bed. She walked over to the swords and picked one from its mount, then held it gently in her palms.

As she examined it from pommel to blade, she heard a bang behind her. Fae turned to see her door wide open and three silver-masked acolytes stormed in. The last one shut the door behind them and all three faced Fae as if ready to fight her. *Light o' Orijin, what the hell is this?* She jumped up onto her bed and grabbed the second sword, then wielded both in front of her. *Have ta do my best ta keep 'em all in front o' me.*

The acolyte to her left stepped forward and swung his blade at her feet, but Fae leapt with one foot and used the other to push down on their shoulder, then jumped past them. She hadn't put her armor on and was sure that all three of them had some type of protection beneath their hooded robes. She decided to swing anyway. *They stormed in here. Can't assume this might be trainin'; they might just be bullies tryin' ta scare me or somethin'.* Her blade whacked against the back of the acolyte she'd just jumped over, and just as it hit, the other two turned and started for her.

She recovered in time to block the strike of the closer one, but the other threw a dagger at her that she hadn't gotten her sword up for in time. It struck her in her left shoulder and she winced but knew that to focus on it would mean sure defeat. She tried to ignore the burn of the blade tearing at her muscle, but its presence prevented her from being able to lift her left arm. As she decided to try and just pull it out, one of the other acolytes punched her in the face with a gloved hand. Fae was surprised at how well she took the punch, as it didn't knock her down, but she still felt stunned.

Before she was able to regain her bearings, another fist hit her in the ribs. She barely had time to double over in pain before more punches rained down and pummeled her. She was crumpled into a ball on the floor within seconds and the punches continued, with kicks added in. The beating was so intense that she couldn't even form a thought, but Fae knew that she wouldn't give them the satisfaction of showing emotion. She guarded her face with her arms and clenched her jaw, desperate to not let a single tear escape her eyes. Her ribs ached, as did her arms and legs from taking the brunt of their kicks. Every little movement caused the dagger in her shoulder to shift, sending searing pain shooting through her arm and chest.

Finally, after several minutes of the attack, the acolytes relented and exited the room without a word to her. They didn't look around for anything or take anything of hers; they simply left as quickly as they'd come in. Fae managed to start processing thoughts again, rather than focusing on her pain, though she stayed in the same position they'd left her in. *What was that? What could they have wanted if they didn't take anythin'? An' were they even acolytes, or are there intruders in the fortress? It makes no sense that they would just come in here ta beat me up. What have I done to anyone here ta piss them off?*

After letting her thoughts dissipate, Fae unraveled herself from the ball she'd curled into, and a new set of aches and pains introduced themselves. As she attempted to sit up, she realized that most of her pain came from her arms and legs. They'd kicked her in the ribs a few times, but not hard enough to break anything or cause serious damage. The same could be said for her arms and legs. She definitely felt agony every time she moved a limb, but nothing was broken. She leaned against the side of the bed. *They were just toyin' with me. They easily could've seriously hurt me or even killed me if they'd wanted ta. I don't understand. Maybe it was some other newcomers who are threatened that I'm advancin' so quickly? But who else would know it's me? Maybe someone followed me around an' figured out where my quarters are. But is it really that serious? It can't be that big a deal fer me ta be progressin' faster than some others. This is stupid, what the hell is goin' on?*

Fae turned and pulled herself up onto the bed. She winced as she put her weight on one elbow and then inched her way back so that she could rest her head on the pillow. Whether she lay on her side or her back, everything still hurt. She settled on her back and closed her eyes, then cleared her mind so all she saw was blackness. *Might as well meditate. Nothin' else will get rid o' the pain.* She focused on the point in the distance and concentrated on only that. As she cleared her mind of any thoughts and simplified her focus, the pain became easier to ignore. She maintained her focus for several moments until a knock on her door disrupted her focus. *Damn. They're back fer more. Just when the pain was gettin' manageable.* She took a deep breath, "Come in. Might as well finish the job." The door opened and a tall, red-masked acolyte entered. *Him again? He's the one who's going to kill me?* "Oh great. Are ya here ta help me or hurt me?"

The tall acolyte shifted a wooden chair on the other side of the room so it faced Fae. He sat down, crossed his arms in front of him, and leaned back against the chair. "It depends on how you look at it, I suppose."

"Right. Well I'm not in the mood fer ambiguous bullshit, so could ya please just be straightforward with me?"

"How do you feel?"

She rolled her eyes, which surprisingly wasn't painful. "Like I've just had the most relaxin' backrub. How do ya think I feel? If yer askin', that means ya know what just happened. Was it you who sent 'em? Why were they so nice about the beatin'? If they were goin' ta attack me, why stab me an' then not do any more damage than just hittin' me in the arms an' legs?"

"Do you feel as though you could fight someone right now?"

"I'm sure angry enough ta fight someone right now. An' yer questions aren't helpin' my mood much." What annoyed her even more was that she couldn't see his face or the countenance that went along with his questions. *Shit. I don't have my mask on. He knows who I am.* "Aren't I supposed ta be wearin' a mask in yer presence?"

"You may do as you please in your own quarters. If you had wanted to wear it, you would have put it on before telling me to enter. And if it's any consolation, I do not care who you are. Identity and background are not important in this fortress. We focus only on what needs to be done, not on what lives we came from before. But you did not properly answer my question. Do you feel as if you could fight an opponent right now, if presented with one?"

My arms an' legs hurt, but if my life depended on it, o' course I could fight someone. Only problem is I still have this dagger in my shoulder an' every time I move, it burns. My left arm wouldn't be able ta help much in a fight. An' if I pull it out, I'll most likely bleed out. So it *was* you who sent 'em, then. Why don't ya take yer mask off so I can get a good look at ya. Yer in *my* quarters, after all."

"It does not work that way. It is up to you to allow me to remove it, if I wish to. But I do not wish to. I will have someone come in to mend your shoulder, at least enough that it would be serviceable in a fight. That being said, it was not me specifically who sent the attackers. But it is the first step in your officer training. Part of being a higher rank than a novice is being able to handle pain while in battle. An acolyte cannot simply guarantee a swift victory in every battle. There will be times in which you will take a beating and yet, you must still be able to deal with the pain while fighting."

"So then yer speakin' from experience?" She wondered when this man had ever had to deal with being attacked the way she had, especially given his size.

"As a matter of fact, I have. Only about two years ago or so, I was being chased by a man who was able to follow my every move. He threw dagger after dagger at me and most of them hit their mark. By the time I had managed to get the best of him, I likely had over twenty daggers in my back, arms, and legs. The only thing that prevented me from continuing on was the amount of blood I'd lost. You never know when you will need your mind to persevere over such self-imposed limitations."

"Self-imposed, huh? Yer sayin' that my mind is stoppin' me from gettin' out o' this bed an' stranglin' ya?"

"That is exactly what I am saying. When I walked in the room, you had just stopped meditating. And as a result, you were able to make your pain tolerable. Your mind was focused enough to drive the pain away. That is what you will need to do in order to climb the ranks as well as succeed in battle. Officers lead by example. You will be asked to do this again in front of others, to show our soldiers exactly what you can withstand while still fighting. If you are unwilling to face such a challenge, then I should know now."

"Will this happen today?"

"No. But it will happen sooner, rather than later. Without any type of warning. Will you be able to handle that?"

If I could handle the pain o' watchin' my friends die, I can handle anythin'. "Anytime."

CHAPTER 12
BROGAN

*From **The Book of Orijin**, Verse Fifty*
Justice is balance. While justice may seem unfair at times, one must consider whether the weight on both sides is the same.

"The guards at the gate were looking at us funny. Do you think they were tipped off by anyone?" Bo'az turned back to face forward after staring behind them. Aurkene and Suriiya rode next to him, while Hansi and Aric stayed a few paces behind. They'd been in the nation of Brogan for a few days, having stayed in the town of Gael for a night, and then in Cauan most recently. Both cities had been somewhat hospitable, despite a lot of looks and stares from the local townsfolk.

Hansi answered him, "Everyone has been looking at us funny since we arrived here. Aside from Suriiya, the rest of us look like we don't belong here. And with my Mark and all of Aric's tattoos, we naturally draw looks from people. That would also be the case in Ashur."

"That's a good point. Still, I don't want to be too careful. If anyone is following us because of Suriiya, then it'll be trouble for all of us." He glanced back at Aric, who seemed oblivious that there was any cause for concern. Aric had been aloof ever since they left Yahaira, though Bo'az hadn't taken the time to ask why. He figured that Aric would open up if or when he wanted to, and Bo'az didn't have the patience with Aric to beg him to share his troubles. *The fact that he's even showing any type of emotion is new. Wonder if he just discovered them.* He focused on what was ahead and realized he'd fallen a little behind Aurkene and Suriiya. He urged his horse forward to catch up to them. "You said we'll get to Yago by evening, right?" He shouted to Suriiya.

"Even at this pace, we should get there before sunset. If you decide you want to get there earlier, we can go faster. Just let me know." Suriiya smiled at him suggestively.

"I'm still tired from last night's adventure. This pace is comfortable for now." The idea of being with her and Aurkene again once they reached Yago, Brogan's capital, was enticing, though he knew he would have to rest before partaking in any such festivities with them. He wished they'd been able to ride in a wagon with a driver again, as they'd done when traveling from Castiel to Yahaira, but those resources weren't offered to them in Gael or Cauan. Despite the fact that the horses did all the running and hard work, riding a horse was still tiring, and uncomfortable even with the nicest of saddles. Riding faster would make his back hurt even more.

"We're all going to need some tender care to our bodies by the time we get there," Aurkene added, as if knowing exactly what Bo'az was thinking. "Maybe tonight we can be gentle with each other; I know I could definitely use some pampering. It's too bad that we couldn't have a wagon. This nation is so primitive to make us have to ride our own horses everywhere."

"They have them in the north, but the southern regions of Brogan are too rocky and woody for wagons, and most of the roads too narrow. But don't worry, I can give both of you a proper rub down tonight after we have had a chance to eat and settle in. By the way, what is wrong with your friend Aric? He looks like his best friend just died. Maybe he should join us tonight? I'm sure it would brighten his mood."

Bo'az shuddered at the thought of Aric joining them in bed. *Light of Orijin, that's disturbing.* "Please don't suggest that again. That's a disgusting thing to imagine. I'm not comfortable being in bed with another man. I know, I know. You'll think it's hypocritical because of the two of you, but other men don't suit my tastes. Besides, even if it *was* something I was into, I don't know if Aric ever developed a personality. He would put us to sleep out of boredom."

Suriiya shrugged, "Very well. Perhaps one night we'll have to get you incredibly drunk to the point that you don't even know your boundaries or inhibitions. And then we wouldn't even tell you about what happened. You'll be none the wiser and will still have enjoyed yourself. Isn't that right, Aurkene?"

"Sure. We could ease him into it and eventually he might even enjoy it. I have seen and heard that drink makes a man do many things. Perhaps it'll make Bo enjoy some experimentation in the near future." She looked over at him and must have seen his horrified countenance. "We're only joking with you, Bo. Don't worry, I would never make you do anything that you are uncomfortable with or don't want to do. Everything we do is about communication."

His shoulders decompressed, "Phew. I was honestly worried. It seems like every city we visit has something else to fog our minds and make us forget many of the night's details. I figured it was only a matter of time before you started tricking me into doing certain things."

Aurkene chuckled, "In all honesty, I feel no attraction to Aric. I don't mean that as a slight against him, but I just feel nothing toward him. Perhaps that's why he's upset? He misses the brief companionship he had back in Hamil Alsamaea. I'm sure it was the first time in a while that he'd had the chance to lie with a woman. We need that type of connection regularly. It's healthy for our bodies and for our minds. As Suriiya stated, sex is a remedy and fixes so many things."

He didn't disagree. Thinking back to how his life had twisted and turned, especially in the past few years, Bo'az had felt his happiest after meeting Aurkene. Even aside from all of the physical enjoyment they'd had, just having someone to share experiences with and laugh with was enough to make him feel better and take weight off his shoulders. It made their intimacy stronger as well.

A thought randomly dawned on him. "Wait. I hate to shift the conversation away from all this, but you mentioned that there is a king and queen of Brogan. Do they know we are coming? Will we be able to just walk into their palace and request an audience? We haven't really thought any of this through, and we'll be arriving there today. We may have been so caught up with leaving Yahaira and making sure we weren't followed, that we kind of forgot to formulate a plan."

"The Brogani king will be receiving subjects tomorrow for requests, complaints, and any other business. He does so once a week, barring a dire situation." Suriiya said. "It would do us no good to request an audience tonight, anyway. King Renan regularly withdraws to his chambers early and rises early in the morning. While he does not bar others from partaking in festivities and the like, he rarely does so himself. If we are intending to reach Yago by sunset, then he wouldn't be willing to see us anyway."

Hansi had rode up to join the conversation as the forest resumed around their path. The trees had lined the road from Gael to Cauan, then thinned around the city. "What is he like, this king? Will he feel threatened by us? Especially by me and Aric for our Marks?"

"He has not been on the throne for more than a few years, but the Brogani seem to like him. I remember there being concern among the Yahairan Senate that he would be like his father, a man who cared too much for control and who tried too hard to push his borders further onto our land. Renan seems to be a fair leader so far, though. We have had peace with Brogan since he took the throne. One part that helps is that Yahaira is much bigger than Brogan, as is our army. It would not be a favorable outcome for them if we ever went to war. I'm sure that King Renan knows that."

Hansi continued, "It must be nice to have a king who sees things for what they are. Back in Ashur, our king had his army search the land for people like me in order to kill us. Imagine that; we are blessed by the Orijin with these miraculous abilities, and one man sees it as a threat, making everyone turn against us."

Bo'az gazed at Hansi for several moments, wondering what would have happened if his own family hadn't been in Haedon. Baltaszar had had no understanding of what was on his face up until their father died. *Would they have found him and killed him if we were living out there in a regular city? Was that why father brought us there in the first place?*

"It must be terrible to have a king like that," Aurkene chimed in. "Kings are supposed to do what's best for their people. Another reason why it's best for Jahmash to invade. Ashur sounds like a savage place to live."

"Indeed," Hansi agreed. "If anything, at least just to kill King Edmund."

Bo'az wasn't sure whether to feel bad about not being able to relate to what Hansi was talking about. He'd spent his whole life in a town hidden away in the mountains and surrounded by forest. They never worried about intruders or kings or armies. People did their jobs, which mostly required providing some type of sustenance to trade with other citizens. In fact, it dawned on Bo'az that his father, or all elders at that, never mentioned the world beyond Haedon. In retrospect, he realized that they'd lived a rather easy life. Tasks were simple and just about everyone knew their role. Nothing was complicated about what they'd had in Haedon. "What happened to his father, the previous king?"

Suriiya turned to him. "Died in his sleep. He wasn't the healthiest of men. Had quite the appetite, for food as well as drink, as his stature showed. That man just always wanted more, of anything. He wanted and wanted and wanted. His servants attempted to rouse him and could not. They say he was blue when they found him. I'm not sure what that means about what killed him, though."

"Most likely the heart," Aurkene replied. "I saw it happen once at a celebration. An older gentleman stood up at his table urgently, clutching his chest where his heart was. All the while, foam was spilling out of his mouth and just wouldn't stop. After a few moments, he collapsed on the edge of the table and then fell backwards onto the floor. Still, he continued to heave a little longer while still clutching his chest, and then all of sudden, he just stopped moving."

"Well, there you have it, then. His heart failed him. Or he failed his heart, you could say. It actually wasn't long after Renan's marriage to Alandra. They say he was a reluctant king. Didn't want the throne at first but then accepted the responsibility. In my experience, that trait makes the best leaders. The ones who don't want to be or who think they are unworthy. They are the ones who do not want to let their people down. It's the ones who want the power that you can't trust. Anyway, Bo'az, I cannot guarantee that Renan will agree to your terms, but he will treat you well regardless. Oh, and regarding a plan, it may be best to use the impending eruption of Infernua as extra motivation for him. There is always the possibility that Brogan could be affected as well, especially if the ash cloud travels west, which is usually the way the wind blows."

"I'll pull out whatever tricks I can to convince him. It would not be a victory unless all three nations of Bisitsad were in support of Jahmash. I hope that doesn't offend either of you, but that *is* the reason for us being here in the first place."

Aurkene rolled her eyes and laughed at him. "Don't act like we fell for some clever trick that you used against us. We're all adults here who can think for ourselves, you know."

Great, here we go again with me putting my foot in my mouth. It's a marvel that any woman stays with a man for more than a month, given how much they mince our words. I need to find someone else who knows what this is like. Hansi and Aric are surely no help. "I know. I didn't mean it like that. I just didn't want you to think I was viewing this all as some conquest." He thought about saying more, but figured that doing so would only provide more words for him to regret.

She shifted her horse closer to his and shifted the reins to her right hand, then reached her hand out to grab his. She squeezed it tightly and smiled at him, "I know how you feel about me, Bo. Don't worry. Sometimes I just like to give you shit because I know it makes you scramble for the right thing to say. But I'm not as sensitive as you think, so you don't have to worry so much about offending me."

Thank the Orijin. Although, she may just be saying that to trap me, and the moment I say the wrong thing, then she will *get offended and use it against me. I don't think I can win at this.* "Thanks," he smiled back at her, "I'll remember that."

She let go and they rode on, side by side. Their journey to Yago continued for a few hours and they stopped for a break and fed their horses, then resumed. They'd paced themselves well, as they arrived at the gates of Yago just as the sun began its descent.

Once they came within a few dozen feet away, Bo'az got a clear view of the entrance to the capital city. Torches illuminated the arched gates from sconces on either side. Two leather-armored men sat out front while several more stood on a bridge overlooking the gates from behind it. Curiously, their leather was dyed a vibrant hue of blue. All eyes were on Bo'az and his company, as no other travelers were around. The two men stood and placed their sword hands on their pommels, while the bridge men simultaneously drew arrows and pointed their bows toward the companions.

Bo'az immediately brought his horse to a stop and put his hands up. The others around him followed suit. One of the two men at the gate yelled, "That's close enough! Stay where you are and state your business!"

"My name is Bo'az Kontez of Ashur. My companions and I are here on behalf of Jahmash, Red Harbinger of the Orijin, and we humbly request an audience of your king and queen at their earliest convenience."

The sentry looked at his companion and then back at Bo'az and the others. "Jahmash, you say? What is your business?"

He took a deep breath. *Why can't they ever just hear Jahmash's name and cower in fear or cater to our every need?* "That is meant for the king and queen to hear first, good sir. We first arrived in Castiel, then Yahaira, and now we are here for the same reason. But our orders are to speak to the leaders of each nation directly."

The guard took a few steps toward them. "And I'm telling you that if you want an audience with King Renan, then you'll have to state your business to me. Your choice, friend. He's a rather busy man, and as you're clearly all foreigners, you can't be trusted to just stroll into Yago and make requests. So what'll it be?"

He wanted to shake his head in dissatisfaction, but it wouldn't serve them well to piss off the first people they met in Yago. "Very well. Jahmash plans to attack Ashur in the coming months and is recruiting armies from the nations beyond Ashur. We are here to formally request a portion of the Brogani army in exchange for a portion of Ashur that King Renan will be able to claim on behalf of Brogan." The guard's eyes opened wide. Bo'az knew there was no way he could have expected that to be their business. "Now you understand why we prefer not to state our business to anyone and everyone. I mean no offense, but I'm simply following orders."

"This is a serious request? Not some stupid ruse? You're really here to arrange a deal with our king on behalf of Jahmash? *The* Jahmash?"

Bo'az stopped himself from rolling his eyes. "Hansi."

Hansi dismounted, then drew his sword and threw it on the ground next to his horse. He walked to the sentry with his arms spread out and stopped when he was about ten feet away from the man. "You see this black line intersecting my left eye?" He pointed to his face and the guard nodded. "It means I am a Marked Descendant of Darian, and the Orijin's Grace is manifested in me. It means that I, specifically, can create illusions of many sorts, to deceive those around me." As Hansi spoke, the scenery around them all transformed into an ocean, with only Bo'az and the others around him standing on the sandy shore. He felt a sudden surge of panic but remembered that it wasn't real. The sentries, however, all screamed as if they were about to fall in the water. Hansi made the facade disappear within seconds, but the guards took several moments to regain their bearings and realize that they were safe.

The guard who had spoken to them had fallen over in trying to regain his balance and fell over two more times while scrambling to get to his feet. Finally accepting defeat, he sat on the ground and faced them. "Please don't do that again; we believe you! We believe you!"

The guard next to him finally spoke up, though he was standing. "Whatever weapons you have will need to be left with us. I understand you may have reservations about being unarmed, but you will be safe within our gates. No one in Yago carries weapons, except for soldiers. Besides, it looks like you don't need swords anyway."

Bo'az commanded his horse to walk, and they all proceeded toward the gates. "Quite astute. But we don't mind leaving them here. As I said, we are here to discuss a deal with your king and nothing more. We intend and expect no violence. However, we have had a rather difficult and stressful journey. We could all do with some tender care."

Some of the other guards descended from the bridge to help collect their weapons, and the second guard continued, "That is a good plan. King Renan prefers to turn in early, so it is too late to see him anyway. One of us will escort you into the city to show you where you can stay, and where you will be cared for. We shall also arrange for two soldiers to summon you in the morning, say two hours past sunrise, to meet with King Renan. I cannot guarantee that he will be free at that time, but he will be made aware of your presence and business."

Bo'az nodded as he rode past, "These arrangements sound ideal. We appreciate your generosity and hospitality."

The guard laughed, "You didn't leave us much choice, even if we weren't going to let you in. Whatever strange magic you have in Ashur, it looks like Jahmash will have his hands full if there are others like you there. I cannot pretend to know the will of King Renan, but I hope for your sake that he agrees to your terms. And if he does, I hope to the Orijin that I'm not one of the soldiers chosen to go there. I'm perfectly happy sitting at this gate."

After they all walked through the gate, the guard untied his horse from the inside wall and led them into the city. They passed several buildings and homes, though the design and architecture of Yago was vastly different from Hamil Alsamaea.

Yago featured many columns and arches, as well as bold colors such as bright yellows and oranges. He appreciated the vibrance of the city, as it brought a certain warmth that lifted his mood. He caught up to Aurkene and slightly leaned toward her, "Did you know the city looked like this?"

She tilted her head slightly, "People talk of its beauty quite often, but I have never seen it for myself. Words don't do it justice, though. Yago is absolutely breathtaking! It makes me so happy just to look around and take it all in."

They continued through the city until the guard looked back and instructed them to all dismount. He did the same and tethered his horse to a rail next to a large stone staircase, then waved them to follow and started up the stairs. "You would not have been able to see it because of all the buildings, but we are renowned for what you will see at the top of these stairs. I know it is a long climb, but I have lived here my whole life and it is worth it every single time." He waved for Bo'az and the others to continue on while he let them pass. "I don't want to be in your way once you reach the top."

Intrigue peaked in Bo'az as he climbed the reddish-brown steps. For a few moments, he couldn't even see the horizon, but after another dozen steps, he saw something in the sky, off in the distance. *What is that? There's no way a statue could be that tall. What could it be?* He continued to ascend and the object started to take shape. It was indeed a statue, but all he could see was the head of it, made of what seemed to be greyish-white stone. A sculpted crown sat atop the head as well. Bo'az quickened his pace, eager to see more. As he ascended the staircase, the neck, shoulders, and torso all became visible. The statue was clearly that of a king, with his right arm outstretched and grasping a scepter, while his left arm hung at his side. He was adorned in flowing robes and looked out at the sea. Once Bo'az reached the top, he realized there was a second enormous statue in the distance, not far behind the first one. The second also bore a crown, but his left arm was outstretched and holding a sword with the blade pointing downward into the ground. "You were right, that is more than worth the long climb. Who are they? And who made them?"

"I told you! They are former kings of Brogan from long ago, Ademir and Damaro. You may not know it, but this region of Brogan existed before Darian drowned the world. Yago has existed for thousands of years. The statues themselves are centuries old. It took sculptors and builders hundreds of years to complete the two statues, as they were originally part of the mountain range out there."

"You said this region predates the drowning of the world? What was different before?" Hansi asked from behind them.

"The southern cities, the ones you likely traveled through to get here, there was no coastline there before the drowning. Some say there *was* a river there, but definitely not to the degree it is now. The islands south of the mainland were also not islands. It is believed that there are whole cities that were drowned in the process, though I suppose we will never know. You said that Jahmash is returning. To what end, if you don't mind me asking?" The guard started walking as they all reached the top of the steps.

Bo'az shrugged, "Get his revenge on Darian, according to him. He said that Ashur is still ripe with Darian's descendants, and he plans to wipe them all out."

"And then what? Hand over Ashur to all of the nations who agree to help him?"

He smirked, "That is for us to discuss with your king, with all due respect."

"Understood. Well, the palace is not far, but as I said, your business will have to wait until tomorrow. There are plenty of inns to stay at, and some of them have amenities such as massages, steam rooms, and medicinal baths. As far as entertainment, the fighting arena would be a thrilling option, but they bring the creatures back to their dens for proper feeding."

Bo'az looked curiously at the back of the man's head as they walked on, "Wait, say that one more time. Creatures? Proper feeding?"

The guard turned and glanced at Bo'az, "Yes. For the fighting arena. They are generally hungry afterwards, even if they win. You know?" He paused for a moment, "Oh, you *don't* know. Do you not have fighting pits with violent creatures in Ashur?"

Bo'az's eyes went wide. He thought about answering, but his shoulders sagged with embarrassment at the thought of having to admit that he'd barely stepped foot in Ashur. Hansi stepped ahead to respond, and Bo'az breathed a sigh of relief. He watched as Hansi saved him. "Actually, we *do* have fighting pits, but I don't believe Bo'az has ever been all the way to Sundari. It's on the other side of Ashur from where he lived. Our pits are entertaining, though. Most of the creatures they bring in are from the mountains of Shivaana, as well as the deserts to the west of it. Giant snakes and vrschiika, I think they're called. Giant things with claws the size of a man and poisonous tails. You can win a lot of money betting against the vrschiika, as they rarely lose. Haven't seen another creature be able to consistently defeat one."

The guard gazed at him for a moment, "In your fighting pits, the creatures fight against *each other*?"

Hansi shrugged, "What other way is there?"

"Ah. Well, actually, in Brogan the creatures fight men." He looked around at all of them, as if surprised he had to point that out. "Our criminals. They are given the choice of death or fighting in the arena. If they manage to win, then they win their freedom. It doesn't happen very often, but I guess it happens often enough that they are still willing to take the chance."

Bo'az almost choked, "You have *people* fighting in there? Do they get weapons? Armor?"

"Of course they do!" The guard smiled, "You think we're barbarians or something? Of course they're given a fighting chance! They get their choice of weapon and armor. Unfortunately, most of the creatures can withstand whatever weapons the fighters choose. And some have claws or talons that can rip through armor. Or breathe certain things that armor can't protect against. Remember, it's criminals that get put in there. Murderers. Rapists, Thieves. Not too many have ever survived, but even then, many survive having lost an arm or leg, or with severe burns or injuries. There are only a handful who have ever been completely successful. They tend to learn their lessons after that, and don't bother anyone again."

They continued walking down a wide street, which was lined with the bustle of vendors and customers. Hansi mused, "I think I would just take death. At least I know what's coming. Seems like too much trouble to fight for my life, especially against those odds."

The guard nodded, "Many of them do choose death. Can't say I disagree. Those creatures are terrifying. We're lucky that most of them don't venture near the cities on their own. They all tend to stay deep in the forests or in the mountains. Anyway, if you're interested, I highly suggest partaking in the spectacle of it all tomorrow. It's worth your while, and you may even make some decent winnings. Obviously, the biggest payout comes from betting on the fighter, but you can also bet on how they die or how fast they'll die. There are all sorts of fun little bets you can make." They reached an intersection and the guard stopped. "As promised, the road up ahead has an inn that offers the amenities you desire. There are two more if you make a right, and then another one to the left. I honestly doubt that you would be disappointed with any of them. Whichever you choose, I'll have two guards arrive in the morning to escort you to the palace."

Bo'az nodded, "Thank you. We'll explore the options before making a final decision. I'm sure they'll all be great, though. By the way, you never told us your name, friend. Might we have the pleasure of knowing it?"

"Of course! I am Thalles. Most of the others just call me Tally. But either one is fine. I'm glad I got the pleasure of escorting you. It's rare that we get the opportunity to show newcomers around. If I don't see you again, I hope you enjoy your stay in Yago and Brogan, and I hope that your meeting with King Renan goes well. All the best, my friends." Thalles bowed his head and put his palm to his chest, then turned back and walked away from them.

Hansi looked at Bo'az, then at the others. "Awfully friendly. You think we can trust him?"

Bo'az took a deep breath, "They could have shot us all at the gate, and didn't. So that has to be something."

"They wouldn't have actually shot us. Especially with me and Aurkene here," Suriiya added. "They knew instantly that I'm Yahairan. It would start a war for them to kill a Yahairan for no reason. Still, you're right Hansi. While they were kind, we should be on our guard."

***

They followed the guard up the palace steps. The building was a marvel in its own right, different from the bright color tones of most of the other buildings and houses. Bo'az noticed that it was built mostly of stone and marble, made up of white, grey, and cream hues. Despite the contrast from the other buildings, it was simple and magnificent, especially with the colossal statues of the two kings in the backdrop. Now that they were in the higher level of the city, the two statues were visible on the western horizon, even with other buildings in their line of vision.

The two guards had arrived at their inn at the promised time, though Bo'az wasn't sure whether he was happy or not that Thalles hadn't returned. He wanted to trust the man, especially given Thalles's candid personality and genuine friendliness, but blind trust based on friendliness was a mark of naivete and he wouldn't let him fall into that trap anymore. It had caused such a mess with Linas and Slade, and with Yasaman, all of which had led to this point. Being so stupid had cost him the ability to be with Baltaszar instead of becoming Jahmash's emissary. *I would never have met Aurkene and Suriiya, though.* He considered the thought for a moment. *Then again, who might I have met in Ashur instead? There have to be plenty of women there that I'm sure would have had a romantic interest in me.*

He shook off the thought to avoid anyone noticing any mental distance he might've been displaying. They walked through the open doors and into the palace. Most of the soldiers they passed nodded to their escorts and eyed them over as they walked by, though no one actually said anything to them. The long corridor opened to a large open room, with two large, white thrones on the other side of it. A man and woman occupied each seat, and their attention was directed toward an older man in tattered clothes. Bo'az couldn't hear the conversation, as the man spoke in a hushed tone and looked around the room before continuing. Whatever the king had told the man seemed to satisfy him, as he bowed his head and put his right hand to his chest, just as Thalles had done to them the day before. The king and queen reciprocated the gesture and the man thanked them before turning and leaving the room.

Once the man was gone, the king turned his attention to Bo'az and his company. As they walked closer to the thrones, Bo'az realized how young the king and queen were. King Renan was a stocky man with a full, thick beard, but he bore a young face that the beard couldn't hide. Bo'az estimated that the man wasn't much older than him.

Younger than I expected. I wonder if that's standard for kings. Then again, I wonder what the King of Ashur is like. The guards stopped a few feet away from the king and queen, then addressed them. "Good morning Your Highnesses. We present to you Bo'az Kontez of Ashur and his companions. They arrived at our gates just before sunset yesterday and have come seeking an audience with you. Bo'az informed our porters that he is here on behalf of the Harbinger, Jahmash. We waited until now to deliver them to you, so that their presence would not interfere with the receiving of grievances and requests."

King Renan and Queen Alandra both stood up and smiled at Bo'az and the others. The king addressed them first, "Greetings, guests. I am Renan Dantas, King of Brogan. You are here on behalf of Jahmash, but what exactly is your business?"

The king's accent struck Bo'az as curious, but only because it was stronger than that of the guards' or others they'd met since arriving. He didn't bother to ask about it, though. *Better to stick to business. Now isn't the time for trivial things.* "It is a pleasure to meet you King Renan and Queen Alandra. I am Bo'az Kontez of Ashur. My companions, Aric Tauren and Hansi Huu, also from Ashur, and I have come on behalf of Jahmash, Harbinger of the Orijin, to request the help of the Brogani army. Jahmash seeks justice from the people of Ashur, who chose to honor the charlatan, Darian, instead of him. He seeks revenge against the descendants of Darian, the false Harbinger who led him on a chase for days, then cowardly trapped Jahmash on an island to live for millennia in solitude, instead of just mercifully killing him. On his behalf, we respectfully request soldiers to aid in his attack on Ashur. In return, Brogan would be given a claim to parts of Ashur to expand its dominion."

The king's eyes narrowed for a moment, as if considering something, then widened again. "I see. As you likely understand, I have some questions about this proposition."

"I would certainly hope so, Your Highness. Only a foolish leader would make such a decision without a clear understanding."

Renan nodded in approval. *Good, he takes to flattery.* "You come from Ashur, but support its destruction? Why?"

Here we go again. "I have barely stepped foot onto the mainland of Ashur. I was raised in a mountain town, hidden away from Ashur, because of its dangers. It is a wild place, ruled by a king who hunts and kills his own people. Many are not safe there and live in fear. I am not saying that everyone in Ashur is evil, but those who would fight against Jahmash and his armies are certainly misguided and disgusting. They must be extinguished."

"I see. Exactly how many soldiers is Jahmash requesting?"

"Half your army, if you can afford it. Otherwise, he will accept what you are willing to offer. Within reason."

"Half of my army would leave us exposed and vulnerable. Anyone could come here and invade us with little resistance. Why would I agree to such a thing?"

"Castiel and Yahaira have already agreed to help. Their ranks will be diminished as well. Aside from them, what other nations would be able to sneak up on you without you having days to prepare?" The mention of Castiel and Yahaira had perked up the king's eyebrows the slightest bit. If Bo'az hadn't been looking him in the eyes, he wouldn't have noticed it. "Furthermore, we obviously came here from Yahaira, and they are facing a terrifying reality. Both of their volcanoes are on the verge of eruption. When that happens, I imagine that the smoke these eruptions create will affect your people here in Brogan. It is rather clear that the wind is constantly moving in this direction. By sending hundreds of soldiers, at the very least, you will create more space for your people to flee the affected areas."

The king waited a moment to respond, "I care nothing of volcanoes. As immense as Infernua is, it poses no threat to Brogan. However, I do not necessarily like how I would look if Castiel and Yahaira send their armies and I do not. I will think on your offer. How much time are you providing me to make a decision? And how amenable is Jahmash to compromising on his terms?"

"We can stand to wait a few days, if you need it. And as long as your requests are reasonable, there is a chance that Jahmash will be open to them."

"Good. We know nothing of Ashur and have never dealt with anyone there. It is not a decision to take lightly. How long was your voyage?"

Bo'az looked at Hansi and Aric and shrugged, "Somewhere around six months or so."

"Right. So my soldiers would have to be willing to stay there if I approved of this."

"They would, but that is why it is part of the offer. You would then have dominion over part of Ashur."

"Over a piece of land that is so far away it could be ripped from us by the time I sailed there to see it for myself."

"If land is an issue, then perhaps there is something else that would make for an agreeable proposition?"

"I shall think upon a suitable offer for what you ask of us. It will involve a large amount of gold and silver, though."

Bo'az nodded, "That can be arranged, though we do not have a quarry of coins that we brought with us. I would have to talk to Jahmash about how soon that could be sent, and how much would be fair to send up front."

"I'm having some trouble understanding the situation, Bo'az Kontez. For whatever we agree upon, you will then have to sail back to Jahmash, discuss those terms with him, then sail back here with your offering. It would then be a whole year from now that our agreement would be finalized. When does Jahmash plan to attack Ashur? Because after you return, it would then take another six months for my soldiers to arrive on its shores. That is a *long* time for such a commitment, Bo'az."

Bo'az wanted to laugh at the man's assumption but knew better. "It will take no time at all. There is a longer explanation, but to put it shortly, Jahmash is in my head. In all three of our heads. He knows our thoughts and can communicate with us on command. As soon as you have stated your terms to me, I will be able to relay it to Jahmash and let you know his response. Once an amount is agreed upon, he will send another ship out here to deliver it to you, which will be about the time that you will send out your armies to Ashur."

"That is… interesting. And you accept such treatment? What does he do with such power? How do you go through your day, knowing that he knows every little thing that you think?"

"It doesn't work like that," Bo'az wished he could sit down. "He is connected, but he is not always present. At first, he was much stricter and wanted to make sure he could trust us, of course. But once we earned his trust, he gave us much more freedom."

"So he is not there right now? As an audience to our conversation?"

"No. He is not. After our agreement with Castiel, he knew we wouldn't betray him. We know our mission and we take it seriously."

King Renan smiled, "So seriously that you have even inherited Casteyan and Yahairan companions. Very well, then. Where are you and your company staying while you are here? I will spend the day thinking about a suitable offer, and I will have these same two guards come to you at this time tomorrow morning with what I have decided."

"Very well, we can wait until then. We are staying at 'O Lobo Pousada', I believe it's called?"

"Ah, yes. *Lobo* is Brogani for 'wolf', our nation's signet. That is one of our best inns. I hope you are enjoying it there. And please take in the city while you are here. I truly hope you do not wait around inside until tomorrow morning. Please enjoy the city and know that you are distinguished guests. I will have one of my King's Guard escort you back and stay with you. None of you are to pay for anything while you are here. There is a lot of history in Yago and we are deeply proud of it. Please take the time to walk around and talk to people while you are here. Try all of the food and the various wines we have to offer. I promise that you will not be disappointed."

Bo'az glanced around at the others, hoping that their faces might give away their true feelings. None of them, however, showed any distrust in response to King Renan's words. They all seemed genuinely accepting of his offer and kindness. "Thank you for your generosity, Your Highness. I would protest, but nothing good could come from arguing with a hospitable king."

"That is smart of you. I have one last question before you all depart. I would imagine every culture has tattoos or symbols that are meaningful to them, and I am curious about the tattoos on the faces of you two." He nodded to Hansi and Aric.

Aric responded first, "My culture celebrates them and sees them as a sign of strength. Even more if you have them on your head or face."

"Mine is not actually a tattoo. There are those of us who descend from Darian, who have manifested the Orijin's grace in the form of magical abilities," Hansi added. "Aric has this same line on his face, except it is partially hidden by his tattoos."

King Renan raised his eyebrows. "I see. Magic, then? I do not mean to offend you, but I do not concern myself with such things. There is always a rational explanation for anything that people say is magical. I am more concerned with real things to have time to worry about it. That is just a personal ideology, though. I am sure your magic has served you well so far."

Hansi countered, which made Bo'az uneasy. "It is my magic that convinced your guards that our mission is real and set their minds to let us in. I would gladly show you what I can do if you'd like."

The king put his hand up, palm open. "That will not be necessary. I trust that your magic is effective, but I am not looking to argue. In fact, I apologize if I've offended any of you. I was simply stating my own tastes and perhaps could have worded things better. But please, go and enjoy yourselves. You have a whole day to take in Yago and you'll likely need it to see and do everything."

***

Bo'az lay in bed and kept his eyes closed. He had been awake for some time but was too tired to move. They had spent the previous day walking around Yago with King Renan's personal guard as their escort. He had taken them to several eateries where they'd overindulged in various delicacies. They'd tried everything from grilled meats, fish stew, soup with various vegetables and spiced sausage, clams in an amazing wine sauce, and a rice and duck dish which was the only thing he could have done without. Everything came with a side of something called "bacalao", which was a diced up salted fish that was fried crispy, and every place they went to had a version of it. After they walked off the drowsiness and fullness of their meals, their escort brought them to a baker who gave them small custard tarts in miniature pie crusts. The sugar on top of the custard was slightly burnt, adding to the flavor. If he remembered correctly, they were called "natas", and they were by far his favorite thing that he'd eaten that day.

After they'd taken in most of the city, the guard had recommended they go take in the fighting arena, which was known as "O Praca". The arena had originally started with criminals fighting bulls, but the guard explained that over time, they were getting better and better at killing the bulls. One of the old kings had ordered hunting parties to capture the most dangerous beasts they could find to keep in the arena and use at random for the fights and had used the most vicious and feral beasts they could find ever since.

Aurkene and Suriiya had shown no interest in going to O Praca, so they went off on their own while the guard brought Bo'az, Hansi, and Aric to watch a fight. The one they watched was over rather quickly, as it pitted a rather short and obese man against a giant bear they called an "Ursa", that was three times as tall as the man and bore plates of armor on its back. Bo'az had asked the guard about it and was told that there was a rare breed that lived in the northern end of the forest. The bear was faster than it looked and stalked the man easily, especially after he lost his sword trying to swipe at it. Bo'az was somewhat glad that Aurkene and Suriiya hadn't come, as the fight ended in a lot of blood.

He eventually returned to his room at the inn where Aurkene and Suriiya were waiting for him. They'd already started enjoying one another before he got there, so he wasted no time getting into bed. They spent hours pleasuring one another until all three of them fell asleep from sheer exhaustion.

He felt sore in places he didn't know existed, and his stomach was practically yelling at him to be fed.

"Mmmm…someone's hungry."

He opened his eyes and saw Aurkene's face a few inches away from his. Not long ago, such a thing would have startled him, but instead he inched closer to her and kissed her. "Can you blame me? Last night was as much fun as it was exhausting. I have muscles aching in places I didn't know I had muscles."

A hand smacked his buttocks and then wrapped around his torso, "Speaking of muscles." Suriiya sidled closer to him from the other side and kissed the back of his neck. "You definitely worked both of us over thoroughly. I think this is the most tired I've been in a long time."

Bo'az sat up at a realization, "The king's guards will likely be here soon. We should request water for a bath so that we can be ready in time."

Aurkene sighed audibly and sat up at the side of the bed as well. He took in her curvy frame and curly hair that fell to the middle of her back. He swiveled himself to be behind her, then sat behind her so that his legs were outside of hers. She leaned back against his chest, and he wrapped his arms around her. She turned her head and whispered into Bo'az's ear, "Can't we just stay here forever? We can let Aric and Hansi go with the guards to receive the news."

Behind him, Suriiya did what he'd done to Aurkene and wrapped her arms around both of them. "It's a lovely idea, but we all know that King Renan, while rather generous, is not someone to be trifled with. He clearly does not want to be perceived as weak, and failing to see him in person would definitely insult him. Bo'az is right; we should start getting ready to be summoned. That being said, perhaps we *could* continue our fun in the bath." A knock sounded on the other side of the door. "Ah. Never mind *that* idea."

Bo'az took the initiative to get up and quickly found his clothes, then did the awkward dance of putting them on quickly. "Just a moment!" He turned to the two of them and raised his eyebrows, "You two want to cover yourselves before I answer the door? Or are you brazen enough to stay like that?" Aurkene and Suriiya both smiled at him slyly, as if they were sharing the same mind. "For the love of Orijin, I wasn't asking to give you a choice. I was telling you both to get dressed. Or at least get back under the covers!"

They relented and drew the blankets over themselves as they giggled. "Happy now?"

"Very. Thank you." He opened the door to see a guard standing a few feet away from it, then stepped out of the room and closed the door behind him.

"Good morning, Master Bo'az. King Renan sent me to call upon you. He has come to a decision and will be ready to receive you and your companions in another hour. He said that he did not want to rush you in the morning or force you out of bed. Please take the time to enjoy your breakfast and get yourselves ready. I will be waiting with another guard outside to bring you to the palace when you are ready." He nodded to Bo'az then turned and walked away.

Over the next hour, they managed to bathe and eat, though the experience wasn't as relaxing as they'd wanted. The bath proved to be more methodical than anything, as they wanted to avoid making the king wait too long. He'd come to a decision, and Bo'az especially wanted to find out what that decision was. They rushed through a simple breakfast of fresh rolls and sausage, then dressed just as quickly and summoned Aric and Hansi after leaving their quarters.

To Bo'az's surprise, as well as the others, the two guards stood in front of a large carriage tethered to two horses just outside the inn. Bo'az walked up to the guard that he'd spoken to inside, "What is this for? We can just walk there, no?"

The guard smiled at him as he opened one of the carriage doors and beckoned for them to get in. "The king has a special surprise for you all. You'll see."

Bo'az looked at him curiously and then at the others. The sound of it seemed innocuous, but it was a strange change in plans, and even more strange for them to ride in a carriage. He took a deep breath and stepped into the carriage as the others followed. *Not like we can do anything about it now. Let's just see where this goes.* Once they were all in, the guards closed the doors and stepped up to the front seat where they commanded the horses to trot.

"I don't like this," Hansi spoke first. "Something seems off." Aurkene and Suriiya nodded, though Aric still seemed distracted and gazed out the window.

Bo'az shrugged, "I agree. But the king didn't give us any reason to be alarmed yesterday. Suriiya, do you have any ideas about what could be going on? Is this something we should be worried about?"

She pressed her lips together then shook her head. "He has always been a rather straightforward man; even jokes are a rarity for him. I'm not sure what this is. Something like this is either very good news or very bad. Either he has something grand planned for us, or he plans to kill us. I doubt it would be anything in between, given the secrecy of all this."

He closed his eyes and tried to clear his mind, hoping that his gut might direct his thoughts one way or another. He decided to try to be positive for the others. *Except Aric. What the hell is his problem?* "Look, it's not bad until we know for sure that it's bad. So far, we've enjoyed everything about this place and maybe this is just a final piece of generosity that King Renan is providing us before it's time for us to go." To his surprise, no one spoke up. He let them process their own thoughts and they all sat in silence for several minutes until Bo'az noticed that they were nearing a large structure as he looked out the window. "Is that…is that O Praca? That's the surprise? Taking in a fight? Maybe he just wants us to sit with him during the match."

Bo'az assumed that the carriage would stop just before they reached the entrance, but they continued on through a corridor as the arena guards parted for them. *What the hell is going on?*

Aurkene grasped his hand, "This is strange. I don't like this, Bo. Something feels very wrong."

To his surprise, Aric finally spoke up. "They're bringing us to the arena floor. They're going to make us fight something."

"And how the hell would you know that?" Bo'az wasn't sure if he was more annoyed that Aric's words made sense, or that those were the first words he'd spoken in over a day. "What if King Renan is on the other side of the corridor and is waiting to escort us to his own royal area?"

"Because that doesn't make sense, Bo'az. We were just here yesterday. You know as well as I do that the layout doesn't make sense for that. Our escort yesterday showed us where the king sits, and it wasn't by this entrance. It was all the way on the other side. I am telling you all, be alert and be ready to fight. I don't know what we did wrong, but this is either a test or a trap."

Bo'az couldn't help himself, "You haven't spoken in two days and this is what you finally have to say? That we're all going to get killed?"

Aric shook his head, "No, I said we're going to have to fight something. Remember that Hansi and I actually have combat training, and even you have a little. We can find a way to defeat whatever they throw at us."

As they came through the other end of the corridor, they were surrounded by sunlight and the roar of the crowd. The carriage came to a halt and the guards opened the doors for them to exit. Bo'az immediately looked back at the corridor, but two other guards were already closing the gates from the other side and locking them. "Thank you for coming, Bo'az and company!" A few paces beyond the other end of the carriage stood King Renan. "As my guard informed you, I have come to a decision. I would like to help you and Jahmash. However, if I must make a sacrifice, then so must you. Brogan will lose many soldiers if we send them to Ashur, and while I want gold and silver in return, I also want to know that you are willing to die for a cause that you are asking my people to die for. So the five of you will face one of our infamous beasts. If any of you survive, then Brogan will help. If you all die, then there is no deal. Is Jahmash in your head right now?"

Bo'az shook his head, "No."

"Then you will have to accept these terms on his behalf. I am going to go to my seat now, and eagerly watch how this all unfolds. I wish you all the best of luck." The king turned and stepped into the carriage that they'd just departed. "I encourage you to use any weapons that we have available. They have been placed at the other side of the arena. And feel free to use the magic you spoke of yesterday. I am sure it will be quite helpful. You'd better hurry to get those weapons, " As he finished speaking, the carriage pulled away to the other side of the arena.

They all looked at one another and around the arena. There were no open doorways to escape, and the walls that separated it from the seats were too high to climb. *There's no escaping this.* He felt his chest begin to tighten and heave, and took several deep breaths to try and calm down. *Now's not the time to panic. Focus.* "Aric, Hansi, since you two have the combat training, what do we do?"

Hansi started to run toward the other end of the arena, "First we get weapons!" They all followed him to the other end and evaluated the inventory of weapons and armor. On the ground at the base of the wall, just in front of the king's area, was a selection of swords, daggers, and spears, as well as a few shields and helmets. "Find a helmet that fits. Even if it doesn't fit perfectly, just take it. Anyone wearing a belt, grab a dagger and tuck it in there. We don't have scabbards, so you'll all have to hold your swords. Also test the shields to see if you can carry one. Remember that you'll have to hold it the whole time, so don't take one if you think it will tire you out."

Bo'az let Aurkene and Suriiya test out the swords and shields first, just in case they preferred the lighter swords. Both of them made their selections and ended up foregoing shields. He wondered what they would end up facing, and hoped that whatever it was, it couldn't do anything like breathe fire or anything of the sort. Once they were all armed, Aric commanded them. "To the center. There are a lot of potential doorways for something to come out of. We have to be ready for this thing to come from anywhere." They did as he said and moved to the center of the arena, keeping their backs to one another in a circle.

Bo'az looked around and noticed a full arena. *Did they all know this would happen, or were all these people going to be here anyway?* To his surprise, the king arose and addressed the crowd. "Citizens of Yago, we have a special treat for you today! Our fighters come from other lands; some as far away as the mythical Ashur! They have requested Brogan's help in their war, and so we demand that they risk their own lives on our soil! We also have a surprise! The beast they will be fighting is a rare treat, and we have *two* of them! Our best hunters and trackers managed to capture two lobisom not that long ago, and now we have them here for your entertainment!"

As the crowd reacted in excitement, Bo'az turned to the others. "Anyone happen to know what 'lobisom' are?"

Suriiya bit her lip and nodded, "They are a myth. At least in Yahaira. The stories say they originated from Brogan, but nobody ever reported seeing one. It was always someone who *knew* someone who saw one."

Bo'az grew impatient, "Yes, but what *are* they?"

"Giant wolves. That walk around like men and are likely just as intelligent. They are said to be very fast and calculating."

The king continued to address the crowd, but Bo'az and the others focused on coming up with a strategy. Aric asked, "Are there any stories about their weaknesses or fears? Anything about them that we can use to our advantage?"

Suriiya shrugged, "It is said that silver can kill them by touch, but that won't help us now. I have also heard stories that they are vulnerable near their heads and hearts. Perhaps if we target those areas, we may have success."

They heard the king must have issued a command, as they shifted their attention to an opening gate to the left of the king's area. After another moment, an enormous metal cage was rolled out by a horse-drawn wagon. Two towering wolf-looking creatures stood inside, snarling and brooding. The wagon driver walked to the cage and detached it from the wagon, then unlocked the door to the cage. As soon as he turned the key, the driver ran back to his wagon and whipped his reins for the horses to rush back into the corridor.

"Light of Orijin, those things are gigantic. And hideous. What are the chances they decide to stay in the cage?" Just as Bo'az posed the question, one of the lobisom pushed the cage door open and walked out while the other followed. Their black fur was darker than the night sky, though their bright greenish-yellow eyes reminded him of stars that lit up that same sky. Once both were out of the cage, they eyed Bo'az and the others and looked them over for several moments.

"They're studying us, trying to figure out weaknesses. Also trying to determine which of us will be the easiest target and which will pose the biggest threat," Hansi said as he stared back at the creatures.

"How do you know?"

"Because they would have attacked already if they weren't. And also, that's what I'm doing to them. Everyone face them and stand side by side. Aurkene, come to my right, then Suriiya to my left. Aric you stand on her left and Bo, you go at the other end. We'll be more balanced that way. And when they get closer, we will split up so that we're on both sides of them. Aurkene and I will move to the right, and you three go left. They'll be easier to fight if we can split their attention."

They all listened to Hansi's command and got into formation. They continued to watch the lobisom and the creatures stared back as they cautiously stalked closer. The crowd made no sound, as if watching every move with breath held. One of the creatures hunched down onto all fours and stuck its long snout toward the ground. It sniffed around while still looking at them, and then the other followed suit. Bo'az assumed a ready stance as both creatures took a few steps closer. They continued to step forward, their eyes shifting with every movement that Bo'az and the others made. As they neared, they started to separate and continued to move apart until the two creatures were on both sides of them. "Damn. So much for splitting up and getting on both sides of them. They beat us to it."

"We can still do the same," Aric responded. "Quick, separate now! The three of us to the left and Hansi and Aurkene to the right. Go!" They split as Aric commanded, though Bo'az couldn't take his eyes off of the creature in front of him. The closer it got, the more he realized how terrifying it was. Its front paws were enormous and each claw was about as long as Bo'az's whole hand. *How long until it decides to attack?* He, Aric, and Suriiya had moved away enough that its back was to the others as it continued to stare them down.

"What now, Aric? Should we attack first?"

"No. Just wait." The lobisom growled at them and then sneered, as if it understood what Bo'az had said. Bo'az eyed a mouth full of long, pointy teeth and froze for a moment. *What the hell did we get ourselves into?* He felt his heart start to pound again and forced himself to take deep breaths. *Calm down. Getting scared will only make things worse right now. Have to focus.* He tightened his grip on his sword and made sure his shield was positioned properly. Suriiya did the same next to him. Just as he secured his shield, the lobisom sprang. Bo'az dashed in front of Suriiya and lifted his shield to block the giant wolf from landing on her. In the process, it came crashing down on him, with only his shield separating them. It cocked its giant paw to take a swipe, but something made it yelp and scamper away. Aric screamed, "I got it! I took off its foot!" The arena crowd collectively gasped and then started to yell. Bo'az rose to his feet and helped Suriiya up, then looked for the injured lobisom. Sure enough, the large black creature had distanced itself and was nipping at its wound. Aric walked over to him and Suriiya. "Wow, that was surprisingly easy. I sliced its foot completely off."

"You did? How did you do that so easily?" They shifted their attention to Aurkene and Hansi, who were in a stare down with their lobisom.

"I don't know and I don't care, as long as it happened." He ran over to help the other two and Bo'az and Suriiya followed. The five of them surrounded the remaining lobisom. Its demeanor didn't change; it only became more wary of everyone around it. Aric yelled to Hansi, who faced the front of the creature, "Maybe you *should* use some of that magic, Hansi! Create something that will confuse it and disorient it, then I can attack while it's confused!"

"Good idea! I'm on it!" As soon as Hansi finished speaking, he took a few steps back from the giant wolf. In a matter of seconds, the scenery around them changed to that of a clear blue sky with no other landscape in sight. Bo'az briefly panicked, just as he'd done when Hansi created the illusion for the guards at Yago's gates. He closed his eyes for a moment to regain his bearing and focused on his feet touching the ground. Screams came from the crowd that couldn't fathom what was happening. Bo'az opened his eyes once more. The lobisom had fallen to its knees and pawed at the ground, as if trying to touch the sky that had magically appeared beneath it.

As it started to test its balance, Aric ran toward it from behind and Suriiya yelled, "Cut its head off! Don't take any chances!" He nodded and then pivoted toward its side, then swung at the beast's neck with all his might. His sword struck its target, but got stuck a little more than halfway through. Aric attempted to pull his blade free, but the lobisom writhed and flailed, and swatted Aric several feet away. Though they couldn't see the actual wall, Bo'az assumed that Aric had hit the arena wall, as something stopped him from hurtling farther.

"Go check on him! I'll finish it off!" Hansi yelled at them as he engaged the frantic creature. Bo'az ran toward Aric, who lay still on the ground. Aurkene and Suriiya ran along with him, getting to Aric first, as Bo'az kept looking back to check on Hansi. He turned to look just in time to see Hansi swing at the lobisom's neck from the other side that Aric had. The stroke of his sword sliced the beast's neck clean off, and sent Aric's sword clanging to the ground. As the crowd screamed even louder, Bo'az fixed his attention on Aric, who was getting to his feet with the help of Aurkene and Suriiya.

Bo'az hurried over to help Aric as well. He was about to put Aric's arm over his shoulder to give Suriiya a break, but Aric's eyes widened at something, and he took off running. Bo'az looked at where Aric was going and saw the other lobisom running toward Hansi. Bo'az blinked several times, "I thought he cut its foot off. How is it running like that? Look at it! It's running on all of its legs! It's got four feet!"

Suriiya stumbled over her words, "I-I don't know. I didn't know it could do that. I saw it scamper away! I swear, I saw its foot. It had to have grown another one!"

"Hansi! Aric! Go for the head again!" Bo'az yelled toward the other two, as it was clear that the other lobisom was running at Hansi, unfazed by the illusion he'd cast. Aric was still farther away from Hansi than the lobisom and was trying desperately to gain ground. Hansi, still looking at the dead lobisom, leaned down to pick up Aric's sword. They all started to yell at Hansi, desperate to get his attention, as the lobisom was frighteningly close and despite Aric's dire attempts, he was actually losing ground in comparison to the beast.

Just before Hansi picked up the sword, he realized what was happening and focused his attention on the oncoming attack. Hansi raised his sword just as the lobisom leapt at him. He slashed at the creature's front paw and managed to slice it clean off. But the momentum of the strike caused both man and creature to fall together. The lobisom landed on top of Hansi's chest, with his shield between their bodies. Hansi raised his hand and only then realized it was swordless. The lobisom shifted its focus from the missing paw to Hansi's hand and snapped at it. It ripped Hansi's hand clean off with one bite, and his screams started the same time as the illusion of sky ended.

The lobisom bit at Hansi's helmet and after only a moment, was able to use its teeth to pull it off of Hansi's head. "Nooooo!!! Ahhhh!!! Please!!!" His screams were cut short as the beast opened its jaws wide and crunched down. Bo'az eyed Aric finally retrieving his sword just as Hansi's body stopped twitching. He swung at the creature's neck as it turned to look at him and separated its head from its body. The blood sprayed everywhere and painted Aric's face and chest. Bo'az barely heard the crowd's uproar as he ran to Aric. *Hansi. No! No no no no no! How? We were so close to getting out of here.* He fell to his knees as he reached Aric. He wanted to look at Hansi's body, but couldn't bear to see his friend like that. Bo'az punched the ground several times until he felt the skin on each knuckle break.

"My friends! I congratulate you on this victory! I know it is not the outcome you wanted, but let's be honest. It had to have crossed your minds that all of you would die. So given the worst possibility, this should be the most bearable." King Renan stood from his seat and walked down to the wall that separated them. "I am sorry for your loss, and I hope you extend the same courtesy and respect to my soldiers who will fight for your cause in Ashur."

Bo'az heard the words, but only realized what the king was saying after a moment. He felt a slight weight release from his shoulders, "I expect that means that you agree to our terms. Perhaps we can discuss that later."

The king smiled, "Indeed. Take all the time you need to mourn and to get cleaned up. My guards will provide anything you request." His eyes shifted to something behind Bo'az and the others. "Who? Who is that? And how did he get in here?"

Bo'az turned to look behind him, curious as to what the king could have seen. He saw a man several feet away walking toward them. The man wore all black and his hair was long and rather stringy. He walked right up to them and spoke directly. "Quick, grab hold of my hands and arms. I can get you out of here. I can help get you fixed." Bo'az didn't know why, but he listened to the man's instructions. The others did the same once they saw Bo'az do so.

I remember him. But from where? Was it at Jahmash's fortress? It had to have been. He was there. Who was he, though? What was his name? "Maqdhuum?"

CHAPTER 13
MASTER JAI

From **The Book of Orijin,** **Verse Two Hundred Ninety-Two**
You were blessed with manifestations to do Our work in your realm.
We have faith that you will use them for what is good and right.

Vasher had held off asking through the whole journey down from Markos, but for some reason he felt more comfortable with Sindha having left for Itarse. They had all stayed in the city of Maramarosa before splitting up, but now it was only him, Delilah, and Krissette. There were two Kraisos with them, but they tended to travel at their own pace and weren't always within hearing of Vasher and the others.

"Del, you know I have to ask and I've waited long enough," he said finally. "What's going on with you and Lincan?"

Delilah mumbled something to Krissette, who was riding next to her. Without saying a word, Krissette fell back several paces behind them.

"First of all, do you know what a relief it is that I didn't have to worry about him being a part of our company?" She looked over at Vasher sternly.

Vasher understood why his friend was so taken by her. Even annoyed, Delilah was a beautiful woman. Now she took a deep breath. "Are you asking for him or for yourself, Vash?" She looked at him from the side of her eye without turning her head.

"Does it matter? By the time either of us sees Linc again, who knows how much time will have passed. This conversation will be a distant memory. So I suppose I'm asking for myself. He's a good man and not the type to get too broken up about how people act. But you really did something to him."

She nodded. "I guess you're right. It's going to be a while before we're all back together again. That's exactly what Garrison was getting at, back in Markos. I'm glad we had the time to enjoy ourselves. He's smart, that Garrison."

"Hey. focus! Answer the question!" Vasher rolled his eyes.

"Right, right. I'm only going to tell you because we've known each other for so long. And also because your mothers are Daughters of Tahlia so you might understand better than others. Vash, I don't really know how I feel. About everything, not just Linc. I made a decision about my life and I don't *regret* it, but I've strayed with Linc and I don't want to keep leading him on. That's my fault; I could've handled it better and what I did was absolutely unfair to Linc. One of these days I'll tell him that and give him the explanation that he's due. You know me, though, Vash. I'm too stubborn to tell people they're right."

Vasher couldn't help but laugh, "Oh don't worry, there are a lot of people like you out there. So what does this all mean? Are you committed to being a Daughter?"

She smiled as well. "Ugh. I know I chose this life for myself and, like I said, I don't regret it. The thing is, it's easier for a lot of the others because they don't necessarily have a taste for men. So there's never any temptation, even after they lay with a man to get pregnant. Me on the other hand, I like to dabble in both. And don't get me wrong, there are definitely other Daughters who like to pretend that no one knows they're bedding men in secret. It's like sport for them. The secrecy and the men. Though you can't confront them about it, or they get all offended. Light of Orijin, I'm one of them. Thinking I'm better than all the others even though I've done it, too."

Wow. She definitely needed to air this all out. Wonder if she knows I'm doing her a favor by asking in the first place. Probably not, too stubborn. "So this all leads me to wonder, why did you choose the lifestyle in the first place? It's not like getting the Mark, where you're stuck in a dire situation. No one forces anyone to become a Daughter of Tahlia."

She turned to him and raised her eyebrows, "Um, excuse me? Have you not seen the dancers in Sundari? What young girl *doesn't* want to be just like them? That in itself makes any girl want to be a daughter. We don't know about sexuality and attraction when we're so little. But since you asked, it was a few things. Definitely those damn dancers more than anything else, if we're being perfectly honest."

"Hold on, so why not just become a dancer? Were you not good enough?"

"Oh wow, Vash. You're just looking to get punched. I'll have you know that I can seduce any man with my dancing. But anyway, it had nothing to do with the dancing. It was the *Mark*. How many daughters do you see walking around with a Descendant's Mark? They didn't have a problem with me becoming a Daughter, but they didn't want the exposure of a dancer having the Mark. They thought it would bring the wrong kind of attention, especially from the Vermillion. Honestly, Vash, I don't blame them. Edmund is dead now and we're still not completely safe. There will always be people who dislike us for what we are."

He nodded in agreement, "You're right. I can imagine both of my mothers having hesitation about such a thing. I still think your bad dancing had something to do with it, but we'll save that for another time. You said there were reasons besides the dancers?"

"Oh right. Well, way back when I started to feel things about other people, I found myself only attracted to girls. I didn't care about boys at all and it wasn't forced. I genuinely only felt something toward girls. I took that as a sign that I should pursue being a Daughter, and wanting to be a dancer didn't help with that. If anything, it helped to push my decision. And then as I got older, I helped a lot with nieces and nephews. That made me realize how much I love children and want my own at some point. It just made sense, you know?"

Vasher navigated his horse around a large rock. The biggest problem with riding from Maramarosa to Sundari was that the road was narrow. Maramarosa was a smaller town and most people weren't hiring wagons to take them down to see all the spectacles of Sundari. "Yeah, I understand where you're coming from. I don't know if I could commit to something so absolute as a child. Hell, even now that would be tough. So I'm curious, and if I'm prying too much, then I apologize. And if we're being honest, Del, I haven't spent too much time around Daughters my own age. So it's nice to be able to candidly talk about these things. A lot of the older ones get so closed off."

"You're telling me. And I already know where you're going with this. Yes. He was. I had been curious for some time, but always felt so guilty about actually doing something. There were obviously a lot more boys at the House of Darian than girls, and being in the company of so many definitely piques one's curiosity."

"Speak for yourself, I never got curious about any of the boys there."

She rolled her eyes at him, "You know what I mean. Anyway, you know Linc. He's a good person and I'm not sure if you can see it as a platonic friend of his, but he can be rather charming without even trying. We worked together a lot in the infirmary, and something about working so closely with someone, especially when emotions get involved, it can lead to things. He did his part in flirting and all that, and I took the bait. Vasher, it was too tempting to just ignore. So I caved and let it happen. It's not all on him; I wanted it, too."

"I don't think there's anything wrong with it, even if you *did* already commit to being a Daughter. If you were that curious, it would have happened at some point eventually. Maybe not with Linc, but sooner or later your curiosity would have gotten the best of you. I think, generally, when we want to do something bad enough, we're going to find a way to do it and nothing will get in our way. I think it gets even worse when we've been curious about it for a long period of time."

"Are you speaking from experience?" She gave him another sideways glance.

"That's generally the best way to speak."

"Oh good; your turn to share then."

"Huh?" He furrowed his brow and looked at her.

"Boy, stop playing coy with me. You know what I'm talking about. Tell me the story of when you caved. I told you about mine; it's only fair."

"I guess. Mine isn't as spicy as yours. It's not even that interesting, to be honest."

"Try me."

He sighed, "Fine. It was a couple of years ago." He didn't have to search for the memory. It had been at the back of his mind ever since the situation had gone wrong. Vasher had never confided in anyone with it, though. He had always been afraid of what someone might say, especially his friends. "So you know about my manifestation. It's not as conventional as many of the others. Ever since I got it, I've used it only in serious situations." They reached the gates of Sundari and greeted the guards as they passed through. "I always wondered what it would feel like to use it to just get my own way with something. You know, like an argument or just to convince someone to give me what I want? But at the same time, I didn't want to stoop to that. It seemed like I would be doing something wrong. So for years that was always my code, I guess you could call it. My boundary. Don't use it for personal gain."

Delilah responded as they continued into Sundari. "Oh this should be good. I can't wait."

"Yeah yeah. Anyway, after the whole thing with Marlowe finding out that he was a target of the Anonymi, he sent me and Savaiyon on a mission to find and question Augurs about any prophecies regarding his death."

"Augurs?"

"Sorry, that's the proper name for Blind men and women. So we were tasked with assembling a team to go around Ashur to find any prophecies that might shed some light on his death. However, Savaiyon wanted me to step up and be a leader, so he gave me the responsibility of choosing who would come with us. I basically picked my friends, and he didn't have much of a problem with my reasoning, except when I insisted that Baltaszar come along. He thought Tasz was too new and unproven. Too much of a risk. I hadn't known him as long as the others, but we got along pretty quickly and I thought it would be good for him to be a part of something like that. So, I opened myself to my manifestation and persuaded Savaiyon to include Tasz. He agreed instantly. We started in Vandenar. I forget what it was, but I think there was an Augur up there that someone was familiar with so we went there first. Everything was fine until Tasz got weird on us. First he tried to fight Des at the inn we were staying at. Then he came to his senses and everything smoothed over. And we assumed he was back to normal. Then he disappeared and we got tipped off that he went north into the Never. Turns out his town was up there in the mountains and forest. Anyway, he ran into a real bad situation up there and ended up setting himself on fire."

"And then Linc and I had to put in hours of work to heal him. His skin was charred in many places," Delilah finished his story for him. "We were most surprised by that because we assumed that, since he could wield fire, he would be impervious to that. Then Linc had a thought. He wondered if there was something in Tasz that he could *fix*, almost like something he could do to make him impervious to the fire. I don't even know what he did, but he figured it out. Once he found that cure, the rest of Tasz's skin that we hadn't healed turned back to normal. It was miraculous."

"Miraculous is one way to look at it. But the whole point of my story is that if I had just listened to Savaiyon, then none of it would have happened. It got Tasz kicked out of the House of Darian. Imagine how much he could've helped when we were attacked. Fire would have been an incredible weapon *and* defense."

"Very true. But you're not listening. That allowed him to become impervious to his own fire. It helped him become stronger. Besides, he still would have been too raw with his manifestation to be much help at the House. There's a good chance he would have set himself on fire there instead of in the Never. And you know what's so incredibly ironic about that whole situation, Vash?"

Vasher looked at her, wondering what irony could possibly exist in the situation. "What's that?"

"That's about the time that everything started with me and Linc. That's when we started working closely together. So while you're beating yourself up over that decision, it also led to me caving to my own curiosities and eventually sleeping with Linc. And before you try to turn that on yourself and say it was your fault, I don't blame you for it. Like you said, if you want something badly enough, eventually you're going to find a way to get it. If it hadn't happened then, it would have happened for me another time, with someone else. And I have no regrets about what happened between me and Linc. I know I didn't handle the situation very well, but I would have been so much worse off if I hadn't done it. You stood up for your friend. You were doing something nice and even though you're saying that it was for personal gain, one could argue that you did it to be a good friend.

And I heard about what happened with Tasz, as far as why he left and what led to him burning himself. I'm sure you did as well. His twin brother slept with the girl he'd been with and got her pregnant. I don't know about you, but I don't know that I'd handle that very well either. You ask me, Vash, that girl's a real piece of work. She then had the gall to show up on Asarei's island pretending to be someone else and even tried to convince Tasz to take her back and raise the baby as his own. If I could wield fire as Tasz does, I don't know how I wouldn't be tempted to just set that girl on fire and watch her burn while enjoying some nice wine. I can't believe Asarei's wife is caring for her now, though I guess it's what's best for her. That kind of crazy shouldn't be roaming around the world. Anyway, I digress. You see my point though? None of that had anything to do with you. Tasz saw the opportunity because he was so close to home. Sooner or later, he would have gone back. You're not responsible for his decisions or actions. If anything, Tasz was being a bad friend by putting himself before the group."

"When did you become so wise?"

"Maybe I've always been this way. You just don't talk to me enough."

He paused for a moment. It would have been easy to confuse her natural playfulness with flirtation. "I can see why Linc is having such a hard time with all this. You certainly have a way about you."

"Aw, thanks Vash. You know, my sister was betrothed to someone and it didn't work out. Turned out that he had a taste for other women as well. She and I are rather alike. I could always mention your name if you're interested?" She stopped her horse and waved for Krissette to do the same. They'd reached the point of the city where they would part ways. "I'm going to see her now, so let me know. You've seen her before, and I can vouch for her character." She must have noticed the hesitation in his face, "I'm not asking you to commit your whole life to her right now, and if things don't work out, I would never hold it against you. But I think you'd be good for each other."

Vasher didn't bother to take long to make a decision. He knew that the longer he thought about it, the more likely he would be to find baseless reasons not to do it. "Go for it. It could be fun. Although I don't know how much time there will be for romance until after this whole war is over."

"Eh, don't get too ahead of yourself. Romance is one of those things that needs to be taken one step at a time. Once you get caught up with what's going to happen years down the road, you lose sight of what's happening right in front of you."

Damn. That's a lot of wisdom. "Good advice. Well let's start at step one then. I'll meet you by the dancers tomorrow morning? We can figure out our next steps then?"

"Good, I'm glad you're willing. Tomorrow morning. We'll be there just after the first dancers begin." She smiled at him with a closed mouth before turning away and commanding her horse to start walking.

***

Delilah thought about what she'd just offered Vasher and a sense of warmth came over her. It would have been easy to be magnanimous and tell herself what an amazing person she was for doing something nice for Vasher, but in truth, she was just happy to make him happy. Despite them not having spent much time together in the past couple of years, he'd always been a good friend. *Always generous, always helpful and accommodating. And Jennikah would definitely approve of him.* She thought of her sister and all the nonsense she'd been through with the man she had been set to marry. *What an asshole.* She drove the thought from her mind. Being back in Sundari was supposed to be a positive thing and she wanted to maintain that mood.

She almost forgot that Krissette was with her. Save for the girl's lighter skin tone, they might have passed for sisters as their builds and hair were similar. "I wasn't eavesdropping, but I overheard you telling Vasher about your sister and her betrothal. Did you two manage to stay in touch while you've been away from Sundari? If so, how?"

Delilah chuckled, "No, not at all. I found this all out when I was here last year. It had just happened weeks before I was last here and, as you can imagine, she was still a wreck. The man's name was Raja Rangajuli. Such a terrible name, and even worse that a man with a name like that could cause such hurt to my sister. Sometimes when I'm pissed off, I like to just say 'Rangajuli' to myself. It's like my own little curse word and it makes me laugh."

"That *is* a silly name," Krissette nodded.

Delilah stayed silent for a moment. It had become clear to her since Krissette had revealed her true intentions back on the island, that Krissette had a habit of deferring to Delilah's opinions and preferences. She tended to agree with Delilah's points of view and opinions, no matter the subject. "Krissette, we'll soon be at my sister's home and then after that, we'll be visiting the Daughters of Tahlia. I need to know that you're your own person and that you have your own wants and preferences. I'm not the best at putting things mildly or buttering things up. So I'm just going to come right out and ask: what do you want out of all this? Out of your time in Sundari?"

Krissette looked at her as they rode alongside one another. Her innocence and naivete were smeared across her face as her mouth hung open for a moment. "I...I told you a while back that, before you, I'd never met anyone else who was like me in terms of preferring girls to boys. And I had a lot of questions about how to navigate that, which you answered throughout this journey and I'm extremely grateful. I don't know. I guess the idea of a community of women who are like me is a rather intriguing one. Del, I've never fully felt like I've belonged anywhere, and that's not meant to be a slight against anyone. My parents are from two different nations with conflicting ideologies about those of us with the Mark. That's one thing. And I just happen to be a girl who bears the mark. That's another issue. Then add to it that I don't follow the same rule of attraction that most of the world follows, and it's a list of things that set me apart that's way too long. And I didn't choose any of it, Del. I'm not asking for your pity, so please don't misinterpret my meaning. It's just that for once, I'd like to feel like I belong somewhere. And I don't even know if the Daughters of Tahlia will be the right choice for me, but at least it's a viable option.

At least it's a group of people who might actually welcome me for who I am."

Definitely naive. "Look, The Daughters aren't some magical group that are going to swarm you with hugs and gifts just because you have an interest in joining their ranks. That's not how it works and I'm sorry to have to break it to you so abruptly. If you want to join our community, then you take an oath that you swear to uphold the rules and all that, and if you break those rules, you're no longer welcome. Well, depending on the severity of the case. There are quite a few Daughters who take liberties."

"Like you?"

"Shut up."

"Sorry."

"No, it's fine. Stop being so meek and innocent. That's the point I was making. The Daughters are like any other community. You'll have some women who will genuinely be willing to help you and answer any question you have. Then you'll have others who are jackasses and who won't give you the time of day, or who will try to *initiate* you by doing mean things to you. You'll have to be on your guard to figure out the difference between all those before you decide to trust anyone."

"Isn't that why I have you?"

Are you kidding me? I am not a wetnurse. There's no way I'm going to coddle you through all this. "Krissette, I don't mind helping you to a certain extent, but I didn't return to Sundari to hold your hand through everything. Remember, I was already coming here. You asked to join me. I have things I must do and people I must see. And yes, the Daughters of Tahlia are part of my agenda while being down here, but again, I have my own reasons for wanting to meet with them that have nothing to do with your needs."

Krissette shrugged, "I understand." She turned to face forward and her gaze fell to the road in front of them.

Light of Orijin, why is this happening to me? Seriously, don't I have enough going on right now without all this? She shook her head and accepted that they would ride in silence until they reached her sister's home. Delilah thought about apologizing, but she didn't really feel like it. And given her annoyance, it likely wouldn't sound genuine anyway.

They reached her sister shortly and Delilah was relieved that Vasher had kept the pack horse with him. All she and Krissette had to worry about were their own horses and packs. She knocked on Jennikah's door, hoping that her sister wasn't in the middle of one of her many naps. Although Jennikah was a well-known seamstress in the city, Delilah marveled at how she was able to complete any of her commissions with how much she slept. Sure enough, Jennikah answered the door after several moments, her eyes still blinking away the sleep and her long, thick hair a mess. As soon as she realized it was Delilah at the door, however, she was wide awake.

"Del! What are you doing here? It's so good to see you!" She dashed outside and wrapped her arms around Delilah. "I didn't think I'd see you again for a long time!"

Delilah kissed her on the cheek and then pulled away so she could walk inside. She beckoned for Krissette to follow. Jennikah closed the door behind them and invited them to sit on the floor with her. "It's not *all* happiness and fun, I should warn you. My people and I, we're starting to prepare the world for Jahmash's return. There are some things that I want to talk to the Daughters of Tahlia about. Speaking of which, I'm sorry for my rudeness. This is Krissette Luuk. She's one of the people who was part of our group once we all got together. She wanted to come and see if the Daughters would be a good fit for her."

Jennikah's eyes grew wide, "Oh. Oh, are you two..."

Delilah realized what her sister was thinking, "No. Not at all. She just realized what we have in common and thought I would be of some help in getting her down here and in front of the right people." She noticed that Krissette was looking down and her countenance bore a half-frown. Delilah took a deep breath. *Am I going to keep having to cater to her feelings?* "Krissette, don't take it personally. You know I don't feel that way about you. Just because I'm the first woman you've met who's also attracted to women, doesn't mean that we're meant to be together. Besides, you'd probably grow tired of me quickly anyway. Be patient."

Jennikah chimed in, "Del is right. She's way too stubborn and curt to be able to bear for more than a week or so. You would regret being with her any longer than that. And I know a thing or two about settling for someone. I agreed to marry the first suitor that came my way, even against the advice of our mother." Delilah's shoulders tightened at the mention of their mother. Once the Mark appeared on her face, her mother essentially disowned her. Jennikah still managed a good relationship with her, though. "I was just so taken by the idea that a wealthy, good-looking man would be interested in me. And I know what you're thinking, Krissette. 'Jennikah is so beautiful; why would she jump at the first man who showed interest?' Well, it's different when someone desires you enough to want to marry you. And somehow I let Raja Rangajuli get the best of me."

"Ranga-fucking-juli." Delilah couldn't help herself. The man's name had become her own personal curse word. "Oh, that reminds me. Have you put yourself back out there yet?"

Jennikah tilted her head and stared at her, "Back out where?"

"Oh stop. You know what I mean. I have a friend who I think would be a good fit for you. He's a Marked Descendant like me, and his mothers are also Daughters of Tahlia. His name is Vasher Jai, and he's a very loyal and good person. Lots of charisma. The only thing is that he's a few years younger than you."

Jennikah rolled her eyes, "Oh great. I've become so pathetic that you need to set me up now? And to a younger man at that?"

"Would you get over yourself? Yes you're beautiful, and somehow your hair gets longer and more stunning every time I see you. But why wouldn't you trust me with this? I know both of you well enough to know what would work for you, and I have both of your best interests in mind."

"And what happens if it doesn't work?"

"If it doesn't work then it doesn't work. It's not like he lives next door. Things wouldn't get awkward."

"You said his last name is *Jai*? So I would be 'Jennikah Jai'?"

Delilah sighed, "Now you're just being ridiculous. That's awfully forward for someone who hasn't even met him yet. And besides, that still sounds so much better than 'Jennikah Ranga-fucking-juli'."

Jennikah pursed her lips, "Yeah that's fair. Fine, you win. So what, is he waiting outside with flowers or something? Ready to rush in and sweep me off my feet?"

"No, not quite," Delilah chuckled. "We parted ways shortly after entering the city. He's meeting with his mothers to seek counsel about something. We didn't actually get as far as how to proceed with this. He only gave me permission to ask you about it. *But,* we're meeting again tomorrow morning to figure out our next steps. In general, not about you. So maybe then I can tell him that you're willing to give things a try and then we'll see where it goes."

"Fine." Delilah knew her sister's facial expressions well enough to know that she was hiding a smile behind her blushing cheeks.

"Good. Then it's settled."

"So what now? You made it clear that you have other business to attend to. What's next?"

"I need to meet with the Daughters. It's easier if I do it today rather than wait until the morning. Krissette, you're more than welcome to come with me if you want to see what they're like. Jennikah is going to make us some spiced tea to ease our aches from the long ride, and then relax for a while before we go." She smiled widely at her sister, who rolled her eyes but was already getting up.

***

Vasher stood against the wall, somewhat in protest of the floor pillows scattered across his mother's floor, but also because being so low would make him feel like a child. His mother looked at him flatly, "Why didn't you just go to Gansishoor first, and then come here once your business was over? You could have spent more time with me that way?"

He shrugged, "I have no idea who I'm looking for. Not even a name. I figured that father might have talked about some of the others during his time as a soldier. Maybe a ranking officer or someone important? Do you have anything you can give me?"

"The only name I can really remember is a man named Harshu. I don't remember his family name, but I know that he was an officer and your father saved his life one time. *However,* you are not to mention or even hint that your mother is a Daughter of Tahlia, or that you know who your father is. You'll have to find another way."

"What? Why?"

She hit her head against one of the cushions behind her. "Stop being daft, Wassa. It would be incredibly easy to connect the pieces if someone up there found out that your father had a son, or sons at that, with no mention of a marriage or a wife. He was awfully close to his fellow soldiers and I'm sure if any of them are still alive, they'll remember him *and* be offended that he started a family without telling anyone."

He shook his head, "So I'm supposed to find this man, or whoever is in charge, and somehow tell them to prepare their army to train militia and defend all of Shivaana?"

The flat stare returned, "Do you not have a whole manifestation dedicated to persuading people to do things you want them to do?"

Damnit. "I do. But I...I don't want to use it for something like that. Not for personal gain."

"How is that personal gain? It is for the best of all Ashur that you would do so. It sounds like you are being stubborn for the sake of being stubborn."

"There has to be a way to do it without tricking people. There *has* to."

"Then try your luck with just talking to them and see where it goes. It seems like a grand waste of time to go through all that and sell yourself short by not using what the Orijin blessed you with."

Am I going to have to come clean here? "It's just... once I start blurring the boundaries of what I use it for, how do I stop? How do I start justifying that I use it in certain instances but not in others? I made a huge mistake with it in regard to my friends and it had huge ramifications. I can't let that happen again."

"Wassa, if we all gave up after one mistake, there would be no progress in the world. No invention, no learning, no success. It is those of us who accept those mistakes and learn from them that put ourselves in a better position to succeed than everyone else."

He nodded, "I understand. But there's more to it than that. Like you said, what I can do is a blessing from the Orijin. But a long time ago, the Orijin also blessed someone else with the ability to bend people's will, whether they liked it or not. And..."

"And you really think that you can put yourself in the same sentence as *Jahmash*? Of all people? The very fact that you are hesitant and scared to use it in such a manner means that you will not go down that path. Keep that in mind. No one else in the history of humanity has done what he did. That is for good reason. You are comparing yourself to a being that has sworn revenge on all of humanity, and you think that using an advantage to help protect the world against that very monster will make you evil?"

Vasher closed his eyes for a moment. He wondered if everyone else's mother was as adept at making their children feel stupid. "Well, I mean, not when you put it like that. But um, maybe you'd be better off going up to Gansishoor instead of me. You're much more convincing than I am." She dismissed him with a wave of her hand. "Also, where is Farzeen? I haven't seen her in such a long time." He didn't have the best relationship with his second mother, but it still would have been nice to see her after such a long time.

"Would it kill you to call her 'Do'maa', instead of by her name? She is deserving of your respect, you know."

While 'Do'maa' was the title for second mothers in the Daughters of Tahlia culture, Vasher had rebelled against it at a young age. Part of it was due to knowing that she wasn't his birth mother. So many of his friends growing up had had one mother and one father, and it bothered him that he couldn't have the same. Over time, he'd come to terms with the reality of it, but Vasher still found himself being somewhat cold toward Farzeen. When he was young, she'd tried too hard to get him to like her, and then once she grew tired of his disrespect and rebelliousness, she stopped trying at all. He knew it wasn't her fault, but he wondered if it would do anything to try and remedy the situation at this point. "At this point, she is used to me calling her by her name. Why change things now?"

His mother's stare reflected more annoyance than playfulness, "Because you are still our child, and you still act like a child. We won't be around forever, you know. Farzeen has tried very hard to make things work between the two of you, and you have always cast her aside. Always made her feel bad for being a part of this family. Your brothers have always been nice to her and you never cared when they told you that you were being out of line. So if you must know, Farzeen is a few houses away, visiting some friends. She will be back shortly, though. Now that we don't see you regularly, the least you could do is be respectful to her."

"You're right. I'm sorry." He pushed himself from the wall and walked over to where she was sitting, then laid down on a few of the cushions. "I'll do better."

They shifted the conversation and talked about happier things, including what his brothers, Seylaan and Chetan were doing, as well as how much his father was enjoying his life on a giant ship. They continued talking and laughing for a while until the door opened and Farzeen walked in. Her eyes went wide at the sight of him. "Vasher, what are you doing here? How are you, child?"

"It's good to see you, Do'maa. How are you?" He stood and walked over to give her a hug. She hesitated at first, and then matched his embrace. While his mother was much shorter than he, Farzeen was of a similar height, which made it a bit easier to hug her.

She pulled back and looked at him, as if studying his face. "I'm doing well, Vasher, I'm doing well." Farzeen was the only one in the family who didn't call him "Wassa." If he remembered correctly, she had for a time when he was young, but then shifted away from it. *Probably around the time I made it too difficult for her to like me. Well, she's probably not going to like me after this either.*

"Come, sit with us. There's something I want to talk about with both of you." He led her to the cushions in the middle of the room and sat down. *Uncomfortable position for an uncomfortable conversation.* "There's something I need to discuss with the two of you and before I get into it, I need you both to understand that I'm suggesting this out of the best intentions. So please don't be offended. Does that make sense?" Both women looked at him curiously, but both nodded. "Good. As you know, war is coming to Ashur. It's only a matter of time and we suspect it may even happen within the year. Even if Jahmash doesn't arrive first, his armies will still be able to get here. There are many of us traversing Ashur now to try to convince nations to prepare for this war and to recruit anyone who can fight. That being said, I want the two of you to board one of the ships in Gansishoor and sail away from Ashur."

"Excuse me?" His mother looked at him incredulously. "Wassa, this is our home. If we are called upon to defend it, then we will. And we will do so proudly. There is no way that we are leaving Ashur."

"You forget that we learned to fight when we were your age. We were trained with swords and daggers, and while it has been some time since we were asked to wield a weapon, it would not take much to familiarize ourselves with them again," Farzeen added.

This is going as expected. "Look, I understand that you're capable with blades and that isn't my point. I care for both of you and my brothers as well. And I plan to have the same conversation with them. Destruction is coming, and the only way to escape it is to not be here when it arrives. I cannot lose any of you, at least not like that. And you can always return once everything has ended."

His mother shook her head, "Absolutely not, Wassa. I understand your concern. I do. And I appreciate it. But it is not your decision to make for us. The Daughters of Tahlia could be valuable in fighting for Shivaana, and how would we look for abandoning the rest of them in Ashur's darkest hour? I know you care about us and you are suggesting this out of love. And I am not offended that you would want this for us. But Ashur is our home as well, and we intend to fight for it."

"Suppose for a moment that we asked the same of you, Vasher."

Farzeen raised her eyebrows at him. "Would you be willing to get on a ship and leave while we fought for Ashur?"

He sighed, knowing that she already knew the answer. "Of course not. It's just..."

Once again, his mother knew his thoughts, "It's just that we are older and you see us as fragile? Not as well-equipped to defend ourselves? You're worried that we will be easy targets for our enemies. I assure you we will not be."

Vasher felt his shoulders, neck, and back grow tense. He knew there would be no convincing either of them to get on the ship. He thought about opening himself to his manifestation, and perhaps persuading them that they wanted to go, but to do so would be wrong and would go against his whole code for using his manifestation. *Isn't this different, though? I'm not using it for personal gain. Not using it for evil. If ever there was a time to make an exception to use it, wouldn't it be right now? To ensure their safety? She's the one who told me not to be so rigid with using it.* He tried to breathe deeply in order to ease the tension, but to no avail. After a moment, he stopped the conversation in his head and opened himself to what the Orijin had blessed him with. He felt the melody course through his veins and the ache in his body went away. He looked at his mother and second mother and smiled at them. "Mother, Do'maa, there's one last thing that I want to say regarding this whole thing."

As he was about to go forth with using his manifestation, a knock sounded at the door. *Blood of a janga. Who the hell could that be?*

***

Delilah waited patiently for the door to open, though the dozens of women behind her and Krissette didn't seem as eager to wait. Still, she was impressed that she even managed to get so many of the Daughters of Tahlia out of their homes and willing to listen to her. The door finally opened and Varana Jai looked baffled, though Delilah surmised that was due to all of the Daughters behind her, rather than her specifically. "Good evening Varana. I was wondering, if Farzeen is home as well, would you both be willing to come out here for a moment?"

Varana looked at her and then around at all the others. "What's this all about? Have we done something wrong?"

A voice came from behind her that surprised Delilah, though

she didn't know why. "No Mata, you're not in trouble. Delilah has business to discuss with *all* of the Daughters." Vasher's head appeared behind Varana, though he looked somewhat annoyed.

"Vasher is right. You've done nothing wrong, but I wanted to be able to speak to everyone, or as many Daughters as I could. It has to do with preparing for Jahmash."

"Ah. Very well." She glanced at Vasher as she stepped outside, "See, Wassa? Perfect timing."

Delilah didn't bother to worry about what that meant. Varana and Farzeen walked out and joined the ranks of the others behind Delilah. She turned around to face them all. Many were engaged in hushed conversations with others. *Why do I get the feeling that this will be difficult?* "Daughters, may I please have your attention? The sooner you hear me out, the sooner you can go back to what you were doing."

Krissette whispered to her, "I didn't realize. Is being a Daughter of Tahlia just a Shivaani thing? None of them look like they come from somewhere else."

Delilah wanted to laugh but held it back so the others wouldn't get the wrong idea. "No. It's just that you can adopt this lifestyle no matter where you live. Many come here, like you, to learn about the lifestyle of the Daughters, and then make the decision on their own about whether to follow or not. But no one is bound to Sundari if they choose this path. They only miss out on the whole dancing with snakes thing. But I guess they could do that at home as well, if they really wanted to. Hopefully that helps with your decision as well."

"Delilah, you have our attention! But you know how these women like to gossip, so you won't have it for long!" Harleen was one of the taller Daughters, and also one of the most skilled dancers. Her light brown eyes were beautiful and reminded Delilah of a doe's eyes.

"Thank you, Harleen. I can always count on you to support me. And to be honest. Daughters, I know we don't believe in a leader, so please don't think that I'm trying to be yours right now. I also know that I have been away for a long time and it is not because I have abandoned you or the lifestyle of the Daughters. However, this Mark on my face bears great significance, and I do not take it lightly. Many of you know that I was at the House of Darian for years. However, what none of you know is that once it was destroyed, those of us who survived came together and turned ourselves into a small army of Marked Descendants. We are the ones who killed King Edmund." She knew there would be murmurs and the Daughters didn't disappoint. She let the mumbles last for a moment and then continued before anything grew from them. "Before you start turning that news into anything farfetched, the throne is now occupied by Garrison, Edmund's son. He has made it the top priority to prepare Ashur for Jahmash's coming, which we believe will happen soon."

"How soon?" Laboni was of an age with Delilah, but much more of a skeptic.

"We believe within a year. We also believe he has armies at his disposal now, from lands beyond Ashur. It is only a matter of time. And that is why I am here today. That is why I came back. Daughters, Ashur needs us to fight for it. Ashur needs as many people as it can get to defend it. Of course, those of you who are too old, too young, or too sick are not expected to fight. However, we are all trained fighters with swords, daggers, and knives. Why waste that on little snakes for drooling men and women when we can make a difference for all of Ashur?"

"And what of the rest of Ashur? Are they joining this fight?" Kinjal was another young Daughter, but Delilah remembered her to be genuine. Her question wasn't meant to be pointed.

"They are expected to. Several of us were with King Garrison before setting out throughout Ashur. We dispersed throughout all of the nations to do exactly what I am doing. In fact, Vasher," she pointed behind her, "will be riding to Gansishoor to have the same talk with the Shivaani military. Others rode to Fangh-Haan, Cerysia, the Wolf's Paw, and Galicea to make the same preparations. Markos has already done so and has armies and militia in each of its cities."

Her friend, Harleen, spoke up again. "Delilah, I am fond of you, so don't take this the wrong way. But why us? In comparison to the rest of Ashur, we are a handful of people who happen to be handy with blades, but how exactly does that make us stand out? Are your associates going to every community and subculture to do this?"

Delilah paused for a moment. She knew what she was about to say was going to sound insane, and some in the crowd might even laugh at her, but it had to be put out there for it to have a chance at being considered. "I appreciate your concern and your honesty, Harleen. Listen, what I'm about to suggest, I know how crazy it sounds. Believe me, the idea first popped into my head when we embarked on our journey down here and it wasn't until we were leaving Maramarosa that I finally stopped trying to talk myself out of it. And even still, I didn't tell any of my travel companions about it." She glanced at Krissette and back at Vasher. "That's how much I believe in it. And that's how out there it is. But if it works, then it's brilliant."

"Well enough buildup already, are you ever going to tell us?" Ojasri spoke up. She'd been known for being impatient, but Delilah imagined it was warranted in this situation.

She took a deep breath. "We put on these shows every day and show off to the world how we can manipulate snakes and get them to do our bidding. While that might not specifically translate on a battlefield, I have an idea of something that could." She hesitated, still nervous to say the idea outright.

Harleen must have caught on, "No. You... you can't be serious?"

She glanced at the tall, beautiful woman and nodded. "If we put our everything into it, I believe we could train bhujanga to fight for us." Her suggestion caused a much more raucous reaction than the news of killing the king.

Ojasri stepped forward, most likely to be heard from the rising din. "Delilah, I don't think the idea is so crazy. But how would we even start such an endeavor?"

She nodded at the girl out of gratitude for taking her seriously, and out of confidence for having thought of that answer. "Thank you, Ojasri. We start with the people who can already do it. The pit masters at the fighting pit must have ways of controlling and taming all of the beasts that they collect. We work with them and learn what commands they use, and incorporate our own that we use when dancing. I understand that bhujanga are enormous enough to swallow any of us whole, maybe even a few of us at a time. That being said, they are snakes. Really large snakes, yes. But still snakes. And Daughters of Tahlia are known for controlling snakes. Look, I'm not kidding about Jahmash, and I'm terrified about what this war will bring. Those of us who set out to militarize Ashur, we all know that we might not see each other again. So we have to take this seriously and we have to use any advantage we can get. And I highly doubt that Jahmash's armies will be bringing monstrously large beasts over the seas with them. So please, Daughters, please tell me that you're with me."

To her surprise, Varana Jai stepped forward and then faced the others. "I am not your leader either, but I am old enough to have seen many of you join our ranks. And in my time as Daughter, I have made friends with just about all of you. Every single woman here is a good woman and is here by choice. None of you did so thinking that you would be asked to save Ashur or fight against Jahmash's armies. "She turned to look at Vasher then back at the Daughters. "But that is exactly what all of you will do. What all of us will do. Young, old, sick, we all fight. We can only hope that all of Ashur will adopt this mindset, but even if not, we fight for the people who cannot fight, and we fight for the future. It is as simple as that. Delilah Fakhri, while we do not believe in having any one leader, you will be our guide in preparing for this next step. And you will lead us on the battlefield, if you are willing to accept that honor?"

Ranga-fucking-juli. What? That wasn't part of the agreement. She hoped with all her might that there was still color in her face. "Of course, Varana Jai, I accept this honor."

***

Vasher walked through the outdoor markets with his two Kraiso companions, Cow and Mutt. He was still getting used to calling them such names, as his first instinct was to giggle every time, but luckily the two of them didn't take themselves too seriously. Cow, a fire-haired girl not much younger than him, explained that the two of them were Slayers, a faction of the Kraisos whose job was to seek out the worst individuals of Markos and either convince them to change, or kill them. Slayers adopted the names of animals, and the other factions had their own themes as well. Vizards were the ones who blended in with the community and made sure that everything was done in a way that avoided corruption. They took on the names of flowers. Coinbearers, who used the names of spices, infiltrated financial institutions, also to make sure that lords and officials weren't stealing or misusing tax money. And the last faction was the Footpads, who handled transporting anything that needed to be moved. They adopted the names of things in nature, such as Mud and Snow. *The whole organization is intriguing. It's too bad everything else about them is pretty much a secret, otherwise I'd ask more questions. I wonder if someone could be a Kraiso, an Anonymi, and a Marked Descendant. They would be unstoppable, right?* He turned to Cow, "Hey, I know everything is a big mystery with what you all do, but let me ask you. Could someone hypothetically be part of the Kraisos, the Anonymi, *and* a Marked Descendant at the same time?"

Cow's freckled face turned quizzical. She glanced at Mutt and then back at Vasher, "Honestly, I don't know. That's a question for the higher ups, not us. I mean, I don't see why not, but then, how would you be able to fulfill your duties to each group? I can only speak for us, but we don't get much time away from our responsibilities. And to be fair, we really like what we do, so I doubt most of us *want* to be caught up with anything else."

"But you're saying there are no rules against it. I was just wondering, not actually trying to join all three. Although it would be pretty amazing to do so. One more thing, where in Ashur do people have hair as orange as yours? I've never seen such a color before."

Cow smiled at him, "That is not something I will share. Kraisos shed our former identities when joining the ranks. I am aware that Wind was willing to discuss his because of the benefits it would have on working together, but there is no reason to share such information with you, Vasher. I will tell you that there are many others with hair like mine in Ashur. You just have to know where to look."

"Speaking of where to look, I think that's the military base up ahead in the clearing." He continued on, feeling more confident than usual because of the Kraisos with him, but also confused about how in the world he'd navigate this meeting. They didn't know he was coming and probably wouldn't take kindly to a surprise visit. He decided to just walk right up to the base, which was essentially a high fence of wooden pikes concealing whatever was inside. A semi-circle of diagonal pikes blocked the gate, but three men stood watch behind them. Before they got too close, Vasher turned to the Kraisos. "Look, they're not going to know what Kraisos are, and they sure as hell aren't going to respect us if I tell them your names are Cow and Mutt." He paused for a second. "No offense. Just go along with what I tell them, even if it means you don't say anything. Got it?" The two Kraisos nodded, though Mutt seemed more bothered by it than Cow. He was far older than her, likely too young to be as old as Vasher's father, but too old to be an older brother.

As soon as the guards spotted them, they all stood and two drew bows and arrows while the other drew his sword. The one with the sword, a muscular man with hints of grey mixed into his black hair and beard, addressed them. "Stop where you are. Lay your sword down in front of you and if you have any other weapons, do the same with them."

"We have no swords or weapons."

"We? Who is we? Who else is with you?"

Vasher looked to his right and left, and Cow and Mutt had

somehow disappeared. *How the hell do they do that? And why would they do it now?* "Sorry, it's just me. I-I'm just nervous and I misspoke. I have no weapons, though." *Do I tell him to search me if he wants? Is that weird? Forget it; I'll just leave that up to him.* "My name is Vasher Jai of Sundari. I'm here to seek an audience with a man named Harshu, if he is here."

The man moved one of the pike blockades and walked to him. He patted Vasher down, "What is your business here and who sent you?" The man finished after a moment and waved for Vasher to walk through the opening in the blockade.

"As you can see by my face, I am a Marked Descendant. If you have not heard the news already, the king is dead and I am one of the people responsible for King Edmund's death. I know how much of a relief it is for Shivaana that he no longer sits the throne. The new king is his son, Garrison. His first order of business is to prepare Ashur for Jahmash's coming and I am here as King Garrison's emissary to ask for your help in militarizing Shivaana. We need for Ashur to be ready in less than a year's time, which sounds far off, but if you think about the time it would take to reach all the capable citizens of Shivaana and properly train them, it is not much. I was told that a man named Harshu was an official of the Shivaani military some time ago, and if that is the case, I hope to speak with him."

The man eyed him carefully, as if unsure of whether to take him seriously. "Get on your knees. And face away from me. Now."

What the hell is this? How is that an appropriate response? "Very well. I have nothing on me that would be a threat here." He knelt down and noticed that they must have been playing "Bones" to occupy their time. It was a popular game throughout Shivaana that used small white rectangles made of white bone that had black dots on them to represent numbers. Judging by the layout on the ground, they were in the middle of a game.

The guard placed Vasher's arms behind his back and then bound them tightly. "Up now." Vasher stood and the guard directed him to turn toward the gate, which was now open. The guard led him through while the other two remained and closed the gate behind them. "You're interrupting our game and I was winning. If they cheat me while we're gone, I will be very angry at you for showing up when you did. Luckily for you, no one really comes to see us anymore except our own soldiers, so at least this is some excitement." Vasher realized once they were inside the walls that the base itself was huge, just not tall. From what he could see of its tan stone walls, it was large enough to hold thousands. "Harshu is inside, but he is not the man who makes all of the decisions. I will bring you to Harshu first, as that is who you asked to see, but I should warn you that he is old and grumpy these days. He may forget all that at the prospect of having some purpose again, but I make no guarantees."

Vasher dared to speak, mostly because the guard seemed to be candid. "I don't think I understand. You keep alluding to the excitement, but what does that mean? What do you all do each day?"

"Oh we train and have schedules and regiments and duties as soldiers do, but our military only continues to exist out of spite for Cerysia. We remain just in case Edmund tries to do anything stupid. We have barely even seen Vermillion lately, much less any other activity, so a lot of us are bored. But if what you're saying is true, then perhaps we'll have some purpose again."

He can't be serious. Surely the Shivaani army hasn't become such a joke? I guess I'll find out soon. "I wouldn't lie about something like that. Trust me, I've already seen people affected by Jahmash directly. It's only a matter of time until Ashur feels his wrath."

The guard looked at him as they walked into the military base, "You're so lucky. All we do here is sit on our asses and wait for things, and usually it's something stupid like someone's neighbor stole their goats or something like that. We used to think that the archers had it the best because at least the best of them could go to Sundari and watch the Daughters dance, even if from rooftops. But turns out the Daughters aren't interested in any of them, unless they want to be fathers, and most people know better than to try anything stupid when the Daughters are dancing so they don't even get to shoot anyone."

"So unlucky for them. Are you required to stay on the base? You can't fulfill whatever duties you were obligated to do and then go home? And then come back if they need you?"

"What kind of life of a soldier is that? Going home makes you soft! Makes you rusty. No one here is interested in that sort of thing." Once they were inside, Vasher realized that a great deal of space was dedicated to training grounds, and the perimeter held the barracks and offices. The guard finally stopped him at a door toward the end of the corridor. "Here we are. This is Harshu's office. Like I warned you, he's been grumpy for a long time, so temper your expectations." The guard knocked on the door.

"What do you want? I'm busy."

"It's Supahi Arthav." Vasher recognized the word "supahi"; it was the title for soldiers in Shivaana. His father had mentioned holding that title for a time, before moving up in rank. "I know you are busy, Kamandar Harshu, but I have a very interesting visitor here who has asked for you by name. He says he may need the entire Shivaani army's help."

"Oh great, another farmer who's lost his cows? Horses? Or was his mother robbed of her jewelry in the middle of the night?"

"Um, no sir. This one bears the Mark of a Descendant, and wants our help against Jahmash."

There was silence for a few moments, to the point that Vasher was sure they'd be sent away. "Send him in. And then leave."

The guard looked at him and shrugged. "Good luck, friend. I know the rest of us would love for you to be successful in there, but it doesn't seem likely." He opened the door, then turned and walked back down the corridor.

Vasher walked into the small room and saw the old man sitting behind a desk. Despite his age, Harshu looked to be in good shape. He was slim and likely all muscle, and most of the hair that he had left sat at his upper lip. He continued writing and didn't look up. "You can sit if you'd like, but I'm sure this will be short. Who told you to come here and ask for me?"

Vasher sat, though it was hardly comfortable with his arms bound behind him. "I have a connection in Sundari that told me they knew someone who knew you a long time ago. They said if I was coming here, I should ask for you."

"I'll let you try one more time. I have no connections in Sundari, save for the rooftop archers who protect the Daughters of Tahlia. I have no family and the only friends I have are either still on this base or dead."

Blood of a janga. What the hell? What do I do now? I can't tell him, can I? That was the only rule that Mata gave me. The hell with it, what choice do I have? "Fine, but only because this is extremely important. If I tell you the truth, can you promise that it stays between us and no one else will find out?"

"Depends on what the truth is. No guarantees." Harshu continued his work without looking up.

This guy was friends with my father? How is anyone friends with him? Damnit, I'm just going to have to take the chance. "Fine. But I'm begging you to keep this secret between us. My mother is a Daughter of Tahlia and the only rule she gave me in coming here was to *not* share this secret. So I'm already defying her by telling you."

"You haven't told me anything yet."

Vasher rolled his eyes. "You knew my father a long time ago. As the child of a Daughter of Tahlia, I'm not supposed to know who my father is, but I do. And you can understand now why I wouldn't want to share that information. My father's name is Albarran; he was in the Shivaani military as a young man. Once he left, he went to Sundari and met my mother there. I asked my mother if he ever spoke of anyone from his time here and she gave me your name."

Harshu calmly put down his quill and slowly looked up at Vasher. "You are the son of Albarran? I see a resemblance, but I wouldn't have noticed it if you hadn't told me the connection. How is he these days? Is he still alive?"

"Yes, he's alive and well. He is enjoying an easy life now that he has slowed down a bit. He's making the most of it."

"Good for him. And good for you that you know who he is. I never understood the whole lifestyle of the Daughters of Tahlia. It seems cruel for a child to grow up without a father, much less not even know who he is. But at least you don't have to worry about that. Now go back to Sundari and make the most of those luxuries you have."

"What?"

"You came here to enlist us to fight against Jahmash? And you think that will be enough? What of the Royal Vermillion? What of the vaunted Taurani? What about the infamous Anonymi? Have you enlisted all of the feared armies and forces of Ashur?"

"With all due respect, you forgot the Ghosts of Ashur."

"Who?"

"The Ghosts of Ashur. That's the feared army that I belong to. There were less than twenty of us when we stormed King Edmund's castle and killed him. Now his son, who is one of us, sits on the throne. We are working with the Anonymi, so yes, we have enlisted them. And the Kraisos as well, but you haven't heard of them yet. That's three, and we're all working together to militarize Ashur and train our people to fight. The last remaining Taurani is one of us as well. Half the Royal Vermillion has turned traitor to Ashur and is helping a group of invaders who sacked Mireya. The other half remains loyal to the new king and will be helping us shortly. I know you think this is a lost cause, but not if we actually make an attempt to save ourselves. There are those of us with the Mark that are as effective as a whole battalion. My manifestation isn't the violent type, but I have friends who can wield fire, move objects with their mind, summon lightning, create doorways out of thin air, and even more. Kamandar Harshu, this is our only chance at saving Ashur. What are you afraid of?"

That perked up the older man. He finally looked up from his work. "Excuse me? You dare walk in here, lie to me, and then accuse me of being a coward?"

"If it's not fear, then what is it?"

"I owe you nothing, especially not an explanation for my thinking. Now leave before I have you put in a cell."

The door crashed open behind Vasher. He turned and saw Mutt and Cow dragging in a large man who looked to be another officer, though much younger than Harshu. Cow smiled at Vasher, "We figured you might need to see the man in charge at some point. Once we knew you were looking for this old cowhide, we thought it better to go off on our own, just in case things didn't go as you hoped. Plus we didn't want them taking all of our knives. Then we heard how willing the guard was to bring you to Harshu, and it made sense that he'd probably just waste your time. That about how things are going?" Vasher nodded but held back a smile. "Knew it. We went and scouted the rest of the base. There are roughly nine hundred soldiers here, and another forty or fifty officers. They were smart about the base. They built down instead of up. There are two more levels beneath this with more training and fighting areas."

"I've been here for five minutes. Definitely no more than ten. How did you do all that in such a short amount of time?"

Mutt looked at him flatly, "We have our ways."

Vasher turned back to Harshu, "These were the Kraisos I was telling you about. See how effective they are?" He turned back to them, "So who exactly did you bring here?"

Cow and Mutt lifted the man to his feet and then nudged him into the chair next to the one Vasher had been sitting in. Cow pointed at him to stay put before answering Vasher. "This is General Prashant. He runs things here. Not the old man."

"Great. What a waste of time. General? I assume you use the Shivaani title, 'Janaral?' Janaral Prashant?" The man nodded. "You don't have to be afraid. My friends here, Cow and Mutt, they had no intention of hurting you. They were just doing me a favor by bringing you to me. My name is Vasher Jai, and I've come on behalf of the new king, King Garrison, to ask for your help in training the people of Shivaana in preparation for Jahmash's coming. Do you think you can help us?"

Janaral Prashant took a moment to compose himself and come to terms with the idea that no one was going to hurt him. He smoothed his uniform and then looked around at all of them. "You people still believe in Jahmash? You need to get on with your lives. No one is coming and nothing is going to happen to Ashur. Stop the delusion and just let it go. Such a pathetic thing to worry about."

"If you don't believe in Jahmash, then how do you explain this line on my face?"

"I have seen many people with tattoos in my life, though not too many stupid enough to tattoo their faces. I know of you Descendants, though. Get over yourselves, you're nothing more than clever illusionists who trick people into thinking you're magicians. Disgusting."

What the...? Did he really just say that? "Light of Orijin, someone's brainwashed you, huh. I've had just about enough of this shit from the two of you." Vasher opened himself to his manifestation and let the melody flow through him. He couldn't tell if it felt sweeter because he was about to teach these two men a lesson. He looked Harshu directly in the eyes, "You're going to take your knife and cut the binding on my hands right now. Then you'll give me the knife." Harshu nodded and walked around his desk. He took his knife from the sheath on his chest and freed Vasher's hands. Vasher then took the knife and gestured for Harshu to sit. The man obliged instantly and Vasher walked around the desk and sat in Harshu's seat. "The two of you are going to stop being cowards. You are brave men who report to me. Do you understand?"

"Yes, sir," they said in unison.

"Good. You will refer to me as Master Jai. Is that clear?"

"Yes, Master Jai!"

"Good. Now. The two of you will send one hundred soldiers to each of Shivaana's six cities. The remaining soldiers will be responsible for fortifying the shores of Shivaana. Make sure our coastline is impenetrable. You have six months to recruit as many healthy and able citizens as possible and train them in combat, both with their hands and with weapons. Do you understand?"

"Yes, Master Jai!"

"I will spend that time traveling throughout Shivaana, making sure that your soldiers and officers are doing their jobs properly. If *anything* is substandard in my eyes, I will find the two of you and cane you in front of your own soldiers. I will stop short of breaking your backs, so that you are able to heal and learn your lesson. Then, if you fail me a second time, neither of you will walk again. Do you understand?"

"Yes. Master Jai!"

CHAPTER 14
CLEARER MINDS

*From **The Book of Orijin**, Verse Two Hundred Ten*
We anointed the Five by looking into their hearts. Despite their
actions, there is always the possibility of redemption.

Marshall took one last glance at his reflection, released his manifestation, and walked away from the riverbank. *I am definitely doing something wrong. What is it supposed to do?* He vividly remembered waking up at the House of Darian a few years ago and looking in the mirror. The shock of not seeing his reflection had scared him to no end, to the point that he broke the mirror. "And now I wish I could command it to go away," he said softly to himself.

He walked through the shambles of his old village, disheartened at the notion that no one would ever rebuild it. Corpses still lay here and there, and he felt a sense of guilt that he hadn't done anything to properly honor them. *Maybe when this is all over, I can recruit everyone to come and help me bury them at their families' trees. Who knows, maybe I can even get some help to rebuild this place.* He paused to look around and tried to remember how everything had once looked. His own home was on the opposite side of the village, but he refused to let himself go anywhere near it. He'd come back to bury and honor his family a while back, so there was no other reason to revisit the pile of rubble that was once his house.

Marshall remembered the soldiers that had attacked under the command of Maqdhuum. *I can't believe he's an ally now. How did he ever convince us to trust him? How do we even know for sure that he's on our side?* He continued to walk through the village. He wanted to enter the forest to find some food, regardless of whether he had to hunt or find some vegetation. He still had a few rations left, but he'd grown somewhat tired of cured meats, bread, and dried fruit. As he walked through the village, he continued to think of the invasion that had destroyed everything. *Changed everything. Where were all those soldiers from? Where did he find so many people who were willing to fight for him? Did he manipulate them all, or did they willingly fight for him? If they could have so smartly and easily have wiped out all of my people, then what might bigger numbers do to all of Ashur?*

He shook his head to try and get rid of the thoughts. They

couldn't afford to think negatively. It was one thing to safeguard against all possible scenarios and correct any weaknesses they had, but Marshall knew they had to remain confident that they'd be able to stop Jahmash. It was the only way they'd be able to rally all of the citizens of Ashur to fight for their homeland. If they were scared, then the war would be over before it began. *I can't afford to take forever with this. I have to have a hand in preparing Ashurians for this. And why did Maqdhuum have to screw things up so badly? He could have helped by telling people about Jahmash. About the Red Harbinger's strategies and commands to his soldiers. Instead he had to be an asshole and mess it all up. I wish I had been able to kill him the last time he was here. So much would have been different.*

The start of the forest came into view and Marshall quieted his steps and walked more cautiously. His preference was to kill something small like a rabbit or two, or a pheasant, but he wouldn't be picky. If a deer happened to cross his path, he'd take advantage. He walked on until he found a suitable tree for perching, then climbed to a branch that could support his weight. Once he was in place, Marshall was roughly thirty feet up and out of sight of any prey. He sat with both legs hanging from either side of the branch, and his feet pressed against the trunk. He pulled his bow from over his shoulder and then grabbed an arrow from his quiver. He knew it would be better to wait until something revealed itself to nock the arrow, rather than having the bow and arrow drawn the whole time. *Easy way to get tired and sloppy.* He'd done enough hunting to know not to shoot as soon as he saw something. More times than not, it would lead to a miss or a poor shot and would send the animal running, which would then lead other animals to run from the area. *If I walk away with nothing today, then it's back to dried lamb and bread.*

A twig snapped far off to his right. It was too far away for Marshall to know what type of animal it could be, but he pulled his arrow and set it on the bow in preparation. As he put the arrow into place, he opened himself to his manifestation and felt the melody course through him. He instantly shrouded himself in a darker shadow than he had previously. It wasn't likely for any prey to be looking up as it walked by, but he wasn't taking chances, especially at the thought of a fresh, hot meal. The situation reminded him of being in the forest as a child and hiding in the tree. It had been what created his manifestation, though he didn't know it at the time. In fact, he didn't realize it until over ten years later. Marshall closed his eyes and focused on listening to his surroundings. Adria had taught him that while training for the siege. Even though his hearing wasn't anything like her manifestation, it was still possible to drown other sensations out and focus only on sounds. The thought of her made him miss her, but he knew he had to be here. By the time she had left with Lincan and the others for Fangh-Haan, Adria knew that Marshall's journey was necessary as well.

As he listened, he noticed an absence of animal sounds. No chirps or buzzing. No real sounds except for the light rustling due to the breeze. *Strange. This kind of silence should mean a predator nearby. Couldn't have been me; I was too quiet to startle anything. What could be out there?* He tried to focus harder and thought he heard footsteps. He opened his eyes and readied his bow. The footsteps were audible even without concentrating. Whatever was coming, it was taking its time and wasn't hiding its presence. The sound grew clearer and Marshall realized it was more than one set of feet. *Two, maybe three of them?* Just as the thought passed his mind, Marshall heard a laugh.

People? Are there people out here? He waited a few moments, holding his breath and wondering who could possibly have traveled this far into the Never. Finally, he saw three pairs of legs. They stepped out into the open with no concern for their surroundings. They all wore loose cloaks of different colors, as if patched together from different pieces of clothing. Marshall was ready to fire a warning shot, but the shock of seeing the three people hit him so hard that he dropped his bow and arrow. Marshall released his manifestation as soon as he realized what had happened. The crash of the bow startled the others and all three of them drew swords. Marshall had already been in the process of climbing down by the time they'd readied themselves. He jumped to the ground and ran to them.

"Eleni? Lumien? Is that really you?" He recognized two of them, but not the third, a girl who looked slightly younger than him.

The man, Lumien, was about ten years older than him. He'd been good with a sword, but Marshall remembered him being more interested in his crops than weapons. He also had twin line tattoos intersecting his eyes, angled diagonally inwards to his lips, then went vertically down to his chin. Lumien stared at him quizzically for a moment, "Who are you? You look familiar and clearly you are Taurani, but I don't know that I remember you." He kept his sword drawn and pointed in Marshall's direction.

Marshall nodded, "I look different now. I am Marshall. And up until this moment I thought I was one of two remaining Taurani in the world. I have so many questions, as I'm sure you do. I remember you, Lumien, and you as well, Eleni." He turned to the other girl, "I apologize for not remembering you."

Lumien waved his hand at the other girl, instructing her to stay quiet. "As you've stated Marshall, we all have many questions. Seeing as how we have been here for years and you only showed up now, we should start with that."

This is going to take a while. He sat down on the ground in the middle of the clearing. "I feel like this may take some time. I might as well get comfortable. I was here when we got invaded. A few of us got into a duel with the general of the invading army and he made easy work of all of us. I was rescued by a few members of the House of Darian and healed there. Apparently the healing process removed all of my tattoos. If you remember, I had so many and I felt like I lost my identity when I lost all of them. What's on my face now, I only got it a few days ago. But to clarify, this isn't the first time I've returned. I came back here twice. Once looking for other survivors and another time to bury my family members at our tree. I didn't see any of you either time that I was here. Perhaps that can be the next part of this conversation? Lumien, I know you are skeptical about seeing me here, but it is quite the opposite for me. I'm thrilled to see the three of you. For the last three years I thought the Taurani were done. Erased from this world in a blink. Have you three been here all this time?"

Lumien walked a few steps closer then sat down and faced him. He waved for the other two to do the same. "For the most part. We have mostly stayed in the forest, unless we have a need for something specific and must search the village. There is too much death there and we do not have the strength nor the mental fortitude to bury everyone."

"I can understand that." Marshall nodded. "Most importantly, how did you manage to survive the invasion?"

He looked at Marshall, as if unsure to answer. "We weren't even in the village for the invasion. The three of us and a few others were on a hunting expedition deep into the Never. We were so far away that we had no idea that it happened until we returned what was likely days later. It all still smelled of ash and rot and death. We smelled it about a day's ride out, but had no idea that it was our village." He tilted his head to his left, "This one here is Vylsia. She is my niece. If you have met her before, it was likely years ago when she probably didn't look like the same person. You know how quickly kids change as they are growing up."

"Indeed." It made him think of his own sisters, Gia and Esha, and what they might look like now. He pushed the thought down and focused on the others with him. "If your group was away during the attack, is it possible that there were others who were away as well? Might there be more Taurani out there?"

"It's doubtful, unfortunately." Eleni responded to him. She also bore the twin line tattoos down her eyes and they extended down her neck and to her chest. She had another line from under her nose down to her chin, and a hoop piercing between her nostrils as well. Her dark hair made her bright blue eyes all the more striking. "We've been near the village for years now and haven't run into anyone since. I would imagine that any Taurani who were in the area would have come back at least once. But who knows. We missed you in the times that you returned, so I suppose it's possible. But Marshall, the question needs to be asked. Why are you here *now*? I understand coming back for your family, but there is nothing here for you anymore."

"Peace. Quiet. A familiar place to concentrate without distraction."

She glanced at Lumien then back at Marshall. "What do you mean? For what?"

Never thought I'd have to have this conversation with other Taurani. But I guess I should be grateful that I can. Here goes. "I…look, what I'm about to tell you is the truth. I have no reason to lie to conjure up a story, especially one that would make our people look so stupid. There were many of us in this village with manifestations. It is the very reason for our tattoos, as they cover up the Mark before we gain a manifestation. You know those trials that we were all forced to do as children?" The other three all looked at him with narrowed eyes, as if he was a traitor, but they nodded in response to his question. "Those unintentionally cause scores of Taurani to develop manifestations without us knowing about them."

"You lie," Lumien spat at the ground as he glared at Marshall.

"Do I?" He opened himself once more and surrounded all of them in darkness. "Surely you remember while you were out on that hunt three years ago that the whole sky went black in the middle of the day? That was me. I did that, just as I am doing this now. I don't know if you remember Aric, but he was with me when it happened, and it turned out that he could see in the dark. I blackened the sky to get away from an enemy and Aric navigated us to safety. In my travels through Ashur, I also happened to meet one other Taurani named Asarei. Lumien, I don't know if you were old enough to remember him while he was still in the village, but he left a long time ago. He also possesses a manifestation. I have seen him use it. Our ancestors didn't trust such things, as they were great warriors and scared of magic. But imagine how much it would have helped stop our own extinction if we had known about them? I think about that all the time. How our people's own stubbornness prevented us from being even better fighters. Look at how many lives it cost."

Lumien shouted through the darkness, "Fine, I see your point! Can you please allow us to see one other again?"

"Very well." Marshall let the darkness dissipate.

Eleni spoke with a strain in her voice, "Marshall, you understand that this revelation is not some casual update on a mundane development. This is life-changing. And despite that, it doesn't answer the question of why you are here."

He explained everything that he'd been through since leaving the Taurani village. Their countenances shifted several times throughout Marshall's retelling, and varied from shock to anger to confusion. "So now we have to prepare Ashur for Jahmash's arrival. My friends have all spread throughout Ashur to ensure that every single nation and every city is trained for combat. I backed out of that responsibility because I want to work on my manifestation. As you've seen, I can manipulate the light and darkness, but I can also control my shadow and reflection. The problem is, I don't actually know how to control them. Bringing the darkness has become easy, because I can just will it to happen. However, it doesn't seem to work the same way for the shadow and the reflection. I came here so that I could be free of distractions and try to focus on how to make it work."

Eleni smiled, "And now you've got the biggest distraction possible, huh."

He shook his head, "No. This is a good thing. I'm elated to see the three of you. If anything, it's motivating. I don't know if it'll help with my manifestation at all, but either way, coming here has been rewarding."

"It's safe to assume you've already been to the water?" Lumien raised his eyebrows in anticipation of Marshall's response.

"Yes, that's where I came from. I needed a break and figured I'd wait in a tree for some unsuspecting dinner. I found you three instead; you must've scared off any animals that were in the area."

Lumien laughed at him, "What happened? You ran out of rations already?"

"No, I just wanted a break from dried meat and fruits. I was hoping for a hot meal tonight."

"Ah, I can understand that. We went through that at first, once we realized we could only cook using fires. We've grown to be rather resourceful in the last few years though. Aside from roasting an animal over a flame, we've learned to make soups and stews as well. Had to forage the ruins to find a large enough pot, though. Our actual camp isn't too far from here, if you're up for the walk. We can definitely prepare you a nice hot bowl of soup. And I know what you're thinking, it's the two ladies who do all of the cooking, but neither of them can cook better than me."

Marshall noticed Eleni rolling her eyes at Lumien's bragging, though she did so with a smile. *There's something there between them. Wonder if they've realized that yet.* "I would be delighted to have some of your cooking. And if there's anything I can contribute, please let me know."

Lumien dismissively waved a hand at him. "You're off the hook for today. Next time you can help."

* * *

Marshall led them to the river where he'd been the day before. After Lumien had followed through on his promise of soup, they all relaxed around a fire and talked about older times in the Taurani village. Marshall had been so full and tired that he fell asleep right in front of the fire. He'd woken up in the morning covered in a blanket that Eleni apparently provided him. "This is the spot. I was here for hours yesterday, to no avail. I don't know what to do or how to make it work."

Lumien eyed him curiously. "I'm not going to pretend to understand how any of this works. Maybe I have a manifestation as well, maybe I don't. Who knows. I wouldn't have the first idea of what it is or what to do with it. But how do you usually control the darkness thing?"

Marshall shrugged as they reached the riverbank. "Normally I just open myself to the manifestation and let it flow through me. Then, to make something actually happen, I simply will it. I free myself of emotion, then think about what I want to do and it happens."

"And clearly that's not working for the other things?"

"Clearly."

"Is there another way to control these things? You said you get rid of your emotions, but what if you control it with your emotions? What if you force it to happen instead of just *willing* it to happen? Suppose you channeled your anger into bending it to your will?"

Marshall shook his head. "Emotions tend to stall our ability to use them. It's not as if different emotions influence these things differently or change how they manifest. Emotions simply block them, as they cloud our focus."

Lumien put his hands up in resignation, then sat on the ground. "I give up, then, friend. As I said, I know nothing about these things. Who am I to give you advice about something you understand better than I do? Or should I say, something you understand but I do not?"

"I appreciate the attempt, Lumien." Marshall chuckled.

"What if you did the opposite?"

Marshall turned around to Vylsia, who was standing behind him. "What do you mean?"

She smiled at him sheepishly. "You said that you normally will things to happen. What if you *surrendered* to it rather than tried to control it?"

Marshall ruminated on the suggestion for a moment. "Surrender to what? It's not like the manifestation has a mind of its own."

"Are you sure? It's your shadow and reflection, which aren't as simple as manipulating light and dark. What if they *do* have their own wills and you have to bend to them?"

He almost wanted to be done with the conversation. Her reasoning made no sense and the longer she tried to explain it, the harder it would be for him to shut her down. "I'm not sure. That seems rather far-fetched."

"Don't dismiss me like I'm some fool, Marshall. I know I am probably a child in your eyes, but only a fool would refuse to take advice when he doesn't know what to do. Last night you told us that you woke up at the House of Darian and your shadow and reflection were both gone, though you had no control over it. So perhaps you unwittingly surrendered to them and they took the opportunity to leave.

Why refuse to try our suggestions when you don't even know how to control your own manifestation?"

Light of Orijin, she's offended that I'm not taking her advice? Who does she think she is? And why would I follow her advice? Because she thinks she has a point? He paused for a moment. *Then again, perhaps it wouldn't hurt to try it. But then do I look weak for taking her suggestion? Maybe it doesn't matter. When it doesn't work, then she'll feel stupid. And then I can put her in her place for talking to me like that.* "Fine. I'll try your way then."

The riverbank faced east, putting his shadow behind him as he turned to the flowing water. Marshall looked down at the clear river and opened himself to his manifestation. He embraced the melody, but did his best to avoid trying to control it. He stared into the water and allowed the melody to consume him, rather than harnessing it as he usually did. Marshall continued to concentrate on the water as he surrendered to his manifestation. The more he let go, the more it seemed to extend beyond him, to the point that he felt like he was connected to the whole world.

As his reach extended, Marshall felt a presence getting closer, as if something familiar was approaching. He continued to stare at the water, where his reflection should have been, as he felt the presence continue to grow closer. After several moments of focusing on the water and letting his manifestation flow freely, his reflection appeared in the water before him. It started off as faint and then quickly became clearer. He'd never paid much attention to his reflection before, though mirrors were uncommon in the Taurani village. Still, seeing himself in the water brought a sense of relief and completion. The reflection mirrored his movements, much to his delight.

He'd forgotten that the others were beside him until Lumien shouted out, "I see it! Your reflection! It's there in the water, do you see it Marshall?"

He smiled at Lumien's excitement, "I do! Trust me, I'm more excited than you are, even if I'm not showing it. The thing is, I'm more relieved than anything else. I feel more complete, if that makes any sense. Even in my mind, it feels like there's more of me there than before." He continued to stare at his reflection as he spoke, nervous that at some point it might stop mirroring him and disappear again. To his surprise, the reflection moved its head on its own, as if looking around, then looked back at him.

The image stared at him and Marshall stared right back, hoping there was some type of connection happening. He wasn't sure if or how it would try to communicate with him, and as if it knew his thoughts, he became aware of it in his mind. There were no words or even images, but somehow he became aware of its intentions and capabilities. *Damnit, it's just like Vylsia said. Mutual understanding. It does have its own will and we have to work together. It's why I didn't die after Maqdhuum stabbed me in the stomach.* Marshall gained a new understanding of what he could do with his reflection and he was certain it worked the same with his shadow. He looked around at the others. "I understand it now. I'm sorry Vylsia, I should have listened to you instead of arguing. You were right; it does have a will of its own and it can go off and do its own thing. Now that I've surrendered to it, I'm *aware* of it and it's like a new part of my mind has been unlocked. And now that I understand it, I realize it works the same way for my shadow as well."

Lumien cocked his head and narrowed his eyes. "So you understand them now. But what is it that they can do? It sounds exciting, but how can a shadow or reflection help with anything?"

Marshall nodded, "I wondered that for a long time as well, and I think maybe that's why I never made it a priority to find out until now. They can attack other shadows and reflections. While that isn't enough to kill anyone on the spot, the consequences can still be dire for anyone who loses their reflection or shadow. Losing either one can cause a person to forget who they are or even slowly remove them from existence. It's almost too bad that you're all friends. I would love to have the opportunity to try them out, but I suppose that will have to wait. Unless any of you are eager to see what happens?" They all shook their heads quickly. "Oh well. It was worth a try."

***

"Are you sure this is necessary? You have them in a cage, for the love of Orijin!" The curly-haired girl yelled at Maqdhuum in a panic. He felt bad for her, for all of them actually. But just as with Horatio, he wasn't going to take any chances when it came to Jahmash.

"Positive. Their minds are controlled by Jahmash. The Red Harbinger himself. It's only a matter of time before he figures out that you're all not in Brogan anymore. So tell me quickly, what was the arrangement with King Renan? Did he already agree to help Jahmash? And what were your names again?"

She looked at him flatly, "I am Aurkene and this is Suriiya. The king said he would help us if we managed to defeat the two monsters that he set upon us. You took us away just as he agreed to send his armies. You have to bring us back so he doesn't think we betrayed him. Ashes of Infernua, why the hell did you take us away?"

"Are you that dense?" He nodded at Bo'az and Aric, who were both locked inside the cell that he'd originally built for Horatio. "Jahmash is in their minds. What could be more dire than that? I know, I know. You both grew up on the island of Bisitsad and have no idea about what Jahmash is planning. Which is why both of your nations agreed to support him, though I'm sure you don't know why. My name is Maqdhuum. However, it used to be Abram. I was there when he turned on us. I lived through it and now I'm trying to stop him. And part of that is getting him out of their heads." He glanced over at Eddis Ebaba, who was standing behind them but off to the side. "You ready? Can I count on you?"

Eddis nodded without much of an expression. "Yes, if I must. Do not let them in. Do not let those two out."

"Good. I should only be gone for a couple of minutes." He looked at Aurkene and Suriiya, "I'll be right back. If you try anything stupid, remember that Eddis can wield terrible magic that will kill you easily. It wouldn't end well for you." He smiled at them and disappeared from the floating island.

In an instant, Maqdhuum was on the outdoor patio of Badalao's family estate. He looked around to ensure that no one else was there, and exhaled once he was sure that he was alone. *I guess I'll have to find what room they're in.* He quietly walked inside and turned down a long corridor with several dark wooden doors. It only made sense to check each one, even if things seemed quiet. *Might be enjoying a midday nap.* He slowly opened door after door on each side of the hallway, but each room had been empty so far. Once he reached the sixth or seventh— he'd lost count—he thought he heard low voices.

He turned the handle slowly, hoping there would be no squeak. He felt the lock move, opened the door slightly and peeked in. *You have to be kidding me. Of all the times, they have to be doing this now?* A woman, whom he assumed to be Farrah, stood naked facing the bed and he managed to see Badalao's legs and arms behind her, though he was still clothed. *I've got to get him while he's still dressed. It'll be awkward otherwise.* He disappeared from the door and reappeared inside the room, right next to the bed. Farrah looked at him and attempted to cover herself, while also squealing, then fainting and falling to the ground. Badalao called out to her confusedly. "I'm sorry Lao, she's fine, but I need you for a few minutes."

"You? Get the hell out of here. Why would you dare come into our room at this moment and think this is acceptable? Are you really that much of an asshole?"

The insult frustrated him, but he couldn't let on. "I'm not, but I'll explain when we reappear. Time is of the essence." *I'm trying to save his friends and hurt Jahmash's cause, and he has the nerve to call me an asshole? Fuck him. Now I'm glad I walked in when I did.* They appeared back on the floating island. He was nervous that the two girls might try something irrational with Horatio, or that Jahmash might try to lure him through Bo'az or Aric. However, Maqdhuum was delighted to see that everything and everyone was the same as when he left.

"Goodness, Meli Ikitenya, that felt like an eternity. You said you would be quick!" Eddis looked at him sternly.

"Seriously? I was gone for two, maybe three minutes. It couldn't have been that bad."

"You know how it is when you are waiting for something. Minutes feel like hours. Besides, I wasn't sure if either of these two would try anything. They look like they're plotting something."

Badalao interjected, "You brought me back *here*? Why? I already got Jahmash out of Raish's head. What more could you need from me?"

"Right. You call me an asshole but then ask idiotic questions. Horatio wasn't the only one under Jahmash's control. Did you think it stopped with him and your girlfriend? There are so many others, and I'm the one trying to find them. I know you all think I'm some selfish bastard, but do you even know who's in the cell right now?" He paused for a moment to let Badalao take in the awkward silence. "That's what I thought. There are two people in there. Their names are Bo'az Kontez and Aric Taurean. If you weren't aware, Bo'az is Baltaszar's twin brother. They haven't seen each other in about three years. Aric is one of the last Taurani in the world. I know this because I led the army that destroyed his village. Back when I was still an asshole. But I've changed since then. And in case you didn't figure it out, Aric and Marshall were friends. They also haven't seen each other in about three years. So I'm trying to fix things. Trying to undo what Jahmash has done. By getting him out of their heads, they're not bound to recruit armies for him anymore. They reached Bisitsad and managed to make deals with each of those nations. However, they haven't gotten to Orol Taghdras yet, and there are six nations there. One nation, Vitheligia, already invaded Ashur on its own, but there are five others and if we can ensure that Bo'az and his company never get there, I'm sure you can see how much that helps Ashur in this coming war." He nodded to Eddis and signaled for him to unlock the cell.

Badalao looked toward him with empty eyes. Maqdhuum noticed the black and purple surrounding where Badalao's eyes used to be. He wondered if the man's face would ever heal, but assumed that Lincan had already tried to do so. Badalao responded, "It would be so much easier if you would appear in front of Jahmash and just kill him. Or are you still too much of a coward to do that?"

Do I really deserve all this shit? Maybe I do, but how long are they going to give me so much grief for it? I'm trying to fix things now. Is he right? Should I just try to end this whole thing once and for all by confronting Jahmash? He would destroy me. Even if I have a chance, it's not worth it to die right now. There's too much to do. He waited until Eddis had completely opened the cell door, then grasped Badalao by the upper arm and shoved him into the cell. Badalao stumbled for a few steps then tripped and landed on his knees. Maqdhuum closed the door and locked it. "I'll consider your advice. Thanks. In the meantime, have at it. The sooner you free their minds, the less chance there is of Jahmash appearing in there and giving you trouble. Better to be quick than to risk anything. Good luck. I did you a favor and bound their hands and legs, and blindfolded them as well. You can either feel around or use someone else's eyes. Up to you." Maqdhuum turned and walked toward the edge of the floating island. He shouted back to Eddis, "Eddis, if the two ladies try anything, you know what to do."

Eddis sighed, "Yes. I will use my *terrible* magic on them."

He reached the edge and sat with his feet hanging over. He looked around and took in the vast landscape before him. The sprawling hills of Domna Orjann looked so small from this high up, but the view took his breath away at times. Having lived for over two thousand years, there were few places in the world that made him feel like he was seeing something for the first time. But every time he looked out at the world from the Deseeti Semai, it felt like the first time he was doing so. Maqdhuum stared off and thought about everything that had happened with Horatio and his mother. He'd been in a different mindset when he used Raya to get to the Orijin. At the time, even though he'd wanted to stop Jahmash, he'd hated so many people and barely saw any of the Marked Descendants as useful. It had been an easy opinion to form, as he'd barely interacted with any of them from the time they'd started appearing throughout Ashur. *They were so fearful of their own abilities. Timid. Looked at themselves as abominations instead of prophets. So easy for the king to hunt them down and kill them. And that idiot Marlowe made them even softer.* He shook his head at the thought of it all.

Wish I had seen the truth sooner. Could have saved more of them. Then again, they all hate me because of this whole Raya thing. And I get it. I fucked up that whole situation. But how do they not see I'm different now? And the worst part is he's right about Jahmash. If I would just grow some balls, I could just confront Jahmash and take him on. Could he really be that much better than me? Actually, yes. Yes he could. Even with me being able to disappear and reappear. He's too smart for it all. He'd kill me. Easily. There's no point in even entertaining it.

He continued to ponder and feel sorry for himself for several minutes until he heard shouting behind him. He sprung up and started walking toward Eddis, who had turned around to face the cell. "Hey! What's happening? Everything alright?"

Eddis glanced at him as he opened the cell door. "I think he's just finished. From the sound of things, anyway."

Maqdhuum looked past Eddis and stepped in to help Badalao out of the cell. "Did it work? Are their minds free from him?"

"Yes. Both of them are free now." He labored with his breaths, as if he'd been running forever. "He had an insanely strong hold on Bo'az's mind, but I managed to root out all traces of his presence. Aric's mind was much easier."

"Good. Thank you. Eddis, can you please lead him inside and the girls as well? Let them all rest for a bit. They've been through a lot in a short period of time. I'm going to unbind these two and I'll let them rest in here for a little while."

They can give me the villain's treatment if they want. Jahmash, I just took two more of your toys away and I know that's going to seriously fuck up your expectations. What are you going to do when you realize Bo'az isn't coming back? When you don't know exactly which nations he managed to get to? I wish I could be there when you realize you can't get into Bo's head anymore.

Maqdhuum went back to the edge of the island and let his legs hang over the side once more. He allowed himself to get lost in his thoughts for a while. The notion of confronting Jahmash crossed his mind multiple times, though he dismissed it immediately each time. He knew doing so would undo everything he'd worked toward for the past two decades.

After getting tired of constantly circling back to one specific thought, he pushed himself up and checked on Badalao. *Good enough. Might as well get him back. Hopefully Farrah's still up for rewarding his efforts.* He grasped the Markosi's shoulder and traveled back to the room in which he'd found him. He set Badalao down on the bed, only to realize that Farrah was sitting on the other side of it, adorned in a thick robe. She turned to them in shock and Maqdhuum noted the splotches covering her face. As soon as she saw Maqdhuum's face, she turned to face him and punched him in the cheek.

"Bloody stones! What the hell was that for?"

"You really don't know?" Her voice cracked as she yelled, "You just show up and take him away without any explanation, especially after what you did? How dare you?"

I'm getting really tired of this. He lunged across the bed at her, grabbing her robe by the neck. He stood up from the bed and lifted her in the air. He was surprised at how squarely her punch had landed. "Listen you stupid groveling little wench, I could easily make you appear in Jahmash's fortress right now. He would have so much fun with you and would pick your mind apart, memory by memory, to find out what you've been doing ever since he put you on that ship so long ago. It must have severely bothered him that you didn't come back."

"And then he'd know everything you've done, too. Fool." She gritted a response, though fear painted her face.

He shrugged, "Very well. Then I can put you in the clouds and let you drop into the sea. If you're lucky, the impact will kill you. Sometimes it's not enough to break your neck. But it would break your ribs. Maybe your hands and feet, too. Makes the drowning all the more excruciating. My point is, if you ever hit me or even touch me again, I will kill you. Am I being clear?" She nodded, which angered him even more. "I'm sorry, I didn't *hear* you."

"Y-yes. Clear."

"Yes, who?"

"Yes Maqdhuum."

"Good." He gritted his teeth and flung her into the wall. Without bothering to check on Farrah, Maqdhuum walked over to the other side of the bed and tousled Badalao's unkempt hair. "Sorry Lao. Shame you two were so brazen. Things would've gone a lot more smoothly."

CHAPTER 15
BLINDNESS AND SIGHT

From **The Book of Orijin,** **Verse Four Hundred Twelve**
Loyalty and agreement are not one and the same. Loyalty to your loved ones will require truth, not flattery.

"We should be at Xuyen in another hour or so." Lincan eyed Adria without turning his head. Her face seemed tight, as if either impatient or concentrating. "You've been quiet for a while. Granted you're not loose with your words, but something's definitely on your mind."

She pursed her lips and looked at him flatly. "Always so intuitive, aren't you, Linc?"

"You know me," he grinned and shrugged.

"Eh, I'm just thinking about Marshall is all. He's been on my mind this whole time, but I've been fighting with myself and doing everything to not turn around and go to him."

"You know as well as I do that that wouldn't go very well. Not only would that seriously complicate things between you two, but he's doing it for a reason. I'm sure the last thing he wants is to be away from you, but he's right. He needs—no, he deserves the time and space to figure out his manifestation. Remember, *we* all had years to figure out our own. He's only known about his for what, three years? Even Asarei tried to help him and it didn't work."

"Linc, I know. Trust me, I know. That's exactly why I haven't left already. It's just that our relationship started while preparing to storm a castle and kill a king. It's not like I was some maiden who caught his eye while shopping at the market. Everything has had to fit in between training or planning or just surviving. I was hoping that this journey would provide some time for us to be together while things weren't tense. Because, I'm sure you know that things will be once we get to Xuyen."

He looked behind him at the two Kraisos and the handful of knights riding behind them. "You have no idea. First I need to see my family. It's probably been about ten years since I've actually been home."

"Hold on a moment. You don't get off the hook that easily. We can talk about your family in a bit, especially because you already told me about how you had to live on a fishing boat for a while to avoid being discovered by the Vermillion. *I* want to know about you and Delilah."

"It's not like there's something to hide." He rolled his eyes. "What do you want to know?"

"Well it's just that one moment you two were a pretty serious thing, and then all of a sudden she was kissing Krissette at Asarei's fortress. I'm sure it's a lot to take in."

"It definitely wasn't as big a deal as it looked. What we had was mostly physical. Anything we had going between us happened at the House of Darian. Once we ended up in Sundari, she told me that it had to end. Sure, it was awkward and uncomfortable for a while, especially since we had to travel together to get to the Tower of the Blind. But honestly, there was no relationship. It was only sex. Obviously it was good since it was me, but that's all there was between us. She had never been with a man and was curious, and I would be a fool to say she isn't attractive. There was barely an opportunity to think about where it could go. So that's that."

"What about now? Would you want more?"

"Truthfully, it doesn't really matter. She stopped it because she wanted to be serious about her life as a Daughter of Tahlia. There's nothing to be done about something like that."

Adria smiled at him, "Don't give me that 'truthfully' nonsense. You didn't answer the question."

Lincan shrugged, "What do you want me to say? She was fun, her personality was great, and she was seductive as hell. Of course I would have liked for things to continue, but like I said, it doesn't matter. It's not like we got into a fight or something. She's chosen a path that forbids her from being in a relationship with a man. There's not much to be done about it." He didn't bother to include that he'd felt spurned by Delilah ending things. It would only lead to more questions and he didn't feel like extending the conversation.

"It's not like she can't ever be with a man. You could have children together."

"That's fruitless. I don't want that for myself. It's one thing to have just a physical relationship when we're young, but I don't want to be a father to children I'll never see. Vasher seems like he turned out alright, but I would never want that for my own children. I would feel too guilty."

"So this whole thing started because you two had to work

together in the infirmary?"

"Yeah. It all started because of Tasz, believe it or not. It was innocent enough at the beginning. Flirting here and there and I'm sure she was drawn to my charisma. After all, she made the first move by showing up at my door. And then *through* my door. With a manifestation like that, it's pretty easy to sneak around. Anyway, I think we've covered everything about me and Del. What about you and Marshall? When did you start to feel like there was something there? Was it back at the House when we first brought him in?"

"Oh, for the love of Orijin, no! He was such a child back then. Do you remember that whole tantrum he threw while we were in the room? With the mirror and everything? There was no way I thought anything of him back then. It was actually during the attack on the House that I first felt something, though I didn't know it at the time. I was shackled to the mast of a ship and Maqdhuum came back and freed me. I didn't want it to be *him*, but I was glad to be freed. And right after he saved me from drowning on that ship, Marshall and Savaiyon appeared a few feet away from us, and then Maqdhuum took me away. I remember being so surprised at seeing him there, and it dawned on me that I must have mattered to him enough for him to be there with Savaiyon. That *I* must have mattered to him that much. I don't think I acknowledged it at the time, given everything that was going on. But I think I *saw* him for the first time in that moment.

"You know me, Linc. I don't like to be the victim. I don't want to be rescued or saved. But being held captive on that ship with no way to save myself, deep down I knew that I would need exactly that. I didn't want to admit it to myself because it would have defeated me. But yeah, Marshall was the one who came for me. And I will always remember the look of horror on his face as I disappeared with Maqdhuum. I knew immediately that he cared about me beyond just trying to do the right thing."

Lincan wanted to chuckle at the irony, but he thought better about potentially insulting her. "I'm pretty sure that there have been at least two dozen men who made an advance at you since you arrived at the House. And all of them would have gladly rescued you"

She stared at him flatly, "Each of them was trying to rescue me from all of the others in a situation where I was perfectly capable of handling myself. Granted, I never wanted any of their attention, but I was quite able to navigate those situations. And it's funny how you've separated yourself from all of *them*, as if you weren't one of the first *boys* to try and pursue me." Her mouth turned into a wry smile.

Damn. I forgot about that. "Well, what do you expect? I was young and eager at that time and, don't take this the wrong way, Mouse, but you've always been pretty."

"Oh here we go with the 'Mouse' stuff again."

"Don't even pretend like you're insulted. You know it's a term of endearment from me. I never belittled you or treated you like you *needed rescuing*. Sure I flirted with you for what, a day? It's not like I pushed for anything once you made it clear that you weren't interested."

Adria raised her eyebrows at him, "Flirted? Linc, you *kissed* me within a week of me being at the House of Darian. Sure you didn't treat me like some damsel in distress, but damn, you were forward like you would have bedded me if you had the opportunity."

He paused for a moment to take in his words. *Wow, was it really like that?* He had definitely been forward with girls from the time he'd arrived at the House, and his advances had worked quite a few times, but he didn't remember being so aggressive with Adria. Or perhaps he hadn't paid any attention to what he was doing. "I'm sorry. I guess it doesn't do much to say I was a much different person back then. My priorities were definitely not the same."

"Thank you. I appreciate that. Honestly, while I obviously remember it all, it's not something that I cried about but it *did* offend me. I just assumed you were like all the others. And sure, I know that you've changed. Once you backed off, it was easy to see that you were a good person. That's sort of why I never bothered to bring it up."

He nodded, more to himself than to her, "I'm guessing you haven't mentioned any of it to Marshall?"

"Nah. He's well aware of how many boys I had to dodge at the House, even Maximillian told him as much, but the names were never really that important. Especially now that so many of them…"

Are dead. "Yeah. I get it." They rode on in silence for a little while. Lincan wanted to say something, but he couldn't gauge whether to be casual, serious, or humorous with Adria, so he said nothing. If anything, the quiet made things more awkward the longer it endured. He focused on the clopping of the horses' hooves as they trotted toward Xuyen. He pointed ahead, "If you focus, you can see the walls of the city far ahead. We should be there shortly."

He noticed her squinting her eyes, but she remained focused and he couldn't tell whether the tension had eased between them. *Should I say something else? Should I just leave it at that? Damn, normally I know exactly what to say in any situation. But this is weird and I'm not used to being the asshole. Maybe a joke to lighten things up?* Lincan chewed for several minutes on the right thing to say. As the gates to Xuyen drew closer, he started to panic about what to say. "So was I at least a good kisser?" He smiled at her awkwardly.

Adria cocked her head at him and narrowed her eyes, "What? After working through all that and then talking about how different you are now, that's what you want to know?"

"No, I was just…"

"You know what? You were terrible. You know why? Because you threw yourself at a girl who barely knew anyone, thinking you could just have your way with me and that I would fall for it because I looked like some weak, helpless girl who you probably thought was desperate for someone to cling to. Fuck you, Linc. How about that?"

"Mouse, calm down for a second."

Her gaze turned into a glare, "Don't you dare call me Mouse! My name is Adrianza Mariako 'Kingsbane' Varela. You can call me Adria or Adrianza, or even Kingsbane. But you *do not* get to call me 'Mouse' anymore." She steered her horse away from him and off the path.

"Wait, what are you doing?"

"I'm stopping. I'm not going with you to Xuyen. You have enough company to handle this place yourself. And I'm sure you'll be fine. I'm leaving and if you try to follow me, I swear by the Orijin, Linc, I'll attack you. So go handle this business for Ashur, and forget about me."

Adria didn't wait for him to respond. She turned her horse around and spurred it to a gallop and raced away. Lincan looked around at his remaining companions. "What the hell just happened?" *Damnit, she's in full armor, too. Where the hell could she be going?*

Asp, one of the Kraisos behind him responded, "I believe you insulted her with your poor attempt at a joke. You see, Adria Kingsbane went into great detail to share her trauma with you, which you had a part in, and your way of trying to ease the tension was to make a tactless joke about kissing. Given the amount of time we traveled in silence, it would seem that that was what you thought was the best option. However, it would have been better to say nothing at all."

Wow. She's straight to the point. "Thanks, Asp." He raised his eyebrows at the knights, "Can one of you catch up to her and travel with her? I'm not certain where she's headed, but if it's where I'm thinking, then she'll be riding for a while. She'll need some company." The knights all looked at each other for a moment and eventually settled on who would go. One of them turned and rode off after Adria.

"Your sarcasm is unnecessary. Why did you not try to stop her from leaving?" The bony girl looked even younger than Adria, though Lincan knew looks could be deceiving.

Lincan looked at her, annoyed. "She barely let me get a word in when I was trying to explain myself. There was nothing I could do!"

"I find your contradictory ways to be quite intriguing, Lincan. The whole quarrel started because long ago, you forced yourself upon her for such a little thing as a kiss. However, now she has put herself in danger by leaving our company, and you offer no force to try and sway her mind. It makes little sense to me."

Lincan shrugged in resignation. As much as he'd always prided himself on his intelligence and wit, Asp spoke circles around him with her logic and there was no argument he could make against her. "You're right, Asp. Happy? Clearly I have a number of things to improve upon. Contradicting myself is one. Adria and I have gotten close over the years, ever since that whole thing. I didn't realize how much it had stuck with her, and I was wrong for what I did. I know I was. I just didn't see it that way at the time and I let myself forget about it because my younger self was too immature to realize how it made her feel."

Asp rode alongside him now, while Moon, the other Kraiso, rode on Lincan's other side. She stared ahead as Xuyen came into view. "These are all good things to say to her when you see her again. Feel free to continue practicing your apology with me. Moon as well. We can both give you constructive feedback, though as you've noticed, Moon doesn't talk much. He's a good listener, though." She turned back to look at the remaining knights behind them. "Are any of you interested in helping Lincan with his apology to Adria? He definitely could use the help."

Lincan didn't bother to look back, as he was sure the embarrassment on his face was visible through the back of his head. "Thank you for being so considerate."

"Lucky you. The knights are not interested. I suppose they are more focused on their duties."

"Lucky me indeed." Lincan took a deep breath. "Why didn't

you go after her to make sure she's safe? All your wit and criticism could have been used more productively to accompany Adria."

She continued to look ahead as her thick, curly, dark brown hair flailed in the breeze. "I do not answer to you or to Adria. My mission, as directed by the Kraisos, is to help prepare Xuyen and the other cities of Fangh-Haan for the fight against Jahmash and his armies. That would still be the same directive if you also decided to leave or if both of you were still here."

They finally arrived at the entrance to Xuyen and Lincan led them all through the gate. He nodded at the sentry while responding to Asp. "Good to know. Thank you for clarifying."

"I'm an intelligent young woman, Lincan. But one thing I have trouble understanding is why you show no remorse for your actions even after your *friend* was so upset with you that she turned and left you, despite how serious this mission is. You offended Adria so greatly that she became incapable of helping to prepare the world for Jahmash's coming. And yet you still have taken no ownership for your actions or words. How sure are you that you are so different from the boy who forced Adria to kiss him *so long ago*?"

Why won't she just drop it already? "Did you stop to think that perhaps I'm still going over it all in my head and I need to take some time to sort out my thoughts? I know I've upset her; believe me I do. But the whole situation is something that I haven't even thought about since it happened. So I could use some time to sit down and think about it all. Is that too much for me to ask? For someone who just met the two of us, you sure are greatly offended for Adria."

"It's just another thing that hasn't occurred to you. You men and boys walk around like you rule the world and want to just take everything by force. Our mouths. Our bodies. Our decisions and independence. You think because you are men, you have a right to do what you wish with us. You never stop to think that just because you can, it does not mean you should. Let me ask you something, Lincan. Clearly you fancy women, but have you ever been with a man?"

"What? No? What does that have to do with anything?"

"My companion here, Moon, fancies men. And as you can see, he is much bigger and stronger than you are. What would you do if he pulled you from your horse right now, pinned you to the ground, and kissed you against your will?"

Damnit. What the hell is going on? "I don't know, I guess there wouldn't be much that I could do."

"And how would you feel about Moon and the whole situation after it happened?"

He took a deep breath. He knew what she wanted to hear but also wanted to answer honestly, "I would be angry and probably afraid of it happening again. I'd probably also want to make him pay for it. I think I understand your point."

"No. The fact that you had to say that means you don't. Because what would you do if this world was full of men who would do that to you whenever they wanted? And acted on those desires more times than not? Do you think you would ever feel safe?"

Lincan paused for a moment. He didn't want to be too eager with his response. He was starting to empathize with Asp, and grasped what she was getting at. "No. I wouldn't. I would probably always have my guard up."

Asp nodded at him emphatically, "Yes you would. So now you have the slightest understanding of Adria's experience. And mine. And I will tell you something. Moon will not harm you. He is a gentle soul. But I am not. And if for one second I think I cannot trust you or I think you might be a threat, I will not hesitate to stab you. And you will not see it coming."

He slowed his horse and paused to consider her words. *Can't let on that she's having an effect on me. She thinks I should be afraid of her.* "I think this is where we're supposed to part ways. I have to see my family before tending to business, and I believe you have some meddling to do. You and Moon can finally be free of me, and I'll take the knights with me."

Asp glared at him for a moment before riding away with Moon. The large man turned back to look at Lincan and smiled at him. *What the hell is that for? Is that a flirtatious grin or an intimidating one?* He didn't bother to let it make him stagnant and continued toward the southern part of the city where his home was, with the few knights in tow. Several people paused as he and his companions passed them, and he was sure it was because the last thing they expected to see was a Marked Descendant leading knights through the streets. Despite the shock, no one said a word to them.

He remembered traveling through the city when he was much younger, though he surprisingly didn't feel as if he'd missed it. Most of the memories involved him traveling in secrecy because of his mark, which meant there were no fun adventures to recall. Lincan could smell the salt of the sea as they reached the southern part of Xuyen. The roads were lined with merchants selling every variety of fish and sea creature imaginable, and Lincan finally felt like he was home again.

After several more minutes, they reached his home, a humble wooden structure not far from the docks. Lincan dismounted, tethered the horse, and grabbed his pack. "I don't expect you to stay with me. Why don't you all go and enjoy yourselves for the rest of the day. There's plenty of sunlight left for you to find an inn and get some rest. You can meet me back here in the morning. I want to catch up with my parents and siblings and, with all due respect, I'd like to do so in privacy." The knights looked at one another and nodded at Lincan simultaneously. "Good, that was easy. Thank you for accompanying me down here. If you happen to catch wind that Asp and Moon have plans to attack me, then please come here right away." The knights snickered and rode off.

As he watched them ride away, Lincan realized he was stalling about knocking on the door. He finally turned to face his home and took a deep breath. Part of him wished he had gone after Adria and not come all this way, but he knew he had to. His parents weren't the warmest of people, but everything they had done had been out of love. And he knew that sometimes that had to be tough love, even if it had been hard to understand at the time. He raised his fist and rapped on the door hesitantly.

The wooden door creaked open after a moment and a head peeked out from the opening. He smiled awkwardly, not knowing what the reception would be. However, as soon as his mother realized it was him, she flung the door open all the way and hugged him tightly. His mother was a short and petite woman, but the force of her arms around him made Lincan forget that. "Maa, it's so good to see you again! I wasn't sure if you'd be happy to see me."

"Oh, Lincan. You must be joking! I have missed you since the moment you left us! Hao! Hao, come! It's Lincan! He's come home! He's in bed; he had a long morning on the boat. Good haul today! Come, come. Leave your bag inside here and come sit down."

He listened as his mother beckoned him inside and pushed him toward a wooden rocking chair with cushions. "Is this a new chair? Is Baa alright? Should I go check on him?"

"No, no. You sit. I'll make us some tea. Baa will be down in a moment. You worry too much. Everything is fine." His mother walked into the kitchen in the next room.

Lincan took a breath and let himself lean back into the chair. It felt good to relax in a comfortable chair after riding for so long, especially after his exchanges with Adria and Asp. He wouldn't worry about that at the moment, though. "Where are Linh and Tien?" He didn't want to let his disappointment show, but was surprised that his brother and sister hadn't come running out to see him.

"Tien is with a friend at the market. They are selling today's catch. He does that now for Baa after they return from fishing. Besides, he's a much better haggler than Baa ever was, so he brings more coin home for us and sells the fish faster. I think the eye accident might have actually helped him with that."

Lincan questioned whether he'd heard her correctly, "Did you say eye accident?"

His mother finally returned to the room with two cups of tea. "Hold on. Those are for you and Baa. Let me get mine." She went back to retrieve her cup and then sat down in a cushioned chair next to him. "It has been a few years now, but your brother had an accident on the boat while they were out. One of the new deck hands tried to cast his line and wasn't paying attention. As he was about to cast, he was only a few feet away from Tien and caught him high on the cheek. Unfortunately, he pulled to send the line out and the hook ripped open his cheek and his eye as well. I was a wreck, but your brother took it all in stride. You know how he is. All jokes even in the face of something like that."

"So did he lose the eye or is it still there?" Lincan regretted that he hadn't been home when the accident happened. He wondered if it was as bad as Badalao's or if his brother was in better shape. *I wonder if he can still be fixed.*

His mother shrugged, "It's still in there, but he wears a patch to cover it up. He's gotten used to it now. Why would you be concerned with such a detail?"

"Well if his eye is still there then I wonder if I can heal him. There's a chance that I could fix it and get him back to normal."

She set down her tea on a small table next to her. "You'll have to talk to him about that. Like I said, he's been doing well for himself in the market and his injury may have improved his haggling abilities. He may not even want you to help him."

Did she really just say that he wouldn't want me to heal him? Whatever, I'll let it go for now. "I'll talk to him about it later. He's coming back here, right?"

"Yes of course."

"Good."

"Lincan! Is it really you?" His father appeared at the bottom of the steps and scuttled over to hug him. Lincan rose from his chair and hugged his father tightly. "Oh how I've missed you, *conjhai.*"

Lincan squeezed his father a little harder. It had been a long time since he'd heard that word, which simply meant "son" in Fangh. "I missed you too, Baa." His father released him and sat down next to his mother on a bigger chair meant for multiple people. He looked down at his father's foot out of habit—the man was missing the big toe of his right foot. They had caught an enormous tigerfish on one outing and managed to bring it aboard. However, in all of its flopping and wriggling, the dying fish chomped at one fisherman's leg, taking a chunk out of it. As it continued to flail, it bit at his father's foot and tore the big toe right off. The giant tigerfish had bitten into the rest of the toes as well, but that was the moment when Lincan's manifestation took shape. He vaguely remembered praying so hard to the Orijin to save his father's life and for someone to stop the bleeding.

In the moment, some of the men on board went to the fish to slit its throat and gills, while a couple others tried to tend to Lincan's father. He knew right away that he could help his father and tended to him. Most of the men backed away once they saw Lincan's face and he realized that the Mark must have appeared. He didn't let any of it distract him, though. He grasped his father's foot and shin, closing his eyes and concentrating, hoping to stop the blood flowing out. After several moments, he opened his eyes and realized that his father's toes had been healed. The big toe was still gone, but the wound had closed.

From the time he was little, Lincan's parents were never the affectionate type. They were always loving and kind, but they barely hugged or embraced, and showing emotions had been a rare thing. When he cried after his father's accident, it was the only time he remembered the rest of his family drowning him in hugs and sympathy. Otherwise, their manner generally was matter-of-fact. He knew it meant a great deal for his parents to see him again. "Where's Linh? I thought she would be home as well."

His parents both looked at him and smiled, and his mother responded. "Oh, Lincan. It really has been so long, hasn't it? Your sister has been married for what, four years now? And she has a son! You're an uncle!"

"Wait, seriously? That's amazing! Where is she, though?"

"Tien and me, and Linh's husband, Ngiem, built a small house for them. It's the next house over, but far enough away for them to have some privacy. Why don't you rest up a bit. Go lay down or take a nap. I'm sure you could use it. I'll walk over there and tell them you're here. They can come here for dinner; Tien will be back soon anyway. Everyone can eat together."

"Are you sure? You don't need help with anything?"

His mother stood up, "What's there to help with? I was about to start cooking anyway, now I just have to make a little more. No big deal. You'll just get in my way. Listen to Baa, go lie in our bed and close your eyes. We'll wake you when it's time for dinner."

"I'm only listening because I'm exhausted." Lincan downed the rest of his tea then stood and grabbed his pack.

"Leave the mug. I'll put it away. You go upstairs."

***

Lincan opened his eyes and blinked a few times. The face of a little boy came into focus and Lincan jumped back. "What the–"

The boy laughed at him and ran out into the hallway, "Maa, he's awake! He's awake!"

My nephew? That's got to be him. What a cute little kid. He sat up on the thin mattress and allowed himself a moment to get his bearings. He heard the pitter patter of two little feet running down the hall, followed by stomping down the stairs. Once the footsteps grew silent, Lincan heard the chatter of his family downstairs and smiled. He jumped from the bed and glided down to the kitchen table. As soon as he walked into the room, his brother and sister both turned and smiled brightly at him. He couldn't help but notice the patch on his brother's left eye, though it did nothing to dim his happiness.

"Hey!" Just as his parents had done, Lincan's brother and sister got up to hug him. While hugs were rare, they were welcome. He pulled back from his sister, "Congrats, *Maa*! Look at you! Married and with a son now! I can't believe I'm an uncle!"

She smiled at him again, "I guess we've all grown up, haven't we Linc? It's so good to see you!" Her husband extended his forearm from behind her and shook Lincan's hand heartily. Lincan nodded to him, "It's nice to meet you, Ngiem. I'm sure Linh's very lucky to have you." He turned to his brother. "And it's good to see you too, Tien. I really missed you. I missed you all. I know we're not the most affectionate family, but there's a lot of love between us and I'm glad I'm here again."

His brother clapped his shoulder, "Speaking of which, I don't mean to make things awkward, but are you back for good or is this just a stop-in before you have to leave again?"

Lincan tried to force a smile. "It's complicated. I'm here for now because I have some business that I have to tend to. And then I'll probably have to leave again. But the whole point of what I'm doing is to make sure that I *can* come back for good sometime soon."

"What business is that?" His brother asked as he sat back down at the table and waved for Lincan to sit next to him.

"I think you should all sit down for this, as it's going to be a heavy conversation." Lincan sat and looked around at everyone. "I don't want to ruin the fact that we're all together again. I knew I'd come back to see you all at some point, and it's safer now for me to travel because King Edmund is dead."

His sister cut in, "It's true? We heard rumors of it but you know how quickly lies can spread. We heard many things, but mostly that he was murdered. Is that true?"

"That's another part of the heavy stuff. He was murdered. I know for sure because it's my friends who did it." He waited a moment for the gasps to finish. "Before you start asking all kinds of questions, let me explain." He broke down the whole process of their agreement with the Anonymi and how they'd planned everything. He also made sure to tell them that he wasn't there when the king was killed, as he knew they'd ask. "So now, Prince Garrison has assumed the throne and the main goal is to prepare Ashur for Jahmash's return." He noticed his sister mouth *the Red Harbinger* to herself. "We don't know exactly when he'll attack, but we know he has armies and we think it will happen within the year. Those of us who have been working together have all split up to travel throughout Ashur to meet with each nation's leaders in order to militarize Ashur. We need armies and militias, anyone capable of fighting, to defend Ashur once he returns. Again, before you ask, the Royal Vermillion Army has turned on Ashur and is aiding in its destruction." He explained about the Vithelegion as well.

Finally his father held a hand up to interrupt him. "So all this, *conjhai,* everything you're doing, is because Ashur is in danger?"

He nodded, "Yes, Baa. We want to make sure there's still an Ashur left after Jahmash attacks. There are nations beyond Ashur from when Darian drowned the world, and some of them have agreed to help Jahmash. Garrison and his general have the loyalty of about half the Vermillion, so at least we have trained soldiers, but they won't be enough. Neither will those of us with manifestations or the Anonymi. We need the people of Ashur to help defend it. So tomorrow morning, there are knights who traveled with me who will meet me here and we will go to the elders to discuss all of this with them. I wanted to see you all first, before doing that."

His mother stood up from the table. "Why don't we take a break from this and eat while the food is still fresh and hot, and then we can get back to it. I know it's serious, Lincan, but I want to enjoy your company while you're here, if that's alright."

"That's fine, Maa. I didn't come home to only talk about this. I wanted to see you all. So we can put all of the other stuff aside for a while and enjoy this time together." The rest of them voiced their agreement and they spent the rest of their time at the table eating rice noodles with various greens and herbs, and roasted fish. Lincan's mother made more tea once they finished eating and they all shared more stories. He had casually mentioned that he could heal his brother, but Tien dismissed the idea as if he wasn't interested, so Lincan let it be. His sister and her husband decided it was time to go once his nephew fell asleep in Linh's lap. Lincan and his brother offered to clean the kitchen after they said their goodbyes and Lincan insisted that his parents relax.

"So this eye thing," his brother said as he grabbed a couple of the plates. "You really think you can fix me?" Lincan followed his brother out to the back of the house where they started a small fire to heat water.

"If your eye is still there, then I think I can. I would at least like to try; I figure I can't make it any worse." Lincan paused for a moment, "If you're interested, why did you refuse so quickly at dinner?"

"I just didn't want to get into it then. I didn't want it to turn into a whole family debate since it's *my* eye. So is it a certainty that you can heal me or are you just guessing?" They continued to bring the wooden dishes out to a basin while the water heated over the fire. "Because it could definitely get worse. You could mess up my face or my other eye."

"No, I've been doing this long enough that I know how to avoid affecting other things. Trust me, Tien, I wouldn't even think about it if there was a chance that I could make things worse for you. But Maa did say that your injury might help with your sales at the market. So if you don't want to do it, then I understand and I'll stop pushing."

His brother stopped walking and turned to him, "I only said that to Maa and Baa so they wouldn't worry about me. I'm sure some people here and there might buy from me because they feel bad and I'm never going to stop them, but you know me, Linc. I can talk to anyone and I have enough regular customers that I don't have to worry about bad days or slow days. We have a consistent thing going."

Lincan smiled and nodded. *I should have expected that from him. He always could turn anyone into his best friend.* "When do you want to do this then?"

His brother put on the thick mitt he'd tucked under his arm and took the pot from over the fire, then poured the hot water into the basin of dishes. "You tired? I'm ready tonight if you are."

"That could work." Lincan took some of the wood ash that was stored in a bucket by the fire and dropped it into the hot water. "I'll need you to lie down and be still. Healing comes with discomfort and perhaps some pain here and there, but we can do it in your bedroom so that you'll fall asleep right after. It generally takes a toll on your body and energy."

Tien smiled. "Perfect." They scrubbed the dishes in the basin as quickly as they could and scuttled back inside when everything was washed. Once the dishes were all set out to dry, Tien raced up the stairs and Lincan followed. Somehow the thought of Adria crept into his head and he stopped at the top of the steps. *Damnit. She'll be fine. I sent the knight to follow her. Besides, there's nothing I can do for her right now.* "Everything alright, Linc? You having second thoughts?"

Lincan shook his head and walked into Tien's room. "No, I was just thinking about a friend of mine. I did something to piss her off and it's been on my mind. I just have to figure out how to fix it is all."

"Need advice, then?"

"Nah, not yet. I'm not ready to get into it just yet." He looked around the room. Once, a long time ago, they had shared the space, though they were much smaller then. That was before Lincan had been relegated to living on his father's boat so no one could see the Mark on his face. *At least I don't have to hide anymore.* "Are you ready for this?"

Tien shrugged, "I guess so. What do I have to do?"

"Lie down on your bed and be still. I'm warning you, this may take a while. For a while, I had the help of someone else because her manifestation made these kinds of things easier. Doing this by myself will take much more time, patience, and concentration. You're lucky, you know. I've learned to numb the area with my manifestation so you won't feel anything." Lincan pushed a small, wooden chair to the side of the bed and sat down. He pulled the eye patch away from his brother's face and assessed the injury. "The scars on your face may have to be done another time. Your eye is the important thing and I'll probably be exhausted once I'm done."

His brother smiled, "Don't even worry about my face, Linc. I just want my eye to work. Whatever you have to do to make that happen is fine. Even if it hurts."

"Got it. As much pain as possible." He laughed at his joke, as did his brother. After a moment, Lincan gently placed his hand on his brother's temple and opened himself to his manifestation. He closed his eyes and let his mind connect to his power. He let the manifestation flow slowly into his brother's left eye, forehead, and cheek. "You should start to lose feeling in the left side of your face. If you feel pain at any point, let me know." His brother nodded slightly and glanced at him awkwardly. *Numbness is starting to take effect already. Good.* He hesitantly placed a fingertip on Tien's eyeball, hoping that his brother wouldn't flinch or shut his eye. "It's a good thing that Maa made such a big meal. These manifestations take a lot of energy and eating a lot of food helps. You don't have to talk, I was just saying."

He focused on the eyeball and let the manifestation flow through his finger. He could feel how the hook had sliced through and, if he wasn't in the middle of healing his brother, Lincan would have shuddered at the thought of the hook piercing his eye. Aside from the veins inside the eye, there were other delicate things that needed to be tended to slowly. "Because of the way your eye was cut, it's better for me to go slow while repairing it. Everything in there is so sensitive and if I try to go quickly, chances are you'll still be blind in the eye. No sense fixing one thing and damaging something else. I know it'll be a pain to have to lie there so still, but like I said, you can always just fall asleep if you're comfortable enough." He placed a second fingertip on his brother's eyeball to get a better feel of the damage.

After another twenty minutes, he realized Tien was asleep. His right eye had shut and his breathing had slowed. *Good. Always easier when they're sleeping.* Lincan had started mending the back of the eye first and he could feel the veins being repaired. He continued to heal the veins throughout his brother's eye and took the time to make sure each one was completely repaired before moving on. *Can't have any scabbing in there; that would be excruciating.*

Once the veins were all intact, he moved closer to the front of the eye. The next step was the parts that Lincan had learned over time controlled the ability to see light and dark and different colors. He took a deep breath and started.

By the time he finished completely and was comfortable that he hadn't forgotten anything, Lincan was sure that it was closer to morning than night. He attempted to rise from the chair, but wobbled and fell over onto the floor. He attempted to form a thought, but everything faded to darkness.

***

"Linc, wake up, you did it!"

Lincan tried to open his eyes and had to blink several times before they'd stay open. "What?"

Tien grabbed his arm and pulled him up from off the floor. "You must have worked for so long that you just fell asleep right there in the chair or on the floor, but you did it! Look! Look at my eye; doesn't it look normal to you now? I can see again! I can see out of both eyes again!"

"Shit! Light of Orijin, I friggin' did it! It really worked!" As they continued to celebrate and yell and scream, Lincan couldn't help but think about Badalao, as well as Adria. *If I can do this for my brother, then there's got to be a way to fix Lao. Maybe I'll have to find him a new set of eyes from someone else? There's no way I can grow him new eyes from nothing; that was my problem before and why it wasn't working. And more importantly, I have to fix things with Adria. Somehow and some way, I have to find a way to make things right.*

CHAPTER 16
BROTHERS

From **The Book of Orijin,** **Verse Four Hundred Forty**
Those whom you love are your family, regardless of bloodlines. The only love stronger than for your family should be for yourself and for Us.

"Finally, the Wolf's Paw is in sight." Baltaszar breathed a heavy sigh of relief. They had traveled for days and the final piece of their journey had been to board a ship in Walde, a city at the south of Galicea.

"Ya better not be tired o' me already. We're still goin' ta be together fer a while longer, Tasz." Desmond stood next to him at the rail on the deck of the small ship. "How ya holdin' up, by the way?"

Baltaszar shrugged. They hadn't talked much about losing all their loved ones since they'd met the others in Alvadon over a week ago. There had been plenty of other things to focus on, especially when the others had been around. He had been relieved to be caught up in everyone else's business, and then Garrison had organized the fighting tournament. "I'm still angry that everyone else knew about this whole Maqdhuum thing and didn't say a word, if that's what you're asking. Just in case you were wondering why I haven't wanted to talk the whole trip down here. Or in case my face didn't give it away. Besides that, I've been so busy trying to process everything that Maqdhuum told me, that I've managed to push thoughts of Anahi to the back of my mind now. Crazy that her death wouldn't be the worst thing I'm dealing with right now." He turned to look at the other side of the ship, where Horatio stood, looking out at the sea. "He's my brother, Des. And then everything that happened with my mother, who I barely remember. It's so much to think about and honestly, it's really hard to address all of the emotions that go along with it."

"Don't worry about me. Ye've barely even spoken ta each other this whole trip. I think it'd be much easier ta deal with the emotions if ya would both talk about things. Don't ya think so?"

"I do, but part of me is angry at him and I don't even know why."

Desmond smirked at him, "A huge part o' ya is just angry in general. Not at Raish specifically. An' I don't blame ya. I'm angry, too.

Probably not at as many things as ya, but I want revenge. Not just fer my family. Fer all o' Vandenar. Fer all o' Mireya. The Vithelegion just came an' took what they wanted with the help o' the Vermillion. That's why this mission is so important, an' why we have ta think clearly. There's too much at stake fer us ta mess this up. So whatever ya have ta do ta get right with Raish, an' with yerself, the sooner the better." Desmond turned and walked away toward the lower deck.

"Understood." Baltaszar nodded at him. While he knew that Desmond was right, acting on it was a much more difficult thing. He turned back toward the water and stared out blankly.

"Hey." The simple word startled Baltaszar until he turned his head slightly and saw Horatio standing a few feet away and looking out at the sea as well. "Sorry, I didn't mean to scare you, Tasz. I just wanted to see how you're doing with everything. I know it's more than you asked for. And I'm sorry for any… trouble my life has caused you. I understand what my very existence means in relation to your family and your… well, *our* mother."

Baltaszar continued to look into the distance. Facing Horatio would send things in a direction that he wasn't willing to take at the moment. "Raish, you don't have to apologize for your existence. That's rather extreme. Look, there's so much that I have to sort out for myself first, before we can have this conversation. And that's not your fault at all. I promise we'll talk about this before leaving Damaszur, but just give me some time to try and make sense of it all."

"Fair enough. Hey, remember when all of you couldn't get me to shut up? Now it's almost a struggle to get me to talk."

"Trust me, I'd take the old way any day. And maybe we'll get back to that one day soon. I think it'll just take time." *And I still don't know whether the prophecy means that I'm going to kill you, Bo, or perhaps a more figurative brother like Linc suggested.* Baltaszar shook the thought away immediately. He glanced past Horatio toward the bow of the ship and realized they were close to land. The captain was yelling for the crew to furl the sails. "Speaking of time, looks like it's time to get ready to dock." They returned below deck and grabbed their packs, then waited patiently for the ship to dock.

***

"I know you're probably thinking that it's a fishing city, and that's somewhat right, but Damaszur is also heavily into mining. That's why we only have one city on the island. Most of the land is used for mining. Apparently there's a huge store of metal ore down there. Mainland Ashur doesn't really know about it, though." Horatio smiled as he explained to Baltaszar and Desmond. He was starting to feel like his normal self after not having control of his own mind for so long. The only problem with finally having his mind to himself was that he was aware of the truth about everything in his life. There was no longer anything to mask any of it, for better or worse, and there were definitely times in which he wondered whether he'd been better off before.

"So then if the city is Damaszur, what's the island called?" Baltaszar rode his horse next to Horatio, with Desmond riding on the other side.

Horatio chuckled more at the thought of his response than the question. "So the island is *also* called Damaszur. It's kind of understood that the city and the island are the same."

"Ya said there's a lot o' minin' done here. What do ya mine an' what is it used for?" Desmond inquired from the other side of Baltaszar.

"To be honest, I know they get a good deal of metal from the mines, though I don't know exactly what kind. They use it for many different things, like bowls and cups, sometimes fancy things…"

"Weapons? Armor? Any o' that sort o' thing?"

He shrugged, "I would imagine they do. Sorry, Des, my mind is still pretty blurry. Even though I spent my whole childhood here, I think I missed a lot of things. Which is why I was hoping we could go to my home first, to see my mother and brother, if you don't mind?"

Baltaszar nodded to him, "That's perfectly fine. I'd also like to learn about your past, especially from your… mother's point of view."

Horatio knew Baltaszar didn't mean any offense in how he'd stressed the word *mother*, but regardless, it was strange to consider the truth that he had a birth mother and an adoptive one. He also knew that Baltaszar must be thinking of their mother and he hoped that any resentment from Baltaszar would fade sooner rather than later. *Of course I feel guilty about what he's been through, but does he actually think any of it is my fault? If it was all undone, I wouldn't even be alive. He already said he didn't hold anything against me. Maybe his head is just foggy because of all this, too.* They turned onto a thin dirt road that, to others, likely looked like it led straight into the sea. "We're almost there. It's near the end of this road." He hesitated for a moment, unsure of how to explain what he wanted to say. "Look. This is sort of embarrassing, but please don't expect much out of my home. We didn't have much and my mother's… her husband died I guess before she even took me in. For whatever reason, most people weren't willing to help her, so our home was basically just walls and a roof."

To his surprise, Desmond tried to comfort him, "Raish, ya know there's not many o' us with the Mark who come from privilege, right? Sure, some o' us live comfortably, but I think that's the point o' us bein' chosen fer the Mark. We're the ones who're in the most danger, an' have ta rely on faith more than anyone else. My home wasn't much either, but it made my family closer because we appreciated everythin' we had."

"And remember, I came from a farm in the middle of a town hidden in the mountains. We lived off our animals and what we could grow. You won't find any judgment from us." Baltaszar turned to the Kraiso riding behind them, "Isn't that right, Wind?" Horatio had almost forgotten that Wind and the other two Kraisos, Sage and Chervil, were with them.

Wind confirmed Baltaszar's words. "He's right, Horatio. It's one of the reasons I left in the first place. My parents didn't have much and I knew I was a mouth they had trouble feeding. It helped to ease their burden. We all know what it's like."

Horatio nodded with a small smile of appreciation and continued on. As the house came into view, his smile disappeared. The roof of his home had holes in it and the outside looked to be one big storm away from collapsing. "Damn. This is even worse than I remember. They must be so busy working that they don't have time to fix anything."

"Look, there are six o' us here who are healthy an' strong. How 'bout before we leave here, we do what we can ta' fix it up a bit?"

He dismounted and the others followed his lead. "That would be great. I appreciate that, Des. Thank you. Let's go inside first and see how they're doing. I haven't been home in about five years, so hopefully they haven't changed much. Then again, my mother might be down in the mines right now. She went off every morning to work there." He decided to knock on the door instead of just walking in. *The last thing I want to do is scare them or have someone get hurt because they got startled.* To his surprise, the door opened and a young woman with thick, curly black hair looked at him. "Um, hello? Are you helping my mother with things around the house or something?"

The voluptuous woman smiled at him and shook her head. "No, unfortunately not." Her accent threw him off; it didn't sound like anything he'd heard before. "My name is Aurkene Ezkerro. My companions and I were brought here and were told to expect you. I think. I'm assuming you are Horatio?"

He looked around at Baltaszar and the others, but didn't bother to wait for the conversation to grow more confusing. "I am. And this is my home, so please excuse me." He brushed past her and walked into his house, and the others followed. "Why would you be expecting us? Who *brought* you here?" As he continued into the sitting room, he saw his mother sitting and talking with a few others around her. Despite his shock at seeing how much older she looked, one of the guests looked exactly like Baltaszar, but with longer hair. "Mother? What's going on here? Who are these people?"

Baltaszar spoke up from behind him, "Bo? Bo'az? Is that really you?" The man he was just looking at shot up from his seat and ran over to Baltaszar.

"Tasz! Holy shit! It's true! He was right! He told us that you would be here and I didn't believe him!"

"Who?"

"His name is Maqdhuum. He rescued us from Brogan and then brought us here."

Oh no. Not Maqdhuum again. No matter what we do, it's like we can't escape him. Tasz isn't going to like that. Horatio decided he didn't want to entertain all that at the moment. He turned his attention to his mother and walked over to her. She stood up and was about to walk to him, but he glided over to her and gave her a tight hug. "I missed you so much. You have no idea how much I've wanted to come back to see you."

His mother squeezed back, though her attempt was feeble. She pulled away and leaned to the side to cough. Horatio held her while she continued her coughing fit for several seconds. She looked at him abashedly once she finally stopped. "I'm sorry, my dear." Her voice was soft and raspy. While she'd never been loud, her voice had never been so frail either. "I haven't been able to catch my breath very well in a while." She paused again, "My chest is very heavy these days. And tight."

He guided her back to her chair. "Sit. Sit, mama. What happened? Was there an accident or something? If it hurts to answer me, then don't bother. I'll understand."

She smiled at him while her eyes still showed sadness. "No, it's fine, dear boy." She let out another small cough. Horatio realized all of the others had reentered the room and sat down in the chairs and on the floor around them. "It's just from working in the mines for so long. It's been happening to many others as well. I just need to rest, is all. The more I rest, the better I feel."

"And what about Leonard? Where is he?"

She offered a slight nod and took a few breaths. "He took my place in the mines. He's been going there every day for the last year or so."

Horatio gritted his teeth and looked away for a moment. He took a deep breath, as if trying to do so for his mother, then looked back at her. "You've been going through this for a year now?"

"Don't you worry about me, Horatio. I'll be just fine. All I need is rest."

Horatio looked down at the ground and then back at her. "Let me take you to your bed, Mama. Go rest for a while. There are a lot of people here and I'm sure it's overwhelming for you. Lie down for a bit and get your strength back, and then we'll catch up a little later." He helped her up and walked her to the bedroom.

"You're always so good to me, Horatio," she said between coughs. She smiled at him as she sat on the bed. "You're right; I just need to rest for a little while. Go be with your friends."

***

Bo'az sat on the scratched wooden floor between Baltaszar and Aurkene. Both of them were people he normally felt safe with, though Aurkene had seemed a bit off since Maqdhuum had taken them away from Brogan. Baltaszar was understandably different than the last time they'd seen each other, especially his eyes, but there was something beneath the surface that Bo'az knew would come to light soon. *He has some things to tell me. Things I'm probably not going to like. I wonder what it could be. After his initial excitement and shock of seeing me, he got quiet pretty quickly.*

Horatio returned from the bedroom and joined them. He sat on the floor, though it was more of a collapse than anything graceful or intentional. "I'm sorry about that. I didn't expect her to be... so sick. It's ironic, isn't it?" He looked at Baltaszar and one of the others who had arrived with them, who also bore the black line down his left eye. "We left our homes because of these Marks, because we knew we'd have to save the world, and yet it's our own loved ones that needed us the most this whole time." He paused for a moment. "Sorry. I know this is an important reunion for the rest of you and I don't mean to ruin the mood."

"You have nothing to apologize for, Raish." Baltaszar comforted him. "You have every right to be upset and nobody here blames you. And if you'd rather be in there with your mother instead, then you should."

Horatio shook his head, "No. She needs to rest and Light of Orijin, it sure seems like there's a lot to discuss out here."

Bo'az took the opportunity to cut in. "I think the first order of business is determining who everyone is and then talking about why we're all here. Maqdhuum mentioned that this was your house, Horatio, but he didn't explain why he brought us here, besides I guess the obvious reason that he knew Tasz would be coming as well. But I imagine there's more to it than that."

A murmur arose among them before everyone quieted down and they went around the room introducing themselves and explaining where they were from. Baltaszar stood up and paced in the little space that he could find. "Fucking Maqdhuum. Did he say whether he'd be back, Bo?"

"No. He hasn't been too outright with the plan going forward. I definitely understand that he can be unlikeable, but why do you have so much anger toward him? What has he done?" He noticed Horatio and Desmond hanging their heads and looking at the ground, though Horatio subtly raised his eyes toward Baltaszar.

Baltaszar turned and looked around at everyone in the room. "I guess there's enough time to explain it all, so here goes." He explained to everyone that Maqdhuum was the Harbinger, Abram, in a new body and with a renewed motive to stop Jahmash. "Bo, I'm sorry that I have to tell you like this, but you might as well find out while surrounded by people who care about you."

What? What the hell could he possibly have to say?

"He's the reason our mother died. These Marks that are on our faces, each of us can do something special because of them. I can control fire. Our mother could travel to the Three Rings. Maqdhuum used her to go there and request a new body and mind from the Orijin. And then after he didn't need her anymore, he handed her over to Jahmash as some type of gift." He paused to look at Horatio, then looked down at the ground and shook his head.

Seriously? That bastard robbed us of our mother? This whole time he had to have known who I was and didn't bother to say a word.

Horatio seemed to take Baltaszar's silence as a signal to continue, "Once she became Jahmash's prisoner, he raped her and impregnated her." His eyes darted around the room for a moment. "I'm the result of that. There's probably a better way to say it Bo'az, but Jahmash is my father and your mother is my birth mother. Jahmash sent me here as a baby to grow up and learn about Ashur. He's been in my head my whole life until a few weeks ago."

Bo'az held his head in his hand and closed his eyes. "This is a lot. I don't know how you two managed to handle all of this. It's going to take me a while to come to terms with everything. But let me guess, Horatio. Someone named Badalao entered your mind and freed it of Jahmash? On a floating island, maybe?"

"Yes. In a wooden cell on a floating island. But don't hold any of it against Lao. He's a good man and has been a huge help to many of us. He's one of us."

"No, of course I wouldn't blame him. None of you know this, but three men came to our home in Haedon looking for Tasz. I pretended to be him, so they took me. Tasz and I grew up knowing nothing of the Harbingers, so I had no idea what it meant or that I should be afraid. And when I finally met Jahmash for the first time, he made one man gouge his own eyes out and cut off another one's ear. He got into my head quickly and basically never let go until a few weeks ago once I guess he was sure I was loyal. The thing is his control was so strong that I *wanted* to do his bidding. I felt happy when I achieved the missions he gave me. And it wasn't until yesterday, when Badalao finally freed my mind and Aric's, that I remembered how horrible he could be." He shuddered remembering the pain of Jahmash controlling his mind and causing him to bleed. "So now what do we do? I understand why Horatio is here, but what about the rest of you?"

Horatio was about to answer him, but Baltaszar interjected. "Well, you already know how Jahmash is hell-bent on wiping out Ashur. We're getting ourselves ready for his attack. There's a faction of us who've been working together to prepare Ashur for his coming, and now we're all traveling to each nation to make sure that anyone physically able can be trained to fight and use a weapon. Speaking of which, Bo, you'll have to tell us what he has planned. What his next moves are and all that."

He's rather cold, isn't he? Does he really only care about those things? "Yeah. We'll have to go over all that. Maybe not right now, though?"

Baltaszar looked at him curiously, "What do you mean?"

"I'm just saying that we all just got here and we haven't seen each other in *years*. It would be nice if we had a little bit of time to catch up and appreciate each other's company for at least a moment. Does that not matter to you?"

His brother took such a deep breath that his shoulders shrugged dramatically. He was about to speak when another voice interrupted. "Doubt it does, Bo'az. He's too filled with anger. Hatred. Too pissed off at everyone else. Especially me." They all looked toward the door and saw Maqdhuum standing there. He looked directly at Bo'az, "But there is some business. Any of you four willing to go back to Bisitsad, now that your minds are free?"

Bo'az looked at Aric, Aurkene, and Suriiya. "Why? What would be the point now?"

"Change the minds of the nations you visited. Get them to reconsider helping Jahmash? What're the chances of that?"

Aurkene responded to him first. "Absolutely not. Castiel gave its word. We were promised claims to land here in exchange for part of our army." She turned to Bo'az, "And that was part of your agreement with my father—that you would bring me here and hold status in the new world. It would bring shame to my family to violate that. Besides, everyone here seems to hate you, Maqdhuum. I've heard worse about you so far than I have about Jahmash." She looked around the room as if thinking something over. "If we betray Jahmash now, who is to say he doesn't direct his attention toward Castiel eventually as well? There would be too much to lose to even have that conversation with the elders."

Maqdhuum shook his head, "Whatever." He nodded at Suriiya, "What about you? Also too much of a coward to ask your senate?"

She stood up at his insult, "Excuse me? Coward? Yahaira's agreement was out of necessity. Those two volcanoes will destroy so much once they erupt that we need a place to go. Preparations are likely already underway. Besides, it would be a death sentence for me to return. I cannot show my face in Yahaira ever again after leaving my husband."

Baltaszar stepped into the middle of the group, though Maqdhuum remained at the door. "Just who *are* the two of you, anyway? I understand that Bo and Aric were sent by Jahmash, and I've just gathered that you're betrothed to my brother, Aurkene. But Suriiya, were you recruited to help them or something?"

Her eyes and mouth went flat as she glared at Baltaszar out of the sides of her eyes. "I have an… arrangement with Bo'az and Aurkene. The three of us are… together, for lack of a better way of saying it."

Everyone's eyes shifted back and forth between Bo'az, Suriiya, and Aurkene. *Well, I guess they would have found out sooner or later. Who cares what they all think of it, though.* Baltaszar shrugged his eyebrows at Bo'az. "Wow. Well good for all of you."

Maqdhuum maintained his focus, "Back to my point. What about Brogan? None of you had a personal connection there. You don't think you could talk to King Renan about fighting *against* Jahmash instead?"

Bo'az stuck out his bottom lip for a moment and leaned forward on the floor. "Honestly, it's hard to say. Our friend died there and shortly after we fulfilled the king's trial, you showed up and whisked us away. I doubt he's excited about that turn of events. Maybe he changes his mind out of frustration, but I don't really want to go back to find out. Especially now that Jahmash is out of my head."

Baltaszar stepped toward the door where Maqdhuum stood. "Why don't you go back there and find out? You've got your hands in so many messes that maybe it's time to start putting out the fires instead of setting more. Why don't *you* go to each of those nations and set things right? We don't need you here, asshole. We've got Kraisos, Anonymi, the Ghosts, and a new king and army. We'll be perfectly fine without you meddling anymore. Why not go to one of the other nations and just live out the rest of your pathetic life?"

Maqdhuum closed his eyes for a moment and balled his fists. However, a moment later he let out a breath and opened his hands again. Despite his attempt to calm himself, he yelled. "You fucking fool. You're so sure that I'm the cause of all the world's problems. Yes, I messed your life up and put it on a much different path. But you have no idea what I've done to help Ashur, long before you or your parents took your first breaths. Who do you all think created the Anonymi? The Kraisos? You think people just came together and did all that on their own? No. It was me. Both of them have existed for centuries, because I started them, knowing that Jahmash would make his move sooner or later. Me. I'm the one who started protecting Ashur when everyone else had forgotten about Jahmash. So fuck all of you and your ingratitude!

Live through what I have and then pass your judgment, you spoiled little brats! Once again, I'll go fix things on my own while you all sit here and cry about your lives over tea!" In an instant, he disappeared from the room and Bo'az and the others looked around at one another in shock and confusion. Murmurs filled the room.

"Tasz, what's he talking about? What were those things he mentioned? What did he do?" asked Boaz.

Baltaszar rubbed his temples with two fingertips. "It's hard to explain. There are two groups we've formed alliances with. One is called the Anonymi and the other is the Kraisos. In fact, Wind, Chervil, and Sage here are all Kraisos. I guess he created both groups a long time ago to start preparing Ashur for Jahmash's return. It's a hell of a claim, but it makes sense that he would be connected to both of them, given their ability to function in the shadows." Bo'az thought he recognized Wind, but there was already too much going on to try and determine from where.

Horatio walked over to Baltaszar and grasped his shoulder. "Look. This is a lot. Maybe we should all just take a break from trying to figure everything out and relax for the rest of the day." He looked around the room, "Can we do that? I don't care if you all want to stay here and unwind, but let's just stop talking about all of the serious things for a little while? We've all clearly been through a lot in the last couple of weeks. I think we could use a break. If you want to leave, there are a couple of inns not far. Feel free to go and drink and then come back when you're done."

Bo'az stood up. "Tasz, wait. We need to talk. Can we go outside for a bit?"

"Sure. Let's go," he nodded curtly. They walked back out to the front of the house.

"Let's walk down a little bit. It's not so much about privacy, but it'll be awkward to be talking while everyone else is coming out."

Baltaszar shrugged in agreement. "That's fine. Whatever you want."

They walked several yards down the road until Bo'az felt comfortable enough to talk. "We can stop here." He waited until Baltaszar turned and looked him in the face. "So. What is it?"

"What?"

"Tasz, we haven't seen each other in over three years and I know we were never the type of brothers who were best friends, but we were still close enough. Yeah, things were definitely tense when we parted ways, but I wasn't so angry with you that I held a grudge or that I would be as cold as you're being to me. So either you've been holding onto that for this long, or there's something else. Either way, what is it?"

Baltaszar folded his arms and then stared down at them for a moment. "You remember those black cloaks we made back in Haedon once we knew we'd have to sneak around? I made this one to be just like them, except more hidden pockets. Not only does it come in handy, but it reminds me of you and father and the farm and all that. There's no grudge, Bo. I was definitely annoyed at you for a few days, but I always wished you were with me."

Bo'az put his arms around his brother and hugged him. In the initial shock of seeing him, he wasn't sure if he'd actually thought to hug Baltaszar, but it felt right in the moment. He released his brother and looked at him again. "I'm not sure if you have more to say, but I need to say this first. I'm sorry. Back in Haedon, after I left you, I went back to our home and it turned out that Yas was there. Tasz, this is going to sound stupid and I don't know if you've been back to Haedon to find out, but she died because of me. Tasz, I pretended to be you and somehow I fooled her and the others for a little while. They all thought I was you." He felt tears welling up in his lower eyelids. "Tasz, I slept with her. I was desperate and I thought we were going to die and I slept with her one night in the mountains, and then the next morning one of the three men pushed her off the side of the mountain, and…" As he looked at his brother's countenance, he realized that there wasn't even a hint of surprise on Baltaszar's face. He wiped the tears from his own face as his emotions dissipated, "Wait. Why isn't any of this shocking or angering to you?"

Baltaszar put his hand on Bo'az's shoulder. "I really wish we were sitting down for this. But here goes. I know the whole story and it's not all your fault. Yasaman used you for her own desires. The thing is, Bo, she's not dead. How she survived is a whole different story for another day, but she survived the fall and made it back to Haedon with several broken bones." *She's alive? She's fucking alive?* Bo'az felt a pit form in his stomach as Baltaszar placed both hands on Bo'az's shoulders. "Not only did she survive, Bo, but she… she had a baby." Baltaszar paused and looked at the ground. Bo'az could see droplets falling from his brother's face. "Your baby. His name is Zane." Baltaszar picked his head back up and looked at Bo'az.

"What?" *He's too emotional about this for it to be a joke. She's alive? And a baby? I'm a father?* "You're sure? You saw it for yourself?" He took a step back from his brother to be able to look at him.

"I saw her lying in her own bed, belly and all." Baltaszar wiped the remaining tears from his face and beard. "That was when I was the angriest at you. And her. In time I forgave you. But not her. Bo, I fell in love with someone else after her, and Yas had the nerve to seek me out on the other side of Ashur and ask me to be her baby's father. To pretend to love her again and be a family together. And after everything that she did to both of us, you know what the worst part is? The woman I loved was killed in an invasion. We talked and dreamed about our lives together once this is all over, and all that was taken from me. But Yas is still alive and well, despite all of her lying and manipulation. I hate her. I fucking hate her. And I'm sorry for that, because you have a son now and you'll have to see the two of them eventually. I know you have this whole… arrangement now, but your son is still more important than that. He deserves better than to spend his whole life with Yasaman."

Bo'az dropped to his knees and punched the ground. *I'm a bloody father? How is that even possible? After just one time? Why did we have to do it? Why did she have to lie to me? Why did I have to lie to her? What a damn mess.* He looked up at his brother, "Tasz. I'm sorry for everything you've been through, especially for the parts that I was responsible for. What do I do now? Do I go to her or stay here?"

His brother kneeled down in front of him. "You know I can't make that decision for you, Bo. But I support whatever decision you make. It comes down to what's most important to you right now. And honestly, I don't think that's a decision that you can make right here, sitting with me in the middle of the road. Let me ask you, how serious are you about the two women in there?"

He grasped a handful of dirt and squeezed it in his hand. "Aurkene and I are betrothed. At first, it was inadvertent and I didn't realize what I'd done. But honestly, the more time we've spent since leaving Castiel, the more I've come to appreciate her and enjoy her company. We get along very well and it seems like our bond grows stronger with each day." *Except for yesterday and today.*

"And what of the other one? Are you marrying both of them?"

"Suriiya? I'm not exactly sure. It started as a whimsical thing and ever since, all three of us have grown incredibly close. It was supposed to be just fun at first, but it kind of worked so well beyond the bed that we agreed to keep it going. That's why she's still with us– we sort of smuggled her out of Yahaira when we left for Brogan. But I don't know what that will look like going forward."

Baltaszar nodded, "Then I think there are a couple of conversations that you need to have. First, figure that part out. I mean, you're all here and both of them are strangers here *and* far away from their homes. Neither can just sail back if they change their minds. And the other thing is that you'll have to tell them about the whole Yasaman and Zane thing. You think they'll be upset?"

"You know what's crazy? I told them about Yasaman and everything that happened on the mountain. Even about pretending to be you. They were understanding and told me that I'm not that person anymore. But that's a much different situation than telling them that I have a child. Holy shit, I just said it out loud. I'm a bloody father." He paused for a moment. "I don't know how that changes things in their mind. But you're right. I have to tell them and I should do that sooner rather than later. Aurkene will know that something's off anyway, and she's been a bit weird ever since Maqdhuum had your friend get Jahmash out of my head." Bo'az stood up and was about to turn around to return to Horatio's house, but something in his brother's face seemed off. *He didn't tell me everything yet.* "What is it? I know there's more. Just tell me."

***

Baltaszar tried to look his brother in the eyes, but he couldn't keep his eyes up. His focus swiveled between Bo'az's face and the ground. "I... I wasn't going to tell you yet."

"You might as well. What's one more thing?"

He tried to smile, but his mouth wouldn't cooperate. "You say that now. Just wait until I say it."

"So then?"

"You should get Horatio. It affects him, too, considering we're all brothers."

Bo'az pursed his lips together and looked off into the distance. "Shit. This is big, isn't it? Fine, I'll be right back."

Baltaszar nodded and waited, hoping that perhaps Horatio had taken a nap or was too busy tending to his mother to have time for anything else. Despite his hopes, Baltaszar saw Bo'az returning shortly with Horatio right behind him.

Horatio looked at him with a tentative smile. "What's going on? Bo'az said there's brother business that you have to discuss with us. I'm not sure whether to be scared or excited. Is there another family secret that I need to know about?"

"Raish, I wish it was some fun and spicy gossip that I could give you. Then again, nothing that I know about our family history has been fun and spicy, so never mind. Anyway, I wasn't going to share this with you two yet, because as you said, we've all been through so much lately. But Bo read me too well and I can't get away with keeping it in. So here goes." He studied their faces, which were both wide-eyed in anticipation. *Why do they have to be so excited?* "Bo, Horatio already knows this, but there are people in Ashur called Augurs, or Blind Men and Women, who have the gift of prophecy. When I left Haedon and went to Vandenar, I met a Blind Man named Munn Keeram who helped me quite a bit, and he gave me a prophecy. Raish, I think I mentioned to you that I had gotten one when we were leaving Vandenar, but I never told you what it was."

Horatio shrugged, "You know how my head's been. I'm sure you did, but I don't remember. I'm surprised I didn't try to get you to tell me."

"No, you didn't. Thinking back to it, I wish I had. At least this wouldn't be such a shock now. Anyway, Munn had a vision that," he took a deep breath and looked down at the ground again.

"Tasz, it's fine. Whatever it is, we'll deal with it." Bo'az tried to encourage him.

"I don't know that you can. But here goes. He had a vision that I would kill my brother." Baltaszar paused for a moment to gauge their expressions. Both of them stared at him. Bo'az's jaw clenched while Horatio's mouth dropped open.

"Before you say or ask anything, I don't know which of you it is. Munn said that in the vision, his point of view was from the person I was about to kill, so there was no way of knowing who it was. But I specifically referred to the person as my brother. Up until recently, I assumed it would be you, Bo. But then I told Lincan about it and he made a point to say that technically, everyone who was at the House of Darian considered each other brothers and sisters, so he thought it could be any of the men who survived the attack. And then Maqdhuum revealed that we're brothers as well, Raish. So now I don't know where or when it'll happen, but Munn did say something about me being angry at whoever it is I'm going to kill."

Horatio mused for a moment. "So then we separate and keep our distance from each other. Right? You can't kill us if we're not near you."

"I don't know, Raish," Baltaszar shrugged. "These things come true whether we like it or not. Again, I don't know who it is, but it's going to happen sooner or later."

Horatio looked at Bo'az and then back at Baltaszar, "Then it looks like Bo'az and I will have to do our best to not piss you off, right?"

Bo'az lifted his head and looked at them, "I'll do my best. I haven't been so good at that so far in my life."

Baltaszar shrugged, "I'm not sure what either of you could do that would be bad enough to drive me to murder. Maybe Lincan is right and it's not my actual brother." He walked past them and patted each of them on the shoulder before returning to the house.

CHAPTER 17
AN ALTERED MISSION

From **The Book of Orijin,** **Verse Four Hundred Seventy-Seven**
Do not assume that you are smarter or better prepared than evil,
simply because you are righteous. Evil will not wait for the righteous
to be prepared.

"They're too far behind for their arrows to pierce our armor!
But they could still get lucky and hit one of our horses! We've got to
keep our pace!" Adria shouted to Harlan, the knight who accompanied
her. The Sanai Mountains were to their right, the river to their left. "I
should have expected that there would be trouble once we got into
Cerysia, but it's hard to tell where the Vermillion are these days. I
thought they were all in what's left of Mireya now."

Harlan confirmed her suspicion, "Agreed. They were all either
in Alvadon or in Mireya not that long ago. Something must have
happened. As you said, though, let's not slow down to ponder such
things."

"If they continue to chase, we'll have no choice but to engage
them, Harlan. How do you feel about the two of us against six of them?"

He raised a fist in the air, "Only six? I like our chances!"

Adria, where are you? I thought you were going to Xuyen with
Linc. Adria flinched at Lao's presence in her head.

Lao, Light of Orijin, where the hell have you been? I could have
used some guidance about a day ago. It's a long story but I just crossed
the Sanai and two of us are being chased by Vermillion. Where is your
sister? I'm riding to her. Please tell me she's on this side of Cerysia and
not to the east.

You're in luck. She just arrived in Maradon this morning. If
you're by the Sanai, though, you're better off going to Magnon first.
Not sure how friendly people will be there, but it's much easier to hide
from Vermillion in a city than out in the open.

Sound advice. Thanks Lao.

Anytime. Turn around and look behind you. Let me see what
you're up against. She did as he said and looked back at the six
Vermillion soldiers riding in the distance, two rows of three wide. *Sorry*
Adria, full armor and at that distance? Guess that's also what's keeping
you from getting pierced by arrows. You won't like it, but your best

chance is to aim for the horses. One well-placed arrow could take out three of them, if not more.

You're right. I don't like it. But there's not much choice. We're still too far from Magnon to keep this going. Thanks for the suggestion; check in with me later in the day. And don't forget!

I didn't forget about you! Maq-fucking-dhuum stole me away to help him just as Farrah and I were about to…you know. I've been busy.

Adria shuddered. *Gross. I'll ask about the other details later. Not the Farrah details, though.* She focused on the Vermillion. "Harlan, if it's you or their horses, what do you choose?"

"Horses any day. I'll feel bad for them if it helps, but their horses aren't going to win the war against Jahmash!" She could almost hear the smile in his voice, even without her manifestation.

"Good enough for me." She rode closer to him so that they were right next to each other. "Grab the reins and steer my horse." Adria handed off the reins to him and carefully turned herself around in the saddle. She pulled her bow over her shoulder and then grabbed an arrow from her quiver. She tried her best to focus despite how fast they were riding. She shot at the oncoming soldiers, but her arrow fell short. *Damn. Too cautious.* Adria nocked another arrow and focused on where the horses would be once she released it. After a moment, she shot at them again and hit the horse on the left in the shoulder. The shot itself wasn't enough to kill it, but the pain sent it into a frenzy and made it frantic. It whinnied and kicked until it crashed into the horse next to it, causing chaos among all of the animals. One of the riders was thrown while another fell off his horse. The others tried their best to stay on and control. "That should do for now." She turned herself back around.

"Nice shot. I couldn't have done that better myself." Harlan handed her back her reins once she was set, and they commanded their own animal to gallop.

"Thanks. Let's just make it to Magnon. Keep your helmet off. I doubt most townspeople will know the difference between a Vermillion ridge and your yellow one, but it would be stupid to take any chances. For now, just play the part."

"Understood. But what about you and your armor? If there are Vermillion there, they'll know something's up."

Adria nodded, "Yeah. That crossed my mind. I'll keep my helmet on to hide my Mark. If anyone ends up questioning us, then I'm your prisoner and you're bringing me to Alvadon."

"The Vithelegion armor is all black. Would it make more sense to pretend you're one of them?"

"I don't think so. All of the reports say the Vithelegion only sent men. There's only so much pretending I can do!"

Harlan laughed, "Alright, prisoner it is!"

***

Adria glanced behind her to ensure no one was following too close. "We're looking for the Golden Blade." Harlan was watching their flank, but she didn't want to be too careful. They'd gotten lucky that they hadn't encountered any Vermillion soldiers in Magnon on Sanai, but that wouldn't last forever.

The sentry at Maradon was an older, white-haired man, and Adria wasn't sure whether to be repulsed or impressed at how drunk he already was so early in the morning. "Rrrr...rrright thra. Right there. Can't miss... you can't miss... j-just go already." He sloppily waved a hand for them to pass and Adria didn't bother to argue. They rode toward the building that the sentry directed them to, though Adria hoped he hadn't been too drunk to mess that up.

Her hesitation continued as they tethered their horses. She spoke softly to Harlan, "Inns are generally bustling and loud, aren't they? Especially those closest to the city gates?"

"Normally, but Maradon isn't exactly a *bustling* town. There isn't much traffic that comes this way. Most tend to stop in Benjam if they are coming from the south. Or if they come from the east, they prefer to avoid the river entirely, so they travel north of Maradon. I've lived in Cerysia my whole life and I may have been to this city once. There isn't much of a draw here."

She opened herself to her manifestation, just to be safe. There were heartbeats inside the inn, but no more than two dozen. "Let's go in, but stay ready. Keep your hand on your pommel." He nodded in acknowledgment as they entered the Golden Blade. Adria looked around the room, which was mostly bare, save for a couple of tables of patrons and a handful of barmaids. "Keep your eyes open for Kiryako and some of your fellow knights."

Harlan nodded his head toward a table in the corner, "That's her over there, but I don't recognize anyone she's with. Might be harmless, might be more Vermillion. It's hard to tell without their armor."

"Also easier to kill them without their armor. But let's be cautious. They have to be invested in their conversation to not even have glanced at the door when we walked in. This place isn't busy enough for that. I'm going to stay back and sit here. It's somewhat away from them so I won't draw attention. Leave your helmet with me and walk over. See what's going on. Kiryako is hard-headed like me; she won't let on that she's nervous or in trouble; you'll have to look for signs. If anything is off, put your hand behind your back and stick out two fingers."

He looked at her for a moment, "Why two? What does that mean?"

"I don't know," she shrugged, "it just made more sense than one finger or a fist."

"One finger if things are suspicious. Two if I need you to come over and help."

"Fine. I guess that's better than what I said."

"Good, then we're set."

Harlan gently set his helmet down on the chair and walked away. *Damnit. Some leader I am. Can't even get hand signals right.* Adria watched as he walked up to the table with Kiryako and the strange men. *Where is the rest of her company? Max, Trevor, Neraiya, the Kraisos? Are none of them there with her, or are they just not visible because of the others? At least one of them should be visible.* Harlan started talking to the group, first to the couple of men standing up and then he looked around at the others. He smiled at them and a few of them laughed at something someone said. Harlan spoke again and the rest quieted down. She realized she should be using her manifestation and opened herself to it and listened to their conversation.

"...and I said enough jokes, soldier. You still didn't tell us what you are doing here." *One of the ones who's sitting. Most of their heartbeats are normal. Just... one that's a little faster. Kiryako?*

Harlan answered, "I was just sent in to join everyone else who was already here. The sentry told me that a group of you were staying here and so it made sense to join you." *Good thinking, Harlan.*

"Strange that you would be traveling alone. Who sent you?"

"The rest of my company was either hurt or killed chasing down Descendants. That's why they reassigned me. It was Easton Grey himself who gave me the order." *Her heartbeat's getting louder. Did he just say the wrong thing?*

A different voice responded to him, "Where were you and your squadron?"

"Down at the Sanai, right by the border between Galicea and

Fangh-Haan." He put his hand behind his back and stuck out one finger. *Already, Harlan? I thought you were cleverer.*

She watched as a few of the men looked around at each other. "The Sanai? I thought Grey was in Alvadon." Harlan stuck the second finger up behind his back and Adria stood up and put her helmet on. She thought about drawing the sword that Garrison and Maqdhuum had given her, but instead pulled two daggers from her waist as walked over to the table. As she counted the men sitting there, Harlan pulled a dagger from behind his back as well. *Five of them. Easy.* She walked up behind the closest one and slit his throat from behind. Before the others could react, she and Harlan stabbed two more and the remaining two attempted to stand up and retreat. One fell over his chair while Kiryako tackled the other to the ground and punched him in the face.

"Here Kiryako, kill him." Adria handed her a dagger and she slit the man's throat immediately. They all looked at the one who remained alive as he tried to scamper away. Harlan rushed forward and kicked him in the torso, knocking the air out of him. The man wheezed and croaked to regain his breath. "Catch your breath; you'll need it." She turned to Kiryako, "What the hell was this?"

Kiryako took a moment to stop staring at the man on the ground. "Sorry, still in a bit of shock. That all happened so fast." She looked around the room, "They were threatening me and these two came to my aid. We'll remove the bodies after we get some answers from him." Adria looked around the room and realized the mess they'd made. *I guess it's the least we could do.* Kiryako turned back to her and Harlan, "First, thank you. They're all Vermillion and one of them recognized me from when we were in Alvadon. I guess they figured that five of them would be a fair fight against me. Seems like they had two agendas: one was to see who had the best chance of bedding me and the other was to get information about Garrison. His concerns were warranted, Adria. They've crowned a new king in Alvadon, Courtland something. They're also building a new castle. He rules from an open-air throne and the high families all support him."

Adria looked at her in shock, "You found this all out from these men?"

Kiryako smiled at her, "Adria, a woman's assets make it so much easier to get information out of men than the other way around."

As they spoke, Harlan made the surviving Vermillion soldier kneel, and place his blade at the man's neck. Adria looked at him flatly, "Is this all true? You've crowned a false king?"

The man hesitated, "No. We've crowned the true king. King Courtland is the rightful ruler of Ashur. Your *king* is an imposter."

Adria smiled at him, "Do you know that my name is Adria Kingsbane? I'm the one who killed Edmund Brighton, right after he killed the queen to try and save his own life. That wasn't so long ago, so I still have a taste for the blood of a corrupt king. I think it would be much easier this time without the protection of castle walls."

The man looked at her suspiciously, as if debating whether her threat was serious. "You'd have to get through hundreds of Vermillion knights. I doubt even you bloody Descendants could do that."

She nodded at him. *He took the bait. That's why we've been spotting Vermillion. They have a new king that they have to protect. And Easton Grey is back in Alvadon. Garrison's going to need to know this. Where the hell are the others?* "Thank you. Harlan, you want his blood on your hands or should I do it?" Without hesitation, Harlan slid his blade across the man's throat and let him fall to the ground. "Wow, good to know you don't blink at things like that. Kiryako, for the love of Orijin, where are the rest of your companions?"

Her cheeks slightly reddened. "Back in Constaniza we discussed starting out in separate factions. I had some Kraisos and knights with me, but there hasn't been much to be concerned about since we've been here. We have had to pick and choose who to speak to in order to win people over to Garrison's side, but we were cautious about that from the start. I hope this doesn't come off as condescending, Adria, but it's much easier to travel through Cerysia unbothered when you *don't* have a black line on your face."

"Damnit, I forgot that you'd all split up from the beginning." Adria shook her head, "This would be so much easier if you were all here. Harlan, can you two ride back to Constaniza? Garrison needs to know all of this and," she eyed Kiryako for a second, "given the state of things right now, it's better that you're with him, Kiryako."

She cocked her head diagonally, "What do you mean?"

"You need to be with him and you need to be safe. I don't mean that as a slight against you; I'm not calling you weak. But we both know of your connection with Garrison at this point. If Vermillion soldiers were willing to corner you here, who knows how far others might be willing to go?"

"I see," Kiryako nodded. "Did you abandon your own mission to come to me?"

Adria almost smiled at the assumption. "No. Something happened and I had to… be away from Lincan for now. I was originally torn between riding up to Marshall and returning to Constaniza. I ended up caving to selfishness. I was going to ride up into the Never to see Marshall when we got chased by Vermillion at the Sanai. If there's a new king in Alvadon, then it doesn't make sense to try and militarize Cerysia, especially with the Vermillion returning. You heard him, there are already hundreds of knights in Alvadon. You need to get back to Constaniza as soon as possible. The next time your brother checks in on me, I'll tell him to have the rest of your company do the same thing. Go and get your things. You and Harlan need to go as soon as possible."

Harlan looked down his nose at Adria, "And what will you do, *Kingsbane*? You talk as if you are staying here."

"I am," she nodded. "I'm going to ride to Alvadon and see what's going on."

Kiryako raised her eyebrows, "Is that wise? I know how accomplished you are, Adria, but is it prudent on your own? Why not ride back with us or wait here for reinforcements?"

"It would take too long. And bringing our own knights to Alvadon would only bring attention to us, which is exactly what I'm trying to avoid. I need stealth. If anything, I may have your brother tell one of the Kraisos to meet me there. Either way, it makes the most sense for me to go directly there, especially before other Vermillion notice that these ones aren't here anymore. What are the chances that we can pay the inn to keep this quiet?"

Kiryako shrugged, "I don't know that they were too fond of the soldiers anyway. When I came down here for breakfast, they were already harassing the barmaids. Lucky for me that I took the Vermillion's attention away from them."

"That's reassuring. Alright, let's clean up this mess, bury the bodies, and then if they need any further reparations, we'll sort that out."

***

Garrison sat out on the sprawling patio. Despite Badalao having warned him about some of the details in Alvadon, it was worse coming from Kiryako. He especially hated that the Vermillion soldiers had cornered her. *She's lucky Adria was there, which is another thing in its own right, but I'll let her tell me about that herself.* He stared out, not focusing on anything in particular. *Cortland Hailstone. I had a feeling. I wonder what that whole process was like. Did anyone else try to make a claim to the throne, or did they all decide on him?*

The door opened behind him and he heard a few sets of footsteps grow closer. Kiryako sat next to him, while Farrah, Badalao, and Wendell faced them. "Wendell, you are probably the only one who doesn't know what's going on, unless one of them filled you in on your way here."

Wendell nodded. "Lao mentioned there's a new king in Alvadon. That's all I know, but I imagine a new king means that Alvadon is swarming with soldiers. So what's the plan?"

Garrison rubbed his closely shaved head, "Ha, that's what I wanted to ask all of you. The easy answer is confrontation. We don't have enough men to ride there and simply fight them. And the longer he sits on a throne in Alvadon, the more credence Ashur will give to his legitimacy. We need to act quickly and intelligently."

"Exactly how possible are quick and intelligent right now?" Kiryako asked. "You need manifestations for any chance at a swift solution, but with all due respect, invention, kissing, and mind control aren't going to do much to help."

Garrison nodded, "You're right. The three of us cannot do much. Even Adria being there already isn't a threat to them. I'm glad that she knows better than to attack, but I wish she had come back with you. Lao, have you reached out to the others to return here? Any response?"

"Yes. I spoke to all of them. Maximillian, Neraiya, and Trevor are all heading back as soon as possible. The Kraisos are staying, which makes sense. They'll be more effective there and they do not need our help anyway. But even with those three returning, none of them can really use their manifestations for some type of grand attack."

"Wait," Badalao took a deep breath, "perhaps our best play isn't in Alvadon right now. I know you want a quick resolution to this, Garrison, but given the state of Ashur, we don't have that luxury. I think time might be our ally in a different way. We have our own people all over Ashur, getting everyone ready. We can spread the message through them that there is a false king on the throne. And we can use our presence to show people that you are doing more as their king than Courtland is. I can instruct everyone to spread that message in every town and city, and show them that the Vermillion is nowhere to be seen and is offering them no protection. If they're all primarily in Mireya and Cerysia, then the rest of Ashur will know that to be true."

Garrison stood up and walked to the railing, resting his arms on it. He closed his eyes and thought over Badalao's plan for a moment. "That is our smartest option. Thank you, Lao. How long will it take you to reach out to each of our people and explain it all to them?"

"Well, I suppose that depends on how many questions I have to answer, but I'd say a couple of hours. I'll likely need to take breaks for my own well-being, and three or four plates of food to keep me going for that long."

"Whatever you need, simply ask for it and you'll have it. Start with the Shivaana group, then Fangh, the Wolf's Paw, Galicea, and save Markos for last. It's unlikely that Courtland is going to send anyone this way anyway, so you won't have much convincing to do. Markos knows who its king is. The sooner you can get started, the better."

With that, Farrah helped Badalao to his feet and led him back inside.

"What do you need from me, Garrison?" Garrison turned to Wendell and smiled.

"Nothing new, my friend." He clapped Wendell on the shoulder, "As usual, you've done so much already and I can't tell you how much I appreciate it. See that the soldiers are ready for anything. I doubt that Courtland would be stupid enough to send Vermillion this way already, but he *is* stupid enough to think he can steal my throne, so clearly we cannot put anything past him. And I'm sure that whoever his council is, they are giving him terrible advice."

"Does any of it surprise you?"

"Not at all. I knew as soon as I spoke to them that something like this would happen. I wonder exactly how they decided on Courtland. Do you think the high families actually agreed on him together, or did they organize some type of tournament to decide who would take the throne?"

Wendell nodded. "That seems more likely. The only level-headed one of the whole group was the one who had no personality. And even he had his moments. I'll leave you to some peace and quiet now, though."

"Thanks again, Wendell."

As Wendell returned inside, Kiryako joined Garrison at the railing of the patio and brushed against his shoulder. "You know, no matter what the plan was going to be, sooner or later Ashur will see that there is no better king for it than you."

He blushed at her words, "I appreciate that, Kiri. Have I told you of my plan for Ashur after all this is over?"

She turned and looked out at the landscape with him, "Tell me again. I love that you have ideas and plans, and that you talk to other people and consider their input. These are all the qualities of an intelligent man and a great ruler."

"I don't know how I came to deserve to have you by my side, but I thank the Orijin regularly that you came into my life."

"Ah, and you can return compliments as well. Another amazing trait. Now tell me your plans."

"I am going to give it all up. I will reclaim Cerysia, and then I shall let all the nations of Ashur govern themselves. What need do they have of a king? Especially a king in another nation. It makes no sense and it's an embarrassing part of my lineage that one of my ancestors thought it to be a wise thing to do." Kiryako placed her hand on top of his and nodded. He glanced at her out of the side of his eye. "And you know what else will be a priority?"

"What's that?"

"I'll need a queen to share my duties. And eventually many, many children to grow up in a new castle, and continue ruling." He smiled again as he continued to look straight ahead.

"And where will you find this queen who will be willing to bear you *many, many* children?"

"I was hoping she might just show up in front of me one day. It would be less work that way. Don't you think? If you know anyone, please let me know." He grasped her hand tightly, and she rested her head on his shoulder as they continued to stare out at the world in front of them.

They stood there in silence for nearly an hour before Kiryako kissed his cheek. "It may be a good idea to practice if you're going to want so many children. What do you think?"

Garrison stopped himself from picking her up and running inside with her. "That is the best idea I've heard in a long time." He was about to tell her that it was better than Badalao's plan, but the last thing he wanted to do was mention her brother before bedding her. *Now's not the time to be an idiot.*

"I was hoping you'd say that. Let me enjoy a warm bath first, and then I'll meet you in your chambers." Garrison nodded as he led her inside. They departed into their respective rooms and Garrison changed into a new set of smallclothes, then waited patiently in his bed.

He tried not to get caught up with thinking about everything going on in the world. Instead, he thought about all of the possibilities of a life with Kiryako and what the future might look like for them. He dared to imagine what their children would look like and how many they might have, as well as how many would be boys or girls. After what felt like ages, he heard the light knock on his door. He jumped up and quickly opened it. Kiryako tiptoed in wearing a thin robe, but let it fall to the floor as she climbed onto his bed. He couldn't help but take in her every movement.

Garrison disrobed as he joined her. They kissed for a while until he knew he would have to initiate things and move forward. He caressed her body as he moved his mouth from her lips down to her neck. Her panting and gasping aroused him even more and he explored more of her body with his mouth.

They continued to kiss and writhe and caress until Garrison couldn't hold himself back anymore.

Garrison. It's urgent, I just…

Lao? What the fuck are you doing in my head right now?

Wait, why? There was a pause in Badalao's voice in his head. *Are you? Is that my fucking sister? Oh, Light of Orijin, why? Why do you have to be doing this right now? Garrison I don't have eyes and now I want to burn yours because of what I just saw.*

"Garrison? What's wrong?"

He pulled himself away from Kiryako, "Your damn brother is what's wrong! He's in my fucking head, trying to talk to me." He sat at the edge of his bed, wondering what could possibly be so urgent. *Well, are you going to fucking tell me what you need?*

I-I, yes. I just finished reaching out to all of our people throughout Ashur. There are ships approaching off the shores of Taiju and Fera! Garrison, it's starting! It's got to be Jahmash's armies!

CHAPTER 18
REUNITED

From *The Book of Orijin*, Verse One Hundred Sixty
To know oneself is to know that you are all on different paths, even if those paths may lead to the same destination.

"You just stand here and watch whenever you feel like it?"

Savaiyon shrugged without turning to look at Khurt Everitas. "Would you suggest a different strategy?" A few drops of rain managed to fall through the gateway onto him.

"Depends on what you're looking for. Are you just making sure they return home?"

He knew Khurt had to be frustrated. Savaiyon still hadn't let the man see his son and that was his only concern. "For now, that is all I care about. However, I am skeptical. As you mentioned, you Master General has to be concerned about the whereabouts of his sons, and it would be perfectly reasonable for him to not want to leave without them." He turned deliberately to face Khurt. "As I know is the case with you. I didn't summon you here to simply show you that I'm watching your people's journey. You have been surprisingly patient in being able to see your son, while still doing all that we have asked. Once you are done here, the guard will escort you to your son's quarters."

Khurt perked up at Savaiyon's words. "Please tell me this isn't some ruse to test my loyalty."

"We do not lie here. Though we may be clever with our words when situations call for it, I assure you that your son is alive and well, and you will see him when you are done here. That being said, I ask for your honesty now." He turned back to the yellow-fringed gateway.

"Of course, what do you want to know?"

"I still do not completely trust that the Vithelegion is returning home, although the fleet has maintained its course for several days now. Is there something that I am missing from this scene below?"

"You do not prefer to get closer?"

"I would rather not alert them to my surveillance. If they are genuinely returning home, such actions may anger them into returning."

"And wouldn't you simply kill them, then? Seems as if you're sabotaging your own plan."

"You're encouraging this?"

Khurt snickered, "No. But it's the most sensible response if they were to reverse course, isn't it? Annihilate them before they can do any damage?"

Savaiyon nodded and let the gateway close. "Very well. Here." He created a new gateway that opened behind the fleet, and was much closer to the deck of the last ship. "Much closer now. Does anything seem off to you?"

Khurt stepped closer and stood by Savaiyon's side. "Well, the deck is rather empty, but given the storm, I would likely prefer to be below deck. Most sailors wouldn't really care about rain, as long as the waves were tolerable. Which seems to be the case here. I'd say that's the only suspicious thing that I see."

Savaiyon folded his arms in front of him and continued to look out at the Vithelegion fleet.. Very well, I shall keep my eye on them more frequently. Just in case. Please notify the guard to escort you to your son's quarters."

"Thank you." Khurt quickly departed and Savaiyon continued to focus on the Vithelegion fleet. He removed his red mask and held it in front of his chin. *How far would they be willing to sail, just to turn around? Would they even know that I'm watching them? That would be the only reason for such a ruse. Otherwise, they're just sailing back home.* He shook his head. *There must be something going on. This doesn't make much sense, especially with all of the ships accounted for. I counted them, counted again, and then a few more times. None of them stayed behind or turned around.* He released his manifestation and let the gateway vanish. One of the things he missed the most at the House of Darian was that Zin Marlowe understood the effects of using a manifestation so frequently. *He always knew to keep me fed and nourished in order to keep using my manifestation.* It wasn't so much that the Anonymi didn't care about his manifestation, but they weren't as self-sufficient when it came to food, so everyone was provided with a normal meal, especially since there were few, if any, Descendants in their ranks besides Savaiyon.

He donned his mask once more and left the room, as the other Officers and Masters would be meeting soon to discuss their next moves. There had been talk of turning their attention to the Vermillion instead. The argument had been made that if the Vermillion were willing to help the Vithelegion, then they were also a threat to Ashur and should be dealt with. Savaiyon agreed with the sentiment and wanted to ensure that his vote was cast.

＊＊＊

Khurt stood outside the door as the guard knocked. A meek voice answered after a moment, "You can come in." The guard pushed the door open for Khurt, then extended a hand to signal for Khurt to enter.

"Thank you." Khurt walked in and shut the door behind him, then removed his mask. He wanted his reunion to be private and genuine, and hoped that the guard wouldn't insist on keeping the door open. "Khenzi?"

The boy turned from eating at a table and his eyes grew wide upon seeing Khurt. He ran to Khurt. "I missed you! They kept telling me that I'd see you soon and I wasn't sure whether to believe them!"

Khurt knelt and wrapped him in his arms and squeezed. He took a deep breath to stop himself from getting choked up. "Are you alright? Did they hurt you or mistreat you at all?"

"No, of course not," Khenzi answered with his head on Khurt's shoulder. "They've been so nice to me here."

"Are you sure? You don't have to pretend if you're unhappy."

Khenzi pulled himself away from Khurt to look at him. "I promise. They've fed me well, let me train with others if I want to, bathe as often as I like, even tour the fortress. I've been enjoying myself. What about you? Where have you been? After everything that happened at that inn, I wasn't sure if I'd ever see you again. But a while after we arrived here, someone in a red mask told me that I'd see you soon."

Khurt thought about giving his son a generalized answer, but he didn't want to lie about the situation that they were in. "Khenzi, I'm going to be completely honest with you. Saol Suldas left me to die at that inn, and some of the Ashurian people found me and took me as a prisoner for a little while. Then, someone in a red mask, perhaps the same one that spoke to you, made a deal with me that if I helped the people in this fortress, I'd be able to see you again. Khenzi, I want you to know, it was Saol and the Vithelegion who betrayed me. They left me for dead without a second thought. And now they're all sailing home and we're stuck here. There's a chance we may never go back."

"Never?"

"It doesn't seem likely. I'm sorry, son."

"I don't really mind not going back, father. Except for Mother and Khaira. Do you think there's a way that we can get them *here*? Maybe we can all live here together while the rest of the Vithelegion stays back at home."

Khurt stood up and walked over to his son's bed. He sat at the side and patted the spot next to him for Khenzi to sit there. As Khenzi sat down, Khurt leaned forward and clasped his hands. He looked straight down at the ground, trying to ignore the fact that his feet still somewhat ached. "You... do not want to go back to our people?" He turned to look at Khenzi's face.

"Not really," he shook his head. "Ever since I can remember, all our people have cared about is fighting, training to fight, and getting better at fighting. I understand why it's important to our people, but it's not important to me. If we weren't caught up in all this, we would still be at home. At *our* home, with the rest of our family. I've had a lot of time to think about things, and the Vithelegion has killed a lot of people since we arrived here. Good people. That inn was full of people who didn't do anything wrong to us. And then the people in the kitchen who found me—they were nice to me. They could have killed me if they wanted to, but instead they rescued me, spoke to me like they cared, and fed me and made sure that I was alright. When they left that town, they brought me with them and treated me like one of their own. Father, I know you said we came here because the people were evil for being followers of Darian, but so far, everyone I've met here has been nothing but nice to me. Who cares who they follow or worship? They weren't bothering us back home anyway. So I'd rather be here, where people aren't so caught up with fighting."

Khurt looked back down at the ground. *Is the boy right? Is our whole culture so primitive and backwards that we only value combat? Have we really lost sight of the important things in life? Even if Saol hadn't commanded us to come here, we would still be at home, training our soldiers and creating new military strategies. And for what? To be stuck in a foreign land with little to no prospects of getting back home?* "For someone your age, you certainly are wise. Saol Suldas and the rest of the generals could learn quite a bit from you. You know that?"

"Are you sure? I'm just telling you how I feel about everything."

"I know. And I'm not upset that you don't care for the fighting or combat."

"Father, I enjoyed it when I was learning it from you. But only because it was the two of us doing all that together. I never wanted other people around for it."

Khurt sat up and looked at him, "I know. Those were my favorite times of this whole trip. The parts that were just me and you. So do you have a plan to get your mother and sister over here?"

Khenzi smiled at him, "No, but I'm sure I can think of something. Maybe get a message to them somehow and they could take a boat here. Or we could sail back and bring them over. I guess we would need a big enough ship for the journey, though."

"Indeed we would."

"I would just want to make sure we could do it together. The worst parts of this journey have been when we've been apart. Getting separated at the inn was the worst, but even smaller things like when you took the envoy boats to go to other ships while we were sailing. I know you weren't going far, but it always made me nervous. And then that last time when Saol pushed you off of his ship." Khurt furrowed his brow. There was something in what Khenzi had said that caught his attention, though he couldn't be sure why. Khenzi continued, "Even if we had to live in this fortress together. I know they also focus on combat a lot, but it's not all they care about. They have other things that they do as well."

Other ships? What was it? Think. Think! He closed his eyes for a moment, aware that Khenzi had finished speaking, but needing to concentrate. "That's it! The damn envoy boats! That's what was off!"

"What are you talking about?"

He stood up and paced around the room. "Before I came to see you just now, I was with one of the acolytes who wears a red mask. They have a magical ability to create these doorways that can open to anywhere in the world. The acolyte has been watching the Vithelegion fleet to ensure that they are returning home. We took a closer look at the ships from a doorway and the only thing that seemed off at the time was that the deck was basically empty of crewmen. However, it *was* raining, so I thought that perhaps they were all just below deck, even though rain never really stopped our crews from being out there. Something seemed off, but I couldn't figure out exactly what it was. *Until* you mentioned the envoy boats that we'd used. I just realized that I didn't see any of them on the sides of the ships. I didn't really think about it because who pays any attention to that. But Khenzi, the Vithelegion would have needed those to return to the ships in the first place, which means they should be there. If not, then the ships are running on skeleton crews while the rest of the Vithelegion is…somewhere else."

"In the envoy boats." Khenzi stood up as well.

"Exactly. And I think I have your solution about how to get the rest of our family here now." He gently punched Khenzi on the shoulder and smiled.

***

Farco stood across from Avenira on his starting point and awaited the instructor's command to start. She had been defeating him more frequently during their sparring sessions as of late, and he could tell that she was becoming much more comfortable with the moves and strategies of the Ranza fighting style than he had been.

The instructor commanded them through several drills in which they alternated attacking and defending. As they went through each exercise, Avenira continued to get the best of him, whether she was attacking or defending. *Damnit, she can take more risks because o' her manifestation. I have ta be smarter.* The instructor had Farco attack again and reminded him not to give anything away with head movements or body positions. He kept the instructor's advice in mind as he advanced upon Avenira. He knew that one of his issues was his creativity, as he'd been trying the same moves over and over again, while Avenira had come to predict what he'd do.

He cautiously stepped toward her, keeping his head straight regardless of where he was looking or where he wanted to move next. Avenira kept her sword up in front of her and took small steps here and there as he moved. It was his turn to attack, so she wouldn't make the first move. *Stupid. Ye don't take turns in combat. Ye look fer yer openin's an' attack.* He sprung on her and came forward with a diagonal overhand strike, but then stopped as his sword was still overhead and spun to Avenira's right and swung his sword horizontally at her back. Avenira had already prepared for the move as she rolled backwards and popped up on one knee with her sword in front of her. *Light o' Orijin. Every single time.*

"Stop." The instructor stepped in between them. "You cannot let your frustration show, just because of a missed opportunity. "Frustration in combat leads to impatience. Impatience is all it takes to leave yourself open to get hurt or killed. You must learn to control your emotions, acolyte. Do you understand?"

Farco took a breath and nodded, "Yes. I understand."

"Good. Both of you return to your starting points and kneel to face me." Farco did as he was told and looked over at Avenira, who was concentrating on the instructor. *What's this now?* The instructor looked at Avenira and addressed her, "Acolyte, tomorrow after breakfast, you will be evaluated to move on from Ranza and up to Nashorn. Be ready and good luck. You are excused to return to your quarters." Avenira nodded and turned her head to Farco, then stood and walked away without saying anything. *She couldn't even acknowledge me? What about me though? Maybe the instructor'll tell me the same thing now.*

He turned back to look at the instructor, who was now facing him. "Acolyte, you are still on the normal pace to advance to Nashorn. Do not compare the successes of others to those of your own. Once you master your patience, you will be well-suited to move up to Nashorn. Continue to practice and take your sparring sessions seriously."

He wasn't sure whether to respond, but couldn't help himself. "I don't understand the point o' takin' turns during sparrin'. "In actual combat, our opponents won't be standin' there waitin' fer us ta attack while they agree ta just defend. Why not just let us spar naturally?"

"Have we placed you into combat, acolyte?"

Farco squinted in confusion, "Um, no."

"Then why are you focused on what to do in combat?"

He was glad for the masks. He was sure the frustration on his face was visible. "Isn't that why we're doin' all o' this? Ta get ready fer combat? Ta be tested once we have ta fight?"

The instructor stood up, but still faced him. "You must first learn the basics of combat. If you do not know the details of how to attack and defend, and the nuances of how to do so in various situations, then there is no point in sending you into combat. Do you think that because you can hold a sword and swing it, that you are ready for combat?"

"Please forgive him, acolyte. He is still new ta this an' still has much ta learn." The voice came from right behind Farco and he already knew who it was. He didn't want to turn around, as he had likely already disrespected the instructor.

"There is nothing to forgive. The acolyte is new, young, and eager. All of those things are useful tools if wielded properly." The instructor nodded to them and walked away.

"Yer bein' a fool, Farco Baek, an' ya need to control yerself."

He turned around and saw Fae wearing her gold mask. It was still strange to see her in one, especially given that he was much taller than she. "What do ya mean?"

"Yer pushin' things too much. It's one thing ta be eager, but yer makin' stupid mistakes durin' yer trainin' an' sparrin'."

He punched his thigh. "It's not fair, ya know. Avenira is bein' tested tomorrow ta move up ta Nashorn. Meanwhile, I'm bein' told that I'm still on the normal pace. So what then, you an' her are so advanced an' I'm just regular?"

"Why are ya so concerned about our progress? Maybe that's the problem; yer so focused on what's happenin' ta us that yer not even takin' the time ta think about what ya have ta do fer yourself. So what if we advance faster'n you? Who said it was a race?"

"It's *not* a race. It's just not fair. Avenira has her manifestation an' I'm sure that helps her with fightin', because she doesn't have ta worry about gettin' hurt. I don't have that kinda advantage, an'..."

Fae cut him off, "An' neither do I. But I've still managed ta advance ta Scorpion before either o' ya even got ta Nashorn. So what does that tell ya about manifestations. Ya sound like a whiny little spoiled brat right now. Stop feelin' sorry fer yerself an' just work harder. Stay focused." She pointed a finger into his chest. "If ya think I'm jokin', just wait. The whinin' doesn't seem like much now, but then ye'll make more an' more excuses about why ya can't an' why we're able ta do things yer not. An' even worse, Near will get tired o' ya blamin' things on her manifestation an' makin' it seem like she's not workin' harder than ya. That's an easy way ta ruin things between the two o' ya. Is that what ya want?"

He gulped. *Is that true? Would she really not want ta be with me?* He looked down at the ground and thought about Fae's words for a moment. He hadn't really thought about what Avenira might think about how he was acting, or about the notion that they might not be together. "No, it's not. I hadn't really thought about it like that."

She pushed her finger harder into his chest. "Well ye'd better start. I've a feelin' that combat's comin' soon an' we're goin' ta need ta be ready."

"What do ya mean?"

"I've been hearin' a lot o' the chatter an' rumors around the fortress. I think havin' the gold mask probably has certain privileges. Anyway, don't go runnin' around tellin' anyone about this."

"Tellin' who? The only people I talk ta here are you an' Near."

"Fine, fine. Well, just in case. There's some concern from the higher up acolytes that the Vithelegion aren't done with us an' might

attack again. They just don't know when. I think they're monitorin'
them somehow ta see if they're actually sailin' home. Not sure how
they're doin' that. In the meantime, there's also rumors that we're goin'
ta turn our attention ta the Vermillion army. I think the Komytii sees
them as a threat ta Ashur, since they helped the Vithelegion." Farco
continued to stare at her for a moment after she finished speaking. He
still remembered both the Vithelegion and the Vermillion being in
Vandenar. He'd assumed that they were fighting each other, but more
and more rumors had swirled in the aftermath that the Royal Vermillion
Army had actually worked with the Vithelegion to destroy the cities of
Mireya. "Ya hear anythin' I said, Far?"

He realized he hadn't responded to her, "Yea, sorry Fae. I was
just thinkin' about Vandenar an' all the destruction they caused. I'll take
yer advice an' get my act together. There's no way I want ta miss out
on combat even if there's a small chance we'll fight the Vithelegion or
Vermillion. I'll be ready, I promise." He wasn't sure why, but he gave
her a hug and it surprised her as much as it did him. "Sorry, I don't
know where that came from." Farco didn't bother to wait around for
things to get more awkward. He scuttled away with what little dignity
he had left.

***

"Hey!"

Lincan walked out of Thanh Thien, the temple that housed the
Elders. His meeting with them had been surprisingly short, as they'd
agreed immediately to prepare Fangh-Haan against Jahmash and his
armies. They had called in the general of the Fangh army, a man by the
name of Nham Kyloon, to instruct him to begin the process. "Hey! Wait
a moment, Lincan!"

Lincan had been so caught up with how easy the meeting had
gone that he didn't realize someone was speaking to him until he heard
his name. He turned around and saw Nham a few paces behind. "Oh,
hi Nham. Or General Kyloon. Sorry."

"No, no, Nham is fine, don't worry about that." He shook his
shaved head, which reminded Lincan a bit of Garrison. "Trust me,
you're the last person who needs to be official with me."

Lincan looked at him and scratched the side of his head, "Why's
that?"

"As soon as I saw you inside, I swore I recognized you. And
then the Elders mentioned your name, I knew for sure. You are part of

the Vo family; your sister is Linh, right?"

Oh no. Where's this going? "Yes, that's my sister. Do you know her?"

Nham smiled awkwardly, "Sort of. We met a few times when we were younger. Teenagers. My parents have a stand at one of the street markets and she would come by for fresh vegetables sometimes. That was a while ago, though."

"Ah, I see. So… uh, was that what you wanted to talk about? Linh?"

Nham scratched his head as well and then looked down for a moment. "Sorry, I guess that was awkward. It's just that I fancied her for a time and I guess…"

No. Not letting this get any more awkward than it needs to. "Hey, Nham, I should break it to you now, Linh is married with a child. I'm sorry, but I figured I should tell you before you get your hopes up or anything."

"Oh. Uh, thanks. Sorry, I didn't mean for this conversation to go this way. I actually did want to talk to you about other things."

Lincan looked away for a moment and then back at Nham. "Look, I think there's probably a better way for me to say this, but this past week has been busy as hell and while a lot of it has been great, there are too many things going on in my mind to try and navigate weird conversations. I'm going to be blunt, you are the most casual general I've ever met in my life and I really don't know how to handle that right now."

Nham looked at him with his mouth halfway open for a moment. His eyes darted around as if trying to direct his lips. "I… uh. Sorry, I swear I'm not usually this awkward. I don't know why I thought that would be a good thing to start with. Can we just forget about all that? I guess it's probably hard to tell, but I'm a good general, I promise. And the Fangh army has grown under my leadership over the past few years."

"By *grown*, would you say that you have enough soldiers to train people in every Fangh city?"

"Oh, easily," Nham smiled. "We have over five hundred men in the army right now, and tensions with Galicea have been minimal, if anything, for the past few years. I wouldn't need to keep that many men at the wall between our nations if they were needed to train more people. But what are we supposed to tell them?"

"Tell them Jahmash is coming to destroy Ashur, and he has

armies with him."

"Lincan, I'm curious. All the stories stated that Jahmash was deathly afraid of the open seas. Would he really come here on a ship?"

"We don't know about him, specifically. But we're almost positive that his armies will arrive before he does. He may not even have to step foot on Ashur to be able to destroy it, though I'm sure he would prefer it that way. How long do you think it would take to prepare our people for combat?"

Nham shrugged, "For basic combat? A couple of months. But if it's armies that are coming and not militias, then they'll need more time to master the sword and shield. We may need more resources as well."

Lincan paused for a moment. He wasn't sure how to ask what he wanted to ask, without sounding selfish. *Isn't it selfish, though? Even if you're trying to help someone else, you're focusing more on what you want than anything else.* "Will you need me around to start any of those preparations?"

Nham shrugged, "I haven't thought about it. Why do you ask?"

"There are a couple of things that I need to do back in Markos and the sooner I get there the better. But I wouldn't be up there for more than about a day, so I would come right back down here."

"I'll be honest, Lincan, it would definitely be helpful to have you here. The perception has changed lately about Descendants, and it would be great for the people's morale to see you working with us to train them. How long would you be gone?"

"I'd say about a week? I would literally go, do what I have to do, and come right back."

"You're not lying to me, right? I know this all started off strangely between us, but please be honest with me."

"No, I promise it's not about that at all. I'm not trying to run away from here. I finally just saw my family for the first time in years and met my nephew for the first time. I also healed my brother's eye and enjoyed every minute that I was with them. Trust me, I *want* to come back here. I just need to go back to do something for a friend, and then I can help in any way that you need."

Nham folded his arms in front of him, "If you're telling me the truth, then tell me what you're going to do."

Damn. How do I explain this? He sighed, "Well, as I just mentioned, I can heal people with my manifestation. It turns out that while I was away, my brother had a fishing accident that cost him his sight in one of his eyes. Well, I healed his eye a few days ago and he's been able to see normally ever since. Are you following so far?"

"Yes. Simple enough."

"Good. Well, back in Markos, I have a friend who actually *lost* both of his eyes in combat. I've been trying to heal him ever since, but since his eyes aren't even there, it's pretty much impossible to heal him. I realized that I can't regrow his eyes for him. But I realized while healing my brother that, perhaps I could use the eyes of someone who died very recently. That way they haven't started to decay yet, and I could work on attaching those eyes to wherever they're supposed to connect. If Lao could see again, it would change so much for us and our fight against Jahmash. Just as you're a great general here in Fangh-Haan, he's been a great leader for us Descendants."

Nham stared at him for a moment. "Wow. You can really heal people like that? With such serious injuries?"

"I can. And if it works with Lao, then when I come back here, I can heal plenty of people here as well. I also must deliver some things to King Garrison. He requested some items that he said can only be found in Fangh-Haan."

"Very well," Nham nodded. "I understand. I think our people could really use your help as well. Especially once we start training people, it will comfort them to know that you can heal them if they get hurt. Assuming it's not too much trouble."

"I think I can handle that."

"Good. I'll see you when you return. We'll have already started training in each city by then. I'll tell my soldiers to be on the lookout for you, just in case I'm not in Xuyen anymore." Nham extended his forearm toward Lincan.

"I can't wait." He grasped Nham's forearm and shook it. "Thanks for understanding. I'll see you soon." Lincan turned and walked to his horse, where one of the knights was waiting and they rode back to his parents' home.

He had already packed his things, knowing that trying to say goodbye would take forever. As he walked into the house, everyone was sitting around the table in the kitchen waiting for him. His mother had prepared a noodle soup with sliced beef and onions. It had been his favorite dish since he could remember. They sat down and ate, and kept the conversation to light topics and memories, and laughed as much as they could. When they finally finished eating, Lincan stood up. "Look, let's not make this long and emotional. I know it's been so long since you last saw me, but I'll be back by the time you're done with this massive pile of dishes. While I'm gone, Nham Kyloon and the Fangh army will begin recruiting and training people to prepare for Jahmash. Please cooperate with them and do as they say. As soon as I return, I will be working with them as well. Understood?"

They all nodded in affirmation, including his little nephew. Lincan went to each of them and hugged them all tightly, before grabbing his pack. Maa, start on another pot of soup in a week. I'll have some as soon as I walk in the door." He could see a tear in his mother's eye as he shut the door behind him

.

CHAPTER 19
SERPENTS AND SECRETS

From *The Book of Orijin*, Verse Two Hundred Eleven
Despite the worst evils that any one of you is capable of, not a single one of you is beyond redemption.

"No, there aren't two kings. There is King Garrison, the actual king, and then an imposter in Alvadon." Vasher took a deep breath and tried his best to not use his manifestation, just to avoid the stupidity coming from Harshu. He continued to watch some of the Shivaani soldiers showing how to shoot arrows with accuracy.

"Then why is the imposter in Alvadon? Shouldn't the true king be there?"

"Light of Orijin, how daft can you really be? Let me break this down for you, Harshu. We stormed King Edmund's palace and killed him. As a result, the palace was destroyed and King Garrison didn't think it wise to rule from there. There are too many people in Alvadon who want him dead, so he decided to rule from Constaniza in Markos. Does that make sense?"

"Stop talking to me like I'm stupid, boy. I understand that. But why is there an issue with him being the king if his father was on the throne before? Why would there be a need for the people of Alvadon to crown a different king?"

"I'm sure you're aware that Garrison bears the Descendant's Mark. As a result, when he finally embraced that and refused to do his father's bidding, King Edmund labeled him a criminal and revoked his princely duties. So now the people of Alvadon argue that Garrison is not the true heir to the throne."

Harshu looked at him flatly, "Look, I am no expert on the laws and affairs of Ashur, but if he was stripped of his title of prince, then he lawfully has no claim. These Cerysians have always taken themselves too seriously, what with their golden skin and pretentious accents and all. Why should we care, anyway? What will change?"

Vasher folded his arms and glanced at Harshu, "You should care. The Royal Vermillion turned on Ashur. Did any of you hear about how Mireya was invaded by people from another nation beyond Ashur? Or were you too busy waiting in your base for something exciting? Mireya was decimated and you know who helped that happen? The

Vermillion. They stepped aside and let Mireya burn. Garrison has his own army that's already traveling through Ashur to help prepare the country for Jahmash. And do you know what he's promised each nation once we manage to stop Jahmash?"

Harshu closed his eyes, "Tea and pastries."

"No you fool," Vasher shook his head. "He has sworn to make each nation in Ashur its own sovereign nation. No more living under the rule of the throne. No more having to deal with Cerysia and their golden skin."

"You're serious?" Harshu finally perked up. "How do you know this for sure?"

"Because I heard it from him myself. I guarantee you that this other king has no intention of doing that."

Harshu offered a rare smile, "Imagine an Ashur where we're not bothered by the whims of a narcissistic king. That would be amazing. Have you told any others of this yet?"

"No," Vasher shook his head. "I only found out about this second king recently."

"Good. Let me be the one to share the news with Janaral Prashant and the others. I would obviously credit you, but I could use a break from being the mad, lazy, old man who doesn't have much to offer."

"Very well. It's your news to share."

"Thank you. Your father would be proud of you for doing me this favor."

Shit. I forgot that he knows about that. Vasher opened himself to his manifestation. "Listen, Harshu. I am a valuable resource to you because of my travels, my manifestation, and my connection to the true king, Garrison. You have no idea that I'm the son of Albarran, or that my mother is a Daughter of Tahlia. Remember, the most important thing is to prepare the people of Shivaana for Jahmash's coming."

Harshu looked at him quizzically, "I swear you look somewhat familiar, Vasher. Did we meet before you came to our base?"

"No, I'd never met you before. But many people have said that I have a familiar face. So don't lose any sleep over it. Why don't you go tell Janaral Prashant about this whole king thing and what Garrison plans to do with the nations of Ashur?"

"That's a great idea," Harshu nodded. "I'll return shortly."

Vasher breathed a sigh of relief. Phew. Hopefully that's the end of that. He turned away from the training grounds and walked for a bit. The island that Agralun resided on had cliffs all around its perimeter, and Agralun sat right at the northeastern edge of the island. Vasher continued to walk until he could see the edge and look out at the sea. *Am I relying on this manifestation too much now? First I almost used it on Mata and Do'maa, even though I promised I wouldn't. I even told Delilah that I didn't want to use it like that.* He knelt to pick up a small rock and then threw it over the cliff and into the water. He was too far up to be able to see it land, but it still brought a fleeting sense of satisfaction.

Hey. Vash. You seemed busy for a while, there. You have a moment now?

Lao? Again? You all must have a lot going on up there, huh?

Yes. Garrison is dealing with a whole mess of things. Which is why I am reaching out again. This is urgent, so the sooner you can take care of all this, the better. First, I've gotten news from Taiju and Fera of ships approaching from the north. Obviously we know that there are other nations out there, but Slade said those are all to the south of Ashur. So we're almost positive that these are Jahmash's armies.

What? Seriously? It's starting already? Have they attacked yet?

No, the scouts spotted them at a distance, but they are steadily approaching. My sister did well to prepare Markos for this exact thing, so there are militias and soldiers ready to defend. Garrison and Wendell also sent knights out to each city to fortify them. But you need to let them know down there that this is happening, and it's likely not long before more ships arrive on your shores.

Understood. We'll be ready. You said 'first'. Does that mean there's more?

Yes. Garrison needs some… ingredients, I guess you could call them. He said he can't get them up here, and most of what he needs is in Shivaana.

Ingredients? What exactly is he… cooking?

He wouldn't tell me. Something about pouches? I'm not sure. I do know that he needs someone to bring the things up here as soon as the ingredients are secured. Do you have someone down there that you can trust?

Trust? I don't know. I could always bring them myself. Now that everything is underway, I don't know how much they still need me around. The military officers are running most of the training, and the Daughters of Tahlia are working on their thing down in Sundari. Just tell me what you need and I'll see about securing everything.

That works. I don't think Garrison would have an issue with that.

***

Delilah stood in front of a group of Daughters in the middle of the arena. She'd done well so far to hide her fears, but she'd cursed herself innumerable times in the past week for coming up with this idea in the first place. *Bhujanga? Really Del? The one who comes up with the idea is always the one who has to lead things. I should have known that.*

The only saving grace was that military officers had convinced the trainers who ran the fighting pit that they had to shut down the arena for official business. The trainers had objected at first, but once they were told the magnitude of things, they slowly agreed to use the arena for training the giant snakes. Delilah had been surprised at how much Sundari had changed in the prior weeks, as all of the Daughters committed to training. There were no more dancers in the streets, and word of it quickly spread. There had been few tourists in over a week as a result, and Sundari was quieter than Delilah could have ever imagined.

While Varana had nominated her to lead the Daughters on the battlefield, luckily it hadn't fallen completely on Delilah to lead the training. Some of the others were far more daring and comfortable around the bhujanga, and were willing to try different methods to train them. Ojasri, who had mostly supported the idea from the start, eagerly took the lead in trying to find out how to get what they wanted out of the creatures. It had taken just over three days, but they finally realized that consistently offering food worked the best. So far, they'd managed to train the snakes to move in certain directions and attack specific targets. They had lost one of the Daughters to a fatal bite on the first day, and another broke her leg after not moving out of the way of an oncoming bhujanga quickly enough, but they persisted and vowed to be overly cautious moving forward.

"We need some volunteers to try and bond with this one! It's a difficult little bastard!" Ojasri yelled from across the arena. The strategy had been to have at least one Daughter bond with each snake, so that it would have a designated person commanding it. Delilah looked around at the others behind her. There were at least two dozen women standing around and gossiping, just asking to be selected.

The problem that Delilah had with them was that none of them would care if asked to try and bond with the giant snake. Except maybe one of them. She eyed Krissette talking to one of the younger Daughters, Anika. Anika was likely a year or two older than Krissette, and her beauty was striking. Her light brown skin appeared to be free of any blemish and her straight black hair shimmered in the sun, showing streaks of dark and light brown. *Light of Orijin, even I wouldn't mind bedding her. I can't really blame Krissette for doting on her.* Delilah quickly shook her head to bring back her focus. "Krissette! Come here for a moment."

The girl smiled at Anika and walked over to Delilah. "Hi Delilah, sorry. I got caught up talking and it won't happen again." *Even when she should be mad, she's apologizing instead. Good luck with that, Anika.*

"Ojasri wants you to try and bond with that bhujanga over there. It's the one behind the gate nearest to her." Every entrance to the arena floor had a gate of metal bars to secure it, and they'd used those to their advantage when bringing out the giant snakes. As menacing as they could be, they could only generate so much power against something in front of them. The trainers from the fighting pits had agreed to stay and help, so they manned the gates and stayed nearby in case of any emergencies.

"Oh really? Will she help me with what to do? I'm nervous that I'll mess it up."

"Yes," Delilah nodded. "Go quickly." Krissette scurried over to Ojasri. Delilah could imagine that she was still smiling as she ran over. *She'll probably smile at the snake, too, and expect the thing to be friendly with her.* Delilah and the others watched as Ojasri instructed Krissette on movements and commands. The trainers opened the gate at Ojasri's command and the giant creature slithered forward. As far as Delilah could tell, the green and yellow-scaled thing didn't look angry or agitated; it likely just wanted the freedom to move about. Krissette called for it to come to her, and the snake turned its head toward her before slithering in her direction.

Good start, girl. Keep it up. Be firm. Don't talk to it like you talk to me. The bhujanga moved closer to Krissette. Ojasri backed away to let Krissette take the lead. It looked tentative in getting closer to her, which surprised Delilah. Would've sworn it would either want nothing to do with her or would just want to eat her. Krissette barked another command at the snake, which caused it to hesitate. It flicked its long, forked tongue in the air a few times and lowered its head slightly, then looked directly at Krissette for a moment. She pointed to the ground emphatically and shouted for it to drop to the ground. The snake continued to look at her and weave its head around until Krissette took a large piece of meat from the bucket behind her and repeated her drop command. Instead of dropping, the bhujanga made itself taller and leaned its head back. Oh no. That can't be a good sign.

Ojasri yelled something at Krissette before backing away even more, but Krissette stayed put and repeated her command. Just as she brought her arm down to finish the command, the snake darted toward her with its jaws wide open. Krissette tried to step back and lifted her arm in the process. The bhujanga bit down on her left hand, which had been holding the large piece of meat and Krissette screamed.

Delilah and the others ran toward Krissette and the snake. "No! Krissette, get away if you can!" Krissette looked directly at her with panic in her face that seemed resigned to her fate. She pulled back from the bhujanga and her arm came out of its mouth. When Delilah finally processed what she was looking at in all the blood, she realized that Krissette's hand had been bitten off, halfway up her forearm. "Daughters! Help her! Wrap her arm tightly to stop the bleeding, then burn the end of the arm! It's the only way to keep her from bleeding out and to save the arm!" She turned to the bhujanga, which was focused on swallowing the chunk of meat along with Krissette's hand. "Hey! Get down and stay! Trainers, can you get it back through the gate?"

The four men standing at the tunnel's opening grabbed their prods and walked toward the giant snake. As Delilah watched, she caught the bhujanga's eyes, locked on hers. They continued to stare at one another until the snake set its head down and slithered slowly toward her. Delilah took a step back, but remembered that snakes generally hadn't attacked them from so low. Despite the chaos going on behind her, Delilah focused on the oncoming snake, which seemed to get slower the closer it got to her. Finally, it stopped a foot in front of her and rested its head on the ground. It maintained its eye contact with her and gave her a slow blink. Delilah froze, unsure how to respond.

Someone whispered in her ear, "Do the same thing back to it. Blink slowly one time. It's a sign of trust and resignation." Delilah did as told and immediately the snake flicked its tongue out at her boot.

"See. This is your snake, Del." Delilah glanced to her left and smiled at Ojasri.

"This is my snake. This is my fucking snake." She paused for a moment, "Holy shit. I have a snake! But it cost Krissette her hand! Kris! Is she going to be alright?"

Ojasri rested a hand on her shoulder, "She's in good spirits. Then again, when have you seen the girl being anything but pleasant? We'll have to have someone with better medical experience take a look at it, but we did what was necessary for now. Cauterized and wrapped before she lost too much blood. And we've been smart enough to have halla milk ever since Chhavi died and Harini broke her leg. We gave Krissette enough that she won't feel any pain for days." Delilah looked at the girl, who sat on the ground, braced against two other Daughters. Anika had already taken her place next to Krissette and was fussing over her.

Delilah smiled, "Looks like she has someone to dote on her. That will help more than anything else."

Ojasri nudged her playfully, "Are you jealous?"

"I'm not sure. I didn't think I would be. But I'm feeling a lot of different things right now, so who knows."

"Your bhujanga is waiting for you. Focus on that first, and later you can let me know if you need help getting your mind off all of those different things." She smiled suggestively at Delilah before returning to the group and checking on Krissette.

Delilah looked back at the gigantic snake that was still flicking its tongue at her boots and pants, and stepped beside it. She knelt down and stroked the top of its head and neck. "You need a name, don't you? How about Raksha? It means protector. Will you be that for me?"

***

"I do not ask because I tire of your company, Meli Ikitenya, but how long do you plan to come and go on this island?" Maqdhuum smiled at Eddis' comment and continued to look out from the edge of the floating island. Every time Maqdhuum had visited lately, Eddis had been kind enough to join him and sit at the edge of the island, and simply look out to take in the view. This time, however, it did nothing to clear Maqdhuum's mind.

"I think one way or another, my time with you will be over soon. I am almost done ensuring that Ashur has everything it needs to be ready for Jahmash, but I am not sure whether Ashur wants my help anymore. I may have done too many wrong things for the sake of what's right in the grand scheme."

"What do you mean when you say 'one way or another'?" Eddis had never been one to get caught up when he started feeling sorry for himself. "It sounds like you have options that you are weighing?"

"Always so astute, Eddis. There are two paths at this point. The first is to stay the course and continue to prepare. It's the safer choice for all of Ashur, but it will likely cost thousands more lives once the war begins. The other choice is… the one that I fear more, but could solve everything quickly if I succeed. It would mean facing Jahmash and fighting him. But that will only work if I defeat him."

"And when will you decide what to do?"

"Soon. I need to check on the forges in Ashur and see what the outlook is with weapons and armor. I'm sure there's only so much they can do. Perhaps I should do that now." He stood up and helped up Eddis, then stepped away from the edge of the island. "I'll return shortly." Eddis nodded at him as he disappeared. He reappeared in Itarse, not far from the base of the mountain range where most of the forges were. He walked between workshops and forges, looking at each blacksmith as he passed. They all toiled away, pounding and shaping metal into swords, shields, and armor. Finally he eyed a shorter person with what looked like a clear barrier in the air protecting her face, pounding a blade with a large hammer. *Wow. Didn't think she was that strong. These Descendants continue to amaze me. Shame I wrote them off for so long. Would've made things much easier if I hadn't.* He walked closer and waited until she was done with her hammer. "Can I bother you for a moment?"

Sindha set down her hammer and adjusted her leather apron. Her eyes had been wide and then thinned once she realized it was him. "Sure. What?"

Oh good. Short. "How are things looking? In terms of supply? How much of Ashur can we help with all this?"

Sindha's expression remained blank. "We? I didn't see you in any of the forges. But then again, I've been so busy making swords that I've barely stepped away from here. We are working day and night, not only to make as many weapons and armor as we can, but others are also in the mines all day, every day, to get the ore. There's barely anyone left in the city between those who are training to fight and those of us who are here." She took a deep breath, "But what have you been up to? The word is you are the one in charge of the Kraisos and the Anonymi.

And so what, you just jump around from place to place checking in on everyone?"

Maqdhuum put his hands up to try and get a word in, "I'm just trying to make sure Ashur is ready." Sindha tried to continue arguing, "Hold on. I'm talking now. I know everyone is angry with me and I have to live with that. But beyond that I'm trying to help."

"Well Ashur is not ready, you idiot. And no, we could probably exhaust everything these mines have to offer and it wouldn't be enough to equip Ashur. So perhaps you can disappear and magically find somewhere else that's able to forge swords and armor and shields. You know, since you're trying to help."

He clasped his hands behind his back and looked down, "Actually, I think I can do that."

"Good. You know what would also make things so much easier? If at any point in the last two thousand years, you summoned the stones to stand in front of Jahmash and fight him. We believed in you, Maqdhuum. We put our faith in you that you were good. Light of Orijin, you were chosen by the Orijin to save mankind, and you ran away because you were too scared of losing. Sure, you can tell us and everyone else that you lived to fight another day and that it made more sense to hide so you could stop Jahmash later. But you did nothing for centuries upon centuries and let him grow stronger. You waited until the Red Harbinger became a threat to the world again before you decided to do anything. And then when you finally did, you stole Baltaszar's mother away and allowed her to be... violated by the only person in this world who's worse than you." Her face was full of tears, but her tone remained firm, "All it would take is one unselfish act from you and you would spare how many lives?"

Maqdhuum disappeared before Sindha could look into his eyes. The last thing he needed was for her to see the tear forming in his own eye. He returned to Eddis Ebaba's island and walked back to the edge where he'd been previously sitting, and shivered. Eddis sat down next to him. "Was it this cold before? I wasn't gone that long."

"There was a chill in the air, but having a weight on our shoulders tends to soften our defenses. That was a rather short trip."

"Indeed. I don't even know whether that went the way I expected it to or not. Doesn't matter. Eddis, I may need the help of Domna Orjann. Actually, Ashur needs its help."

"You know I do not speak for this nation. I am one Nerisi on a floating island, who rarely leaves for the mainland."

"I know," Maqdhuum nodded. "But I am the Meli Ikitenya, remember? You can vouch for me in Tafari. Could we at least try to speak to your council to get their blessings?"

Eddis looked down from the edge of the island and sighed, "This is not some casual request, my friend. The Mikiribet is made up of nice people, but they take their procedures quite seriously."

"Eddis, there's no time for procedure. This is urgent. Ashur needs their support and given how long it would take to get everything there, this needs to be discussed now."

Eddis sighed again and wiped the sweat from his brow, "Then what choice do I have? Let us go while it is still light out. I can only help you if I can see where I am going." Maqdhuum nodded and extended his arm to Eddis. Once the other man grasped his arm, they appeared just inside the gates of Tafari, the capital city of Domna Orjann. Eddis let go of Maqdhuum's arm and cupped both of his hands around his mouth. "Citizens of Tafari! I am Eddis Ebaba, the Nerisi of Hulet Island of the Deseeti Semai! Be warned that I have an outsider with me! He is not a threat to you, but dear Birabiro, conduct yourselves accordingly until we are gone!" As soon as Eddis finished speaking, a series of whoops could be heard through the streets for several moments.

Maqdhuum looked at Eddis incredulously, "What the hell was that?"

Eddis smiled as he walked, "We have secrets in Domna Orjann that even you do not know of, Meli Ikitenya. Now come, let us go so that you can get me into more trouble. The Foq Mikiribet is just ahead." They walked on for another minute or so until they reached a tall, rectangular dark grey building. "This is it." He paused and briefly put his palms to his face before turning to Maqdhuum. "Perhaps you should enter first. At least then, it would make your impatience more apparent."

"Very well." He didn't want to be short with Eddis, as he knew the man was doing him a favor and was clearly uncomfortable about it. *Wonder what big secret they're all hiding here. And how have I not found it out in the last two thousand years?* He shook off the thought to focus on the building in front of him. He pushed the door open and entered a small foyer, with Eddis right behind. There were staircases on both sides and a hallway in front of them. "Which way do we go?"

"Up, my friend. Either side will work." Maqdhuum heard a lot of noise, almost like buzzing and things being flicked or fluttered about. He hadn't realized that Eddis was such a heavy walker, as the man practically stomped on every step up the stairs. By the time they reached the second floor, everything had gone quiet.

"Is this it?" Eddis nodded to him. "Good. Those stairs are steeper than they look. Also, what are Bira…"

"Don't worry about that. It's an explanation for another day. The Mikiribet chamber is this door right in the center. They may already be meeting with someone, though."

"Shouldn't they have guards, then?"

"Not when everyone in Domna Orjann understands the rules and follows them. We are an old nation, my friend. And we understand what has made this nation work well for so long. Our people work hard and are rewarded for it. Those who may be facing hard times are still taken care of. There is no reason for anyone to break the law, as they will be provided for as long as they follow the law."

"So you're saying there are no corrupt people in all of Domna Orjann?"

"What need is there? Corruption comes from a need that you cannot fulfill on your own. It happens when there is something that you want or need that is beyond your reach, so you break your own sense of morality to attain it. But that is not necessary here. This nation is fair to everyone, to the extent that people's wants and needs are always within their reach."

"How lovely for you. If only all the other nations were as wise. So what do you want me to do here, knock or something? You know what, never mind." He knocked loudly on the tall wooden door, waited barely a moment, and then impatiently pushed it open. The room was large and rectangular, with colorful tapestries on each of the incredibly high walls. At the other end of the room, several people sat at a crescent-shaped table, all facing a woman who stood in the middle of the floor. "I'm sorry to interrupt your business, lady, but I guarantee you that my reason for being here is incredibly more urgent."

The lady turned to him and stared for a moment. She was older than he'd thought, and taller than him. Her copper skin wasn't quite as dark as Eddis', but it reminded Maqdhuum of the bronze metal common in the nation of Rhagavi. "You are not one of us. Why are you here in the Foq Mikiribet?" She looked at Eddis, "Outsiders are not allowed in here. You know that and yet you would break our sacred laws?"

Maqdhuum moved so that he was between the woman and Eddis. "It is not his fault. I am not a true outsider, at least not in the way you think." He turned to the Mikiribet, "My name is Maqdhuum, though you may better recognize my former name, Abram Feroze, Harbinger of the Orijin. I am here because I need your help and I have nowhere else to turn."

The woman stepped several paces back. "Oh, I would dearly like to hear this. Esteemed members of the Mikiribet, I will gladly allow this man to approach you ahead of me, if it pleases you."

The nine members of the Mikiribet stood from their seats and Maqdhuum took in their elaborate outfits. They all wore loose white robes embroidered with swirling patterns of bright colors. Each of them wore a silver piece that covered the tops of their heads and came down to their eyes, with slits for each eye. What caught his attention the most, though, was the silver pieces lining their entire earlobes from top to bottom, with thin chains extending from the bottom of each earlobe to each side of their noses. From what he could tell, the mix of men and women was almost even, with four women and five men. They all looked at the older woman and nodded to her, then shifted their attention to Maqdhuum. The woman at the far right of the table spoke to him first.

"We have heard legends that you still exist, and there have even been rumors from time to time that you have visited the Deseeti Semai. However, we do not generally concern ourselves with half-truths and matters that are not verified. But before we would even be willing to engage with you, it would be prudent for you to prove that you are who you say you are."

Maqdhuum nodded. "If you are familiar with the stories of me from the past, then I might assume that you know what the Orijin blessed me with?" They all nodded in response. "Good." He didn't wait to disappear and reappear several times throughout the room until the older woman grew faint from watching him. He stopped and caught her before she fell down, then eased her to the ground to get her bearings. "Sorry. I tend to only do that around people who know that I can do it. I hope I didn't startle you." She nodded and waved her hand dismissively for him to go back to what he was doing. He approached the crescent table again, this time getting a little closer.

The man at the center addressed him, "Thank you for cooperating." The man looked at Eddis, "You are Eddis Ebaba of the

Hulet Island of the Deseeti Semai. Do you vouch for this man and confirm that he is who he says he is?"

"I do," Eddis responded meekly from the other end of the room.

The man looked back at Maqdhuum, "Very well, Harbinger. Please be direct with your business. It is our rule to finish our responsibilities before nightfall, and that shall be upon us soon."

Maqdhuum nodded, "If there's one thing I am, it is to the point. So I'll get right to it. Ashur is in danger. And the only reason it hasn't reached out to anyone else for help is because almost no one there knows that other nations exist."

"How could they not?" Another man asked from the table.

"Because two thousand years ago, Darian drowned the world when everything was still Iman Qaja. Once the world drowned, the people who were left there had no reason to believe that there was anything else. So they resigned themselves to life there. With what they knew. Just as you stated you do not concern yourselves with half-truths, they focused on what they knew for sure, and that was their lives there. As I was saying, though, Jahmash intends to attack them soon. And he has the backing of Castiel, Yahaira, and Brogan. Vitheligia has already attacked Ashur, albeit for different reasons, so they have already been compromised. Right now, they are training anyone who is able to fight and fortifying themselves in preparation for this attack. But they need help and I don't know who else can help them."

"Have you sought an audience with the nations of Orol Taghdras? Besides Vitheligia? The other five nations refused you?"

Maqdhuum shook his head, "I have not. The nature of my request isn't for people. It is for resources. The Ashurian people are exhausting their mines and ores to make weapons and armor, but frankly it will not be enough and they know it. That is why I have come to you. Domna Orjann is notorious for its mines and metal, especially its swords. I have come to you to ask if you might be so generous as to share your resources with them."

"You may or may not be aware, but we are a nation that keeps to ourselves." The man at the left end of the table spoke to him. "We do not concern ourselves with the affairs of other nations, for better or worse. This has been known to every nation in Bisitsad and Orol Taghdras, and as a result they do not bother us. To aid another domain would be to directly oppose many of those other nations, making us a target. We need nothing from Ashur, so why give up our resources?"

He looked down for a moment, then back at Eddis, before

looking at the Mikiribet again. "Honestly, if I had taken the time to think this all through, I'd probably have a better answer for you. You are right. There is nothing that Ashur can offer you. And I understand, likely better than anyone else in this world, that when we're asked to make a sacrifice for someone else, it's only fair to expect something in return. Even if that something is less valuable. And that isn't the case here. But Ashur is filled with good people. And magic. There are direct descendants of Darian there who can wield magic in dynamic ways. They have blind men and women who can see visions and provide prophecies."

"If they have magic at their disposal, why do they need armor and weapons from us?"

"It won't be enough. There aren't enough Descendants to stop what's coming. Magic requires energy. They can only use it for so long before it saps them of energy. If they don't get help, thousands upon thousands will die. I ask that you put yourselves in their position. Their only crime is that they exist. Jahmash is so obsessed with revenge against Darian that he wants all of Darian's descendants wiped from existence. They have done nothing wrong. Just like you, they have kept to themselves for millennia. So put yourselves in their position for a moment. Imagine that one day, the nations of the other islands decide that they want your land. Or they want something that you have here. And they all decide that they will work together and come *take* what they want. What will you do? Would you not wish for an ally in your darkest hour? Would you turn away a selfless nation who offers help?"

He looked around at all of them for a moment. "I know I don't have much time, but I humbly ask you to consider empathy in making your decision."

"Given Ashur's distance from us, it would take several months to sail there even if we had everything ready right now. How do you know that we would make it in time?"

He shrugged, "I don't. I am just hoping. And asking that you make your decision soon. But please consider the entirety of this in making your choice. I am a Harbinger of the Orijin and even I have nowhere else to turn. I am helping Ashur in every way that I can, and I don't think it will be enough. And that is why I'm here speaking to you."

Another woman at the table responded. "We understand your need for urgency, but this is not a decision that we can make lightly. It will take some time to consider all of the possibilities that would go along with this."

"How long will you need?"

"Give us three days to come to a decision."

Three days? Three fucking days? He hoped his face didn't reveal his frustration. "Very well. I don't like it, but I am not in a position to argue. I'll return here in three days."

"You may return on the morning of the third day, if it pleases you. We shall not be entertaining requests from our citizens that day, so you will not have to wait."

"Thank you." He nodded and walked back to Eddis. "Let's go." They disappeared from the room and returned to Eddis' home. Maqdhuum sat on the ground and leaned back against the wall. "What do you think, Eddis? Will it work?"

"I wish I could tell you one way or another. But I wouldn't get my hopes up if I were you. This request is unprecedented. They will not take it lightly."

"These times are unprecedented. It's not like a rogue Harbinger returns for revenge very often." He paused for a moment. "I'm sorry. I don't mean to take it out on you. Thank you for your help, Eddis."

"I am always willing to help, as long as what you are doing is good for the world. So will you be staying here until it is time to return to them?"

Maqdhuum smiled. He wished he'd had Eddis' moral code. "No, there's too much to do. I may come and go just to have a comforting place that I can return to. I can even sleep in that cell, now that it's not needed anymore. Hey, I've been meaning to ask this for a long time. I never did because I'm worried that it's a stupid question. You Nerisi are on every island with homes and everything. How did you get it all up here? And how do you normally leave your island when I'm not around? There's no way you're jumping from island to island like it's a giant staircase."

Eddis laughed at him. "It's just another one of Domna Orjann's secrets that I am sworn to protect. Perhaps I will tell you when you are minutes away from death."

This place and its damn secrets. "I'll hold you to that."

CHAPTER 20
FORESIGHT

From **The Book of Orijin,** **Verse Four Hundred One**
Trust that those whom you hold dear care for you and heed their wisdom.

"With all due respect, Garrison, you still need protection here. We cannot just send every soldier we have and leave you exposed." Wendell had refused to sit, despite everyone else doing so.

Garrison stood up to join him. "Who is coming here, Wendell? Exactly what threat are you worried about?"

"We don't know what Courtland is capable of, and he knows that you are here. What if he sends the Vermillion here to eliminate his competition? What will you do then? You are a great swordsman, Garrison, but not that great."

"We'll have reinforcements here soon enough. Lao said that Max, Neraiya, and Trevor should all be back soon. Not only that, but Adria will be in Alvadon shortly. Lao can check in on her regularly to find out what Courtland and the Vermillion are doing. Even if she must stay out of sight, it will be obvious if a contingent of his army mobilizes. Wendell, you are my best friend and I hate to use this tactic on you, but I am your king and this is my command. Our entire army needs to be sent out. The majority goes to Taiju and Fera, and you will send the rest to Darling Harbor and Pyrrha. Jahmash's armies cannot succeed here in Markos. This is the start of the war for Ashur, and we cannot lose the first battle. If we can stop this wave, it will make it much more difficult for them to attack the rest of Ashur." He leaned back against the patio banister and looked at the others.

"Very well." Wendell sat down with the others, "King Garrison. But I still do not think it is wise for Adria to be in Alvadon. What good could possibly come from that? Do you think she'll get close enough to learn any information? She's a Marked Descendant, Garrison. She won't exactly blend in."

"I have asked Lao to have her test the waters in Alvadon. See what Courtland is doing and gauge how receptive he is to his citizens and how much he wants to actually help Ashur. If it seems that he cares for everyone's well-being, then Adria will approach him and ask for the Vermillion's help in Markos."

Wendell glared at him, "You cannot be serious."

"I'm aware of how backwards that may seem. Trust me, Lao and Farrah both responded much more vehemently than you, but Ashur is the highest priority. If he wants to be the King of Ashur, then he has to be willing to protect Ashur. No matter what he decides in this, it will help my cause. If he agrees, then all the better for Ashur and he helped because I asked him to. If he disagrees, then he is willing to let Ashurians die while his domain comes under attack. Neither scenario makes him look good."

The rest of them grew quiet for a few moments until Kiryako spoke up. "Garrison, I know I'm relatively new to this group and there are certain topics that I'm completely unaware of, so what are these pouches that you've all been mentioning?"

He finally smiled for what felt like the first time all morning. "Well, you know how my manifestation allows me to invent and create things. Years ago when I was still leading the Vermillion, I had a workshop near the military quarters. I started playing around with various—I guess you could call them ingredients—to see what would happen if I mixed them together. After months and months of trial and error, I was able to consistently create certain combinations that resulted in various reactions once mixed with a catalyst, such as water or blood. Once I ended up in the dungeons of the House of Darian, I suppose I forgot all about them. But now that things are starting to stabilize and I am in control of my destiny, there is time to make them again."

Kiryako nodded. "And how will you use them? Are you planning on joining in any of the combat?"

Great. Is she starting a fight as well? Did she and Wendell agree to ambush me or something? "My hope is that Vasher and Lincan can bring back enough of what I need so that I can parcel it out to various squadrons throughout Ashur. I should probably have mentioned to all of you that Vasher and Lincan are returning here as well. See, Wen? Even more protection."

Wendell rolled his eyes at him.

"But Kiri, I am not going to lie. At some point I am going to have to face Courtland to settle who will be king. I'm not looking to turn it into a full-scale battle by bringing a squadron with me. The pouches will help me in that regard as well. If I remember correctly, one was able to cause tremors in the ground, which would come in handy right by his new throne."

This time it was Kiryako who stood up, "And when do you plan to do this? What point is there in declaring yourself king if you get killed before you can even be recognized as the king?" Her eyes grew thin and she crossed her arms in front of her.

"Look, I don't even have what I need to make the pouches yet. And when I do, it will take time to remember how to make everything again. It will be some time before I go. But either way, unless you are all willing to siege Alvadon again, this is the plan."

Wendell rubbed his face with his palm. "Fine. I'm not going to bother arguing with you when we both know how stubborn you get once you've made up your mind. But why send for Vasher and Lincan? I thought the whole mission was for them to be in their locations so that they could oversee things. Are you changing the plan again without telling us?"

It was Garrison's turn to fold his arms. "You two really woke up this morning ready to attack me. Lao reached out to Vasher and spoke to him about securing the ingredients, and also asked about sending someone trustworthy back. Vasher confirmed that the Shivaani army and the Daughters of Tahlia have everything under control, and that there isn't much for him to oversee, so he volunteered to return with what I need. As for Linc, he... well he thinks he can heal Lao. Apparently he managed to heal his brother's blinded eye and is positive that he knows what to do now. So he wants to return as soon as possible to do that, and then he will return to Xuyen. He made it very clear that he will only be here for a day or so before leaving again. It stood to reason that since Linc was coming up here anyway, I should ask him to retrieve the things I would need from Fangh-Haan." Garrison knew enough about himself to accept that he was stubborn, but it bothered him that they didn't see the wisdom in his choices.

"He said he needs eyes to be able to help me."

Kiryako looked at Badalao incredulously, "He said what? Eyes? What do you mean?"

"Linc needs a fresh pair of eyes to be able to heal me. He said most likely from someone who is recently deceased, and I guess a comparable size to me."

"These manifestations are something else. Magical pouches, dead people's eyes." Kiryako stood up again, "I need a break from all this. Perhaps I'm too tired to properly take it all in. I'm going to go take a nap and hopefully things are a bit more normal once I wake up." She turned and went inside.

"So now what, Garrison?" Wendell asked. "Shall I send the whole army away now?"

"Yes. The sooner they get to their destinations, the better."

"You know, the whole reason that we're disagreeing with you is because we care. You are King Garrison, I know. But that does not mean that I have to agree with every decision that you make. And it also doesn't mean that all of your decisions are wise. Now if you'll excuse me, I'll go and give them their orders."

"Yes, please do your job and let me do mine." *Damnit.* Garrison regretted his words immediately. He couldn't help but get the last word in. *I need to be better about that.* He thought about apologizing to Wendell, but his friend had already turned in disgust. Let me wait until both of our heads have cooled. As Wendell walked away, Farrah rose from her seat and helped Badalao toward the door. Garrison walked toward them, "Wait, Farrah. Lao, might I have a word with you? I can help you to your quarters once we are done."

"Very well, I'll see you inside, Lao."

Garrison grasped Badalao's forearm and led him back to the chairs, then helped him down into his seat. "I, um. I thought that we should talk after, you know."

"Please don't remind me of that whole thing. It's bad enough that the memory is burned into my mind. I don't want to have to imagine it. Garrison, I could infiltrate your mind and find out what I want to know, but obviously that wouldn't be fair. So give me an honest answer. What exactly do you want with Kiri? This is the only time I'm going to ask without being angry."

Without pause, he looked at Badalao, "I want her to be my queen, Lao. I want her by my side through everything. I haven't told anyone else this, but I brought the prince's crown with me. I retrieved it from Donovan's quarters before we left Alvadon and I want to keep his memory alive by using it as my king's crown. Once we have won this damn war, I plan to marry Kiryako and have a matching crown made for her."

Badalao hadn't moved or changed his expression since Garrison had started speaking. "You're serious about this? And she knows your intentions?"

"She does. We spoke of it not too long ago. I'll spare you the specifics of our conversation, as there may have been some flirting and suggestions made that you will not want to hear about."

"Thank you," Badalao smiled. "I'm happy for you. I needed to know that this wasn't some casual affair for you just to relieve your stress. She is too good for that. And for what it's worth, Garrison, I'm glad that we didn't kill you when you reached the House of Darian. I know many people wanted to, but I'm glad that Marlowe put you in the dungeon instead."

Marlowe. "Do you want to know something funny? Apparently Zin Marlowe was my great grandfather. That is why he put me down there. He was protecting me and I had no idea the whole time."

"Seriously? Wow! That's unbelievable. When did you find out?"

"Right before the funeral procession back in Alvadon. My uncle told me. It feels like such a wasted opportunity, you know? If I had known years ago, I could have done so many things differently, and my time at the House would have been so much more fruitful."

"Don't get caught up in what could have been. It's a path that never ends. It's only recently that I've come to terms with losing my eyes and that's what I did the whole time. I kept asking myself, what if we'd known about Horatio earlier? Would things have turned out differently? There's no way of knowing whether things would be better or worse. We can only make our choices based on the knowledge we have at the time, and then live with them."

"That's good advice. I'll keep it in mind. Speaking of which, do you think Wendell and your sister are right about leaving soldiers here?"

"Do you want my opinion even if I disagree with you?"

Garrison laughed, "It wouldn't be anything new! Just tell me."

"I kept my mouth shut because I didn't want Kiryako to fight with me. I thought about your plan and then thought about what I would do in your position. And I would do the same thing. So I understand your reasoning."

"Thank you." Garrison took a deep breath, "It's nice to have some support. I should go find Wendell now. I don't want things to stay sour. But thank you again."

"Anytime. I am always happy to offer advice."

Garrison stood up and helped Badalao to his feet. "Good. Might I offer you one piece of advice as well?"

"What's that?"

"The next time you want to talk to me through our minds, please check first to survey the situation before jumping all the way in and killing the whole mood." Badalao punched him in the chest as they returned inside.

***

Lincan sipped his ale from the mug, hoping that the draught would spur his intentions into an actual plan. Four Vermillion soldiers sat a few tables away, though they'd left him and Vasher alone for the time being. He was sure that it was simply due to them not seeing him. Vasher had been in Linchester for a couple of days already and Badalao had instructed him to wait for Lincan there. He knew he would have eventually seen Vasher in Constaniza, but he'd told Badalao that he'd try to find eyes to use before arriving. He eyed Vasher returning to the table after surveying the room. "Anything of note?"

"Of note? Who are you, Garrison?"

"We're in Cerysia again, we have to speak properly in order to fit in."

Vasher raised his eyes at him, "Between my brown skin, your barely tan skin, and these black lines on our faces, the last thing we're doing here is fitting in. Trust me." He took down a gulp of his drink. "Anyway, there's nothing of note. Those Vermillion soldiers are likely only here to establish a presence now that they have a king in Alvadon. I'm sure there are more in the city, so we'll have to make sure not to draw attention. Have you come up with anything?"

Lincan shook his head and lowered his voice. "We're obviously going to have to kill someone, though. I figure the most sensible thing would be to separate one of the Vermillion from the others, perhaps draw one outside, and then do the deed."

"How do we get only one to follow us?"

"Maybe you could walk over to the table and use your manifestation? Pick the one that looks closest in size to Lao."

Vasher sat quietly for a moment and continued to drink his ale. Finally, he nodded in agreement. "So you'll be waiting behind the inn then? And how will we kill him?"

"I suppose it can't be anything too obvious like stabbing him. They'll definitely go looking for whoever did it. I might be able to use my manifestation to make him sick enough to kill him. I don't think that would affect his eyes anyway."

"You leave first, then. Find someplace secluded that won't draw too much attention. When you see us come out, just whistle to let me know where you are."

Lincan downed the rest of his ale then tried his best to casually walk out of the inn. There were a handful of cooks and maids working behind the building, so he walked farther out toward a stable several feet away from any other people. He climbed over a short fence made up of three horizontal wooden beams and ducked. He waited a few moments before the anticipation began to build. *Where the hell is he? Come on Vash, we can't take forever with this.* He took a breath. *Patience. There are a few of them that he has to talk to and maybe that just takes more time.* Finally he noticed two figures walking around the side toward the back. He whistled as loud as he could and the two of them shifted their course toward the stable. He stood up once they were close enough to recognize. "What happened? Was it tougher than you thought it would be?"

"Basically. They got tense as soon as I walked up to the table, so I had to push a little harder than I would. I didn't bother to get any names. I figure it's easier to… you know, if we don't know anything about him. Hey, let's climb over and go into the stable for a bit." Lincan nodded and assessed the Vermillion soldier. He maintained an innocent smile as if he had no care about anything. *Damn. We're really going to do this.* He paused as doubt started to creep in. *Stop. This is for Lao. It has to be done.* He let his manifestation flow through him and looked at the unarmed soldier blankly. Vasher whispered to him, "He's already been told to listen to anything you say. So whenever you're ready, just do what you have to do."

Lincan looked at the man for another moment. *The night's not going to get any darker. It has to be done now if it's going to happen.* He took a deep breath and exhaled slowly. "Can I see your arm, my friend?" The soldier extended his left arm out, and Lincan took the opportunity to push the man's sleeve back. *This is so awkward.* He grasped the man's forearm and closed his eyes. He let his manifestation take over and kept his eyes shut, not wanting to have to look at what he was doing.

Vasher whispered to the man, "Everything is fine. You don't feel any pain. Nothing is wrong." Lincan knelt down as the man started to lose control of his body. He opened his eyes and saw Vasher bracing him so he wouldn't fall.

After another moment, Lincan felt no more life in the soldier. "It's done. You can let him go now."

Vasher let the man fall to the ground and then stood to look at him. "So now what?"

Lincan shrugged, "I guess we take his eyes out and then… oh shit. Oh no."

"What?"

"We have no way of transporting the eyes. They need to be kept fresh and intact, and these ones will have decayed some by the time we get to Constaniza."

"Are you sure? We can make it there in a day if we don't stop."

Lincan shook his head vehemently. "These things start to decay within an hour. By the second day, they would already be withered and incapable of vision. Vash, we killed him for no reason."

Vasher raised an eyebrow, "We? You killed him and I made sure he didn't fall down."

"Seriously, Vasher Jai? This isn't the time for that. We need a new plan."

"Why didn't you think of this detail before? You know what, fine. But you're saying we have to what, wait until you're basically ready to start healing Lao in order to kill whoever's eyes we need?"

How did I not think of this? Damnit. We murdered someone for nothing, even if he is a Vermillion soldier. "Yes. Whoever it is that I'm going to use, we have to swindle them into coming with us to Constaniza and then kill them right before I start. Any ideas?"

Vasher stared at him for a moment. "Well, there are three other Vermillion inside. I say we just bring them along. They're already under my control, so it wouldn't be too hard. Maybe if you don't need to kill all three, Garrison and Wendell can use the… um, leftover soldiers for something."

"That's actually not bad. Because then we'll be left alone while we still travel through Cerysia. What do we do about this one, though?"

"Leave him here. It's dark and he died of sickness. Someone can find him in the morning."

***

As they sat at the long table, Lincan noticed everyone glancing back and forth at the three Vermillion soldiers. He and Vasher had informed Badalao of what they were doing, but seeing them in person was surely different. Of everyone in the room, Garrison seemed to be the most uneasy. "You are sure that your influence will last, Vasher?"

"As long as I'm here with them, I can continue to influence them. My manifestation tends to last for a few days, at the very least. Even then, they generally don't remember what happened after they snap out of it."

Garrison nodded, "If you say so. Lincan, what do you need from us in order to do this?"

"I need a place with no distractions, where Lao will also be comfortable. I'll also need all three of the soldiers to be bound, and probably gagged as well. The sun is already setting; I don't want them screaming if this goes late into the night."

"No tools or equipment?"

He smiled. "I am the tools and equipment. It's… fortunate, I guess you could say, that Lao's face ended up the way it did in order for me to do this. With how much of his face is missing, I won't have to force the eyes in there." He thought for a moment, "Actually, I might need a knife or something flat that will help me pry the eyes out. That way I don't break or damage them. Towels as well. There won't be any bleeding from Lao, but no guarantees on the others." Farrah turned her head away from the table at that. "That reminds me, no one in the room except me, Lao, and these three. Lao, do you have a preference of where we do this?"

"No. Wherever is the easiest place for you to work a miracle is fine with me."

Lincan nodded and looked around at the others. "Any objections to using this room then? The table is quite large and will allow me to set things down without them getting in the way."

Garrison stood up, "If Lao is fine with it, then it works for the rest of us. I know that I've taken over this place temporarily, but it is still your home, Lao. I'm glad that you'll be back to normal soon. Linc, do you need anything else? Food or water?"

"No, thank you. I'll eat when I'm done here. I'm sure it will take a lot out of me, so I'll worry about it then." Vasher, Garrison, and Kiryako wished him luck and left the room, while Farrah had Badalao wrapped tightly in her arms. She kissed him on the face and head several times and then hugged Lincan and thanked him on her way out of the room.

Garrison and Vasher returned shortly and bound the three Vermillion soldiers' hands behind their backs, then bound them to their chairs. None of them put up a fight or struggle, and happily sat there through it all. After they were securely bound, Vasher gagged their mouths as well.

He looked at the three of them and pointed, "All of you are

happy to be in here to watch what is going on. None of you will feel any pain or be upset about what you see. You will be calm and happy the entire time. Right?" All three of the soldiers nodded in agreement. "Good. Then I'll see you soon and we'll all be friends." Vasher nodded at Lincan and smiled before he left again.

Garrison placed a few towels on the table and placed two spoons and a knife on top of them. "This was the best we could find. The spoons are thin and dull, so they should work, but I'm sorry if they'll be difficult to use. I brought the knife just in case."

Lincan smiled, "Those should work just fine. Like I said, I just need something to scoop them out. I don't know why I didn't think of spoons in the first place. Thank you."

Garrison nodded and grasped Lincan's shoulder. "I appreciate what you are doing, and the fact that you thought it urgent to come up now to get it done. You're right, Lao will be so much more helpful if he can see properly. Thank you."

"Save all that for when I'm done. We have to see if it works first."

"Lao has enough faith in you to let you try, so that means I believe in you as well. I'll see you in the morning."

"I'll see him first!" Badalao stood up laughing.

"Yes you will. Until then."

Garrison left and Lincan turned to Badalao. "You ready? All I need you to do is lie on the table and be still. Do you still have feeling in your face or did it go away again?"

"I can still feel everything from the last time you worked on me."

"Good. Well the first thing I'm going to do is numb your face so that there's no pain for you." He placed his hand over Badalao's forehead, eye sockets, and nose, and took a deep breath. He searched for what he was looking for in Badalao and let his manifestation start working. After another minute, he took his hand away. "Can you talk?" He watched as Lao tried to move his mouth but only unintelligible grunts and sounds came out. "Good. Then it worked. I should warn you, Lao. This will take a lot of energy out of you as well. So I'm going to advise that you don't fight the sleepiness when I'm done." Badalao nodded.

Lincan walked over to the three Vermillion soldiers and studied them for a moment. The one on the left. He didn't hesitate to place his hand on top of the soldier's head. *So much easier to kill him when Lao is right here, waiting for the eyes.* He concentrated on shutting down the soldier's brain and after a few moments, the man slumped in his chair without a sound. *Easy. Let's get those eyes now.* He pushed the man's head back so that his face was pointing upward, then grabbed one of the spoons on the table. *Damn, I'm hungry. I should've let them get me some food.* He shook off the thought and pushed the tip of the spoon into the crease between the man's left eye and its socket. With a little wiggling and force, it popped out of the socket, though it was still connected to the inside of the man's face. *Wow. That was easier than I thought it would be.* He proceeded to do the same to the right eye, which proved to be a little tougher, but it came out with a struggle.

He went back to Badalao and inspected the inside of his blackened eye sockets. He remembered that he'd left most of the inside of Badalao's eyes intact, though scar tissue had formed over the openings. He took the knife and gently cut into the scar tissue to remove it from each eye socket, being careful not to cut too deep. He was looking for what connected Badalao's eyes to his brain, and he put the knife down after the incision was large enough. Lincan used a finger to search the back of Badalao's right eye. *There it is. Phew; this is going well so far.* He stopped from getting too ahead of himself and wiped the knife off on a towel, then severed the dead soldier's right eye from its connection.

Here's the hard part now. "Here we go, Lao. I'm about to start connecting the right eye. You won't feel a thing." Badalao held up his left hand and gave him a thumbs up. He brought the eye over and placed it gently into Badalao's eye socket. It fits! It fits! He smiled as he closed his eyes and let his manifestation guide him. Reattaching it take a while, as he wanted to make sure that everything was connected properly on both ends and that nothing was left disconnected. He worked intricately on it for over an hour to ensure that it was all done properly, then healed Badalao's eye socket and skin. *Shit. Shit! He has no eyelids!* Lincan walked back over to the dead soldier and inspected his face. *This might do. I guess I'll have to figure it out once I'm done.* He severed the left eye and brought it over. As he placed it into Badalao's eye socket, he realized that his friend was already sleeping. The thought of it made him yawn, but he shook his head and continued on.

Before he started working on connecting the eye, Lincan briefly thought about sitting down and taking a break, but the excitement and desire to finish spurred him on to keep going. Even as his stomach continued to rumble over and over again, he ignored it and focused on connecting the left eye.

The left eye proved harder to attach, as the piece he was trying to connect it to kept moving. *Even if it's the slightest bit off, that could be the difference between sight and blindness, or vision issues. I'm sure the last thing he would want is a worse problem.* Lincan continued on for another two hours until he was finally sure that the left eye was connected properly.

He placed his hand on Badalao's face once more to numb it again, just in case it was about to wear off. *Damn eyelids. I'd be done already if not for those.* He yawned again and walked over to the dead soldier with the knife. He dared to glance at the other two soldiers before he started cutting, and they simply looked on at what he was doing as if he was giving the man a shave. *I have to give it to Vasher. He's good at what he does.* He started trimming off one of the upper eyelids and cleaned it off on a towel, then brought it over to Lao. *Eh. The skin tone will be different. I doubt that'll matter to him too much.*

It took another couple of hours to attach the eyelids and Lincan was happy with the placement of each. He looked at Badalao's face for a few moments and realized that until now, the extent of the damage had made his Descendant's Mark almost completely invisible. He yawned deeply and braced himself against the table for a moment. After he felt stable again, Lincan moved back over to Badalao's face. Only thing… only thing to do is. He lost his train of thought for a moment and shook his head to try and focus. Have to make sure there's no infection. He sat down in the chair behind him for a moment, trying desperately to fight off sleep. *Can't stop now. Most 'portant part and... almost done.*

After what felt like an hour of trying to stand up from the chair, Lincan leaned over and placed one hand on Badalao's face and the other on his head. He tried his best to keep his eyes open so that he wouldn't be tempted into sleep. Inspecting Badalao's body for any infections proved meticulous and he knew that using the same knife for both bodies could cause some issues. It was close to another hour until he detected nothing in Badalao that would cause any sickness or complications, but he was so exhausted that he couldn't even form a thought.

He kept slumping over onto Badalao's torso, and each desperate attempt to push himself upright drained him of more energy until he had nothing left in his body to move. Lincan tried to lift his head, but even the thought of moving was more energy than he had. As his legs gave out and his body slid down to the floor, Lincan heard the most beautiful melody.

***

Badalao awoke with a startle, though his eyes were still shut. *My eyes are closed? They're closed! I can feel them! They're there!* He was almost too scared to open them, but he slowly braced himself onto his elbows and sat up. *Here goes.* He opened his eyes and blinked several times. At first, he only glimpsed light and blurry colors around him. As he continued to blink and try to focus, he realized there were three figures sitting at the other end of the long table. "Who is that? Hello?" *Wait, those are the Vermillion soldiers.* He continued to look at them and realized that the first one was dead, sitting with his face up, dried blood caking it. "I have your eyes now, bastard." *Those two must be sleeping. Vasher had told them not to make a sound. Where's Linc?* He continued to look around the room and finally felt confident enough to stand, when he noticed a body on the floor. "What the... Linc?"

A rush of energy surged through him and Badalao jumped off the table. He scooped Lincan's body in his arms, but everything about him was limp. "Somebody help! Linc, you have to wake up. Linc, wake up! You're asleep, I know you are! Orijin, please! Not like this! Not like this!" He opened himself to his manifestation and tried to enter Lincan's mind, but there was nothing there. Badalao concentrated on the others and sought out as many people as he could. He wasn't sure how, but he'd managed to enter all of his friends' minds simultaneously. *I need help! Anyone, please come to where Linc was working on me! I don't think he survived healing me!*

CHAPTER 21
A KNIFE IN THE HEART

From *The Book of Orijin*, Verse Three Hundred Fifty-One
Trust in those who are willing to help in your fight. Though you may be blessed with Our Grace, you are not expected to fight alone.

Marshall turned back to ensure that the fire had been properly snuffed, then pushed his horse ahead. He didn't really care whether Lumien, Eleni, and Vylsia attempted to keep up. After hearing about Lincan, the last thing he wanted to do was talk to any of them. He'd told them about what happened and the details he knew, but he'd also made it known that he wasn't in the talking mood. *I still can't believe it. How could that have happened? It had to have been preventable. Light of Orijin, what the hell were they thinking?* He tried to stop himself from drowning in a sea of questions that wouldn't be answered for days. There was no way Badalao would provide intricate details through their mental connection. He wondered how the others had been dealing with it, especially Adria. She had traveled with him all the way down to his home, and would probably be feeling guilty for letting Lincan return to Constaniza without her. *Damnit. Why?*

Lumien shouted from behind, "Marshall! How do you plan to get around the wall? Surely there will be soldiers there if your sources are correct that there is a new king!"

"Damn. The bay." Marshall slowed his horse to let Lumien catch up. "I used the raft to get across when I came this way." Generations before, Taurani had built two rafts large enough to carry a horse and a few people across the bay that was north of the Cerysian Wall. The docks for them were far north, close to where the bay let out into the Sea of Fates. "It will take a few trips, but there's no way in Opprobrium that I'm going to the wall or south of it. Think everyone can handle that?"

"It's not the people that I'm worried about. I just don't want the horses to get skittish."

"It's our best option out of a few and none of them are great. We'll ride there and if anyone has a better plan, then we'll consider it. This way *is* the fastest way back to Constaniza, though."

"Understood. How are you holding up? Our people have been surrounded by so much death, but that doesn't make it any easier to deal with."

"I'm fine." Marshall reconsidered whether to be truthful or not. *He knows I'm not fine. Who would be?* "No. Truthfully, I'm so angry that I want to punch a tree until I knock it down. Linc was a good friend. A good man. He was part of the group that rescued me from here and then he healed me and basically brought me back to life." He paused for a moment to temper his emotions.

Lumien helped him by filling in the silence. "Life is strange that way, isn't it? To an extent, we can accept that people will die in combat or during wartime or from sickness because it's expected. It's the norm. But when our loved ones die in such an unexpected way, there is no way to come to terms with it. Especially when we weren't there for it. There are so many questions. Always so many questions." They both rode in silence for a few moments.

Marshall chewed on Lumien's words for a moment. "When our village was attacked, even though so many friends and family died, the emotions were different. I remember saying my family's names over and over again to remind myself who I was living for and getting revenge for. And I still do that from time to time. Not because I need to remember their names, but because it helped me to direct my anger. *Most* of the time. But for Lincan's anger, this feels different. I don't know who to be angry at and I feel like I'm angry at *everything*."

"The way you feel about Lincan's death is how I felt about our people. We came back to dead bodies littered everywhere and of course, no explanation as to why. We didn't know who did it, why, or how, and I was angry at everything. I definitely unfairly took it out on the other two. And even though that anger diminished somewhat over the months and years that followed, it was always there. It wasn't until you arrived and explained to us what happened that at least we had something specific to direct our anger to." Lumien paused for a moment. "You know, Marshall, it's all one and the same as far as who is responsible. If not for the Red Harbinger, none of this would be happening. Everything that you've explained about you and your friends and all that you've been through, it all traces back to Jahmash. Even these manifestations are a direct result of him. Direct your anger toward him."

Marshall considered Lumien's words. "That makes sense, my friend. However, at the moment it's too difficult to get past his loss to try and direct my emotions just yet. I just feel so... destructive."

Lumien didn't offer a response and Marshall was glad for it. The last thing he wanted was for anyone to tell him that his feelings were right or wrong, or what to do with his emotions. He was also tempted to access his manifestation and see what happened, but being so emotional wouldn't help. *Either nothing would happen, or I'd do something by accident that I'd likely regret. It's not worth it.*

They rode on for a while and slowed to a trot once Eleni mentioned that the sun was starting to get lower. Marshall had kept the pack horse riding next to him while the others rode just behind. "How far to the dock? Can we make it before nightfall?" Vylsia had directed the questions toward the other two, but neither of them knew.

Marshall turned to her, "If we're all willing to push our horses, we can definitely make it. We have about two hours until it hits the horizon." All three nodded in agreement and Marshall commanded his horse to run. He was tempted to see if his manifestation might work to maintain daylight, but he wouldn't even know where to begin and he didn't trust that things would go as planned given his emotional state. They neared the edge of the forest as the sun still hung low and Marshall noticed another light in the distance. "Stop!" He held up a fist as he slowed his horse. "There's a fire up ahead. Right where the forest end meets the bay."

Lumien pulled up next to him. "Who would it be? It doesn't make sense that it would be Vermillion all the way out here."

"I don't know. You're right, though. It wouldn't make sense for it to be Vermillion. What are the chances that it's more of our people?"

Lumien's eyes widened for a split second and then he shrugged. "While I hope that is the case, it doesn't seem likely. We almost certainly would have crossed paths at some point in the last few years out here."

Marshall nodded, knowing that it was most likely a futile thing to hope for. "Then we need to be extremely cautious. Ashur has already been invaded once in the past year and Garrison told us that Jahmash's armies are nearing Markos. Perhaps this is a faction of them."

"What should we do, then? They're blocking our ability to get across."

Marshall took a deep breath. *Damnit. I'm going to have to do something.* "We'll wait here. I'll send my shadow out to survey the area. I just have to hope it works properly."

Vylsia walked her horse up to Marshall's. "Is that wise? Will you be able to control it?"

"We don't have much of a choice, do we?" He opened himself to his manifestation and just as he'd practiced regularly since learning the ability, he surrendered himself to his shadow. It took him some time to clear his mind of thoughts and emotions, but finally his shadow separated itself from him and moved toward the light in the distance. Marshall had made sure to hold up a dagger. He'd learned different tactics while practicing, and realized it could "carry" weapons as long as he created a shadow of whatever he wanted. "We'll see how this goes. Hopefully I have some answers before the sun sets."

They dismounted and waited near a group of dense trees for a while. Marshall knew it wouldn't take long for his shadow to investigate the area. He had become familiar with it and communicating had proved to be strange but easy. The shadow didn't use words, but somehow relayed images and visions to Marshall's mind as it moved around. Marshall closed his eyes and focused.

It investigated the area before taking any action. While Marshall could "see" what the shadow was doing, its vision was more blurred and dependent on light to create the images. "There are people there. Several dozen, looks like all men. No horses. Hard to say who they are though." He waited for the shadow to move around more and hopefully get a better look at the men. "Black armor. Can't be Ashurian." He waited a little longer for his shadow to move around more. "Weapons as well. Lots of them." *Attack them. Do what damage you can while their shadows are still visible.*

He kept his eyes closed as his shadow navigated the camp. Many of the soldiers sat or stood around fires, either cooking or staying warm against the cold breeze. The shadow crept alongside many of them and slashed at their shadows while they remained oblivious. Marshall had yet to see his shadow actually attack anyone and he wondered whether the process of hurting them would occur immediately or whether it would take time. The shadow continued to move from one man to the next and swipe at them until finally the sun was too low to attack anything specifically. Marshall felt it getting closer again until finally it was a part of him once more. As soon as it reattached to him, his knees buckled and he fell back against the tree that was behind him. A wave of exhaustion came over him as he dropped to the ground.

Lumien noticed first and quickly knelt down next to him. "What is it? Did something hurt the shadow?"

Marshall took a moment to catch his breath. "No," he paused. "Using one's manifestation requires energy—the brain's energy. I didn't realize it would sap so much out of me so quickly. I just need to rest for a moment."

"Are you sure?"

He nodded. "My shadow didn't get everything. And I don't know how long it will take them to be affected. Either way, there are still more. We have to take care of them if we want to cross the bay."

Vylsia stepped in front of him. "Look at you. That's a terrible idea. I'd be surprised if you could even mount a horse, much less attack a camp of soldiers.

"Why are you always so angry?" Marshall focused on the other two. "Can one of you please bring me something to eat? That will help me regain my strength more than anything else." Lumien and Eleni brought him some dried meat and cheese from their rations as Vylsia continued to glare at him. *This whole act is getting old. They've tolerated this from her the whole time? Best option is just to ignore her.* "Thank you. Don't worry, I'm sure they have food in camp that we can take for ourselves. This will hold me over until then. By any chance, do either of you know how to fight?" Every Taurani had been raised to learn combat, but none of them had ever faced anything real.

Lumien and Eleni looked at one another and then back at Marshall. "I haven't even sparred with anyone since before the invasion. But before then, I was serviceable."

Damn. That won't help. "Then I need the three of you to stay here while I finish off the rest."

"I just said that I was serviceable. I can help you,"

"Serviceable isn't enough, Lumien. You and Eleni are together, yes?"

"Yes."

"Then you stay here. It is likely that you two are the last hope of a pure-blooded Taurani. I know you mean to help and I'm sure you would fight well, but I wouldn't dare risk your life for this. I promise you I can handle this. I've already seen what the camp looks like and the longer we talk about it, the harder it will be for me to see anything." He finished the last piece of cheese and pushed himself up off the ground. "I'm feeling better already. I can handle it." Lumien was about to argue when Eleni put her hand on his shoulder and shook her head. Marshall checked his inventory of daggers before leaving. *I wonder if Vylsia is quiet because she thinks I'm right or because she wants me to die. I'm sure she wouldn't tell me either way.* "I'll be back shortly."

He stalked toward the camp in the waning light, letting the shadows and the dense trees cover him. As he approached, Marshall heard shouting from various parts of the camp. *That's too chaotic to be shouting orders. They're all over the place.* Marshall hid behind a tree a few feet away from one of the campfires. Men dressed in dark clothing ran in various directions as if something had scared them. Marshall furrowed his brow as he noticed some men running away from others. *What the...? Unless? Could it have worked so quickly?* He dared to step out from behind the tree and crept closer to a group of men, but stopped as he noticed he could somewhat see the fire *through* the men. *If I hadn't known it was possible, I would also be running away.*

Marshall continued on quietly, still not wanting to disturb anything. Despite the men being affected by the shadow, he didn't know for sure whether they could still hurt him. *Only one way to find out.* He walked up behind one of them with his dagger ready and stabbed the man through the back. He almost jumped when he realized that the dagger hadn't cut into anything. It went right through the man as if he was air. *Great. I won't be able to tell who's actually a threat and who isn't. Going to have to make this quick.* He swiped at all of the others by the fire and the same thing happened. Some opened their mouths to yell at him but no sound came out.

He didn't bother to waste time thinking about their limitations in such a state. Instead, Marshall stealthily continued on. He crouched and crept behind more men and as he went on. Some were like the previous group while others were flesh and blood. He did his best to stay behind them so he wouldn't have to engage in combat. As the men continued to yell in panic, Marshall heard some of the words they were saying. *Vithelegion. They definitely said Vithelegion. Tasz, Des, I hope some of these men I'm killing are the same that got your loved ones.* He got angry as he considered the notion that these men had come to Ashur and destroyed an entire nation. *With the help of the Vermillion, at that. They can rot in Opprobrium.* He refocused and hewed down man after man as they ran through their camp in confusion.

Some were trying to don their armor while others looked for weapons. Eventually there were shouts for everyone to return to the boats. *Boats. That makes this easier.* Marshall waited a few moments and crouched down behind a tree as several Vithelegion ran northbound toward the bay. Once it seemed as if all had passed him, Marshall ran behind them and cut them down one at a time. He'd killed at least a couple dozen when one turned around and engaged him. The move briefly surprised Marshall and the man threw a knife at him. The blade grazed his leg as he tried to pivot and he wasn't sure if he was actually feeling pain or if the expectation of pain had just made him wince.

The man ran at him and pounced on him as he reached for his sword. He landed on his back with his hand still behind him, pinned under his shoulder with the weight of the man on him. He struggled to free it but the man put his knee on Marshall's shoulder. He grimaced. "I am Bragha, Sixth General of the Vithelegion. You are not worthy of life, you disgusting Ashurian." He reached for a dagger at his belt and Marshall tried to fumble for one of his own with his free hand, but Bragha blocked him. Bragha held the dagger up for Marshall to see. "Would you prefer it in your head or in your heart, you worm?" He waited, as if expecting Marshall to actually answer him. "Heart it is. The pain will last longer."

Just as Bragha finished his sentence, an arrow pierced him in the left cheek and sent him reeling off Marshall. Marshall didn't wait to look around. He got up and drew his dagger, then walked over to Bragha, who was on his knees, trying to pull out the arrow. He didn't notice Marshall standing right in front of him. As he let go of the arrow, Marshall stabbed him in the heart. "The pain will last longer."

He shoved Bragha to the ground with his boot and turned around. Standing just behind him was Lucien. "Vylsia said you'd probably die out here by yourself. Not sure if she would have been too upset, but I would've felt bad. I suppose being *serviceable* isn't so bad."

***

Baltaszar stared out into nothing as he crouched down. Bo'az and Aric had offered to load up the pack horses and get everything ready. Based on how frequently he'd found himself stopping in the middle of something and getting lost in thought, he figured they were doing themselves a favor as much as him.

It had been over a day since Badalao had informed them all of Lincan's death and for some reason, this hurt much differently than the other losses he'd had to deal with. He knew why Lincan would have done what he did. *Why am I so angry at him, though? There had to have been another way to heal Lao instead of sacrificing himself. It just doesn't make sense.* He found himself going back to that thought quite often, to the point where he almost wished he could hide. *I hope they can't see us from the Three Rings. I hope he doesn't know that I blame him.* He took a breath and wiped a tear from his eye. *Light of Orijin, Linc. I know you ran into it without thinking things through. And I'm sure you had a great idea, but I'll also bet that you didn't ask for any help either.*

Bo'az nudged his shoulder, to his relief. "Tasz, we're all set. Time for goodbyes."

He stood and nodded to his brother. He turned around and Horatio and Desmond were already standing behind him. Horatio had wanted to go with them, but his mother's health was more serious than she had let on and his brother worked as much as he could to pay for food and medicine. "You sure you'll be alright, Raish?"

Horatio half-smiled at him. "We have six knights and six Kraisos with us. Des is probably better off with you than with me anyway. I know he's angry and emotional right now, but who purposely burns their own hand? Besides, there's a chance you're going to kill me, so I'm still safer here." Desmond had been smoking tambaku from his pipe when Badalao had told them all what happened. In his state of shock and anger, Desmond had turned the pipe onto his hand and the hot chamber burnt the back of his hand. He was so emotional in the moment that he didn't care about the pain, but the wound had reddened and calloused over the course of the day and the rest of them knew it was painful for him to deal with, even if he was pretending it wasn't.

Baltaszar smiled and glanced at Desmond. "Yeah, that was something. But emotions get the best of all of us from time to time." He looked back at Horatio, "How are you doing with all the, um..." he pointed to his head, "you know."

Horatio shrugged and looked down. "I still blame myself. If Lao wasn't blind in the first place..."

"I know, I know. But that doesn't fall on you. That's all Maqdhuum and Jahmash. Remember, if it wasn't for you, Lao would have been dead, not blind. Focus on that part. Who knows how much worse the siege would've been if you didn't hold off Jahmash from doing worse?'

"I guess. I'll do my best to not dwell on it. Working to get the islands ready will help to keep me from focusing too much on it all. And then when that's done, if anything, I can talk to my mother about it. When she's doing well, she talks just as much as I do. I'll have as much company as I need to help me get through this. I think it will be a while before any of us are in a good mindset anyway."

Baltaszar hugged him tightly. "I'll miss you, brother. I really do hope that we can enjoy a peaceful life together once this is all done." He patted Horatio's shoulder before turning away. He mounted his horse and rode away ahead of the others. *Are you there? I need your help. I don't know if you've been paying attention this whole time, but I could really use your help right now.*

"Tasz, can I talk ta ya fer a moment?"

Baltaszar had been concentrating so deeply on his own thoughts that he didn't realize Desmond rode up next to him. "Of course, Des. What is it?"

"I know *I* was pretty daft with how I handled things yesterday, but I've been known ta overreact from time ta time. I just wanted ta tell ya that I'm proud o' ya."

What? "What do you mean? Proud of what?"

"Ya know. How ya have handled things an'..."

"Don't! Des, don't you dare." He wanted to shout, but he also didn't want Bo'az and the others behind them to hear everything. "I know what's coming next. You're going to say you're proud of what, how far I've come? Everything I've been able to accomplish and overcome in the past few years? Because what, you didn't expect that much from me?" Desmond raised a hand to try and respond, but Baltaszar wouldn't let him interrupt, "Look, I know my place in this whole group, alright? I'm not a leader like Lao or Adria. I'm not the king like Garrison. I understand.

"I'm the little brother who's always trying to catch up to the rest of you. I learned about Ashur late. About my manifestation late. Got to the House late. And yes, I've been immature. *So* immature that I was banished from the House and didn't even get to help defend it while you saved everyone all by yourself. So exactly what the fuck are you proud of? That I didn't do anything stupid after finding out about my mother and Jahmash and all that? Or about Raish? Or Anahi? Or Linc? Which one? The hell with you Des. I know I'm the group's little pity case, but you don't have to throw it in my face." He pushed his horse to go faster and rode ahead. He was thankful that Desmond didn't try to catch up to him again.

It wasn't until they boarded the ship to take them back to the mainland that Baltaszar finally let himself decompress.

Are you calm now?

The voice surprised him. He hadn't been the Jinn would

actually respond to him. *Yes. Yes, I'm calm. Sorry. As you may know, there has been so much going on.*

We are aware. It is important to mourn the loss of those close to you. However, it is also important to remember not to take out unnecessary aggression simply because you are in an emotional state.

You are right. But that doesn't mean Desmond was in the right, either. I knew what he meant and it wasn't a compliment.

We shall think on this. You will need to return to us soon. The war for Ashur has already begun. There is much for us to discuss. See to your affairs with your companions and then return to us.

I will. Thank you. Baltaszar closed his eyes for a moment. *Lao mentioned that there were ships approaching some of the Markosi cities. I wonder if they've attacked yet.* He shook off his thoughts and enjoyed the peace of the sea by himself for a while.

***

"Still prefer to be alone?"

He glanced at Bo'az, who stood next to him at the rail, then looked back out. "Nah, I just had a bunch of things going on in my head. I've managed to sort some of it out, though. What about you? Are things still complicated with them?"

"Eh. You could say that. Aurkene insists that she is just going through some things in her own head and that it will be fine in time. I don't know whether I fully believe her, though. I know the change in plans definitely impacted her, but I had no control over that. Maqdhuum literally appeared out of nowhere and whisked us away. I didn't ask for your friend to free us from Jahmash's control, but my mind is finally my own after over three years. Why would she be upset about that? I can finally live without fear of him. You'd think she would be happy about that."

Baltaszar shrugged. "Women are an incredible mystery, Bo. And you have two of them to deal with. If that wasn't enough, you're on your way to see a third. I don't envy you. But the best advice I can give you is to just be honest no matter what happens. For better or worse, it's the easiest way. Your *whole* mess started on a lie and, to be fair, if you hadn't lied to Yas and Slade in the first place, you likely wouldn't have gotten caught up in any of this."

"No lectures. It's not like it's all been bad. I went from thinking Haedon was the whole world to seeing places that the people of Ashur didn't even know were real. And I know we were doing Jahmash's work and how bad that is, but we also got to experience wonderful cultures and meet amazing people. Don't get me wrong, the king of Brogan is an asshole, but we got spoiled in Brogan before he showed us his true colors. And you know it's not as simple as me telling a lie. Either way, I went back to our house and people came looking for you. While Slade might have tried to help me, knowing I wasn't *you*, the other two would've likely just killed me for wasting their time. I was never going to leave with you, Tasz. I was too stubborn and closed-minded to do that, so honestly, that lie saved my life."

Maybe he's right. Baltaszar stayed quiet for a little while. "We definitely had our issues before everything happened in Haedon and even though I missed you, I was angry at you for a long time. I know I have my shortcomings and I hope that I've outgrown some of them. I guess what I'm trying to say is that I'm glad you're here, alive and healthy. That's all that matters to me."

"Good. Well then just don't kill me." Baltaszar knew his brother was trying to make the prophecy not seem so bad, but sooner or later it would see itself to fruition, and he hoped that somehow there was some grand misinterpretation on Munn's part. "Sorry, I know it's not a joke. But making light of it makes me feel a little better about the whole prospect of you killing me."

"I understand. I just do my best to try and not think about it. It's going to happen sooner or later and the situation will arise whether I like it or not. So, best not to dwell on it.

"Good point. I'll try that."

"Have you figured out what you're going to say to Yas?"

Bo'az chuckled. "No idea. But I figure it will help to introduce Aurkene and Suriiya right from the start. At least it'll avoid any confusion or anything like that."

"You'd be surprised at how little that might matter to her. Like I told you, she came and asked me to be a stand-in father, even though I told her I was in love with someone else. She ignores the things that don't suit her needs."

"That being said, how are you with all this? Of course she manipulated me, but I still had a part in all of it."

Baltaszar took a deep breath. "Listen, I was so angry at both of you for a while. So much so that I set myself on fire when I found out. That part's on me; clearly I had some problems with being able to handle my emotions. I even wondered for a little while whether that was what would make this stupid prophecy come true, but the truth is that there's nothing in this world that would make me mad enough to want to kill you."

"Well, thanks for that. Have you thought about life after all this? About what you'll do when this war is all over?"

In truth, Baltaszar hadn't considered what life might look like ever since Anahi died. At first he'd dwelled on the life that he would be missing out on and once he finished obsessing over that, he turned his focus to what needed to be done to prepare Ashur. "I haven't, to be perfectly honest. I was supposed to enjoy an easy life with Anahi. Settle down, have children. Enjoy each other's company and that would be enough. I think now, I'll just see how I feel when this is all over. First I have to kill Khurt Everitas. Then we have to stop Jahmash. After that, I'll be able to think about it."

***

It had taken them a few days to ride through Fangh-Haan and Cerysia, but Baltaszar told Bo'az that Shipsbane wasn't far off. They'd spent much of the journey reminiscing about life before their father's conviction and confinement to the farm. Being back in Ashur, even though it was completely unfamiliar, brought hope to Bo'az that he might be able to enjoy life again. He hadn't spoken to Aurkene much beyond superficial topics, even at night when they were in bed. He was thankful enough that the three of them were still sharing a bed, even if there hadn't been anything pleasurable about it. He'd wondered whether Aurkene would turn her attention to Suriiya and ignore him, but it hadn't happened.

He turned from atop his horse and caught Aurkene's eye, then waved for her to ride up next to him. As soon as she brought her horse next to his, he reached his hand out to her. She looked at him and then at his hand, and grasped it with a soft smile. "Things have been strange ever since we arrived here, Aurkene. You mentioned at Horatio's house that you were worried we wouldn't be able to fulfill the deal that I made with your father. Is that why you've been so distant?"

She looked down at her saddle for a moment and then straight ahead. "It is. In a sense. But it is more complicated than that." She let go of his hand, but Bo'az didn't sense any malice in the gesture. "I left everything I know behind on the promise of a great life here, with status and land and money. I expected to travel to the nations of Orol Taghdras after we were done in Brogan, and all of that was taken away from us in a matter of minutes. I understand that Jahmash did not always treat you well, Bo'az, but you clearly switched sides upon our arrival here, and that is not fair to me."

"Wait. I was under his *control*. I was never on his side. I was tricked into going to him in the first place and then forced to be his emissary. It's not that I switched sides, it's more like I was finally able to choose for myself."

"And where does that leave me? And Suriiya? We joined you based on a promise that apparently was never yours to make. Then beyond that, it turns out that you have a child with a woman whom you said betrayed you. Bo'az, how do you expect me to feel about all this?"

He stopped himself from answering immediately and saying anything stupid. After a moment, he looked at her again, "Confused. Out of place. But you knew since Yahaira that Jahmash was controlling me and that I wasn't completely in agreement with what he was doing. I told you then that he was making me suffer to make sure that I fulfilled the mission. As for Yasaman and my child, how was I supposed to know about any of that? I slept with her one time and thought she died the very next day. But the reality is that I have a son now and I have to own up to that."

"It's just… so much to try and grasp."

"Aurkene, despite everything that has happened, I love you. I understand that the dynamics of our path have changed, but I don't think that should affect how we feel about each other. Do you?"

"I don't know. Suriiya said that I should be wary of you. Now that you are in your homeland, you might be different and we might not matter as much anymore."

There it is. Suriiya. Is she being serious or is this sabotage? "I literally just said that I love you and that nothing is going to change that. No matter where we are or who else is around, or which side of this war we're on. My feelings for you are still the same. Aurkene, what we have is more than just a deal I made with your father. I was smitten with you from the moment I looked at you. And the way we've gotten along since, can you deny that that has been anything less than genuinely magical?"

She shifted her mouth around for a moment as if unsure whether to answer. "It *has* been wonderful, Bo'az. And that is part of the problem. I do love you and how we are with each other, but what happens when the Casteyan armada arrives on these shores and starts attacking? Will you fight against them?" She looked at him, waiting for an answer. Bo'az sighed and pressed his lips together. "See. You do not know. How can I accept how things have changed when there is a possibility that my future husband will be opposite my people on the battlefield?"

"I don't want to fight with you about this. And honestly, I'm not a warrior in the first place. I highly doubt that my place will be on the battlefield once the time comes. But can we worry about that another time? For the time being, we have love and I really need for that to be enough right now. Is that possible? In a day's time, we will likely be face to face with a woman who manipulated me almost as severely as Jahmash himself. And I don't want anything to do with her except to be a father to my child. But I'm going to need your support and have you by my side when that happens. Can we put all this aside to do that?"

Aurkene dabbed at her eyes. "I do not know, Bo'az. I will think about it all and try to find some clarity before we leave Shipsbane." She let her horse drop back behind him again and Bo'az rode the rest of the way in silence.

Once they reached town, Baltaszar and Desmond led them all to the Tall Tale Inn, which they'd said they'd been to before. They'd hoped for three rooms but only two were available, so Bo'az shared a room with Baltaszar, Desmond, and Aric, while Aurkene and Suriiya shared the other. Baltaszar insisted that he take the bed, which he gratefully accepted. Despite the comfort, Bo'az spent most of the night wondering whether anything happened between Aurkene and Suriiya while he wasn't there. He knew it would be hard to be visibly upset about it, as they'd all agreed to share each other. But he also knew he would feel a sense of betrayal if Aurkene was being intimate with Suriiya while unsure of her future with Bo'az.

The following morning, Baltaszar led Bo'az, Aurkene, and Suriiya to the edge of town where a small boat awaited them. He helped them all board and provided instructions. "The way's much easier if you have the Mark, so unfortunately you'll have to sail out to the island. Rooster, your captain here, is one of us. He's a Kraiso and will take you to the fortress, but you'll have to help him row out until the wind catches your sails. The lady of the fortress is Canda. She knows you're coming and will have everything arranged for you to see Yas."

"Does Yas know we're coming?" Bo'az felt a flutter in his stomach.

Baltaszar smiled at him. "Are you kidding, Bo? I wouldn't do that to you. She has no idea. So do what you have to do and I hope that things go well. Personally, I never want to see her again, but I know you'll have to. Once you're ready to leave, Rooster will bring you back here and another Kraiso will escort you all up to Constaniza. I can't guarantee who will be there when you arrive, but Badalao can connect with your mind, so we should be able to keep up with what you're doing. Any questions?"

"No. Aside from wondering how the hell I'll navigate this whole mess. But I know you can't help me with that."

"Of course I can. Just be honest. With yourself and with her. I'll see you soon." Baltaszar turned and walked away.

They sat down and Rooster instructed them each to grab an oar. Bo'az and Aurkene sat next to each other behind Rooster and Suriiya. "Sorry. Our presence on the island's a secret, so we can't use a bigger ship or hire oarsmen. It won't take long to get out into the open."

They rowed away from shore and Bo'az leaned closer to Aurkene. "Did you manage to get any clarity on things?"

She shook her head, "I am still unsure of how I feel. I just need more time. But as you said, let us focus on what needs to be done here and hopefully we can sort it out later." He wasn't sure whether *later* meant in the next few days or some other unspecified time in the future. Bo'az didn't bother to ask, though. Instead he glanced at Suriiya and then down at the floor of the boat. "No, nothing happened last night," she whispered to him. "I do not think it would be appropriate to be intimate with her while I am still trying to make sense of everything. While we all agreed upon sharing one another, it feels like it would be a betrayal to you. We *did* talk, but that is all."

He nodded and remained quiet. They eventually arrived at the island where a woman old enough to be his mother awaited. She smiled as they departed from the boat and walked to her. "Greetings. I am Canda; you must be Bo'az."

"I am." He tried his best to smile. "It is a pleasure to meet you."

"You really are Tasz's twin. Despite the hair and no Mark, you have the exact same face. Come, all of you. Rooster will take care of the boat. You all can follow me. The fortress isn't too far. Do you all have the same business here?"

"Technically the business is mine, Canda. But Aurkene, Suriiya, and I are all *together*, so my business is theirs."

"Aha. Very well. I'm sure Baltaszar confirmed with you that Yasaman doesn't know you are coming. I should tell you, though. Despite all the craziness that happened when she arrived and confronted your brother, Yas has calmed down quite a bit. She did admit to me that you are the father of her child and while she has resigned herself to the idea that she'll never see you again, she hoped to be a family more than anything. My daughter and I have been helping her, especially with the baby. She explained extensively about what her life at home had been like and, if I'm being perfectly straightforward with you, I can somewhat understand why she's as troubled as she is. All I ask is that you be gentle with her."

"I understand. I didn't come here to fight. I only found out about Zane about a week ago and I want to meet him."

"Good." They reached a stairway that led down under the ground. Canda led the way and walked them through several corridors lit by torches on sconces. After a few minutes they reached a set of closed wooden doors. "Are you ready?" Bo'az nodded and Canda opened the door. They walked into a large stone room with several thick rugs covering the floor and a dining table in the middle. Someone sat at the table with their back to them. Canda waved for them to follow her.

"Is that you Canda? I'm just feeding Zane; we should be done soon."

That voice. So intoxicating and revolting at the same time. They followed Canda to the table. "Yas, there are some guests here. One in particular is here to see you. I'll let you all have your privacy." She walked back toward the doors and left them.

Yas turned her head and her eyes went wide. Bo'az did his best to smile and hoped it didn't look too awkward. "Bo'az? Is it really you? How? What happened and how did you find me?"

"It's a long story." He walked closer to her and Aurkene and Suriiya followed right behind him. "I... I thought you were dead. I saw Gibreel push you off the side of the mountain and I got so angry that I pushed him right after."

"That's a long story as well. Speaking of that day, though, I found out not too long after that I was pregnant." She turned completely around and Bo'az realized she was breastfeeding the child. "This is your son, Zane. You wouldn't know about him because you continued on and left me to die."

What? "Yas, you were thrown off of a *mountain*. Did you expect me to jump after you? And how was I supposed to know you'd be pregnant? You made it clear that you knew I wasn't Tasz and that you'd just used me for pleasure. Have you ever stopped to think about what that was like for me?"

"No, Bo'az. I didn't have time to. I was pushed off a mountain and broke several bones. When I finally returned home, I was bedridden for months as I grew two babies in my body, only to have one of them be stillborn. So no, I didn't have a chance to consider your feelings."

"Yas, I'm sorry. I didn't know."

She waved her hand dismissively. "Who did you bring with you?" She looked down her nose at Aurkene and Suriiya, then back at Bo'az.

"This is Aurkene and Suriiya. We are together."

Yasaman flinched, "Excuse me? You hadn't even been with a woman before me and now you're parading around with two harlots at the same time?"

"Don't do that, Yas. You don't know what our situation is like."

"Situation? Your situation, Bo, is that you have to be a father to this child and a husband to me. Your family is sitting right here. *We* are your *situation*."

Aurkene stepped forward, "Listen…"

"Stop. I don't want this turning into a fight." Bo'az looked at Aurkene and tried to plead with her with his eyes. She backed down after a moment. "Yas, you are out of line with how you're speaking about them. I have no problem being the boy's father, but there is no way in Opprobrium that I could ever be your husband. You are too self-centered and manipulative. Tasz told me what you tried to do to him, even after he told you he loved someone else."

Her eyes narrowed, "So what? Did you come here to take my baby away and leave me with nothing?"

"No, of course not. I came to talk. And to see him. And see what we could work out." He walked to the table and sat down next to her. "Can I have some time with him?"

"No." She shook her head. "I am going to put him down for a nap and you'll just have to wait until he wakes if you want to talk to him."

Bo'az took a deep breath, then glanced at Aurkene and back at Yasaman. "I'm right here. You're saying I can't sit with him for just a minute?"

"That's exactly what I'm saying. His nap is important and as his father, you need to understand that." She pulled Zane from her breast and her voice became saccharine in an instant. "Are you all done, my dear?" Bo'az studied his little face and saw hints of himself and Yasaman in it. The boy had her eyes and complexion, but his nose and mouth.

Zane smiled at her and clapped his hands, "All done Mama!"

"Good, now it's time for your nap, my little baby."

"Nap! Nappy nap!"

She stood up and looked at him. "I'm going to set him down and I'll be right back. Wait here."

As soon as Yasaman left the room with the boy, Aurkene looked at him incredulously. "Are you kidding me, Bo'az? You expect me to stay silent and peaceful when that *bitch* is sitting there talking to you like that? I don't even care that she insulted me, but she needs a good slap in the face to reset her attitude. And she refuses to let you be with your own son?"

"Please. Please just stay calm. Remember that this is my fight, not yours. I just need you to support me, but I can handle this." Aurkene glared at him. "Aurkene, promise me that you'll let me handle this?"

"Fine. But please put her in her place."

Before Bo'az could respond, Yasaman returned to the room. "Now where were we?" She sat down next to him once more. "Bo, you have to see that you need to be with your family. You've already missed so much; you need to be a part of his life. A part of *our* lives."

"I think you need to fix yourself before you can be with anyone, Yas. You have some serious issues. We're going to leave this room and wait for Zane to wake from his nap. When he wakes up, I want to spend some time with him and talk to him. You didn't even tell him that I was his father. And yet you want us to be a family? You sure don't act like it." He didn't bother waiting for a response. Bo'az got up from the table and nodded to Aurkene and Suriiya to head for the doors.

"And you don't act like a man. You come here out of nowhere with your two whores, trying to tell me that you'd rather be with them than with your wife and child." Aurkene and Suriiya both looked at him tight-lipped. He put up a hand to tell them not to do anything.

They exited the room, "Thank you. I know I'm asking a lot and that it takes an incredible amount of patience to not do or say anything to her, but please let this end without any incident." Aurkene agreed as they continued on, and eventually they walked up the steps that led out of the fortress. Bo'az took a deep breath and was glad to be able to distance himself from Yasaman for a while. He turned around and was surprised to only see Aurkene. "Where did Suriiya go?"

She squinted, "I thought she was right behind me. I have no idea."

"That seems a bit off."

"Give her a moment, I am sure it's fine."

Bo'az nodded in agreement, wondering what could have possibly happened to her. After another few minutes, Suriiya appeared at the bottom of the steps and walked up with her hands behind her back. "Why are you smiling?"

Once Suriiya reached the top of the steps, she revealed a bloody knife in her hand. "I stabbed that stupid little charlatan right in the heart. You're free from her wrath now, Bo'az."

CHAPTER 22
BROKEN

From *The Book of Orijin*, Verse Four Hundred Seventy
The greatest evils will sometimes come from your own minds. Do not succumb, as such damage will be greater than anyone else can inflict upon you.

Adria lay tangled between sheets and blankets. She was barely aware of anything beyond her bed, except that the blurriness of her mind was starting to fade and she would need to get back to that feeling soon. She had spent so much time in the past few days alternating between crying and drunkenly falling asleep in her bed, that she couldn't be sure how long the crusts in her eyes and at the corners of her mouth had been there. One thing she was glad for was that there was no window in the room. Sunlight would have been an unwelcome guest.

Although she hadn't eaten in over a day, the pit in her stomach fed more on her emotions than food. *Ale is enough. Need more ale.* She knew that the very fact that she was able to form cohesive thoughts meant that she needed to drink more. After fighting with the blankets for a few minutes, she fell off of her bed and found a way to stand up. The tactic proved short-lived, as she put her hand down on the bed to brace herself. Adria blinked her eyes barely open and found coins on the nightstand, then attempted to walk to the door. The swaying made her stop before opening the door and she rested her head against it, hoping it would somehow sober her up enough to get downstairs. She stayed there for several minutes until she was sure she could walk properly enough to make it to the common room of the inn. She eventually made it to a table and sat down with a thud.

A few minutes later, a barmaid approached her. "More ale, honey? You're lucky we only care about your money. Between your constant state of drunkenness and that Mark on your face, most other inns would've booted you out in a heartbeat."

She closed her eyes for a moment and thought about a smart response, but her brain couldn't come up with anything. She held up two fingers and mumbled, "Two please."

"Oh, are there two of you here?"

"Mmhmm. One's for me... down here. And... the other one's...

for me… upstairs."

She barely perceived the barmaid shaking her head. "Just don't kill anyone else or yourself while you're here. Got it?"

"Of course," she nodded. The barmaid left and returned a few minutes later with two mugs of ale. Adria gulped down the first one in a matter of minutes and tried to stifle a burp, but it came out anyway. She was already feeling her mind get blurry again and swore that it was someone else who burped. "That's… so rude." She left the coins on the table and walked back upstairs, holding the mug close to her chest. A quarter of the mug spilled by the time she got back inside her room, and she cursed whoever it was who'd drank some of her ale.

Adria sat at the side of the bed and took another gulp. She could feel her mind going numb again and she smiled as she closed her eyes. She took another gulp knowing that it was only a matter of time before she couldn't hold herself up anymore, and then a few more until the mug was empty. It fell out of her limp hand as she let herself fall back on the bed. She woke up a few hours later and continued the same pattern for the next day.

Hey. Listen you drunken fool, you're not helping anyone by doing this, least of all yourself.

She recognized the voice, but her skull was so sore that it pounded against the insides. *Stop… yelling at me.*

I'm not yelling at you, dummy. Get it together. I know Linc is dead and knowing you, you probably think it's your fault. But it's not. And I need you to get up and act like a functional human being. Can you do that?

"Hey. Who… who is that? Who's there?"

Damnit, Adria. I can't help you if this is all you're going to do. Listen, there's a Kraiso coming to you. She's going to accompany you to Alvadon so you can scout what's going on there. Are you hearing anything I'm saying?

Adria moved her head from under a few pillows. "Who's there?" She tried to open her eyes but they felt like they were glued together. "I can hear you. Are you in the room? Get out." She let her head fall back down.

I'm in your head, Adria. This is really how you want to deal with this? This is so unlike you. I need you. We all need you.

She barely heard anything Badalao was saying to her, and was understanding even less. She tried to shift her body to get comfortable enough to fall asleep again when she felt something wet beneath her.

"Shit. What is that? Did I waste some of my drink?"

That's not ale, you dummy. You know what, I'll try this another time.

Adria sat up in the bed. She had a vague notion that something was wrong with her bed, but she wasn't sure what. She finally forced her eyes open and rubbed away whatever was covering them. She could have sworn someone was just talking to her, but she scanned the room and no one was there. As she shifted her hands to brace herself and get her bearings, she felt more moisture coming from the mattress. The sensation gave her a rare moment of sobriety, "Oh no. That's not ale, is it."

"Afraid it isn't. Lucky for you, nobody is around for you to be embarrassed. Except me, obviously. But I don't count. Sorry. This whole thing is rather awkward and I tend to ramble in awkward situations. If I'd known about your… thing, I wouldn't have come in yet."

Adria trembled at the voice and sight of someone else in the room. Standing in front of the closed door was a tall, thin woman in a dark cloak. Despite her height, her face looked even younger than Adria's. She took a deep breath. "Are you real?"

"Yes. Definitely very real. Why don't you um, get changed and everything. I'll just turn around until you're done." The girl was about to turn and face the wall when she stopped herself. "Wait, sorry. I'm Orchid. Lao said he told you that I was coming here?"

"That doesn't sound right. I feel like I would've remembered that." She shifted herself to the side of the bed. "So why exactly are you here?" Her voice sounded deeper than usual. *Ugh. What the hell is wrong with me?*

"He can connect with me as well. He literally just told me a few minutes ago that he told you I was coming."

Adria shrugged. "That's strange. I don't remember having a conversation with him. Maybe he connected with someone else by accident, thinking it was me."

Orchid squinted at her in confusion. "I'll just turn around now."

Adria eyed her curiously and pushed herself up from the bed. Her head was still groggy, but aware enough to know what she was doing. She quickly stripped off her clothes and then pulled out a new set from the dresser. She tried to get everything on quickly but got her foot caught in a pant leg and ended up hitting the ground with a thud.

"Ow."

"I don't want to make this even stranger, but do you need help, Adria? You seem a bit... off. I was only told to meet you here and then we would go."

Adria sat up and braced herself against the side of the bed, then pulled her pants all the way up. "Sorry. Oh, you can turn around now." She sat and tried to organize her thoughts for a moment. "Wait, what? Where are we going?"

Orchid hadn't finished rolling her eyes by the time she turned around to face Adria. "Look, I'm trying to be very patient with you, but you need to help me out a little here. I understand that your friend died and believe me, I know how hard that can be. But drinking so much that you piss the bed isn't going to make anything better for anyone. I'm sorry if that's harsh, but I don't really know how to make things sound all flowery. Do you even know where you are?"

She wanted to respond with something snarky, but as she started to sober up, she understood more and more just how far gone she'd been. "I-I'm pretty sure this is Maradon. The marbaid, sorry–barmaid, made it clear that they were willing to keep taking my money no matter how much I drank."

"We are going to head downstairs and you will eat something. Your face looks... empty. And your eyes are surrounded by darkness. Will I have to carry you down or can you make it on your own?"

Damn. I'm a far cry from Adria Kingsbane. "I can make it. I promise. Just lead the way, please." She pushed herself off the ground and standing came a little easier than the last time. Orchid opened the door and Adria followed her out and down to the common room. The Kraiso picked a table away from most of the others and asked a nearby barmaid for two cups of tea. "Tea?"

"You really thought I would get you more ale?"

"Well, no. But I wasn't expecting tea. Did I also miss the conversation about where we're going and what we're doing?"

"Apparently." Orchid paused for a moment and kept her voice low. "The plan is for us to go to Alvadon as scouts to see what Courtland and the Vermillion are up to. Lao and King Garrison want to know how many Vermillion soldiers are in the city and whether the palace has been rebuilt. Adria, we are not to be seen and right now, there's a good chance you're going to mess this all up."

The barmaid placed the mugs of steaming tea in front of them. Adria took in the aroma and sipped at it after blowing on it for a moment. "I won't. I promise. I know you think you understand what I'm going through, but you don't. Trust me. It's more than just losing a friend."

Orchid shrugged. "I'm easy to talk to. Try me."

"I don't really want your comfort right now."

"Ah, I see." She took her braid from behind her shoulder and started to fidget with it. "What you really mean is that you blame yourself and you're too stubborn to let go of that, because you *need* to blame yourself. Otherwise, who would you blame?"

I can't even tell whether I like her for being smart enough to see through me or whether I hate her for being so blunt about everything. Maybe it's both. "Good for you, you think you've figured it out. So the plan is to just walk into Alvadon and do surveillance?" Orchid didn't seem bothered by Adria sidestepping the question, which bothered Adria even more.

"No, it's more involved than that. We go into Alvadon unnoticed and do all that. But we also have to pay attention to the townspeople and their attitudes."

Adria wasn't sure if the tea was working or if she was just getting back to normal. "To gauge how they feel about Courtland on the throne."

Orchid nodded, "Good. You're not useless anymore."

"Apparently." She smiled at Orchid as she sipped some more tea. "Can we eat before we go? I'll be even more useful with some food in me."

"You sure?"

"I think I would have liked you so much better if you hadn't first seen me as a drunken mess."

"I think I would have, too. Oh well. I'm hungry. Let's eat." They ordered hearty breakfasts and grabbed Adria's things before leaving the inn. Adria felt guilty for the way she'd left the room, so she left some extra coins on the nightstand for whichever maid would have to clean it all up. Orchid gave her an extra cloak to wear that hung over the top of her face. "Garrison said that they would know your face in Alvadon. If you get noticed, we are likely both dead."

"I thought you Kraisos were good at being stealthy and appearing and disappearing quickly."

"We are. But I was specifically ordered to not leave your side. So that kind of ruins my ability to come and go as I please. Or pretty much do anything I want. But don't worry, based on what I've seen from you so far, I'm sure you'll be great at staying out of trouble."

The ride to Alvadon took almost a whole day and Adria spent most of that time thinking about Lincan and specifically their last conversation. *Why do I have to dwell on this now? Why did I have to storm off and leave him? Things would have been much different if I'd just stayed. Some leader I am. Some friend I am.* She yearned for another pint of ale. Or two or three.

"Hey. Focus on what you're doing. We're about to enter the city and the last thing we need is for you to be staring off into the distance and showing your whole face. Save the regrets and the what-ifs for when we get back to Markos."

"It's almost like Lao lent you his manifestation or something."

"Ha. It doesn't take magic to figure out what's going on. Your last interaction wasn't on the best terms and you feel guilty about it. And you think you could have done something differently."

"Basically. That doesn't mean I'm wrong, though."

"Doesn't mean you're right, either. Let's say the two of you got into an argument or a disagreement, right?" Orchid paused for a moment, "I'm doing my best here to not be harsh, but there's no way to not be blunt about this. Just because Lincan died doesn't mean that whatever you were feeling in that argument was wrong. Does that make sense?"

"Maybe. I don't know."

"There's no point in talking about all this right now. You don't want advice yet anyway. Let's head toward the palace. See what shape that's in." They dismounted and tethered their horses at an inn, then walked to the palace.

Adria did her best to keep her head down and her hood low. *Doesn't this just make me look more suspicious? I guess it's better than not having anything.* A large crowd was gathered around the front patio to the palace, or what was once the palace. Savaiyon had made the palace collapse upon itself before leaving them, but all the rubble was now completely gone. Dozens upon dozens of workers were off in the distance moving stones and hammering things in place. "Wow. They're moving quickly on this."

"Shh. Look. Grey is addressing the people."

Adria tried to peek through people and around them and instead pushed through the crowd with Orchid in tow. *Easton Grey. We can't seem to ever get rid of him.*

"We have learned that Garrison has moved his base to Markos, which only further proves that he is a false king! The throne rules from Alvadon and always has! King Courtland will continue the strong rule of previous kings and with your help, will bring order back to Ashur! There have been rumors fluttering around about Ashur being in danger. Those Descendants want you to believe that Jahmash is coming to destroy Ashur, that your lives are in danger if you do not follow Garrison! Fellow Cerysians, that is simply not true! What *is* true is that there are nations beyond Ashur and we found an ally in one of those nations called Vitheligia! They came here to help us destroy the Descendants—the very people that *murdered* King Edmund!

"The Vermillion learned that many cities in Mireya were harboring these Marked Descendants, even though they are trying to destroy our home! We worked with the Vithelegion to root out anyone helping them, but that turned out to be so many Mireyans that most of their cities were decimated! We will do the same to any nation or city that is helping the downfall of Ashur! So if you have information about anyone hiding or protecting Descendants, please let us know! The glorious Vermillion Army has returned to Alvadon to protect you and the rest of Cerysia. They will hunt down any Descendants on sight! From today forward, King Courtland has officially decreed that Descendants are once again criminals and should be killed without hesitation! Starting today, every Cerysian city will have soldiers at every gate, checking for Descendants. And we need more soldiers and knights in order to do so! We request anyone of appropriate age and health to come to our barracks and join our ranks! We need your help! Ashur needs your help!" Grey paused for a moment and roars and cheers instantly filled the streets.

Shit. Adria grabbed Orchid's forearm and pushed through the crowd, away from the patio. She couldn't find an opening fast enough, especially while trying to keep Orchid with her. *I really hope the others managed to beat Courtland to it by spreading Garrison's word. This is going to be devastating for us.* She continued through, though the throng of people seemed to grow more and more dense as she tried to leave. At some point, Adria realized that she was no longer holding onto Orchid. *Damnit. Alright, just get out of here and hopefully Lao will check in again soon. He can help us find each other.* Adria pushed and squeezed between people until she finally made it into an open space. She adjusted her hood to make sure it was still covering her eyes and walked along the side of one of the quieter streets. She turned to face the street to keep an eye out for Orchid when something pulled her backwards and covered her mouth.

"Don't say a word. I'm trying to help you." The voice was a woman's, soft and trying to sound reassuring. Adria opened herself to her manifestation as she was pulled into a dark room. *Her heartbeat's fast. So is her breathing.* "If you scream, you will only make people notice you and I know you do not want them seeing that line on your face." The woman let go of her once she managed to shut the door.

Adria could barely see her in the unlit room, but there was enough light coming from outside for her to see that the woman wasn't much taller than her and her stature was anything but imposing. "Start talking then. Who are you and what do you want?" She kept her fingers on one of the daggers at her waist under her cloak.

The woman stepped closer to her and pulled down her hood to reveal a beautiful face. "My name is Vanna Wynchester. I am biding my time because sooner or later, Courtland will likely have me killed and I want to help dethrone him."

"Why would he kill you?"

Vanna folded her arms in front of her. "I do not have the best reputation in Alvadon. Some of that is my doing and most of it is due to gossip that has gone too far. I was Garrison's lover for some time before he was branded a criminal. After that, I may have seduced a few other highborn men in Alvadon as well and one of them was Courtland Hailstone. In fact, after a little while, he was my only lover up until recently. He discarded me like a runt once he felt confident he would become the next king. You know, his reputation and all. But he got word that I slept with some other highborn men, including Garrison. It is only a matter of time before he tells Easton Grey to find me and kill me."

Crazy. Descendants and whores are going to feel Courtland's wrath. What's her motive? I have to find Orchid. "So are you asking for my protection? What exactly is it that you want?"

"Ale's still clogging your mind, Adria? She wants us to bring her back to Constaniza."

Adria looked behind her and saw the tall outline of Orchid a few feet away. "How... never mind. You wouldn't tell me anyway." Adria looked back at Vanna. "Is she right?"

"She is," Vanna nodded. "I can help. Men tend to be loose with their tongues when they are being pleasured, or when you make that pleasure a little harder to get. I know things that can help Garrison's cause."

"And why would you be willing to help Garrison?"

"Honestly, in part to see Courtland fall. But Garrison was generally nice to me. Even when he tended to be short, he always apologized and did not judge me. The last time I saw him I threw a lit candle at him out of anger and he still did not cast me out. Look, I am not asking for any charity and I am not looking to seduce him. I need to leave Alvadon and going with you will accomplish multiple goals."

Good. He won't want you now anyway. "There are likely Vermillion already at the gates. How will we get out of Alvadon without any trouble?"

Orchid stepped up beside Adria. "Vanna, we have two horses tied up down the road." She turned to Adria. "As of right now, you're the only one who would be stopped at the gates. Which means Vanna and I will ride the horses."

Adria looked at her quizzically. "And what will I do?"

"Fortunately, you are small enough to fit in one of the larger packs. Think you can stay still and silent until we're out of the city?"

You can't be serious. I'm really about to be smuggled out of the city in a piece of luggage? She took a breath. "If I have to. If it'll keep me alive."

"Good. Vanna and I will go retrieve the horses. You wait here." Orchid didn't bother to wait for a response. She nodded to Vanna and they left the dark, empty room. Adria waited around for several minutes, crouched behind a shelf just in case. The other two finally returned and Adria tentatively peeked out to ensure it was them. Orchid opened the pack and emptied it, then waved for Adria to get into it. Adria scowled but complied and once she was in a position she found comfortable enough, Orchid placed some clothes back on top of her and strapped the pack shut. Adria wasn't sure why she'd closed her eyes, as everything was dark anyway. She felt Orchid lift her up and carry her to the horses, where she strapped Adria to the beast. "We'll ride slowly, don't worry."

Sure enough, Adria slightly bounced around but the jostling was manageable. After a few more minutes, she heard Vanna talking to Orchid. "Should we stop now to let her out?"

"No. She deserves to be roughed up a little bit. Let's go a little faster and then maybe we'll let her out."

You have to be kidding me.

***

"If I had not seen you do that already, I would be much more surprised by your appearance." King Renan smiled at Maqdhuum as he watched his every move. His knights stepped forward to initiate an attack, but Renan commanded them to resume their posts. Maqdhuum had appeared in the throne room, far enough away from the thrones to not pose a threat.

"Good. Then you know that I don't intend to hurt you. By the way, my name is Maqdhuum. In case I was too rude to introduce myself the first time."

"I would argue that you already have hurt me, Maqdhuum. I was in the middle of securing a deal with some new friends before you took them away. Now I don't know where we stand."

"That's why I'm here now. I'd like to renegotiate the agreement, if possible."

King Renan eyed him suspiciously. "You also speak on behalf of Jahmash, then?"

Maqdhuum smiled, "Not at all. I speak in opposition of Jahmash."

"I do not understand. What is it that you want?"

"I want you to send your armies, just as you and Bo'az agreed. However, you will send them to *help* Ashur. Jahmash has only recruited Castiel and Yahaira so far. Because I stole Bo'az and his companions away, they were never able to go to Orol Taghdras to recruit more nations. Jahmash has recruited his own armies over the centuries. Made up of pirates, sailors, criminals, and anyone else who might've gotten caught in his web. But he only has two nations supporting him. Brogan could be the nation that turns the tide. That saves Ashur."

"And why would we do such a thing? We would immediately make enemies of our two neighbors. If word got back here, they would surely attack us."

"You would have new allies in Ashur. And I would inform Fah'Zavan of your efforts as well. As we speak, Domna Orjann is developing their own plan to aid Ashur as well. What threat could Yahaira and Castiel pose against all that? Besides, there is word that Yahaira will soon be covered in ash. They have bigger concerns than to attack you. If anything, they might soon be asking you for *help*."

King Renan leaned forward in his throne. "You are lucky that the room is empty of my subjects now."

"Call it strategy. Not luck."

"Semantics. I still have no reason to trust you."

Maqdhuum walked closer to him and extended his forearm. "Let me show you why you can trust me. Come. Take my arm for a moment."

King Renan studied him for a moment before stepping down from his throne. The queen stood in protest, but he raised a hand to silence her. "Do you mean to make me disappear as well? I am rather curious about how it all works."

"Good. Then let me show you. I promise I'll bring you right back. But there's something I want you to see." Renan hesitated, then grasped Maqdhuum's outstretched forearm. Maqdhuum smiled as they made contact and promptly made the two of them disappear from the room. They reappeared atop a giant stone, hundreds of feet above the ground. "Do you know where we are, Your Grace?"

Renan's eyes widened and he clutched Maqdhuum tightly. "Why are we up here?"

"Who are we standing on?"

"We are standing on the statue of King Ademir! But why?"

"You are partially correct. We are standing on a statue of *me*."

"I don't understand."

"The reason I can travel like this is because a long time ago, I was known as Abram. Harbinger of the Orijin. You see, I never died. The stories said I did, but they lied. I have lived many lives these past two thousand years and I've had many names. One of them being King Ademir of Brogan. The key has always been to find a way to make people believe I'm dead before they wonder why I'm not getting old. But back to the point. I could very easily leave you up here by yourself. Or let you fall off. That is, if you have an issue with my request?"

Renan's face paled as Maqdhuum stepped away from him. "No. I accept your terms. I accept. I ask that you please offer something in return."

"Don't worry. You'll still get your gold. I'll make sure of it. But I can return to your castle at any time to check in. If I have any reason to believe that you are dishonoring me, I can put you right back up here."

Renan shook his head vigorously. "I'll give you no reason to doubt me. You have my word. My army and my ships are yours. Please bring me back!"

"I'm glad we're in agreement." Maqdhuum smiled at him.

***

He sat at the edge of the island as the sun began its ascent. The vibrant shades of pink and purple and orange traversed the sky differently at various levels, to the point where he couldn't stop looking at it. He'd let Eddis sleep in, as he'd felt guilty for asking so much of the man, but he'd gotten so used to his friend accompanying him when sitting at the edge of the floating island that he felt lonely. *I should just wake him up. He won't be mad. But he deserves to sleep. What kind of friend would I be to take that from him? Two more days. Just two more days and I'll know for sure.*

The Mikiribet would notify him of their decision soon, but he was growing too impatient to wait that long. He desperately wanted to go back and demand an answer, but doing so would likely work against him. *I should go back to Ashur. Tell them I'm working on helping. They won't care though, will they? Guess it depends on who I talk to. Most of them hate me by now.* He went through the names of everyone who'd spurned him already and who might still be willing to talk to him. *Garrison? He might be the only one left. Is it worth it?* He continued to stare out and tried to restrain himself from leaving. *Everyone thinks I'm worthless now. Except Eddis, bless his soul. Maybe I should just stay here and the two of us can live out our days together. Shit, he's only got a few years left.*

He got up from the edge and walked toward the cell that he'd built for Horatio. It had been constructed of logs and was sturdy enough to keep someone in. *But with the right tool, it could be destroyed.* He went inside and retrieved the axe that he'd used to chop the wood in the first place, then started swinging at the cell. After an hour or so, most of it had been reduced to a pile of wooden rubble. As he stood and took in the destruction, he realized he would have to put it somewhere so that it wasn't a bother to Eddis. *Damn. Should have thought that through. Breaking that down didn't offer as much satisfaction as I thought.* He folded his arms and stared at the ground for a moment. *Which one makes more sense? Helps things more?*

In an instant, Maqdhuum traveled to Constaniza, to the patio where Garrison and his companions loved to spend so much of their time. Garrison was already sitting there along with Badalao and Farrah, though all of them were facing away from him. *Good. At least they can't attack me right away.* He thought about eavesdropping and joining their conversation as he'd done so often before, but changed his mind. "I'm sorry. I don't want to interrupt." All three turned around, including Badalao. Maqdhuum twitched at the sight of Badalao's face. "Wow. You're healed? How?"

"Lincan did it." Badalao's tone was much more somber than he expected.

"You sound sad. Isn't that a good thing?"

Badalao leaned forward in his chair and looked at the ground. "He died in the process."

Shit. No. Died in the process? Had to have overexerted himself. Lincan, you fool. That was avoidable. Why take that risk so close to the start of this war? "I'm so sorry."

He turned to Garrison. "I do have some encouraging news, if you'll hear me out for a moment?" Garrison nodded without a word. "Sindha has informed me that the forges in Itarse won't be enough to properly equip Ashur for what's coming. I went back to Domna Orjann and requested weapons, armor, and reinforcements from them. They'll let me know in two days of their decision."

Garrison tried to smile at him, "Thank you. That will be helpful if they agree."

"*If* they agree. You don't even know for sure yet?" Farrah scowled at him. "Why even tell us then? What if they say no?"

"It's killing me to wait for an answer. I thought at least the prospect of it would offer some hope."

"What good is hope right now, you fucking imposter? The Red Harbinger's army is already on our shores and attacking Markosi cities as we speak! What have you done to help that?"

He thought about actually answering Farrah's question, but knew it wouldn't matter. "Look, I know you all hate me and I promise you that I'm doing what I can to help."

"Do you realize that Lincan died because of *you*? If you hadn't manipulated Baltaszar's mother in the first place, then Jahmash would never have been able to force Horatio into hurting Lao and killing Malikai. The same people you think you're helping are *dying* because of you."

"I know. And I'm sorry."

Garrison stood up. "Maqdhuum, I know you're trying to help. But you should go. We're all still dealing with Lincan's death and as much as I hate to say this to you, you're only making things worse by being here."

Farrah stood up as well, "And by being alive. Go away."

Wow. He thought about trying to argue but there was no argument to make. *They're right.* Maqdhuum disappeared and traveled to the Stones of Gideon. He sat in front of the stone that was once Gideon and stared at his old friend. "How is it that you were so brave? How did the Orijin look into my soul and see anything but a coward? Gideon, what do I do now? They're right. Lincan's death is my fault. The only one of them that was able to heal people. Dead. That only helps Jahmash's cause. What the fuck am I doing? Even when I try to help, I'm still fucking things up." He sat in silence, wondering what Gideon might say if he could actually respond. "I know. It's not your problem. You were noble from the start. Sacrificed yourself to try and end things. Me? I ran away instead. You get to rest in Omneitria forever and I had to beg the Orijin to let me into Oblivion. I won't even get to see you again." *Unless.* "I wonder if I sacrificed myself, if the Orijin would reconsider."

Maqdhuum stood up and wiped his face, then pulled his three swords from the scabbards on his back one at a time and inspected each one. *Sharp enough to kill with one blow. Who knows, maybe I'll get lucky.* He put one of them back in its place and held the other two in each hand. He looked at Gideon once more and took a deep breath. "You've inspired me more times than I can count over the past two thousand years. I hope this time it's enough to help me win." Maqdhuum wrapped his arms around the stone remnant of Gideon, swords still in his hands, and hugged the piece of stone. "I hope I'll see you soon."

He let go and traveled to the island that he'd become so familiar with. He appeared in the sitting room where Jahmash usually spent his time. He held his swords with the blades crossed in front of him, ready for an immediate attack. A few men were in the room, sitting around and talking. Once one of them noticed him, he jumped up and reached for his sword. Maqdhuum dashed toward him and slashed his throat before his hand could pull the blade from its scabbard.

The other three men shot up and engaged him with their swords drawn. Maqdhuum stepped to one of them and pretended to attack, then reappeared behind him and stabbed him through his lower back. He used his other sword, the one that he'd carried since his days of being a Harbinger, to slice the man's head clean off. The other two men grew visibly more afraid, but duty possessed them to keep fighting. "So honorable to your cause." They flanked him on either side and tried to confuse him with their movements. "Have you not learned anything?"

Once again Maqdhuum disappeared and reappeared right behind the one to his right. He brought his blade around the man and slit his throat. The last one looked as if he wanted to cry, but he held his sword in front of him awaiting Maqdhuum. Maqdhuum reappeared behind him, but once the man turned his head, he disappeared and reappeared in front of him again. In a split second, his blade was through the man's heart.

As soon as the man's body hit the ground, Maqdhuum heard clapping behind him. *Here we go.* He turned to face Jahmash, who was smiling widely at him, dressed in all black just as he was. He'd kept his hair shaved close to his head, but his beard and mustache had grown long. "I didn't think I would see you again, Abram. Have you really come to fight me?"

"I figure if I die in the process, at least Ashur is ready to face you. I'll watch you lose from the Three Rings."

"Oh I'll be happy to kill you my friend. But stop it with the Three Rings. We both know it's all a fairy tale. The Orijin has nothing waiting for us. He sold mankind a dream. A fantasy so they would behave. Because He couldn't bear to watch His great creation continue to disappoint Him. Over. And over. Again."

"I've been to them. Seen them with my own eyes. How do you think I got this new body?"

"The Orijin has many tricks. If the Rings are real, why didn't you stay? Say hello to Darian and the others whom you love so much?"

Maqdhuum shook his head. "It doesn't work that way. You don't just float your way into the Three Rings."

"Of course not. You have to die first, right? And then you get the mighty Orijin's reward. It sounds so perfect, doesn't it? The Orijin creates us with gifts and flaws and virtues and desires and free will. Whether we asked for any of it or not. And then we're the ones who get punished when we don't live our lives perfectly according to the Orijin's set of rules. The Orijin should be the one who gets punished for using us as these little playthings to move about on a whim. For giving us things like sickness and suffering. For making mankind violent and lustful and greedy. For allowing parents to have to bury their own children. No one in this world ever asked for their life. It was forced upon each and every one of us by the Orijin and then we're forced to live it according to a set of rules that we never agreed to. You're telling me that that's the divine plan, Abram? That's the point of our existence?"

"I don't know," Maqdhuum shrugged. "All I know is that I've been a bastard and a coward for a long time. And I've grown tired of it. Are we going to fight now?"

"You seriously *are* here to challenge me?"

"Definitely didn't come to listen to your feelings about the Orijin. So let's go." He lifted his swords in front of him and assumed a ready stance.

"Very well. What should I do with your body when I'm done hacking it apart?" Jahmash pulled one of his swords from his waist and held it in front of him with two hands.

"Eat it. And choke on it." Maqdhuum took a couple of steps to his left. The center of the room remained mostly open, except for the bodies of the men he'd just killed. "You think you'll beat me with just one sword, huh?"

"We'll see. Once you start disappearing and reappearing, I might draw the other one. Haven't decided yet whether it will be more satisfying to kill you with Darian's sword or my own."

Maqdhuum didn't bother to wait to see if Jahmash was done speaking. He'd grown tired of the banter and had no idea why Jahmash insisted on talking. He rotated his wrist so that one of the swords moved in a circle, then advanced upon Jahmash. As he played with one sword, he struck with the other, but Jahmash readily defended it. He struck with the other sword and as Jahmash used his blade to block it, Maqdhuum swiped at him with his first sword. Jahmash quickly spun out of the way and grasped his sword with both hands once again. He smiled at Maqdhuum as he awaited another attack.

He's always ready. For everything. Maqdhuum stalked him with both swords vertical. *He's not going to attack me. Doesn't think it's worth his time. He knows he can beat me like this. Is he toying with me?* Maqdhuum traveled and reappeared behind Jahmash, then struck at him with an overhand diagonal swipe, but Jahmash stuck his sword behind his back with both hands to block it and rolled away to avoid Maqdhuum' second attack. Once again, he smiled. *I can't travel fast enough to be able to get him.*

"Didn't take long to start traveling, did it? Come, let's keep going."

Maqdhuum shook his head. He studied Jahmash for a moment, then went at him again with a series of strikes that Jahmash either parried or dodged handily. He thought about resting for a moment but went after the Red Harbinger again with both swords. Jahmash continued to defend himself well, but one swipe got through and cut Jahmash's forearm. Maqdhuum felt a tinge of pride, but knew he couldn't let up, especially once Jahmash smiled at him again.

His next volley was even faster and angrier, though nothing was able to get through. Once again, Maqdhuum disappeared, reappearing farther away from Jahmash to throw him off. He traveled once more and appeared at Jahmash's left, away from his sword hand. Just as he was about to strike, Jahmash used his hand and pushed Maqdhuum's head back, causing him to take a couple of steps backward. Jahmash still didn't take the opportunity to attack him. *Why won't he just attack me? This doesn't make any sense. He wants to toy with me. I get it. But for how long? Why not just kill me and get it over with? Is he that lonely?*

"Are you done already? Unfortunately, I don't think that one cut will cause me to bleed out."

"Why don't you attack, then?"

Jahmash nodded, then drew his second sword. "You have a preference for which one cuts through your midsection?"

Maqdhuum advanced again without responding. This time, Jahmash moved like he wanted to attack. He directed several strikes at Maqdhuum, which he was able to deflect. But Jahmash followed with another flurry of strikes that Maqdhuum knew might be too fast for him. He disappeared and reappeared behind Jahmash, but the Red Harbinger had already switched his grip on one of his swords and used it to strike behind him without turning around. The blade went right through his side but Jahmash pulled it back out quickly. *Damnit.* He knew such a strike would bleed a lot, but he couldn't focus on that. *Need to try to get him quickly before this gets bad.* He disappeared once more and reappeared a few feet away in front of Jahmash. He started his next sequence before Jahmash could begin one, but the man spun to his side once more and directed a strike at Maqdhuum's left arm. Maqdhuum disappeared before the blade could hit him and reappeared to the right of Jahmash.

Jahmash quickly became the aggressor and stalked Maqdhuum down with a series of slashes. He was too slow for the last one and it caught his thigh, though not deeply. Maqdhuum traveled once again to the other side of the room so he could inspect it. *Stings, but that one will be fine.* He looked up as Jahmash advanced again. Maqdhuum didn't wait for Jahmash's attack this time. He stepped forward and struck at the other man, going high and low at the same time. Jahmash deflected both strikes, hitting the blades away and managed to recover from the momentum before Maqdhuum did. He thrust one of his blades forward and caught Maqdhuum in the right shoulder.

"Are you ready to run away yet?"

"Not happening this time. Either I die or you do."

Jahmash stared at him for a moment. "Why? From my point of view, it looks like that will be you. And rather soon at that."

"And then what? You'll find a way to Ashur and kill everyone? What will make you satisfied?"

"Oh it's not just about killing Darian's descendants. I will use my Orijin-given abilities to make sure that everyone who survives loses all of their belief in Him. All their belief in the Three Rings. Think about it, Abram. If you need the existence of some immature, judgmental higher power to tell you that you should be a good person, then you are not doing good deeds for the sake of being a good person. You are doing them for a reward. You're being bribed. What kind of god would be so petty?"

By the time Jahmash had finished speaking, Maqdhuum had already advanced on him, plunged his ancient blade into the Harbinger's midsection and hefted it as far up Jahmash's torso as he could. As Jahmash collapsed to the ground holding his chest, Maqdhuum fell back in shock. *I did it. For the love of Orijin, I killed him.* "You have the nerve to shit on all of existence, but you're so arrogant that it blinded you. Maybe I'll see you in Opprobrium. Who knows." *I can't believe it. I just saved Ashur.*

Maqdhuum sat for a moment and smiled, then realized he should return to Eddis to be healed. He traveled back to the floating island and sat at the edge for a moment, looking out at the horizon.

So simple. Aren't you? How did you ever get chosen?

No. How?

Why don't you come back and I'll tell you.

Maqdhuum closed his eyes in horror and tears poured down his cheeks. He forced himself to slip from the edge of the floating island, hoping that he would die instantly upon the impact below. Deep down, he knew the attempt was futile, but he had to try. It was the only thing that would save Ashur.

So desperate, aren't you? Did you really think that would work? Just as Jahmash's voice finished pounding through his head, he saw the vivid colors appear all around and something inside him forced him to travel back to Jahmash's fortress. He appeared in the very same room in which he'd cut down Jahmash, except that the man stood right in front of him with no injuries save the slice on his arm. "It's so nice to see you again so soon, Abram. You see, when you're stupid enough to let me touch you, then you've already lost. And my abilities have grown a great deal since our days as Harbingers. Which is why your mind told you that you'd killed me. Because I told it to."

"Kill me. Please. I'm begging you." Maqdhuum tried to move but his body was frozen in place.

Jahmash's voice got deeper and more guttural inside his head, like a monster. *You already know that will never happen. Tell me, why didn't I know you were Abram the first time I was in your mind? The first time you came to me?*

"I still have the mind of the other man whose body this is. You had access to his mind, not mine."

Clever. I'm so proud of how smart you can be. And so grateful for how stupid you are. Centuries of waiting for a way back to that cursed realm. Waiting for the right person who could help me find a solution for crossing the sea. I thought it would be the Kontez boy. I would have had him burn away the sea for me. But you. You are about to take me to Ashur in an instant and nobody is going to know.

CHAPTER 23
INFILTRATE

*From **The Book of Orijin, Verse Two Hundred Fifty***
The Five have always been capable of greatness and of chaos. There are lessons for humanity even in the chaos they create.

Savaiyon stared out through the yellow-fringed doorway at the ships below. He'd been studying them for nearly an hour, watching for activity and creating new doorways every time they got too far away. *There has to be something that I'm missing here. A small detail. What is it? What's not right?* He'd been doing the same thing over and over again every chance he'd gotten since his last meeting with Khurt, which had been a few days before.

Khurt had requested to see him again; he wondered if the man had another request or was going to make things complicated. He'd grown to appreciate Khurt since bringing him to the Anonymi fortress. There was something admirable about his devotion to his son, that he was willing to sacrifice everything just to keep them together. *We never got that luxury, especially once Edmund became king.*

He wondered how the others were doing, especially in the aftermath of the siege and the prospect of a fight for the throne. Part of him wished that he could be with them, taking action more visibly and freely. But it was an important time for the Anonymi. They would be needed out in the world in full force soon, and everyone needed to be trained and battle ready.

"Hello again, acolyte. I hope I'm not interrupting?"

Savaiyon turned. Khurt's voice was different. He noticed that Khurt was wearing his mask this time; the gold mask of a soldier. "No, I am continuing to monitor the Vithelegion. Something about them still eats at me and I am determined to solve it. Why are you wearing your mask here? I have never required it from you."

"I am to be tested later to advance to Monkey style. I wanted to be prepared. Shall I remove it?"

"If you wish. I have already seen you, so I shall cater to your comfort." Savaiyon turned back to the doorway over the sea.

Khurt walked up next to him and removed his mask. "I've figured it out. I know what's wrong." Savaiyon looked at him and nodded for him to continue. "However, I have a request in exchange for this information."

"I meant your comfort in regards to your mask. Now you think blackmail is suitable?"

"It is not blackmail. If anything, my request is meant to help me further support your cause and immerse myself as an acolyte. I am asking you to let me continue to help you."

"I see. And what is this request?"

"I would like for you to bring my wife and daughter here. To the fortress."

"For what reason?"

"My son does not want to leave. He has come to hate the Vithelegion lifestyle and wants to live a life free of combat and war."

Savaiyon glanced at him then continued to watch the ships. "Are you sure that the timing is best for that? War is coming to Ashur and it will be virtually unavoidable. Why bring them here before all of that begins?"

"For that very reason. Who knows how long we have? I do not want to rush off into combat having not seen them again. And the same for my son. He misses his mother and sister. If something happens to him, I would never forgive myself knowing there was a chance he could have been reunited with the rest of his family."

"This fortress is not an inn. We made an exception for your son because you are both outsiders and you promised to join our ranks in exchange for being reunited with him. It was a special agreement."

"So then put them in the same room for now." Khurt's voice grew louder. "Look, I am literally telling you that I will give you the solution to the very thing you cannot solve on your own, and all you have to do is bring my family here. Two people. A kind woman and a little girl. Please."

"Very well. Do you have a plan for how to retrieve them?"

"That's why I'm asking you. I thought you could simply create a doorway that would lead to my home."

"It is not that simple. I need to have seen the destination before I can create a bridge that leads to it. I cannot blindly find the destination." Savaiyon thought back to how he'd worked with Badalao and Garrison to get to the dungeon and rescue Baltaszar. *If only it could be that easy this time.* Savaiyon wished Badalao had tried to reach out to him at any point since he'd left Alvadon, but he understood that he was likely refraining in order not to bother him. *I wouldn't mind being bothered, Lao. Especially right now when I could use you.*

He looked down into the water and at the ships and tried to think of an alternative. He followed the progress of the ships for a few moments. *That's it.* "I have an idea. But it will be tedious and will take great patience on both of our parts. Do you have any concept of the route that you sailed to come here?"

"I have a general idea, yes. We sailed northeast from Vitheligia. Why?"

"I can create a series of doorways high over the sea and each one will be farther out than the previous, until we locate Vitheligia and your home."

"As long as you think it will work, I'll do whatever you need."

They worked together for over an hour to find the correct path from Ashur to Vitheligia, using dozens upon dozens of doorways. Savaiyon knew he would have to eat soon in order to regain his energy, but Khurt had pointed out land in the distance. "There. That shoreline is my nation. It should only take a few more doorways." Savaiyon created another doorway closer to the coastline, then let the previous doorway disappear.

Khurt directed him closer to his home. "Keep the doorways lower. I don't want anyone there to wonder what's going on. I want my family to leave without a trace, for people to think they just disappeared. No one else will have any idea what happened to them."

Savaiyon did as he asked and continued to get closer until the final doorway opened to a grove of trees behind Khurt's home. "Is this close enough?"

"Perfect. Now, may I walk through and retrieve them? Do you trust me enough?"

Savaiyon nodded. "Seeing as how your son is still here, I am not worried about you trying to flee. Besides, I control the bridge. I could simply walk through and find you."

"This is true. It may take some time. I will have a great deal of explaining to do to my wife, and likely some convincing to get her and my daughter through the doorway."

"Understood. Take your time. Just remember not to touch the borders of the doorways. They will hurt you. And one more thing—no names. For your family, no one here should know their names. Not even me."

Khurt carefully walked through the doorway and disappeared as he turned the corner. Savaiyon took a few steps back to be able to keep track of Khurt's door and the one watching the Vithelegion ships. He knew that Khurt would tell him what was going on, but he was determined to try and figure it out for himself. He stared out at the ships for nearly twenty minutes until Khurt's voice made him aware of his surroundings once more. After another moment, Khurt appeared in front of the doorway with two others behind him who looked annoyed and confused. He guided them through slowly and all three stood before Savaiyon. "Thank you, acolyte."

Savaiyon closed the gateway once they were all through. "You are welcome. Have the guard take them to your son's quarters. Also instruct him that they should be taken to the bath and stretching chambers as well. I am sure they could use some relaxation and it will help to see that this place is not so scary." Khurt's daughter whimpered at the sound of Savaiyon's masked voice and she buried her face in Khurt's leg. Savaiyon turned to Khurt's wife, "You will be safe here. Your husband will return to you shortly to explain things in more detail. Right now he needs to help me with an urgent matter." Khurt nodded and showed his family to the guard waiting outside the door. Savaiyon heard him trying to calm down his wife and daughter.

Khurt returned after another moment. "You see the sides of the ships and how there's nothing there where all those ropes are? All of our ships are equipped with envoy boats on each side. None of those ships have them. The Vithelegion would have needed them to get back, which means these ships that you are watching are likely running on skeleton crews. The rest must still be close to Ashur somewhere."

"You're sure of this?"

"It's the only thing that makes sense. There's no other explanation for the decks to be so empty. It means there are only oarsmen aboard. And likely the bare minimum. I'm telling you, those boats are not far off the shores of Ashur. They won't be able to hold much food so they'll likely have to come ashore every so often. Scan the perimeter of the island. You'll find them."

"Very well. Go be with your family. I don't need you here to do that."

"Thank you."

"And thank you for helping me. And for your honesty. I appreciate that I can take you at your word." Savaiyon turned back to his open gateway as Khurt left the room. He closed it and thought for a moment about where the Vithelegion might be. *Let's try south first.* He opened a gateway over the shores of the Port of Granis in Galicea, high enough that he could see miles of the coastline. *Nothing.* He continued to create gateway after gateway over segments of Ashur's perimeter and started to get frustrated by the time he started checking the coast off of Shivaana's islands. *Still nothing. Was he lying? Why would he when he knows I could send his family back in a heartbeat? I have to keep trying. I've already gotten to half the island. There's only so many places left that they could be.* He continued to follow Ashur's eastern perimeter north, creating a gateway each time. Finally, as he studied the waters off of Darling Harbor in Markos, he noticed something. He opened a gateway a little lower to get a better look, but still kept it at an elevation of hundreds of feet up in the air. "Those are definitely boats and there are many of them. Traveling south."

***

Maqdhuum appeared inside one of the smaller rooms of the Anonymi fortress. He stood still as he took in his surroundings and noticed Savaiyon facing one of his gateways, talking to himself. From where he stood, Maqdhuum got the feeling that Savaiyon was looking at something from very high up. *Looks like sky. Must be looking at something from above.*

Good. Disembowel him and kick him through.

Maqdhuum quietly stepped forward with his sword already drawn. He found himself excited to carry out Jahmash's command and made sure he did nothing to give himself away. He crept within a few feet of Savaiyon, plunged his blade through the tall man's back, and tried to lift it up while it was still inside his body. Savaiyon gasped and Maqdhuum kicked him forward so that the man fell through his own gateway. Maqdhuum watched him fall for a moment and then turned away.

Doesn't that feel good, Abram? That's what you wanted to do to me. I'm so glad that you got it out of your system.

It does feel better, Jahmash. Thank you for giving me the opportunity.

It's my pleasure, Abram. I want to make sure you are happy.

Thank you for your generosity.

Now go. Infiltrate the fortress. Create chaos.

Maqdhuum exited the room and the guard at the door turned around. He stabbed the acolyte immediately and continued down the corridor. Within a few steps, several other acolytes noticed him and yelled out in unison, "Intruder Protocol! Engage and evacuate!" They were upon him in seconds, swords in hand. As they advanced, every other door opened and scores of Anonymi poured through the corridor in both directions. Maqdhuum lifted his sword and hacked through the oncoming Anonymi. He cut through a few of them before the corridor became too crowded for sword combat. Maqdhuum pulled two daggers from his belt and continued to stab any Anonymi within range. He disappeared and reappeared throughout the corridor as the chaos continued, stabbing at random.

You created their training process and taught them combat, and yet you are able to cut them down so easily.

I didn't teach them everything. That's poor strategy.

You are so smart, Abram. One of the smartest people I know.

Thank you, Jahmash. He continued to disappear and reappear, cutting through everyone until the corridor only contained lifeless bodies. Maqdhuum took a deep breath and basked in the silence of all the dead Anonymi at his feet. A strange feeling of sadness almost crept into his mind, but something pulled it back right away and he smiled once more.

He walked through more and more corridors, checking rooms at random for signs of life. As he continued on, he became more obsessed with finding anyone alive. He checked every room, each one was empty of people. He turned down another corridor and continued to go into every room. With every empty room, he grew hungrier to find signs of life. He finally opened a door and saw a woman and two small children inside. The woman leaned forward in a chair, a sword in her hand. The two children sat huddled together against the far wall. "Well, you're definitely not Anonymi. Your skin. Vithelegion? Why would you be here?"

The woman pointed her sword at him. "Don't come any closer. If you know we are Vithelegion, then you know I am well-trained to fight you."

He took a step forward and she stood up; her sword still pointed at him. "The last time I spoke to Vithelegion, it didn't go very well. You see, my name is Maqdhuum. But it used to be Abram, as in *the* Abram, Harbinger of the Orijin. I walked into a tent where all of your generals were talking and planning, and introduced myself. I foolishly assumed that they would readily accept me and follow me, seeing as how you people have been rumored to be *followers* of Abram. And you know what they did? They circled around me and stabbed me. So I'm not too fond of you and your people. You're awfully simple-minded in my experience."

"I am sorry for the slight against you. But please go on and leave us alone. My children are young and afraid. And they have not wronged you in any way."

"That is where you are mistaken. I am Jahmash's assassin. And all of Ashur has wronged Jahmash. Your very presence here is an offense against him. The penalty for that is death." He was about to advance on her when he heard footsteps coming closer.

***

Farco ran frantically through the corridors after the tall acolyte, Fae and Avenira right behind him. They'd all been outside at the training grounds when several acolytes relayed the order of the Intruder Protocol, which caused them to return inside and be ready to fight. The tall acolyte had returned inside just before them and immediately sprinted through the corridors, though he hadn't drawn a weapon, ignoring the possibility of an intruder. Farco knew that, for anyone to completely disregard the Intruder Protocol, there had to be someone they cared about inside and he knew of only one person inside the entire Anonymi fortress who fit that description. *Khenzi's father. He must be rushing back to* him. He was too far away to be able to do anything to Khurt Everitas, but still close enough to follow his every turn. As they ran through corridor after corridor, Farco couldn't believe how many bodies of acolytes littered the floor. *Who could've done this?* The man eventually stopped at an open doorway that Farco assumed was his own chamber. *Why wouldn't Khenzi have just left?*

"Sabina! Sabina! Get away from them, you damn vappa!"

Farco and the others arrived at the doorway just in time to see an unmasked man turn to face Khurt. He had a slender face with long, stringy black hair and was dressed in all black. Farco thought he noticed dried blood caking the corners of the man's eyes and mouth, as well as underneath his nose, but he couldn't be sure. The man smiled at Khurt, "Goodness. Vappa? I feel so honored to have such old insults thrown at me. But my name is Maqdhuum, not Vappa. You Anonymi aren't supposed to be so emotional, you know. You must be new to this."

To Farco's surprise, Khurt removed his gold mask and revealed his face. "Anonymi or not, you will die if you harm my family."

Maqdhuum looked back at the woman behind him and the children huddled behind her. Farco wondered when the rest of Khurt's family had arrived and why. One of the most stringent rules of the

Anonymi fortress was that family and loved ones were not allowed. *He must've made a deal. Wonder what they agreed on.* Maqdhuum laughed at Khurt's threat. "I assumed you ran over and around all those bodies to get here? I did all that. And you think you'll stop me? Come. Try." He glanced at Farco and the others behind Khurt. "Why don't *all* of you come in and try to kill me?"

Farco nudged Khurt's arm. "Don't fall fer it. He wants us ta fight him. It's not worth riskin' yer family. Or yerself."

"Of course I want you all to fight me. But his family is at risk even if you *don't* fight me. I have no problem killing any of them."

Khurt took a step toward Maqdhuum as Avenira grabbed his arm and stepped in front of him. "No. Let me. Trust me, I can beat him." She looked at Farco and nodded. He knew exactly what expression she was making under her black mask as she lifted her sword and walked into the room. "Fight me first. An' if I win, then ya have ta leave."

Maqdhuum didn't acknowledge her offer. Instead he swiped his sword at her. Farco panicked as they started fighting. "Near! Be careful!" He knew she'd already accessed her manifestation and as long as she avoided a hit to her midsection, she wouldn't be seriously hurt. They dueled in the center of the room and Khurt's wife moved back to block the children. Farco could see Maqdhuum growing frustrated as his attacks weren't getting through. He managed to cut Avenira once but she barely flinched at it.

"I should go help her." Khurt said to Farco.

"No. She's doin' well. Her bones are unbreakable. He won't be able ta do any real damage ta her. Or else I'd already be in there. Ye'd only make things harder fer her." Khurt heeded his words. As they watched the fight, Avenira started to get more confident with her attacks and came close to hitting Maqdhuum a few times. Just as one strike was about to cut into Maqdhuum's side, he disappeared and reappeared behind her. *What?* Maqdhuum grabbed Avenira by the back of her neck and threw her into the wall. Although her bones were unbreakable, she didn't get up right away. "Now! We have ta help her!"

Khurt stormed into the room with Farco and Fae right behind. They swung at Maqdhuum relentlessly and he continued to disappear and reappear in various places in the room. Khurt's wife joined the fray as well, but Maqdhuum's ability to vanish combined with his swordsmanship made it near impossible to hit him. *He's been toyin' with us the whole time. We can't beat him.* Farco didn't say anything to the others. He knew they had to play the man's game and hoped that things could unfold without anyone getting hurt. They continued to attack, sometimes in unison and other times taking turns, but Maqdhuum evaded everything and toyed with them even further by reappearing and kicking or punching them. None of them were in armor and every hit that Farco took hurt. One punch stunned Farco as Maqdhuum hit him squarely in the back of the head. Farco dropped to one knee and as he dropped, Khurt swung his sword at Maqdhuum's chest. The man disappeared again, but somehow Fae predicted exactly where he would be. She thrust her sword into an empty space, right where Maqdhuum appeared again. Her strike wasn't perfect but it cut into his shoulder at the joint. He grimaced and disappeared again.

They looked around at each other for several moments until Sabina broke the silence. "I think that might have done it." She lowered her sword and walked over to Farco. "Are you alright?"

He stayed kneeling but nodded at her. His head throbbed and he rubbed it a bit to try and ease the pain, but knew it would likely take some time. Avenira came and sat next to him. "What exactly is goin' on? Does anyone know why he attacked?"

"All o' us were out at the training grounds an' I'm assumin' ye and yer children were here in yer room. Did ya happen ta see or hear anythin'?" He looked at Sabina and then at her children, who were getting themselves up from the floor.

Sabina shook her head. "We only heard a commotion and announcements, but we didn't know what any of it meant. So we stayed in here, thinking this is where we would be safest. And then he flung the door open and looked at us like he was ready to kill us all."

"I was." They all looked toward the children. Maqdhuum was standing behind them. Before any of them could react, he put his hands on each one's shoulder and they all disappeared from the room.

"NO!" Khurt ran toward where they were just standing. "Khenzi! Khaira!" He looked around at the rest of them frantically, "Where did he take them? Where did they go?" Sabina ran to him and kept her eyes on where her children had just been standing. Her sobs filled the room and she fell to the ground and rocked back and forth.

Farco looked around at the others. "We don't know. We don't even know who he is. But I think we should leave the fortress. Aside from Fae's strike, he handled us rather easily. If he came back, he might kill one or more o' us. We shouldn't be here if that happens."

Khurt knelt down to hold his wife. "Let him come back. I'll kill him myself. I need to find my children."

"I know ya do," Fae walked closer to the rest of them. "But that won't happen if either o' ya kills the other. If he wanted ta kill yer children, he would have just done that here an' left. He wouldn't take 'em away just ta do that. I agree with ya, we have ta find them, but that's not goin' ta happen in this room. Or this fortress. They're somewhere else."

Khurt considered her words for a moment while he rubbed Sabina's back. "What do you suggest?"

Fae looked at Farco and Avenira. "The Intruder Protocol requires us ta disperse ta Fangh-Haan an' Shivaana. My gut tells me most o' the acolytes will have fled ta Fangh cities. I think we should head east inta Shivaana. We probably won't have as many numbers there an' they'll need our help. What do the rest o' ya think?"

"I think we should follow yer lead," Farco replied. Yer the most advanced o' all o' us, an' we still have duties ta fulfill. Just because the fortress was infiltrated doesn't mean our responsibilities as Anonymi are done. Let's go ta Shivaana an' we can tell people there what happened. Maybe someone there knows who Maqdhuum is an' can tell us where he mighta gone."

They looked around at each other before Fae spoke again. "Look, I know yer worried. But what ya don't know is that the three o' us are the ones who protected yer son when he was left alone in Vandenar. We remember ya; we thought ye were dead. We took yer son in an' brought him here ta keep him safe. We'll do what we can ta find him again. But ya have ta trust us. Can ya do that?"

Sabina looked up at them, confused. "What is she talking about, Khurt?"

He shifted his focus to the ground. "I got knocked down the stairs during our attack in one of the cities we attacked. Saol and the others left me for dead. That's why I ended up here. I know I told you I would explain it all in time. This is the story. I was taken to a dungeon and I made a deal with the Anonymi to help them if they would reunite me with Khenzi."

"What do you mean 'help them,' Khurt? Help them do what?"

He pressed his lips together. "There's no way to make it sound good. I turned on the Vithelegion. I am a traitor to our people. But before I even made that choice, Saol betrayed me on our voyage here. He's left me for dead twice now, all because I wanted the Vithelegion to show mercy and not kill everyone. I was angry at him and willing to get revenge. So I agreed to face him as an Anonymi. And I did defeat him. I cut off both of his hands in front of all of his generals. I made another deal to bring you here. The Anonymi thought the Vithelegion would return home after Saol was defeated, but they used the envoy boats to stay while the ships are all sailing back home. The acolyte that you saw, the one who made those doorways, he was looking for the envoy boats. I hope he located them before all this happened."

"Oh Khurt. That is why you brought us here?"

"No. What I told you about Khenzi is true. He doesn't want to go back home. He wants us all to stay here. So can we please listen to these people who saved Khenzi once before? They are our best chance of surviving and finding our children."

Sabina looked at Fae. "Very well. We will follow your lead."

Fae stood up. "Good. Gather whatever weapons an' supplies ya think we'll need. Let's gather food as well. We'll have ta cut through the mountains ta get ta Shivaana an' since none o' us has been there before, it could be days until we find a city where we can rest."

CHAPTER 24
WORLD ON FIRE

From **The Book of Orijin,** **Verse Five Hundred**
O Mankind, your greatest test is nearly at hand. Have faith in Us and in yourselves. There is no creation of Ours that can defeat you as long as you have faith.

Rhadames Slade took another gulp of his iron ale, for which the inn was named. The draught was heavy and strong, and he guessed that was what had earned it its name. While he'd spent time in Galicea decades ago when he and Joakwin Kontez had originally come to Ashur, he'd never spent any time in the city of Eris until now. It had proven to be a relatively quiet and simple town made up mostly of farmers, making it somewhat complicated to train the people for combat. Most had no interest in giving up their farming responsibilities, especially for a war they believed wouldn't reach them.

He tried to reason with many of them, as did Asarei, Manjobam, and Ahvedool, that Jahmash's war wouldn't spare any town or any person, and that everyone would be affected. Still, most of the people of Eris wanted to focus on their lives as they knew it.

Asarei sat across from him and nodded. "Shame, isn't it? We've been so successful in Galicea so far. Most of these cities have wanted to be able to fight and defend themselves. This place, though. They don't believe anything will happen to them. They're like the weak link in the chain."

"You can't completely blame them," Manjobam responded. "They live far away from the coastline and have very simple lives. Look at this inn. It's tiny compared to most others throughout Ashur, and the only other people here are likely townspeople who just want a drink after a long day. What fears could they possibly have of the outside world and why would they listen to a strange group of men like us? I'm surprised they haven't asked us to leave already."

Slade shrugged, "So what would you suggest, Bam? Accept our losses and move on?"

"Why not? If they're unwilling to fight, how much will they be able to help? These are the type of people who will panic in the face of combat. People were responsive to the threat of Jahmash and war in the other cities. You can train people like that. If people don't want to defend themselves, there is nothing you can do that will make them want to until it's too late."

"What do you two think?" Slade looked at Asarei and then Ahvedool.

Asarei finished his drink and set his mug down. "He's right. We can't beg people to want to defend themselves. It's a waste of our time and energy. Liezen is the only city we haven't visited and the sooner we finish our business there, the sooner we can go back." Slade glanced at Ahvedool, who nodded in agreement.

"Seems like it's settled, then. We'll get a good night's sleep knowing we did everything we could, and then we'll leave in the morning. Let's make sure everything is packed and ready before we go to sleep. I want to be able to eat and go. No need to stay here longer than necessary. That work for you, Dool?"

Since they'd arrived in Galicea, Ahvedool had been intent on bedding as many girls as possible in each city. The issue was that he had a habit of being awkward in trying to flirt. It wasn't until they'd reached the Port of Granis that Ahvedool had found success and that was only because Manjobam had helped him with speaking to a woman at one of the inns. Manjobam had made it clear to Slade and Asarei that the woman likely would have flirted with any man who'd walked up to her, but he didn't have the heart to tell Ahvedool that. They let him enjoy the experience without any shaming.

"I'm ready to go. This doesn't seem like the type of place where I'll have success anyway."

"Good idea. Then it's settled. As I said…" As he spoke, Slade noticed two men walk into the inn and for one of the first times in his life, he regretted being so tall. He ducked down at the table so that Asarei blocked him from view and whispered, "Shit. Everyone stay still. Whatever you do, don't turn around or look toward the door. We have some real trouble."

Ahvedool, who was sitting next to him, tried to speak without moving around much. "Is that Maqdhuum? What's he doing here? And who's that with him?"

"It's Jahmash. I would recognize him anywhere. We have to find a way out of here without being seen. Jahmash will recognize me and it's bad news if Maqdhuum is walking around with him. He'll recognize any of us. Don't look, but there are streaks of dried blood all over his face. Eyes, nose, mouth. That screams that he is under Jahmash's control. If we don't find a way out, then we'll either be killed or suffer the same fate as Maqdhuum."

Slade managed to catch the attention of one of the barmaids and she walked over. "Anozher round of drinks for all of you?"

"I'm afraid not. We have an emergency and we have to leave. But we can't be seen doing so." He took all of the coins out of his pouch and placed them on the table then eyed the others for them to follow. "Do you think you can help us?"

She eyed the pile of coins on the table. "Vell, zhe kitchen is zhis vay," she nodded behind Slade. You can go zhat vay and leave from zhe back of zhe inn."

"Please, let's do that. I'll go first, the rest of you follow one at a time. Remember, be discreet. If anyone is discovered, you'll wish you were dead." He looked at the barmaid, "Pretend you're helping me to the kitchen. It'll be too easy to notice me if I don't hunch over." He got up from the chair and kept himself doubled over as the barmaid escorted him into the kitchen.

"Go straight back and zhen turn right. You vill see zhe door."

"Thank you. Please help the others. You're a godsend."

She smiled at him and nodded, then walked away. Slade didn't waste any time hurrying through the kitchen. He reached the door quickly and walked outside. Over the next few minutes, the others met him out there one by one.

Manjobam was breathing deeply and gently pounding his chest. "What the hell was that? What's going on, Rhadames?"

"I don't know. It looks like somehow Jahmash got control of Maqdhuum again and the only way that would be possible is if Maqdhuum traveled to Jahmash's fortress. I can't imagine that he would've turned on us. Maybe he tried to confront Jahmash and it didn't go well? There's no way of knowing for sure."

Manjobam nodded, "We need to get the hell out of here just in case they noticed something. Best for us to be far away."

Slade was about to agree when he paused. "Wait, no. Chances are Jahmash or Maqdhuum saw at least one of us leaving. We're all either too tall or too noticeable to have been able to sneak away without drawing some eyes." He looked around for a moment to survey what options were around. "Those wagons over there. We need to get in them and be as still and as quiet as possible." He saw Ahvedool looking at him, confused. "Just trust me. It's the one thing we have to do if we want to get away." He ran to the wagons without waiting for any of them to agree then lifted the cover and jumped in. Slade saw the others standing at the side and whispered, "Two of us in here and two in the next one. Hurry. Don't move. Don't make a sound." They did as he said and laid down in the wagons. Ahvedool pulled the cover back over as got into position.

After another moment, Slade heard voices coming near. "Would they have gone this way, dear?"

"Yes. Zhis vould take you tovard zhe ozher side of Eris. Zhe only ozher vay vould be to leave zhrough zhe front. But zhey vould have passed you." Slade recognized her voice as the same barmaid who'd helped them. *Did he just know or is he in her mind already?*

"They wouldn't be far ahead at this point. Abram, slice her throat. Her mind is too simple to be of any further use." Within seconds, Slade heard a loud thump on the ground. He was surprised that Ahvedool didn't flinch at the sound. Jahmash continued. "Let's travel a little farther ahead. See if we can find them. She saw their faces. Rhadames Slade was one of those men and I would love to find out why he betrayed me." The night fell silent but Slade gripped Ahvedool's arm, hoping he'd get the hint to wait another moment or two. Finally, once he pushed away any remaining paranoia, Slade sat up. "Come. We have to go the other way. It's too risky to go in the same direction." He sprinted toward the front of the inn and unhooked one of the horses. He turned it around and the others followed him away from the Iron Ale Inn. As they rode out of Eris in silence, Slade pondered how he'd just managed to outsmart the Red Harbinger.

***

Jahmash commanded Maqdhuum to reappear inside the inn and within a moment they were back. The small crowd inside barely looked up and went back to what they were doing. He had hoped they would be more impressed by them appearing out of nowhere, but most of the people seemed uninterested. Jahmash took matters into his own hands by circulating the common room and gently touching each person on their shoulder or head, accompanied by a smile or greeting. Once he was certain he'd gotten to everyone, he returned to where Maqdhuum was standing.

"My friends! I am so sorry to bother you while you want to relax and enjoy yourselves. But please, gather around as I have important news to share." He was inside most of their heads, so the announcement wasn't necessary but the showmanship entertained him. He'd rarely gotten to do such things in his own fortress. "Come, come. There are rumors that people are going around, trying to tell you that Jahmash is coming. That you need to drop everything you are doing so that you can train to fight. Is this true?"

One man in the back responded. "Zhey vere just in town tozay. Trying to scare us avay from our farms. Zhese Descendants zhink zhey can go around and tell us vhat to zo just because zhey have magic."

"Indeed they do. And you are right. They are just trying to scare you. The truth is that there *is* no Jahmash. He died centuries ago and Ashur is perfectly safe. There is nothing to fear regarding Jahmash."

Another person spoke up. "I knew it! Zhose damn people trying to make us worried. Vhat good does zhat do anyvone?"

"Right. They are only trying to make you all worried. And do you know why? It's because these *Descendants* are the real threat to Ashur. They walk around with their magic and those lines on their faces as if they are superior to everyone. But they are abominations and need to be stopped. Do you know what they have done in the other cities of Galicea?" The crowd looked at him with anticipation. "They spoiled everyone's crops. All of the crops are rotten and had to be burned. They diseased all of the animals! Go to your farms! They have destroyed your crops and infected your animals! Everything you have tried to harvest has gone bad! You need to burn everything and put your animals out of their misery before they go mad! Go now! Before all the rot and disease spreads too far! Burn everything!"

He watched as everyone in the common room grew frantic and left the inn in a panic. He smiled at the prospect of being able to turn Ashur into a wasteland. It would start here in Eris and then over time, it would be all of Ashur and no one would even know it was him behind it all. Jahmash knew that sooner or later, he would have to come up with a name to give people, but he was still unsure of what he would call himself. He sat down at one of the tables and gestured for Maqdhuum to join him. Despite being in Maqdhuum's head, he'd decided to give him a sliver of autonomy. It would be no fun if the man was completely his slave with no personality.

"You really messed up my plans for recruiting armies. Tell me, where are Bo'az and Aric? You had the Majime boy free their minds and the last you saw of them was at Horatio's home. Would they have stayed there?"

"It seems likely. Horatio and Baltaszar and the others were down there to prepare the island cities for combat. Bo'az was finally reunited with his brother after how many years? It stands to reason that they would stay together down there until the job is done."

"You had me fooled the first time. I really thought you were someone else. Even when you brought the woman to me so long ago, I should have known, what with all the concern about me seeing the others in the Three Rings. Why decide after all this time to go against me? You've lived with all of this just as long as I have. Why wait until now?"

Maqdhuum looked at him sheepishly. "You can find all that out in my mind, you know."

"Yes, but I want you to say it. Coward."

"I had stopped thinking about you and all of the Harbinger stuff for a long time. Tried to be normal. Moved from nation to nation and formed relationships and friendships. Continued that for a long time. I got to experience a lot of great things. I was even a king for a while. It all left me empty, though. It was too much. I was always leaving people behind. Families. Children. And how do you explain it to people when you don't show any signs of aging? Finally I remembered that you were still around. There were rumors in Ashur that you would be coming back. Once those black lines started appearing on people's faces and it turned out they could do things, I knew it was probably connected to you. Even still, I hated those Marked Descendants for a while. Felt like the Orijin was spitting on us by making them special. Then I realized that, just like us, they didn't get to choose either. And so many of them were trying so hard to just live normal lives and be good people. Made me realize what an asshole you are."

"Ah, be careful my friend." Jahmash pressed his mind until blood ran from his nose. Maqdhuum was about to wipe it, but Jahmash stopped him. "No. Leave it. Let it be a reminder."

"I will. I'm hungry. Can we eat something here?"

"No. You are not hungry. You no longer need food to be satisfied."

"You're right, I'm not hungry."

"Good boy." Jahmash hadn't let him eat all day. He wanted to see how far he could press the man before he started to show any ill effects. "You do realize that you've cheated me out of the backing of perhaps five more nations? I am going to have to find a new emissary to recruit them now. And because I can count on you to travel quickly, you will have to accompany that person."

Maqdhuum continued to look down at the table. "Please spare

Bo'az. He was never meant to be caught up in all of this."

"Do you have another suggestion, then?" Jahmash let his mind reach out to all of the people who had left the inn not too long ago. They were all at their farms, doing their best to inspect their crops in the dark. With the onset of winter only a few weeks away, the amount of crops that would be affected would be limited. *It will still be effective.* He would start with what was already there and would deal with the aftermath when it was time. He knew that the whole process of creating famine would be a slow one, but the reward would be watching people experience it and being in their minds throughout the whole thing.

"Not at the moment."

"That's perfectly fine, Abram. Why don't you take some time to think about it? I have some ideas, but I will listen to your suggestions."

"Thank you. So kind." Maqdhuum licked some of the blood that had been trickling out from his nose.

"What do you think, should we go to the next city now or wait until morning?"

"I'm a bit tired. Today has been rather exhausting. We should wait until morning."

"Ah, you're not tired. Come. We'll ride out for a little bit and take in all of the fires being set throughout Eris and then you and I can travel to the next city. Where should we go?"

"You're right. I'm *not* tired. That's so strange. Penzaedon would be fun. It's a bigger city. More people to talk to."

"That's perfect. You know, I could use a friend or two." Jahmash thought about the notion for a moment. In truth, he couldn't remember how long it had been since he had a true friend to confide in. Over the years, there had been some followers whom he'd grown close to and with whom he could have genuine conversations. But over the course of two millennia, those types of people had been a rarity. More often than not, people were afraid of the mere mention of his name. He wasn't naive enough to believe that anyone would feel sorry for him about it, or that anyone was aspiring to become friends with him. *Still, it would be nice to have someone I could trust, who I could talk to and confide in without having to control their mind. It's too bad I can't trust Abram any longer.* "Let's go to Penzaedon. We'll have a little fun and cause some late night panic for the people there."

They left the empty inn and untethered two horses from out front, then rode through town. Jahmash saw at least a dozen fires all around them and every now and then he could hear the bleats of dying animals in the distance. *Good. Let it all burn.* They rode around through Eris for several minutes until he was satisfied with the amount of chaos happening. "Let us travel to Penzaedon now, my friend." He grasped Maqdhuum's arm and in an instant, they were riding on the street of a different, much calmer city.

"Are we going to go to every city in Ashur to do this?"

"I doubt that those who want to stop me will let that happen. Sooner or later your friends will take notice of what I'm doing. But if I can make enough of Ashur go hungry before their war begins, then I'll have already won. These Descendants require a great deal of sustenance when using their manifestations. So they'll either die trying to stop me or they'll have to fight me like regular people. That does not bode well for them. But as far as *we* are concerned, you will stop traveling with me at a certain point and I will do the work on my own."

He could sense Maqdhuum's tension. "What will you do with me?"

"Abram, I already told you that I need your help in recruiting more armies. You will be in Orol Taghdras convincing the leaders of those nations to send their armies right away. Have you thought about who you'd like to bring with you as my emissary?"

"You only brought this up a short while ago. I haven't had time to think about it."

"You are right. I'm just excited about the prospect of you helping to recruit more armies for me. Are you not excited?"

"Yes. I'm excited."

"I need more emotion than that."

"I'm so excited to help you!"

"I knew it. I'm glad you are. You will come along with me for the first few cities and then I will send you off to Orol Taghdras." Jahmash smiled to himself. It was little games like this that kept him entertained. He'd learned long ago how boring it was to just be in people's minds all the time. When the Orijin originally granted him his abilities, it was such an intriguing thing to know what others were thinking. Learning things that he wasn't supposed to know, even if they had nothing to do with him, was a novelty that wore off quickly. Most people didn't have interesting thoughts. Even the ones who had questionable morals or who intended to do wrong. They always thought they were the victims. They always insisted that other people or the world owed them something. *Entitlement. Only cowards like you, Abram, believe that you are entitled to anything, that you deserve something just for existing. You have to work for what you want, even if it takes time. Even if it takes two thousand years, you have to be willing to make it happen yourself.*

Aside from the entitled, he found so many that possessed no ambition whatsoever. They were happy with the droll routine of their lives without ever challenging themselves to achieve a goal or improve upon themselves. He found these types of people to be the most dangerous, at least back when he was still young. These people only talked about other people and consumed, whether it was gossip or news or trivial information, it was the only thing that simple people did. *That's why I grew bored of people so quickly. Most never think of the unattainable or push their imaginations to the limits. Focus only on what is, rather than what could be. That is why it will be so easy to destroy this wretched place. They are all sheep here, waiting to be told what to do and how to think.*

The streets of Penzaedon were busier than Eris' streets, which brought a smile to Jahmash's face. The ability to walk freely through a town and not be recognized or hated was refreshing beyond anything he could have anticipated. For so long, Jahmash had thought he would have to return to Ashur on someone else's terms. But to be able to roam around and have a vessel in Maqdhuum that would allow him to travel wherever he wanted, even back to his own fortress, was almost as if the Orijin was favoring him.

As they neared one of the inns in Penzaedon that appeared to be busy, Maqdhuum asked, "Will you not try to sway them without forcing their wills? Why not let them decide for themselves?"

Jahmash leaned over on his horse and punched Maqdhuum's arm playfully. "Decide for themselves? Abram, these people have been told the same story over and over again for their whole lives. They've been told of a god that loves them and wants to reward them and forgive them. They've been told myths of four righteous Harbingers and one evil one, and how he turned on his own brethren out of jealousy. Isn't that brainwashing as well? Ashur has been conditioned and brainwashed for thousands of years about what the *truth* is. And I'm the asshole for using a literal gift from the Orijin to change their minds?"

"But you're not exactly telling them the truth."

"Truth? I don't see you running around to everyone, telling them that you ran away from our fight and have been alive for the past two thousand years. If you're so concerned about the truth, then please share it with the world."

"I have told... some people."

"Because you needed them for your own agenda. Because you're a coward and only recently started to feel guilty about your actions. Don't pretend to be self-righteous around me. You are the worst of us because you couldn't pick a side. Now tether your horse and let us go in. But please keep your opinions to yourself." As they dismounted and walked to the entrance, Maqdhuum licked the blood trickling from his nose.

"I understand."

"Thank you for being so open-minded. I appreciate it. Now let us go inside." He let Maqdhuum walk in before him and much to his delight, the common room of this inn was bustling. People were sitting and standing everywhere he looked, laughing and talking and drinking. "I like this place much better than the last. Is there anyone in here that puts you off? Someone that just looks like they could use a good punch in the face?"

Maqdhuum looked around the room for a moment until his gaze became fixed on a towering muscular man in the back. "Him. That one over there."

"Why?"

"Men who look like that tend to need a good punch in the face. And his beard annoys me, if I'm being perfectly honest."

"I like it. I'll be right back. Stay here." He walked over to the large man and brushed against him as he passed by, and muttered an apology for doing so. The exchange was forgettable enough, as the man didn't even look twice at him. He returned to Maqdhuum and they both continued to survey the room. "Now we need an aggressor. Someone ironic. Small. Meek. Would you like to choose this one as well?"

"Yes please."

"Good. Let me know who your champion is." He waited as Maqdhuum looked around the room again.

"There. That little wiry one whose poor excuse for a mustache looks like a patch of dirt."

"Oh that's a fine choice. I was tempted to take wagers from the room about the outcome, but I doubt I'll have much need for coin while

I'm here." He nudged Maqdhuum to follow him and they walked up to the young man who Maqdhuum had selected. Jahmash grasped his shoulder and smiled at him. *Walk over to that large man in the back and punch him in the face as hard as you can. Then continue to punch him wherever you want until he falls to the ground.* The young man smiled and set his drink down, then did as Jahmash had instructed.

He walked over to the other man and instructed him to lean in so he could tell him something. As soon as the larger man leaned close enough, the smaller one violently raised his fist into the larger one's jaw. The larger man's head snapped back and the smaller one continued to pummel his midsection until he doubled over and fell to his knees.

"You see, Abram. This scene that is unfolding before us is the same lie that the Orijin has fed humanity. 'Follow my word and you will be protected against any evil and against the greatest threats. Live according to my rules and you will be able to overcome anything.' But while He gets to hide from humanity, He forgets that human beings have to actually live a life filled with weakness, desire, flaws, emotions, and inequality. They're fed the Orijin's lie from the beginning, but then there are no instructions for how to navigate once things fall apart. For instance, watch what's about to happen as I release both of these men from the lie." Jahmash released his hold on both men's minds. After a moment of uncertainty from both of them, the larger man got to his feet and grabbed the other one by the neck. He threw him down and then relentlessly punched the smaller man in the face until it was a bloody mess. "Do you see what happens to the meek once the higher power abandons him and leaves him to his own devices? When the higher power is too bored or selfish to step in and protect his creation? You've spent all of your years around many different people. Do you mean to tell me that people were consistently rewarded for putting their faith in the Orijin?"

"I don't know that I ever really paid attention to that."

Jahmash rolled his eyes. "You are useless. You know that?

"And yet you are using me."

"Oh shut up. You see? Now I don't even want to talk to these people. I'm too wound up to try and be charming and charismatic anymore. I can't even *talk* about the Orijin without being in a bad mood. Damnit. Let me just get this over quickly." He walked around the room again and came into contact with as many people as he could. Once he returned to Maqdhuum, he closed his eyes and reached into all of their minds, and told them all to go home, burn their crops, and kill their animals. After the people left, some remained whom Jahmash hadn't physically touched the first time around. He repeated the process again and once the inn was empty, he signaled for Maqdhuum to follow him out. "Now I feel a little better. Still no thoughts on who can assist you in Orol Taghdras?"

"I still haven't had much time to think about it."

"You are right. I'm sorry. I'm just so excited about getting the rest of my army. You know who would make a great companion for you? And someone who you already know well enough? Horatio. Oh the adventures you two would have. We shall go to him shortly to share the good news. First, we should go back to those two children that you decided to abduct. They must be scared and lonely."

CHAPTER 25
TWO CROWNS

From **The Book of Orijin,** **Verse Three Hundred Five**
O Chosen Ones, Our Grace is manifested in you in various ways.
Each of you possesses miraculous potential through Our Grace. It is
your responsibility to learn the limits of your potential and unleash it.

"He said he was only in Taiju. The bigger part of the army was there, rather than in Fera, so Wendell took more men up to Taiju. They defended themselves well in both cities, but both are reporting many casualties." Badalao looked at his sister, "Kiri, he told me that you prepared the cities well; the militias fought admirably and were a big part of overwhelming Jahmash's armies. Speaking of which, it has been confirmed that they fought for Jahmash, though the captives would not reveal anything about Jahmash's intentions or timeline for further attacks, even when tortured. It isn't much to go on, so we will have to be prepared for the next attack to be anywhere. I know most of us are back together again, but we may have to disperse again in order for me to stay updated on what's going on throughout Ashur. The Kraisos are now all in place to be able to best help prepare Ashur as well."

While the armies and militias in the northeast of Markos had staved off the attack, Badalao knew there were likely many friends of his and his family who'd lost their lives in the process. He tried not to focus on that part of it for the time being, but the only alternative was to talk about Lincan instead. He looked around at everyone on the sprawling patio, which made it even harder to bring up Lincan. Surprisingly, everyone waited for him to continue speaking, even though he wished that someone else would speak up.

They'd all been mourning Lincan's death for the last few days and it had taken most of them until that same morning to get their emotions together long enough to be out and around each other. Even still, just about everyone looked like they'd spent the morning crying.

"Look, I know this is tough, but it's a conversation that needs to be had. Some of you were here when Linc returned and you can attest to how excited he was to help me. I will be grateful for what he did even when I'm dead and somewhere in the Three Rings. The man left his family and rode all the way here, just so he could fix me. That type of friendship, that type of bond... those aren't the types of things that everyone gets to have in their lives. For those of you who don't know, Linc came back here and refused everything we offered him before he started to heal me."

"What do you mean?" Adria asked between sniffles.

"We asked him if he wanted food, drink, rest, even encouraged all of it. But he swore he needed to heal me first and told us that he would worry about all of that once he was done. To be completely honest, all of us who were involved were stupid for how we acted, and I suppose ignorant. None of us have seen anyone stretch themselves too far, when using a manifestation, to the point that it killed them. Even with Desmond it was different. That was too much power for him to handle. But Lincan? We were so foolish and we need to learn from his death. All of us here have to be more careful with our manifestations. We've seen what can happen when we become so focused on something that we put our well-being aside. And now we won't even have Linc to heal us if we try to do the same.

"We are at a crucial point in Ashur's history. Everything is vital now, especially our lives and survival. We have to be more careful, and smart, and less stubborn. We have to be willing to ask for help and to accept help when it's offered. Lincan's sacrifice can't have been in vain. Look at me. He gave me my sight back and I can assure you all that I am back to my normal self. I can see properly and I feel like my old self again. Fortunately, that means that Farrah will not need to wait on me hand and foot all the time anymore. But that also means that we have to let this be the end of our mourning process. I am not telling you how to deal or how not to deal with his loss, but Linc's sacrifice restored my ability to function properly and I feel as if I owe him at least that much to make sure that Ashur doesn't fall to Jahmash. We can only guess where Jahmash's forces will show up next, so we have to be ready on all fronts. I will relay the same message to Delilah, Sindha, Horatio, and Slade so that they know to be ready."

"Tell them what we talked about, Lao." Marshall spoke up from Badalao's right. He was sitting with his newfound Taurani friends. There had been a great deal of confusion when the four of them returned, even after Marshall explained their story. They'd almost come to accept that Marshall and Asarei were the only Taurani left in the world. Once the initial shock had worn off, everyone rejoiced at the notion that Marshall's people had a better chance of continuing on. The news offered a small light in the darkness they'd all been trying to navigate.

Badalao nodded to Marshall as many of the others glanced at him and then looked back at Badalao. "Yes. There have been some other developments as well. While Marshall and his new companions were traveling back here, they encountered a squadron of Vithelegion camped out on the northern shore. Marshall informed me that he and his company managed to kill enough of them that the rest retreated to their small boats and sailed away. However, there are likely more who were still out at sea. We don't know when or where they will attack, but it will no doubt be coming soon as well. Ashur is facing multiple enemies and it just reinforces my point that we have to make sure that all nations are ready to defend their lands. I was hoping that with Savaiyon returning to the Anonymi, they would have eliminated them and we wouldn't have to worry about them anymore, but that does not seem to be the case." He had wrestled with the decision of whether to reach out to Savaiyon to see how successful the Anonymi had been with the Vithelegion, but he felt as if he'd be bothering the man during something important and the last thing he wanted to do was be a pest.

* * *

Baltaszar pushed the door open impatiently with Desmond and Aric right behind him. Over a dozen people were out on the large patio with Badalao standing in front of them. The guards in front of the manor had informed Baltaszar that the group was there and offered to arrange to have their packs brought to their rooms. There was a tightness to everyone they encountered and Baltaszar knew it wasn't just from the loss of Lincan. Badalao had told them all that armies were on the verge of attacking certain Markosi cities and those left back in Constaniza were likely anxious for their friends.

As they stepped out onto the patio, everyone turned to look at them. Marshall jumped up and walked toward them. "Aric? Aric, is that you?" Marshall rushed to him and hugged him before Aric could even respond. "I can't believe it's actually you! After all this time, you're alive!" Marshall turned to the rest of them and pushed his hands through his hair. "This is Aric, another Taurani survivor. I haven't seen him since I was still in our village. We fought Maqdhuum together, along with another Taurani, and he cut me down and left me for dead. All this time I assumed the same had happened to Aric."

Baltaszar smiled. It was the first thing he was genuinely happy about in days. "Why don't you two catch up for a bit. I have to talk to everyone about my next steps anyway." Marshall nodded to Baltaszar and thanked him before putting his arm around Aric's shoulders and walking inside. Baltaszar walked up to Badalao and faced the others. "It's too bad that we're all here under these circumstances, but I am happy to see you again. Horatio's mother is ill and he's focused on tending to her. He also blames himself for all this, so it's just another reason for him to stay away. I told him it's a ridiculous notion that any of it would be his fault, so I can only hope that he heeded my advice." His mouth contorted a bit as he forced the words out. "Maqdhuum showed up again while we were at Horatio's home. He rescued my brother from Jahmash's control and brought him back to Ashur."

"That's amazing, Tasz! Where is he, though?" Vasher shouted from his seat.

"Well, most of you here know about the whole situation with Yasaman. He went to handle that. I brought him to Shipsbane and arranged for him to go to Asarei's island. Hopefully it all goes well. What makes it even more… fun for him is that he's betrothed to a woman from another nation and they have another woman who's part of their relationship."

"Wow, lucky him."

"We'll see. That seems like a lot of responsibility. Not something I would want, but to each his own." Baltaszar thought about Anahi for a moment. He wondered how anyone could desire more if they'd met a person like her, who made them feel like they could achieve anything. A person so good that no one else could ever measure up to them. He'd been dreaming about her almost every night lately, to the point in which her voice was constantly in his head. Baltaszar forced himself to focus on everyone else around him. "But back to Maqdhuum. We didn't welcome him very warmly down there, which I'm sure comes as no surprise. But in his frustration, he told us that he's the one who created the Anonymi and the Kraisos. Both trace back to him and the more I've thought about it, the more sense it makes. Both groups are just like him, but in different ways. It's like he took whatever good parts of him he had and put that into them."

The revelation created a lot of murmurs in the group, but most of the others ended up in agreement with Baltaszar. They weren't mad at the Kraisos or the Anonymi. They weren't even mad at Maqdhuum for creating them. They all agreed that his tactics and foresight had been smart. Baltaszar finally spoke again after things quieted down. "When will we bury Lincan?"

Badalao cleared his throat, "Tomorrow morning. On my

family's property."

"Very well. And what happens afterward? With us, I mean?"

Garrison stood up, "We continue to prepare for Jahmash. Why, Tasz? Do you have some ideas or plans?"

"I do. I think we've sat back long enough. I think between everyone here we can handle a fight against Jahmash. I plan to ride back into the Never and meet with the Jinn. Find out how to connect with their minds and then I'll ride north to the edge of Ashur and burn the sea away. Give him a path to get here and then we'll be waiting for him. Maybe we can even get Savaiyon here to help us."

Badalao shrugged, "I've been hesitant to connect to his mind for a while now. I don't want to interrupt anything he's doing. But I can make that happen. It will be tougher to face him without Linc, but I agree that we're ready."

"Good. Then that's what I'll do. Desmond and I were thinking about something else. The Vithelegion is done in Mireya. We think it's time for the Mireyan refugees to return to their cities and rebuild. They should be allowed to resettle if they want and bury their loved ones. And if they so choose, prepare to fight. It's not like that side of Ashur will be spared by Jahmash's armies. We might as well prepare it for battle."

Garrison walked up to him and Badalao. "Your plan for the Mireyan refugees makes sense. I'm ashamed to say that in the chaos of everything else that has been going on, I haven't thought about that very much lately. But they have spent way too long cooped up in the Tower of the Blind. You are right, Tasz. They deserve to return home, bury their family and friends, and rebuild. We can initiate that soon. However, I don't whole-heartedly agree with a face-off against Jahmash so soon. We have to be smart about this. Tasz, once you create a pathway for him to come here, there is no reversing that. We've only recently lost hundreds and hundreds of Markosi soldiers between the attacks on Taiju and Fera. Let us get some idea of their strategies and methods before committing to the next step."

***

Garrison watched as Badalao nudged Baltaszar for the two of them to sit down. He was grateful that Baltaszar didn't turn his response into an argument in front of everyone. A part of him was itching to face off against Jahmash and end things once and for all, but he knew there was still much to do before that could happen. *Jahmash isn't acting alone. There are armies coming for us and we have to be ready for that as well.* "I know we're angry about Linc but we cannot let that cloud our judgment. Jahmash didn't kill him, neither did his armies. It sounds good to say that we want to fight Jahmash and feel confident about facing him, but Jahmash has armies behind him and we don't know how many will come or where they'll land. We need to be patient and smart. And I think we also need to leave this place."

Adria looked at him in shock, "What do you mean? This house? Or Constaniza?"

"I mean Constaniza. Lao and Kiryako know that I mean no offense to them or their family. I have been thinking about this for a while now and I do not think Ashur will recognize a king sitting in an estate in Constaniza. Especially not while someone else in Alvadon calls himself the king at the same time. Courtland is a threat that needs to be eliminated as soon as possible. Now that I have everything I need, I think I can finish my pouches in the next few days. At least enough to bring with me."

Adria questioned him again. "Do you mean to say that you're going to Alvadon soon?"

He glanced at Kiryako and then back at the others. Garrison wasn't sure whether to be happy that Adria asked the question. He knew he would have to come out and say it at some point but he was hoping to dance around it for a little longer. At least with Adria asking, he had a way of bringing it up that wasn't out of nowhere, although that wouldn't guarantee that some people wouldn't be mad at him. "As soon as I can. No offense, Adria, but why else do you think I asked you to scout the situation there? Between your information and everything that Vanna has told me, I know exactly what needs to be done."

Adria tilted her head forward and looked at him. "And what exactly needs to be done?"

"It's rather simple, actually. I plan to ride to Alvadon with Kiryako, Badalao, and Farrah as soon as I have enough pouches ready. Then I plan to openly challenge Courtland in front of all of his subjects, for the right to sit atop the throne. Vanna has informed me that Courtland has no plans to face me in person. Instead, he's criminalized Marked Descendants again and he plans to turn all of Ashur against us. Even though all of you have helped spread the word throughout Ashur that *I* am the true king and Courtland is the imposter, I know people will become confused once the Vermillion starts telling them otherwise and they find that Courtland is sitting in Alvadon while I am not.

"Again, it is not meant as a slight against Markos. Staying here was a solution to a problem, but I was never sure whether it was a temporary or permanent solution. And if I plan to relinquish the throne's rule over all of the nations of Ashur, then it is only right that the throne stays in Cerysia. Now, there is another matter that is important once I retake the throne in Alvadon." He glanced at Kiryako once more, though she looked at him plainly. "One aspect that will make my rule vastly better than Courtland's is that my counsel will be immaculate. And while I have already appointed many of you to be my advisors, there is one title that has yet to be fulfilled." The others looked at him attentively. "The most important person to a king must be his queen—the woman who will keep him grounded and humble, yet brave and bold. And speaking of humility, Kiryako, I humbly ask that you would be my queen and sit beside me."

She sat in her place for a moment, staring out into space. Garrison wondered whether she'd heard him or if she was actually considering her answer. He was about to call her name again when she blinked several times and stood up, and then walked to him. "Yes, of course I will, Garrison. Light of Orijin, I'm sorry. As soon as I heard your words, my mind just wandered to a daydream of what it would be like to be the queen. I think every little girl dreams of being a princess or queen one day and now that dream has become a reality for me. Thank you, I would be honored to be your wife and queen." She kissed him on the cheek and hugged him.

As she turned to face everyone along with him, Farrah stood up and revealed that she'd been holding two silver crowns. She walked up to them and stood in front of Garrison. "Thank you for holding onto these, Farrah." Garrison took the crowns and Farrah smiled at him and Kiryako, then returned to her seat. He addressed the group once more. "Lao and Farrah are the only ones who know of this, but this crown was my brother's. It's the only thing I cared to save from our palace. I had a duplicate made to fit Kiryako a few days ago, with the hopes that she would be willing to be my queen. Now that she has accepted, the two of us will lead this war against Jahmash together. The first order of business will be to walk into Alvadon together and reclaim what is ours. Adria, I know you are Kingsbane, but I would like to try my hand at it this time. At least against the imposter."

Adria smiled at him, "My hope is that my days of killing kings are done. Don't give me a reason, Garrison. Congratulations to both of you." As he quietly laughed at Adria's joke, he heard a strange but familiar noise to his right at the corner of the patio. Everyone else must have heard it as well, as they all turned to look at the source at the same time. Hovering in the air in the far corner where the railing should have been was a yellow-fringed doorway. Garrison and the others looked around at one another, expecting Savaiyon to walk through at any moment, but nothing happened and no sound could be heard from the other side. Garrison finally took it upon himself to walk toward the gateway to inspect it and found himself confused as the gateway seemingly led to the heart of a grove of apple trees. As he peered through, Garrison noticed a strange looking house in the distance.

Badalao asked, "Where is that? I don't think I've seen that part of Ashur before."

"Neither have I. Perhaps it isn't Ashur at all. And more importantly, where is Savaiyon?"

EPILOGUE

Baltaszar rode to where he remembered the Jinn to be. He could feel their presence growing closer and closer until he swore he saw a pair of bright red eyes looking at him from a distance in the black night. The nights had grown significantly colder since the last time he'd seen the Jinn and he hoped more than anything that they could keep him warm. He walked further into the forest for barely a few minutes when they revealed themselves to him and surrounded him as they'd done the last time.

You have matured a great deal since we last saw you. He felt the scar on the right side of his face grow warm, as well as the part of his chest where they'd stabbed him the last time. The sensation remained warm, though, rather than becoming hot or uncomfortable. *Much of that is due to how you have handled the obstacles you have faced. You have overcome serious tragedies in your life up to this point, and especially since we last saw you, you have handled all of them with great maturity. Because of that, we are ready to help you in two ways. First, we are aware of the dreams that you have been having. We know of her presence in your dreams and her significance to you. Because of your devotion to her and her strong existence in your dreams, our voice will now be represented by hers in your mind.*

"What? You mean when you speak to me, it'll sound like Anahi's voice?"

Yes. We know how difficult her loss has been for you. It is a comfort that we believe will make your journey easier going forward. Is that acceptable?

Baltaszar paused for a moment. The thought of being able to hear Anahi's voice again made him drop to one knee. *What I wouldn't give to be able to talk to her again.* He stared at the ground in contemplation for a few more moments. "No. I appreciate your offer, but it wouldn't be real. I would love to hear *her* voice again, but it wouldn't be the same if it wasn't really coming from her. Besides, I think I have an idea of what sacrifices must be made in order to defeat Jahmash, and being reconnected with her is what fuels me to do what is right and what is necessary. Turning your voice into hers would make it feel… cheap. Thank you for thinking of my well-being, but it will do more harm than good at this point."

Good. That is further evidence of your growth. You must

continue to sharpen yourself like a blade if you are to defeat this adversary. To be weak in mind is to assure defeat.

"I understand. What is the second thing?"

We have deemed that you are ready to connect to our mind. We must warn you that once you are connected to us, you will be connected to ALL of us. Our very nature allows us to function as one collective mind. However, this is not how your kind functions. We do not know how long it will take for your mind to completely connect to our hive, but the change will likely be uncomfortable at first. We have only completed this process with one other of your kind, though he was much older than you by that time, and much more hardened as well. However, once you are one of us, you will be completely equipped to face your adversary. You will simply need to learn how to wield these new tools.

Baltaszar looked around at all of the creatures around him. He remembered being deathly afraid of them not too long ago, and now they were about to share the same mind. *What could this possibly entail?* "I guess I'm ready when you are. What do we do?"

Relinquish yourself. Submit. And we shall do the rest.

"I don't understand. Like with my manifestation? Just open myself up to it?"

Do not access it. Surrender yourself. Relax your body and your mind. The last one of your kind lay down on the ground in order to do so. You can try the same method.

Baltaszar did as they suggested and lay down, then shut his eyes and slowed his breathing. He tried his best to relax and clear his mind. A giant hand gently grasped his head and he took in its warmth as if it was a blanket covering him. The warmth grew into heat and pierced through his skull and into his mind. As it grew stronger, the heat felt like it was swearing him like hundreds of hot needles pressing into his mind. *It hurts. It hurts so much.*

That is part of the process. We need to create pores in your mind so that it will connect to all of us.

He tried his best to accept their words and tolerate the pain. *You've had worse. You've had worse. You can take this.* The heat continued to pierce his mind, stronger than any fire he'd ever experienced or created. The intensifying pain caused his arms and legs to twitch. More hands grasped his limbs and held him down so firmly that he couldn't move. The pain became almost unbearable until finally the heat vanished and his mind felt cold. The sensation lasted for a mere moment until a new warmth came flooding in. It felt like hundreds upon hundreds of pieces of thread being sewn through the new holes in his mind until he became aware of what each thread was connected to. Baltaszar felt the voice of every single Jinn and while he was aware of all of them, they all shared the same voice.

The other one needed several days to recover from this process. We will grant you as much time as you need to do the same.

WE are all the same now. I am one of you and I am ready.

Good. Go back into your world and finish preparing it. Return to us when it is time to lead your army.

APPENDIX

Acolyte - an Anonymi apprentice

Adria Varela - A Marked Descendant and a Ghost of Ashur. Her parents are from Markos and Galicea. She grew up in Fera, Markos. Her manifestation is enhanced hearing.

Ahvedool Bain - A Marked Descendant, one of Asarei's followers. Lives on Asarei's island, originally from Maramarosa, Shivaana.

Alamar of Talha - A Yahairan senator

Anahi Yeon - a former maid at the Happy Elephant in Vandenar. Died in *The Ghosts of Ashur*.

Anika - A Daughter of Tahlia in Sundari

Anonymi - an ancient organization that resides in the underground of Fang-Haan and works secretly to maintain balance in Ashur.

Aric Taurean - A Marked Descendant and Taurani. Currently under Jahmash's control.

Arild Hammersland - A Marked Descendant from decades ago. He was able to receive messages from the Orijin, and used them to transcribe the *Book of Orijin*.

Asarei Taurean - A Marked Descendant and Taurani

Asp - A Kraiso working with the Ghosts of Ashur

Augur - Commonly referred to as a Blind Man or a Blind Woman. Capable of receiving prophecies.

Aurkene Ezkerro - A citizen of Castiel and daughter of an Elder

Avenira Gwonahn - A Marked Descendant, resident of Vandenar. Her manifestation makes her bones unbreakable.

Azar of Fatyan - A Yahairan senator

Badalao Majime - A Marked Descendant and a Ghost of Ashur. Highborn from Constaniza, Markos. His manifestation is the ability to mentally connect with anyone he touches.

Baltaszar Kontez - A Marked Descendant and a Ghost of Ashur. Grew up with father and twin brother in Haedon, in the Never.

Bhujanga -Ggiant snakes that live in the mountains of Shivaana and the deserts of Fangh-Haan

Bisitsad - An island of nations to the southwest of Ashur.

Blastevahn Handschuh - A Marked Descendant and a Ghost of Ashur. From Eris, Galicea. His manifestation was the ability to mesmerize others by singing.

Bo'az Kontez - Twin brother of Baltaszar, son of Joakwin. Originally from Haedon. Currently under Jahmash's control.

Book of Orijin - A sacred text transcribed by Arild Hammersland, using words direct from the Orijin. The text provides directions to normal humans and Marked Descendants about the proper way to live.

Bragha Drusus - Sixth General of the Vithelegion, native to Vitheligia.

Brogan - A nation on the island of Bisitsad, southwest of Ashur

Canda - Wife of Asarei. Originally from Roaldon, Cerysia.

Castiel - A nation on the island of Bisitsad, southwest of Ashur

Cerys - One of the original three Harbingers, who predated the Five.

Chervil - A Kraiso working with the Ghosts of Ashur

Chetan - Vasher's older brother

Chhavi - A Daughter of Tahlia in Sundari

Courtland Hailstone - A Cerysian highborn vying for the throne in Alvadon.

Cow - A Kraiso helping the Ghosts of Ashur

Cyrus Baek - Owner of the Happy Elephant Inn in Vandenar. From Vandenar, Mireya. Uncle to Desmond and Farco. Died in *The Ghosts of Ashur*.

Dafne - Daughter of Asarei and Canda, lives with her parents.

Darian - One of the Five Harbingers. Could control and manipulate water, had multiple wives. Darian led Jahmash away from civilization and summoned the seas to create an island in order to trap Jahmash, sacrificing himself in the process.

Darvel Valoran - Son of Davala. Native to Vitheligia.

Daughters of Tahlia - A group of women in Sundari, Shivaana, who follow Tahlia's example. A Daughter of Tahlia takes a woman for a life partner and forms agreements with men for the sole purpose of procreation. Once Daughters of Tahlia bear a child, they cease their connection with the father of the child.

Davala Valoran - Fifth General of the Vithelegion, native to Vitheligia and father of Darvel.

Deacon Drahkunov - A Marked Descendant, nephew of Jesper Drahkunov. His manifestation is the ability to not feel pain. From the Port of Granis, Galicea. Currently under Jahmash's control.

Delilah Fakhri - A Marked Descendant, a Ghost of Ashur, and a Daughter of Tahlia, from Sundari, Shivaana. Her manifestation is the ability to alter her cellular density in order to move through objects.

Descendant - 1) any person from the many lineages of Darian. Because of Darian's numerous wives, a descendant can have a vast array of physical features. 2) Marked Descendants are descendants of Darian who bear a black line down their left eyes, signifying that they have a manifestation and can wield magic given by the Orijin.

Deseeti Semai - A group of floating islands in Domna Orjann

Desmond Baek - A Marked Descendant and Ghost of Ashur from Vandenar, Mireya. His manifestation is the ability to levitate objects and move them around.

Diya - The midwife who helped Yasaman give birth, from Haedon.

Domna Orjann - A nation on the island of Fah'Zavan, south of Ashur

Donovan Brighton – Former prince of Cerysia and Ashur, and younger brother to Garrison. Died in *The Ghosts of Ashur*.

Dorana - One of Savaiyon's mothers and a Daughter of Tahlia, from Sundari, Shivaana.

Drahkunov (Jesper) - A former general from the Port of Granis, Galicea during the Galicean/Fang War. Currently a general of Jahmash's armies.

Durr'an of Alderete - A Yahairan senator

Easton Grey - An officer for the Royal Vermillion Army, from Alvadon, Cerysia.

Eddis Ebaba - A healer in Domna Orjann and friend of Maqdhuum

Edmund Brighton - The former King of Ashur, Garrison's father. Died in *The Ghosts of Ashur.*

Eleni Taurean - A Taurani who survived the attack on the Taurani village

Ezera Albes - Seventh General of the Vithelegion, native to Vithelegia.

Fae Miyung - A maid at the Happy Elephant in Vandenar. From Vandenar, Mireya.

Fah'Zavan - An island of nations to the south of Ashur

Farco Baek - Apprentice to Munn Keeramm, an Augur in Vandenar. From Vandenar, Mireya. Nephew to Cyrus Baek and cousin to Desmond Baek.

Farrah Shokan - A Marked Descendant and Ghost of Ashur whose parents are from Markos and Galicea. Her manifestation is the ability to release venom from her lips.

Faryal Hammersland - Daughter of Hugo Hammersland and younger sister of Vilariyal. From the Port of Granis, Galicea.

Farzeen Jai - Vasher's second mother, normally addressed as "Do'maa."

Garrison Brighton - A Marked Descendant, Ghost of Ashur, and former prince of Ashur. From Alvadon, Cerysia. Previously renounced title as heir to the throne.

General Grunt - A resident of Asarei's island and source of stress relief for those on the island.

Ghosts of Ashur - A group of Marked Descendants, whose mission is to kill King Edmund.

Gibreel Casteghar - A former soldier of Jahmash, who perished during the journey to bring Bo'az and Yasaman to Jahmash. Native of Castiel, a nation beyond Ashur.

Gideon - One of the Five Harbingers, who sacrificed his life to end a war between nations. Gideon could turn things to stone.

Gunnar Richteven - A Marked Descendant from Wasseron, Galicea, who was captured by Maqdhuum for Jahmash. His manifestation was heightened vision. Gunnar was killed by Farrah on a ship, on the way to attack the House of Darian.

Hansi Huu - A Marked Descendant from Zebulon, Fangh-Haan, who can create illusions with his manifestation. Hansi is currently under Jahmash's control.

Hao Vo - Lincan's father

Harini - A Daughter of Tahlia in Sundari

Harleen - A Daughter of Tahlia in Sundari

Harshu - A general in the Shivaani army

Hector Calidus - Second General of the Vithelegion, native to Vitheligia, father to Hector.

Hemeretzi - The Elders of Castiel

Hernan Calidus - Son of Hector, native to Vitheligia.

Horatio Mahd - A Marked Descendant and Ghost of Ashur from Damaszur, Wolf's Paw. He can summon and create lightning with his manifestation.

Hugo Hammersland - deceased father of Vilariyal and Faryal, and brother of Raya Hammersland. From Galicea.

Ibarra of Jalidah - A Yahairan senator

Iman Qaja - The nation that existed before Darian drowned the world and created Ashur.

Imanol - The language of Iman Qaja.

Ihsan Adin - Deceased father of Yasaman. From Haedon.

Jahmash - One of the Five Harbingers. Killed Lionel, fought Abram and Darian. Can control and manipulate others' minds after physical contact. Trapped on an island north of Ashur.

Janaral Preshant - A general in the Shivaani army

Jaya - Jahmash's former love interest, from the time of the Five Harbingers.

Jelahni - A Marked Descendant who was killed in the attack on the House of Darian, from Shivaana. His manifestation was the ability to communicate with animals.

Jennikah Fakhri - A Daughter of Tahlia and sister of Delilah. From Sundari, Shivaana.

Joakwin Kontez - Father of Baltaszar and Bo'az, originally from the nation of Semaajj. Raised sons in Haedon and was publicly hanged before Baltaszar left Haedon.

Kadoog'han Valatteir - A Marked Descendant and Ghost of Ashur from Kharza, on the Wolf's Paw. His manifestation allowed him to camouflage his skin based on his surroundings. Died in *The Ghosts of Ashur.*

Khaira Everitas - Daughter of Khurt Everitas, native of Vitheligia

Khenzi Everitas - Son of Khurt Everitas, native of Vitheligia.

Khurt Everitas - Eighth General of the Vithelegion, father of Khenzi. Native of Vitheligia.

Kinjal - A Daughter of Tahlia in Sundari

Kiryako Majime - Highborn girl from Constaniza, Markos. Sister of Badalao.

Kraisos - a thieves guild that operates in secrecy beneath Taiju, Markos.

Krissette Luuk - A Marked Descendant and follower of Asarei. Lives on Asarei's island, parents originally from Cerysia and Markos.

Laboni - A Daughter of Tahlia in Sundari

Leonard Mahd - Older brother of Horatio, from Damaszur, Wolf's Paw.

Linas Nasreddine - soldier of Jahmash who was tasked with finding Baltaszar and eventually brought Bo'az to Jahmash. Blinded by Jahmash for his mistake. Native of Castiel, a nation beyond Ashur.

Linh Vo - Lincan's older sister

Lionel - One of the Five Harbingers, had the ability to speak any language. He was killed while fighting Jahmash, in an attempt to help Darian flee.

Lincan Vo - A Marked Descendant and Ghost of Ashur, from Xuyen, Fangh-Haan. His manifestation is the ability to heal others.

Lobaton of Massar - A Yahairan senator

Lucena of Banafsaj - A Yahairan senator

Lumien Taurean - A Taurani who survived the attack on the Taurani village

Maarida of Alderete - Wife of Durr'an, a Yahairan senator

Magallan of Hamdin - A Yahairan senator

Magnus - One of the original Three Harbingers, who predated the Five.

Malikai Aitos - A Marked Descendant and Ghost of Ashur from Taiju, Markos. His manifestation was the ability to change the texture of his skin, depending on the threat. Died in *The Ghosts of Ashur.*

Manifestation - an ability given to those chosen by the Orijin. Manifestations tend to be given when a person is between the ages of five and eight years old, and puts their utmost faith in the Orijin during a dire situation.

Manjobam Gidda - A Marked Descendant and follower of Asarei, originally from Agralun, Shivaana. His manifestation is enhanced strength.

Maqdhuum/Abram - One of the Five Harbingers as Abram, and disappeared while fighting Jahmash. During present times, has been granted a new body and changed his name to Maqdhuum. Currently allied with the Ghosts of Ashur, has the ability to teleport to anywhere.

Marika Taurean - A member of the Taurani civilization, which descends from Taurean, one of the original Three Harbingers. She was the mother of Marshall Taurean, and died while helping Garrison travel to the House of Darian.

Massi of Garsiyya - A Yahairan senator

Maximilian Eddington - A Marked Descendant and Ghost of Ashur from Benjam, Cerysia. His manifestation is the ability to absorb energy and redistribute it to other people or living things.

Meli Ikitenya - Eddis Ebaba's nickname for Maqdhuum. It is an Ojanni word that translates to "prophet".

Melina Shokan - The younger sister of Farrah, who was killed at the hands of Garrison's soldiers while Garrison was still hunting down Marked Descendants.

Moon - A Kraiso working with the Ghosts of Ashur

Munn Keeramm - An Augur from Vandenar, Mireya. Died in *The Ghosts of Ashur.*

Mutt - A Kraiso working with the Ghosts of Ashur

Neraiya - A Marked Descendant and follower of Asarei, who resides on his island. She is originally from Darling Harbor, Markos and her manifestation is the ability to breathe underwater.

Nerisi - Healers that inhabit the Deseeti Semai in Domna Orjann

Nham Kyloon - General of the Fangh army

Oblivion - One of the Three Rings, reserved for those who chose inaction over good or evil.

Ojasri - A Daughter of Tahlia in Sundari

Omneitria - One of the Three Rings, reserved for those who lived righteously.

Opprobrium - One of the Three Rings, reserved for those who lived evilly or unjustly.

Oran Von/Vitticus Khou - A Galicean man who is currently the Chancellor of Haedon. Originally from Penzaedon, Galicea.

Orchid - A Kraiso working with the Ghosts of Ashur

Orijin - The god of this universe.

Rabarrah of Razin - A Yahairan senator

Raffa Canus - First General of the Vithelegion, native to Vitheligia, father of Ravindra.

Raiza Malleolas - Fourth General of the Vithelegion, native to Vitheligia.

Ravindra Canus - Son of Raffa, native of Vitheligia

Raya Hammersland - A Marked Descendant from Galicea. Mother to Baltaszar and Bo'az Kontez, and wife to Joakwin Kontez. Her manifestation was the ability to travel to the Three Rings. She disappeared when Baltaszar and Bo'az were very young.

Renan Dantas - King of Brogan

Reverron Maidenfield - A Marked Descendant and Ghost of Ashur from Alvadon, Cerysia. His manifestation was the ability to move quickly via bursts of speed. Died in *The Ghosts of Ashur.*

Rhadames Slade - A former soldier from the nation of Semaajj, and former friend of Joakwin Kontez. Pretended to be loyal to Jahmash, but is now working with the surviving Descendants.

Riha Simalti - Older sister of Savaiyon. Lives in Gansishoor, Shivaana.

Roland Edevane - Uncle to Garrison Brighton and a Marked Descendant from Cerysia, whose manifestation is the ability to create astral projection.

Sabina Everitas - Wife of Khurt Everitas

Sabouros Majime - Father of Badalao Majime, from Constaniza, Markos.

Sadie - A maid at the Happy Elephant Inn, in Vandenar, Mireya. Died in *The Ghosts of Ashur.*

Sage - A Kraiso working with the Ghosts of Ashur

Sagrajas of Aban - A Yahairan senator

Salken Suldas - Older son of Saol Suldas, native of Vitheligia

Saol Suldas - Commander of the Vithelegion, native to Vitheligia

Savaiyon Simalti - A Marked Descendant and Ghost of Ashur from Shivaana. His manifestation is the ability to create yellow-bordered gateways to any location he has been before.

Saymon Suldas - Younger son of Saol Suldas, native of Vitheligia

Semaajj - A nation on the island of Fah Zavan

Seylaan Jai - Older brother to Vasher, from Sundari, Shivaana

Sindha Taravari - A Marked Descendant and Ghost of Ashur from Itarse, Shivaana. Her manifestation is the ability to create force fields.

Sivika - A former Daughter of Tahlia, and Savaiyon's birth mother. From Sundari, Shivaana.

Sopira Majime - Mother of Badalao Majime, from Constaniza, Markos.

Stones of Gideon - A historical location on the outskirts of Alvadon. This is where the Harbinger Gideon turned a battlefield to stone, including himself and all of the soldiers, in order to teach humanity a lesson.

Stream - A Kraiso working with the Ghosts of Ashur

Suriiya of Aban - Wife of Sagrajas, joins with Aurkene and Bo'az

Taali of Ihtizaz - A Yahairan senator

Taurean - One of the original three Harbingers, who predated the Five. The Taurani people were direct descendants of Taurean, as was the Harbinger Darian.

Thiel Aquilas - Third General of the Vithelegion, native to Vitheligia.

Three Rings - The domain of the Orijin, where souls are sorted after their departure from the world of flesh.

Tien Vo - Lincan's older brother

Trevor Nightsmythe - A Marked Descendant and follower of Asarei. Lives on Asarei's island, originally from Shipsbane, Cerysia.

Vanna Wynchester - A young woman from Alvadon, Cerysia, and Garrison Brighton's former love interest.

Varana Jai - A Daughter of Tahlia, and Vasher Jai's birth mother. From Sundari, Shivaana.

Vasher Jai - A Marked Descendant and Ghost of Ashur from Sundari, Shivaana. His manifestation is the ability to persuade through speaking.

Vermillion - The Royal Army of King Edmund, named for the red-dyed crest of hair on their helmets

Violet - A maid at the Tall Tale Inn in Shipsbane, Cerysia.

Vikram Bhoodoo (Wind) - A young man from Haedon, in the Never, who was friends with, and of a similar age as Baltaszar Kontez. Now a Kraiso working with the Ghosts of Ashur.

Vilariyal Hammersland - Daughter of Hugo Hammersland and older sister of Faryal. From Galicea.

Vithelegion - The Army that hails from Vitheligia.

Vrschiika - giant scorpions that live in the mountains of Shivaana and the deserts of Fangh-Haan

Wendell Ravensdayle - best friend of Garrison and Donovan, general of Garrison's army

Vylsia Taurean - A Taurani who survived the attack on the Taurani village

Yasaman Adin - A young woman from Haedon, in the Never. She was previously the love interest of Baltaszar Kontez, but is currently carrying the child of Bo'az Kontez, Baltaszar's twin brother.

Yahaira - A nation on the island of Bisitsad, southwest of Ashur

Zin Marlowe - The former and final Headmaster of the House of Darian. Marlowe was originally from Maradon, Cerysia, and perished during the attack on the House of Darian.

ACKNOWLEDGEMENTS

I would like to once again thank my friends and family for their ongoing support. Their encouragement took many forms over the years. It started with asking when I'm ever going to get started on the book that I keep talking about, which has evolved into anxiously asking when the next book is coming out.

Over the course of the last few years, I've made it a point to absorb as much superior writing as I can, in whatever form. That ranged from television shows, movies, books, poetry, music, and anything else that could inspire me. I don't know if any of that shows up in this novel, but I'm so grateful to all of the other artists out there who are unafraid of sharing their work with the world and letting humanity see them for who they are. The world needs artists more than ever these days, and I'm proud to be among the ranks of people who are brave enough to create.

I would be remiss to not mention Emmanuel, a fellow writer who is relatively new to the craft. It's been such a pleasure these past couple of years to talk about writing all the time and to share my process and what's inspired me and guided me. Thank you for not being afraid to ask questions and for all the genuine conversations.

Lastly, I would like to thank you readers. There are so many moments in the writing process in which we writers question ourselves and whether it's worth it to continue. But oftentimes, all it takes is the smallest question or comment from someone who's given our writing the time of day to put us back on course. Sometimes it's a text to yell at me for killing off a character. Sometimes it's enthusiastically listening to me explain my story at author events. And sometimes it's donating a softball bat to my daughter with the expectation of Book 3 in return. I'm infinitely grateful for all of you who've read the first two books. It's because of you that I was able to write *World on Fire* with such enthusiasm. Thank you.

ABOUT THE AUTHOR

Khalid Uddin is an author from New Jersey who began dreaming up the Drowned Realm Series back in college. His biggest inspirations have been comic books, fantasy novels, historical events, religious mythology, and various cultures.

Along with his love for writing, Khalid also loves music, donuts, coffee, and obviously his family. He is currently working on the fourth and final installment of the series. Feel free to reach out to him on Instagram at @khalid.uddin.author or email him at khalid.uddin23@gmail.com

www.ingramcontent.com/pod-product-compliance
Lightning Source LLC
Chambersburg PA
CBHW031731180726
48283CB00005B/1460

* 9 7 8 1 7 3 6 5 9 7 9 8 9 *